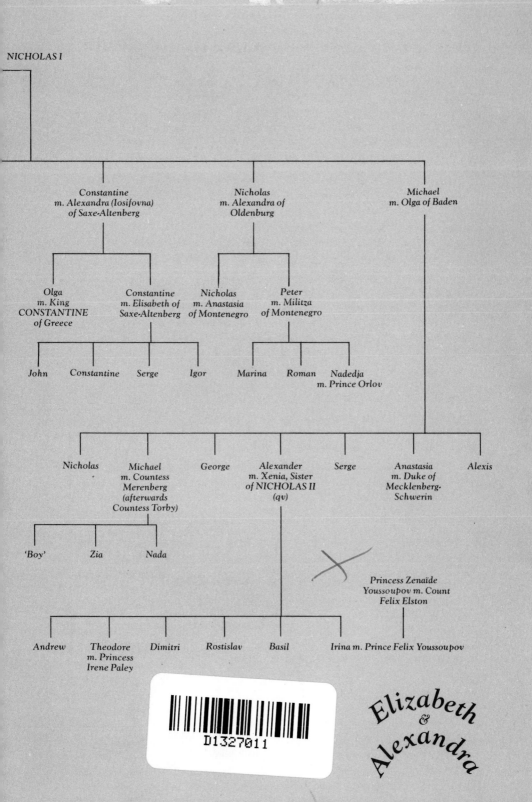

Elizabeth & Alexandra

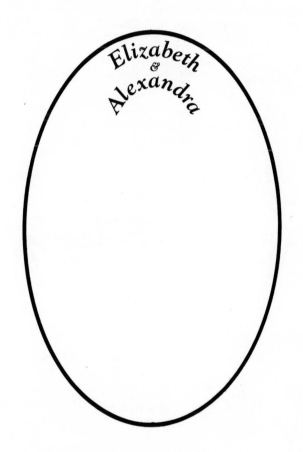
Elizabeth
&
Alexandra

Elizabeth & Alexandra

Antony Lambton

Ω

Quartet Books
London   Melbourne   New York

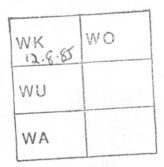
First published by Quartet Books Limited 1985
A member of the Namara Group
27/29 Goodge Street, London W1P 1FD

British Library Cataloguing in Publication Data
Lambton, Antony
   Elizabeth and Alexandra.
   I. Title
   823'.914[F]   PR6062.A48/

ISBN 0-7043-2530-6

Phototypeset by AKM Associates (UK) Ltd.
Ajmal House, Hayes Road, Southall, London
Printed and bound in Great Britain
by Mackays of Chatham Ltd, Kent

For Claire

Acknowledgements

I would like to express my thanks to Lady Celestria Noel for her help with the first part of the book. And to Mr Peter Ford, who has guided the book through the press and offered much valuable advice. Like any other writer on the last days of the Romanovs I am also extremely grateful to Mr Anthony Summers and Mr Tom Mangold, whose research on the ultimate period for their book *The File on the Tsar* unearthed forgotten evidence which added immensely to the public knowledge of the supposed fate of the imperial family. I am also grateful to the Duke of Beaufort for giving me the papers of Sir William Lambton, which add to the scanty evidence relating to King George V's opposition to his government's offer of sanctuary to the Tsar and his family. I would like, too, to thank my friend Dr Roger Williams, who put me in touch with Dr John Burton, who in turn put me in contact with Professor David Bowen. The opinions of these eminent members of the medical profession may be read in Appendix 7. I can only sincerely thank Dr Burton and Professor Bowen for their great kindness to a stranger. I am grateful to H.R.H. the Princess Paul of Yugoslavia, who must be the last living member of the European royal families to have played with the ailing Tsarevich Alexis when he was a little boy. And to H.R.I.H. the Archduchess Ferdinand of Austria, granddaughter of the Archduchess Helen who appears in this story. And finally to Prince Alexander Romanov, grandson of the Grand Duke Alexander who married the sister of the last Tsar. These relations of the Romanov family have helped with their own memories and stories told in their childhoods, but all have remained silent about the role played during this century by the Archduke Ernest Louis of Hesse. And lastly my thanks go to Miss Vicky Gillespie, who unsparingly devoted herself to receiving dictation, typing and correcting uncomplainingly for ten months.

Contents

Part One
1864–1884

1

She was christened Elizabeth but called Ella. The first thing she could remember was the excitement and celebrations of the birth of a new baby, though whether it was Irene or Ernie she did not know. Her memory of places was confused because, when Princess Alice had built the nurseries in the new palace in Darmstadt, she copied the materials from her mother's various houses in England. When, as a young child, Ella woke up, she might have been in either Hesse or England.

She was certain of one thing: a perpetual terror of getting lost, either from an experience or from a dream which haunted her early years. She would be out walking at Windsor or Heidelberg and find herself alone in a wood, defenceless should wild animals wish to eat her. Terrified, she would run and run, crying out in terror until at last, exhausted, she would lie down by a tree and fall asleep, only to wake up safely in her own bed.

Every summer, the whole family travelled to stay with Mama's mother, Queen Victoria. The early visits left one clear memory in her mind: a huge urn on a pedestal that stood at the end of a passage at Osborne. A housemaid told her it was full of the secrets of the world and that naughty children would perish who tried to look inside. Nobody in the world was allowed to climb up and learn them except the Queen of England. It did not occur to Ella for years that in no circumstances would Grandmama have climbed up a ladder to look inside the urn.

The clearest and most important of her early recollections which influenced her youth was a visit to Marburg, a hundred miles north of Darmstadt, to the church of her ancestress, St Elizabeth of Hungary. Her nanny, Orchardson, always called Orchie, was indignant at her father's taking her without even a maid in attendance, but he silenced Orchie's objections with the brusque words: 'She's called after the saint, so doubtless her namesake will look after her.'

They went alone. Her mother was in the last stages of one of her many pregnancies. To Ella's surprise and annoyance, they stayed in a castle bigger than her father's. On the journey, she remembered sitting in a train and then driving in an open carriage, so it must have been in spring or summer. On the way, her father told her she should model herself on the queen whose faith and courage had made her the beloved patron saint of Hungary and Ella's most illustrious ancestress.

She remembered wearing a white frock and bonnet and driving in an open carriage before stopping at the door of a huge church to be greeted on the steps by a man dressed in a woman's white dress. Her father jumped out, swung her over the side and put her down at the stranger's feet. The steps up to the church looked high and difficult to climb, and she felt forlorn and tearful, but at once her father whisked her up into his arms again and she was secure and safe. Inside, they stopped before a huge white statue of her ancestress and Ella thought how sad and odd it was that St Elizabeth's right arm was broken off at the wrist. How doubly good she must have been to have done so much for everyone with one hand. When Ella cut her finger once she could not even hold her knife. Later she was cheered to see on the paintings on the wall that the saint had two hands. Perhaps, when Elizabeth became a saint, her broken arm grew again. Her father spoke to the man in the woman's dress and pointed to a painting of the saint tucking up a poor leper in her bed.

'What is a poor leper?' she asked.

'Oh, a very sick man, I suppose.'

'Is it a good thing to put a sick leper in your bed?'

'Yes, you see, it has been remembered for hundreds of years.'

Ella paused, puzzled, before asking in a serious voice: 'Would Orchie think me good if I put a sick leper in my bed?'

To her surprise, both her father and the man in white burst out laughing, but neither of them answered her question.

After they left the church, her father allowed her, as a special treat, to ride on his shoulder as they climbed a hill. Once again they stopped and she was shown the exact place where food for the poor, hidden in her ancestress's apron, had turned into roses. Ella was confused and wondered whether, if food could be turned into roses, roses could be turned into food. If so, wouldn't the flower beds look funny? But she did not dare to ask another question in case they laughed at her again.

At some point she fell asleep and remembered waking up, still in her father's arms, but this time they were in another church, walking between dark pews like those in the church at home. She looked about her and saw a beautiful young girl, wearing a handkerchief over her head so you could not see her hair, looking down and moving her lips as she read a little book. As they drew near, the girl looked up and Ella noticed she had lovely, sad, dark eyes and the whitest skin she had ever seen. As they passed, her father looked down, noticed the girl too, changed his step and bent his body and Ella forward as he gave a surprised bow. Outside the church, she asked him what the beautiful girl was doing. After a few seconds he replied solemnly: 'She is preparing herself to be a bride of Christ.'

This was mysterious news, and she would have asked more questions except that her father took out of his pocket a little book telling of the saint's life which had a coloured picture of her walking downhill with her apron full of flowers. Ella slept with the book in her hands that night and held it firmly in the train all the way home, where she gave it at once to Orchie and made her read it aloud, and the next day made her mother read it again. She could not get over the beauty of the story or have it read often enough, until at last not even tears could make Orchie or her mother open the book. By that time she knew the

4

legend by heart, and often imagined herself becoming a saint, which made her feel holy, important and happy.

A month later, after endlessly dwelling on her ancestress's life, she decided that true saints did not just think, they performed miracles. She would try herself and prove she was a worthy descendant of St Elizabeth. It was the evening of Ernie's first birthday party, although he did not appear to enjoy himself and was put to bed at the usual time. Orchie was downstairs, and knowing the night nursery to be empty, Ella crept in and carried her baby brother from his cot along the passage into her bedroom, and placing him carefully in her bed, went down on her knees and prayed he would turn into a leper, but only for a short time: not long enough for him to feel ill or uncomfortable but long enough for her to become a real saint. When her prayer was finished, she jumped happily into bed, curled up beside him and went to sleep. There was a terrific fuss when Ernie was missed. Orchie went downstairs again to see if, by any chance, Mama had taken him. Then Papa and Orchie came into her room, and when Papa saw Ernie in her bed he was very angry and scolded her but, to Ella's amazement, Orchie turned on him and said slowly, in a stiff voice she had never heard her use before: 'It's no good, sir, you blaming the child. It's all the fault of those who fill her mind with Roman idolatry. I never knew such silliness in all my days', and swooping on Ernie, she walked out of the room, her bonnet trembling.

Ella looked at her father, who she thought was at least God's brother, and wondered how he would punish Orchie for daring to speak to him so crossly. To her surprise, he only shuffled his feet and, with a shrug of his shoulders, kissed her goodnight. She thought Orchie was more important after that. She was short and plump with a long, rather severe face, and always wore a white bonnet. But you felt safe with her. If she punished one of them, it was always for a good reason, and she always insisted that the children finished their food. They respected and loved her, but in a different way from Mama.

Ella's game of playing saints did not last long, though she never forgot the beautiful bride of Christ and thought he must be a wonderful man if such a beautiful girl wished to marry him. She knew the girl in the church had brought her closer to God, and when she said her prayers she felt He was listening, which made her decide to try and please Him. After careful thought, she decided the best way was to improve her character, behave better and make promises which He would help her to keep; to be good and kind. She set herself a high standard, and if ever she failed, she asked to be forgiven and gave herself punishments. Even if she cheated at racing demon, she was not happy until she had told God, slapped the guilty hand and promised not to do it again.

At first, Ella would shut her eyes when she made one of her frequent pleas for forgiveness, having found it difficult to be perfectly good, and her sisters and mother would ask her what on earth she was doing. She did not like the questions, and wild horses would not have dragged the true answer out of her, but she was determined not to give up her plan and, instead, prayed with her eyes open and punished herself by offering to look after the baby or helping Irene with her ABC. Her change of character, for she had been considered difficult, surprised her mother, who said she had turned into a kind, thoughtful

5

child, and although her elder sister, Victoria, was scornful, her father was pleased. To her disappointment, Orchie wasn't grateful and often looked at her as if she was trying to decide what was wrong. One day Ella heard her say to Mama in a worried voice: 'I'm sure I cannot make out what's come over the child. I would rather she was her naughty old self.'

Gradually her fervour declined and she gave herself fewer punishments, and since nothing happened if she forgot, she slowly stopped judging all her actions, though for years she continued to hope that one day she would be good enough to be a bride of Christ.

2

One sunny morning in 1872, when Ella was eight and Victoria nine, their governess, Miss Jackson, said that since they had worked so hard she would, if their mother agreed, allow them a half holiday and they could go for a ride in the park at Kranichstein. They had looked at each other and Victoria had said: 'Ella, run and ask permission. Mama will give it to you, not to me.'

Ella had sighed and thought of protesting, knowing perfectly well that Victoria was lazy, but the idea of a ride on a lovely morning was such a wonderful treat that she decided not to waste time and, dashing out of the room, hurried upstairs and breathlessly knocked and opened her mother's door with one movement.

To her surprise, Mama, who was standing by the window, turned round in tears. Ella felt embarrassed and guilty not to have waited after knocking, but her mother did not correct her and sat down, openly wiping her eyes.

'What is it, dearest?'

Frightened by this unaccustomed docility, Ella explained awkwardly, 'Miss Jackson is so pleased with our work she says, if you agree, we can have a holiday and go riding.'

'Certainly,' Mama said, smiling. 'I am glad you have been good girls. Come here a moment and let me kiss you.'

Ella bent down and her mother kissed and hugged her, pressing so closely that she felt her wet cheeks. Astonished at such behaviour, Ella looked at Mama and thought how small and frail she looked, except where her stomach stuck out, how white her skin was, how thin her hands in which the blue veins showed. And surely her mouth had once been larger than the thin line it had recently become?

'Is anything wrong, Mama?' she said, taking her mother's hand.

'Yes,' said her mother, looking up and smiling, two tears running down her cheeks. 'My dear friend, Dr Strauss, is leaving today. You know how he has been my solace here as we have talked together every day for the last five years. He has opened my mind to many things and, though Mama in England won't hear a word of good of him, and your Papa has never liked him, he is a good, innocent, clever man who has taught me that the only true religion is to be kind to others. You know, some people think that if they call themselves Christians and go to church once a week, they will get to heaven however arrogant they are

7

on earth. He has taught me many other things you would not understand yet, and perhaps never will. He is a clever, clever man and the only person I can talk to here, for I cannot stand the etiquette and the dull old stories.'

She continued crying as she talked and appeared to be about to say something else when, looking up and catching the horror on her daughter's face, she sat back with a jerk and finished quickly, 'But run away, my sweet, and both of you have a lovely ride. Please don't say a word to Victoria, and when you grow up, perhaps you will understand what it means to lose a true friend.'

Ella said nothing to Victoria, who was over a year older than her and understood many things, and thought how strange life would be without Dr Strauss, since he came every day, whether her mother was in Darmstadt or Kranichstein. Their conversation was terribly grown up, and she had not understood the little bits she heard, but then adult conversation was always difficult to make out. She also remembered how Papa often called him 'a damned heathen', causing a look of weariness to come over Mama's face, the same look as when Papa told one of his long stories which they all knew so well, or described every detail of a day's shooting, when Mama would tap her fingers on the table. Ella did not tell Orchie either; it was nice to have a secret with Mama. But if Dr Strauss went away, might not Orchie go as well? It was hard to imagine life without her for, although she was strict, they all loved her, and if any of them felt ill or even had a pain, they told her at once. The idea stayed in her mind. She knew that Orchie annoyed Papa. He often talked scornfully about her 'English ideas'. Ella put her arms around her and whispered one night as she was tucked in and kissed goodnight, 'Orchie, please don't leave.'

A look of surprise came over her nanny's face as she said indignantly, 'The very idea! How would you all get on without me, I'd like to know?'

She remembered a further mention of Dr Strauss soon after he disappeared for ever. One day at lunch her father said in his loud voice, 'Thank God we are rid of the heathen.'

Mama at once left the dining room. Papa followed, looking upset and mumbling as he went out, 'God, what a fool I am, I cannot help saying the wrong thing. The trouble is, Alice is too damned clever for me.'

His last words made Ella think, and had the same effect on Victoria, for they had a long talk that evening and decided the self-criticism was correct. Papa was exceedingly slow and clumsy and did always say the wrong thing and, if there was trouble, it was always Mama who put things right. They also wondered why their parents never spoke to each other when alone with their children, except about the weather or Grandmama or Prince Bismarck, who, Papa always shouted, was 'more evil than the devil'. On the other hand, with Dr Strauss, Mama had talked and laughed and argued, though in a different, friendly way, and they had looked at books together, which, of course, Mama could not do with Papa, as he said again and again that the only book worth reading was the *Almanach de Gotha*.

Later on that year, Orchie explained that they must play quietly for a week or so. Everybody whispered, and Victoria was the first to guess that another baby was coming. When it arrived, she was a little girl called Alix, and now there were six of them.

A year afterwards, on 29 May – she would never forget the date – a terrible event happened. The three elder girls now, each morning, took lessons together with Miss Jackson in a sitting room next to their mother's bedroom. Before starting work that day, they went in as usual to kiss their mother as she lay, having breakfast in bed, her three younger children playing around her on the floor. As they left, the two little boys, Ernie, aged five, and Frederick or Frittie, aged three, raced after them to the door while little Alix sat on the floor by a French window, one of two which opened on to small balustraded balconies. Ella felt a pang of jealousy. Mama looked contented and happy as she watched the young ones playing, while now she and her sisters had to go and learn boring geography.

For years she remembered clearly every detail of the remainder of the morning. When the three of them sat down before starting their lesson punctually at 8.45, Victoria asked Ella coldy if she had found her lost crayon. It was all so silly, but the day before Ella had needed a red crayon to colour a drawing of a dress and had borrowed one of Victoria's, who missed it and asked if her sister knew where it was. Ella said no, but admitted the theft to God, gave herself a trifling punishment and decided to keep the crayon until she finished her colouring since it was exactly the right shade and she knew her sister would not lend it to her again. That morning, when she said 'no', Victoria called her a little liar, but Miss Jackson told them to be quiet. It was time to start a geography lesson on the puzzling source of the Nile.

As they examined a map of Lake Rudolph, they suddenly heard the sound of Ernie's screams coming from their mother's room and looked at each other in frightened amazement. Then the door opened and Orchie came in carrying little Alix, a nerve throbbing in her forehead. She shut the door quickly behind her, but not before they heard the sound of gasping sobs. Miss Jackson forbade them to move and went out with Orchie as they sat white-faced, too frightened to think, listening to doors opening and shutting and sounds of grief coming through the windows. After that, at one moment, she and Victoria went into their mother's room and found her sitting on her bed still in her dressing gown, her blue eyes the only living thing in her face. Then she turned away and leaned over something hidden on her bed. A maid hustled them out.

In the nursery, Ernie was lying, his head buried in the sofa, sobbing his heart out, while Orchie sat with little Alix on her knees, tears running down her cheeks as she murmured, 'Oh, my poor little darling, you don't understand, do you, you don't realize what you have done, do you?'

By the end of the day, all they knew was that somehow Frittie had fallen out of the window and was dead. But what had little Alix done? Whenever Ernie was asked, he burst out crying. Miss Jackson ordered them to stay upstairs in the nursery and keep quiet. Ella went and found the crayon and gave it to Victoria, expecting her to be angry and call her a liar again, but instead she only reached out, pulled Ella to her, and they sat crying, clasped in each other's arms.

Years later the children agreed that Mama was never happy again. Frittie's death killed something in her, and whenever she asked about their lessons or tried to play with Ernie, the elder girls could see she was trying, with a broken heart, to pretend nothing had happened. They also noticed that when she nursed Alix she always put her down quickly, and for weeks did not have her on her bed, which was strange, for how could a baby of one who could hardly walk have made Frittie fall over the balcony?

Two years later, Mama had another baby girl and her treatment of her fifth daughter showed how much she had changed. She did not stare at May in the same way as she had at her other babies, when she had appeared to be restraining herself with difficulty from crushing the life out of their bodies with love. Instead she held her as if she was carrying out a duty, and never looked regretful when she was taken away.

Life at the new palace was quieter after the tragedy. The servants walked softly; their mother lay in bed; their father was always away shooting; the children made frequent visits to relations. They liked best staying at Heiligenberg with their Uncle Alexander of Hesse and his wife and rough children who were inexplicably called Battenberg. She sometimes asked why they had a different name, but the truth was not explained for many years. Aunt Marie, the tired, sick Empress of Russia, was often staying with her brother. Her huge children terrified Victoria and Ella. She liked Serge the best, although he was ten years older. Perhaps it was because nobody else liked him and that he once stopped to pick her up when she fell off her pony.

In 1875, when Ella was eleven, they paid a long visit to Grandmama in England while Mama stayed at home, and after a month at Windsor, spoiled by daily lessons, spent three weeks at Osborne on the Isle of Wight. She would long remember the big house with the high tower, up to which she and Victoria would creep together when nobody was in sight to open the tower door, lock it again, and climb to the top where they could see everything in the garden. Half of the fun was never to show themselves, and no one ever saw them or found out that they had discovered a hidden key. Afterwards Ella thought how at that age they took their grandmother for granted. But the old lady was often kind to them. In fact, Mama said she was much friendlier to her grandchildren than she had ever been to her children, and that she had softened with age.

On their last day in England, the Queen sent for the two elder girls and, after kissing them and patting their cheeks, asked them to sit on the sofa as she wished to speak privately. They sat erect, longing to know what she was going to say. She was looking cross, which made them exchange frightened glances, and started off by discussing the selfishness of all men and how sad was the lot of married women. They listened agog as she continued: 'Doubtless you have noticed how thin and pale your mother has become, not that it is surprising. Apart from having seven children, she had all the worry and expense of finishing the new palace at Darmstadt and paying many of the household expenses. Her life was not eased by the German wars, of which I strongly disapproved. In the first war, Hesse, instead of minding its own business as I advised, chose the losing side and consequently lost a large part of land and revenues. Neither, to my everlasting regret, has your mother received the religious consolations I had hoped. Her choice of companions, Doctor . . .'

Here Grandmama paused and closed her mouth into a firm, thin line as if she had said enough, before continuing sternly, frowning, 'I wish you to be discreet and watchful and to look out for little ways and means by which you can help your mother, who has always been so good – too good, I sometimes think – to you children, in the running of her houses and with her charities and duties. You are old enough to realize that she is overworked, especially as she has to plan the management of two establishments, the difficulties of which even the best of men . . .' and here she sighed again, '. . . never understand. You are both good girls, if somewhat thoughtless, and I have only spoken because I have observed the firmness of your characters. In any event, I hope that in the future you will help your mother and enable her to regain her strength.'

Grandmama stopped talking and looked up. They immediately rose to their feet. She gave both their hands an extra squeeze as she kissed them goodbye, as if to say 'I am relying on you now', which caused the girls to burst into tears outside her door. For the first time they realized that Grandmama was undoubtedly the dominant figure in their lives, although she was so small and round and often looked unhappy. Whatever she said was law, even if it contradicted what their father or mother had said the day before. Everybody was different when she was in a room, and even Papa, who was so big, talked in a low voice and never took his eyes off the little figure who always wore the same black clothes.

They had loved Windsor. Off duty, the courtiers there laughed and played jokes on them, whereas at Darmstadt Papa's attendants never for a moment laid aside their dignity. After having a long talk about it, they decided that their mother was tired, which was why she rested all day without even going into the garden. Years afterwards, Ella thought that her grandmother had taught them an important lesson: the necessity of thinking of others. How like her to show them this truth by making them feel grown up. Directly they arrived home, they went to see their mother and stayed a long time talking with her. She wished to know every detail of their visit, exactly how her mother looked, the number of her dogs, whether any of the servants had changed and every detail concerning their English aunts and uncles.

The next day, Ella showed Mama a personal report from the Windsor governess, who had written:

I find the Princess is a difficult child to understand. She is sensitive and charming in her manner and occasionally perceptive, often reaching the correct conclusion by instinct rather than logical deduction. For example, while she is religious and says her prayers with regularity, I found it impossible to teach her scripture. A task learned one day is forgotten the next. The same applies to all subjects in which I tried to excite her interest. I believe this forgetfulness is not caused by want of effort but through lack of interest. She is, however, practical, kind and good-natured and has a pleasant wit.

Her mother read the report, smiled, put it aside and never mentioned it again.

11

3

During the next three years, Ella followed her grandmother's advice and tried to help her mother – who often said 'I wake up tired, which is a nuisance as I have so much to do' – by spending time in riding or walking with the younger children. The death of his brother had made Ernie excitable and nervous, and he often woke the others up by screaming in his sleep, while Orchie said he often woke up sobbing, crying out that he did not want to die alone like poor little Frittie.

Alix was difficult even as a baby, and Ella noticed months after the accident how Orchie as well as Mama continued to treat her in an odd way, both unconsciously keeping her outside the circle of intimacy which bound them and the other children together. She remembered trying every way she could think of to make a close friend of her baby sister, but she was a strange little girl, and while the townspeople called her Sunny, it was not an accurate nickname, for even when Alix was hardly more than a baby, the way she clung to her toys as though the rest of the world were anxious to take them from her suggested forlorn uncertainty. Could her mother and Orchie's early coldness have made her feel deprived and unloved? Ella tried to get her brother and sisters to understand that Alix was an unhappy girl and to be nice to her. Her advice was disastrous in Ernie's case, since he was so affectionate that Alix came to regard him as one of her possessions and screamed whenever he spoke to anyone else.

Ella, however, did not have much time to worry about Alix, as she was always busy with her own lessons, the other children, and helping her mother who, tired but resolute, tried to continue to stimulate the improvement of schools. One effect of the activity was to push Ella's interest in religion into the background, causing her two young Romanov cousins, Serge and Paul, to call her 'little mother' instead of 'holy mother' whenever she saw them at Heidelberg, where her Aunt Marie, the Tsarina, spent more and more of her time. The sisters could not help comparing their aunt unfavourably with Grandmama. Everybody was deferential enough to her, but never frightened. Papa spoke to her in his usual loud voice. Her children did not obey her, yet nothing happened. It was strange, for on their maps her kingdom looked huge, and they liked their aunt best when she told them of far-off Russia, which the Hessian children regarded as a land of romance with its great, onion-domed churches, immense forests and colossal palaces.

Even in Hesse, the Tsarina's household was exciting to visit. Outside her door stood two huge, fierce Cossack guards in red coats criss-crossed with bandoliers, who wore beautiful, wrinkled, soft leather boots which made no sound and frightened the maids to death. Victoria was fascinated by two Russian officers who were always in attendance and whose fat faces and sparkling uniforms made the frail old woman seem very small. Incessantly the girls tried to make the fading Tsarina tell their favourite story of her coronation, when her regalia and robes weighed so much that she was a prisoner unable to move until eight maids of honour lifted her velvet train. Once she had told them of the rediscovery of a monastery in the limitless countryside where the priest used unknown words and prayers that had not been used in the Orthodox Church for five hundred years. Each story was told with little sighs, as if now that she was safely in Germany, every memory of her alien life, to which she would soon return, was painful. With the pitilessness of a child, Ella often thought how stupid the frail little woman was to grumble so often about a country which sounded so wild and barbaric and in which, as Empress, she could do anything she liked. It was no excuse that she was small; she was bigger than Grandmama.

As Ella grew up she began to hear strangers remark to her mother that her second daughter (which was herself) had a beautiful face. Other relations would tell her, in joking amazement, that she was no longer ugly, and young men stared at her in a very embarrassing way. Mama by now tired very easily, but Victoria and herself, young and strong, retained the satisfying belief that to be busy was to be good, and lived happy lives. There were, however, times when they felt puzzled and upset at the differences between their lives and other people's.

One day Ella accompanied her mother on a visit to a hospital in Darmstadt. In one of the new wards lay four members of a family in a row: first, three little children with arms like sticks whose white faces under their black hair merged with the white sheets; beyond them, the mother, a thin woman whose black hair fell over a hawky little peaked face as she lay asleep, grey with exhaustion. The matron of the ward explained how the family had been picked up at the gates of the town, having come from 'God knows where, all nearly dead from cold and starvation'. Ella asked what would happen to them, and was answered by a shrugging of shoulders. It was not thought that the two younger children would live, but the mother, who was only twenty, and the elder daughter might pull through. The sight made a tremendous impression on Ella, and she never forgot how, looking back from the door, all she could see were four black mops of hair. It was as if the bodies had fled and left the hair behind. She stood staring, in case she had made a mistake, but the faces remained invisible. She hurried on to where Mama stood talking to the matron.

That evening, Ella knocked on her mother's sitting room door. The younger children had gone to bed and it was a time of day in which, by an unwritten law, the elder children gave Mama 'a little peace'. She was sitting at her desk but jumped up in surprise with a look of intense worry as if dreading a further calamity, and asked nervously, 'What is it, my darling?'

13

'Oh Mama, I wanted to ask you something which worries me.'

'Of course, sit,' her mother said with a smile.

It was the sweet welcome Ella always received from her, however tired or ill her mother looked. Whenever her young children came to her sad or worried, she would give them kind attention and make them believe she was pleased they had come to share their doubts with her.

'Mama, how is it right that we should live in this palace with other castles to go to whenever we feel like it, and every day have more food than we can eat, when poor little children and their mothers are starving to death? You saw those four today; all thin and pale and looking half-dead. How is it right for us to have so much when they are starving?'

Her mother looked at her steadily before she answered: 'Please do not repeat what I say, but royalty is in itself ridiculous. No man or woman is better than another. One day it will be time to do away with us all, but for the moment we serve a valuable purpose and should behave in a fitting manner to earn the respect which enables us to help the many poor people who look up to us as protectors. Much needs to be done, but nothing can be done in a hurry. People cannot be forced, only persuaded, to change their minds. It takes time. You know, my Papa's belief was that no kingdom could survive sudden changes successfully. In England, his examples and reforms gradually changed age-old ideas and made councils and local authorities build hospitals and schools. He educated people out of their old-fashioned selfishness, and I have done what I can here. We have now eight hospitals in the Duchy and the number of schools is increasing, but things can only be done slowly, too slowly for my liking, though this is better than haste and bloodshed. Your grandmother has been very helpful and generous to me by sending money from England, but there is still not enough to do all the things I would like, and to help all the poor as they could and should be helped. That is why I am so glad you both are thoughtful of others. Remember, it is one of the uses of royalty that snobbery gives us influence over the middle classes, who only think of themselves, and enables us to get money from the rich, who often call themselves liberals but are very conservative with their own fortunes. You know, at your age I was full of ideals and thought anything not absolutely straightforward was wrong, but when you get older you will find you will not get what you want all at once, only a little of it, slowly, and I fear you will learn by experience that we live in a hard, cruel world. Now leave me to my letters, but I am glad you came and I am glad you are questioning the injustices of the world. It makes me happy.'

She smiled as her daughter gently closed the door.

About this time her uncle died and Papa became Grand Duke. It made no difference to their lives as Mama had always considered herself to be the first lady in the dukedom and positively refused to alter her life by adopting ridiculous formalities. Ella had recently come to notice that, while her mother was good and kind to the poor, she was always short with the courtiers and did not hide her opinion that they were of little consequence. Ella thought she was happy with the poor, and happy working, but bored to tears with the formalities which the courtiers loved.

On 9 November 1878, Victoria woke up with a sore throat. The doctor diagnosed diptheria. Orchie and her mother told the children not to be frightened; one of them was often ill. Three days later, Alix was feverish; the next day May, who was four, Papa, Ernie and Irene all collapsed. In the afternoon, May died.

Ella was doing her lessons in the schoolroom when Mama came in and stood with her back to the door, holding the knob with her hand behind her back, and quietly said: 'May is dead.'

Ella's first impulse was to jump up, run over and throw herself into her mother's arms, but Miss Jackson put a restraining hand on her arm, whispering: 'Don't speak.'

She soon saw why as Mama, white and shaking, with black rings under her eyes and on the edge of tears, was exerting her will not to break down and waste the strength she needed to nurse her husband and children. Ella felt proud at having restrained her own feelings and made it easier for her mother. They exchanged a look of silent understanding as, with a little smile, her mother asked her to be a good girl and closed the door.

That night, in her white nightdress, Ella knelt by her bed, placing her palms together upright in what she considered to be the most respectful position, and prayed to God to be merciful to her good family, telling Him of the clever and kind things all the invalids had done, giving Him examples of their goodness and innocence and asking Him to balance these against all their little faults. If one of them had to die, it should be herself. She prayed and prayed and wished and wished with all her heart for her family to get well.

Years after she heard how Sir William Jenner, whom Grandmama had sent from London, thought, after visiting all the patients, that he would look at the remaining healthy child. A maid took him up to the top floor and showed him to Ella's new room. He opened the door quietly and at first could see nothing. Then a bit of coal fell forward and a little forked flame illuminated the slumped figure of a girl on the bedside rug. Alarmed, he lifted her with difficulty into bed, and turning on the gaslight, looked with his reflector down her throat. Further reassured by the coolness of her brow, he piled coals on to the fire and turned out the gas. The next day she was sent to Kranichstein.

Separation from her family was unbearable. Sir William had given orders that she should have as much fresh air and exercise as possible. Every morning she was sent out riding with a groom in the woods. To begin with, she rode sullenly at a walking pace, not bothering to make her pony even trot, but on the third day, as she was walking down to the stables, she heard two maids discussing the burial service of May on the previous day in Darmstadt. Ella nearly burst with rage. Why had her mother sent her away? It seemed so unkind. She mounted, keeping her eyes averted from the groom, and gave her astonished pony a terrific blow with her whip. Her groom cursed and shouted at her to stop.

The pony bolted down a narrow, little-used ride with low, overhanging branches. The groom, terrified she would catch her head on a branch and be killed, flogged his own horse alongside and, seizing her pony's head, pulled him up. For a moment he was too angry to speak, then told her what he thought of her for nearly killing both of them, and shouted that he would inform the head

15

of the stables and ask never to go out with her again. She only smiled. The averted danger of the low-branched path was a pleasing memory, showing she would not have been afraid to help her mother and was not afraid of death. But by the time they had got back to the castle, she felt guilty and apologized to the groom, offered to shake hands and asked could they be friends again? She never knew whether her mother ever heard of her wild escapade.

Every day she wished herself back at Darmstadt, and once planned to escape home by riding through the night. She put on a riding habit, wound a thick scarf around her neck and crept down to the stables, only to find all the doors locked. The next day she heard that the patients had improved. Victoria was the first out of danger, and gradually Alix, Papa and Irene grew stronger, although for a long time it seemed as if poor little Ernie was likely to die. He lay on his bed crying all day, and sometimes screaming for his little dead brother, Frittie.

Ella was told her mother spent most of her time with Ernie and seldom rested as she had no faith in nurses taking care of her beloved. Without respite or thought for herself, haggard and pale, she would pass from patient to patient. As Orchie wrote: 'She is lucky if she has a little sleep in an armchair in Ernie's room at night.'

At first Mama had not dared tell Ernie that May was dead. Then, one day, he sent his little sister a fairy tale which he had written and illustrated. It was too much for Mama. She let it drop on the floor, crying out: 'My dear little boy . . . you will have to know sometime. She is dead.'

Ernie let out a terrible cry of pain and threw himself sobbing on the bed as if his heart would break. Mama, in despair, sat beside him, pulled him on to her lap, pushed back his hair, and with an irresistible impulse to comfort with love, kissed him on the lips. A few days after this forbidden act, the Queen again sent out Sir William, but in vain. On 14 December, the anniversary of the death of Prince Albert, Mama died of diptheria.

Ella's first thought was that she would never be happy again, but then she tried to think what her mother would have wanted her to do and decided she would have wished her to devote herself to looking after the younger children. For the rest of her life she nursed a grudge against Lord Beaconsfield, and never spoke to him at Buckingham Palace or Windsor, for, after her mother's death, he had made a wicked speech in the House of Lords:

'My Lords, there is something wonderfully piteous in the immediate cause of her death. The physicians who permitted her to watch over her suffering family enjoined her under no circumstances whatever to be tempted into an embrace. Her admirable self-restraint guarded her through the crisis of this terrible complaint in safety. She remembered and observed the injunctions of her physicians. But it became her lot to break to her little son the death of his youngest sister, to whom he was devotedly attached. The boy was so overcome with misery that the agitated mother clasped him in her arms, and thus she received the kiss of death.'

Ella had never liked the old Prime Minister. She thought he was a hypocrite, playing with her grandmother in a sly, artful way, praising her, telling her what she wanted to hear. He was like an actor, emotional, amusing, serious or upset, whatever suited his immediate purpose, although his eyes remained calculating. Who but an actor, when her mother died, would have descended to bathos and so cruelly, callously, thoughtlessly blamed her little brother?

Years later, when Ernie was staying at Windsor, he received an anonymous letter addressed to 'The Grand Duke Ernest, the Kiss of Death'. It said:

I suggest you go back to Germany. You have done enough harm in England. I and many others hope you will not try to kill the Queen before you leave.

Ella was allowed to come home for her mother's funeral and to sleep again on the top floor. Sadness overcame her as she drove up to the palace so full of memories of her mother. She walked upstairs feeling forlorn, and found a wonderful surprise – Victoria. The two sisters looked at each other as strangers: sadnesses borne apart had separated them. But soon, as they discussed the terrible past few weeks, the odd feeling vanished and Victoria told her a little piece of membrane had crossed May's throat and killed her immediately, how Papa had never stopped complaining, and that, despite Orchie's warnings, Mama refused all help and rest and worked herself to death. Ella felt again the pain in her heart she had felt at Kranichstein. Why was she alone excluded? Why had she been sent away? If she had stayed in Darmstadt, perhaps she could have helped her mother, shared her burdens and saved her life. She said nothing except how happy she was to see her sister, but after supper it was all too much and she went crying to bed. At ten o'clock, Victoria came in and said how greatly they had all missed her, which made her cry even more. Exhausted, she fell asleep as they talked of the best way for them to bring up the children.

In the middle of the night she sat up with a start. Had a voice called 'Ella'? In a limbo between wakefulness and sleep, conscious of her movements, unconscious of logic, she walked along the passage and down the stairs and slowly approached the door to her mother's bedroom. It was open. She peeped round the door and saw, in the firelight, four candles standing at each corner of the coffin, nightlights on side tables and, on either side of the fire, piled high with coal, two ladies-in-waiting in black lying fast asleep in armchairs, their slippers off, their feet on footstools with toes extended towards the flames. She walked on tiptoe to the coffin where her mother lay surrounded by white lace and lilies, looking less frail and tired in death than in life. That pleased her. She stared down on one she could never imagine dead, leaned forward and kissed the icy cold forehead. The chillness, the faint smell of decay, horrified her. Determined to prove her selfless love, she made herself bend down again and place a quick kiss on the little mouth above the sloping chin. This time she was conscious of no chill or smell. In her imagination, the lips seemed alive. Dumbfounded, she resisted a wicked wish to wipe her mouth. She turned and tiptoed out and never stopped running until she reached her room. Lying back, she thought contentedly that if she died it would be proof she loved her mother, and it was a comfort to know she had risked her life to prove it.

After the last of the children was considered innocuous, they went to stay with their grandmother at Windsor. Desolated by the death of her beloved daughter, Grandmama again and again reduced them all to tears by relating little instances of their mother's childhood and the way she had nursed the Prince of Wales back to health. She also, to their surprise, informed the two elder girls, now fourteen and fifteen, that she regarded them as her children and was already looking out for suitable husbands. They both noticed a different look come over the old woman's face as she gave them the amazing news. Her eyes sparkled, she looked younger and seemed to be eyeing them both with an appraising look as she examined their faces and figures.

Victoria said one day: 'Ella, do you know something very odd, Grandmama looks at us sometimes in the way men do at dances!'

Perhaps to illustrate that they were growing up, Grandmama made them perform 'the cercle'. They had to put on their best dresses and each in turn walk 'naturally' around the room while she sat upright in her favourite armchair with, in her hand, a wand which she continually rapped on a table, telling them to hold their backs straight and forget their hands existed. Then she made them sit still and watch a lady-in-waiting carefully, whom afterwards they would have to copy without a mistake. She rapped her wand and the lady-in-waiting immediately started walking around the room, addressing the furniture as people, gaily telling a bust how well she was looking, asking hopefully whether her children were in good health; turning to a desk, curtseying and saying, 'What a pleasure to see you again, Aunt Helena'; putting on a sad voice and saying with genuine sorrow to a flower vase how sorry she was to hear of her cousin's grievous loss. Afterwards she pretended she was in a cottage asking a poor Scots woman whether she had enough oats to last through the winter before gracefully accepting a cup of tea. When this performance was over, Victoria and Ella had to go through the whole programme. It was embarrassing curtseying to a desk, especially when all the time their grandmother was correcting, rapping her wand and saying: 'Be more natural, my dear. Say words as though you mean them. Manners are of the utmost importance, ensuring respect and winning friends which, as you will find out, is very necessary in life.'

They practised 'the cercle' three more times in the next few weeks. The last time was the worst, as Ella had to perform first instead of the lady-in-waiting, and Victoria had to copy her. Their grandmother was sparing of praise and said, 'You have a long way to go yet before you move correctly. I shall speak to Miss Jackson. You should continue to practise at home.' Otherwise they loved the visit and made friends of the courtiers, who behaved quite differently, almost like other children, when the Queen was not present.

After two months, the family took a tearful farewell of their grandmother and returned to Darmstadt. Victoria was determined to concentrate on her studies, for she was horrified how little she understood of the conversations at her grandmother's court. Ella went home, anxious to make up to the younger children for their loss, to continue her hospital visiting and ensure that her mother's good works continued. She knew that if she was to do good it would be by hard practical work since she had always accepted she was not a clever girl. In those days, she never could understand the great political issues which caused such furious arguments and family divisions. She never dared speak when Schleswig-Holstein was mentioned, despite hearing endless explanations, as she could not make out why it caused such bitterness. As for Bismarck, her father and mother had hated him because he had stolen half their Duchy, while their Aunt Vicky in Berlin approved of the robbery but hated him as well: it was so confusing. And the Balkans! She never could keep pace with the endless rebellions, enthronements, murders and massacres, or understand the relationship of Turkey to Bulgaria, and what such phrases as 'nominal suzerainty' meant; nor why, if the Tsar, Uncle Alexander II, was furious with England and Disraeli at the Congress of Berlin, he did not care who was King of Bulgaria so long as he was not a Russian prince; or exactly where Serbia was – although she had been told many times – unless she looked at an atlas; or why it was important to have a Prince of Montenegro, which was so small you could hardly see it on the map; or why Russia wished to expand into Europe and support countries where everybody spent their time killing each other.

After their return, they felt flat and gloomy, but in the spring Papa pulled himself together and made a great effort for the second time in his life, organizing picnics and long walks in the great beech woods, where they found marvellous clumps of violets and lilies of the valley whose scent almost made the children faint. Later on, the summer was filled with golden days when Papa came down to breakfast and shouted to his eldest girls to put off their appointments and drive with him south in a carriage to where the wheatfields stood blue with cornflowers or red with poppies. At other times, he would take his whole family north into the great plain to his little hunting lodge, where they would mount their horses and gallop down the sandy tracks, wild with excitement and love of life.

But of all the new places they came to know on their excursions, Ella's favourite was Hexenalle, a long avenue between huge old yew trees. She never knew why it was known as the Witches Avenue, but the name suggested magic and romance. Sometimes Ella and Victoria would nod to each other and break away from Irene and their grooms and gallop off to tie their horses to a near-by pine tree (yew would have killed them), enter the avenue, climb up the twisted branches and sit and discuss secrets of their home life: the loneliness of their father; why Grandmama said he could never marry again; how tiresome and possessive Orchie was becoming; whether it mattered that Ernie was not like other boys, crying if you only teased him a little and happier arranging flowers than climbing trees; whether he should be sent to Eton as Grandmama wished or educated in Germany; and lastly and most frequently, what their future was to be and whom Grandmama would choose for them as husbands, and what could be done if they did not like her choice.

When winter came, Miss Jackson made them perform 'the cercle' once a month. They found it much easier without Grandmama's keen little eyes picking out every fault and became rather pleased with their carriage. In wet or snowy weather, to perfect their style, they took riding lessons in a rundown building grandiosely called The Riding School but also used for auctioning cattle on Wednesdays. The riding master was an impecunious, withered little baron whose boots shone like glass. Irene had once offended him by asking him if he was the auctioneer as well, and to her distress, not only did he refuse to teach her for six months but she also received a sharp reprimand from her father for being rude.

'But how was I to know?' she asked in tears. 'Cows *are* auctioned there!'

They lived unrestrained lives and walked unattended about the town, often showing visitors the houses where Goethe and Schiller had stayed. In the shops, they were greeted with little bows and curtsies, but once these were out of the way their relationship with the shopkeepers was friendly and informal, except, of course, for a few ridiculous old women who would address them formally. They always disliked intensely their Aunt Schönborn, who was a terrible stickler for etiquette and complained incessantly about their manners every time she came to Darmstadt. The children politely ignored her, while their father was so bored by his sister that once, when she was telling him details of her husband's ancestry and how he should be made a prince, he fell asleep.

Ella loved the scents and smells of the town's old gardens, hidden behind high walls or overhanging winding, cobbled streets. Sometimes she would be overwhelmed by the smell of lilac or madonna lilies, and on one occasion she had stood stock still, her nostrils recognizing the beloved scent of lilies of the valley. Afterwards, whenever she smelt the little white flowers, she remembered the exact place inside a gate where they had grown in Darmstadt.

On her fifteenth birthday, Ella, following her mother's plan, began nursing lessons in the hospital. But when Grandmama heard she wrote to her father: 'Ella should not at her age be shown sights quite unfitting for one so young.' As a result, her father spoke to the doctors in the hospital, who restricted her to observation and help in the women's ward. All arguments were in vain. Her mother's wish was disregarded. Papa was terrified of Grandmama. Ella was not squeamish about the sight of blood and agreed with her mother: it was ridiculous to believe women should not nurse men.

One day, although she hoped she had not shown her feelings, Victoria made her happy. She had looked at her, sighed and said in a joking way, 'Oh dear, it's so annoying my being a year older than you, for after I have been presented I will make friends and admirers and next year you will come along and take them all away and I won't have anyone to dance with.' And while Ella stood flushing, embarrassed, she continued, 'I don't know why you are so beautiful. It is not that your features are better than mine, as photographs of us show, but it's some combination of your auburn hair and the way your skin looks, and a peculiar glow which makes you look like a beautiful fairy. I think it's very unfair that kings nowadays don't choose their wives by paintings because then one would marry me. As it is, they will see us both and marry you. It's most annoying.'

Victoria's casual joke had effects on Ella. The first was that, having stared at herself in the glass from every angle, she had to agree that she was pretty; the second was to recognise that Victoria was not pretty but handsome. Immediately she admitted these conclusions she found herself blushing with shame at her conceit and her unkindness to her beloved sister. She put her hands over her blushing face and wished and wished that, whatever happened to her, Victoria would love and be beloved and have the happiest marriage conceivable. Victoria's remarks also made her understand that their family as she knew it was coming to an end and they would all soon be separated. Of course, she had

20

realized this before but never believed it. Ella tried to explain her discovery to Irene, who could not understand what she meant, which made her realize with a shock that Irene never understood anything. She pulled herself up again; now she was being nasty about Irene, but honesty made her admit that Irene was slow and pleased with herself, which was an irritating combination.

Alix had not improved either. She was so shy that if a new friend came to tea she would sit in dead silence and knock over the milk. If she was told not to be silly or to stop sulking by her brother and sisters, she would grow red with fury and lapse into silence. She loved Miss Jackson, who the other children had never loved like Orchie, and Miss Jackson loved her. Victoria, as usual, saw why.

'It's because she doesn't have to share her. It's the same with her dolls and toys and kittens. She will scream if any of us pick one of them up. It is the same with her friends. She is perfectly furious if we try to be nice to them. She has got Miss Jackson to herself, which, as far as we are concerned, is perfect, but that is why she loves her.'

Ella knew why Victoria was angry with Miss Jackson, for she had arranged with Grandmama, without saying a word to them, for their cousin Willy to come to stay. They had never liked him. Even as a little boy he was arrogant and conceited. Their mother had agreed. However, Grandmama was determined that all her descendants should be friends, and Miss Jackson, to curry favour with the Queen, had arranged the visit. She said firmly that they must understand he had a withered arm and as a result was always trying to assert himself. They discussed revolt and not speaking, but Victoria remembered their mother had once said: 'Try and imagine how you would feel if you were a boy – and it matters more in boys, they are more naturally competitive – if you had a crippled arm. You only have to see the way he hides it behind his back and rides with his twisted fingers concealed to understand he is always thinking of his sad liability. You should be sorry for him.'

They tried hard to be nice despite Willy's awfulness, but from the first moment of his arrival he would do and say things which made them dislike him. Ella hated his conceit and condescending patronage and the way he constantly hinted that, if she was a good girl, he might consider one day making her Empress of Prussia. She pretended not to hear. Victoria was bored by his frequent boasts that he was heir to the greatest throne in Europe while they were only a grand ducal family and poor relations who should do everything he wished.

4

Ella sometimes thought she would have liked to have been a nun, but shied away from the idea of a passive existence. She wished to do good and preferred hospital work and teaching to parties and social life. She realized that she had a curiosity which would not be satisfied by her devoting herself to contemplative religion. In that case, who could she marry, which made her ask herself who was kind to her? That was the first time Ella thought of her cousin Serge as a possible husband, for he was nice to her, although he was ten years older.

She had always found him interesting. As a child, she was flattered and grateful when, while the other great giants, his elder brothers, totally ignored her, he helped her to walk. And later, when she had halted, frightened, he had lifted her over a stream. Last summer, she had felt sorry for the brutal manner in which his elder brothers spoke to him, imitating his voice, tightening their coats to imitate his slim corsetted waist, which they considered a germanic affectation. They sneered at his friends, thrusting him back for company on his younger brother Paul, who, because he was four years younger, adored him. She never could make up her mind what she felt about Serge. He would do her a kindness, she would thank him and look into eyes which looked back at her with such iciness that she wondered what cold thought was passing through his mind.

Nothing had prepared her for the extraordinary drama which took place one summer morning when she was sitting in the shade in the garden at Heidelberg, rehearsing her first public speech. She sat, repeating the last words of her vote of thanks, without being able to convince herself that she sounded natural, wishing bitterly that she had entered more enthusiastically into the lessons of 'the cercle' her grandmother and Miss Jackson had given her.

Ella had decided she sounded so stiff and unnatural she would address a tree as the chairwoman and see if her words sounded better, when she heard a bellowing and screaming which made her jump up and stare through the bushes at an extraordinary scene which had her standing motionless. The three Romanovs were fighting, or rather his two elder brothers had pinned Serge to the ground and the gigantic Vladimir was sitting on his legs while Alexis was pulling his brother's arms back over his head as he steadied himself by pushing his feet against his shoulders as if he was rowing. Vladimir, still sitting on Serge's legs, was aiming with a pair of shears at his brother's stomach. Terrified, she thought that surely not even Russians would cut up their brother in a garden. Serge's yells and the brothers' bellows of laughter suggested a rough game. Suddenly, with a roar of triumph, the two let go and Vladimir stood to attention, saluted and handed a broken, bone corset to Alexis, who pretended to imitate Serge's walk while their victim ran away sobbing. It had been awful to see his tears as he ran past her.

After a while, miserable at his unhappiness, Ella walked nervously down the path and found him lying on a bank, convulsed with sobs. To her own surprise, she went up quite naturally and stroked the back of his head. He started up, thinking it was his tormentors, but seeing his little cousin, lay back, his face on the grass, and sobbed for perhaps a quarter of an hour while all the time she gently continued to stroke the back of his head. She was surprised at herself afterwards for behaving in such a forward, indecorous manner, but all she had done was try and comfort him; she knew no other way.

Then Serge lay still and she could feel him wiping his eyes with a handkerchief. At the same time his body stiffened. The weeping ceased. He stood up, closed his coat over his slashed shirt and looked at her with cold eyes.

'This is to be forgotten, never spoken of again.'

He turned and walked, erect, away.

She was driven into Darmstadt after lunch and later made her little speech to an audience, not of peasants, but of well-to-do shopkeepers and officials' wives, the inevitable audience of any meeting which members of her family attended. She felt uneasy at telling these fat women to take precautions against smallpox which they had already taken, and silly pretending she was doing good when she knew she was wasting her energy.

She arrived back at Heidelberg next day before lunch and had time to change and do her hair before joining the assembly – her father had revived the custom after their mother's death – in the hall for the progress into the dining room. To her surprise, she saw Vladimir, Alexis and Serge standing together laughing as if yesterday's fight had never taken place. She sadly walked away, knowing any little thing would make her cry, and stood by Victoria, who, realizing something was wrong, went on talking while she squeezed her hand.

At luncheon, she sat between Serge and her cousin Louis of Battenberg. During family gatherings she had, from the age of twelve, eaten, as part of her training, with the grown-ups. Louis was in the British Navy, and told her interesting things about ships and his voyages, which was lucky, for Serge, after the coldest of nods, turned his back and never spoke to her. How she blessed her grandmother's training which had taught her to smile whatever her thoughts.

She continued to try, although deeply hurt, to keep a bright face while she asked Louis about Malta, the wonders of modern shipping and how much closer the opening of the Suez Canal brought England to India. She was only half-listening as, although she nodded and smiled, her mind was trying to solve the puzzle of Serge's behaviour. Could the brothers have boasted of their exploit and Serge have blamed her? If so, oh how unfair! Would he give her a chance of explaining, or would he go away thinking her a malicious, shallow gossip? That would be so unjust. Not for anything would she have uttered a single word. She had been so pleased to share a secret with him. Ella half-turned to be faced by the thin, rigid black, and wondered why, if he were so thin, he wore stays. The cropped head remained adamantly away from her. He had judged her guilty. In no way could she explain her innocence and loyalty.

She turned back, and putting on what she hoped was a natural smile, asked Louis about China. He answered at length and she put on her listening face, but when he had finished she could not think what to say next, for although his explanation had lasted the whole of one course, she simply did not know whether he had actually been to China or not. She racked her brains. He was looking at her inquiringly, as if expecting a reply. Panicking, she decided to do what Victoria called an 'Uncle Ernst', which means that when you were asked a question you did not want to answer, or had been thinking of something else and did not know what the conversation had been about, or even if you simply wanted to rest a little, you brought up the name of Uncle Ernst, who was, in fact, the Duke of Coburg, the elder brother of Prince Albert. Immediately attention was given, the last subject forgotten. Reactions depended on the age of your neighbour. A member of the older generation would give you a surprised, shocked look and ask, in a critical voice, what a little girl like you could know about Uncle Ernst; to which you replied that you knew only what you had been told; at which a throat would be cleared and, since the favourite subject of conversation in Germany was too fascinating to drop, you would then hear a long discourse on his sins, with – as Victoria said – all the interesting parts left out.

If, on the other hand, your neighbour was young, you would hear a catalogue of interesting facts. Cousin Henry, for instance, had once told her with pride the names of the mothers of thirty-six of his illegitimate children. The trouble was that, with a huge family of cousins of all ages, you grew up knowing all the facts of other people's lives while nobody ever mentioned the facts relating to your own, the consequence being that you half-understood a lot of things but really understood nothing, remaining innocent about the one thing you should have known.

When luncheon was over, Serge disappeared without a glance in Ella's direction, and that night the Russian cousins took the train east. Ella was bitterly hurt. The injustice of Serge's behaviour and the belief that he thought she had betrayed him made her feel sad for days.

She was still suffering from hurt feelings a week later when her father asked her to go for a walk in the public gardens. She knew he enjoyed these walks, the ceremony of taking off his hat to a delighted subject, the pleasure of remembering the names of those he had only seen once before. While they walked, she found herself thinking of the unkindness of Serge and she heard herself ask, 'Papa, are the Russians a barbaric nation? Miss Jackson said the other day that if you scratch a Russian you will draw barbaric blood.'

To her surprise, her father jumped with embarrassment and looked at her with keen interest.

'My goodness, my girl, what do you know of these things? Who has been talking to you? I suppose it has got to come out, though don't say a thing in public. Trees have ears. Come to my room when you have taken off your galoshes. We'll discuss the question.'

24

Ella had no idea what Papa was talking about, but as he often had odd ideas, she wasn't worried, only amused. He was so put out that he passed two gentlemen of his acquaintance without mentioning their names before looking at his watch and saying it was late when it was early, turning round and walking quickly home, only occasionally slowing down to take off his hat. As the front door closed, he asked her to come into his library as soon as she could, in the manner of a good-natured man who wants to get an unpleasant scene over. She hurriedly got ready and knocked on the door. He was sitting by the fire, his feet extended, twiddling his thumbs in embarrassment. She noticed how the oil lamp by his side was turned down but the light by the armchair opposite turned up; clearly he wished to watch her carefully. Why? She sat down, beginning to feel nervous, on the extreme edge of her chair, and watched her father fiercely poke the fire before he came out with, 'But my dear child, how did you know, who told you? I thought it was a closed secret between Aunt Marie, the Tsar, Alexis and myself.'

She sat silent, wondering what he was talking about. It was not her fault if she was stupid and had not the faintest idea what he meant. 'What secret?' she asked at last in a distressed voice.

Her father looked angry and shouted, 'This damn plan you should marry Alexis!'

'Marry Alexis?' she gasped, thinking of the bearded man pulling Serge's arms back and roaring with laughter.

'Marry Alexis? Why, Mama always said we would never be forced to marry against our inclination, and he's old and horrible and cruel,' she said, thinking again of the scene in the garden. 'I would rather die than marry him.'

'Of course, not now,' her father said, ignoring her last remark. 'But next year you are sixteen and can be engaged and married the year after. All he wants is my agreement to an understanding.'

'Not next year or any year, never,' she replied, ungrammatical in her concern.

Her father was silent for a moment before he said in a relieved voice, 'Well, I am glad. It never worked, you know. My aunt was never happy and the other marriage did not work either. Anyhow, the Tsar does not think Alexis should marry you, which is lucky, although it shows he is a damned fool. I will go and see my aunt tomorrow and tell her you are against it, I am against it, the Tsar's against it, so nothing . . .'

He got up, leaving his sentence in mid-air, and gave the coal a terrific kick to rid himself of his anger. Ella stood up and went and gave him a kiss. He returned it like a sheep pecking, which had the effect of knocking her away from him. With her head still awhirl in amazement, she went upstairs and on the way up decided to say nothing to Victoria. She might think it rude for Alexis to have proposed to the younger and not the elder sister. But then she changed her mind, as she knew that nothing on earth would make Victoria marry him either, and after they had discussed the proposal, which her sister refused to take seriously, she went to her room to think. Alexis's behaviour was so different from a German's or Englishman's that she could not get over it, but perhaps Russia was different, and certainly her cousins always behaved in an unexpected way. Surely it was odd for him to ask for her hand without once mentioning that he had any tender feelings, apart from staring at her like a bear, which was a habit common to all the brothers.

Although her father had said she was safe, the threat still hung over her. She knew how weak he was, but a thought came to her causing instant relief: Grandmama would never allow it. Victoria always said you could learn a lot by watching Grandmama's mouth: if she were pleased it remained straight, if angry the sides dropped. Ella was pleased to remember that whenever Alexis's name was mentioned at Windsor, the mouth turned down into a half-circle of disapproval. Ella, however, also realized that her grandmother would soon be producing suitable prospective husbands. The choice was, she knew, confined to European princes. The year before she had found Victoria trying to write down a list of eligible suitors; together, they had gone carefully through the *Gotha* and found forty-three suitable names. Ever since, they had looked at each other laughing whenever they heard of a crime being attached to one of the 'suitables' and delightedly crossed the name off the list. Alexis had been one of the first to go, and here he was, offering to marry her. But why had Victoria crossed him off? There must have been a reason. She suddenly remembered, jumped up and clapped her hands. Alexis had secretly married one of his mother's ladies-in-waiting.

Ella and Victoria laughed at the idea of the huge Alexis living in such fear of his father that he could not face telling him he was married, and thought how furious the Tsar would be when he found out. Victoria stopped laughing and said, 'But you know, Ella, have you ever thought of what is going to happen to the others when we are married? Of course, Irene will never be a problem. She always does as she is told, tries hard without success at her lessons and is never a nuisance. Ernie is another matter, and has never recovered – I don't think ever will – from the deaths of Frittie and May and darling Mama. Orchie told me the other day that he still wakes up in the middle of the night crying out, "I only wish I could die and go and be with them!" '

Although Ernie was still young, it was obvious that he could not be treated like an ordinary boy, and Miss Jackson for once openly disagreed with the Queen and said it would be fatal to send him away to an English private school and, later, to Eton, and so he stayed at home with tutors who without exception found him unreceptive, except in music and art, in which he was passionately interested. Miss Jackson was dubious and his father disgusted when Ernie discovered a new interest: arranging flowers and spending endless happy days in copying patterns on wallpapers and curtains. His father thought it utter rubbish, and said it was time the boy started to shoot, but when Ernie refused to kill anything, he shrugged his shoulders and said, 'I give him up.' His elder sisters thought their father was unkind and spent more time with Ernie, trying to make up for the sadness which they realized still haunted him. He was easy to talk to and interested in their dresses and how they did their hair, and after a time they realized that they talked to him exactly as if he were another girl, which was hardly right. In spite of their intentions, they could not help keeping on speaking to him in the same way, and when they wondered why, decided it was quite simple: he was more like a sister than a brother. Would he manage when he grew up? His moods changed like the wind: one moment he was hilarious, the next sitting in a corner sobbing. He certainly would make a strange grand duke, and for once they agreed with their father when he said, 'Ernie worries me to death.'

Alix had grown still more possessive. As a small child she had clung to her toys and Ernie, but now she was jealous of anyone and anything. When Ernie once repeated one of her confidences, she shut herself in her room, locked the door and would not speak to him for three months; then screamed and screamed and said she could not live without her beloved brother. He was the only one who made her forget her shyness, which was so acute she could not answer strangers. Her only other close friend was a little girl called Toni Bauer, the daughter of a patron of music, whose father owned a house near Kranichstein and gave, in the summer, musical evenings which Miss Jackson encouraged the girls to attend. Alix would sit for hours talking to Toni, smiling and whispering, but if they even said hello to Toni, her face and hands would turn a violent red and, looking miserable, she would relapse into an agonizing silence. The others found it difficult and tedious to have to remember not to say good morning to their host's daughter.

5

In 1881, their childhood was to end officially with a ball in Darmstadt for Victoria and Ella. Afterwards, their father was taking them to England for the summer season. In one way, they looked forward to an exciting new life, but in another sense, they regretted the end of their own little private world.

A few weeks before the ball a momentous event occurred which changed Ella's life. Every Friday morning at nine o'clock she attended surgeries for female outpatients. One day she was late and heard the doctor examining a poor peasant woman who had come about her knee, which, she sobbed, was causing her unendurable pain. To prevent embarrassment during examination, her whole body was shrouded in a 'nameless sheet' with four openings cut to allow the relevant limb to be thrust into view while the face and the remainder of the body remained completely covered.

Ella closed the door softly behind her and walked quietly towards the inspection couch on which a thick, old woman's leg was sticking through the sheet, while a man, his back half-turned to her, was feeling the knee with long fingers. She watched, unnoticed, fascinated by the most beautiful hands she had ever seen, curved at that moment like a crab's pincers, the joints slightly enlarged, the skin intensely white. As she watched, he ceased his probing and, flattening his left hand, rolled it gently backwards and forwards over the wrinkled knee cap, asking at the same time whether the woman felt any pain. It must have been difficult for him to tell as the grunts from under the 'nameless sheet' might have meant anything. Ella paid no attention to the patient and watched with absolute fascination the rhythm of the doctor's movements. After a moment he shrugged his shoulders and said, 'You have a complaint known as housemaid's knee. I can only recommend treatment which will be of little comfort; put up your knee and rest. I fear this may be impossible for you.'

She often thought about his words afterwards. The sentence was not particularly sympathetic or kind, but he spoke with feeling, showing he understood and sympathized with the woman's life, conveying that he knew her day started early and ended late, that she had to feed the poultry, the pigs, dig the vegetables and cook large meals morning and evening for her family. Was it her imagination, or had he really conveyed these things? For the next two years she would analyse, write down and dwell on every word she ever heard him say.

She only saw him on her weekly visits to the surgery. She scarcely spoke to

28

him. Occasionally, in the operating theatre, he casually asked for an implement or together they might help an infirm patient. Once, in the street, he said good morning; once, during a musical evening at Toni's, he said good evening. She uselessly tried to avoid looking at him in the hospital. Her eyes, against her wishes, followed his every movement. She knew every detail of his slim figure, his face, the clipped, dark beard and moustache, the short nose, the upper lip, the wide generous mouth. The first time she saw his grey eyes in the operating theatre, she felt sick and giddy, and when he had finished examining the peasant woman, she apologized for feeling ill and walked home, her heart thudding.

Her life changed. From then on she thought of him day and night. In the evenings, when she said her prayers, she would try to think of God, but his face would intrude. She knew the exact shape of his ears and once or twice drew them, only to screw up the paper immediately and throw it away. She argued that her love was innocent, her thoughts pure.

She knew that not by the remotest chance could they ever marry and that it was adoration on her side alone, as the next Friday she heard he was engaged to a pretty girl in Düsseldorf. The news did not make her jealous or alter her feelings. No action of his could have destroyed her love. She would have died for him far more willingly than she would have kissed him. Her love made the whole rest of her life seem meaningless.

After their dance, of which Ella remembered little, Victoria had admirers and flirtations and many young men fell in love with both of them. Victoria was pleased. Ella was unmoved, although she loved dancing, caring only whether her partners danced well. She treated her admirers with great kindness, knowing herself the pains of hopeless love, and asked about their lives and families, never flirting or ceasing to think of the doctor. Every moment of the day, she wondered where he was. When it thundered, it was a link between them to hear the same noise; when it was hot, she thought with pleasure how the sun was shining on them both; when it rained, she hoped he wore galoshes to keep his feet dry.

She lived for the present. To think of him was to live a life of romance exalted by the purity of her feeling. She never confided in Victoria, who would not have understood. On the never-to-be-forgotten occasion when he asked her to bring him an instrument to hold open the nostril of a child, she felt a thrill of almost ecstatic pleasure, as if she was sharing with him a momentous event instead of handing him a little blunt pair of tongs. Was she dishonest with herself? How could she have pretended that her love was spiritually pure when she nearly fainted with joy the only time she touched him? An old woman had slipped on the inspection floor. They had gone together to pick her up; she had put her hand behind the trembling old peasant and, dispassionately, he had put his hand on hers. Together they had supported the old woman to a couch. Ella felt as if she had received a physical shock, and when their hands separated, dispossessed, as if he had taken hers away for ever. He must have sensed emotion as he gave a little start. Their eyes met and stayed together and she was sure his expressed astonished admiration. He did not move towards her, but, with a look of faint surprise, turned away. A little later, she heard the poetic phrase 'in thrall'. She felt it exactly described her situation.

29

Soon, while admitting that she was in love with him, she convinced herself it was a harmless, pure love. She asked no more than to see him once a week. After they had looked into each other's eyes, she dared to wonder if he loved her. She hoped not; her love was selfless adoration and she wished him eternal happiness. Her love was her religion. She entwined herself with the beautiful nun in the church at Marburg and persuaded herself she would never know happiness.

Ella's confusing life circled around Fridays. In the preceding days, she was governed by a gathering excitement which made her repeatedly count the hours. On the day, she would with difficulty restrain herself from running as she drew near to the hospital. Her reward was usually no more than to see him set a broken leg or arm or lance a boil. She watched him with a breathless interest. Above all, she loved and admired his attempts to diagnose the exact cause of a pain felt by an old peasant stiff with fear, unable to string two words together. All his humanity and natural kindness came out in the gentle, sympathetic way he put his patients at ease and gradually coaxed them into a state of lucidity which enabled him to understand their muddled fears. These occasions gave her an almost ecstatic pleasure. The experience of love had awoken in her body a desire to live, marry and bear children to teach and inspire, and these wishes were incompatible with her withdrawal from the world.

Her behaviour puzzled her Grandmama, who began to think her a cold, unnatural girl who never took the slightest notice of the good-looking princes carefully placed next to her. She never flirted innocently like Victoria, and took care never to dance twice with a young man, and when they expressed feelings of eternal love, she talked to them kindly but gave them no hope. What gave her great pleasure was to sit next to a young man who Grandmama told her had exceptional charm, and find that however hard she tried she could only compare him unfavourably with her beloved in the hospital at Darmstadt.

One Friday morning, two years after his arrival, Ella, carefully dressed to look unobstrusively beautiful in case he glanced at her during his morning surgery, noticed with interest that his left bootlace was untied. She wondered why as she carefully watched his hands examining an old woman's arm. She had never known him untidy before. Usually every detail of his dress was neat, his hat well brushed, his boots well polished. Why now the trailing lace? She had never seen him in a hurry. What other reason could there be?

Her mind was still dwelling on the puzzle when she heard one of the nurses say casually that it was sad the doctor was leaving in ten days to be married shortly, before joining in a partnership with two successful general practitioners in Hamburg. With difficulty she controlled her face, giving no sign of pain. But, making the excuse she was needed at home, she walked out of the hospital and up through the town to the ruins and found a place overlooking the plain where at last she could cry unobserved. Relieved, she wiped her eyes and admitted that her beautiful but insubstantial dream was over. It was painful to know the truth, and each heartbeat hurt her so intensely that, but for her unhappiness, she would have cried out in pain. Her gloom lifted when she remembered that she would see him again next Friday and fix a picture of him in her mind which would remain with her until she died. Comforted, she carefully wiped her eyes and slowly walked down to the old palace.

That afternoon, Ella accompanied her father, Victoria and the other children to Kranichstein, where they found a dashing young Hungarian, Count Czernin, who was known to be looking for a wife. Immediately he started talking to Victoria, and Ella heard them discussing getting up a four for tennis near the house. She went up to her room. It was a lovely day, and after a time she decided she could not sit and do nothing but would walk to one of her secret places in the woods where she had often found comfort for an unfair punishment as a child. The path ran behind the tennis court. As she turned a corner, she found Victoria kissing the young man. She felt herself blushing with embarrassment but Victoria only laughed and, in the evening, told her with amusement that he had asked if the discovery would mean they would have to get married. She said it meant nothing of the kind and went on: 'It is strange, you know, kissing a man with a moustache – it's like brushing your skin with a clothes brush.'

Ella wished she could be as natural and honest as Victoria.

That night, thinking of the doctor with a sadness beyond tears, she found herself wondering for the first time what it felt like to be kissed. How extraordinary of Victoria to say it was 'like brushing your skin with a clothes brush'.

She turned uncomfortably in her bed, her mind racing from the doctor, to Count Czernin, to her clothes brush. She could not imagine why Victoria had made that strange, rather coarse remark. She felt hopeless, unable to sleep, and after straightening her pillow and turning over at least ten times, climbed out of bed, walked over to her dressing table, sat down and looked in her glass. The face she saw looking back at her was white, with black rings under the eyes. After a moment's hesitation, she picked up a clothes brush and gently drew its bristles across her lips. Immediately overwhelmed by shame and embarrassment, she threw it on the floor, jumped into bed and buried her face in the pillows.

As Friday drew near, she pretended she might not go. Should she or should she not see the doctor for the last time? But all the time she was preparing for the last meeting and, when Friday came, she washed her hair before breakfast and went with her heart thumping so hard that she felt it must be heard by passers-by in the streets.

The doctor was performing a small operation on a forester who had a large splinter in his leg a few inches above the knee. It seemed a curious repetition of the first time she had seen him. Once again, a leg was sticking through the hole of a 'nameless sheet', but this time not the bandy leg of a woman but the thick hairy leg of a man. The doctor was using a pair of pincers, and after extracting the splinter he allowed the wound to bleed to clear away the poison. Then he carefully washed the shaved section of the skin and swabbed the wound as if he knew his work was well done. At the same time, he kept his eyes on the nurse dressing the wound and winding a bandage around the leg. Ella thought he looked so clever, good and capable, that she could imagine no better memory to carry away. Without looking back, she left the theatre.

Ella cried herself to sleep every night for the next two weeks until she persuaded herself that she was behaving self-indulgently. But she could not help feeling lost and sad. Victoria, although she never asked a question, was particularly nice, and Ella often wondered whether her sister had guessed more than she pretended. It was at her suggestion that they went to stay at Heidelberg with Uncle Alexander.

6

The first night she put on her best dress and sat wondering if the doctor was now married. Looking at her watch, she saw she was late and ran downstairs and into the drawing room where, to her amazement, the first person she found was her cousin Serge, who had turned his back on her two years before. He strode up, looking grim as ever, and said he was pleased she had been placed next to him at dinner. When they sat down, he turned to her and talked as if he were delighted to see her, the past forgotten, and she thought how curious he was. He spoke in a sharp, curt voice, asking her one question after another: when had she been in England; how was her grandmother; was Ernie more satisfactory? He paused and, without the slightest warning, asked her if it would be convenient for the Tsar, on his behalf, to ask the Grand Duke for her hand. She was so astonished that, without thinking, she said, 'Oh, you are exactly like Alexis. You have not spoken to me for two years.'

She realized immediately that it was tactless because it would remind him of his humiliation. He said nothing for a moment and she saw he was pale. She noticed, for the first time, how his eyes had flat pupils like a cat's. Despite her interest, she was embarrassed and frightened and turned away without answering.

That night, he asked her again. In her confusion she replied it was not to be thought of. He stared, shrugged his shoulders and walked away.

She could not get his image out of her mind. She liked his tallness – he was six foot four – his elegant slimness accentuated by his, to her mind, detestable bone stays, and was fascinated by her fear of his sudden rages and silences. They different distinctly from the doctor's gentle capability. She knew she did not love him, would never again feel the same wild excitement she had known for the doctor whom she couldn't have married. But did her interest justify marriage? She did not know what to think and half-hoped, half-feared that her definite refusal had put him off. Or had there been a frightening persistence in his cold eyes?

After a few days, Serge turned up at the New Palace and asked Ella again. Again she said no. He was kind to her, but she could never love him as she would always love the doctor. He paid her obvious attention and when Victoria questioned her she made a little face. Victoria's face fell and then brightened as she said she was in love with Louis of Battenberg and, what was more, if Papa agreed, their engagement would be announced and they would marry in the spring. She was sure she loved him. He was straightforward, diligent and hardworking, and very highly regarded in the British Navy, and Grandmama had promised he would soon get promotion.

The news was upsetting. It made Ella feel guilty that her love of the doctor had filled her mind to such an extent that she was unaware of her sister's feelings, and at once she felt insecure at losing her beloved sister on top of her unadmitted lover. Pulling herself together, she hugged and kissed Victoria and thought how lucky she was never to be troubled by fervent beliefs or to have thought of becoming a nun. She had flirtations, but they never made her unhappy. Everybody liked her. She was never shy, never had doubts. Now, placidly in what she called 'love', she was going to be married.

Nothing went wrong with Victoria or ever would. She would always remain her dearly beloved sister whom she knew she could always ask for advice and on whom she would always rely, but at that moment she admitted the inadmissable. Her sister had no doubts because she lacked passion, desire for adventure and depths of feeling. She was safe and limited and would always be happy, serene and contented. But she would miss many things and never have allowed herself to love the doctor, believing that to waste affection on a man you could never marry was a waste of time.

Victoria's engagement was unsettling, indicating the final break-up of the family; next year there would be a strange brother-in-law staying in the house. It was a disturbing thought. At the same time, Ella wondered what had happened to their father. He seemed livelier, sprucer and better dressed than at any time since her mother's death. His walk had a certain jauntiness she had never noticed before, and wasn't it odd that he hadn't noticed Victoria's affection for Louis? Ernie, who was becoming perter every day, said it was the effect of Countess Kolemine. She told her brother to be quiet.

One evening, a week or so after Victoria's startling announcement, Ella went for a long walk through the woods at Heidelberg, following a narrow path she had loved as a child. At one place it led up a hill between pollarded old oaks and came out on a circle of cut grass – a favourite place for picnics. The track continued on the other side of the clearing down the hill, through a wood of tall, silver-barked beeches rising out of a bare carpet of brown leaves. It was a lovely evening, but a slight chill in the air showed autumn was near. At the bottom of the hill a wooden seat overlooked a stream into which, as a child, she had often thrown little bottles, wishing them luck as she sent them off on their journey to the sea. Today she watched the running water and thought how pretty it was beneath the surface, with the mosses streaming before the current. At last she started to walk home.

As she climbed the hill to the clearing, she noticed the evening sun shining above her, cutting straight lines of light through the leaves, and remembered it was a place where, for years, she had played a game with Victoria. The rule was that they stood on a path at either side of the clearing a little way down the slope so they could only see each other's heads, and then walked forward, trying to meet exactly in the centre of the clearing. She could not remember how the game had started, why they played it so long nor when it stopped, but whenever she walked on either path, she expected to see her sister walking towards her.

Smiling at her inevitable memory, she walked up towards the circle of bare grass, the sun shining in her eyes, and stood still in amazement. As Victoria in the old days had walked, so now a figure came towards her, the sun behind casting a long shadow forward. As she watched, the face turned to the right, and the profile, illuminated by the light of the sun, glowed as if on fire. Her dazzled eyes saw the head of the doctor. But how could he be here? She felt her heart beating as the figure reached the summit of the little hill, when she saw, by its thinness and height, that it was Serge. She did not move as he walked quickly towards her and stepped to one side so the sun shone in her face. As she stood, half-blinded, he put both hands on her shoulders, looked down at her and said in a commanding voice: 'You are to marry me.'

Was it because of the strangeness of the meeting, the fact that her heart had leapt when she thought the stranger was the doctor, or simply that the unexpected apparition coming out of the sun seemed to her an irresistible force? Whatever the reason, she said yes. He bowed to her, took her hand and kissed it, but made no attempt to hold her arm as they walked back side by side.

Serge immediately told her father, who curiously appeared to be neither surprised nor interested. Afterwards, they sent telegrams off to her grandmother in England and her other relations. She still did not know why she had said yes and regretted it that night in bed. It was too late. She knew she had committed herself. As usual, she prayed to God, asking Him to help her be a good wife worthy of her husband.

The engagements of the two sisters were announced after the Queen had given her approval, doubtfully in Ella's case, and it was settled that Victoria would be married in the spring in Darmstadt, while Ella, as a result of the Tsar's insistence, would be married in Moscow in June. She would go through two wedding services, the second Lutheran, as her father, showing a belated interest, made her reluctantly promise not to join the Orthodox Church for seven years. Pastor Sell shook his head with pretended dismay, but looked pleased when she told him he would join in the Lutheran service. She saw he would enjoy telling his wife.

The spring and summer consisted of letter writing to friends and numerous new relations she had never met or heard of, but who wrote when her engagement was announced. Every letter was an effort, as often she had to answer questions from unknown relations about other unknown relations. The envelopes needed to be correctly addressed, which was tedious, as Ella could never remember who was a Royal, Serene or Imperial Highness, and Papa, who was trying to be correct again, said it mattered dreadfully; you must be accurate if you do not wish to give offence.

As the day of Victoria's wedding drew nearer, numerous delegations came daily from Hesse, bringing illuminated scrolls of good wishes. At the same time, Ella had to help her sister with letters of thanks for the presents which started to arrive in Darmstadt. Everything seemed to be going well, and the accommodation was fixed for all the visitors, strictly according to precedence, when their mother's brother, Uncle Leopold, died of haemophilia in Cannes. The Queen could not come. The Queen would come. The Queen came.

On the day, her sister looked happy and lovely. The rest of her relations, after strutting around grandly at the wedding ceremony, suddenly, at the reception, turned into school-children producing false noses and comic hats, playing endless practical jokes and roaring and roaring with laughter. Ella walked around smiling. It was hard to laugh uproariously at jokes she knew by heart, but Victoria was happy, which was all that mattered.

Ella was in her room resting when Ernie, who was now fourteen and going through a precocious stage, came prancing in without bothering to knock.

'I say, Ella, have you heard the news? You won't believe it, but Papa has married the Kolemine.'

'Why?' said Ella, who could not think of any sensible comment to make.

'Can't say,' he replied, jumping about in excitement. 'But there is a wonderful row going on. Uncle Bertie was told by Uncle Alexander and insisted Lady Ely told Grandmama, and she is livid, and sent a telegram to the Kaiser, and the Crown Prince is going home in a huff. They are going to make Papa give her up. I hid behind the curtain in Uncle Bertie's sitting room, that's how I know. You should have heard the sort of things they called her! I had no idea she was that bad, and really, it all comes down to their thinking she's not good enough. Apparently they all knew she was what's called a "friend" and that was perfect. But marriage, no. It all drags us down to her level, you see,' and he burst out laughing.

Ella felt sorry for her father. Why shouldn't he marry? But she could not get a word in as Ernie went on in a loud, squeaky voice, 'I can't tell you how funny the conversation was in Uncle Bertie's room. I think I am going to live behind curtains in future. You would not believe what they said about Papa. Uncle Bertie said he was a bloody silly ass, at which Uncle Alfred said he could not understand how Louis could be as stupid as he is, when Uncle Alexander and the Battenbergs are so different and such good fellows, at which, would you believe it, Uncle Bertie burst out: "Of course it isn't strange, you fool – everyone in Europe knows Alexander and the Tsarina are the children of a courtier called Augustus von Grancy. Their mother had not lived with her husband for years and Alexander, as a boy, was packed off to Moscow when his sister married the Tsar. All I can say is that I would rather be a bastard Battenberg than a Hesse. All they have is huge hips and no brains." Wasn't that unfair,' Ernie giggled. 'I haven't got big hips at all and am rather clever. But the comic thing is that Uncle Alexander and all the Battenbergs never stop talking about "our ancestors". Now it turns out that they are not *their* ancestors at all. I can't wait to tell Victoria. It will be useful to her to shut Louis up if he gets pompous, and if he's ever rude to me again I will just tell him he's a bastard-Berg. That will be a good joke, don't you think?'

Ella tried to tell Ernie he should be discreet, but he only laughed and skipped away. It was no good being cross with him. He was either in the wildest of good spirits or in tears. Anything was better than tears.

The Queen was adamant that the marriage should be annulled, and sent telegrams off in every direction. The Emperor of Germany and the Empress Augusta agreed. Poor Papa was treated like a schoolboy and dressed down and bullied until he agreed to an annulment. It was a shame. Ella was sure that her mother would have wished Papa to marry 'the Kolemine' and be happy. Now he would lose both his elder daughters and the woman he loved, all within three months. It was cruel. The relations went around murmuring that it was sad Victoria's wedding was ruined by such an unpleasant scandal, but Ernie said: 'That's nonsense – it is the only good wedding I've ever been to, and nobody's enjoying it more than the relations who, despite pursing their lips and tut-tutting, spend their time in corners whispering juicy bits into each other's ears.'

After a pause, the preparations for Ella's own marriage began. Although she never said a word, she thought that Serge behaved strangely during their engagement. Apart from occasionally kissing her on the forehead, he never touched her. She was glad he respected her shyness, but at the same time felt vaguely disappointed. She did not wish him to kiss her, yet was offended he had not and wondered why.

When Serge arrived at Darmstadt with a leather Gladstone bag stuffed with enormous jewels, she was speechless as she looked at the tiaras, bracelets and the biggest parure of emeralds she had ever seen. Her prospective mother-in-law sent necklaces, more diamonds and pearls in strings so long a single strand reached to the ground. Ella felt sorry that Victoria, who loved jewels, should have had such comparatively mean presents, and was glad her sister was not there to see her Gladstone bag.

Serge took Ella and Irene into a bedroom, where he asked his future wife to put all the jewels on at once. She demurred, and almost angrily he banged on her head the huge tiara of emeralds and, one by one, put on the huge matching jewels. With an excited look, he hung round her waist string upon string of pearls until she had protested that it was ridiculous to wear so many, like an African woman. He paid no attention, almost roughly forcing bracelets on to her wrists and hanging in her ears huge earrings which painfully pulled down her lobes. At last she was so covered with precious stones that she could hardly stand, and Irene said she looked like a Christmas tree, but Serge, his eyes shining brightly, paced up and down, staring at her from every angle, turned her round, looked at her from the back, gave his funny, thin smile and left the room. Ella, Irene and her maid had a terrible business getting the jewels off as they could not find the clasps.

In May, she paid her last unmarried visit to England, where her reception by the Queen, though by no means enthusiastic, was not as dampening as she had feared, although Grandmama was exceedingly dubious about life in Russia and informed Ella she should know something of that barbaric country. She had therefore arranged for her, the next morning, to meet at luncheon a gentleman from the Foreign Office who had a considerable experience of Russian life.

'This is wise, because only too often my children and relations have, as young brides, arrived in their new countries without an understanding of the people and consequently made mistakes both unnecessary and unfortunate.'

The Queen added: 'I gather that Sir Harold – who is a baronet and not a knight, for I would not have knighted him – is a man of great knowledge and understanding but is considered . . .' she paused, and it appeared to Ella that she put relish into her next few words, '. . . both peculiar and indiscreet, which has prevented him from reaching the highest positions in the Foreign Office.

Nevertheless, his knowledge of Russia is considered unsurpassed and his indiscretions may give you an understanding which will prevent your following *his* footsteps and talking too freely.'

Her grandmother, as she was speaking, put her head on one side like a wren and suggested that, although it was wrong of the unknown baronet to be indiscreet, it was sometimes helpful for sovereigns to have such advisers. Ella thought how her grandmother frequently surprised her. On this occasion, she had shown an extraordinary sympathy with a man she would have expected her to dislike. Often she appeared severe and narrow-minded but, if she was interested, she would often show tolerance, sympathy and a sense of humour which suggested she had a wider understanding than was believed. Her appearance changed with her mood; if she was intrigued, the little round body became transformed. You forgot the elderly woman in a chair and faced a clever, understanding mind.

Next morning, a lady-in-waiting told Ella that she, the Queen and Sir Harold would eat at one end of a dining room with Lady Ely and two ladies-in-waiting at the other end in case of emergencies.

'What emergencies?' asked Ella, wondering what on earth Sir Harold was expected to do.

She received no answer and wondered why. The truth was equally startling, for when she followed Grandmama into the dining room, to her surprise Sir Harold was already sitting down, an unheard-of situation which the Queen must have expected, since she said good morning quite naturally and showed no concern as, still sitting, he lowered his head among the silver. He looked definitely odd and was dressed in an orginal style, a silver brocade waistcoat showing through the front of his tail coat. His side-whiskers grew down under his chin, and he had a long, drooping moustache which hung down almost like that of a Chinaman beneath a broad, red, hooked nose which nearly reached his mouth. Ella's confidence was not increased when she looked into lively little eyes that darted up and down, expressing blatant admiration. Grandmama looked at him with interest, and he seemed determined to behave in a manner which showed he was not impressed by his surroundings. The Queen started the conversation by saying her advisers informed her that Sir Harold had unrivalled knowledge of the Russian royal family into which her beloved granddaughter was going to marry, and she wished him to give her an account of the members of the family among whom she would live.

'That, Your Majesty,' said Sir Harold, bowing his head among the silver, 'is a good idea, as it is difficult to ask members of the Romanov family questions about themselves since it is their fixed belief that those who do not know every detail of their lives are rudely pretending ignorance.

'To begin with,' he said, turning to Ella, 'as you certainly do know,' and his eyelids closed as if asking her to excuse him, 'the head of the family is your future brother-in-law, Alexander III, an enormous man' – he stretched two unusually long arms apart – 'and it is one of his proud beliefs that he and his brothers are reincarnations of the giants of old Russia.

'I would point out that the connection is tenuous. The Tsar is only one sixty-fourth Russian and, as you know, princess, a relation of yours. Also you should know, but never mention, that although the family like to consider themselves Romanovs, they are, in fact, through the male line, Gottorb-Holsteins. This information is factual, not critical.'

During the last sentence, the Queen's mouth had begun to curve down, and Ella saw Sir Harold pause a moment as if he was reconsidering his future remarks before continuing in a hurried voice: 'Again, as you will know well, the late Tsar Alexander II, the Grand Duke Serge's father, freed the serfs twenty-three years ago, but they still remain a subject race whose primitiveness is hard for you to imagine. You should prepare yourself for a shock. While the late Tsar was spasmodically motivated by liberalism, the same cannot be said of his successor. He is an autocrat and rules by autocratic methods which you, princess, may dislike, but as Her Majesty' – and his head went down once more – 'has asked me to give you honest advice, I would like to suggest that you keep to yourself any opinions born of repulsion which you may naturally initially feel as a consequence of your upbringing in the gentler communities of Hesse and England.'

Sir Harold now screwed up his eyes and spoke with especial emphasis: 'The autocratic family of Romanov bitterly resent any criticism and show a brutality to newcomers which you would be wise to avoid bringing down upon your head. And anyhow' – he gave a quick smile – 'it is always wise to begin on the right leg. Of the Tsarina, I can only say that she is a sister of our Princess of Wales, although,' he said smiling again, 'she is not one half as beautiful.'

His expression was so comic that the Queen looked at him, threw back her head and gave her silvery little laugh, a sure sign of approval.

'The second living brother, the Grand Duke Vladimir, is also a man of gigantic stature who realizes that his intellect is far superior to his elder brother's. You will also know how the Tsar, having spent his early years in the shadow of a prodigy, his elder brother, now alas dead, whose betrothed he married, quite understandably dislikes his intellect to be unfavourably compared with that of his younger brother. The unfortunate consequence is the exclusion of this able man from the inner circle of government advisers. The Grand Duke has reacted by concentrating on the arts and leading a life which on occasion verges on the bohemian. The coolness between the two brothers has been increased by his wife, Marie, born a duchess of Mecklenburg-Schwerin, a clever woman with that assertiveness found especially in northern Germany among the smaller courts whose dukedoms are, in many cases, lesser estates than those possessed by certain British baronets.'

He paused almost defiantly, and Ella stole a glance at her grandmother, though to her surprise she still sat smiling, nodding her head. Sir Harold continued: 'The consequence is, in short, that you will find the Grand Duchess Vladimir – Miechen to her family – a clever, difficult woman of considerable secondary importance. As she is also the possessor of an exceptionally sharp tongue, I would be so indiscreet as to advise you to tread carefully in your relations with her. She can do you little good; she could do you great harm.'

At that moment, a secretary came up and whispered in the Queen's ear. Ella caught a few words: '. . . foreign secretary . . . immediate decision . . . urgent . . . dangerous consequences . . . only five minutes'. The Queen looked pleased at whatever crisis threatened and walked out of the room after quite obviously telling Lady Ely to keep an eye on Sir Harold, who, now that they were alone, stared at Ella in a manner which made her lower her eyes.

'The third living brother is, as you know, the Grand Duke Alexis, whose huge strength is equalled by his great simplicity – yes, I think that is the correct word – which enables the Tsar to consider his brother of no account and has caused the great autocrat, preferring obedience to talent, to give this indolent brother positions of state which would have been more successfully filled by the Grand Duke Vladimir.'

His eyes sparkled with excitement as he spoke defiantly, 'Also, the Grand Duke Alexis is fond of Paris.'

The little man paused, smacked his lips, looked at her keenly from under his eyebrows and changed the subject while she sat very still, showing no emotion.

'The fourth living brother is fortunate enough to be your future husband.'

Ella could not help noticing that his eyes, which he used to convey nuances of meaning, dropped when he mentioned Serge; it was unfair.

'The last grand duke of this generation is Paul, whose acquaintance I have never had the fortune to make, but I understand he is a pleasant young man and will make a helpful friend for you, princess, in your new and, I am sure, happy home.

'I have spoken of the immediate imperial family, excepting the children, who are too young to mix in society. But the Romanov family is large and all the grand dukes are possessors of enormous wealth. The Tsar's most notable cousins are the Grand Duke Constantine Constantavich and the Grand Duke Nicholas Nikolaevich, of whom the latter is the stronger personality. Although little older than yourself, he has already displayed an independence which has caused resentment.

'There is another danger which I should bring to your attention. Although you will find the family riddled with jealousy, rifts and cabals, any impoliteness to any member of the family by an outsider is considered to be an insult to the Tsar. This fact has not been realized by certain people, who have paid for their ignorance.'

He smiled. 'I am not fatiguing you?'

'Oh no, do go on.'

'Outside the royal family, but allied to them by blood through the female line, are the families of Leuchtenberg and Oldenburg, who are called, in a jocular manner, "the half sovereigns", which anglicism perfectly describes their position and explains the real, sometimes roughly declared feeling of superiority held by the imperial family for these cadet branches.

'That, my dear princess, is all. I hope you will forgive my frankness and any indiscretions.'

At that moment the secretary returned with messages to say that the Queen was detained and to thank Sir Harold for his valuable information. Immediately the strange little man thanked the princess for her kind attention, stood up and walked to the door. To her amazement, Ella saw that he walked with the greatest difficulty, with two sticks, and that while his chest was of normal size, his legs looked tiny and malformed and the back of his tail coat brushed the floor. With every step, the shoulder opposite the foot which he put forward rose and later fell, giving his receding body a strange, jerking, puppet look. She understood his desire to show off and impress, and tried to follow him especially to thank him for explaining to her so cleverly the pitfalls at the court of the Romanovs, but Lady Ely stood up and spoke for fully a minute about the weather.

Half an hour later, a message arrived to say the Queen wished to see her. She had barely sat down before she was asked her opinion of Sir Harold.

'He was most helpful and kind, Grandmama, and very informative concerning the imperial family and all the difficult problems I will have to face.'

'And was he forward or embarrassing in his conversation when I was called away?' the Queen asked sharply, but with, it seemed to Ella, a hint of probing interest in her voice.

Ella felt very protective about the little man with his crippled, dwarfed legs and acute sensibility, which must have made him self-conscious and unhappy. To tell the truth, he had shocked her by the manner in which he had mentioned Paris, but as the last thing in the world she wanted was to cause trouble for the little man, she merely smiled and said, 'Oh no, he was very informative, that was all.'

Her grandmother looked disappointed. Ella wondered afterwards why, and could think of no answer. It was strange, but then Mama had always said that Grandmama was very puzzling.

Two days later, she sadly said goodbye to her beloved Grandmama and her other cousins and friends, and was annoyed at their sad farewells, suggesting 'this is probably the last time we will ever see the poor girl'. She found the attitude maddening, but understood that everything in England was so secure it made Russia appear to them a savage wilderness. The farewells left her more determined than ever to make her marriage a success.

In Hesse, it was even sadder. Delegations came from schools, workhouses and old people's homes and hospitals, bringing presents and illuminated scrolls, and little old women would appear with a horseshoe or an amulet to keep her from harm in the frightening East. She cried herself to sleep on her last three nights, but after days filled with farewells it became at last a relief to set off for Russia.

Part Two
1884–1891

1

Ella travelled with her father by ordinary train until they reached the frontier, where a guard of Serge's Preobrazhensky Regiment escorted them on to the imperial train. The difference was extraordinary. Instead of travelling in an ordinary first-class carriage, a captain in full dress uniform led the way up wide iron steps into a state room with armchairs and sofas and little tables, and, behind, came a dining room to seat at least twelve. Next came their own private sleeping car, which had a large double bedroom and bathroom that she insisted her father used, a smaller double bedroom for herself, four single rooms and a bathroom. Adjoining was a carriage with numerous small bedrooms for members of the duke's household, which consisted of an ADC and his valet.

Further back in another carriage, Countess Olsoufiev, her future Mistress of the Robes (she did not like to say she had not got any robes) was to be found with three Maids of the City (she did not like to ask which city), who continually asked her if there was anything they could do. As she had nothing to do except undress and have a bath and dress again, she could never think of a suitable reply.

The train was completed by two carriages: the first contained four officers; the other, two platoons of fully armed soldiers who embarrassed her acutely before the train started by walking up and down outside her carriage with fixed bayonets. What was much worse, every time she looked out a passing private would snap to attention, fix blank eyes on her and present arms. She tried sitting on the other side, but that was no use, since soldiers patrolling the railway lines immediately caught her eye and went through the same process. She had no alternative but to turn away from the windows, look her father in the face and talk about the amazing flowers. Luckily, this was easy. When she had stepped into the state room she was dazzled at the blaze of whiteness and overwhelmed by the scent of lilies. On either side of both the double beds stood great bowls of lilies of the valley, her favourite flower – out of season, she had thought, so the surprise was a delight. The dining room was as enchanting. On the centre table stood no less than six vases of lilies, while four great bunches of white lilac filled vases on the walls of the corridors. Even in the bathroom, a white orchid hung in a wire frame from the ceiling. Her heart was touched. How kind of Serge to have provided such a beautiful surprise.

After they settled down in the travelling greenhouse, Countess Olsoufiev, an apologetic lady with mousy hair, a thin face and, despite powder, a red nose, came and tapped so gently on the door that for a long time they did not hear her. When at last she ventured in, she brought alarming news: the train was to stop twelve times before Peterhof. At each, the future Grand Duchess would make a short speech, receive principal citizens and accept little gifts from her new countrymen. Ella was horrified. She had practised Russian for six months, but her accent was still bad. At once the countess said she would write down phonetically a few sentences of thanks. The result delighted the elders. As for the peasants, they stared at her open-mouthed in dead silence, holding their caps in their hands. Afterwards, she was told that they thought she was the most beautiful princess in the whole world.

The stops, on Serge's orders, lasted exactly ten minutes. As the train steamed out, she sat by the state room window and waved goodbye. Her instinct told her that the arranged welcomes were false. The crowds behaved quite differently in England, waving and cheering, full of jollity. Here, at each stop, they only whispered as the train steamed away. What with her uneasiness and dislike of saying meaningless words, she was glad when the journey was over and the train arrived at Peterhof.

Ella found the splendour of her bedroom overwhelming. Neither did her new family put her at ease. She felt shy with the huge, surly Tsar, the smiling Tsarina, the unlikable brothers Vladimir and Alexis, and Vladimir's wife Marie Pavlovna, who, unfriendly on her earlier   sits to Hesse, was now as openly resentful as Sir Harold had prophesied. Ella was confused by the countless officials who surrounded the royal family. Many of them looked alike and she could not make out who was who. What was the function of the Minister of the Court, the Grand Cup Bearer or the Grand Esquire Trenchant? She was relieved to encounter the Master of the Imperial Hunt, as he was the one man her father wished to meet. But it was confusing again: 'hunting' in Russia was called 'shooting' in England. The ladies of the court perplexed her even more. Everything seemed confusingly nonsensical and unnecessarily complicated. Her father was still in low spirits, and   ten sighed as he looked out of the window, and later, whenever she went to see him in his gigantic sitting room, Ella knew he was sadly missing his second wife, from whom he was separated, awaiting the humiliating divorce. He had now grown stout and his cheeks baggy. All the life had gone out of him and she knew he longed for the ceremonies to be over so he could return to his beloved home.

A few days after her arrival, Princess Galitzine, the Tsarina's Mistress of the Robes, called and politely handed her diagrams of her position in imperial processions and the names of the functionaries of her own court. She was surprised to learn that she was to have her own chamberlain, but did not like to ask what he did, or interrupt as the old princess muddled on for half an hour with details of protocol and the names, which she could never remember, of her attendants and ladies-in-waiting.

Her greatest surprise came when she learned that she was expected to provide the master of ceremonies with the names of her dancing partners at balls, since no grand duchess could be casually asked to dance. Ella was dismayed and conceived herself spending endless evenings alone unpartnered. She only knew the Tsar and his brothers by name, and she would not dare write down their names. A further distressing thought struck her – how embarrassing it would be if she wrote down the name of someone who did not wish to dance with her. She explained her doubts to Countess Olsoufiev, whom she now called Sandra, who smiled and replied: 'In Russia everybody wishes to dance with a grand duchess.'

After a week of near imprisonment at Peterhof – she was not allowed to see Serge until the wedding – in which her gaolers were dressmakers, she was allowed unofficially, as a special favour, to visit St Petersburg to choose furs to wear in the coming winter. Accompanied by the inevitable Sandra, she travelled by train. When they arrived, a Cossack captain stood outside her carriage and saluted her as she alighted on to the platform. Formally introducing himself, he asked if she would inspect her escort. Outside was a troop of twelve Cossacks in a row, six on horseback, six standing level with the horses' heads. They looked smart and fierce. She inspected them in silence, and afterwards wondered if she should have complimented their smartness. They escorted her to a carriage, which set off to the furriers. At the door, six men dismounted, threw their reins to their mounted companions and placed themselves, three a side, in a guard of honour between the kerb and the shop door. Only when they were standing in position, swords drawn, was Ella permitted to step down and to walk towards the shop.

As she put her foot to the pavement, she saw a little man, oblivious of everything except his thoughts, come hurrying head down along the street towards the guard of honour. He was only a few yards away and looked certain to bump into one of the standing Cossacks. Fearful of the consequences, Ella cried out in English: 'Look out!'

The man stopped dead and looked at her, his eyes slowly returning to the present, as she carefully examined his expensive suit, new shoes and plump, white, gentlemanly face. Suddenly, without warning, he spat at her. A Cossack moved forward, lifting his sword.

'No, no!' she cried in Russian, and the Cossack stood motionless, his sword in the air.

The little man did not back away, but stood still, looking at the Cossack. The expression on his face changed and she saw his lips moving and knew he was going to spit again, this time at the Cossack. Terrified of the consequence, she called again to the man in German, with despair in her voice: 'Please, please don't!'

Did he understand German? Did he realize her fear was for him? Slowly, his surprised eyes looked at her. Then, after taking a step towards the Cossack to show he was not afraid, he turned and walked quickly away. The whole scene took perhaps half a minute. She relived it many times in agony, wondering why the man hated her. He was well fed, well dressed, obviously well educated – why had he spat? If the Cossack had cut down the little man she could not have stayed in St Petersburg.

At Peterhof she mentioned the incident at dinner. Afterwards, the Minister of the Court drew her aside and said she should have let the Cossack cut the man down. 'You never know whom he might spit at next,' he added, shaking his head. She thought of Sir Harold's advice, bit her tongue and said nothing.

2

Ella moved from Peterhof to St Petersburg officially the day before the wedding, on 14 June 1884, and was met at the station by the Empress Marie in a coach made for Catherine the Great with panels by Boucher. All the city stood in the streets to welcome her, and even the windows fluttered with waving hands. She stayed the night with her family at the Winter Palace, but never had a free moment with them. So many last-minute instructions had to be heard, or Uncle Bertie wished to see her with a message from the Queen, or the dressmaker wanted a last fitting, while all her jewels had to be tried on again.

As she was to be married in the chapel of the Great Palace at ten o'clock, she was woken at dawn and, after a struggle with an unknown maid, shut herself in a bathroom and put on her own underclothes. Afterwards, in her dressing gown, she was led into the robing room. On the table lay the Romanov crown jewels, worn by every imperial bride since the reign of Catherine the Great. She examined them with care, but did not dare to touch the gigantic stones.

The ceremony began. A long train of silver cloth was wrapped around her as if she was a Christmas present. The maids curtsied and retired, to be replaced by the stooping, dandified old official hairdresser with a wizened face and a large wig of fair, human hair, who placed her standing in front of a cheval-glass, ran up some little wooden steps and attached to each side of her head two long, dark ringlets of hair which lay like two dead snakes on her shoulders. Next he coiled golden rings around her ears and on them, beneath her lobes fastened two long chains holding up two swinging, perfectly formed, large round diamond cherries. They hung low, half-way down her neck, and when she moved her head sideways to look into the glass, a cherry knocked beneath her chin.

He stood back to look at the effect of his artistry and, satisfied, placed on her left wrist a huge bracelet of matching diamond cherries. Finally, with infinite respect, he climbed up his little ladder and hung around her neck the cold, huge, heavy, double-diamond necklace which had, over the last hundred years, weighed down so many brides. To complete his ceremony of adornment, he placed on her head a giant diadem, in the centre of which sparkled a huge, pink, triangular diamond.

Looking at her glittering reflection in the glass, she pinched her left arm to see of she was awake. The hairdresser, with profuse expressions that he had never adorned a more beautiful bride, bowed himself out, and it was the turn of the 'ladies of the palaces'. They came in one by one, introduced by a formidable lady wearing a diadem nearly as big as Catherine's. Serge had introduced her during the week, but Ella had forgotten her name. Under her direction, the ladies fussed around Ella, placing on her head a lace veil in which they quickly stitched little sprigs of fresh orange blossom especially sent from Nice. To keep the veil in position, a small crown, again Catherine's, a name she never wanted to hear again, was placed behind the diadem on her head, and finally, with everybody pushing, pulling, lifting together, the enormous velvet mantle with a cape and edges of ermine was laid over her shoulders. As if the velvet and fur were not heavy enough, they fastened her train with a huge silver buckle. Every detail had been ordered by Catherine to be worn by imperial brides. The custom would never be changed.

She was now unable to move, and when she tried a step forward could not put her foot down and nearly fell over. All at once, she felt unhappy. It was so unlike other weddings, where the mother and sisters dressed the bride. Here she was all alone, her sisters dressing far away in their own rooms, but she had no time for mournful reflections. The door opened and in came the imperial family, and in the procession led by Tsar Alexander III, her imminent brother-in-law, were her father and brother. Her heart gave a leap of relief to see them. But she was still terrified of the remainder of the ceremony, in most of which she knew she would be accompanied by Alexander, an enormous man with an endless receding brow. When he had called to see her with the Tsarina at Peterhof, his ungainly bulk filled the room. While his wife Marie was easy and welcoming, he had stood silently looking out of the window, obviously anxious to go. When asked a question, he gave a monosyllabic reply and appeared totally un-interested in her. As she was curtseying good-bye, the door was opened by a gruff equerry, and he jumped and looked quickly around, his eyes darting here and there. Ella was amazed that such a huge man could look so vulnerable and frightened.

The memory passed through her mind as the Tsar left the procession and, with great ceremony, handed the thirteen traditional hairpins to the Mistress of the Court, who placed them under Catherine's crown. This was his traditional role in officially fixing on her head the symbol of imperial royalty. To her delight, her brother and father walked over, looking very solemn, though Ernie winked, which was not the right thing to do as now, with his father, he had to play an important part in the ceremony and lead her over to kneel before the Tsar and be blessed with two holy icons which stood upright on bookrests by his right hand.

Papa took her right arm, Ernie her left. The weight on her shoulders eased; her train was lifted. She was told to move forward with small, slow steps. Certain she would fall over and her father and brother would let go, she tottered forward and stood before the ancient holy icons of two saints with long noses and narrow eyes. They reminded her of the pictures of St Elizabeth at Marburg, and the same feeling of ecstasy began to fill her mind until her father whispered in one ear: 'Down', as if he was talking to a dog while, to her horror, Ernie said, almost out loud: 'For she's going to marry yum yum, yum yum.'

Both at the same time pushed her on to the floor. Frightened, she implored

49

her brother to behave, and at the same moment smelt spirits. Horrified, she turned to her father to tell him to make Ernie behave, only to smell spirits again. There was no escape; they had both been drinking. She looked at the Tsar in terror. What if he flew into one of his terrible rages? But, apparently, noticing nothing, he lifted one of the two icons, made the sign of the cross over her head, put it down as if he was in a hurry, lifted the other and quickly repeated his blessing. Rubbing his hands together, the huge man came and stood over her, smiling, sure of himself, fearless, before bending down, placing his hands beneath her elbows, and lifting her up like a feather.

The procession to the chapel came next. Looking over her shoulder she saw, bending down to pick up her train, a whole flock of unknown train bearers, and again had to cling to her father at the change of balance when the train was raised and nearly pulled her over backwards. Once again she moved forward, hot and tired, wondering what would happen if she fainted. The chapel was boiling hot and she concentrated all her efforts on standing up and kneeling down at the right time. Beyond these worries, she later remembered silver and golden chasubles moving backwards and forwards, and endless comings and goings by bearded priests and bishops who looked all so similar that she could not tell them apart, any more than she could make out what they were doing, which was not surprising, as she could not understand a word of their chants. But when the communal singing started again, it was much better, and she felt infinitely touched by the many voices raised to God asking for her happiness.

Of the crowning and the remainder of the service she remembered nothing, and was amused when she was afterwards praised for her beauty, poise and dignity; which was reassuring, for she had not the faintest idea how she had behaved and was only aware of being married when, after three and a quarter hours, she left on her husband's arm to be married again in the Lutheran church.

Just before six, after ten hours of standing, the reception came to an end. Given a merciful reprieve, she was allowed to retire to an apartment, take off her robes and have a short rest. Dinner followed at a table the shape of a horseshoe. To enable every guest to see the bride, she sat to the right of the Tsar with Serge on her own right. Looking round anxiously, she saw Ernie talking excitedly, which was dangerous, and her father looking very sleepy. Dinner was not easy. The Tsar grunted when she spoke to him but otherwise was silent; Serge spoke only to the Tsarina. At last the meal ended, and on the Tsar's arm she led another procession to the ballroom. As they entered, the orchestra played the first notes of a polonnaise, a dance which Ella had practised all the previous week. The dancers went three times round the room, holding each other's hands, delicately bowing and curtseying at the beginning and end of each round before changing partners. The Tsar opened the dance with Ella, and was strangely light on his feet for such a big man, which was a pleasant surprise, but it would have been nicer if he had spoken an occasional word. She had asked for Ernie to be her partner for the second round. The request violated protocol, as she should, by tradition, have danced next with her father, but he hated dancing, moved like an elephant and would have trodden on her dress or brought her down. No official had the authority to grant her request.

50

Eventually, it went to the Minister of the Court, who brought it to the attention of the Tsar, who, after some hesitation, agreed.

Now she wished that she hadn't made the request. Anything would be better than dancing with Ernie, who, clearly drunk, was at times laughing loudly and at other moments standing still with a glazed look on his face. As he faced her for the beginning of their round, she willed him to behave. She curtsied, he bowed, as they touched hands he winked again and sang: 'It's true my prospects all look blue but don't let that unsettle you. Never you mind, roll on.'

She paid no attention, and at the final bow he said again stiffly: 'Never you mind, roll on.'

'Oh please, please, Ernie,' she whispered, looking at him imploringly, but he only winked back.

She danced the last round with her brother-in-law Paul, and saw to her horror that Ernie was standing opposite the Grand Duchess Constantine, a terrifying-looking old lady who, Serge said, lived in the past and was exceedingly old-fashioned and disagreeable. Paul moved beautifully, although by this time she was so tired that she thought she could fall asleep as she danced. The polonaise ended. Paul bowed, Ella curtsied and looked round for Ernie to see his partner backing away from him, a scandalized look on her face, while he followed, looking fatuous, trying to explain a funny joke. It was no good. She stalked away and Ella died a thousand deaths for her brother when she saw that the Grand Duchess had stopped by the Tsar, rapped out an angry sentence, turned and pointed an accusing finger at Ernie. A look of surprise came over the Tsar's face as he looked intently at her brother. What on earth was going to happen? Why, why had stupid Ernie made a fool of himself? At that moment the silence broke. The Tsar bent forward like a broken tree, and out of his huge frame came a gigantic bellow of laughter. There was a moment's silence, followed by a hum of relief, and she noticed how all the weak-looking men burst out laughing as if they alone appreciated the imperial sense of humour.

The Grand Duchess Constantine stood for a moment, aghast. Then, with a look of indescribable disdain, she turned from the Tsar with only the faintest bob and stalked across the room to collect her husband, leaving Ella's new brother-in-law thundering with laughter and holding Ernie with his huge left hand while, with his right, he clapped him again and again on the back, each blow causing her brother's head to go backwards and forwards. Ella thanked God that her new brother-in-law had a strange sense of humour and, looking round to change the subject, pointed to a little wooden-legged card table surrounded by old chairs which stood unused at one end of the room. Each time she passed the odd little group of furniture she had stared, wondering who was going to play cards on such a shabby table for, although it was covered in velvet, the material was now creased, threadbare and faded. On either side of the table lay piles of ivory and gold fish counters and two little slates with golden edges on which were thin, newly sharpened pencils of solid chalk. In the centre, lay a pack of immensely old, warped cards. The chairs stood on either side, one straight-backed, uncomfortable; the other the size of a sofa, upholstered and torn, with faded old blue silk and, beneath it, a large tattered footstool. At one side stood another little gilt table with a round, malachite top on which stood a silver jug and a magnificent jewelled Byzantine cup.

'Who plays cards there?' she asked Paul.

'Catherine the Great,' he replied, a smile of ineffable superiority on his face as if he sympathized with her for not having such traditions in the lowly Hesse family.

Shortly afterwards, Serge drove her and the Tsar to the Old Palace where the Empress and Vladimir received them on the doorstep with bread and salt on a silver platter. She thanked God that these were the end of the customs and ceremonies and that she was now allowed to retire to prepare herself for the night journey by imperial train to Moscow.

When they left, the young relations threw handfuls of rice and tapioca at her as hard as they could. She was too exhausted to feel pain, and never knew how she climbed into the train, but she was certain she fell asleep before her head touched the pillow. Where Serge slept, Ella never knew.

3

In Moscow, they stayed in the Kremlin. The colossal walls convinced her that she was in a prison and, despite the excitement of seeing such an amazing town, she was pleased when, the next afternoon, they drove off to her new home, Serge's country house, Ilonskoye, twenty-three miles to the south-west. She had been surprised by photographs, which made it look like a large, *nouveau riche*, pretentious house similar to many large villas on the Thames which she had noticed from her grandmother's pony cart during the drive from Windsor.

As they drove along, she occasionally turned her head and saw Serge sitting unmoving, hunched up in his corner. She thought she had never seen his long, thin frame look so crooked before, and wished he would speak. Perhaps it was the fault of her stupidity. They stopped once to change horses, and to her astonishment the posthouse was immediately surrounded by hundreds of peasants who, as she stepped down, murmured before prostrating themselves. An officer was waiting and handed Serge a telegram. Ella fidgeted, embarrassed and self-conscious as the two men continued to talk. After staring at the ground, she looked desperately at the crowd and smiled and noticed, not for the first time, the difference between the men and the women. The men gazed at her fixedly with unblinking eyes, exactly as they had done at the railway stops, and the fact that they paid not the slightest attention to her smile disconcerted her and made her feel uncomfortable. The women, on the other hand, gazed openly, taking in her dress, her hat, her pearls, their eyes darting brazenly from one part of her dress to another as they whispered laughing to each other, their eyes bright with excitement and interest and, she hoped, kindness.

The posthouse was exceedingly dirty, and to avoid sitting down and catching the famous fleas, Ella walked back and forth while Serge, his conversation finished, looked silently out of the window. She wasn't sorry to get back into the carriage again, although once more Serge disconcerted her as he rudely ignored the crowd, never once looking out of the window. Ella smiled good-bye, and at once all the peasants bowed from the waist, their noses nearly touching the ground.

When they arrived at Ilonskoye, the under-agents, farm bailiffs, the head of the dairies, grooms, foresters, keepers and so on stood drawn up in a long line beside the front door and, at the other side, between two policemen holding truncheons, stood a large crowd of workmen, and behind them a mass of women and children. Once again, their arrival was greeted with dead silence, and Serge, without looking round, led an inspection, walking unbending in front of her, introducing her to the heads of departments in a harsh voice, giving her only time to shake hands quickly. Without a pause, they walked in the same way down the rows of employees. The introductions appeared so cold and rude that twice she waited behind her husband, first to say a few words to a forester who turned deathly white, and secondly to speak to an old gardener who leaned on his stick and was, she learned later, blind. Each time Serge waited impatiently, looking back at her with irritation. When the inspection was finished, she stood on the steps with Serge and ate the traditional bread and salt before waving to the crowd of women and children, who sang a melancholy hymn. She did not understand a single word, but tried to wave cheerfully again and followed Serge into the house. In the hall stood another line of household servants, and again she saw that Serge was irritated. The housekeeper gave a low curtsey and presented to her the keys of the house.

'Thank her and give them back,' said Serge.

She did as she was told and they walked upstairs and turned down a long passage to the southern end of the house, which looked over the garden and the river to an endless plain. He then spoke for the first time since leaving Moscow, telling her how his mother built the house in 1870. Upstairs, every bedroom was furnished with a large mahogany bed, dark velvet curtains and numerous black oil paintings. Serge told her that, with three exceptions, she could do what she liked with the house, and in the next few days to make up her mind and tell him her wishes so he could give the orders. Her bedroom luckily had a brass not a mahogany bed, but it was surrounded by tables and chairs and icons so dark she could not make out who or what they portrayed.

Ella made up her mind to copy the bedrooms at Darmstadt and Kranichstein, copied, in turn, from Osborne and Windsor, with their chintz curtains and white-painted walls. She could not wait to do away with the mahogany, the icons and the heavy velvet. Once the gloomy place was more like her old homes she would, she hoped, feel less lonely and far away from her family. As she stood looking out of the window, two maids came in and curtsied and started taking off her coat. Serge looked at his watch, announced that dinner would be ready in forty minutes and went to change.

Ella had always loved clothes and jewels and her second trousseau from the imperial family staggered her. She could not believe that any girl could have so much. How lovely it would be to put on a new dress every day. As for her jewels, which filled two large cases, she had never let them out of her sight since leaving Moscow. It seemed like a dream to be the owner of such pearls, rubies and diamonds, and the most magnificent emeralds in Russia, so splendid that her sister-in-law, the Tsarina, had said to her in a laughing voice: 'Please say when you are going to wear your emeralds so I will know not to put on my own poor stones and be outshone by my beautiful sister-in-law. Not that, my dear, your beauty doesn't outshine me already. I think my brother-in-law and Russia are lucky to have you as his wife.'

The maid knocked at the bathroom door and asked to come in and dry her. She said no, adding that she never wished her maids to enter her bathroom. She had never dressed or undressed before anybody, except her sisters, and she found it strange the way her husband's relations allowed maids to come into their bathrooms and even, it was said, wash them while they lay motionless in the hot water. The idea was mortifying. Surely it was demeaning to treat people as if they had no feelings or refinements of their own.

Ella dressed simply, without a necklace, for the first evening in her new home and found it rather a relief not to be weighed down by precious stones. Looking in the mirror, she saw that the excitement of arrival had brought colour to her cheeks and that the many gas lights in the house lit up her gold auburn hair which, catching the reflections, gave her an aura of fire. It annoyed her when she saw, in the looking-glass, how pretty she was looking and how badly she photographed. Her nose and chin were both too pointed. As Victoria said, her prettiness lay in her expression, colouring and smile, and you could not go on and on smiling at photographers. It would look too silly for words. She looked at herself again. Her auburn hair grew in thick waves. Her skin was a dazzling pink and white. A woman of great beauty stared doubtfully back at her. She could not help being pleased and stared at herself, satisfied at what Serge would see.

Serge returned in exactly forty minutes, pleased she was ready to go downstairs. Dinner was not an amusing meal. Her husband sat silently at the other end of a long table, looking down at his plate, sampling without enthusiasm the endless courses. She flushed for his bad manners, but at last, in the same cold, disinterested tones which he had used to introduce her to the servants, he explained to her in French that she had made a serious mistake on arrival, and when, in future, they inspected nurses or school-teachers or local officials, she was never to stop to talk on her own initiative but to wait until he told her she should. In future, he would touch her hand and say quietly, 'Two ahead.' On these occasions, she was never on any account to have a conversation which lasted more than half a minute. She blushed, apologized and smiled at him. He looked at her with staring eyes that, she was sure, saw through her, and said in a cold, harsh voice: 'You are the most beautiful woman I have ever seen, but I wish you to wear jewels for dinner. Please do so in future.'

He seemed about to say something else, but changed his mind and kept on staring at her in a way which made her wish to look away and wonder whether dinner would ever end.

At last it was over, and Serge led her around the downstairs sitting rooms, which pleased her by their unexpected simplicity. The rooms looked far nicer than the grand, overwhelming, high-domed state rooms in St Petersburg and the Kremlin. As they went out of each room, he said: 'Do what you like, but inform me of your wishes and I will give the orders.'

She was pleased and quite understood that he should wish for his own bedroom and sitting room and the billiard room to remain unchanged.

When the tour was finished, he excused himself, saying he would return in exactly one hour, and left her sitting by the fire in her sitting room. She was not frightened, but she felt different. Surely it was not Ella sitting there, a girl who all her life had eaten with her father and family, but an unreal stranger alone in a house which was now her home, waiting for her husband.

55

She sat, remembering details of her childhood, and woke up with a start, not knowing where she was. It was late. In horror, she ran upstairs and rushed along the passage, but before she had time to undress, Serge came in and said, without emotion, it was time for bed and went out again. She sent the waiting maid away – she really could not bear these strange young women hanging round her all the time – and went into the bathroom, put on her nightdress and dressing-gown, and going back into her bedroom, quickly jumped into bed, pulling the sheets up to her chin. Serge came back in a few minutes, a small case in his hand, and climbing into the other side, lay back and looked at her as she lay trembling, giving him a half-smile. She was not certain what was going to happen, for although Victoria had told her how wonderful marriage was, they had both blushed and shirked discussing details. She was determined not to be silly.

Nothing happened. Serge gave her a faint, impartial smile, opened his case, read through some papers and, one by one, laid them in a neat pile on his bedside table. She looked at him now and again and saw the pile of papers growing, and the next thing she knew it was morning and another maid had come in to ask her whether she wished to breakfast in bed or downstairs. She said, 'Downstairs, of course,' and later spent the morning going round the house with men from shops in Moscow whom Serge had sent for without bothering to tell her. The agent asked her always to write down all her wishes to enable him to ask the Grand Duke to initial her requests. She spent the next few days choosing carpets and curtains, looking at pictures and testing the new French box mattresses which had just come into fashion.

After a week, she did not know what to think. Their relations remained unchanged. Her mind was divided. In one way, she did not wish, although he was her husband, for Serge to kiss or touch her, but, at the same time, she was married; and although she did not love him, she had married him, and longed for children, and hated the embarrassing uncertainty of not knowing what was to happen to her. As she had nobody to confide in, she wrote to her family, saying how wonderfully happy she was with her kind and thoughtful husband. After tea each day he arranged for her to write thank-you letters for their wedding presents and laid down the length of her letters. To kings or presidents she should write at least two pages, to princes and grand dukes one and a half, to minor royalties a page, to the nobility a few words of appreciation, and to the thousands of people who had sent her little things like apples or egg-boxes, she should sign her name on a printed form of thanks. She tried at first to ignore the last instruction and write to all those who had sent her pathetic little presents, but she could never write two thousand letters, and soon gave up. Every evening Serge kissed her goodnight. Every morning he had left her room before she was awake and bowed to her politely at the breakfast table. Increasingly fearful that she had somehow behaved stupidly, she went on writing to almost unknown cousins, saying how happy and lucky she was. She could not hide from herself her worry, but consoled herself by remembering that, in a few days' time, they would leave for the Crimea to stay in a house belonging to their country neighbour, apparently the most beautiful woman in Russia – Zenaïde – whose father, Prince Youssoupov, had lent them his villa. Surely there her life would change. During the long drives and silent meals, she examined her husband carefully. He was certainly good-looking, but his cold eyes dominated his face and she wondered what he was thinking. However firmly she put the doctor out of her mind, he crept in again, but she found at the same time that she was more often thinking of Serge, which was what she had prayed would happen, and was surely a good sign; and she only hoped that she had not in some way offended him.

One evening he said that he planned to drive the next day to a distant estate and inspect the woods. Ella was enchanted, and obtained his reluctant consent that she should arrange the picnic. He wished to start early in the morning in a dog cart he had imported from London, which made her homesick for her childhood. But she was up before dawn and, to the chef's amazement, insisted on preparing the picnic herself. She packed the wine, fruit, eggs, butter, and a little spirit stove on which she was to show off her skill to Serge, who was astonished and shocked that she could actually cook. He expressed intense disapproval of her mother's insistence that her children should be brought up to look after themselves.

It was a lovely, faintly misty morning, promising a hot day, and as Serge drove away, a young kitchen boy came rushing out, and running as fast as he could, overtook the dog cart and handed a parcel to Serge, who, without a word of thanks, threw it casually under the seat.

'What is it?' she asked.

'Oh, it's just jars of caviare and *foie gras* in case you are not as good a cook as you think – I want to ensure I have something to eat.'

She looked at him with a smile and was about to say it was unworthy of him to be so distrusting when she saw that he was perfectly serious and meant exactly what he said: he wanted something good to eat for lunch, and there was nothing the faintest bit funny in his distrust of her or the precaution of taking alternative luxuries. Ella gave a little sigh, and they drove on in silence.

'That is the way to Arkhangelskoye, the Youssoupovs',' he said, pointing to a turning just outside the park. All she could see was some distant trees. There was a faint wind, and the rather thin crops of corn on either side of the road rustled. Far away on a small hilltop he pointed to a castle, a rarity in Russia, and remarked in an angry voice how ridiculous it looked. She wondered why, but did not like to ask.

A few miles further on, they passed, on their left, great gates leading to another house, which, he said, belonged to one of the oldest families in Russia, the Cherentevs. Ella would meet them on her next visit. He hoped she would behave with decorum. She flushed with anger. It seemed to her that everyone in Darmstadt, even the poorest, behaved with more decorum than these despots, but she said nothing.

After driving another two or three hours through the endless sparse, thin-stalked corn – she had never seen corn look sad before – she began to wish desperately for Serge to say something. She was disappointed as they drove in absolute silence until, at last, they reached a huge pine forest and a head forester waiting by a pony trap, cap in hand, to greet them. Serge gave a nod, the man jumped into his light cart and led the way down a sandy track. From time to time they passed foresters along the road who, although ignored, abased themselves before Serge like slaves. The pine trees looked identical, but Serge occasionally stopped, measured their girth, made notes in a little book and drove on before repeating the process. Ella wondered which was the saddest, the pine woods or the endless flat, thin cornfields, both of which made her long for green trees and valleys and the thick, rustling fields of wheat which grew on the plains north of Darmstadt.

At last, at 12.30, Serge said he was hungry and told the forester to lead them to the centre of the forest, where he planned to eat. Suddenly, to Ella's delight, the pines ended and they drove through a parkland of widespreading oaks separated from each other by patches of bramble and bracken. At last the sandy road ended in a perfect grass circle surrounded by lime trees, dissected by avenues. In the centre stood an enormous, perfectly shaped oak, resembling a huge mushroom.

Serge dismissed the forester without a word of thanks after he had dropped a boy who, while they watched, took the pony out of the shafts, gave it a nose-bag, tied it in the shade and vanished. Serge strolled off without speaking, and Ella, looking around, was entranced to find two little seats cut out of the living wood at the base of the tree with a small, rough table facing them. She unpacked the stove, which was, to her relief, unbroken, laid a white tablecloth on the table, put out knives and forks and lit a little fire to make toast for Serge to eat with his *foie gras* and caviare. Then, behaving professionally, she broke six eggs into a bowl, whipped them up, cut up mushrooms she had picked in the woods the day before, opened the white wine from the Tsar's estates in the Crimea and, when Serge returned, said proudly: 'Everything is ready.'

He nodded, sat down without speaking, spread his toast with a thick layer of butter, covered it with *foie gras* and spread, over the two, a thick layer of caviare. She did not like the look of such richness and was relieved that he only ate one piece of toast. The great moment had now arrived: the preparation of the omelette.

Everything went right, and as the eggs bubbled in the frying pan she dropped in the slices of mushrooms. Even the turning over went well, and the omelette was unbroken when she put it on to a large white plate. Serge nodded and said nothing. To her surprise, he ate the whole omelette, leaving none for her, and washed it down with glasses of white wine, of which he also offered her none. But she did not mind as long as he was happy, and the fact that he had eaten the omelette must have meant he liked it. Nevertheless, she admitted to herself that she would have liked him to say one word of thanks.

Afterwards, they moved round the tree, away from the dining table, and sat on two more seats cut in the wood. Serge produced a book and said he would be grateful if she would read to him while he rested after the meal. She could not remember what the book was called, but it dealt with society life in St Petersburg and Paris. She could hardly stay awake, let alone understand what it was about. Both of them must have fallen asleep at the same time, for when she woke up an hour later, Serge was still contentedly snoring with his head slumped forward. Very quietly, Ella stood up and washed and dried the plates, packed up the stove and stacked everything away neatly by the cart so Serge wouldn't be kept waiting. At last he stretched himself, stood up, walked over to examine the pony, cupped both hands to his mouth and shouted loudly for the boy to put it in the shafts. When their lunch was packed away he climbed into the cart first, and she did not even have time to sit down before he roughly jerked the reins and brought the whip down on the pony's hind quarters. The boy, ignored, remained behind, and as the pony, swishing his tail, careered down the road, Ella wished she was not always finding fault with her husband.

Although it was the hottest part of the day, Serge, without consulting her, continued on his apparently endless inspection of the plantations. Ella tried to find it interesting, but could not possibly think of anything to say about the pines. As she was becoming exhausted, they stopped and drank cold milk in a woodman's cottage. Revived, she felt contented and happy as they drove slowly home, although Serge had not said a word since lunch.

At dinner, he did not speak to her either until, in desperation, she asked him if he could get her a copy of *Anna Karenina* in French as wherever she went, and especially at Miechen's, she was asked her opinion of Tolstoy, and she felt stupid at having to reply that she had never read a word of his books. Serge frowned and said it was, in his opinion, not a book for her to read, and he would buy her other novels if she had not enough to do in the house and garden. Again she felt a flush of anger, but told herself to be quiet and obey her husband while a small, sly voice said: 'Read the book without telling him and then everybody will be happy.'

Over the next two days, they drove to other estates, once lunching with the bailiff, but on the second day she fried him hot sausages and chicken in breadcrumbs. Ella felt positively flattered on the second picnic, as he brought neither *foie gras* nor caviare, but she would have been happier if he had only said a word of appreciation.

Time passed quickly as she became absorbed in making plans for the house and garden, and she was amazed to find that their visit was nearly over, and that the next evening they would travel south to stay at the Youssoupovs' house in the Crimea. All at once she was excited again, and in her imagination conceived the Crimea as a romantic Isle of Wight. The way in which Serge ignored her was surely a phase, and perhaps it had been a mistake to go to his country house where he was so busy. She was certain that he would change in the south and all would be well.

But, despite her determination to look on the bright side of her marriage, Serge's neglect worried her more every day as she was beginning to think that instead of drawing closer they grew further apart. She had heard her father say that his aunt, Serge's mother, was too weak to bring up and discipline her children. Remembering her frail old great-aunt, she was sure her father was right. Obviously Serge was never denied anything, or taught that he could not reach out and take whatever he wanted without either politely asking or expressing his thanks. She hoped she was not being disloyal to her husband in deciding that she would bring her own children up in a very different way.

4

Ella was awake before dawn on the morning of their departure, first to Moscow and later, by night, to the Crimea. She was too excited to stay in bed and was dressed by the time a maid called her. Her sadness at leaving Ilonskoye did not stop her enjoying the journey to Moscow and their lunch with the Governor-General, but all day she looked forward with childish pleasure to the beginning of the journey south, where, she was sure, her hopes would be fulfilled. She could hardly contain her elation as the time to catch the train drew near. Her pleasure must have improved her looks, for on the way to the station Serge stared at her with admiration and said slowly, 'You look beautiful today.'

She flushed with pleasure and impulsively clasped his hand, feeling utterly happy, certain that his neglect was over and enchanted at having their own imperial train to take them on the long journey to the Crimea. Serge had further news: from now on she would have in attendance her Mistress of the Robes, Countess Olsoufiev, and six ladies-in-waiting, but only Countess Olsoufiev and two ladies would be coming to the Crimea on the train. He would probably have five gentlemen in attendance, consisting of three officers of the Preobrazhensky Regiment and two civilians. They would be introduced the next morning. Tonight he and Ella would eat alone in the dining room.

'Your two ladies-in-waiting,' he added, looking at a bit of paper, 'are Princess Natalie Oblensky and Countess Anna Tolstoy.'

Ella had wondered who Anna was and asked, 'Is she the great writer's daughter?'

'Great writer?' he said in a cold voice. 'Leo Tolstoy is not a great writer. He is an instigator of revolution and my brother should send him to Siberia.'

Momentarily she was too discouraged to answer, but Serge continued, his voice losing its coldness, to tell her the names of his officers and gentlemen in attendance. She could not understand his pronunciation and, anyhow, all the names sounded so long and complicated that she would never remember them.

Her pleasure dimmed a little by the idea of so many unknown attendants, Ella stepped out of the carriage at the station to find before her a roped-off space lined by soldiers standing a yard apart, holding with one hand rifles with fixed bayonets and the rope with the other. All round the ring stood knots of men and women, collected together by curiosity to watch the departure of a member of the imperial family. Ella was looking with distaste at the military scene when she suddenly saw, looking over the rope between two soldiers, a familiar face. The big nose, the loose mouth, the clean-shaven, running-away chin and the long, dark, greasy hair which she could see hanging down under a big black hat could belong only to one person.

'Oh, it's Jacob Rubinstein!' she cried. For three Septembers running the Russian pianist had played at concerts in Darmstadt. She had met him often at the house of Toni Bauer's parents. Sometimes he had helped her clumsy efforts, but always afterwards, as if to wipe the memory of her discordant sounds away, played for a few minutes to himself. Realizing the unbridgeable gulf between them, she had sighed, 'I wish I could play like you.' He would stand up and walk away smiling. Never was he unkind or superior, and even Miss Jackson liked him.

The memories passed through her head and, remembering Jacob Rubinstein's kindness, she ran between the soldiers, reached over the rope and took his right hand in both of hers, saying, 'I am pleased to see you – we must meet again. Tell me quickly where you live.'

Then she felt her left arm gripped and, turning round, saw Serge towering above her, trembling so much that she wondered if he was ill. At the same time, she noticed the soldiers had dropped the rope and turned their bayonets towards poor Rubinstein, who, dismayed, quickly took two steps back, the crowd moving with him.

'How dare you speak to this filthy little Jew,' Serge said slowly and distinctly. 'Follow me.'

She had not much choice, for his fingers half-lifted her over the platform. Hot with shame and horror at his behaviour, she was helplessly jogged along.

When they reached their carriage, Serge, still cold with anger, dismissed the station master and attendants without a word of thanks, and told the stewards to go away. As soon as they were alone, both still wearing their overcoats, he told her that the Jews had murdered his father and tried to kill his brothers several times. He knew that one day they would kill him. Never should she forget how these people had spilt Christ's blood and plotted the Empire's ruin.

She sat down in one of the armchairs fixed into the floor and said she was sorry, but Rubinstein had never and would never shed anyone's blood. She realized she knew little of the actions of the rest of the Jews in Russia, and understood how Serge must feel about the race who had killed his father.

Hoping he might recover his temper, she went to change, but all through dinner Serge spoke of the crimes of the cursed race; how they battened on and ruined the peasants; how they organized revolutionary movements dedicated to the overthrowing of the Empire; how they smuggled in anti-imperial propaganda; how they manufactured bombs and carried out ritual murders. She was astonished by how little she knew of Jews, except for the polite men in black who had always bowed when they saw her in Darmstadt, and the gentle musicians. She did not argue with Serge, and sat silent, but she couldn't make herself believe his diatribe. He appeared to sense her doubts and stood up after the coffee, excused himself and stalked off to his cabin. Ella prayed that she might understand him, for it was the duty of every wife to help her husband, but she knew she would really have liked to slap his face.

After a long, tedious journey, with Serge still sulking, they arrived at the station. As she stood on the platform, she smelt the faintest scent of roses. In the open carriage sent to meet them, she was overwhelmed by the rich beauty of the countryside and the extraordinary caressing warmth of the air. Prince Youssoupov had lent them Kolutz, a large black and grey house which reminded her of Cliveden. She could not wait to walk through the garden with Anna, and was astonished at the number of terraces, which were lined with statues and fell, one after the other, towards the sea. They passed Dianas and Davids, gladiators, lions, bulls, Apollos, fierce Tartars and, when at last they reached a jetty, found to their amazement, with an owl on her shoulder the size of a baby, an enormous woman who Anna guessed to be Minerva. Beyond the goddess, a hundred yards from the land, a sea nymph sat on a rock. Ella sat down and looked across the water and then back up the hill to the confusion of statues and flowers, and thought that surely such a place was made for happiness, and that she had made a friend of Anna, admiring her fresh skin, natural red lips and kind, pretty, round face, while knowing she would never feel at ease with the dark-haired Natalie Oblensky, in whose narrow eyes she could never read a meaning.

The richness of Russia shocked and amazed Ella. In this property belonging to a man who was not even a member of the imperial family, she had seen, while walking through the gardens, more labourers than her father employed in all his country houses. She wondered whether this plethora of riches was not the cause of Serge's boredom and coldness.

During the first two days, she saw only glimpses of her husband as he was busy from morning to night, but on the third morning she received on her breakfast tray a letter saying he would not be back that night but would, on the next day, meet her at a country inn for luncheon, from where they would travel into the hills to spend two nights at another house of the Youssoupovs – Kokuz, an imitation Tartar palace. There, if she liked, she could imagine herself a Tartar beauty, but not the heroine of the house's legend: a beautiful kidnapped girl who had cried herself to death and was commemorated by stained-glass weeping eyes set in the top of every window. She did not like the idea, but was excited to hear she could wear Oriental clothes provided by the Youssoupovs. They sounded romantic and exotic and exciting. Her heart beat as she persuaded herself that the plan was a romantic idea of Serge's to bring them together.

Ella awoke the next morning feeling excited and joyfully deciding it was going to be the happiest day of her life. She thought that the birds were singing to her and the air purposely blowing sweet breezes. She jumped out of bed and knelt, her body upright, her white arms triangular, in prayer. She thanked God for her good health and her good fortune, asked him to preserve her father and family and asked him, above all, to help her honour and love her husband and bless her with children. Then, putting on her dressing gown, she walked cheerfully out on to the balcony, stupid with happiness.

Anna came in and told her they would meet the Grand Duke at an inn twenty miles inland. Count Merskey, one of his aides-de-camp, would accompany him. They would leave at ten o'clock as the road was winding and narrow.

They left precisely on the hour and, as they drove out of the park, she decided that the endless rows of statues reminded her of a graveyard. On every side grew vines with a blooming rose bush planted at the end of each row. The vines looked taller, the ripening grapes larger, the leaves greener than those on the Rhine. The Tartar peasants looked happy, and their houses upright and clean, comparing favourably to the hovels she had glimpsed at Ilonskoye. But why should she make comparisons when she was happy? She remembered a sentence she had heard in Moscow during a discussion of the beauties of the Crimea. A Count Galitzine had said: 'Up to now you have only seen the cold, cruel, poor north with its splendours and poverties. When you are in the south you will be happy there for ever. After a time, you will wish for plainer fare and miss the north's harsh truths and realities. But, of course, when you come back, you will long with all your heart for the south again. It is one of the characteristics of us Russians – we cannot be happy wherever we are.'

Ella felt excited and, without reason, laughed out loud. Anna Tolstoy relaxed and smiled in sympathy, her pretty round face beaming. Count Merskey, Ella saw, was in love with her and stared as if he could not believe his eyes. She did not mind or feel guilty, but smiled at him and he smiled back. They all felt alive, young and happy.

On the front seat of the open carriage sat a huge, clean-shaven coachman with double chins falling down on to his waistcoat. He had small eyes, like currants buried in the fat of his self-contented face, and looked the personi-fication of responsibility and stodginess, but, to their astonishment, provided entertainment which fitted in with their mood. Although the expression on his face never changed, it was obvious that the sight of a chicken transformed his character. With amazing skill and accuracy, he attacked every one he saw. Strutting conceitedly in his harem, a cock would find himself whirled into the air and left a bundle of outraged feathers. Hens peacefully feeding found their tail feathers plucked out as if by a devil, and scuttled away to safety. The coachman's surprising attacks delighted them and, although for the last two hours they drove through precipitous woodlands, they arrived at the inn in high good humour.

In a garden facing south, they were shown a table, laid on wooden trestles and covered with a dazzling white cloth, beneath a pergola of twisted wisteria, sheltered from the road by a high hedge of roses. Fussing about, four clumsy footmen in Youssoupov livery hampered the innkeeper and his family. Easy chairs, which she recognized as coming from Kokuz, stood in another wooden pagoda hanging with green grapes over a table laden with drinks and buckets of snow ice.

They quenched their thirst with cold lemonade, before sipping a bottle of the landlord's fresh cold white wine, and relaxed, idly talking until they were disturbed by the sound of horses' hooves on the road and the clattering noise of dismounting. The aide-de-camp at once jumped to his feet and excused himself. He was a pleasant-mannered young man, but he puzzled Ella. She liked him, yet, despite his obvious adoration, a look of inexplicable uneasiness would pass from time to time over his good-looking face. She had sensed beneath his admiration, politeness and efficiency a carefully concealed resentment, no less annoying because it was hardly discernible and might have been a figment of her imagination. Was she also imagining a freemasonry from which she was excluded? It was not the same with the other equerry. He came from Bessarabia and looked like a hawk.

She dismissed her worries and waited for Serge, taking out her glass to see how she looked. Pleased, she waited for her husband. Instead, the Bessarabian appeared and bowed and said it was the Grand Duke's wish she should take her place at the head of the table. Surprised, she sat down at one end of the trestle. Still no Serge appeared and she looked round, startled by even louder noises of banging and shuffling in the inn. They grew louder, until into the garden four men came staggering under the weight of a mimosa tree in full bloom in a large terracotta pot full of earth. With difficulty the men advanced and put the bush down next to her so the flowering branches rubbed against her face and clothes. She looked at the men with astonishment. What had they done? The confusion was increased by the arrival of another mimosa tree which was jammed up against her other side to make her a prisoner of yellow blossom. Ella was wondering if she had gone mad when she heard her husband's voice asking if everything was ready. At last he came into sight. Immediately he saw her he stopped, bowed and asked gently: 'How do you like the prison I have enclosed you in, my pretty?'

But gradually the pleasure left his face and, in a harsh voice, he called angrily to the carriers to stir themselves and push the plants closer to the Grand Duchess.

'I hope you like the scent of mimosa. The variety is "Quatre saisons". I saw them yesterday on an estate by the road and borrowed them for the day. They arrived by cart this morning. I hope you are happy.'

An aide-de-camp sat beyond them on either side of her, while Serge sat between her ladies-in-waiting, facing her at the end of the table. Ella felt confused as the mimosa was now enveloping her body, brushing against her cheeks and dropping blossom in her hair, but it was undeniably exciting and the scent was so strong she wondered if she was going to faint. When she saw Serge leaning forward, bright-eyed and staring with unblinking admiration, her embarrassment became so acute that she leaned backwards and disappeared into the heart of the tree.

'Come out, come out, come out!' Serge called in a loud voice until she leaned forward and guessed, by the eyes of the men, that she looked beautiful, her hair crowned with broken flowers. She blushed and half-laughing protested: 'Let's eat – I am hungry. And please, all of you stop looking at me in such a silly way.'

She drank another glass of wine.

They had a simple meal of toasted wholemeal bread, butter and caviare, and lamb cooked in the Tartar way, which she did not like, but she hardly knew what she was eating, it felt so strange to be enveloped by a tree whose pollen was making her feel increasingly dizzy. She began to wonder if she was not growing out of the soil. A soft breeze caused the branches to stroke her face and bare skin and gently comb her hair, tempting her to lean back again into the green security. All the time Serge sat, eyes shining, eating nothing, staring. Ella felt weak, as if the branches had sucked out her strength. At last the carriers hauled back the tubs. She was free and stood up, took a few little staggering steps and leaned, breathing heavily, against a support of the pergola. Serge came up and said quietly as he held her hand: 'Oh, my little one, I hope you enjoyed your lunch. You looked so wonderfully beautiful intertwined with those branches.' He gripped her hand. 'Goodbye, my love. I will ride on and meet you at Kokuz.'

She fell asleep the moment she sat back in the carriage, and woke up with no idea where she was. Looking around, she was amazed to find they were jolting down a steep road surrounded by dense, dark pine trees through which the carriage wound down in semi-darkness. Without warning, they came upon a gap and saw below, on a hill in the centre of a valley, a large white house with minarets and towers sticking out of a pitched, sloping roof of pale green slates distorted by the sun into the colour and texture of sea water. A clump of dark-green cypresses pointed upwards beyond the towers, and rivulets ran down the hill into a flat-roofed, white Tartar village. In the garden, she saw fountains spouting among the trees and bushes, while the house appeared to be half-built of green leaves and white, pink and blue flowers which fell from balconies, twined up pillars and ran along the walls.

As they drew near the door, hordes of manservants in baggy trousers and white waistcoats ran out with welcoming cries and struggled for their luggage. No sooner was Ella shown into her bedroom than the door opened and in came laughing maids, carrying robes of velvet and silk embroidered with gold and silver, which they laid out on her bed. Ella had to sit down and laugh. They wouldn't go away until she had selected the finest costumes, which they hung carefully in the cupboard before giggling away. As she wished to be alone, she decided to go for a walk and followed the course of a little stream which ran by the house into an orchard filled with perfectly pruned peaches and apricots, apples, pears and plums and opened on to a lawn planted with magnolias, leading to a circular lemon garden with Versailles tubs. Beyond lay an area of greenhouses with orchids hanging down in mossy wire baskets above beds of pineapples and strawberries. Often she saw gardeners downing their tools and vanishing as she drew near, making her believe that she was a fairy queen who had found her palace. She had never imagined a place so beautiful, so peaceful; it could only mean that she was standing on the edge of a new life.

She walked slowly back to the house, washed, dried and combed her long auburn hair in the evening sun, then lay down and slept until the housekeeper knocked on the door and told her dinner would be served in an hour. Serge had arrived and, at the request of the head gardener, gone off to shoot an elk which had broken into the garden. Ella dressed and walked downstairs into the hall where, for the first time, she noticed a peculiar waterfall of drops of water dropping from the ceiling into one stone cup after another, imitating, the housekeeper told her, the tears of the beautiful prisoner. Momentarily depressed, she walked around the house, never out of the sight of the stained-glass eyes looking down on her from the top of every window.

Turning a corner, she faced a mirror, and once again was delighted by her beauty. She cheered up and sat on a stone seat in the courtyard, enchanted by the scent of valerian and sweet-scented geraniums.

Serge, having shot the elk, was in a good humour at dinner, and for the first time she found herself perfectly at ease. Everything he said was original and she often burst out laughing, which pleased him, as several times he smiled and told her she was both beautiful and humorous, a rare combination. For some reason, even this remark made her laugh, and he smiled back, showing his teeth. After dinner, Tartar musicians with curious instruments came in to sing strange, plaintive songs. At half past ten Serge stood up and briskly dismissed them. They looked so disappointed that Ella, who wished the whole world happiness, asked them to come and play the following night, and walked up to her room. Slowly she undressed, putting on a white cotton nightgown embroidered with gold, and stood in the window looking down on the stream. The water made a gentle rippling sound. She closed her eyes, imagining herself flowing gently with the current on and on for ever. She climbed into bed, thinking how gracefully she moved, wondering why she had never noticed her elegance before, utterly content to be in a beautiful house surrounded by lovely trees. She lay back, closed her eyes and tried to remember how the garden had looked in the afternoon.

Immediately she saw again, with peculiar clarity, the circular lemon garden shaped like a bowl, adorned geometrically with Versailles tubs, which she had admired in the afternoon as she had stood fascinated, examining the carefully trained trees with Persian roses tied to their stems, their branches formed into cupped fingers pointing upwards. Ella was thinking sadly that she had come too early for the second flowering of the roses, as she remembered exactly how the garden had looked, and precisely where each lemon tree, with a rose beneath it, had stood in its tub, when she saw with pleasure and without surprise a rosebush starting to grow, the buds swell and burst out and blossom so that soon the tree turned into a tangle of yellow lemon skins, delicate pink roses and white lemon flowers. As she stood watching, each tub in turn stirred and blossomed before standing still, waiting for its neighbour to follow. When the last tree had bloomed, she sighed. She knew she would never see anything so beautiful again. Looking back, she saw that her footsteps were marked on the grass by lilies of the valley. She walked on for twenty paces, looked around, and saw she was still followed by footsteps of the flowers, which bowed as their little white bells started gently ringing. She put out her hand and bent down to examine them. At once the bells stopped ringing and bent away in fear. Again she tried gently to touch them, again each flower recoiled, but stood upright when she moved her hand away. A large white petal fell on her head, and to her surprise she saw that the magnolia trees in the garden were flowering, and as she stared upwards, buds burst, white flowers opened and expanded until the petals gently fell around her feet.

A harsh sound broke into her dream comparable to a fist smashing a windowpane. Dazed and sad to leave her flower-strewn garden, she saw the door had opened and that Serge, his right hand behind his back, stood looking at her. She made a sign to be quiet and beckoned him unselfconsciously to come and share in her dream. His nervousness disturbed her peace, and she looked at him as if she had never seen him before. His skin was sallow, his mouth small and his eyes withdrawn. She could only see into one at a time, and then it was like looking down a bottomless well into blackness. He suggested menace. She looked away, but as she turned, caught a glimpse of his cropped head on which every individual, fair, coarse hair stood upright. She shut her eyes, hoping he would vanish, and turned to lie on her side as the moonlight shone on her through a blue stained-glass eye. She stared back and knew it was not the moon looking at her but the eye of the weeping girl who had come to comfort her and say all was well. The girl was about to say something important when Serge spoke: 'Pass me a glass of water from the bedside table.'

She turned and reached out her right hand, but as she was about to pick up the glass three things happened: her bedclothes vanished, her face was brutally thrust into the pillow and she felt a blinding pain. Jerking round in dismay, she saw Serge kneeling, his lower lip hanging down so she could see his teeth, his upper lip stretched stiffly downwards like the flap on the back of an envelope, his eyes almost closed, while in his right hand he held a horsewhip which, as she looked, he brought down with all his force across her legs, eight inches above her knees. She thought he had gone mad and twisted herself upright to try to jump off the bed, but, catching a foot in the sheets, she fell, her shoulder hitting the tiled floor before her head.

The next thing she remembered was lying dizzy and weak with no idea of where she was or what had happened. Serge was bending over her, wiping her brow with a wet, cold sponge. She felt the cold water running down behind her eyes on to the pillow. His hand was shaking as he gave convulsive little sobs and tears ran down his cheeks and dropped on to her face. When he saw her eyes open, his face softened as he bent down to kiss her. Every part of her flesh reacted. She sat up, calculating how she could defend herself, but when she looked at him again, he had turned into a sad, dim old clown, powder-white, crinkled and despairing. He had dropped the whip. She was no longer afraid. He fell on the bed beside her and beat his chest with his fists and told her things she would never let her mind recall, relating facts she found impossible to believe but explaining the doubts of her father and the concern of Grandmama. She stared at him as he went on with confessions that were only interrupted by himself asking again and again for an understanding she could not give. 'Can't you understand, love is pain?' he shouted desperately against her silence.

He ranted and screamed, dredging up his past, throwing in her face obscenities, vices and cruelties which did not belong to a civilized man, until at last she realized at some point in his incoherence that he must have given her an eastern potion to put her into a frame of mind to enter his own sad cruel world. How lucky his scheme had purified, not possessed her. She shut her eyes and thanked God that she had escaped him now and forever as he grasped both her wrists, shouting: 'Can't you understand I love and hate you, love and hate you?'

Shock gave her an unexpected strength. She withdrew her hands, although he was holding her with all his force, walked to the cupboard, pulled on a light travelling coat and, once she had fastened the front, stood at the end of the bed and looked down on her sobbing husband. Her first emotion was one of unutterable distaste, but slowly her anger turned to sorrow. He looked desolate, defeated, a broken man in need of help. He was her husband. Could she ever leave him to destroy himself? Was it not her duty to stay to help? With a little shudder, she forced herself to do something against which her physical instincts again protested. She sat down beside him on the bed, lifted his head, put it on her lap, as she had done years before, stroked it as she gently told him she would forgive him, never leave him, never let the world know their relations were anything except those of man and wife. But he must understand he could never touch her; she would only stay on that condition. He clutched her hand and nodded his head. She told him to lie still. The secret would be theirs alone. He must try to change, as she believed he did not realize the magnitude of his sins in the eyes of God and she was sure that if he repented and led a good life he would be forgiven. She repeated that it was her duty to live with him, pray for him, help him in every way, and that he in return must try and change his thoughts and actions and try to be forgiven for the cruelties of his past.

He turned over and sat up and told her that his hatred for the revolutionaries who had killed his beloved father had warped his life, demanding revenge, and how he would never waiver in his fight against the powers of evil.

She addressed him as a child, explaining gently that she understood his hatred of terrorists, and even his desire for revenge, but that this had nothing to do with inflicting pain on children. Couldn't he see how he was destroying his own soul, inflicting vengeance on himself, not on his enemies, and committing mortal sins by corrupting and torturing the innocent?

Ella was surprised that she was able, in a detached manner, to speak unashamedly of subjects which would normally have caused her to cover her face with her hands. Somehow this inconceivable conversation did not embarrass or shock her, and she ended by saying in an ordinary voice, without an echo of distaste or disapproval: 'In the short time I have lived in this country, I have come to see that its customs are entirely different and, indeed, incomprehensible to one who comes from Western Europe. I will only ask you to say no more. Please go to your dressing room for the night.'

She took his hand firmly and led him to his room, shut the door, went back, locked her own door and prayed by her bed to have the strength to live with a man who could never be her husband, to help him overcome the weaknesses of his nature which had made him commit acts contrary to nature and the will of God. She stayed on her knees, cold and chilled, until five o'clock before climbing stiffly into bed. Not for a single moment had she believed her own prayers, never overcome her belief that she had, in a moment of madness, made a terrible mistake in promising to stay with a husband who was no husband, to remain married but unmarried, and sacrifice her life-long desire for children. Bitterly, she admitted that she had made a promise she could not break and so committed herself to a life of useless misery.

The next morning she woke up with a splitting headache and a feeling of nausea which forced her to jump up and run quickly into the bathroom. It was only when she got back in bed that she clearly remembered the events of yesterday. She put her head in her hands in an agony of embarrassment and wondered what had happened to her; why and how had she entered into a dream which now, looking back, held no magic but rather the faint smell of corruption. Certainly the garden was beautiful, but the flowers springing up in her footsteps, her affinity to nature, her belief she was a part of every blossom and blade of grass must surely have been some extraordinary fancy. Had she been drunk? No, she had only had three glasses of white wine at lunch and less at dinner. The agony of the conversation with the sobbing Serge became a nightmare that belonged to another world.

She rebelled in horror at the idea she had calmly accepted last night that Serge had given her a potion to make her comply with his terrible vices; but if he had not, what had been the cause of her entrance into another world? She knew she must leave, be alone, make up her mind and decide whether the promise she, or rather her unreal self, had given bound her to a man she now despised.

She pulled the bell-rope and ordered breakfast without mentioning her determination to leave. She realized how strange it would look, and what talk it would cause. She lay fretting, dreading a meeting with Serge, rehearsing what to say to her ladies-in-waiting, conscious of a sickness at heart and a desperation to escape that she could not see how to fulfil. Events came to her aid. The maid brought in a little note from the Grand Duke's aide-de-camp saying His Imperial Highness was recalled to St Petersburg. He would call on Her Imperial Highness before he left.

She sent a message back:

If His Imperial Highness is leaving it is my intention to go rather than remain alone. I am particularly anxious to return to Ilonskoye and plan the redecoration of the house. I will leave tomorrow.

Then she waited in agony for Serge. What would he say? Would he talk about what she had already put out of her mind? She lay, clutching a handkerchief, rolling it up into a round ball. Then Serge came in perfectly dressed, as if nothing had happened. His mouth was tight, his eyebrows a coarse white-blond, his eyes small and dark and, when she quickly glimpsed them, showing nothing. He stood at the end of her bed, looking down, and said: 'Dear child, I am sorry I have to go but I am pleased that you are going to begin work at Ilonskoye. After two weeks I will expect you in St Petersburg.'

He made no apology. She thanked God for that. At the same time, she could not but look at him with horror, as last night she had bound herself to him with a promise from which she now feared there was no escape. Directly she saw him she knew she was trapped by the strength of her inherited conventions and that her only joy would be the fulfilment of meaningless duty. She hardly paused before saying yes, she would be in St Petersburg in two weeks, and when he came nearer, stretched out her rigid arm to its full length, an object to kiss and, at the same time, a bar to intimacy.

She did not see him again and stayed in bed until lunch, hoping her head would stop throbbing. Before Serge left, she sent him another note, asking to be allowed to stay at Ilonskoye alone without Sandra or a lady-in-waiting. He wrote back, granting her request on this occasion, and ending: 'Countess Olsoufiev will take you to Ilonskoye and fetch you at the end of your visit to escort you to St Petersburg.'

After lunch she felt better and longed to get out of the cursed house, but not into the garden. She asked the young housekeeper to recommend a beautiful afternoon drive. A carriage appeared at two o'clock to drive her and Anna to an

69

eyrie in the mountains. They set off, going uphill all the way. After a few miles, they changed horses and climbed up and through woods to stop at last outside a little house with footmen and maids standing at the gate. Shown down a passage, they came out on a balcony and saw that the house was grafted on to a rocky cliff overlooking an enormous valley of unbroken forest.

They ate cakes and drank tea and sat looking down at the wild and beautiful view. The footmen and maids consulted together, leaned over the edge, pointed and shook their heads. One of them went into the house and came back with the coachman, who was clasping several large stones to his stomach. These he put down before, shading his eyes with his hand, peering over the parapet down the precipice. At length he gave a grunt of satisfaction and beckoned to Ella and Anna to join him. Nervously, they also peered down but could see nothing except a few crooked trees clinging to the cliff-side. The coachman smiled complacently and swung a large stone on to a ledge some hundred feet below. Immediately a brown object detached itself from the cliff and fell like another stone towards the forest but, before hitting the trees, opened wings, glided outward and soared vertically upwards past them into the sky to circle above their heads. The coachman took aim again, and two more huge birds dived, skimmed, soared and circled. Satisfied, he rubbed his hand on his trousers and with pride told them that the house was called 'The Eagles' Nest'.

Looking up at the grace of the three huge birds, Ella envied them their freedom and cried the whole way home. When they arrived at the front door she thought, with desperate sadness, of her happy hopes when she had arrived only the day before; now the future held nothing but darkness.

5

Ella was met by a carriage at Moscow station and, to her surprise, taken to another large house called Usovov on the other side of the river, in the park at Ilonskoye, which Serge usually moved into at the end of the summer. Every room had a fireplace and a huge stove. It was not the usual time to move, but Serge had given orders that Ilonskoye should remain unused so it would be easier for her to plan her desired changes there.

It was melancholy, sleeping alone in a strange house, but the next day, as she went round Ilonskoye, Ella felt her spirits rise, her mind taken off her troubles by what she supposed was the hereditary practicality which she inherited from Mama and Prince Albert. She made herself go from room to room, deciding what to keep and what to discard. After she had toured all the rooms, she walked downstairs and started all over again. She had dreaded the work of changing furniture, but it turned out easier than she had feared as she was accompanied by two maids and four strong young outdoor workmen in spotless white tunics who moved and changed the furniture around with effortless ease.

In the middle of the morning, they were joined by a famous upholsterer and a carpet maker from Moscow. The upholsterer, who also supplied wall materials and papers, understood her wishes before she spoke them and was so quick and clever that she soon saw it would be possible to transform the heaviness and ugliness of Russian taste into replicas of the private rooms at Windsor, Osborne and Darmstadt.

Far into the evening she made plans and notes of her requirements for each room, and wrote a friendly but firm letter to the carpet maker saying that unless he could provide her exact order, she would write to kind Sir Frederick at Windsor and ask him to send out a man from Axminster.

It was past twelve by the time she put away her pencils and notebook and drove back, supperless, to bed. The sun was shining when she woke up in the morning, and she was lying back in her bed, thinking what a noise the bees made in the garden, when suddenly all the awfulness, the sheer horror of the unmentionable but unforgettable returned; she ran into the bathroom in tears, knowing nothing could ever be the same again.

After breakfast, she felt better, and as usual when she was sad started to write letters emphasizing her happiness. It was no good and she tore them up. Oh, for Victoria! But she must not mope and despair and, determining to put sadness out of her mind, she resolutely continued to plan the redecoration of the rooms at Ilonskoye. Again she was unable to concentrate and found to her dismay she could not face another morning's planning. She sent for the gardener and suggested that climbing roses should be planted against the house, but her enthusiasm waned when she realized they would never be at Usovo in the flowering season. It was the last straw. She sat in the drawing room and cried. Then, to her surprise, at eleven o'clock a footman brought an invitation from Princess Zenaïde Youssoupov, who hoped they had enjoyed their honeymoon and regretted that Serge had been forced to return to Moscow. Ella was so pleased to get a letter which broke into her depression that, without even reflecting, she replied she would be pleased to come for the night and would arrive before dark, but hoped the Princess would not think her rude if she returned early tomorrow as she had to supervise the alterations at Ilonskoye.

She set out at four o'clock. The house was only three miles away and, after a few minutes, Ella's carriage arrived at a classical arch and drove into a huge, magnificent park, divided by an avenue leading, in the distance, to a mass of white buildings which grew into a small town as she approached. The Princess was waiting at a side-door, and Ella immediately recognized her as the prettiest woman she had seen at her wedding. At second sight she was even lovelier, slim, elegant, with long, shining soft black hair, a faintly olive complexion and sparkling blue eyes. They liked each other on sight, and Ella knew that here was the friend she desperately needed and asked her at once to call her by her Christian name. They talked like old friends as they walked through the gigantic pillared hall which made the rooms in the royal palaces and castles at Darmstadt look like cupboards. The furniture was of a magnificence to equal the house, and she wondered how anyone could live in such overwhelming splendour.

It was a lovely afternoon, and Zenaïde said they would take tea outside in the warmth but out of the hot sun. They walked through the biggest library she had ever seen and out through the open doors of a round ballroom, and sat on comfortable cushioned wooden chairs under a canvas awning overlooking a garden full of vistas and statues fading into the distance.

Ella was flustered when a footman offered her no less than four different kinds of China tea. She had no idea which to choose. But the fright jolted her memory, and she remembered other details of this beautiful girl's life. Zenaïde was the sole heiress to a stupendous fortune. Her father had hoped she would make a great marriage and, although every German prince proposed, she had turned them all down for love of a young, good-looking officer, Count Elston, whose father, Serge had told her in a scornful voice, was the illegitimate grandson of William IV of Prussia. She remembered his lips curling as he had said: 'To be a Hohenzollern is bad enough, but to be an illegitimate one . . .'

They sat and talked with the familiarity of old friends. Zenaïde spoke proudly but humorously of her young son and how she could not prevent herself from showing him to every visitor who came to the house. Ella found her natural, gentle and charming, and felt safe and at ease for the first time since her marriage.

After dinner they sat in a small sitting room upstairs. Zenaïde lit the fire and said, quite naturally, 'Ella, how is Serge?' as if she understood her new friend wished to confide in her. Ella told her everything, walking up and down in the little room, and Zenaïde sat still, never interrupting, her sparking eyes growing bigger and bigger as she sympathetically nodded her head. At the final horror, Ella burst into tears and her new friend came and put an arm around her shoulders, led her to her bedroom and said she would send her up some hot milk and come and say goodnight.

Later, as they talked in the bedroom, Zenaïde lay on the bed, leaning on her elbow with the complete naturalness of youth and beauty, and said: 'I'm so sorry. But should you deny yourself children? You know, nowadays wonderful doctors understand those sort of things and perhaps they could change Serge's character.'

When Ella held up her hand to push away such an idea, Zenaïde didn't argue but said with a gentle smile: 'In any case, whatever you decide I am sure we will always be dear friends. I will never ask questions, but always tell me if you are unhappy.'

After she had kissed her goodnight, Ella thought how reassuring it was to have a normal friend who spoke the truth, was full of sincerity and kindness, and, bored by the continual round of parties, only wished to stay with her son. In the morning she was reluctant to leave and agreed to stay four nights, going only for the morning to Ilonskoye and coming back each day for lunch and explorations in the extraordinary house and park. Arkhangelskoye was full of surprises. In the library sat a wooden effigy of Jean-Jacques Rousseau in eighteenth-century clothes, writing at a table. When Zenaïde touched a spring, the arm at once began to move and his pen scratched across the paper.

The private theatre was twice as large as the public theatre in Darmstadt. Acres of greenhouses grew every conceivable fruit out of season. Black swans swam on the lake, tigers roared, gazelles and giraffes walked among the trees.

The next morning, before Ella left for Ilonskoye, Zenaïde said that a charming young painter called Serov was coming to lunch. She hoped he would paint her new friend, but, she added, smiling: 'There is a snag. If he doesn't like your face he will refuse. A famous beauty once forced him to paint her on condition she sat in private and did not see the painting before it was exhibited. Arriving in triumph with her friends at his exhibition, she found to her fury that the painting was of a large hat and her chin. Turning on him in a rage, she was silenced by his simple reply: "The hat was the most interesting part of the subject." '

The story frightened Ella, who begged Zenaïde not to ask him. Her friend laughed and insisted that he would want to paint Ella; and he did, and asked her to sit for him that afternoon. Sadly, he was dissatisfied with his work and destroyed the canvas. Ella was not surprised and told him how her looks vanished in photographs and paintings, which made him stare into her face intently for a long time before saying slowly: 'Yes, I see why, your beauty lies in the delicacy of the shade of your colouring and the continuous change of expression. And while the two make you matchlessly beautiful, I can't see how I or even Raphael could ever capture your mobility. Your face changes with the flow of your blood and the intensity of your moods. You are one of the most beautiful women in the world, but when you are dead, nobody who has not seen you will believe it.'

His remark made her both pleased and sad, but she laughed and said that anyhow it was a compliment he had not covered her face with a hat.

At dinner Zenaïde said, 'I have a surprise for you. Have you ever heard the gipsies sing?'

'No.'

'Well, it is extraordinary. I wonder what you will make of them. You know, a lot of rich young men ruin themselves sitting night after night paying for enormous quantities of champagne. One of the Radishchevs is said to have gone to them every night for three years until he was penniless and now works in a government office and lives in rags in a garret eating bread and salt, his only purpose in life being to save enough money to hear them three or four times a year. He lives for nothing else.'

Ella had heard, even in Hesse, about the magic of gipsy singing and excitedly asked, 'Do they come and sing to us in here?'

'Oh no, they sing in the theatre.'

'Who else hears them?'

'Why, nobody, of course. We are all alone. Whatever do you mean?'

Ella paused before her words came out in an embarrassed rush: 'Oh, at Darmstadt we always asked all the household servants and anybody from outside who wished to come. It was a great treat,' she ended apologetically.

Zenaïde was surprised. 'Servants sitting watching with us – what a curious idea. I have never heard of such a thing. And you think they'd enjoy it? Perhaps. Why not, I suppose. Well, if you like,' and she told the butler that anyone who wished could come and hear the gipsies in the theatre. The butler looked so amazed she had to repeat herself and add: 'The three front rows can be left empty so that we have room to breathe.'

Ella truly loved her new friend, but was shocked by her attitude to her servants. Zenaïde's behaviour had nothing in common with her mother's belief that the only difference between the classes was education.

Ella thanked her hostess, who remained doubtful, as if she had taken a dangerous decision. But, on entering the theatre after dinner, her friend's doubts turned to blank astonishment when she saw that all the seats, except for the first three rows, were filled with expectant dependants, who jumped as one to their feet and clapped and bowed as the ladies took their places. After a dark face had peeped round the curtain, all the lights in the theatre went out and they sat in shuffling, whispering darkness. Ella was as excited as the audience and was only afraid that the famous, glamorous Russian gipsies might resemble the dirty vagrants she had seen at fairs in Darmstadt.

She wasn't disappointed. The stage lights came up and a man appeared, wearing a dark-blue blouse, baggy trousers over high top boots and a wide-brimmed black hat that shaded eyes which, to her delight, definitely flashed. He was followed by a woman whose body swayed in an undulating manner, who wore a long, black, gathered skirt and a scarlet shawl, and whose long blue-black hair was tied behind her head by a piece of dark blue silk. Her face was striking

74

rather than beautiful, and she looked down all the time, so that Ella could not see whether her eyes flashed. At last she looked straight at them and began to sing, in deep bass tones of singular sweetness, beauty and sadness, to the soft cords of her companion's guitar.

Ella immediately felt the words enter her heart and make her think of what she had been told foreigners always thought of: the endless plains of Russia. At first Ella thought that the gipsy was singing for her alone, but on second thoughts decided that she was merely taken in by the skill of a great artist. When the song ended, the last note lingering and slowly dying, not a sound was heard before Zenaïde began to clap politely. At once the tension broke. Hands banged together, feet thudded on the floor and women sobbed. The singer gave a little nod and the guitarist struck up again as the gipsy sang:

> 'They say my heart is as the wind,
> I to my love am never true.
> Why then do I forget the rest
> And my heart but remembers you?'

Again the applause was terrific, and altogether she sang eight songs with two encores. At the end both performers bowed, as much to the audience as to the Princess, and walked proudly off.

When Ella kissed Zenaïde goodnight and thanked her for the lovely treat, she replied: 'Oh Ella, I would like to say what a good idea it was to have an audience – it would never have entered my head. You know, I never heard them sing better and I will always fill the theatre in future. The strange thing about gipsies is that they understand us better than we do ourselves and treat us as half-cruel peasants and half-sentimental children, which I suppose is what we are.'

Ella feared that her last evening's entertainment, a dinner for distinguished neighbours, would be less enjoyable. But she was flattered to some extent when Zenaïde said: 'They would never forgive me if I kept you to myself. They are mad with anxiety to see you out of your wedding robes, and my life would not be worth living if you left without meeting them. As you will have to visit their houses later, it will make it easier if you have met, but that, of course, is an excuse. Forgive me, I could not face their fury. I have only asked the nicest.'

Ella said she quite understood and asked who was coming.

'Oh, the two old Galitzines. You will find you can't have a dinner anywhere without a Galitzine – they breed like rabbits. But as these are relations, I could not leave them out. Then there are the Cherentevs, who have two houses near here which you will love. Not a thing has changed in either of them for two hundred years. You would not believe it, but nobody ever dies in their service. Their butler is said to be a hundred and eleven and claims he was too old to fight the French. Another man I hope you will like is Prince Shcherbatov, who is old and courtly with beautiful manners. Anyhow, I hope you will find it interesting to step back into the past.'

The dinner was very different from their early, laughing meals, but she liked the polite, friendly old people. It was pleasing to think that she would not be lonely at Ilonskoye. One conversation stuck in her memory. She was standing in the drawing room, talking and laughing with Zenaïde – at that stage of their friendship, anything made them laugh – when Prince Shcherbatov came up and, bowing to each in turn, said: 'I see you two are close friends. I am not surprised. Let me tell you that it is difficult for beautiful women to have close friends unless they are also beautiful. As you know . . .' and he made an apologetic bow, '. . . women are the most jealous creatures in the world, and when a plain woman – or, worse, a pretty woman who is plain by comparison – smiles and flatters a beauty, she will be looking for faults, listening for gaffes to trump stupidity with perfection. But when two beautiful women are friends, they look at each other with admiration, realizing how they compliment each other's beauty. They admire instead of criticize, and so beautiful women have beautiful friends. In your case, I cannot imagine two more beautiful women, so you should be close friends.'

They had both laughed, but Ella wondered if there was not something in the argument as several women in Russia, including her sister-in-law Miechen, looked at her with unreasonable dislike.

6

Sandra Olsoufiev and Anna Tolstoy arrived the next morning at Ilonskoye, although Ella had told them to meet her in Moscow. They talked all the way back, and Ella felt she would get on well with her Mistress of the Robes, who she now knew was forty and married, without children, to a General older than herself. Nothing upset or shook her loyalty and complete discretion, and she behaved as if the visit to the Crimea, which she must have known was a disaster, had never happened. Anna was pretty and hinted that she might marry soon. Ella was sorry, but told Sandra that she insisted her replacement must be pretty as well. Sandra shook her head and said with a smile: 'Of course, but, you know, pretty girls *will* get married.'

'I don't mind, I can't bear ugly people.'

A little later, she saw Sandra surreptitiously examining herself in her hand glass and could not help laughing and saying: 'Of course, I didn't mean you, you're perfect.'

Sandra looked happier and, putting the glass away, ended the conversation by saying: 'I am not perfect, but I will try as hard as I can to please you, I can promise that.'

In St Petersburg, Ella faced the dreaded task of moving into Sergei Palace, a grand, gloomy house purchased by Serge, full of dark rooms. She was glad when he agreed that they could each have for everyday use apartments of little private rooms on the first floor with low ceilings. These, she knew, she could make warm and comfortable in her own English manner, which her new acquaintances told her Miechen had described as 'Ella's housekeeper's taste'.

She had dreaded her next meeting with Serge, but mustering all her courage she walked up and kissed him. He accepted the kiss and held her at arm's length, leaning backwards to examine her.

'Yes, you are as beautiful as I remember,' he said in a satisfied tone. Considering what had happened, she found his examination acutely embarrassing, since there was a genuine gleam of appreciation in his eyes and his face had exactly the same look as when, at the Hermitage, she had seen him stand in front of a picture in the Rembrandt Room. He held her prisoner for a full minute before letting her go as if he had thought of something else. She felt relieved that the dreaded meeting was past, but could not get over her husband's insensitivity and ability to behave as if the nightmare at Kokuz had never occurred.

Immediately, she was forced into an unending round of dinners, parties, receptions and balls. To begin with, Ella felt excited at being able to order anything she wanted. The dressmakers, understanding her passion for mauve, went to endless trouble to find her the most sumptuous silks, satins and velvets. Cost was irrelevant, they said. The Grand Duke wished her to be the best-dressed woman in the capital. Ella was overjoyed, but after her spartan upbringing, also continually felt like a spoilt child.

As Zenaïde had warned, it wasn't easy to make friends. The Tsarina was polite but distant, not nearly as enchanting and funny as her sister, Aunt Alexandra; Miechen was crushing; the great hostesses patronizing. Her life was saved by the officers of Serge's Preobrazhensky Regiment. He was intensely proud of his position of Colonel, and the officers, especially the younger ones, seemed very fond of him. He was relaxed with them and teased the younger officers with a familiarity which surprised her. Sometimes he would perform with them, and they would cling together, singing music-hall songs which, for some reason, surprised and embarrassed other visitors. She could see no reason why Serge should not be interested and encourage young men and join in their entertainments.

Mysteriously, he was immensely proud of her beauty and as jealous as he was proud. After a few weeks, she began to resent his wish that she should stand by his side, beautiful, obedient and silent. Out of deference, she pandered to his whim and appeared happy and obedient, and she did not object when she noticed, after a kind hint from Miechen, how a man followed her wherever she went. After all, she had nothing to hide. Serge was pleased with the universal praise of her charm and beauty and told her what the pattern was he had decided their life would follow. In St Petersburg, they would have different apartments, but in Ilonskoye they would always share the same bedroom. She consented, as she knew he would not break his promises, and strove to please him by her faithful demeanour as she could see that beneath his rude manner there was the desire of a weak man, wounded by himself, to tell the world he was master of a situation which did not exist. It was piteous, but her sadness was tempered by gratitude for the jewels and beautiful flowers he never tired of giving her.

Despite her good intentions, Ella found it impossible not to be irritated by his reaction to her love of dancing and at the system which had amazed her on her arrival. Nobody, however suitable, could ask her to dance; she, as a grand duchess, had to decide. To begin with, Serge decided on her partners, but after the first five dances she found, to her dismay, that the list was always limited to – apart from Serge himself and his brother Paul, who always claimed two dances as a 'brother-in-law's right' – old generals or ambassadors who had no idea how to dance and who ruined her evenings by tearing with their clumsy feet her beautiful clothes. Irritated beyond endurance by his sixth list naming the usual old clodhoppers, she asked Serge if she could not dance with some younger men. He looked furious.

'Please,' she said, pretending not to notice, 'I would like to dance with some of those nice young boys of the Preobrazhensky Regiment. You have no idea of the difference between dancing with a good dancer and some awful old man who slobbers on your dress and tears your clothes.'

As she spoke, she noticed Serge was looking at her with a set, angry face, but she met his glare, serene in the innocence of her reasonable request. It was unreasonable of him not to grant it.

'Surely you cannot be worried by my dancing with officers under your command – you must know my honour too well for that.'

Gradually, as he stared at her, his face softened and a curious cynical smile showed on his lips as he said, almost laughing: 'Yes, my dear, I can see no reason why the Colonel's wife should not dance with some of her husband's officers.'

That was better. The elegant young men whom Serge chose suited her as, apart from their skill, they never tried to slobber or to squeeze her hand like the old generals and ambassadors. Nevertheless, she wondered why Serge had smiled, and noticed that his eyes never left her or her partners.

The difference, though, was immense and, innocently enjoying herself, she could often forget her sorrow, although by Christmas the endless receptions, official balls and private parties satiated even her love of dancing, and she began to long to do something, almost anything, which would mitigate this tedium of endless entertainment which was gradually making her feel she was becoming a useless, purposeless object. Guilt at her uselessness reawakened her religious beliefs, and finding no more comfort in her Lutheran pastor than she had in Hesse, she began to study with fascination the beliefs of the Orthodox Church in the hope that they would one day provide, apart from satisfaction in their splendid ritual, confession and absolution to salve her conscience and direct her life and stimulate her dormant love of good works. Her friendship with Zenaïde, much as she loved her, was not enough, and the constant cruelties and brutalities of everyday life made her long to organize the mitigation of all the poverty and sickness which she saw, carelessly neglected by the circle in which she now moved. Bound by the promise to her father, she was forced to wait another six years before she could join the Orthodox Church, and she felt it would shrivel her to have to live that long without the solace and stimulation of a belief. She asked for the name of the most suitable religious teacher she could consult. Surprisingly, the Tsarina heard of her worries and spoke tactfully in front of her to Serge, suggesting that his wife should take a first step towards understanding Orthodoxy by visiting Father Ivan. Serge looked surprised, but agreed.

A week later, on a cold winter morning, she set out on a private pilgrimage to see the miracle worker at his church on the island of Kronstadt. She took Anna Tolstoy, the least formal and the gayest of those whom Serge called 'her women'. They drove in one of Serge's sleighs to the local land's end, although in winter it was not possible to see where the land ended and the water, or rather the ice, began. To her surprise, the road over the frozen sea was marked alternately by Christmas trees and large poles set upright in the ice, and the strange avenue could be seen until it disappeared in the white distance, overhung by black clouds.

They transferred outside a wooden hut into a lighter vehicle, driven by an old coachman who was covered from head to foot in thick, greasy old furs. Having tucked them in the back, he stood waiting by his horse, occasionally looking over his shoulder. It was tedious standing still in the cold, and Anna leaned forward and told him to start. He looked surprised, but after one last doubtful look over his shoulder whipped the horses on to the track between the trees. They sped over the packed snow at a speed which made the cold air cut into their faces as they sat otherwise warm beneath several huge furs. Almost immediately, Anna produced two strange-looking fur hats, one of which she gave to Ella. It was lined with astrakhan which had holes cut for the eyes, and it fitted tightly over her head and the bridge of her nose before falling loosely over the furs, allowing her to breathe warm air. After a few hundred yards, they passed over a piece of emerald-green ice swept clear of snow by the wind. It looked colder than anything she had ever seen. She shivered with excitement, but under the fur rugs and her strange hat she remained warm while the wind appeared to be playing tricks, bringing them from the east cold air and from the north-west little flakes of snow out of the blackness which hung over the avenue and which grew larger and larger until it enveloped them.

Inside the cloud was a maelstrom of snow. At times, huge flakes would come roaring from behind them, racing past the sleigh as if to sweep it along. At others, they would momentarily enter a pocket of absolute silence in which the snow fell slow and straight, covering them and the carriage and the horse with a thick white blanket until suddenly whirled off by a whirlwind that tried to lift them into the air and carry them away. Without warning, the wind would change again, blowing directly in their faces, covering their eyes, forcing the horse to lower its head and walk. The driver shouted uselessly, his words blowing back over his shoulder. Ella was both frightened and exhilarated by the insignificance of the sleigh in the storm. She had never felt so inconsequential but at the same time so much a plaything of an irresistible elemental force.

It was disappointing to return to a dull world as they arrived at a lighted wooden hut, out of which a man ran waving a red lantern and bawling incomprehensibly to the coachman, who, in turn, repeated the unheard over his shoulder. Seeing that they looked blankly at each other, the old driver with difficulty heaved out of a large side-pocket a slate and a piece of white chalk and started laboriously writing. When he had finished, he turned the slate round and they saw, written in large, shaky letters, the word 'VOUGA'. Their astonishment increased. Even Anna had no idea what it meant, and they looked from one to the other in bewilderment. At last the coachman turned round to them, stretched out his arm and swivelled it forward, waited a moment, wrenched himself round and pointed backwards. The question in his gestures was simple: forward or back?

'On, on!' Ella cried, pointing both hands forward.

The coachman shrugged, his expression unchanged, and, leaning forward, hung a bell over the front bar of the sleigh, snapped his whip, and off they drove back into the storm to the cracked sound of an inaudible warning. Ella thought it exciting that she, brought up in the middle of Germany far from any ocean, should be driving over the Baltic ice in a snowstorm which told her that, although she was utterly unimportant, it was splendid to be a part of nature.

Stimulated, she forgot everything but the magnificent and terrible storm.

It was soon plain why the man with the red light had advised them to turn back. The wind changed its sound to a whistle, covered their horse, the coachman and themselves with snow, threatened to blow them over so that even the coachman hunched himself into a ball as they settled deeper into the warmth of the rugs.

'Oh,' Ella cried, ecstatic at the surrounding whiteness, the noise, the loneliness. 'What fun this is! How I love Russia. This could not happen anywhere else in the world.'

She and Anna reached up with their gloved hands to catch the snowflakes, looked at each other and laughed. Anna was Ella's favourite lady-in-waiting, never cross, always laughing whatever happened. Despite knowing that Serge would think it improper, Ella put out her fur glove and gripped her companion's hand as they smiled and drew closer to each other.

Without warning, the horse stood still and pricked his ears, listening. The driver cracked his whip without effect, the animal stood immovable, turning his obstinate head from side to side. Ella listened, but could hear nothing, until suddenly, swerving to miss them, another sleigh shot out of the white darkness, travelling fast in the opposite direction. The drivers waved their whips as the sleigh disappeared, but this time the wind brought to them the sound of a bell which seemed – to Ella's over-excited mind – the music of the driving snow. She wanted, as they started again on their journey in an invisible world, to sing from sheer joy of living, and without thinking began: 'Good King Wenceslas' and heard Anna repeating in Russian the same carol.

They looked at each other, delighting in the words, although they could hardly hear their own voices above the sound of the wind and a new loud booming which rose from under the ice. When they finished they sang the carol in German, and, trying their hardest to defeat the elements, hit with their hands at the passing snow, feeling triumphant, as if they had won a victory. The sledge stopped again in a pause in the storm, and to Ella's amazement she saw in front of them a break in the ice and, to both sides of them, a river of moving, grinding ice producing the underwater thunder which they had heard. A number of thick wooden boards covered the break, making a bridge over which the driver uneasily guided their sleigh. The horses broke into a gallop, and again the storm engulfed them. Now Ella, listening intently, noticed the variations of sounds as the wind whirled the snow in ever-changing patterns, and wondered fearlessly what new adventures lay ahead. She was not disappointed as, in the distance, she heard the sound of a bell and found her stimulated imagination transporting her back to Windsor where Ernie as a young boy, dressed up as a pirate, was reciting to Grandmama and his aunts and uncles 'The Inchcape Rock'. She saw her brother again in a huge pair of boots, his shrill voice reciting:

> 'They hear no sound, the swell is strong;
> Though the wind had fallen they drift along,
> Till the vessel strikes with a shivering shock –
> "Oh Christ! it is the Inchcape Rock!"

'Sir Ralph the Rover tore his hair;
He curst himself in his despair;
The waves rush in on every side,
The ship is sinking beneath the tide.

'But even in his dying fear
One dreadful sound could the Rover hear,
A sound as if with the Inchcape Bell,
The devil below was ringing his knell.'

The performance was meant to end with the boom of a local church bell, especially arranged by Uncle Bertie. Unfortunately, the bell rang too early, but Ernie had bravely continued and Grandmama had patted his head in praise.

The memory faded as the bell rang louder and louder and they dashed to a rest area where lamps shone on an open space surrounded by temporary buildings. A man covered with snow was tugging at a rope and tolling the bell, hung on a cross to guide lost travellers to safety. The driver half-turned to Ella to see if she wished to stop. Such an idea was, in her present mood, unthinkable, and Ella waved him imperiously on back again into the storm. She sat silent and content in a whiteness which blocked out the rest of the world and made her forget her fears and troubles. Once more the horse slowed his pace, this time to pass two peasants trudging on foot towards Kronstadt. The man was carrying a large bag strapped on his back and the woman a bundle to her breast. Ella knew it was a baby. Both plodded wearily along, the man carrying a long stick, white with icy snow. The magic of the day disappeared. Why, as soon she loved an aspect of Russia and decided it was the most beautiful country in the world, was she always subjected to a sad display of poverty or cruelty which ruined her pleasure? But Anna, unaffected by the cold, struggling pair, continued laughing with the joy of life. After all, she had been brought up to think of poverty and misery as the lot of the poor, and the tragic figures in the snow, bringing a sick child to Father Ivan, left her unmoved.

They passed another lighted resting place, where Anna glimpsed Ella's serious face and became immediately solemn. Then, without warning, they drove out of the storm into the daylight, and Ella saw against the sky the outline of a church and beyond, to the left, the vast ramparts of the fortress. On land again, the road sloped uphill and stopped in front of a modern well-built house of considerable size. No one was waiting to greet them, but after the driver had gone in, a young novice with long, flaxen hair came running out, bowing and lamenting that he could not have guessed Her Imperial Highness would be so brave as to drive through such terrible weather.

He led them through a number of rooms on the way to see Father Ivan. The lack of order was surprising. One hall was full of waiting peasants and the wives of working men drinking cups of tea. Another room looked like a casual hospital, except that a number of fully dressed peasants, their legs still covered with frozen snow, lay snoring on beds. At last they came to a chapel where, before the altar, knelt a tiny little priest. The flaxen-haired guide bowed them on to the foremost bench in front of several peasants who sat passively waiting.

Despite their disinterest, Ella was embarrassed and wished that Father Ivan would hurry up. After a long wait, the little man finished his prayer, stood up, turned to face the congregation, made the sign of the cross and retired to the sacristy. But soon he came out again and, walking towards Ella with a surprised expression, bowed and said: 'I had not expected you. No member of the imperial family has ever faced the Vouga before. It kills many. You were brave to come – you two by yourselves.'

Father Ivan was a surprise. She had expected a grey-haired, benign, saintly old man. Before her stood a commonplace, perky little priest who, a good foot shorter than herself, further confounded her by leaning forward, standing on tiptoe and, without a word of warning, ruffling her hair with his fingers before making a rough sign of the cross on her forehead. She heard oohs, ahs and envious intakes of breath from the sitting peasants. He then blessed Anna, shocking Ella by the brevity of his welcome, and led them towards his private rooms, but left Anna outside sitting on a hard chair. Ella, feeling very young, followed the saint into a little whitewashed, unbearably hot cell which had a huge stove in the corner. He sat her down on one side of a table and placed himself opposite in a high chair, folded his hands on the table and stared at her with impartial interest.

He was, she knew, about fifty-seven, but he looked younger. His beard was beginning to grow grey and his pale-brown eyes had, not the ascetic look of a priest, but the healthy, curious, sly sharpness of a farmer or prosperous tradesman. There was a growth of some kind on one side of his forehead, and as he leaned forward, staring at her, she saw hanging round his neck beneath his chin the Russian Orthodox Cross with the second short bar slanting upwards to reach the shortened foot of Christ. She wondered why Christ was often portrayed as lame in Russia. With the aid of a dictionary, she explained haltingly that she had come for help and aid as a fellow Christian, although not yet a member of the Orthodox Church, of which she would like to know more. When she first looked into his eyes, she saw understanding not pity, but when she looked again, she had a fright. He was, she felt certain, looking into her mind, reading her thoughts with ease and clarity, and occasionally nodding to show that he understood and was not shocked by her position.

She looked down, overcome by shame. It was surely not her imagination. She looked up again. He was smiling at her.

'There is no need to be ashamed,' he said in a brisk voice. 'We are all sinners, every one of us. The Grand Duke Serge, myself, you doubtless. All of us are born to sin. Unless you are an admitted sinner, you cannot be redeemed. You ask my advice. I will give it to you now because, looking into the future, I see you will become a member of our Church, which is the only true Church of God on earth,' he added fiercely. 'You have made the right decision and you must keep to it. Remember, the Tsar is the Protector of the Church and the link between the people and God. Any action of yours which hurts this holy connection would be an unforgivable sin. Looking at you, I see you will lead a good life. You will be revered at your death, but that's a long way away. You can see me whenever you will. When you are ready for entry into the Holy Church of Russia, come again. Meanwhile, obey your lawful husband, with whom you are one flesh in the sight of God and our Holy Church. Do what he tells you. Do not, as you are doing now, resist him. Help him, agree with him. That is God's wish.'

Then, as suddenly as he had ruffled her hair, he pushed forward his right hand as if he was going to hit her. She bobbed back, felt silly and leant forward to kiss it. She thought he was a good man and wondered if she would be able to make herself obey his wishes, which puzzled and confused her.

The storm was over, and they drove back without incident under a cloudless sky which transformed the seascape into a featureless flat plain. Serge showed no interest in Father Ivan, but was furious that she should have crossed without a military escort. Was it on purpose? Once he was convinced of her innocence, he left the room abruptly. The next day she noticed that her follower was changed. Later she received a letter from a woman, begging for the Grand Duchess's intercession:

It was not my husband's fault a runner broke on his sleigh. He has weak health and a long stay in the fortress of SS. Peter and Paul will certainly kill him. I ask for mercy for myself and my children.

Without comment, she showed the pathetic letter to Serge, who crumpled it up and threw it in the fire. She prevented herself from criticizing him and could not make up her mind about her visit to Father Ivan. Apart from telling her to obey Serge, he had given her no practical advice or spiritual comfort, though he had taken away restlessness and disquiet at her useless life as if he was a private Romanov magician who could read her thoughts, know her past, and tell her what she had never ceased believing: that a wife is in God's eyes the same flesh as her husband. Was it her duty to forgive and obey? She decided to do as he told her, at least to the extent of continuing uncomplainingly to live with Serge. The decision made, she was again enchanted to buy new clothes, to plan combinations of colour to match the many sets of jewels, and generally to revel in the fact that she, who had been brought up with spartan simplicity, had now her own Court Chamberlain, Mistress of the Robes and ladies-in-waiting dressed in her own colours. Once again she felt free to enjoy the effect of her beauty and the pleasures of adulation.

7

Her life followed a regular pattern. She was called at eight o'clock every morning with breakfast. At nine o'clock, she would discuss with the Mistress of the Robes her appointments and plans. Nearly every day the dressmaker would arrive with, perhaps, the finest Chinese silks, or maybe a roll of old velvet from Genoa, or jewellers would bring a magnificent clasp or necklace which the Grand Duke had added to her collection.

Daily they gave a lunch at the Sergei Palace or went to one of the Grand Dukes or the Youssoupovs. In the afternoon, old acquaintances of her husband would call in for tea, and sit making conventional conversation for an hour, leaving her two hours in which to prepare before the evening's entertainment. She never ate alone at home, or read in bed. She hardly had time to think, so intensely busy was she doing nothing. Now and again, she found herself thinking of the doctor, and could never make up her mind whether her unhappiness made her remember him or whether she was unhappy because she remembered him.

Serge's new policeman followed her movements, but she never gave him even the faintest nod of recognition, having grown used to his predecessor, who she hoped was out of prison. That spring, the Tsarina gave three official balls which put Ella's dressmakers into an absolute frenzy of excitement. For the preceding weeks, she had daily fittings with the jeweller and the dressmaker to discuss the precise distance the dress should be off the shoulders, the exact position of her necklaces and earrings, and which parures should be worn with her new dresses. Obediently, at every ball, she checked her dancing partners with Serge and gratefully accepted his choice of young officers. At receptions he never left her side, gazing proudly around as he told her that she was the most beautiful woman in the room. But if ever, pleased by his compliments, she thoughtlessly aired an opinion, he would tell her to keep quiet. Again, she was saved by the young officers of the Preobrazhensky Regiment, who behaved naturally, unlike courtiers, who thought carefully before they spoke, or Serge's family, who lay in wait for her to make a mistake or to say something silly so that it could be carried off immediately as a prize to be repeated to her sisters-in-law. She liked hearing that she was the most beautiful woman in Europe, and that some young officer would love her for ever. It always made her laugh happily. She liked best the young men who looked at her and hardly dared to speak, trembling with admiration and flushing scarlet if they caught her eye. She would ask them about their mothers and fathers, their estates and their childhood, comparing their childhood to her own. When she realized that they were hopelessly in love, she treated them gently, without hurting their feelings.

Father Ivan had made her see that she should replace the silly romantic ideas of her youth with her duty to her husband, and so she thanked God that she was so busy. At the same time, she became spoilt and began to accept the admiration and endless praise as her right. In May, when the time came to move for the summer months to Ilonskoye, Serge told her that she would not be 'under observation', and she and Zenaïde travelled alone to Moscow and then on to their neighbouring houses to prepare for the arrival of the summer guests. She was pleased to find, as if by magic, that the house was now her own. Chintzes had replaced the heavy velvet and brocade curtains, and light wooden furniture stood in place of the heavy mahogany cupboards and marble tables. Dressing rooms had turned into bathrooms, carpeted from wall to wall, the gilding was painted white, and Ilonskoye had, for all the world, turned into an unpretentious English country house.

Ella explored the park with Zenaïde, who approved her redecoration of the main house and the six dashkas for guests. To her surprise, she discovered another dashka she had not seen on her last visit, which the housekeeper said was to remain unaltered by order of the Grand Duke. The furniture in it was heavy, the curtains velvet, while at the head of a huge mahogany dining-room table stood a soft chair, big enough for a bullock to sit on. In the sitting room was a gigantic settee, and in a downstairs bedroom three huge mattresses lay on the floor in place of a bed. In the other bedrooms were photographs of strangers and unknown houses while, in the cupboards, hung everyday clothes. Amazed, Ella had asked Zenaïde, 'But who lives here? I feel like Goldilocks.'

'Oh,' she said laughing, 'this is the house of your husband's friends who stay every summer. They sing, act, play cards or just laugh and keep everybody happy. And as for the mattresses and large chair, they can only belong to Princess Vasilchikov who is the biggest woman I have ever seen and who weighs twenty-three stone, with arms as big as a man. Do you mean to say that Serge has never told you about her? She dines at least three times a week and reaches out and picks up guests who think themselves important, like my husband, who is one of her favourite victims, and settles them on her knee, holding them with a grip of iron and treating them like a baby. She torments Felix so much that he won't come here if he knows she is dining, because he cannot bear to see me laughing at him.'

Ella stammered, 'But what an extraordinary thing. Will she lift me up? I would hate it.'

'No, no. She will treat you with deference, otherwise, she knows, Serge would send her away.'

'But are the others huge freaks as well?'

'No, no. She is unique. The others are called "the menagerie" and are really old-fashioned jesters.'

'They are all,' interrupted Sandra, as if to make the matter respectable, 'nobly born.'

'What happens to them in the winter?' Ella asked.

'Oh, they all go off and live on their own country estates, but they all prefer the company of Serge and prefer living for five months as butts in an aura of royalty to staying on their own properties.'

The idea of this huge fat woman living in a house with companions whose sole purpose was to make Serge laugh shocked Ella. She could not conceive her grandmother ever treating her subjects in such a way. She was determined not to criticize Serge, but she knew she would find it difficult to laugh at people whose function was to make themselves ridiculous. The idea was disgusting.

Despite her fears, it proved to be a gay, light-hearted summer in which Serge's menagerie was genuinely funny and talented and the huge Princess's antics so comic that Ella could not help laughing. She was surprised by Serge's kindness to his menagerie. He never said anything to hurt their feelings, and while he frequently corrected Ella, he never said a word to them.

Victoria and her husband Louis came, and Ernie, who delighted in the menagerie and at once acted in an amateur theatrical, playing the part of Cinderella, while the fat Princess was one of the ugly sisters. At other times, he would sit on the huge woman's knee and pretend he was riding a horse as she jogged him up and down until, with a final huge jerk, she would throw him – to everyone's delight – on to the floor.

When Ella first saw Victoria again, she flung herself into her arms, forgetting her sister was pregnant, but drew back horrified at her instinctive reaction of envious hate which the touch of her sister's stomach made her feel. How could she hate anything to do with the sister she loved best of all her family? And as the two stood together, their hands clasped, she realized that while her love would always remain, they had become and must now always remain separated by divided loyalties, and on her part by a secret she felt she could never confide.

Serge's strict rules, however, placed limits on plans for any series of entertainments. No guest could go on a picnic without his permission, or order a horse or visit any neighbour. He alone decided upon the picnic sites, and even chose the exact places where rugs and cushions should be placed against trees, and defined the area in which guests could wander before and after lunch. Occasionally, when Serge was resting, Ella had to make a decision. Once she allowed Ernie to go out in a dog cart, but when Serge heard of the harmless trip, made without his authority, he was publicly rude to Ella. Victoria one day asked her if his autocratic manner caused her pain. She thought seriously before answering and said, 'No, I am an obedient wife and he is my husband. I know he loves me in his way. I would hate anybody to pity me.'

The sisters looked at each other and Victoria said she would never again worry about her sister, and promised to tell Grandmama Ella was happy.

Her family stayed at Ilonskoye until the third week in August, after which the guests gradually drifted away. Once Victoria had left, Ella realized that her pride had put up a barrier between them. It was sad.

She deeply missed the happiness of country life after their return to St Petersburg, where she hardly had time to think between dressing, undressing and attending endless imperial ceremonies, which she found so long and tiring that she learned the knack of falling asleep while standing up with her eyes open. It would have been so much pleasanter if Serge's family had welcomed her. Vladimir made it plain that he considered her a brainless fool. Miechen was changeable: often she was downright rude, but occasionally showed flashes of kindness and generosity, which was confusing, since Ella never knew what to expect. Open unpleasantness would have been easier to deal with than the uncertainty of not knowing whether she was to be welcomed or snubbed. On the other hand, while she grew increasingly fond of Paul, Alixis never spoke to her and still seemed to bear a grudge that she had refused to marry him. As for the Tsar, he seldom left the safety of Peterhof. Serge once told her, when he was drunk after a regimental dinner, that his brother was a coward who lived in terror of assassination. The next morning he told her sharply that on no account was she ever to repeat any opinions which he ever expressed upon any member of his family. Afterwards, she watched the Tsar – only with great difficulty could she think of him as her brother-in-law – carefully, and noticed how he constantly looked about him, showing the whites of his eyes, as if he was expecting a stab in the back. His wife Marie behaved perfectly on every occasion but, after her initial kindness, clearly thought of Ella as a member of the family to be smiled at but kept at a distance, thus to avoid any tiresome intimacy which might impinge on the happy private life at Peterhof.

The general unfriendliness made Ella turn increasingly to Paul. He gave to a lonely girl, starved of affection and missing her family, a natural friendship and kindness that made her regard him as her only true friend. She guessed that he loved her in a youthful way, and was very careful never to give him any encouragement, and constantly said how she regarded him as a loved brother. Serge's reaction to her friendship with his brother puzzled her. He would gaze at her with cold eyes without speaking, and there were times, as she and Paul laughed together, when she would see her husband staring at them both. Yet he never spoke a word of criticism and positively encouraged their friendship by asking Paul to use their houses as his own.

This precious friendship was ended by a stupid misunderstanding at a ball given by Miechen at Tsarskoye Selo. The evening had started well. Ella was happy, Serge in a good mood and she, wearing her favourite colour of mauve with her diamond parure, knew that she looked beautiful. It was a grand occasion and for once the Tsar and Tsarina, despite their dislike of Vladimir, had agreed to attend for a short time. Ella danced first with Serge, next with a major in the Preobrazhensky Regiment, who said, as he did at every dance, that he had never seen her looking so beautiful. That evening she believed him. As she danced, her feet scarcely touched the ground. Everything was perfect. The Tsar was complimentary in his rough way and the Tsarina charming. Even Vladimir, who Serge said later was tipsy, praised her loudly in front of the whole room and insisted that they drink two glasses of champagne together.

Late in the evening, Paul asked her to dance a waltz, and as he put her hand around his back, she felt an extraordinary sense of physical elation, as if she could dance for ever. She wondered if it was her imagination that his arm was holding her a little tighter than usual. If so, it was pleasant; she felt her back consciously relaxing. The romantic music of the dance was so overpowering that she shut her eyes and, for perhaps half a minute, dreamed she was guided by his slightest touch. She opened them, still dancing, aware of a message of antagonism, and saw, as Paul turned her round, that Miechen's eyes were fixed on her, her whole face expressing satisfaction as she said goodbye to the Tsar and Tsarina, who both stood staring at her with shocked surprise.

Three days later, on the morning of Countess Kleinworth's ball, Ella was, as usual, deciding with Serge who her partners should be, when she realized that he was looking at her with a set face, waiting for her to suggest dancing with Paul. She knew, by his coldness, that he was aware of her innocent, momentary indiscretion and was angry and jealous. It was annoying.He must know that she would never have considered anything but a brotherly love for Paul. It was maddening that the music of the waltz should have made her give in to the momentary impulse to close her eyes and float around the ballroom, and now Serge would never forgive her. She decided it would look odder not to ask to dance with Paul than to suggest his name naturally. Serge looked at her, his manner exaggeratedly cordial, and said: 'Yes, my little one, you may dance with my beloved brother, but I would like you to know that your beloved husband will be watching your every motion, so do not give way to foolish fancies which embarrass your beloved husband, the Tsar and Tsarina, cause gossip and give great pleasure to your sister-in-law, who, as far as I know, is not beloved of anyone.'

Ella never found out who spoke to Paul, but when he next saw her, ease and innocence were replaced by restraint and embarrassment. She felt sad and insulted, but chiefly sad – she had genuinely taken to him. Their friendship was innocent, they were both young, liked each other, dancing and talking together. That was all.

Two months later, Paul was sent on a long journey. The next time she saw him he was engaged to Marie of Greece.

Part Three
1891–1905

1

In the years following her marriage, the pattern of Ella's life was outwardly unchanged. She spent the winters in St Petersburg at the Sergei Palace, the summers at Ilonskoye. Every year she visited England or Hesse, and insisted that she was happily married and Serge the best of husbands.

Alexander and Marie spent more time at Peterhof and Livadia, and each year made fewer public appearances as the battle continued between the police and the terrorists. Gradually the authorities, by ruthless persecution of any man, woman or child who showed the slightest support for change, or who even read forbidden literature, began to gain the upper hand, but at the price of internal dissatisfaction, for a thoughtless word could easily send a guiltless man on the road to Siberia.

Alexis divided his time between the affairs of the navy and visits to Paris, and it was a common joke in St Petersburg that the ladies of Paris cost at least a battleship a year. Paul was happily married to his Greek princess, who had a little girl in 1889. Vladimir and Miechen took advantage of the imperial withdrawal to establish a rival intellectual court, scornful of the Tsar's simplicity. Ella emptied her mind of bitterness and regrets and devoted herself to Serge, never contradicting him, never arguing, accepting all his actions as irreproachable. When he quietly announced to her an arbitrary decision, she would accept without reproach. Pleased, he would gently pinch her ear and tell her she was a clever little girl.

She never gave an order in her own house unless Serge was away or asleep. When he was cruelly critical, she never argued or defended herself, but apologized for her stupidity. Every night she would pray she might forget Serge's confessions and will herself to put them out of her mind. Every night she prayed that he might become her normal husband, once he had confessed his sins and repented. Knowing of the rumours concerning their marriage, she wrote annually to her grandmother, her brother and all her relations to express happiness and emphasize the goodness and kindness of her husband. She wondered whether she was indirectly telling the truth and took pleasure in martyrdom. Miechen, scornful of her placid acceptance, annoyed her by saying in a light, unpleasant way, 'Ella. You know, you are a masochist.'

She laughed, not knowing what the word meant, but was angry when she looked it up in a dictionary. She thought Miechen was mean in suggesting that her emotions were twisted by sensuality, and disliked her sister-in-law so much that she prayed not to be guilty of malevolence.

The consequence of her dance with Paul had made her realize how she was a prisoner, her life hollow and empty. She had a Mistress of the Robes, six ladies-in-waiting, a husband who made every decision, and nothing to do. She was not even allowed to visit the poor. She disliked reading, and when she tried to read a book by Dostoyevsky, she could not understand what he was writing about. She did not like poetry. She could not understand the beauty of pictures. She was thrown back on what she thought, sadly, was the only thing she was any good at: looking beautiful. To this end she dedicated herself, and found it surprising how much time she was able to devote to what, as a girl, she had thought of as an irrelevance. She neglected no detail, even making herself the face cream of cucumber juice and sour cream which she rubbed into her skin at night. She had bought a little pot on a stall at her annual sale at Ilonskoye during her first year in Russia. Finding, to her surprise, that it suited her skin, she asked Anna Tolstoy to track down the old peasant who had sent it to the stall and to buy the recipe. Afterwards, she improved the original mixture by using sour Jersey cream, into which she poured the juice of skinned cucumber crushed with a pestle. She also made her own powder from iris roots, which she dug up from her own flower beds and ground into the finest conceivable consistency before mixing it in with scented Persian powder.

Wishing for perfection, she made changing for dinner a complicated ceremony lasting three hours. The rites never altered. A maid would run her bath, and when it was the correct temperature (taken by a special red enamelled thermometer from Fabergé), would scatter over the water a spoonful of oil of roses and rose petals – in summer fresh, in winter dried. A huge, soft towel from Witney in England would then be placed loosely on a chair by her bath. Finally, before the maid left the bathroom, she would fill a wash-basin (Ella had two in all her houses) with warm water diluted with essence of verbena grown by the Tsar's head gardener at Livadia. After her bath, which lasted exactly ten minutes, Ella would immerse both hands in the verbena-scented water and stroke her bare arms, shoulders and neck to leave behind the faintest elusive scent. After ringing a little silver hand bell to prepare her serving women for re-entry, she would return to her bedroom, where the mistress of her wardrobe and her maids stood waiting among pairs of shoes, stockings, neatly gilded petticoats, and cambric lace-bordered linen in a basket lined in rose satin. They would dress and attend to every detail except her nails. These she manicured herself, intensely proud of the manner in which they curved in Chinese fashion around the end of her thumb and fingers.

Sitting on a mauve, silk-covered stool, she examined herself in a triptych with infinite care, her grey-blue eyes anxious for imperfections. By seven o'clock, she always knew whether she was satisfied with her effect or not. If not, she still had forty-five minutes to change her dress. Otherwise, she would continue to make minute changes and improvements. At a quarter to eight, Serge would come in to watch her select and put on her chosen jewels from the ever-increasing stock which he lavished on her, on view in glass cabinets running around two sides of the room. At exactly eight o'clock, they would go down to dinner. He could not abide unpunctuality. As they walked downstairs, he would show, by admiring looks, his pride in her appearance, and above all in her jewels. And for the first seven birthdays of her marriage, he gave her a parure to match every colour she could conceivably wear.

She often wondered whether her intense self-interest was wrong. She could not help loving beauty, admiring herself despite her merciless self-criticism, but her happiness in her appearance was, she soon realized, literally skin deep. However beautiful and self-satisfied she might feel at the beginning of an evening, she often went to bed angered at the coarse remarks of Vladimir and Alexis or upset by their callous jokes about the persecution of Jewry or the Poles or the Armenians, which made her long for the tolerance she had known in Darmstadt and England before her marriage.

Her anchor remained the Preobrazhensky Regiment. Serge said with pleasure how the whole regiment was in love with her; it was scarcely an exaggeration. She was fond of many of them, and of their wives and children. It was a world apart from St Petersburg, where endless gossip about the scandals and rivalries of the great were the only subjects of conversation. In the little regimental world, she knew she was dealing with human beings who had the problems and illnesses which she had faced so often and learned to understand in the hospital at Darmstadt. She was godmother to child after child. She prevented rash marriages and encouraged wise engagements. It was a consolation to know that she could go and see a young girl who was having her first baby and, in comforting her, comfort herself. Her friendship with so many of his officers' wives puzzled Serge, who commented, 'I understand your wish to dance with good dancers, but why bother with their wives? They can't dance with you.'

Her 'regimental friendships' made her realize the artificiality of the imperial court and its dangerous detachment from everyday life. The division between the classes, the poverty, the daily cruelties she heard spoken of as irrelevant made her feel as if she were living among strangers with whom she had nothing in common. What she considered amazing was to them mundane. She was literally astounded by the attitude of the imperial family to the two Montenegrin princesses who appeared like strange comets in the spring of 1889.

2

It all began when, in the interests of Pan-Slavism, the Tsar and his advisers decided that a member of his family should marry a royal Slavian princess. The trouble was to find one. Bulgaria was ruled by a Coburg, King Ferdinand, and Romania by a Hohenzollern. Serbia was suitable, but, alas, the national habit of murder had thinned the Obrenovich princesses down to an old witch of sixty who even the most obedient members of the family would have declined to marry.

The imperial policy looked like coming to a standstill, but the situation was saved when Count Lamsdorf remembered Montenegro, a minute mountain princedom smaller than Wales, where the ruling prince maintained authority over his brother bandits by brute force. Few Russians had visited the tiny mountain state, and those who had considered it to be a barbarous and primitive wilderness. Rumour stated that the Prince's palace was the only two-storey building in the capital of the country, Cetinje. However, the country possessed one distinct advantage: the Prince had several daughters reputed to be handsome, if dark, and the Tsar's special representative met with no difficulty in persuading the Prince that Militza, his prettiest daughter of marriageable age, should be affianced to the Grand Duke Peter Nikolaevich. When the engagement was announced, the Tsar was considered to have made a shrewd move in the Balkan game.

Unfortunately, a hitch occurred. One evening after dinner, as the Russian representative was calmly smoking his pipe and sipping plum brandy as he sat on his tin-roofed balcony which fronted his bungalow on the main street, a dishevelled, scarlet-faced Princess Militza burst into his room, her large lower lips unusually swollen, shrieking that on no account would she be separated from her sister, Anastasia. The next moment two members of the Prince's guard also charged in and dragged the screaming princess away. On the following day an almost illegible letter from the Prince was handed in at the newly opened Russian legation:

I have floged my daugta three times she is stuborn and will not leve the cuntry without her sistra. I plan to have her robed in chain and sent with you. I advis you to be sever with her if she stay stuborn.

The terrified representative, conceiving his career to be ruined, sent his account of the situation by mule and telegraph to the Tsar, who, horrified at the appalling effect a bride arriving in chains would have, both on Slav policies and his own European repuation, forbade the Prince to send any of his daughters unless they came of their own free will. Fearful of becoming a laughing stock, he searched round his relations and found a further cousin, the Duke of Leuchtenberg who, while he did not like women, would have done anything for the dowry which the Tsar promised to settle on Anastasia. The first stage of the matter was therefore happily concluded, and the Prince and his two dusky, unchained daughters arrived with their father in St Petersburg to meet their future husbands.

The old-fashioned members of the imperial family protested in horror at an alliance with the member of a family half bandits, half black priests. This was an exaggeration, but not a great one. Miechen inspected the Princesses Militza and Anastasia like horses and described them as 'dusky to say the least of it'.

Of course, neither the Grand Duke Peter Nikolaevich nor the Duke of Leuchtenberg had met their future wives, and since, the day after their arrival, Prince Orlov was giving a ball, this occasion was naturally selected as a fitting opportunity for introducing the two brides to the court. The Empress found out their exact measurements and sent by her Mistress of the Robes two white dresses. To her surprise, they declined the gift, saying they intended to wear their own gowns. Princess Galitzine replied tartly that their refusal to wear the Empress's gifts was unthinkable and would cause great offence.

By now the Montenegrins had become the sole subject of conversation in St Petersburg. It was common knowledge that only imperial persuasion and a large dowry had made the Grand Duke Peter agree to the marriage, and even the poor Duke of Leuchtenberg, a pensioner used to obeying the Tsar blindly, was said to be having second thoughts. Excited by the rumours, which turned them into savages eight feet tall who, for breakfast, ate raw meat in their fingers, everybody pushed and shoved to see the frights and a general disappointment was shown when it was seen that they stood barely six feet high. Their bird-like faces, distorted by large underlips, were, however, some consolation, and it was agreed that these features denoted passionate natures.

The two girls danced with gipsy abandon, which was hardly surprising as they said, openly, that this was the first indoor dance they had attended, though at home they danced every Saturday night under a large tree in Cettinje. Both, in the end, wore the Empress's white dresses, which unfortunately accentuated the swarthy tint of their flesh, which was nearly hidden by the longest white gloves the old dowagers had ever seen and white shawls draped over their shoulders and upper arms. Eyes probed beneath their finery, and within a few moments the ballroom knew that the Montenegrins were covered with black hair.

Alexander, to whom the gossip was reported, stared at them with distaste and sent for his special representative. The two men retired into an inner room, where the trembling diplomat was asked in a voice of thunder why he had not informed the court of this malformation. The poor man, almost dead with fright, replied that he had never seen any part of the girls' bodies before, since the Prince of Montenegro followed the Turkish custom of keeping his daughters covered. He had insisted on seeing them on three occasions, when they had appeared, demurely dressed, in national costumes which covered their necks, backs and the tops of their arms.

'I had enough difficulty persuading my cousins to marry these women when you stated they were beautiful. How can I make them marry these monkeys?' the Tsar shouted in a rage. 'Cannot you understand that the cancellation of the marriages will be regarded as an insult to Slavs throughout Europe and confound our foreign policy?'

At that moment a volley of shots was heard from the ballroom, but when guards rushed in and hurled themselves on the culprit, it turned out to be the Prince of Montenegro who, drunk and conceiving himself to be back home, had seized a young, nervous Princess Lvov, hurled the terrified girl into the air so that she fell and hurt her knee, and then himself made a tremendous leap, blazing away with his revolver into the ceiling. The Tsar, pale with fright, was furious and was not satisfied with the Prince's explanation that he was only performing his national dance. The one fortunate part of the whole affair was that later that night the Prince discovered the gipsies, with whom, in a state of constant intoxication, he afterwards spent his whole time.

It was said that the Duke of Leuchtenberg asked the next day to be allowed to break off his engagement, but the Tsar forbade him to change his mind, on peril of perpetual banishment from court. The Empress was asked to help, and called together all her ladies and, pledging them to secrecy, asked if any of them knew a cure for this diplomatically unfortunate hirsuteness. By good fortune, a young lady-in-waiting had heard of a mendicant vet, famous in the town of Tambov, near her father's estates, for removing moustaches and unsightly hair from the faces of wealthy provincial ladies. The Tsarina told the Tsar, who put the matter in the hands of the Colonel of the Chevalier Guards. Meanwhile, the two Montenegrins were packed off to Peterhof under the excuse that it was necessary for them to learn Russian, and the bridegrooms were asked to take into consideration, before requesting the end of their engagements, that the Tsar was doubling the dowries of the two beauties.

Ella had met the two ungainly girls at Prince Orlov's and, feeling sorry for their plight and cruel reception in a foreign country, travelled with the best of intentions by train to Peterhof and was shown into a sitting room where two old ladies, looking like fortune tellers, crouched by the window over a table covered with dirty playing cards. They hobbled off to fetch the Princesses, who came rushing in, wearing Russian-style blouses of purple and dark red, and resembling, Ella could not help thinking, two excited parrots.

'Oh, what a pleasure,' Militza said.

'Yes, truly,' added Anastasia, 'such a pleasure.'

'We admired you at the ball.'

'We thought we succeeded and everybody liked us.'

'Of course, speaking French helps. Russian we are finding difficult. But how kind of you to come.'

'Yes, very kind.'

At last Ella managed to interrupt to ask if she could be of any help.

'We would like to see more of our intended.'

'Yes, both of them. We only had two dances each with them. We understand, though.'

'Yes, men are passionate. Our father shot five men at home. We had never seen two of them so we could not understand what they had done.'

'Six men, dearest.'

'No, five I am certain. I know all their names.' She started counting on her fingers.

'Six, my dear. You have forgotten the window cleaner.'

'That is true, but window cleaners don't count, even if he was an Italian. You see, we have no window cleaners at home as there are so few windows. He was sent from Trieste. He had six children. But Papa forgot who he was and shot him off his ladder. He fell down, flop, stone dead. It was too comic, for he had never even seen us.'

'Too comic for words.'

Ella asked again if there was anything else they wanted, explaining sympathetically that, before her own marriage, she had spent two weeks at Peterhof without once seeing Serge.

'Foreign customs are difficult – always hard to understand.'

'We are happy to train. We like training – we had never seen one before. But we are locked in.'

'And we don't know where father is. We have not seen him since we came here.'

'No, not since the ball. We hope he has not been shot.'

'Or knifed, we hope very much he has not been knifed.'

They looked at her inquiringly. Fortunately, she was saved from explaining that the Prince of Montenegro was in no danger, except from the effect of a fortnight's sodden drunkenness, by the old women playing patience near the window breaking their silence with cackles of delight and beckoning to the girls, who jumped up in excitement.

'It's out, it's out!' they screamed when they saw the cards.

'Our fortunes are made – both aces, diamonds and hearts – and the death card at the very end. But we have all to die anyway, haven't we, some time?'

A few days later, Serge told Ella the end of the story, which had caused immense amusement at every dinner party. The Colonel sent three picked young officers by train to the province of Tambov to find the 'hair remover' and bring him to Peterhof. They eventually ran him to ground, made inquiries and were assured that the effects of his muttered charms and manual rubbings with a secret ointment was nothing short of miraculous, and that in disposing of unwanted hair he was much sought after by the wives of rich merchants.

Returning to the inn, they held him for a quarter of an hour under a cold pump before taking him to collect his balm. Since his clothes stank, they put a sword to a tailor's throat and forced him to cut and sew two suits. The next day the three officers returned in triumph to St Petersburg with their terrified, sober prisoner, who was told he would lose his head if the Montenegrins did not lose their hair. A few days later, the whole town knew that his remedies had worked. The two marriages would take place and the Tsar had only, after all, increased their dowries by half again, claiming that the girls now looked presentable and attractive.

Serge thought the affair very humorous. Ella smiled so as not to anger him, but persuaded herself she was shocked by the gloating cruelty of society to poor girls little better than natives. Then she remembered the screaming parrots at Peterhof and burst out laughing, realizing she was as unkind as Serge.

Gradually the fuss died as the sisters' persistent politeness and habit of telling every woman they met that she was a beauty won them many friends. Yet Ella disliked their sly eyes and mischievous personalities, and doubted their sincerity, although at the same time she felt sorry for them as Miechen laughed in their faces and appeared to get a peculiar pleasure in making fools of them by encouraging them to play unsuitable charades and act ridiculous scenes at her parties. Ella thought her unkind and believed it was poetic justice when Miechen and Vladimir became involved in a scandal which made them, and not the newly christened 'Black Perils', the chief subject of the gossips.

Miechen and Vladimir gave a dinner in the Bear Restaurant to honour the presence in the capital of the distinguished French actor, Lucien Guitry, and his beautiful French wife. Vladimir drank even more than usual and paid extravagant and unwelcome attentions to Madame Guitry, eventually becoming so over-excited that he lost all restraint and publicly embraced the surprised Frenchwoman, to the consternation of the waiters and amazed diners. Miechen, angry but perfectly controlled, pretended nothing had happened, but Lucien Guitry, not educated in the same school of manners, unfortunately vented his fury by jumping on her and behaving in the same manner as Vladimir had treated his wife.

While the Grand Duke thought it perfectly permissible for himself to seize Madame Guitry, Guitry's attack on his wife appeared to him an unforgiveable act of lese-majesty, and, pushing Madame Guitry aside, he tried to hit him. A mêlée ensued, with the Grand Duke on his feet furiously shouting that he would kill the actor. After an undignified argument, the head waiter separated the two men and an attempt was made to hush the matter up. This was unsuccessful; too many had seen the incident. By midday the next day the scandal was the talk of St Petersburg. Before evening the Tsarina had given the Tsar an account of the undignified brawl which sent him into such a rage that, it was rumoured, he could not trust himself to speak for three days. This could not have been strictly true, as the Guitrys found themselves on the first train to Paris at the same time as the Tsar was interviewing his younger brother.

What was said at the meeting was unknown, but within a week Vladimir and Miechen had left for a long holiday in Nice. Ella could not help feeling pleased. Ever since her arrival, Miechen had gone out of her way to make her sister-in-law feel inadequate by semi-public references to her inability to please Serge, by repeating scornful jokes concerning her stupidity and ignorance, and referring to her, in patronizing terms, as 'the beautiful innocent'. How could the eclipse of such a malevolent enemy not have pleased her?

3

Ella waited with impatience for the summer holidays in Ilonskoye. She had grown to love the house and associate it with family reunions. Victoria and Irene came every summer, and her father to Usovo in September for the shooting, and one year Serge's sister Marie brought her four children to stay. Her eldest child, also Marie, who was the prettiest girl she had ever seen, adored her, refusing to go to sleep unless Ella kissed her good night. Ella was never sure whether such affection made her happy or unhappy.

That year, Serge was more relaxed in the country than in Moscow, although the usual restrictions prevailed, which made what could have been pleasant informalities into military operations. Once permission was granted, they jumped helter-skelter into the formal ranks of boats tied up at the back of the house and floated downstream. But there was no choice. It was the same old story. At a certain point a footman on the bank halted their progress and forced them to land for a delicious picnic, prepared on linen-covered tables, with iced wine, tea and coffee. If, after eating, they strolled among the trees, rugs would be laid out in the places where Serge had elected they should rest.

One afternoon, the picnickers received a message that the Grand Duke wished the party to return at six o'clock, 'so please would all re-embark immediately after the meal is finished'. Ernie asked if Serge locked his sister in at night. Nobody laughed, and Victoria changed the subject.

Serge's sacred habit of resting undisturbed for two hours every afternoon had one advantage: it gave Ella a period of freedom. Occasionally, she would sit in the shade, drawing ideas for new dresses, but usually, if the weather was fine, she wandered in the woods to favourite places where she could think, as she had as a child at Kranichstein. During these walks, she occasionally saw, in the obscurity of the woods, flutters of colour among the distant trees, which turned out to be the bright skirts of village girls collecting the mushrooms which grew after rain. The peasants, even after five years, remained strangers. Ella tried to interest herself in the lives they led in the squalid villages, outside the gates of Ilonskoye, but if ever she spoke they would stand silently, looking at her with unresponsive, uncomprehending eyes.

Every year she organized, on behalf of the local peasants, a bazaar at which she expected that her neighbours and the friends staying in her house would help to sell exciting goods collected in the Crimea, St Petersburg, and even

England and France. It caused great excitement in the locality, and Serge arranged for the profits to be used for the good of the villages.

Even on these occasions, the gulf between the peasants and herself appeared, unlike in England and Hesse, to be unbridgeable. Ella found it unpleasant to be regarded with terror, but this was the only contact which Serge allowed her with his employees. He turned down her ideas for a school and hospital, saying it would be throwing good money after bad. Forgetting her resolutions to obey, she pointed out the savagery of wife beating and the number of child deaths.

He shrugged his shoulders and remarked laconically: 'You will learn it is one of the sacred traditions of our peasantry to beat their wives every Friday night. You do not understand our history.'

'And what about the children, the murder of unwanted babies?'

'That, as far as I know, is not a problem which concerns you.'

She had blushed scarlet. How could he say such unkind words?

She was surprised when Serge, without telling her, appointed a medical officer in their district. She thanked him and received the cold reply: 'I do not deserve thanks for wasting time and money.'

When she visited Zenaïde at Arkhangelskoye, and saw the manner in which their peasants lived, she knew that Serge was wrong. The Youssoupovs had built four model villages with, at their centre, a bath-house, a reading room and a chapel, while, at the edge of their park, there stood a large hospital under the direction of a doctor from Moscow. Zenaïde's husband, a typical soldier, inspected with martial efficiency the buildings and instigated a system of three warnings to slothful peasants which, if ignored, resulted in their expulsion.

As a consequence, the four villages – which altogether perhaps included six hundred houses – stood spick and span. The houses looked clean and well kept, and the hospital decreased the childbirth deaths. But the Prince's educational theories shocked her. He believed in teaching children to read and write, but afterwards they had continuous lessons in husbandry and practical farming. When Ella asked: 'What if they wish to do something else?' he replied, in surprise, 'What else is there for them to do? After all, they must do as they are told.'

Serge laughed at such a waste of money, would have nothing to do with any similar expenditure and was delighted whenever trouble of any kind occurred on the Youssoupov estate.

Three of the villages consisted of simple-roofed peasants' houses with attached stone pigstys, but a pianist in the Youssoupov orchestra designed the fourth village in original and constrasting styles, each house having an architectural symbol of the inhabitant's occupation. He had built houses for librarians, picture restorers, piano tuners, musicians, actors, dancers, singers, stage painters. Once a year, Zenaïde gave a concert, followed by a dance, to which she asked what she called 'my cultural employees' with their wives and daughters. Every year, a party drove over from Ilonskoye and stayed until dawn, with the exception of Serge and his cronies, who always went home early, muttering about 'filthy Jews'. Serge considered it bad taste to give a party for actors and musicians, but was mollified and a little amused, considering she had put the artists in their right place, when Zenaïde told him that she copied the idea from the servants' ball at Sandringham.

The concert always took place in September, after the harvest and the bazaar at Ilonskoye. By 1890, the year of the fifth party, Ella had met many of the musicians and once unsuccessfully tried to learn the mandolin. It was no good. She had no talent. Late in the evening, she was surprised to find herself followed by a violinist she knew by sight. Having hovered around her, he at last plucked up courage, approached, bowed, made a nervous remark, began to say something else, lost his nerve and walked away. Later on, he again stood hovering. She beckoned him and said: 'Anton Yashnin, I have known you for five years; you have come several times to play in my house. I know you wish to speak to me. What is it? Tell me, please.'

He was a nervous little man with long black hair, a bald patch at the back of his head and dark soulful eyes. He appeared taken aback and blurted out: 'Your Imperial Highness, you once came to take lessons in the village on the mandolin. Might I ask you if you will allow me to give you lessons on the violin?'

Ella was surprised into a silence which further confused him, and he added, speaking quickly, 'But please give me two or three weeks' notice before you come.'

She was puzzled. He was a sincere, sensitive man who passionately resented the anti-semitic laws in Russia and dreamed of emigrating to the United States. She looked at him with interest. Why, after nervously hovering around, had he dared to make such an unusual request? She was sure there was something more to it, but what could it be? Her curiosity was aroused. She replied, speaking very slowly, 'Yes, I will come for a lesson in two weeks' time.'

Her reply surprised her and made her doubt whether she had answered of her own free will or was being guided by an instinct over which she had no control. In the same way, she had accepted Serge's offer of marriage, and now, also without knowing why, she had committed herself to visiting a musician's house at a period when she knew her husband was away. On the day, to show she had nothing to conceal, she ordered a groom to drive her over in a pony cart, having previously sent a message that it was necessary for her to return by 5.30 to change for dinner.

4

Anton Yashnin and his wife stood waiting in their best clothes outside the front door and led her, with apologies for its simplicity, into the house. To her surprise, stained-glass windows on either side of the porch displayed violins, and in the passage hung prints by Burne-Jones and Alma-Tadema, which she remembered from her English youth. His wife curtsied and fled into the kitchen while he led her through a small drawing room with a wooden fireplace with coloured tiles, again stirring memories of England, into a small, dark room separated from the rest of the house. Similar rooms with sound-proof doors had been attached by Prince Youssoupov to every one of the musicians' houses out of consideration for their wives. He had explained their purpose in his loud, jocular voice: 'I can't imagine anything worse for wives than to have to hear their husbands continuously practising. The constant noise would make them either kill their children or ruin the lunch.' He was very pleased with this joke, and repeated it whenever he graciously showed guests over his model estate on Sunday afternoons.

Anton led Ella to the double doors and stood aside. The only light in the bare room came from a single stained-glass window and she thought she was alone until she saw, in the right-hand corner, a man bowing. Anton waved his hands, muttered an introduction, grabbed at the door handle and ran out, but immediately came back, flung himself at her feet and gabbled: 'I must tell Your Imperial Highness at once I am a wretched liar and brought you here under false pretences to allow a friend to give you an account of the suffering of my people. In case you think I am biased, listen to him. He does not belong to my race but wishes to tell you certain truths. Please forgive me.' Sinking to his knees he seized her reluctant hand. 'My people are suffering. Cruelties are forcing them to rebel, making them hate Russia. Forgive me, oh forgive me. I have put my life in your hands. If you tell His Imperial Highness, not even the Prince can save me.'

She never knew why she had not gone home. She had decided to leave, for to stay was monstrously disloyal to Serge, but instead she sat down and Anton quietly closed the door behind him and started to scrape away at his violin. The man in the corner, without moving, said: 'I am honoured to meet Your Imperial Highness.'

It was difficult to see what he looked like in the darkened room, but, straining her eyes, she thought he was coarsely made, of medium height, running to fat, with a puffy, unhealthy face, a wide mouth and black moustache below a spreading, coarse nose. His hair was thick and oily. Altogether, his general appearance resembled that of a butcher, but he spoke in melodious tones compelling her to listen; forcing her against her inclinations to stay and hear charming, dangerous sentences which would, in ordinary circumstances, have made her leave immediately. He explained that the love of Russia ruled his life, but that he was worried that the present policies of the Tsar would lead to revolution.

'You cannot, in the enlightened world of the nineteenth century, repress a whole nation, bury its ambitions, trample on its ideals, imprison, banish or kill all dissidents and insist that every man and woman do exactly what they are told without redress, justice or appeal to any elected assembly.'

'Who are you?'

The man, still in his corner, replied: 'I am a patriot who serves Russia in my own way. May I tell you why I asked my friend Anton to bring you here today, imperilling his life and mine? It is because I think I know your character and believe myself to be safe in your hands. Anyway, I am prepared to take the risk and consider it my duty to tell you of events which, unless checked, could lead to your husband's death. Your know, despite your goodness, you live in a golden cage. I wish to tell you what is happening outside it.'

She feebly lifted her hand and said it was her duty to pass on everything she heard to her husband, adding: 'I can and will not promise to hide anything from him.'

He spoke almost impatiently. 'Please listen before you decide. When you have heard certain facts, I believe you will understand why I am here.' He paused. 'I do not believe you realize the danger which your husband faces when he is appointed Governor-General of Moscow next year.'

'What!'

'Ah, you see, you are unaware of this appointment. Let me assure you, the final details will be settled when your husband returns from Moscow in three days' time. He will tell you he has accepted out of loyalty to the Tsar, who believes that the only way to combat terrorism is by firmness. He will not tell you that the Tsar plans for the Jewish population of Moscow – who he considers to be the enemies of the State – to be expelled from Moscow next spring. The announcement may be made before your husband takes up his appointment, but he is in agreement with the proposal and intends to enforce it with all his powers as Governor-General. I do not believe you realize the strength of his anti-semitism or the implications of his appointment. With great respect, I think you should. I do not wish your husband to be killed.'

Astounded at the disclosure of an imperial secret of which she had heard no word, Ella could think of nothing to say or do. The surprise made her feel weak. She stood up, moved forward and sat down again. The stranger bowed.

'Well yes, if you wish, I suppose,' said Ella in confusion.

'I am deeply grateful. Today, despite Anton's predictions, I do not wish to discuss the Jewish problem. With great deference, I hope to give you an impartial view of this Empire's plight, of which, with respect, I believe you know nothing, explaining why brutality, born of fear, is an everyday event. Before 1500 , Russia was the size of France. In every suceeeding century, it has grown, swallowing its neighbours one by one. And today, almost unnoticed, we have become the greatest, or at any rate the largest, empire the world has ever known. The danger of our conquests is that we have ceased to be a country and have become a disorderly mass of discordant peoples. However, the Tsar believes that we can regain our old unity by what his favoured adviser, Pobedonostsev, calls Russification. This policy has now become confused with nationalism and religion. Finns, Armenians, Uzbeks, Tartars, Poles, Balts, Jews, Moldavians, Azerbaidjaniis and countless other minorities are to be persuaded to give up their traditional faiths and become Orthodox Russians, accepting the primacy of the Holy Synod. As further encouragement, every possible disadvantage is to be heaped upon those who refuse. Having made the Tsar agree to the Russification of his alien subjects, it is logical for Pobed-onostsev, the actual director of imperial policy, who is nothing if not logical, to ensure that Russians who deviate in their beliefs should conform.

'But here he comes up against an insuperable difficulty, dissent, which has always divided the Orthodox Church without affecting the practice of the faithful or the loyalty of the peasant to the Tsar. Alas, to explain, I fear I shall have to give you a lecture on the religious history of Russia, unless, of course, you decline to hear me.'

Ella was so astonished by his unexpected, half-comprehended remarks and her submission to this strange, ugly man's personality, that she could only weakly shake her head. He continued in sentences that rose and fell with a monotony superior to interruption.

'As you will know, the Russian Empire accepted Orthodoxy as the official religion in the tenth century. As our western empire grew and repelled the invasions from the east, so our religion was accepted by the inhabitants of the ever-increasing imperial territories, but, during this period, illiteracy was common and dogma and beliefs frequently passed from mouth to mouth: and services and prayers differed in various districts. This was inevitable, considering the geography and climate of the country. In the spring, seas of mud prevented, even more than nowadays, the already distant communities leaving their immediate areas. In the few months of summer, the peasant had and has no time to move. Even today, he spends all his time working to make hay, grow enough grain and plough and sow before winter comes again, which makes communication difficult. Consequently, a nationally accepted dogma and liturgy as existed in the countries of Western Europe was unknown in Russia. Only in large cities were the precise tenets and liturgy of the Orthodox Church, based on Greek Orthodox practice, known or understood. In many country districts, the wording and stories of the gospels and the names and actions of saints became altered, while different spelling of Jesus abounded and were considered to be a private matter, sometimes related to a legend of the locality.

'When, in 1650, the Patriarch Nixon insisted on a standardization of services, his reforms created dismay and confusion. In isolated regions, religious practices, originally passed by mouth and altered by hundreds of years of local practice, bore no relation to the rigid rules and dogmas of Byzantine scholarship suddenly being thrust down their throats, and so open rebellion broke out. How, priests complained, could they possibly convince their parishioners that God's son had changed his name, that the local saint, to whom they nightly prayed and after whom they called their children, was no longer accepted? The use of troops to standardize belief had a certain success in the vicinity of Moscow and the few centres of population, but in the remote countryside, standard Orthodoxy was unaccepted, and the dissenters continued to worship the old names and saints, and proudly called themselves the Old Believers.

'The cynic would say that the persecutions they suffered over the years stimulated their faith but was not consistent enough to disband them. At any rate, these Old Believers elect their own priests carefully, lead decent, sober and discreet lives and have thrived in business. Today, the whole grain trade of Russia passes through their hands. Unified in their disunity, they may occasionally suffer local persecution, but they are too powerful to be crushed into Orthodoxy, and although the Holy Synod will not admit it, they numbered, at the last official census, approximately nearly 40 per cent of those whom the State claim to be Orthodox Christians.'

He stopped. 'Am I boring you?'

'Oh no,' she said. 'You have made me realize for the first time that I am still an ignorant stranger here. Please go on.'

He nodded, almost as if he had taken her agreement as a foregone conclusion. 'I would now like to digress again and speak further of the effect which climate and distance have on the Russian peasant's soul. If you live in a community that is only periodically in touch with its neighbours, and is lost for eight months of the year in a sea of snow with only a few hours of light, then, to survive, the peasants have to believe. And if you add the ill-effects of the climate, and the almost total lack of any medical aid, I think you will understand that it is an essential part of their character to conceive that a better world lies the other side of death, justifying their triumphs over the miserable circumstances of their lives. Their belief in another, gentler world causes the peasant to cast a critical eye on the local priest, the distributor of the Host, the conveyor of the thoughts of God. The Orthodox Church, now little more than an arm of the State, offers the peasants little outside the theatrical churches of Moscow and St Petersburg, since the country priest, very different from his sophisticated, celibate city brother, is hardly more than a hereditary official and blackmailer satisfactory to his employers, provided he costs no money and keeps the peasants quiet by uncomprehended rituals which become habit rather than demonstrations of belief. In every village in the great land mass of Russia, country priests are not men of God but sons and grandsons of priests who pass on their careers to their sons in much the same manner as a money lender. The prospective hereditary priest is brought up in poverty, in the words of a Russian apophthegm, "an inch above the peasant, a foot below the rest". Before their ordination, they are "finished" in religious colleges and taught, not the meaning of the gospel or the love of man preached by Christ, but the rites of the Orthodox Church and how much they can charge peasants for performing their parish duties.

107

'They have to know which icons should be displayed and worshipped on various days, the correct form of words to be used to praise saints on their name days, the customs and prayers of Christmas, Easter and holy days. That is all. In other words, they learn what might be described as the technicalities of the Orthodox Church but nothing of the message of the gospel and the teaching of Jesus, so it is not surprising if many of them regard the Trinity as levers to extract money from their parish.

'When they are considered to have gained sufficient knowledge of these technicalities, they are shown, in the library of their college, volumes of books describing the characteristics, age and inclinations of daughters of other priests. They take their choice, marry them and set off for their new parishes, where their only payment is what they can extract from the peasants at times of illness, weddings, christenings and funerals. Despite this, and especially if the local priest is a man of kindness, he will live in grinding poverty. If his wife dies, he is not allowed to remarry, although when he employs a housekeeper to look after his motherless children, she is expected by the villagers to satisfy his carnal needs. This is not criticized, but frequently results in numerous illegitimate children who add little to his dignity.'

He paused at the look of horror on Ella's face. He was right. She wished to challenge some of the aspersions on the Church which she planned to enter, but, realizing she knew nothing of the subject and that her objections would sound ridiculous, she closed her mouth, wondering whether these frightening statements could be true. The stranger seemed to have read her thoughts as he continued.

'Don't think I am exaggerating. Recently a report was made on the priesthood. It has, of course, been suppressed as it brought out the almost universal disrespect in which the brotherhood is held, and cited thousands of cases illustrating their degradation. I will send you a copy.'

'Oh, please don't,' Ella interrupted in a panic.

If the Orthodox Church was demolished, where could she go for refuge?

'All right,' he said inexorably. 'Let me give you a few examples. Villagers nearly beat to death a priest caught stealing money from beneath the pillow of a dying man; another was turned out of his village after receiving a payment for christening a dog. In a twelve-month period, over two hundred priests became involved in drunken fights, and twice, in recent years, have killed opponents, using the cross of their profession as a bludgeon of death.

'The report was critical of the system of hereditary priesthood as bringing annually into the service of God men with no religious vocation or knowledge. But the priest's ignorance is more resented than his sins. The Russian peasant is, as I have said, by nature religious, and a holy man lives in nearly every village, devoting his life to reading the gospel. He is held in universal respect, his knowledge often superior to the priest's, which encourages parishioners, starved of religion, to accept with excitement his beliefs founded on some sentence of the gospel which the priest can neither contradict nor explain. The inevitable consequence has been the perpetual dissatisfaction and the mushroom birth and death of local prophets whose beliefs, upon occasion, spread beyond their own districts and momentarily establish unlawful religions.

'I will not go into the confusing history of these segments of Christianity, but merely say that their beliefs are intense and sincere. Their only sin is that they are unorthodox and prepared to die for Jesus and God. To prosecute and murder such men is folly. They are not protesting, as the Synod argues, against the Church and the Tsar. They are protesting against the bleakness of their lives and the stupidity and ignorance of their Orthodox priests, as they have done for the last eight hundred years.

'The history of Russia is the history of dissent, and dissent is a personal protest and in no way implies disloyalty to the Tsar. To try and hustle dissenters into the Orthodox Church is as stupid as attempting to turn the minorities into Russians. But such is the policy of Pobedonostsev. The consequence is the destruction of loyalty and the creation of revolutionaries. The Church may officially swallow and destroy poor, irrelevant, stagnant tribes, but in assaulting the Jews and the Old Believers, it is creating enemies of quality, brains and ability who make natural leaders of the dissatisfied and without whose help I doubt if revolution will ever succeed.

'I consider that you should know the story of Jewish persecution, and why, unless there is a change of imperial policy, Jewry will play a catastrophic role in the future of the Empire which the Old Believers could never play. I would like to explain why, so I hope I will see you again. But return now to Ilonskoye. Your allotted time is over and a longer visit would excite interest. Please do not tell your husband of this meeting. It would be a poor way of thanking Anton, to send him and his family to Siberia. What good would that do? As to myself, I ask you to believe that I have come to you out of admiration and in good faith, to try and save your husband's life. My extraordinary behaviour I may one day explain.'

He bowed and stood in silence. Ella could not make up her mind what to say or do. If what he said was true he must be in a powerful position. If not, who was he? Her one idea now was to get out of the room and bring order to her thoughts, and she stood up, putting her hands behind her back, determined not to make a formal gesture of farewell to a man who had turned her world upside down. When she spoke, her voice sounded, she was glad to hear, clearer and calmer than her thoughts: 'You have given me information which I do not believe. If I am wrong, I will return here in a week, having ascertained the exact truth from my husband. If you are misinformed, I swear I will never mention this meeting, not that I care what happens to you, but I don't wish to send a harmless musician into exile.'

Without even nodding goodbye, she turned and left the room. The sitting room was empty, but she heard a noise coming from the kitchen, and, opening the door, saw Anton trying to comfort his wife, who was screaming and sobbing as she beat her head on the kitchen table. Anton looked up white-faced, the picture of misery, with tears in his eyes. Ella walked towards him, avoiding looking at the weeping woman as she took his hand and said slowly and loudly: 'Lies may have been told in your house which could result in your ruin. I do not believe you are responsible. I will say nothing.'

Gently, she put her hands on the woman's head and, pulling the hair away from the brow, gently stroked her forehead, saying in a voice which she tried to

109

keep calm: 'I promise, you have nothing to fear.'

Gradually, the woman stopped crying, and Ella bent forward and kissed her brow before walking out of the room with her head averted to prevent Anton seeing the tears in her own eyes.

On the way back, she tried to gather together her thoughts. Could Serge really be planning to expel those poor people? Should she be responsible for sending Anton to Siberia? Should she – if Serge was planning to follow this course – not try her hardest to stop him? She could say she heard from the Youssoupovs that he was going to be Governor-General and find out the truth. If the news was inaccurate, the stranger was a braggart to ignore. If he was correct, she had no idea what to do.

When Serge returned from Moscow, he was in a strange, elevated mood, and watching him, she noticed that he did not listen to his neighbours at dinner nor smile afterwards when the huge Princess pulled a footman over her knees and smacked his behind. Directly after dinner, he went to the library. She pleaded a headache and went to bed.

At midnight, Serge came in. He paced up and down the room in an unusual manner, and when at last he climbed on to his side of the bed without a dispatch case or papers, he sat upright, obviously intent on speaking to her. Tactfully, she put down her 'approved' novel by Octave Feuillet and asked if he was worried.

'No,' he said loudly, 'I am not troubled, but I must tell you that your life will change. I have agreed to my brother's request to become next Governor-General of Moscow.'

Ella was too relieved to speak. She had constantly thought how she could tactfully find out if the story was true. Now, without her asking, he had told her what she wanted to know. In relief, she said the first thing which came into her head, and asked him if he would not mind leaving his beloved Preobrazhensky Regiment.

'I give it up,' he replied, talking quickly, 'because Pobedonostsev has persuaded me it is my duty to help to contain the undermining of our fatherland by alien elements who conspire to create revolution, disorder and kill my brother, who is not only the Emperor of Russia but Protector of the Russian Church.'

Then he started attacking the Jews.

She waited until he had finished and said: 'I think I have always shown you my loyalty. If I ask you with my whole heart to refuse this position, will you grant me that one favour?'

'No,' he said, 'it is my duty to preserve my country, its form of government and religion which have made it the greatest empire on earth.'

'Please,' she said, 'I am afraid that if you become Governor-General you will be killed.'

'If I have done my duty, I will not have died in vain. You have no idea how the plotters have infiltrated even into my brother's house. Once a week, for the last year, messages threatening his life have appeared upon his pillow or desk or in any obvious place. This means that although his household has been checked and rechecked and every possible precaution taken, there is, even in Tsarskoye

110

Selo, a killer planning to assassinate my brother as another killed my father.'

He was staring straight in front of him now, his eyes blank.

She put out her hand and held his and said: 'Of course, if you feel you should take this position do so, but take care.'

He paid not the slightest attention, and when she took her hand away, he remained looking into the distance.

That night, before she fell asleep, she wondered if she should have stayed and listened to the stranger; who could he be to know imperial secrets? How could he wish either of them harm if all he had done was to try and prevent Serge from becoming Governor-General and warn her he would be killed? And whoever he was, surely he was right that Serge's faults made him unfit to hold a position of unlimited power, especially if it was his intention to expel thousands of Jews from Moscow? Was she wrong to believe in the sins of those cursed people? She must know the truth, and decided at once to go the next week to Anton's, if Serge gave permission for her to have another music lesson. When she asked, he nodded, without showing the slightest interest, hardly appearing to hear her question. She understood the reason for his unusual carelessness. At the moment, he was so concerned with his own career and involved in the future that, for the first time since their marriage, he simply had not time or interest to bother about her movements.

5

She lunched with Zenaïde before her second 'music lesson', and at three o'clock, with her heart hitting her ribs, arrived at Anton's house to be met again at the door by the musician, who looked at her with tears of gratitude in his eyes. This time she dismissed him, walked alone into the little practice room and once again closed the door to the faltering sounds of Anton's violin. The stranger, who was standing in the same corner, bowed, without making any attempt to approach her. She sat down and told him, without looking up, how Serge had conveyed his intention to accept the Governorship of Moscow and her unsuccessful attempt to dissuade him. There was nothing more she could do.

'You said last time that you would tell me the history of the Jews in Russia. Please do so, but don't ask me ever again to try to influence my husband – he never changes his mind.'

She kept her eyes fixed desperately on her hands, nervously locking and interlocking her fingers. He stood silent, waiting for her to look at him. She continued to examine her hands until, at length, he began to speak, and she found herself unable to keep her eyes down any longer.

'I am sorry that your husband has agreed both to be Governor-General and to persecute innocent people. I will be brief and concentrate on essentials. Forgive me if I appear spasmodic and carried away by my own words, or if I digress – I have only two hours to give you an impression of four hundred years of violent persecution. I will not bother you with the first contact between Russia and the assimilation of the Jewish kingdom when many Jews took up residence in the principality of Kiev. All we are certain of is that, from the eleventh century, a perpetual conflict existed between the Jews and the increasingly powerful Russian Orthodox Church, but that, at the same time, religious tolerance was practised and many persecuted Jews from eastern Europe found sanctuary in Moscow and continued freely to practise their faith. It was not until the fifteenth century, after the final defeat of the last surge of eastern invaders and the consolidation of our territorial gains, that Russia became what is in this century called nationalistic, and began to organize its territories and institutions into the form of an empire. From that moment the Jews, tied to their traditional religion, came into increasingly violent conflict with the Russian Orthodox Church, which justified persecution whenever the State needed money from the murderers of Christ. Gradually the Jews, whose ostentatious religion and dress made them a 'nation within a nation', split into two distinct groups, the rich and the poor. The former shrugged persecution and the anti-semitic laws off as unavoidable blackmail, the ill-effects of which could be averted by the payment of money. But the latter, originally crammed into slum ghettoes, were, after the influx of Jews at the partition of Poland in 1722, banished into a number of eastern states known as "the Pale", where life was and is a ceaseless struggle to survive, while those who broke out of this hereditary prison became illegal immigrants, subject, if arrested, to the severest penalties.

'In the early part of the nineteenth century, the territorial additions to the south and east and the increase of population in the west frightened the Tsars into reviving the policy of Russification, which had limited success in the privileged classes of the minority groups, many of whom paid lip service to Orthodoxy and accepted Russian citizenzhip to avoid legal liabilities and financial demands. This success had an effect – at the time unnoticed – detrimental upon the Russian social state, dividing the country into those who had possessions and those who had not, uniting the first against the second, destroying the position of men of all races who stand in the middle between the rich and the poor, and ensuring that, after emancipation, the peasants changed from feudal serfs into economic slaves.

'But I have strayed. Let me return to the anti-semitic brutalities which have stained the last century of Russian history. I will give only one typical example of the type of persecution which the poor Jews suffered. In 1827, legislation forced Jewish boys of the age of twelve to serve in military training battalions. If the arbitrary numbers of cadets fixed by local authorities was not produced, the law forced the heads of Jewish communities to produce, themselves or by chosen proxies, enough children to bring the battalion up to strength. As few Jews could face the task of sentencing their friends' children to a few months' living death, they chose careless proxies who cheerfully selected boys of twelve, and if they had difficulty finding the necessary numbers, pressganged younger children. A Russian writer in 1835 described, in the following words, a terrible glimpse of a child battalion on the move.'

For the first time, the stranger moved towards her, taking a paper out of his pocket, but he stopped by the window and, putting on a pair of spectacles, read:

' "This was one of the most terrible scenes I have ever witnessed. Poor, unfortunate children! The boys of twelve or thirteen managed somehow to stand up, but the little ones of eight or nine . . . No artist's brush could paint the horror. Pale, emaciated, frightened faces looked out of the ludicrously clumsy soldiers' uniforms, casting about helpless, pitiful glances at the soldiers. From their blue lips and the blue veins under their eyes, it was obvious that they were suffering from fever and exposure. A sharp wind was blowing, and these sick children, loveless and helpless, were marching straight to their graves. I grasped the officer's hand, and crying 'Take good care of them!' flung myself into the carriage choking with tears."

'Nicholas I, the author of the deliberate murder of these children, was without concealment practising a solution favoured over the centuries by anti-semites – genocide. But the sight of infants blue with cold, dropping dead

113

hundreds of miles from their homes, was unpopular, and when Alexander II became Tsar, he appeared to reverse his father's brutal policies. The conscription of child soldiers ceased. Jews could obtain the right to live in districts in which they had served and frequently married. The most welcome of all his liberalizations was the ending of strict limitations on education. The Tsar was conceived a hero, and a wave of relief swept through the Pale and the thousands of Jews living illegally in Russia. Their optimism was misconceived, for Alexander was guided by two ambitions: to be loved and to modernize the Russian state. He knew that if his second ambition was to succeed, it was necessary to utilize the best brains in industry and government to overcome the stagnant conservatism of the nobility, and that since the acutest brains in his empire belonged to members of the Jewish race, to continue to deny the right of open competition would leave Russia at the mercy of those whose inertia and inefficiency defeated progress. That, not liberalism, was the reason why he opened the doors of education to the Jewish race.

'They grasped their chance and, within a few years, monopolized the leading positions in the legal and medical professions, thrived in government services and became the most daring and successful industrialists. Without intention, the Tsar had unconsciously aided the policy of Russification, for, to the dismay of the rabbis, the successful Jews began to drop the public extremities of their religion and follow the advice of one of their radical poets, ''Be a Jew in your tent and a man in the street.'' Many went further and began to assimilate freely and merge with the professional Russian classes, dropping their religion and becoming Russian citizens. The consequence to Russian Jewry was disastrous: their élite forsook the tradition of standing by their countrymen and distanced themselves from their less talented brothers and relations in the Pale, who, legally contained in towns, remained unemancipated, devoted to their ancient religion, under the sway of the rabbis, squashed like sardines into the filthy, squalid, overcrowded areas of the Pale, subject to disease and malnutrition and suffering the worst aspect of containment to a Jew: the lack of opportunity to work.

'Alexander, unintentionally, by offering opportunity to the élite who accepted his bait, succeeded in weakening Jewish unity by robbing the starving, discontented masses of the east of their natural leaders and spokesmen and incorporating them, to the infinite advantage of the empire, into the establishment. Yet at the moment when, to Russia as a whole, the success of his policy had begun to show material benefits, he was assassinated. His death was greeted with sorrow by both liberals and Jews. Idealistic and autocratic in turn, he was inconsistent and easily influenced. However, even in his last years, he had not tried to destroy his Jewish subjects and many of his reforms remained unchanged. He overlooked illegal practices which enabled them to work in the biggest cities by registering as artisans but following other trades, while, in 1880, the governors of the provinces west of the Pale received instructions not to expel Jews living illegally within their jurisdiction. When he died, his Jewish subjects wept because, inconsistent as he may have been, the Hebrew community was, at the end of his reign, competing equally with Russians in the professions and public services.

114

'The present Tsar had not received the education of a presumptive ruler. As a second son, he was intended to follow a military career. When he came to the throne, apart from certain fixed prejudices, he had no ideas and was under the sway of his former tutor, Pobedonostsev, who can be accurately described as the Torquemada of Russia. The Tsar was taught to believe in the purity of the Russian race, and that even when minorities joined the Orthodox Church and became assimilated into the Empire, they should be treated as inferiors while the conduct of affairs of State remained in the hands of élitist pure-bred Russians. His answer to the Jewish problem was simple: force them, by persecution, to emigrate.

'I cannot go too fully into the details but within a year of the Tsar's succession, a series of pogroms broke out in the south-west. They followed a simple pattern. Instigators arrived in a town and fanned anti-semitic prejudices never far beneath the surface because of the superiority of the Jews to the Russians in commerce. A local death would be exaggerated into a ritual murder, followed by the arrival of a group of strange young men ignored by the police. The next day, further accusations would be made against the Jews. Again the police would do nothing. Tension would rise, followed by thuggery, looting, rape, murder and wholesale destruction of Jewish property. Eventually, public opinion would force the hand of the local authorities and a few rioters would be arrested and given light sentences. The remainder would disappear, to reappear in a few weeks in another town where the parody of justice would be repeated. The placidity of the local authorities and police encouraged the local citizens and surrounding peasants to believe that the destruction of Jewish property and personal attacks on harmless men and women with whom they had lived on neighbourly terms for years was official imperial policy. Abroad, the Tsar received the blame as chief instigator of the pogroms. I have reason to know that the accusation was unfair. The massacres occurred over a thousand miles from St Petersburg in the south-west, and it is unlikely that he knew the actual culprit was his own mentor, Pobedonostsev, who, working with Count Ignatiev – appointed Minister of the Interior in 1881 – cleverly organized the affair by making money available to numerous bands of anti-semitic 'pure Russian' royalist societies who believed that their orders came from the Tsar. But to instigate mob rule is dangerous. Disorder spreads, and soon the Tsar replaced Ignatiev by a conservative Count Tolstoy, who insisted on order and discipline and, to Pobedonostsev's dismay, momentarily crushed the Sacred League and the Black Hundreds, or whichever names the purist anti-semitics had momentarily given themselves.

'The Pahlen Commission was set up in 1883 to consider the Jewish question, but when, after five years, they recommended emancipation, the report was ignored because, in the meantime, the Tsar's hatred of the Jewish nation had overcome his caution. On the advice of Pobedonostsev, the methods of persecution changed and the police savagely enforced anti-semitic laws deliberately ignored by Alexander II. Jews who had lived all their lives in a town suddenly heard it reassessed as a village, making it necessary for them to move. Freedom of movement was curtailed. 'Illegal' Jews, who had happily lived for years outside the Pale, received notice that they must sell their businesses and

115

move within three days. The poorest Jews had less time and often left in chains without their families. Doctors who had served in the Army in the Turkish war of '78 found themselves out of work, as not more than 5 per cent of a regiment's medical officers could be Jewish. The reason for their dismissal was designedly insulting: for their 'adverse influence on hygiene in the army'. It would be difficult to conceive of a crueller way of dismissing men who had risked their lives on active service for their country, and it illustrated the spiteful venom of the government. Lawyers, doctors, civil servants received equally brutal treatment. An order in council dismissed judicial officers and denied civil servants further advancement, and an order in St Petersburg prevented Jews from teaching their sons trades, while all Jews who lacked permission to live in the Empire received a command to return to the village in which they lived six years before. More dangerous to the welfare of the country was the assault on the younger generation emancipated by Alexander II. To encourage them to emigrate, the number of Jews accepted by secondary schools and universities was drastically reduced. In the Pale, the educational authorities could only allow 10 per cent of their entry to be Jewish. In St Petersburg and Moscow, the limit was 5 per cent; in other areas $2\frac{1}{2}$ per cent.

'I could continue indefinitely with anti-semitic examples. But I have spoken enough, I hope, to show you that imperial policy was and is to drive the Jews into the Pale and ultimately out of the country by public humiliation, while denying to the younger generation the right of education which their race had enjoyed for twenty-five years. The lucky few who manage, by especial fortune or the wealth of their parents, to obtain a university education, find their future curtailed in professions in which their fathers shone. The policy is madness.

'Three years ago the Tsar appeared at least to be listening to protests and shocked opinion in England and America, until, in 1888, fate played a cruel trick. In October, the imperial train was wrecked at Borky and the Tsar held up with his own hand the collapsing roof while his family miraculously escaped. Pobedonostsev, knowing his superstitious nature, set out to convince him that God had saved his life to enable him to purify Russia by the expulsion of the Anti-Christs. He succeeded, and on the death of Count Tolstoy in 1889, appointed P. D. Durnovo as Minister of the Interior with V. Plehve as his assistant. Both men detested Jewry and used and twisted the laws to satisfy their hate. I will tell you of only one method they are using, which will show you the depths of pettiness to which they descend.

'The Chief of Police in St Petersburg issued an order that signs on Jewish shops should bear, in large letters, the name not only of the owner but also of his father. When the signs appeared, other inspectors came and demanded that the signs should be rewritten in bolder letters. When the ordered alterations were completed, a different inspector informed the shopkeepers that the capitals exceeded the correct size and must be reduced. Judge for yourself the effect on those tormented in such a way! Alexander III has undone the Russification of his father and reunited the rich and poor of the Jewish nation against the imperial family. His assault has just begun. Next year, as I have told you, it is planned that your husband will organize the expulsion of all Jews from Moscow and make enemies of a newly created class of young and bitter men who have (except for the very richest) no career open to them apart from revolution. He has given them no alternative and they excel in intrigue.

'Certain of my comments will be unacceptable to rich Jews. I have kept to essentials and avoided discussing the doctrine of the Haskalah, the policies of the Maskilim, the decline of ostentatious beliefs, nihilism and socialism, all of which played their part in their emancipation. But I have tried to give you an accurate personal résumé of the policy towards the Jews in this century, and especially in the last decade when the policies of the Tsar, conceived by Pobedonostsev, have been to drive them out of Russia. It is a policy of lunacy to drive out brains which have, in twenty-five years, created our thriving new industries. What is, in the long run, more serious for the imperial family is the donation of intellect to the revolutionary movement which, without it, is a disordered, inefficient mass. I repeat, the next attack will be carried out by your husband next year. If you could have stopped him accepting the Tsar's post, you would have saved both humanity and the Empire and saved the destruction of many innocent lives. But I understand that you can do no more. Please forgive my original request.

'This is all I have to say, except that may I continue – in your interest – to keep you informed when danger threatens the Grand Duke?'

Ella sat silent. Her leave-taking was similar to their first meeting, but this time Anton and his wife, with looks of servile adoration, bowed her to the carriage.

6

A week later, Ella left for Hesse. The imperial train took her to the border, where she changed into an ordinary sleeper. She looked forward to this return home with certain reservations. To begin with, she had to break to her father her intention of joining the Orthodox Church the following spring. She knew that he would object and probably shout at her. She could not understand why he minded. His attendance at Lutheran services was regular, but she could clearly remember him sitting with glazed eyes during the address, and he had never shown the slightest interest in the alternatives of religion. His position was clear: 'As far as I am concerned, it is Lutheranism or nothing.'

Now she understood why his narrow-mindedness wearied her mother: he was unable to sustain a logical argument. His mind was closed. He would never be able to understand how, to Ella, the Church should be a living body in which she wished to participate by confession, punishment and absolution. She understood the necessity for the creation of a protesting Church in the Middle Ages, but surely the indulgences and scandals at which Luther and his early followers protested had long ago disappeared? A protesting Church which has gained its ends becomes an anachronism. Both Churches had the same God. What did it matter how you worshipped him?

But she knew that logic was no good. Her father would consider her to be an apostate and would never understand her need for the splendour of the Orthodox services with their dazzling robes and triumphant singing which made her sense that she was in touch with both the Father and the Son, while in her father's church she only felt the discomfort of the wooden seats.

She knew that her father would believe she was only following Serge's wishes, which would not be true, although there had been a look of pleasure in her husband's eyes when she had told him her decision, as if to say, 'I was right not to interfere – I knew which way you'd go.'

In fact, she had been more embarrassed by Serge's request that she should forward the romance between Alix and his nephew Nicky, who had fallen in love with Alix at Ella's wedding when she was twelve. It was ridiculous, but the attachment lingered on. Although Nicky was having a love affair with a ballet dancer, he often said, 'Alix is the only person I will ever marry.'

The idea of such a marriage displeased the Tsar, and he told his son to look elsewhere 'than the disease-ridden Hesses', while the Empress Marie carefully examined the prettiest princesses in Europe. Alix, now an intense Lutheran and possessive of Pastor Sell, frequently declared that she would never marry outside her Church. She loved Nicky, but would never marry him.

Ella thought her loyalty to the Lutheran Church a pity. Her sister would, with all her little faults, make a true and loyal wife, and she had a strength of character which poor Nicky lacked; and surely, as she grew older, she would become less shy and gauche. She was prepared to persuade her sister to have second thoughts, but she knew it would not be easy.

The visit started badly. In Hesse, her whole family was staying at Wolfsgarten, now her father's favourite country house, and Ella had hardly entered before she was involved in a family quarrel. Ella could hear Alix sobbing in her room. But Ernie, who was, Ella saw to her annoyance, gaudily dressed up as a lieutenant of the First Prussian Footguard, seemed in a state of high excitement.

'It was only a joke. Why has Alix no sense of humour? If anyone has the right to cry it's me, the way everybody snaps my head off for a little prank any normal person would have laughed at.'

Ella sat down and asked Ernie to tell her quietly and slowly what had happened and why her sister had locked herself in her room in floods of tears. He was about to answer when the door opened and in came Alix, her face and hands bright red. They were upsetting, these red hands. Orchie had said it was only childish embarrassment when she blushed down to the ends of her little fingers, but at the time she had been a child. Now, at eighteen, it looked most unsightly. Once Alix had given Ella a formal kiss, she turned on Ernie, clenched her fists and sobbed: 'That you, of all people, should do this to me. You, whom I have always trusted!'

He jumped up in his clanking Prussian uniform and, seizing her red hand, knelt before her, himself choking with tears as he pleaded, 'Oh, Alix, Alix, it was only a joke. Please don't go on crying or I'll cry too, I promise you I will. It will serve you right.'

Ella told her brother and sister to be quiet and tell her what had happened. At last it all came out. Ever since their mother's death, one of her sister's 'possessions' had been Miss Jackson, and it was a family joke that Alix ended even the shortest note to her with 'A good long kiss from your very loving P.Q. No. III'. P.Q. stood for Poppet Queen. The elder sisters had always told Miss Jackson that it was rude of Alix to call herself P.Q. No. III when she had three living elder sisters. Why wasn't she P.Q. No. IV? Miss Jackson never seemed to like the question or to answer it, and they only brought up the joke when she needed teasing.

It turned out that Ernie had written a breakfast-time note saying that he had forgotten their aunt and uncle, the Erbach-Schonbergs, were coming to lunch, and that Alix had better dress up and behave well, as she knew what dreary, critical 'stuck-ups' they were. He sighed the letter 'S.I.L.L.Y. A.S.S., Ernie.' This idiotic note was the cause of all the tears and trouble, and now Ernie was on his knees in that ghastly Prussian uniform saying he was going to cry too. It was ridiculous.

'Really,' Ella said, 'how silly you both are – Ernie to write the letter and Alix to mind it.'

This made Alix burst out crying again: 'What's silly about signing oneself by a loving name to a person you really love? She always loved me best, you know she did.'

'Of course. She did then and she does now, and so do we both love you, even if Ernie is a silly ass. But run to your room, Alix, and powder your face and . . .' but she just stopped herself saying 'hands'. It had been curious how this unattractive detail worried her. It was a grievous fault to care so much about grace and beauty. 'And Ernie was right. Make yourself pretty and smart, otherwise we will all be criticized.'

The next day, she kept her word to Serge and spoke about Nicky's wish to marry Alix. Her sister coloured and said it was impossible. She would remain unmarried rather than change her religion. Ella waited a moment and then confessed that she was about to enter the Orthodox Church, adding, as she held her sister's hands, 'You know, Mama always said that if there is a God He will not mind what you call yourself as long as you believe in Him. If He minded that sort of thing, he wouldn't be worth worshipping.'

Although Alix continued to shake her head and insist she would never change her mind, Ella noticed how pleased she was to hear of Nicky's faithfulness and how she repeated her intention of remaining a Lutheran in the tone of one reiterating a lesson rather than expressing a passionately held belief.

Ella's interview with her old, ill-looking father was as embarrassing as she had feared, but after she had kissed him he calmed down and resignedly said he was disappointed in his children.

'Look at Ernie. Why did he leave his Hessian regiment and become a Prussian soldier when Prussia stole half my dukedom, and why does he ingratiate himself with young Willy who still has filthy manners even though he's become Kaiser? I feel an old man and don't understand these things. What puzzles me most is Ernie's extraordinary friends – all actors and painters. He does not show the faintest interest in even the most beautiful girl. Would you believe it, he still goes into flower shops in Darmstadt and rearranges the window displays? It was bad enough when he was a boy, but it is ridiculous in an officer. I think I have stopped him, for I said yesterday that I would tell Willy if he did it again, and that frightened him. He is a snob, you know.'

She found Ernie very pleased with himself, and underneath the veneer of his prattle and Prussian uniform as nice and kind as ever. She agreed with her father that he was an unusual young man. How could he have nearly burst into tears over that ridiculous incident with Alix? Would he ever be stable?

After Russia, everything at Darmstadt and Wolfsgarten and Kranichstein, which had loomed in her memory so large and impressively, now seemed small and insignificant. After two weeks, she left for England, where she knew that, whatever else happened, her Grandmama would remain unchanged.

7

Ella arrived at Windsor late on a Wednesday afternoon and, feeling like a schoolgirl, ran again across the drawing room and, to the astonishment of a new lady-in-waiting, threw her arms around Grandmama, who was sitting in a push-chair guided by a stately Indian wearing a turban.

The Queen had said: 'Now, now, my dear,' when she saw her granddaughter running towards her, but as Ella bent forward, she put her arms around her neck, pulled her towards her and kissed and hugged her, tears running down her old cheeks. After wiping her eyes, she told Ella brusquely that she must go immediately to her bedroom and change. They ate in forty minutes, and the Prime Minister and his wife were staying the night. Ella ran up to her room, to have a bath and change and dress. How nice it seemed to be able to have only half an hour to get herself ready, instead of the two or three hours she always left herself in Russia. Already she had received one disappointment: Grandmama had changed. Age had at last taken some of her strength away. For the first time, Ella felt sorry for the Queen. In the past, she would not have dared to run and kiss her. Now she seemed smaller and rounder and sadder. She put such thoughts out of her head as she bathed and changed.

It occurred to her, as she ran downstairs, that she did not know the Prime Minister's name and felt frustrated at her ignorance. Who could he be? It could not be Lord Beaconsfield, because she remembered her guilty feeling of pleasure in his death some years before. She had never forgiven him blaming Ernie for Mama's death. Could it be Mr Gladstone, or was he also dead? Anyhow, it couldn't be him, or the Queen would not have sounded so pleased. The fact was that she had no idea. She was always ashamed and irritated by her ignorance of politics, especially of those in England, where the two parties seemed to stand for the same things.

As she walked into the drawing room, she wondered if she could ask, but whom? Grandmama was out of the question; anyhow, she was surrounded by strange faces. How quickly the court had changed. At last she was relieved to find Lady Ely, but was in such a state she had not listened as the other guests were introduced. At the beginning of dinner, she still did not know who the Prime Minister was. It could not be the two men on either side of the Queen, since both were German cousins. The man on her own right she thought was called Stoner, and the man on her left, although he looked vaguely familiar, was unlikely to be the Prime Minister, since his bow tie was askew and his waistcoat was buttoned up in such a way that the top button had no eye to go into, the bottom eye no matching button.

He was a large-featured, thick-set man with a big, bushy beard who stared down his nose intensely at his plate. At last he turned and looked at her hard, obviously trying to remember whether he knew her. She wondered if she should say who she was, but decided he might think her pushing. At last he said deliberately, 'I hope you will forgive me. I was kept in London and do not think I have the honour of your acquaintance, but if I have, please forgive me. As my wife says, quite rightly, I am hopelessly vague.'

She told him he was correct that they had not met, which was not surprising, since she lived in Russia. At once he became interested and asked her whether 'our Ambassador is right in thinking that the Emperor remains resentful of England's treatment of Russia, believing his country to have been perfidiously treated at the Congress of Berlin'. Ella, seeing an opportunity of saying who she was, replied: 'My brother-in-law, I think, does believe that England behaved badly.'

As she spoke the words 'brother-in-law', a concentrated look came over his face, and after a pause he said, giving her a little bow: 'I think I must have the honour and pleasure of sitting next to the Grand Duchess Serge.'

She bowed in turn and said how pleased she was to meet the Prime Minister.

They talked, or rather he talked, of the Congress of Berlin and the strength of British public opinion, and how he had admired Count Shchouvalov. This embarrassed her yet again, for she did not know which Count Shchouvalov he was talking about. She knew two, and if she mentioned the wrong one, he would think her a perfect idiot! But luckily, and very deliberately, he stated: 'I am no enemy of Russia, no, no. If I was I would have followed the advice of many of my hot-heads and declared war over your advances on the borders of Afghanistan and your plans to conquer Pamir. They argue that you intend to march down into India. It is nonsense, you know, nonsense. No general could go down that way to India. The supply problems would be insoluble.'

Gradually, she understood that he was talking to himself and not to her, as he continued: 'You know, the British Empire is said to have weak foundations because it is scattered all over the world, while the Russian Empire is an unbroken land mass. Yet, you know, I would prefer to rule a scattered overseas empire to a contiguous empire. With our scattered possessions, we can vary our policies. One colony scarcely knows or cares about the existence of another. Your Tsar calls his colonies Russia and pretends to rule a nation. Our nearest Moslems live two thousand miles away. Yours are close neighbours and fellow countrymen. One day it will be seen that Russia is an empire not a country. We can suffer losses and survive; you will not. I am certain that one day in the far future the Russian Empire will collapse under the stress of pretending to be what it is not – a united country – when it is a collection of dissimilar races bound together by force of arms.'

Lord Salisbury looked down again at his untouched plate, deep in thought. Ella listened, her eyes wide with surprise. It was extraordinary, puzzling and troubling to hear the Prime Minister of England repeating views so similar to the stranger's.

On this visit, and to her disappointment, she sensed for the first time the breakdown of the secure England which she had known as a child. Was it because Grandmama no longer frightened Uncle Bertie and her aunts and uncles as she had done years before? One day she received a message to go and see Grandmama about a certain matter 'on which the Queen requires information'. Ella guessed that the matter must be Ernie, and she was right. Sitting in the wickerwork chair pushed by the Indian, Grandmama shot one question after another at her as they sedately proceeded around the garden.

'What is Ernie up to? Why has he joined the Prussian Army? Who are his artistic and musical friends?'

She was unable to answer, but tried to reassure her grandmother by saying her brother was as kind and good as always, and after all, he was very young. To change the subject, Ella remarked that she was worried about her father's health.

'So Louis is ill, is he?' said the Queen with a little smile, and Ella saw how his second marriage would never be forgiven. They sat on in silence, and Ella stared sadly at the Queen, trying to fix her appearance in her mind, for every time that she saw her she wondered if it would be the last.

'But, my dear, I can assure you I am in the best of health,' the Queen interrupted her thoughts. 'You have no need to look so sad,' and she had given a rich little silvery laugh of enjoyment at her blushing granddaughter's embarrassment.

At that moment, a footman appeared with a message on a silver tray. The Queen read it and looked annoyed, saying: 'There is something further I wish to say, but I see it will have to wait.'

On her last morning in England, when the maid brought in her cup of early-morning tea, Ella saw a letter on the tray, addressed in a copperplate clerk's writing and delivered by hand the night before. She opened it carelessly, expecting yet another invitation she would have to decline. Inside she found a letter from a committee in Moscow, stating itself to be the first of many. The authors regretted writing to a good and saintly woman, universally respected in Russia, but, they asked, how could she remain married to a man who practised diabolical cruelties on young Jewish girls? Was she aware that a large number of young, unregistered Jewesses in St Petersburg had been given assurance from the police that they could stay in St Petersburg provided they went through the *formality* of receiving a pink prostitute's ticket? The alternative facing them was expulsion to the Pale. Did she know that the police had arrested four of these girls, and taken them to a house for an interview with the Grand Duke, who had outraged and tortured them, one so severely that she was in hospital? Apart from these atrocities, the Grand Duke had committed other acts of cruelty of a nature too indecent to mention. How could she, a good woman, stay with such a man?

The letter went on to say that the writers knew of the Grand Duke's acceptance of the Governor-Generalship of Moscow and of his determination to persecute the whole Jewish community. She should therefore know that the

Moscow Jews had formed a Committee of Defence, one of whose first actions was to bring to the attention of the Grand Duchess her husband's past behaviour in the hope that she might curb further brutalities against harmless children. She should also know that when the four ruined children complained to magistrates, each had been asked if they were registered prostitutes, and that when they truthfully replied 'yes', had it explained to them that the law could not inquire into the way they managed their business. Two hundred of these girls remained in St Petersburg, and now, each week, the police arrested a number, questioned them brutally and took them to strange houses, where they suffered violation. It was known that three district police chiefs used the girls for their own personal profit to satisfy the perverted desires of aristocratic libertines.

The writers did not wish to associate her husband with these crimes, but the listed four girls, three of whom were sixteen and one fifteen, had identified, beyond the shadow of a doubt, the Grand Duke as their violator and torturer. At the foot of the letter were given the names and addresses of the four girls.

Ella shut her eyes in agony. The story could only be a tissue of lies, but when she read it again, she had to admit that Serge's absences during the past year had puzzled her; and had she not occasionally seen on his face a look which reminded her of her own terrible experience? Could she be imagining things? Serge was, in his way, kind to her, and he always went out of his way to be nice to children. She shuddered. What should she do? Of one thing she was certain, she would hide her doubts from Grandmama, to whom she had repeatedly spoken of her happiness with Serge and with her life in Russia, although she was unsure whether she had succeeded in convincing the Queen. Often she noticed how, after ending her praises, her grandmother's little eyes would continue to peer and the corners of her mouth turn down as she said: 'I am very glad to hear of that, my dear;' but the tone implied regretful doubts, as if she was thinking: 'Ella does not know what I have heard, but she is a brave girl, and is doing the correct thing to pretend happiness. I can only pray and hope that her husband is not as bad as I have heard.'

Ella had to keep up her pretence, since so many of Grandmama's schemes for her children and grandchildren had gone awry and she did not wish to add to her regrets. The farewell was surprising. This time, when Ella came to say goodbye, her grandmother told her Indian attendant to wait outside the door, and when Ella leaned forward to kiss her, the old lady took her granddaughter's head in both hands and held it down, whispering: 'Tell me, dearest child, are you really happy all those miles away?'

It took an immense effort for Ella to say, 'Please don't worry, Grandmama, I assure you I am very happy and Serge is very, very good to me – in fact, so good that I feel I must join his Church, although he has never ever pressed me to do so.'

The information had the desired effect of changing the subject, and the Queen exclaimed in horror: 'Ella, dear, I cannot get over you becoming a Greek Catholic. What would your poor mother have said?'

It gave her a wonderful chance, and Ella said, as she gently withdrew her head: 'I am sure Mother would not have minded. She always told me that it did not matter what religion you followed so long as you worshipped God.'

As Ella looked down, she thought how the Queen's little figure grew smaller every year.

The Queen was now in a vexing dilemma. Even where she had found fault with her children during their lifetime, once they died, they became saints. Her daughter Alice was now remembered as the personification of goodness and efficiency for the way in which she had nursed the beloved Albert, and later Bertie. This time it was her turn to change the subject and, after looking doubtfully at Ella, she patted her hand and said: 'Well, my dear, I am sure you will be a good Christian whatever you call yourself, but I do not like Catholicism of any kind, and never will, nor did your beloved grandfather.

'There is another matter which I wish to mention before you go, despite what you said the other day before we were interrupted. I hear all sorts of things about Ernie from my minister in Darmstadt. I am told that he gives numerous parties, attended by undesirable friends, and spends large sums of money on art nouveau – whatever that may be – and his house. Although I am sure I don't know where the money comes from, as dearest Alice received nothing from Louis's German estates. I have given the matter serious thought, and it is time he married and I consider Ducky would be a most suitable wife.'

'Oh,' Ella said, 'she is only sixteen, isn't she?' visualizing the little Victoria, Uncle Alfred and Serge's sister Marie's second daughter.

'That is not the trouble,' said the Queen tartly. 'In my view, she is ideal in every way, and what is more, she is Ernie's first cousin, so we can expect well of her.'

She finished the sentence on a hesitant note, and Ella wondered what was coming next. She soon heard.

'The trouble is that her mother, Marie, your sister-in-law, always disliked England and made such difficulties here that I had to arrange for Alfred to go to Malta, and since then, you know, she has gone to Coburg, and although Alfred is good and kind, he is weak and regrettably does everything his wife tells him. She, I am certain, will do exactly the opposite to anything I suggest for the good of her children, forgetting they are also my grandchildren. You know, there was an understanding between Missy and Georgie in Malta, and I am sure that they were very fond of and well suited to each other, but Marie at once stopped it and made Missy write to Georgie a hurting and unkind letter. And now poor Missy, as you know, has married Ferdinand of Romania, who sometimes does not answer when I speak to him, and the poor child will have to live for years in a barbarian country where, I am told, the King insists on having his own way, so we will probably never see dear little Missy again.

'As to Ducky, I know that Ernie is agreeable to such a match, but if it is believed that the suggestion comes from here, Marie will say "no" at once. So I would be pleased, my dear, if on your way back you would visit her. After all, she is your sister-in-law and aunt and your father's first cousin. Tell her that you are speaking on Ernie's behalf, but stress how, in your opinion, Ducky is too young. Don't forget,' the Queen said, looking out of the corner of her eye, 'that when you want to get Marie to agree with you, argue against your own wishes; she is exceedingly contrary.

'Now, my dear, I would be grateful if you would telegraph Serge explaining to him that you have to go to Coburg. It is an ideal marriage, and from what my minister in Darmstadt tells me, respectable people in Hesse are beginning to worry about Ernie's levity and all the money he is spending on art nouveau houses, so his decision to marry will be greeted with relief.'

Ella was not too pleased at the request. The stout Marie, Duchess of Edinburgh and daughter of Tsar Alexander II, was even when she came to Ilonskoye, fierce and abrupt, and she had placed Ella in the enemy English camp, to be treated with disdain. The Duchess detested England and regretted having married a younger son. The food, the fogs, the mourning court, the necessity of giving precedence to the Princess of Wales, all produced endless quarrels and discontent, and having escaped from England and reigned in Malta, where her good-natured husband, the Duke, was in command of the Mediterranean fleet, nothing would make her return with him to Plymouth. She had settled in Coburg, awaiting the death of her husband's uncle (Prince Albert's elder brother, Ernest), whom he was to succeed as Duke of Coburg. As the Queen had said, her grandson Prince George had wanted to marry the beautiful Missy, but, despite Alfred's wishes, his wife refused to consider an English marriage.

Now it was Ducky's turn. Marie was known to be carefully examining German princes. The most curious aspect, Ella thought, was the impossibility of keeping any plan secret. Europe was ruled, not by separate dynasties, but by one huge family who relayed to each other every aspect of local gossip. The consequence was that everybody knew everything, and Marie would certainly have heard how her sister-in-law was travelling on the Queen's behalf to fix up another of her marriages. Ella decided she would be likely to receive a frigid reception.

8

Ella disliked the tedious train journey to Coburg but, even though it was getting late in the year, the sun shone in an Indian summer. She arrived at the pretty little castle of Rosenau to find Marie, large and square, sitting under a chestnut tree. The Duchess, dressed as usual in the oddest clothes, stood up to welcome Ella. She positively declined to follow any fashion except her own eccentric taste, a fact which had always infuriated Queen Victoria. She was wearing, beneath an old, round, tattered straw hat, a coarse linen blouse buttoned up at the wrists, overhanging a long, indefinite-coloured plaid skirt, from the bottom of which stuck out a pair of square boots especially made in Moscow so that either boot could fit either foot.

Ella felt both shy and cautious, not having seen Marie for three or four years, but after a few minutes' silence, broken only by the click-clack of Marie's knitting needles the size of pokers, Ella became embarrassed and remarked, in what she feared was a feeble voice, 'You are looking well.'

Marie, without looking up, replied brusquely, 'Fat,' to which there was no polite reply. They continued sitting in silence until a sudden breeze fluttered the trees and lifted one side of Marie's hat, standing it on end at a rakish angle above her head. Moving swiftly, she seized the offending side and, pulling it down, held it firmly in place. Ella, thinking she must be uncomfortable, asked if she could go in and get her a hat pin.

Marie turned on her fiercely. 'You shall do no such thing. I learned in Russia only to put a pin on the right side of my hat, and what I learnt in Russia I stick to. Alfred has always tried to make me put pins in the left side of my hats, but I refuse to copy English habits.'

Ella nodded and smiled as if approving a clever decision, but could not help thinking that her aunt must be going a little mad and wondered whether this was a favourable moment to discuss a marriage between Ducky and Ernie. Remembering that she had promised her grandmother, she at last plucked up courage and began the dreaded conversation by asking: 'Is Missy well?'

'I am sure I cannot imagine why she should not be well. Have you ever known her ill?'

Ella shook her head and smiled again, but her remark had unlocked Marie's silence and smouldering resentment as she looked angrily at Ella and growled: 'I heard you were coming, and I wish to make it plain that I will not consider any of my daughters marrying Georgie – or any other Englishman,' she added as a definite afterthought.

'Oh,' said Ella, smiling with pleasure at the opportunity offered by Marie's mistaken belief that the Queen had sent her to try and arrange a marriage – now that Missy was no longer available – between Georgie and Ducky.

'Oh, I am glad, for Ernie is very anxious to marry Ducky and asked me at Wolfsgarten if I would call here to see if you would agree to his visiting Rosenau to get to know her better.'

Marie was taken aback by her miscalculation, and a more civil expression came over her face, replacing her set, obstinate look.

'Why, I didn't know Ernie wished to be married. I thought he liked . . .' She paused and changed her sentence rather lamely, '. . . he was happy with his music.'

'No, he feels he needs a wife. The only thing is,' Ella added, remembering her grandmother's advice, 'I suppose she is far too young.'

'Certainly not. Girls should all marry young. If they reach twenty without marrying, they get complicated ideas of their own and think too much. Besides, an unmarried princess has no position. Princesses must be married, and if Ernie is sincere in wishing to marry Ducky, I am sure she will marry him.'

Marie spoke with the absolute conviction of one who knew her daughter would obey, and Ella gave a little sigh. Ernie seemed so feckless and volatile, she wondered if he was ready to be a husband to a young girl who knew nothing of the world.

Although Marie now looked more friendly, she did not speak another word until, at last, looking at her watch, she said: 'When Uncle Ernst heard you were coming, he decided to abandon protocol and come to lunch. So, my dear, perhaps you would like to go and put on your best clothes. I shall not change.'

Ella was rather disappointed: she would have liked to have seen another outfit but as she walked upstairs she thought what fun it would be to be able to write and tell her sister Victoria what their Great-Uncle Ernst, the Duke of Coburg who had been the forbidden ogre of their childhood, was really like.

It was a small lunch party, consisting of the three of them with a nervous-looking equerry of Great-Uncle Ernst's and an equally nervous-looking lady-in-waiting of Marie's. When Uncle Ernst came in, he lived up to all her expectations: his enormous body tightly buttoned in a bursting black frock-coat and exceedingly tight trousers which looked as if they might explode every time he moved. His face was huge and red and pimply, and marked by large black liver spots, and from his upper lip hung down, on either side of his mouth, a long, nicotine-stained moustache which curled upwards amazingly at the ends. A few strands of long hair stuck to his bald head, failing to hide his warts. He jumped when he saw Ella, and giving Marie a perfunctory greeting, waddled over and softly caressed her hand with his old, clammy fingers before lifting them slowly to his wet lips, kissing them twice, rubbing his moustache on her skin and keeping her imprisoned fingers close to his mouth while his eyes, whose lower lids resembled drooping pockets of blood, plainly conveyed his passionate admiration. Ella wondered whether she was going to be sick, and glanced in desperation at Marie, who was watching with a satisfied expression on her face, delighted at the embarrassing scene. Having reluctantly released her hand, Uncle Ernst behaved quite decorously, except for pushing his leg against hers, causing her to finish the meal sitting sideways.

To her surprise, Marie told Uncle Ernst that a marriage had been arranged between Ernie and Ducky. He nodded his head with enthusiasm, winked at Ella and said it gave him immense pleasure to become an even closer relation to his beautiful great-niece.

When he left, Marie suggested in a spiteful tone that Ella should write to her grandmother in England and say how well and active the Prince Consort's elder brother was looking. She did not answer, but Marie continued to look puffed up with pleasure at having produced Ernst, whom she knew the Queen of England detested.

To begin with, on her long journey back to Moscow, Ella felt rather clever. Her success in arranging the marriage would please Grandmama. But then, as usual, her elation was followed by gloom. Had she actually done a wicked thing in arranging for Ducky, still only sixteen, to marry her wild younger brother, who had never paid attention to any other girl?

Ella felt homesick for a week after her return to Russia, and decided she disliked intensely the attitude of her servants and even of her Mistress of the Robes and her ladies-in-waiting; their manner was so ingratiating. In England, all the courtiers were terrified of the Queen, but in a different way. Her discontent made her long to enter the Orthodox Church, and now that her father knew, she asked Serge if she could choose a suitable instructor. To her annoyance, he said that that was the business of Pobedonostsev, from whom she would doubtless hear in a few weeks.

Two months passed and nothing happened until one evening, as she and Serge came downstairs on their way to a reception, she noticed an altercation in the hall, where a footman was angrily trying to push the door shut as he shouted at an unseen visitor that it was impossible to come in. To some unheard remonstrance, he repeated crossly that it was 'absolutely impossible'. At that moment, two other menservants pushed him aside and flung open both doors for Serge and herself to walk down the steps to their carriage.

In the centre of the doorway stood an old, bent priest with a long white beard who, under the impression that the door had been opened for him, walked in, his eyes cast down, and almost ran into Serge, who asked him sharply who he was and what he was doing. He replied in a gentle, sing-song voice that he had called on the orders of the Holy Synod to prepare the Grand Duchess for entrance into the Holy Russian Church. He spoke quite naturally, unabashed by the splendour of his surroundings. Ella took his hands in hers and said how she had looked forward to his coming, but regretfully, that evening, the Emperor was holding a reception, otherwise nothing would have stopped her from talking to him and she hoped he would come tomorrow as early as he wished.

'The Emperor,' he had sung. 'Of course, it is the duty of all who serve the Defender of our faith to wait upon the Emperor. I will return tomorrow.'

He bowed and turned and walked out of the hall in front of them. This lese-majesty, Ella saw, infuriated Serge and she asked quickly whether

Pobedonostsev always had good judgement. He thought for a moment before answering: 'The best in Russia.' She felt the muscles in his arm relaxing.

The priest came again early next morning and told her that his name was Father Constantin. She thought him a curious choice to be her adviser, as he appeared to know nothing of liturgy or the history of the Holy Russian Church, and when she asked him to define the difference between Russian and Greek Orthodoxy, he first of all lifted two of his fingers, lowered them, lifted three and shrugged his shoulders as if the problem was beyond him. Ella sat silent with disappointment until, without any warning, he began to tell her stories of Russian saints and their miracles and never drew breath until, in the middle of an anecdote concerning St Cyril, he walked out of the room. Ella was angry, realizing that Pobedonostsev had chosen a soft-headed old story-teller to express his contempt for her intellect. She knew it would be no good complaining to Serge. He would simply say that she should, if she wished to enter the Church, trust the Holy Synod.

After a week of legends and fairy tales, Ella felt she must have an adviser who would explain to her certain simplicities of which Father Constantin seemed unaware. It would really be ridiculous if, on the day she was received into the Church, she could not answer the most elementary questions. She plucked up courage and asked Serge if she might change her useless, kind instructor. As she expected, he refused and said that Father Constantin was specially selected for her by Pobedonostsev at the request of the Emperor, and that to change him would be a deliberate insult to both. Later, Ella was glad, and used him as a guide, for she found that, to her delight, he knew every shrine, chapel, monastery and hermit's cave within a day's drive of the capital. It was fun setting off to visit a toothless hermit living on charity in some dark cave, or the tomb of a saint surrounded by old peasants on their knees with looks of bliss and faith on their faces. She would kneel with them, receiving satisfaction in prostrating herself in such simple company. After a time, she came to believe in many ways that Father Constantin was, by introducing her to the poor, preparing her more sensibly than any pedantic ritualist could have done.

Nevertheless, with her conversion only a few months away, she remembered the invitation and prophecies of Ivan of Kronstadt, who was to receive her into the Church. She decided to go and explain to him that she was entering her new faith as a sinner seeking salvation, having a passionate desire to believe in the tenets of Orthodoxy. But he must realize that, thanks to Father Constantin, she knew little of the way in which she was expected to behave and was not even sure which responses she needed to know. Her ignorance was so embarrassing that she decided to go without a lady-in-waiting so that none would hear of Ivan's scorn at her ignorance. A week later, she set off across the ice, accompanied by a troop of mounted Cossacks whom she found waiting at the edge of the frozen sea. The crossing bore no resemblance to her previous adventure. The sun shone in a cloudless sky. No bells tolled, the wind blew gently and the crossing appeared to take only a few minutes.

Father Ivan, with a self-satisfied smile, received her in the same little room and told her he was pleased but not surprised as he had foreseen her conversion. As for Father Constantin, he was, of course, a brainless old fool, but a good man, and she would learn from him the simple faith and beliefs of the peasants. Without pausing, he then asked about her relations with the Grand Duke and whether she was pregnant. These staggeringly private questions made her feel faint with embarrassment, and she shut her eyes and thought how typical it was of uncivilized Russia that saints like Ivan of Kronstadt could say what they wished. She looked down and replied, 'No,' hoping he would leave it at that.

But he continued remorselessly: 'By your wish or his?'

She could only shake her head. After all, she had come to ask him about her correct responses, not to be persecuted by indecent questions.

'You must remember, as I told you before, that God is represented in Holy Russia by the Tsar, and his brother is near to God. Is it not your duty to have children?'

Her irritation at his impertinence made her look up, appealing to him to end this distasteful conversation, but all she saw in his eyes was an obscene twinkle that only increased her anger. Noticing her obvious distate, he laughed and said, 'I see you dislike poor old Father Ivan, but isn't it your duty to fall in with your husband's wishes?'

Horrified, she whispered, 'Surely I should not commit sins?'

Her remark infuriated him and he shouted, 'How can a man repent unless he has sinned? Again and again we are told to repent. How can you repent if you have not sinned? Remember Christ said, "Joy shall be in heaven over one sinner that repenteth, more than over ninety and nine just persons which need no repentance." Tell me, Imperial Highness, did he not mean that man must sin to be redeemed, otherwise he is worthless, and if Our Lord did not mean that, what did he mean? Tell me, tell me, tell me, tell me . . .' he shouted louder and louder, his eyes glaring, his face red with the exception of the sponge-like patch on his forehead.

'Have you ever considered that to sin and repent is better than not to sin? Remember again, Christ said, "I am not come to call the righteous but sinners to repentance." You think because you go on your knees for a few moments every morning and evening and, whenever anything goes wrong, pray to God, you are a good Christian. It is not so – you worship at your own shrine. Look at your day: you lie in bed in the morning and spend hours adorning yourself before the mirror, tampering with your beautiful face. You eat lunch, visit friends, sit as president of a committee, return and again gaze at yourself before a glass. At dinner, laden with jewels, you sit next to a visiting prince who, after staring with astonishment, cries out that you are the most beautiful woman in Russia. You deny the truth, return to your bed, pray and fall asleep, to wake up and start all over again. What is Christian in such behaviour? I say to you, it is better to sin, even against your inclination. Anything is better than the useless, wasted empty life of pretence that you are serving God when you are serving yourself. But say something, say something, say something!' he shouted again.

She was stunned and hurt by this savage attack, so totally unexpected, so unfair, and yet so little different from her own opinion of the uselessness of her life. Somehow, she had to explain to this dreadful man that it would not be right for her to encourage her husband in his weak, cruel habits. But it was impossible to put her thoughts into words.

'Oh, I can't,' was all she feebly said.

'Make yourself, make yourself,' shouted Ivan, leaning over the table. 'You need to sin, you are full of pious self-satisfaction. Sometimes I am the same. Those old women you see here listen to every word I say, praise my actions, pretend healings, and hang on to my words until I think I am a good man. When self-satisfaction has crept on me unawares and filled my soul with vanity, I know the time has come to mortify myself, admit to God the wickedness within and pray for redemption.

'Years ago, when I was younger – although I loved my wife – at such a moment I would sing and drink and commit carnal sin. The next morning, when I awoke, I knew I was a miserable sinner, the servant of the devil, not fit to wash the feet of a beggar. I would weep and fast and scourge myself until I knew I was forgiven. But those days are over and I practise other depravities or admissions of my original sin, which otherwise would remain in my heart and corrupt my soul.'

The little man sat back, a look of seraphic self-satisfaction on his face as he continued: 'Do you know what I did last year? A young man came here with heart disease. Looking into his eyes, I saw death and told him there was no escape. He must die. I decided to play a prank on him, and told him to wait, and walked into the storage room and asked Father Ralph to pack him up a shroud in a small parcel with orders that on no account should he open it until he received a further gift, when he was to open both in the order he received them.

'Two weeks later, when I was still full of pride and vanity, I remembered the young man and sent Father Bulat with a second present to his house in St Petersburg. He found him lying on a sofa reading, looking a little better and flushed with pleasure at my kindness. Remembering my orders, he opened my first gift.'

Here Father Ivan burst out laughing.

'Father Bulat told me he had never seen such a look of horror on a face in his life as my shroud fell out. He sat down on a chair and put his hand to his forehead and said: 'What can it mean?' To soothe him, Father Bulat gave him my second parcel, and out fell four corpse candles which rolled all over the floor.'

Father Ivan's eyes gleamed with excitement as he leaned forward, pointing his forefinger at Ella as he came to the climax of his story.

'And do you know what happened? The young man fell down stone dead, as if shot by a bullet, too quickly even to receive absolution. Father Bulat came hurrying back here, pale and trembling, and told me the story in a frightened voice. Do you know what I did? I laughed with pleasure, for I knew I had committed a terrible sin, and for a month I fasted and prayed and whipped myself and asked the forgiveness of God for a miserable sinner. During twenty-nine days, no food passed my lips until God forgave me and my powers returned.'

He sat back with a contented look, before saying in a stern voice to Ella, 'Your mind is full of the sin of another, compared to whom you believe you are a good woman, but no man or woman is good until they repent. The evil stays in them. You should repent of hypocrisy, the original sin which has never left you.'

He stopped and sat back, looking tired.

Ella could not think of anything to say to a man who could feel so self-satisfied after playing such an inconceivably wicked trick, and looked at him with detestation. He walked over, blessed her, made the sign of the cross and gave her a sweet smile which did not belong to the man who had played the cruel joke. He looked so full of goodness and holiness, she wished to go down on her knees before him. He must have noticed her change of mind, for he gave her a smile as if to say that he was not going to take advantage of her, which made her admire him even more.

But on the way back her horror returned, and all the way across the ice, as the Cossacks trotted behind, she thought of his early remarks, which made her ache for the security of the Lutheran Church in which a sin was a sin and not, as in this savage country, a step to salvation.

After her second visit to Father Ivan, she could not get herself to show Serge the letter she had received in London. Instead, she tore it into little pieces, rejecting by her action Father Ivan's opinion that it was her duty to share a manner of life with Serge which she could not believe was right. But as soon as she had destroyed the letter, she began to feel guilty and wonder if she was disloyal and whether she would ever again know peace and contentment.

9

On 22 February 1891, two items appeared in the St Petersburg newspaper. The first stated that the Grand Duke Serge was to become the next Governor of Moscow; the second announced the expulsion of 30,000 Moscow Jews. Serge was jubilant, and Ella found it hard to control herself when, at the balls and receptions that marked their last few weeks in St Petersburg, red-faced old generals would come, and having abased themselves before her husband, express the hope that he would rigorously enforce the anti-semitic laws which at long last gave the crucificiers of Christ their fitting desserts.

She had to travel south to see their new, bleak official residence before Serge took up his appointment, and once again was fortunate to find a floor consisting of small rooms which she planned to redecorate in her favourite English country-house style, associated so closely with the happiness of her youth. As usual, she heard how Miechen scoffed at her housekeeper's dullness and lack of taste.

Ella found her last week in St Petersburg unbearably sad, and feared she might break down at the farewell party to their Colonel, given by the officers of the Preobrazhensky Regiment. She knew that she would miss these people, who had treated her with touching kindness. They and their wives and children had become her closest friends. She had known their family dramas and helped many of the younger officers with the problems of their married lives. They had softened her own unhappiness, and without her interest in their lives she would have led a dull life in a country where she was otherwise treated as an unwelcome stranger. The day before she left, she gave her many little godchildren presents, and at the farewell dinner was touched nearly to tears by references in all the speeches to their beloved Colonel's wife. At the end of the evening Serge said goodbye to all his officers, and as they filed past, kissing her hand, she knew she would never again have a collection of such kind friends of all ages.

Moscow greeted its new Governor and his wife with another incessant round of balls, and she found that in fact she preferred the old capital's society to that of St Petersburg. Her hosts appeared to be more old-fashioned and perhaps duller, more staid and less gossipy than those in St Petersburg, but they had a quality of self-assuredness without conceit which reminded her of her grandmother's court in England.

Serge was very busy, and she heard rumours of Jews starving in the street and of gangs of soldiers nightly gathering up fugitives to pack them off to the Pale. Since he refused to listen to her opinions on the exodus, she tried to put the matter out of her mind and be as dutiful and obedient to her husband as possible and not irritate him with doubts and fears.

Winter ended earlier than in the north and, during a warm spell of May weather, she stayed in Usulov on the Ilonskoye estate for a week with Serge. She was surprised at his unusual good humour; he never lost his temper as they discussed the new flowering trees which she wished to plant on the estate.

Two days before their return to Moscow, she went for a walk in the woods and was startled, on turning a bend, to come upon a young boy pressed up against a fir tree, his arms encircling the stem. She looked at him and as she did so noticed that his head was thrust against the bark. Staring with curiosity, she saw how he was sobbing and clinging to the tree with the desperation of a lost child. She walked up and gently touched his shoulder. To her surprise, he jumped back with a terrified look and put his hands in an attitude of defence as if she was going to hit him. When he saw her sympathetic attitude, the fear slowly faded from his face and he stood silent, looking at the ground.

She recognized him as one of two pale, dark-haired boys she had noticed when Serge showed her around the stable yard on the day after their arrival. They seemed out of place and somehow different from the other thick-set, red-faced country lads. She had wondered, but not bothered to ask, where they came from. Now she asked him gently why he was unhappy. He replied, still looking down, 'I miss my family.'

She asked where they lived, and he said, after a moment's hesitation, in a voice of tremulous sadness: 'I do not know. They were taken away from Moscow in different trains, where to I cannot tell. As they do not know where I am, I have had no letters.'

Horrified, Ella tried to change the subject by asking where was the other little boy who was with him in the stables. He shuffled his feet, blushing with embarrassment, before saying in the voice of a pupil repeating a lesson: 'He tripped on the top of the stairs, fell to the bottom and hurt himself badly.'

She said she was sorry, and he was not to worry, as she would speak to the Grand Duke Serge on his behalf. At the mention of her husband's name, the boy shook so much that she thought he was going to fall down. This annoyed her, since she knew how carefully Serge looked after his workmen, but she hid her anger and, telling him kindly that she was sure he would settle down, continued her walk.

The sight of the unhappy boy stuck in her mind, and that night she asked Serge if it would not be kinder to reunite him with his family, who, she presumed, had left for the Pale. Serge told her coldly that it was no business of hers what happened in the stables. She apologized, and said he knew she never interfered in any way with his affairs, but since the boy was crying and desperately unhappy, she thought it her duty to tell him as she knew he was proud of the conditions of his workmen. Serge said nothing, and during the last two days of her visit she never caught any further glimpses of the boys. Although Ella tried to avoid hearing accounts of the expulsion, she could not help hearing her ladies-in-waiting talking or stop herself from overhearing excited conversations at luncheon and dinners related to, what was according to the opinions of the speakers, the terrible tragedy or just retribution of the forced exodus. She gathered that, within three days of the original proclamation, nearly nine thousand Jews had been, often separated from their families, packed into trains and carried off to different districts of the Pale.

As usual, the matter was more complicated than the simple expulsion order suggested. While another ten thousand poor Jews had gone into hiding – many of them to gain a few days in which to sell their businesses and get some money to take away – the authorities had granted exemption orders to another ten thousand of the richest families. One of Serge's aides explained the anomaly quite simply: 'The rich can stay and pay, the poor must go.' Gradually Ella understood how, to those belonging to this fortunate group, the order was nothing more than an inconveniently heavy tax, and that their position was by no means desperate. The same could not be said of the second group in 'hiding'. Every day police searches decreased their numbers and filled the trains to the provinces of the Pale, and every night young bloods, encouraged by Serge, engaged in a new sport: Jew hunting.

Ella could not avoid knowing the details, since Serge was constantly congratulating young volunteers for their skill at the new game, while they, in turn, poured into his delighted ears details of how they had scoured the back alleys and taverns of the old town, breaking down doors and smashing their way into poor houses in search of 'foxes' who, when caught, were shoved into special carriages attached to trains that carried them off west to start life again, penniless.

Ella, standing silently by her exultant husband, sensed in other quarters doubts concerning the sport, for many of the older generation looked nervous and unhappy and tried to change the subject whenever possible, but without success. As Serge could talk of nothing else, his conversation made her evenings nightmares, especially in their own house, where every night his disciples shouted new stories. She found it extraordinarily difficult to sit uncritically opposite her husband, internally sickened by sadistic tales which made him roar with laughter.

One morning in May she opened an envelope stamped with the crest of the Preobrazhensky Regiment and, seeing a letter without beginning or end, knew by instinct that here was another warning. She put it down and shut her eyes. Was her whole life to be a series of secret letters, each one uselessly stabbing her, for what could she do? She wished she had shown the Windsor letter to Serge. This time she would make no mistake, and she put it unread in a drawer beside her bed, but almost immediately realized that she could not give it to Serge without reading it. What if it mentioned the Windsor letter? At any rate, it would excite her husband's curiosity, and if he questioned her, she might break down and tell him all her secrets, which would mean that poor Anton, his wife and child would all end up in Siberia, and she would never forgive herself.

The simple note was from the Windsor writer:

Your husband's personal cruelties have continued and he has badly injured a

136

boy at his country house who is still in hospital. In view of his murderous private habits the Committee has decided to end the life of this 'man of evil'. We beg Your Imperial Highness to avoid riding in his carriage.

Enclosed with the warning were the hospital cards of the four girls in St Petersburg and one boy from Moscow. She carefully put the letter at the back of the drawer and sat down to try and decide what to do. Should she tell Serge that his life was in danger? She would have to tell him everything or nothing. What of the accusations against him? She already had an inkling that the story the little Jewish boy at Ilonskoye had told her about how his friend received his injuries was untrue. He had spoken in such a queer, artificial way. Neither could she ignore the fact that the names and addresses of the injured girls sent to her at Windsor matched those on the hospital cards. She could not doubt that Serge was to blame, and for the second time allowed herself to loathe him with her whole heart. But what shocked her even more was the way in which she had hidden her knowledge from herself and refused to believe the obvious: what a wretched, cowardly hypocrite she was. Even now, after the pretence was over, she knew that her upbringing and hatred of a public scandal would prevent her from leaving Serge; convention, not loyalty, would make her stay. She was too weak to make a bold decision. These reflections made her realize that she was a detestible, weak woman whom she should despise as much as she did her husband. The shock of her self-admission sent the blood rushing to her head, and she fainted at the moment the housekeeper came into the room.

That efficient woman, jumping to the conclusion that she was pregnant, sent for the doctor. He diagnosed fatigue and shock and gave her a dose of laudanum which sent her to sleep for sixteen hours. When she woke up, the first thing she saw was another letter by her bed. Horrified, she shut her eyes, but when she opened them again, the letter had not moved. She tore it open and found inside a cutting from the previous day's newspaper reporting the arrest of a nest of six Jewish terrorists in a cheese shop stored with hidden explosives. They had resisted arrest, wounding a policeman in the chest. The police had shot four of the terrorists and severely wounded the other two. On a piece of paper were printed in capital letters the words: 'I regret I did not know before that these men had the barefaced impertinence to trouble you. They will not have the opportunity again.'

The note was unsigned, but she had not the slightest doubt it was from the stranger. She lay back and thanked God, which she realized was wrong, as *four* men had died, but the Windsor letters had hung over her from the moment she woke up until she fell into uneasy sleep. At last she felt at ease, unthreatened.

A few weeks later, she was accepted into the Orthodox Church and heard, with disappointment, the Holy Synod had decided that Father Constantin was to remain her confessor. The decision was an anti-climax which damped her enthusiasm for an event from which she hoped so much. But before long she found relief in exploring the sixteen hundred churches in the city and praying for two hours every afternoon that she would be forgiven for her lack of courage in confronting Serge, and in promising that if she was ever released from her bondage, to which she was tied by upbringing and traditions stronger than

137

herself, she would gladly give away all her worldly possessions and devote her life to the unfortunate.

After one afternoon period of prayer, Ella had felt sure that if she only asked Serge, he would allow her to involve herself directly in charitable work in the Church and to go into the poorest districts since her interest in good works would increase his popularity. Praying on her knees, she was certain that he would agree, thanked God for his kindness and sat back smiling and happy. She tried to maintain her feeling of certainty in her carriage, but found her faith in his consent weakening, and when, late at night, she asked him if, now that she was a member of the Church, she could move freely among the poorer districts, he gave her one of his hard looks and said he had informed her she could not. He had not changed his mind, and the matter was not to be mentioned again.

Conscious of how she would deteriorate into a bitter woman unless she filled her empty days, she concentrated for the second time on her beauty, painted pictures of dresses for her friends and designed settings for the jewels which Serge gave her on her birthday or name day, at Easter or at Christmas. She also again tried hard to listen to her reader, but found it very difficult to get through Russian books. She liked some of Turgenev's short stories, but was not allowed to read his novels or anything which Count Tolstoy wrote, and when Serge allowed her to read a book by a man called Shchedrin, she found it so grim and sad that she could not face the end. She was happiest when her reader would sit gently reading English books. She found the stories of Ouida so exciting that she could hardly wait for the next chapter, and she loved Mrs Henry Wood and *Cranford* and *Our Village*, which made her cry, but when her reader tried *David Copperfield* and *Vanity Fair*, she fell asleep after five minutes and could never follow the plots.

She decided it would be diverting to entertain, and when she suggested to Serge that, as 'viceroy of the south' – as she had heard Pobedonostsev describe him – he should entertain all distinguished visitors to Moscow, he asked her sharply why she called him that. When she replied, 'Pobedonostsev', a look of intense pleasure came over his face, and he at once agreed that her suggestion was sensible.

She sent for a list of visitors and found, to her surprise, how a large number of vassal chieftans and khans were continually passing through the city on their way north to St Petersburg, which sounded entertaining. To begin with, she enjoyed outdazzling their oriental magnificence but found conversation so difficult that she invented a way of pleasantly shortening the evenings. She would dress in her full splendour, wearing a diamond parure and overwhelming her guests with her beauty and grandeur, but at eleven o'clock would leave the ballroom, go upstairs, change her costume and put on her emerald parure and descend to more excited admiration. By such diversion, she filled the days and nights of her first year in Moscow, and closed her ears to politics and persecution. After all, she tried to persuade herself, there was nothing she could do.

The brutal expulsion of the Jews from Moscow shocked world opinion. Ella received a sharp questioning note from her grandmother, and even her sister Victoria wrote critically, but Serge, determined not to call off the chase, was strongly supported by Pobedonostsev, who came down to visit him every month. Her reader told her that he was the original of the husband of Anna Karenina in Count Tolstoy's novel, but as she still wasn't allowed to read the book, the remark was meaningless. It increased her desire to know what Serge's *éminence grise* was like. At their occasional meetings, he appeared dull and cold, and she shivered when his eyes looked at her through his gold-rimmed, thin, egg-shaped spectacles. Neither was his reaction to polite conversation reassuring. He would stare at her, reflect a moment and turn away as if she was of no importance. His rudeness, of course, made her wish to get to know him, to find out what lay behind his arrogance and success. His power was now undisputed. He ruthlessly ruled the Church, displacing bishops without a moment's thought. He was said to be the only man of whom the Tsar was frightened, and both Serge and Nicky hung on his words. Miechen said she was sure that he was more powerful than the Tsar, because he actually believed in autocracy, whereas the Tsar and Serge supported the system out of frightened self-interest and found comfort in the certainties of a brilliant, logical, analytical supporter who gave substance to their instinctive but uncomprehended beliefs. Ella did not quite understand what she meant, but wished to try and win the sympathy of the man whom Serge worshipped, and at the back of her mind, despite all her disappointments, admissions of self-deceit and periods of detestation, she still hoped that her husband might change his life.

She gave a start of pleasure when Serge casually said one day that Pobedonostsev was coming to lunch and Nicky would be the only guest. She at once thanked him for his kindness in enabling her to meet the man whom she wished above all others to get to know. Turning away, he said: 'I would like you to be aware that the purpose of this meeting is for the chief of the Holy Synod to explain certain questions of the precise relationship between the Holy Synod and the Tsar which Nicky does not yet fully comprehend.'

Before lunch, she examined the Procurator carefully, noticing his long, perfectly manicured, bony fingers and how, when he spoke, his Adam's apple jerked up and down his thin neck as if it was trying to jump out of his throat. As she sat down, she wondered what she could say which would not sound silly, but before she had a chance to speak, he turned to her and said in a bleak voice: 'I gather, Your Imperial Highness, that the Tsar's support of the Holy Synod's attempt to control some of the excesses of certain minorities meets with your disapproval. Do you support the antics of such sects as the Skopzi or Podpolniki?'

She was outraged at his scathing attitude, especially since she had never heard of either of the sects, and knew that if she admitted her ignorance, Pobedonostsev was sure to tell the Tsar, who, ignorant himself, was always delighted to hear of other's stupidity. Should she decline to discuss a question on which she had never given an opinion? Anger at his ill manners made her independent upbringing assert itself, and she replied coldly: 'I was brought up to believe that people should choose and follow their own beliefs.'

His eyes remained unblinkingly fixed on hers as a scornful look spread over his face, as if he were now sure that she was even stupider than she looked. At last he spoke.

'Might I inform Your Imperial Highness of the practices which the Skopzi follow: they mutilate themselves and their women are encouraged to cut an artery in their chests – I do not speak precisely – which results in constant bleeding, and ensures that they lose blood daily for the remainder of their lives. If they have children, these are brought up in their parents' faith. They justify their mortifications by the twelfth line of the nineteenth chapter of St Matthew 'which had made themselves eunuchs for the kingdom of Heaven's sake'. I fear I have shocked your sensibilities, but in view of my factual information, I wonder if you still disagree with the Tsar's support of the Holy Synod's decision to outlaw the custom of parents malforming their womenfolk and emasculating their sons?'

Ella sat in silence; what could she say?

The Procurator continued, an edge of triumph in his voice: 'As for the Podpolniki, I must inform you that they believe . . .' He stopped, and looking at her sarcastically, murmured: 'But please tell me if I am tiring you by impartial information of which you are already aware.'

Ella shook her head.

'Thank you. I will continue. The Podpolniki believe that the sun is the eye of the devil, and at one time they considered it a foot on the ladder to heaven to be buried alive in the walls of new buildings. This custom was autocratically outlawed by a former Tsar, doubtless you conceive wrongly, and today, as their savage sacrifices have been condemned, their present-day prophets live underground in pitch-black caves, kept alive by their followers, who are forced to waste long periods of each day stumbling about with food and drink in complete darkness, attempting to find these modern martyrs whose rights I gather you support.'

Ella flushed and felt idiotic, especially as Serge was listening with a satisfied look on his face. The Procurator spoke in such scornful, sarcastic tones that it was obvious he wished to crush an ignorant meddling fool, and she had to admit he had succeeded. How could she have known how, in innocently proclaiming her belief in the freedom of religious choice, she was laying herself open to be accused of supporting such horrific rites? How could she imagine such people? Who, in Hesse or England, would think of mutilating their children or believe that the sun was the devil's eye?

But Pobedonostsev had not finished with her yet.

'I could inform Your Imperial Highness of other sects with customs too brutal and lascivious to mention, and you will forgive me for asking whether it is Your Imperial Highness's belief that sects practising such barbarisms should be encouraged.'

Ella knew she was defeated and could again only shake her head, although she knew she was right about freedom of belief. She realized that Pobedonostsev, by citing extremists and avoiding the real issue, had made her look a tongue-tied fool.

The Procurator bowed, said he was always at her service if she wished for further information, and turned to answer a question from Nicky, who luckily had not bothered to listen to a word she had said. Ella sat in silence, hating the trumphant eyes as they glistened behind the gold-rimmed spectacles, and felt how she would love to slap his silly, conceited, self-satisfied face.

That evening, she complained to Serge of the Procurator's unfair behaviour. 'I thought he was unbearably rude.'

'Oh, did you, little one? But I think you are mistaken – Nicky said he was very nice.'

He leaned forward and flicked her ear, a patronizing gesture which she detested. Afterwards, she decided never again to ask to sit next to one of the Tsar's administrators, and looked forward, with intense desperation, to the middle of July and the annual move to Ilonskoye.

10

Every year she loved her annual holiday more and for months looked forward with excitement to seeing those she loved most in the world. Sadly, her high expectations ended this year in disappointment. She still needed and always would need Victoria, but they no longer confided in each other. How could they? Childnessness remained a barrier; she could not help resenting the way in which her sister dwelt on children, their illnesses and baby clothes. She felt silly, listening to other young mothers, but how could she join in? That was her first disappointment. Papa was the second. She knew from the moment he arrived that this would be the last time he would ever come to Ilonskoye. Nobody else appeared to notice how he had changed and how his enthusiasm had vanished. Usually partridge shooting made September his favourite month, but he only went out once. Otherwise he sat all day with a book or paper in his hand, slumped in his chair, doing nothing.

She asked if anything would amuse him. He shut his eyes and gently shook his head from side to side. She was sad to see the man who had once loved walking and the countryside never leaving the house. One day, after lunch in the woods, she insisted that her father took his gun, but he held it listlessly, his head down, looking so utterly unlike the man she remembered, always ready to shoot a robin or a wren, that she knew he was ill and said so to Irene, who had sat in silence next to him at lunch.

'Oh, is he?' was all she said. 'I have noticed nothing.'

Ella never could make out why her sister was so stupid; she knew she was not clever herself, but, compared to Irene, she was both brilliant and tactful. If there was anything which should not be said, Irene would say it. Her excuse was always the same: she was worrying about one of her poor, sickly little babies. Irene was the one member of her family of whom Ella could not think with pleasure, so she tried never to think of her at all.

Ella realized that children weaken old ties which, if you are childless, you only cherish more. She was sad about Papa. Victoria, who had formerly loved their father more than herself, was so busy with her own young family that she noticed neither his decline nor her loss of affection for him.

Ernie was so excited by his engagement to Ducky that he could talk of nothing but his marriage next spring, the flowers in the church, the style of his tail coat from Savile Row, the costumes and pink dresses he was designing for the eight pages and twelve bridesmaids, the art nouveau room he was designing for his future wife, the dozen pairs of soft-heeled Cossack boots which he would wear in the evenings. He pestered Ella to design him cufflinks for the boys, and 'V'- and 'E'-entwined platinum diamond brooches from Fabergé for the girls.

Nicky came and openly expressed his love for Alix, who was in such a rage over Ernie's marriage that she did not even bother to be polite. Ella did not wish to agree with her jealous sister, but she was forced to admit that the marriage she had helped arrange was unlikely to succeed. Ducky, still only sixteen, was a strange girl, one moment full of life, the next moody, passing in an instant from a phase of wild hilarity to one of deep depression. How could Ernie, who, as far as she knew, had never been in love, manage such a wild, dangerous, passionate girl? He was still a child: vain, gay, witty, kind, and a lover of social life, and at his happiest dressing up in new army uniforms, despite his hatred of war. His character had none of the force or strength needed to deal with a daughter of the tough and worldly Marie Coburg. Ducky would soon hurt his gentle, brittle nature.

There was one unfortunate incident which added to her fears. Prince Wittgenstein, a dashing young Cossack officer, arrived at Arkhangelskoye with a magnificent, brown wild Cossack horse called Marsyas, who would allow none but his master on his back. Vladimir, who had come on from the Youssoupovs, said the horse had stepped out of mythology, and that when he snorted he looked as if he were blowing fire. The Prince had taken a bet that, given four hundred yards' start, his stallion could, without breaking out of a trot, not be overtaken by a galloping horse in a five-mile run. Ducky, who admitted she liked horses better than people, insisted that they rode over to see the prodigy, and a party went over to Arkhangelskoye after lunch.

In front of his proud owner, Marsyas was led out into the stable-yard where, held by a nervous lad, he backed and turned, lifting a hind leg up and down as if deciding whom he was going to kick. At that moment Ernie and Ducky, who had started later, rode into the yard. She was, with complete confidence, riding side-saddle a pale, flashy chestnut with a red ribbon on his tail, while Ernie sat uneasily on a fat old bay hack. When Ducky saw Marsyas, she threw her reins to a groom, leapt to the ground and ran over to stare with open admiration.

'Oh,' she said, her eyes shining with excitement, 'I would die to ride him.'

'That is quite unnecessary,' said the Prince, putting his hand to his high fur cap and smiling. 'If you can make him stand still and lead him once around the yard, you may take my place in tomorrow's race, and I will back you to win.'

'Oh, thank you,' she said, flushing scarlet with pleasure.

'Thank you. I am grateful for your appreciation of beauty. I can see you are a true lover of horses.'

'Darling, don't be silly!' cried Ernie. 'It would be like riding a tiger. I never saw such a brute in all my life.'

Ducky gave him a scornful look, did not reply and continued to thank the Prince.

'Please, wait before you say too much,' said the latter, 'and remember, my terms are that you must make him stand still and walk him around the yard. I warn you, I am so far the only person he has allowed to get on his back. I hope you succeed.'

Ducky, without a moment's hesitation, walked up to the trembling animal and stood staring into his eyes. At first Marsyas pushed out his head and laid back his ears. As she stood gazing unabashed, a look of interest appeared in his eyes. He stopped trembling, slowly lowered his head and, at last, pricked his ears and appeared to stare back at her with equal interest. Slowly, despite a shriek of protest from Ernie, she put her hand out and gently rubbed his nose.

The Prince said slowly, 'Be careful,' but Marsyas looked pleased. At any rate, he stood still, even when she put her mouth to his nostrils and whispered a few words before rubbing noses and leading him quietly around the yard.

The Prince, who had watched with admiration, said quietly: 'Bravo, you win,' and taking her side-saddle off the chestnut, put it on his horse and gave her a leg up. She sat erect and beautiful while her mount arched his neck with pleasure.

The next day, Ducky, with a start of four hundred yards, won the race, and when the losers, driving their horses into the ground, galloped up the little hill to the finishing point, they all jumped off and prostrated themselves before their conquerer. Flushed with pleasure, she looked around for Ernie. He was not to be seen, but as the heroine lead her vanquished rivals home, they found him stuck on an island between two small streams.

'The beastly thing won't move,' he shouted.

Without a moment's hesitation, Prince Wittgenstein leapt his horse over the brook, turned the hack, backed and brought his Cossack whip down with all his strength on its quarters. Surprised out of its life, the fat animal shot into the air over the water and Ernie, as surprised as his mount, banged his face on the back of his horse's neck and sat forlornly holding a handkerchief to his bleeding nose. Ducky ignored him as she tried vainly to make the Prince sell Marsyas to her.

Serge told Ella that Ernie had cut a sorry figure, adding, 'Alix will never accept Ducky as the first lady of Hesse. She will have to marry Nicky, you'll see. I have sent for Father Yanishev. He is the most skilled convertor in the Empire.'

By the evening, Ducky appeared to have forgotten her triumph, and Ernie, with a swollen nose, was only slightly subdued. But Alix was livid and declared loudly her detestation of 'showing off'. She went to bed immediately after dinner, leaving Nicky sadly playing solitaire.

Towards the end of her visit, after her family and most of the guests had gone, Ella decided to call – it was a compulsion she could neither understand or resist – on Anton. For the second time, she felt ill at ease and sat on the extreme edge of her chair while he picked up his violin, cocked his head and started to play.

'Oh please,' she said desperately.

He stopped, but looked at the window as if to warn her that a silent house would arouse his neighbours' curiosity.

'Play later then, but tell me, have you any news? Is there a letter for me?'

'Yes,' he said, 'I was instructed to give to Your Imperial Highness this note if you called.'

He passed her a letter and went with his violin into the little room where she had first met the stranger. Against the background of his music – she loathed violins now – she read the note which had neither address, beginning nor end:

I had hoped to see you, but events have necessitated a journey abroad. In Moscow, my forebodings have turned into facts and some 17,000 Jews have been, up to now, expelled from the city; the remainder of those unable to bribe are hunted down. Enemies have been made of men of determination who are organizing themselves into revolutionary societies motivated by hatred and revenge. I was able to help you last winter – I will try to continue to do so. It will be increasingly difficult. Are you aware that the Tsar is seriously ill? I expect no trouble until his death.

She read the words through twice and thought that he must be exaggerating about the Tsar's illness, but his words about the persecution gave her a shock. How wicked she was, to allow Ernie's marriage to put the suffering of these poor people out of her mind. She walked up and down, her guilt making it impossible for her to sit still. If only she could do something for somebody. It was unendurable to have become so corrupted by a life of pleasure that she could ignore horrors for frivolities. Meanwhile, the mournful strains of the violin grated on her nerves, irritating to such a degree that she would have liked to smash the instrument on the floor. She endured it for more than ten minutes and then left without saying goodbye. She smiled, as she walked down the path, at what his neighbour must think of Anton continuing to play after she had left. But perhaps they would sympathize with her for walking out!

The date of Ducky's marriage was fixed for the end of April 1894, when she would be just seventeen, but in October Ella received a telegram to say that her father had died. She was ill, and could not go to the funeral, but shortly afterwards felt relieved that Ernie was to be married, for, according to Mr Buchanan, he paid scant attention to the formalities of mourning and 'had plunged into his "new art" building programme as if he had been waiting, indeed preparing, for his father's death'.

The Queen wrote:

I cannot but deprecate his lack of propriety and thoughtless insensitivity. He certainly has not inherited his weakness from dearest Alice.

But England and Darmstadt seemed a long way off, and every year Ella felt her Western ties grow weaker. The news of the continuous persecution of the poor Moscow Jews gave her a distaste for social life, and three times during the winter she saw soldiers escorting ragged bands of men down the street. Each time she looked away and dug her nails into the palms of her hands, guessing that race was their only crime. Her depression was aggravated by Ernie's telegrams. He was constantly bothering her to go to Fabergé's Moscow shop to change the design of the cufflinks and the diamond brooches, or to order enamel pencils for the ushers. Aunt Marie added to her irritation with a letter asking her niece to make out a list of Russian courtiers and officials who should be asked to the wedding. Every day seemed a waste of time.

Ella was bored to death by the weddings she had to attend every few months. Each followed the same tedious pattern: numerous relations would arrive by train at a German court to be met by a harassed chamberlain. Then the quarrels commenced. Every guest would spend his or her first day ascertaining whether relations of inferior rank had received a more respectful welcome. Recriminations followed. The next row inevitably concerned placement at State dinners, and it appeared to Ella that nearly all her relations lay in wait to tell her that while they personally did not care where they sat, they minded the slight to the honour of their country.

By the time the pre-marital celebrations ended, the court chamberlain would be at his wits' end, and some grandee would either have taken mortal offence or – in rare cases – have left. Close friends would not speak, and the bride's father would have on his desk a pile of personal notes reminding him of happy past days, asking him to correct what the writer hoped was a careless mistake and not a deliberate insult.

As Ella feared, Ernie's wedding looked all set to be no exception to the pattern. The usual mistakes occurred, the usual protests were lodged and sides chosen with bitter relish until suddenly, overwhelming all niceties, there came Alix's startling announcement that she would marry Nicky. Serge merely smiled and said: 'I told you she would never stay here, ceding precedence to Ducky,' and certainly Alix's one idea was to get out of Darmstadt as quickly as possible. She had already accepted the Queen's offer that she should spend the next few months in England and receive religious preparation for her new life. Her instructors included Father Yanishev and the Bishop of Ripon, Dr Boyd Carpenter, who had caused a stir a year or two before by preaching a sermon claiming a close affinity between the Russian Orthodox and Lutheran Churches. Ella was amused as she remembered how Grandmama was surprised and shocked at the time, but as things turned out, she obviously considered that the Bishop's opinions could now be useful.

Every secret decision immediately became common knowledge, to be discussed and embroidered, and Ella noticed that although the relations expressed delight, their voices sounded insincere, which was not surprising, since she knew how her family's splendid marriages caused irritation and acute jealousy. But at least the engagement stilled the usual petty quarrels and made the prelude to Ernie's wedding unusually peaceful.

The Queen attended the service, but retired immediately afterwards to rest. Ella sighed; she knew that after her Grandmama left the horseplay would begin. She was right. The wedding lunch had hardly started before George of Greece attacked his fat aunt, the Duchess of Würtenberg, and roughly tore off her tiara and false hair. This traditional witticism was greeted with shrieks of laughter, which redoubled when he put the tiara on himself. As they waited for the bride and groom to leave, George again attacked his aunt, jamming his top hat on her head and knocking off and breaking her spectacles. This was considered especially funny, since she was almost blind. Beside herself with laughter, the Princess of Wales ran and whispered in the old Duchess's ear that her assailant

146

had been a correct young British courtier standing beside her. The angry old woman at once turned and hit the young man on the head with George's hat. The scene was considered memorable.

The bride was pelted with rice on her way to the waiting carriage and as she drove away Nicky, to the horror of his detectives, burst through the crowd outside the door, ran round the corner, caught up with Ducky and Ernie, ran alongside and threw a bag of rice and a shoe into Ducky's face. Catching the shoe, she hit him again and again on the head until he stopped, choked by laughter, to be immediately surrounded by stolid German detectives who hemmed him in like an escaped lunatic.

Ella found these antics tedious beyond words and, what was worse, knew it was a beginning and not an end. Countless stories would be told and retold, illustrating George of Greece's wonderful sense of humour and the scintillating wit of the enchanting Princess of Wales when she caused the Duchess of Würtenberg to belabour an innocent young courtier with a top hat.

11

Two months after their return to Moscow, Serge received a report from Count Fredericks: 'The doctors believe the Tsar's illness to be incurable. He has not long to live.' The news came as a shock to Ella, despite the stranger's warning and her knowledge that the Tsar had lost weight and looked thin and ill, yet it solved one problem which worried Serge: why his brother had suddenly agreed, despite earlier opposition, to allow Nicky to marry Alix.

Ella spoke aloud her secret thoughts. 'But how terrifying that Nicky should be Tsar. He is only a silly boy, and you have always been worried by his naïvety and inexperience.'

Serge turned to her and said in his coldest voice: 'You forget that in the last two years I and Pobedonostsev have coached him, and that, whatever happens, he can be relied upon to retain the system of autocracy without which the Empire would disintegrate. He may look silly, but is wise enough to accept advice from those with knowledge and good judgement.'

Ella did not reply, but silently wondered how could an ignorant boy like Nicky and a girl like Alix, who was not clever and who was obstinate and proud, govern Russia. Serge interrupted her thoughts by saying triumphantly: 'You see the wisdom of the trouble I have bothered to take with Nicky. Vladimir always said I was a fool to waste time on the boy. Now I will enjoy showing him how I backed the right horse.'

The next day they took the train south. At Livadia, Serge hardly recognized his brother. Alexander had shrunk, his voice grown thin, his face grey. Nicky had already arrived from England, and when the Tsar realized he was dying, he asked that Alix be sent for and suggested that the pair be married immediately. Startled by the unexpected summons, Alix set out, Victoria coming with her as far as Warsaw. At Kiev, she was met by Ella and Serge, who had the task of explaining the changed situation. An impatient Nicky was waiting at the station in unexpectedly good spirits. He explained that his father, although bedridden, was certain to recover, but once they arrived at Livadia the truth could not be side-stepped. The Tsar was waiting to greet his son's future wife in the drawing-room, sitting fully dressed by the window, his huge, bony hands grasping the sides of his chair. With enormous difficulty he pulled himself to his feet, leaned forward, kissed Alix's hand and fell back with the satisfied look of a man who has reached a mountain top. Shortly his smile faded. His eyes closed and, at a sign from the Tsarina, they left the room.

The next day, Marie Feodorovna gave a lunch for the commanding officers in the Crimea and asked Serge, Ella and Alix to support her. They stood in a room, waiting to be ushered into the Empress's presence. When the door was flung open, Ella, with a polite gesture, beckoned Alix – who would in a few days be the wife of the Crown Prince – forward. Alix had taken a tentative step when Serge roughly pulled her back and pushed Ella forward, remarking in a stern voice: 'Until you are married, remember my wife takes precedence.'

Alix turned bright scarlet and drew back, and Ella knew how her sister would never forget this unnecessary insult. It was no use speaking to Serge; he would neither understand nor apologize. The harm was done. It was one of those moments when she hated her husband's insensitivity.

Nicky was entranced at the arrival of Alix, and gazed at her every moment of the day, careless of his father's health and his imminent succession. Serge was satisfied by his nephew's ignorance and stupidity, imagining how he would continue to dominate the simple young man. Ella believed him wrong, and that once she was married her possessive sister would choose her husband's friends.

The next day, Father Ivan arrived. Ella tried to keep out of his way, but when they met in a passage he gave her a sly look and said, with his lascivious smile, 'Ah, I see things haven't changed. Remember, you won't be redeemed without sinning,' and the horrible little man winked and strutted on.

Ella knew she should reprimand his impertinence, but no words came out and she stood blaming her inadequacy. Yet afterwards, she was glad she had not spoken. How could she have insulted a man of God who had come to comfort and absolve the Tsar on his deathbed?

On 1 November 1894, Alexander III, in the presence of the imperial family, died. Serge insisted that Ella should be present, but all she saw was a skeleton ceasing to breathe. They all kissed the back of his widow's head as she knelt in tears by her husband's bedside. The Tsar's death set in motion a strange sequence of mourning and celebration lasting for three weeks. The beginning was surprising. Alexander's body disappeared overnight without pomp or ceremony into the parlour of an embalmer, and appeared two days later, the face plump and rotund, lying in state in Livadia Cathedral.

On the morning following the death, Ella was asked to dress in white and accompany her sister to be received by a pensive, solemn Father Ivan into the Orthodox Church. Although Alix had prepared herself for conversion, she was flustered by the suddenness of the ceremony coming on top of the Tsar's death and Nicky's succession, and was reluctant to accept her new faith in such strange circumstances, but Nicky implored her to carry out his father's last wish.

During the afternoon, the Tsarina Marie Feodorovna asked Ella to come and see her. She found her calm and tearless, but with icy cold hands and a set, rigid expression. The Tsarina quickly disengaged herself from Ella's embrace and, walking over to the window, stood silently looking over the Black Sea. After a few minutes of silence she turned and said: 'I think Nicky should marry Alix tomorrow or the next day.'

Ella was so surprised that she said the first thing which came into her head, although afterwards she realized it must have sounded shallow and silly.

'She can't. She has not even got a wedding dress.'

'Oh, that can be arranged,' was the reply in the tone of one who knew that, to her, everything was possible.

'But really,' Ella said, 'I don't think she is in the right mood to marry, and neither's Nicky.'

She spoke the last words as an afterthought, to reassure Marie Feodorovna that her son regretted his father's death, although he gave no signs of grief and only appeared to be sad when events separated him from his beloved Alix.

'My own view is the quicker the better, but I suppose I cannot alone make the decision. I will call a family council. Try and persuade Serge to support me, will you?'

Ella repeated to her husband Marie Feodorovna's exact words without comment. The brothers immediately met and decided against an early wedding. It was their unanimous view that it should be a public spectacle which could not be held until the Tsar was buried. The body stayed at Livadia until the 8th, when it sailed out of the little local port to be transferred to a cruiser escorted by battleships of the Black Sea squadron and carried to Sebastopol.

The journey to the port began in the early morning, led by the coffin draped in the darkest purple, followed by the widow Tsarina alone in a carriage. Behind her rode Nicky and his four uncles, and then came another carriage with Miechen, Ella and Alix. Behind these rode or drove visiting kings and princes. The way to the port from the cathedral, 'The Route of Mourning', was covered with branches of cypress and laurel, some of them so large that they jolted the carriage uncomfortably. Ella later heard Serge tell Alexis that the sound of the wheels of the gun carriage crushing branches was like the noise of breaking bones. Marie Feodorovna, despite her drawn, sad face, smiled and bowed unceasingly to the silent crowd. But Alix sat upright and stiff, never glancing at the peasants who lined the route, hats in hands, bowing low or prostrating themselves as the cortège passed.

The journey by sea was uneventful, but when they reached Sebastopol both Ella and Alix thought that the train looked like an enormous coffin: every carriage was draped inside and out with black. The dead Tsar travelled alone in the first coach covered with flowers; the imperial family and chief mourners slept in the carriages behind. Alix was a reluctant traveller, especially after she saw the pitch-black train, and begged to be allowed to return to England and come back in the spring, but Nicky, for once determined, would not hear of the idea and implored her in tears to stay, refusing to listen to his uncles when they argued that it would be considered an ill omen by the superstitious peasantry if his bride arrived in St Petersburg behind a coffin.

The journey north appeared endless and was marred only by one incident. After a stormy night, the train crossed a railway bridge and Ella, looking out of her window, saw a boat caught by the current being washed downstream towards the train, despite its peasant owner's desperate attempts to row himself to the side. As she thought what a nuisance it would be for the man to be washed

150

miles downstream, she saw him fall backwards, struggle to get up and then fall again and lie motionless at the bottom of the boat. A moment afterwards, a soldier passed along outside the carriage, and later she heard that a possible assassin had been shot, trying to blow up the bridge. She did not say anything but she could not rid her mind of the picture of the poor man desperately rowing against the current with his fishing nets in the stern; surely no one could have believed he was trying to blow up the bridge. The soldier who fired the shot would, Serge told her later, receive a decoration.

Again and again the train would stop at a platform in the depths of the country for local priests to hold services that never lasted less than three hours. At every station, guards stood on the platform, keeping back thousands of peasants who had walked miles across country to pay on their knees in the bitter cold their last respects to one whom Serge said they coupled in their minds with God. Each evening, for some incomprehensible reason, the train would draw into a siding, to remain motionless until dawn; and one clear, moonlit night Ella, looking late out of her carriage window, saw, beyond the guards, a kneeling army of silent peasants, their countless black figures obscuring the snow and stretching into the distance. Tears came into her eyes as she thought of their faith and devotion.

She could see that her sister was becoming depressed. Alix was seldom alone with Nicky and was shy of the other travellers, most of whom, like the Prince of Wales, were becoming increasingly irate and bored. Serge told his wife with pleasure how her Uncle Bertie ceaselessly complained that he had never expected to spend his fiftieth birthday 'on a damned train behind a coffin without even a pack of cards'.

'I can't think why the hell they don't bury Alexander,' remarked the Prince of Wales. 'After all, it is not as if travelling two thousand miles at ten miles an hour is going to bring him back to life.'

At long last the train reached Moscow, where the corpse lay in state in the Kremlin. The visiting royalties saw their chance, rebelled and refused to stay in the train for yet another endless journey, this time to St Petersburg. The rebels included Ella's Uncle Bertie, who, hearing that it was planned to hold fifteen memorial services in the capital before the final burial, wired for his son George to come over immediately and stand in for him on the less important occasions.

Many of the imperial family also made excuses of pressing business, but the group reunited when the train ended its long journey a few days later. Ella could not help comparing her own triumphant entrance ten years before with Alix's four-hour crawl behind a coffin to reach the church of Saints Peter and Paul, the burial place of the Romanovs, joined to the full and famous prison, many of whose inhabitants, Serge had told her once with relish, were 'slowly rotting to death'.

Tradition necessitated the holding of two memorial services a day during the lying-in-state, each of which Alix attended, although she could not understand a word. She seldom saw Nicky, and despite all Ella's attempts to cheer her up, she was obviously cross, lonely and unhappy, while her hard set face won her few friends.

At last, on 19 January, the Tsar was buried. Ella never forgot the beginning of the service. The whole congregation was kneeling with unlit candles in their hands when, as if by magic, monks appeared with burning tapers. Slowly, almost like the sun rising, the church lit up. Afterwards, every dignitary in the empire insisted on playing his part, and she thought the lamenting would never end. The ceremony over, the new reign officially began, and as the carriages full of relieved mourners drove away, bands played, soldiers fired volleys into the sky and the thunder of canon celebrated the beginning of the new Emperor's reign.

Ella asked Serge why it has been necessary to torture Marie Feodorovna by keeping her husband unburied for nearly three weeks. He repeated his unchanging reply to her critical comparisons: 'A little country like Hesse has different customs from the great Russian Empire,' and added: 'I wish that, as her sister, you would inform Alix she should look happier.'

Ella for once retorted angrily: 'Do you think it has been fair to subject a young girl to an engagement in which she has either had to go to memorial services all day or otherwise spend her time shut in a train behind a coffin? All I can say is that I am glad we have different customs.'

When her sister came to stay at the Sergei Palace, Ella found, to her surprise, that Alix had made two new friends, the Montenegrin sisters. On second thoughts, she was not surprised; the Montenegrins abased themselves and agreed with every word her sister said. They had also established themselves as the leaders in St Petersburg of what was known as the 'mystic set', which appealed to Alix, who had always enjoyed séances and table-turning. She appeared to be amused by their endless chatter, which was more diverting than the pretended grief shown by hypocritical old courtiers. The 'Black Perils' called daily and stayed for hours.

One day, when Alix was out trying on her wedding dress, they met Ella in the hall and rushed up to her with their usual enthusiasm.

'How beautiful!'

'Too beautiful for words.'

'We are sorry to miss Alix, but can nothing be done about the unkindness?'

'What unkindness?' asked Ella, who could never follow the sisters' trains of thought.

'Oh, what people are saying!'

'Yes, people you would not expect to say such things; that it is unlucky to enter her capital behind the coffin, that ill fortune will follow.'

'Is it widely said?' Ella asked, surprised into curiosity.

'Yes, widely.'

'And openly, and believed.'

'Of course. Dearest Alix encourages such talk, looking so sad and dispirited.'

'Yes, dearest Alix. We are so sorry for her.'

Ella lost her temper, already frayed by endless dreary periods of mourning. She turned on Militza and said coldly: 'Please do not discuss your future Tsarina's appearance. She would not like it. And please discontinue your habit of relating unpleasant facts.'

She turned away, but not before seeing a venomous look pass over Militza's face. But it was unfair to blame Alix for looking sad after the train journey and service. Now she had to fit clothes all day and learn a strange language every night. And tiresome as Alix could be, she was not going to hear her being unfairly criticized by these hairy gipsies.

A week later, a strange, grim marriage service took place in the Winter Palace with an unhappy looking Marie Feodorovna dressed for the day in white. The sudden change from ostentatious grief to ostentatious celebration grated on even the insensitive and gave the ceremony a stark, forced gaiety. Ella warned her sister of the weight of the Catherine robes, but, during the endless ceremony, Alix once tried to move at the wrong moment and nearly fell over, exactly as she had done herself twelve years before.

There was no honeymoon, and – builders thronging their own new quarters – the newly married couple moved into six pokey little rooms in Alix's mother-in-law's palace, which was all that Marie Feodorovna felt she could offer. It seemed to Ella to be a deliberate display by Nicky's mother of her power over her son and of her contempt for her daughter-in-law. But neither of them appeared to notice or care and they lived in total happiness together.

The wedding and the funeral over, Ella thought that she would have a respite from ceremonies. She soon learned her mistake: preparations for the coronation began immediately and Alix begged her not to return to Moscow. Ella felt she could not leave her sister, as there was little doubt that the gossip of Militza was true. One by one, Ella's ladies-in-waiting told her how their relations wrote asking why Alix has been allowed to arrive behind a coffin. As to the peasants, they believed that death followed death, and the manner of her entrance to her future capital and her marriage following a funeral were considered the worst of omens.

To her surprise, Serge told her one evening that Pobedonostsev was concerned at the universality of forebodings, for the peasants' belief in coming misfortune was shared by the Tartars and other minorities. He later wrote to Serge, saying that the rushed wedding had wasted an opportunity for showing to the public, who should have shared in the celebrations, the grandeur of autocracy and the sacred relationship of the Tsar to the Orthodox Church.

> The peasant is both deeply religious and impressionable, and an admirer of displays of splendour which maintain his opinion of the Tsar as a ruler chosen by God. Instead, the sudden unprepared marriage under the shadow of death has resulted in the unknown, uncrowned Tsarina becoming known as 'The Coffin Bride'. The past can neither be altered nor recalled, but every effort should be made to change public opinion by preparing a coronation of unequalled magnificence, excelling all the splendours of our past, exciting both imagination and loyalty and illustrating that the revolutionaries, for all their boasting of public support, are a despicable minority.

As usual, Pobedonostsev had his way, and Nicky ordered celebrations to be staged all over the Empire. The news of Alix's pregnancy, while deferring the coronation, added to the enthusiasm. Serge was, as Governor-General, anxious that the celebrations in Moscow – the site of the ceremony – should transcend all others, and at an early date he decided that the mementoes, which it was customary for Tsars to hand out on the Khodynka Fields, should be of lasting value and eclipse the miserable little gifts which earlier Tsars had distributed to their subjects.

Moscow, conceiving itself momentarily to have regained the position of capital of the Empire, which it lost under Peter the Great, welcomed Serge's grandiose plans. After the first Coronation Committee meeting, he told Ella with exultation that he had ordered a million small metal mugs stamped with coloured reproductions of portraits of the Tsar and Tsarina, adding, in a contemptuous voice, that the idea was one of the few good things which ever came out of England.

He had noticed the popularity and quality of the Queen's Jubilee mementoes which he had seen displayed on the mantelpieces of every cottage he entered while shooting in Scotland or Norfolk. He admitted, with a smile, that he had borrowed another idea from England: the creation of a committee to plan the celebrations, and he had chosen its members – society women, senior officials, local governors and many of the city's richest merchants. When Ella asked if any of them had put forward good ideas, he replied that the committee was not identical with its English model. In Moscow it had three purposes: to do as it was told, to provide money, and to ensure in Moscow the presence of peasants from all the adjoining provinces to witness the enduring strength and splendour of the Romanov family.

Serge appeared to carry everything before him. One day he came home to say that the brewers had offered to provide beer at cost price for 500,000 people and that the coopers and timber merchants had presented free two hundred huge oak barrels to hold the liquid. Another time he brought news that the sailmakers of St Petersburg would provide free canvas for the roofs of the stalls. Ella's services were not neglected; she was sent to call on the enormously rich Ivan Blok, a convert to Christianity, to ask him for a donation. Serge laughed when he asked her to go: 'You may get something out of him. I would get nothing. He's a convert, but remains a Jew.'

She was surprised at the noble-looking old man sitting in his library. She explained, in some embarrassment, the purpose of her visit. He nodded, wrote a large cheque and stood up. 'I have given you what you came for. Please do not think you need stay out of politeness.'

Understanding that although the old man was prepared to give her money, he did not wish to prolong a conversation with the wife of the tormentor of his people, she stood up and spontaneously held out her hand, which he gently lifted to his lips, gazing up at her from beneath his eyebrows. Looking into his eyes, she saw that there was a mutual sympathy and admiration. As she was shown out of the front door, he bowed deeply. Tears came into her eyes, and she thought what a fool she was to cry so easily.

It was soon apparent that the coronation was arousing immense interest and that Alix's pregnancy had regained her her popularity. But Ella remained worried about her sister; certainly she had received a cruel baptism in her new country. The death of Alexander III, the gruesome rites in Livadia, the terrible train journey, the endless incomprehensible memorial services, the rushed marriage and the degradation of being squashed into six little rooms would have embittered the most generous of characters, and Ella understood he resentment. Even so, Alix appeared unnecessarily stiff and unyielding, and found it impossible even to smile at the crowds who cheered as she drove past.

Ella decided to visit her. To her surprise, she was shown into Alix's bedroom, her sister explaining that Nicky usually needed the sitting room for audiences and business. Again Ella was amazed at the behaviour of Nicky's mother, cramming her newly married son and his wife into so few rooms, although they appeared to enjoy living in conditions which ensured they were never more than a few feet apart. Alix looked beautiful and happy, and it seemed a good opportunity to convey gently that she should appear more relaxed and friendly to the court and public.

Ella waited until her sister had, with a laugh, told some ridiculous story of the effects of their crowded life before she interrupted, talking more nervously than she wished, 'Alix darling, you are so beautiful and so lovely when you are laughing. I wish you would smile more in public. I know how silly it feels to be in a coach with crowds gaping at you, but, you know, if you smile at the crowds, especially the peasants who have come for perhaps hundreds of miles to catch a glimpse of you, they will treasure the memory for the rest of their lives. You know, I have lived here for eleven years, and have experienced how jealous the rest of the family can be, always looking for things to criticize. And you see, if you put on a severe face, they make up stories that you and Nicky are unhappy. And if Miechen gets hold of them, she tells everybody and they are believed and quoted and passed on. It took me years to learn the lesson of looking pleased, but now I smile all the time and people say I am happy, which is not always the case, as you know. So, darling Alix, smile even if you don't like the look of people, for anyhow you have such a lovely smile.'

Ella had become rather confused by the unchanging look on her sister's face and ended rather weakly and ungrammatically. To her surprise, after she had finished, Alix sat in silence and began to turn red, a sure sign that she was angry. Then she stood up and walked, with pursed lips, up and down the room as if she was trying to contain her anger. At last she asked Ella: 'When are you going to England?' – a clear hint it was not her sister's business to give advice.

Ella felt sad. If Alix was not going to take advice from a loving sister, who would she listen to? How would she ever learn what and what not to do?

They kissed goodbye with affection and, just as Ella was going out of the door, her sister hurriedly asked her to come again. She said, 'Of course,' but after Alix's exhibition of anger at the gentlest criticism, she was sure that Nicky would soon be taking advice from his wife. It was a pity. Marie Feodorovna had faults, but she was cautious and knowledgeable, while Alix was possessive and jealous and had never shown the slightest interest in politics. Ella knew that ignorance wouldn't stop her sister from giving advice and it was clear that she now regarded Nicky as a personal possession, as Toni Bauer and Miss Jackson had been, which meant that nobody except herself had any right to him. How could she make a calm, wise wife, and how could a Tsar of Russia belong to his wife alone?

Ella saw Alix directly after Olga was born. Her sister was so happy to have a baby that she did not mind it being a girl and nursed the child with such loving concentration she did not notice when her sister left.

12

Despite Serge's blunt refusals, Ella continued to long to carry out the practical work which, she had always known, was her vocation. However hard she tried to enjoy doing nothing and concentrating on herself, idleness gradually began to poison her life and to spoil her interest in the charity committees, even in the plans for her sister's coronation. She thought life was unfair. She had saved Serge from destruction and received no thanks. Now they lived together like strangers. Her only chance of happiness lay in freedom to try and mitigate the horrors and sicknesses of the slums, and Serge would not allow her to move a hand. She was discontented and sick to death with her own beauty, her jewels and her dresses. She knew that Serge was incapable of change. For the first time in her life, Ella gave in to bitterness, and was in a state of despair when she received a letter from Miechen who wrote that she and Vladimir wished to come and stay in Moscow for a week, as he was anxious to examine certain old churches in need of restoration. Ella at once felt better. Vladimir was a challenge and she decided that Miechen was not as unpleasant as she had thought. So she planned to do everything she could to try and please them. It was only their second visit since her husband had become Governor.

On the second afternoon, as they sat together in Ella's small sitting room, Miechen, without the slightest warning – they had been laughing at the Montenegrins – said, speaking quickly: 'Serge wishes you to have a baby. Why he has consulted me, I cannot imagine, but he has sworn me to secrecy and I haven't told Vladimir. I find it an extraordinary business, as it is nothing to do with me, and twice already I have refused to give you this message, but he says I am the right person. Why, again, I do not know. Anyhow, that is what he wants me to tell you. Although I can't think why he can't tell you so himself. I apologize. Please, now that this unpleasant task is over, let us never mention it again. As far as I am concerned, this conversation never took place.'

Ella had not known what to do or say. Surprised and shocked, she sat in silent thought, unaware of her sister-in-law's presence. Ever since the dreadful night in the Crimea, Serge had never made any suggestions to her, although sometimes he had looked at her in a curious way. How could he have approached her on such a subject in such a circuitous way? How could he think, when he had not changed his ways, that she could give herself to him now, after ten years of icy companionship, after she had accepted childlessness as a part of her life and her husband as a formality only proud of her beauty. Could she be wrong? The cruel criticism of Ivan of Kronstadt came back to her mind. Was she a miserable coward? Would it be nice to have a baby? After all, she was only thirty-one. How could Serge have asked Miechen to approach her – even though her sister-in-law, today, had behaved with a nobility which made Ella realize her duality of character. The import of the message overwhelmed her, and she burst into tears, reverting to her childhood, and buried her head in her sister-in-law's lap.

Miechen put one hand around her forehead and gently stroked her head with the other. The effect was infinitely soothing, and she could have kissed her sister-in-law for not speaking. Drying her eyes, she stood up and looked in the mirror. Miechen came and kissed her on the back of the head, and without a word of pity or kindness, neither of which she could have borne, quietly went out of the room, leaving her in a state of utter confusion.

In the evening, she could not look at Serge, but during the following weeks – for he made no move of any kind towards her – she constantly, if quietly, examined him critically. Certainly he was good-looking, although she could not abide his stays and wished that, now he was over forty, he would throw them away.

She was unable to forget the strange, cruel private life which he had told her about in the Crimea and which she knew he had not abandoned. Again and again she wondered whether, if she sacrificed herself, as Father Ivan suggested, and had a baby, it would soften and change her husband's nature? After all, Serge loved children, and strangely enough, despite his fierceness, they loved him. If he had a son, would the baby work a miracle? She decided that it might and prayed, asking God's advice. She thought she received a welcome answer. Or was she persuading herself of what she wanted to believe because she wished to have a baby? The idea had stirred something inside her, brought back a potential purpose to her life, made it possible that the future could be full with happiness rather than with discontent, selfishness and increasing disbelief in herself. Gradually she persuaded herself that she should have a child. But how? She could not conceivably make the first step. She thought of using Miechen as a go-between again, but the idea was so absurd that she burst out laughing and felt better. What was to be done?

She was still filled with doubt and embarrassment when they went to St Petersburg for a dance given by their beloved Preobrazhensky Regiment. Before they left for the ball, Ella took a last look in the glass and thought, for once, that she looked so nice that she would not mind if Serge was in a distracted unobservant mood. Determined to enjoy herself, she drank several glasses of champagne and danced with intense enjoyment, sometimes closing her eyes, as she had on the fatal occasion with Paul, but this time she knew that she was queen of the evening and there was nobody to criticize her. She danced for hours with a joy she had not known for years, and when, at three o'clock, Serge said it was time to go home, she found herself humming tunes and tapping her feet gently on the carriage floor while he sat in his usual silence beside her. In the bedroom, she stood still and he leaned forward and kissed her on the mouth for the first time in their lives. She relaxed in his arms and, shutting her eyes, wondered what would happen.

Nothing happened, except that Serge drew away, looked at his watch, said he would be back in five minutes and walked out of the room. She knew he was wrong, and that had he stayed everything would have been all right. They had, for a moment, moved close together, but then he had gone. Perhaps the moment would be recalled – she had to accept him now. Throwing her clothes on the floor, she put on her nightgown, turned down the gas and lay still. Was this a mistake? Serge must have thought so, for as he returned he turned all the lights up and walked over to her jewel case, took our her parure of emeralds and threw the pieces one by one on the bed, adding to them a thick belt of diamonds as he said: 'Take off your nightdress and put these on. I will give you . . .' looking at his watch, '. . . three minutes,' and picked up her book and walked to his bedroom.

His behaviour drove her to the verge of hysteria. How could he be so insensitive and behave so tactlessly, if not viciously, but she fought against every instinct of repulsion, knowing this to be her last chance.

Slowly, her excitement evaporating, she did as she was told, her heart sinking lower every moment, thinking how extraordinarily silly she must look, covered with jewels. Serge was as punctual as ever and came in with his dressing-gown open. With determination, she looked at his face and kept on looking as he pulled back her bedclothes. Then a terrible thing happened. As she lay there bejewelled, at his mercy, he lifted his hand, his mouth went funny and she knew he was going to hit her for the second time. Screaming, she jumped out of bed and pushed him so hard with both hands that he staggered back against the door, hitting his head, with a crack, against the wood. Filled with panic, she turned round, ran into the bathroom, locked the door and tore her jewels off, breaking her diamond belt, not caring whether she broke the clasps or that blood was pouring from one of her ears. She sobbed as she had done years before, but now with a deeper bitterness, and lay on the bathmat, welcoming the cold air in the hope that she might be found dead in the morning.

After an hour or two, cold and self-consciousness overcame despair. How could she explain to her maids her bloody nightdress, torn ear, the broken clasps, the diamonds scattered all over the bathroom? She took off her nightdress and, soaking it carefully in cold water in one of her basins, wiped the blood off the floor and decided to say that she had torn her ear taking off her earring. She examined the jewellery – only one clasp was broken, and this she could hide beneath the other jewellery and produce later. As for the broken belt, she collected all the diamonds into a heap and decided to tell her maid to have them reset. There was no alternative.

She felt better once she had tidied up the bathroom and made the neat, shining pile. When she climbed back into bed, she thought again of the scene and was filled with depression. It may have been that Ivan was right and she was a stupid, weak women, but her natural instincts could not accept Serge's habits. Ella knew that if she had once allowed him to hit her, she would have gone out of her mind. The look in his eyes and his aura of corruption appeared to her as the essence of depravity, and to join wih him in this would have been to associate herself with dirtiness and vice and to condone his cruelty to the young and innocent.

Miechen had once hinted that marriage to a Romanov was difficult and that Ella should not think she alone suffered from their vices. But that was her business. Ella could not allow herself to be corrupted; it would have destroyed her soul. She would, she supposed, go on living with Serge, but she could not now pretend that one day everything would be all right, and the hope which had lingered in the back of her mind for ten years now lay dead. Curiously enough, she was kept awake by worrying whether her maid would believe her story about the diamonds.

For the second time, Ella knew that she would have to go away. Perhaps, in a month, she would feel strong enough to see Serge, but before her return she would write to him and say that if he ever touched her again, she would leave him in the clothes she stood up in.

At the same time, whatever he said, she was determined to involve herself in practical social work, which meant that she would go where she wanted when she wanted, since she had to have an occupation beyond adorning herself. If he disagreed now, she would not return. If he disagreed later, she would leave. Ella sighed. How easy it was to make firm resolutions, how difficult to carry them out. But she was angry and wrote the letter at once, walked along the passage and pushed it with venom into Serge's private mail box.

In the morning, she sent a telegram to Victoria in Germany, saying that she was sorry to hear her niece was ill and would be arriving in two days' time; she knew that her sister would understand. Victoria was, as usual, pleased to see her, and asked no questions, and Ella rested and walked and tried in vain to like her little niece, Maud, who was so exceedingly plain that she found herself averting her eyes whenever she looked at her. She received a surprising letter from Serge, agreeing to her requests, but asking her to restrict her activities until after the coronation, because her wanderings in Moscow would put an unwelcome strain on the police and might tempt terrorists to try to mar the ceremonies.

The great ceremony was to take place in May, and Ella had to admit that Pobedonostsev was right: the interest was immense, and was added to by the womens' pleasure at her sister's little baby girl, while the Tsar's popularity was shown by the working men's disappointment when the child was a girl. The whole of Moscow became united in a frenzy of excitement, and Serge was very busy controlling the arrangements, although Count Vorontzov-Dashkov had equal powers; but when Ella saw them together Serge never listened to a word the Count said and treated him as a useless old fool. As Minister of the Court, the other was nearly always in St Petersburg, which pleased Serge, and Ella understood that he wished to receive undiluted credit for his magnificent organization.

Preparations continued smoothly, and Serge estimated that more peasants would see the coronation than ever before. The Tsar's presentation of the gifts which he had chosen so carefully was to be made the morning after the wedding on the army parade ground of Khodynka. Hundreds of booths had been erected, and behind them stood the huge barrels of beer to ensure that every visitor could drink the Tsar's health. Ella noticed how Serge was jealous of any interference with his plans for the great spectacle, despite insistent warnings

159

that the crowd might get out of hand.

He was particularly sharp at lunch with Count Vorontzov when the latter asked Serge whether he was sure so many people could be peaceably accommodated and received the cold answer: 'Have you any better plans than I have made? If so, please let me hear them.'

The old man apologized.

The most convincing doubts, however, came from an unlikely source: the Tsar's brother-in-law, Alexander, a huge man with a loud voice who always thought he knew best. Serge disliked him intensely since he was always poking his nose into other people's business. Nicky having no mind of his own, and Alexander being his brother-in-law, the latter was often able to get his way simply because he was the last person Nicky saw.

He came to lunch, as loud as ever, some weeks before the coronation, after visiting the Khodynka Fields, and said, in a loud, pompous voice which made Serge turn white, 'I told Nicky I would make an informal inspection of the site, and I must say I am worried. The roped space is too small, and you know what the peasants are like – they go mad with excitement if they think they are missing anything. Unless the space is enlarged, they will stampede and crush each other to death. For God's sake, Serge, give them more room.'

Serge, who clearly regarded his interference as a meddling impertinence, waited a whole embarrassing moment before replying coldly: 'Peasants are used to close contact and the deliberate containment of the area of celebration is to enable all visitors to have the opportunity of seeing the Tsar.'

'But,' Alexander shouted, 'there will be over half a million people packed together like sardines!'

'I think,' said Serge, with a superior smile, 'there will be many more than that. Will you please change the subject? I am not used to discussing tedious arrangements in front of my wife.'

Alexander opened his mouth but shut it again and sat eating in angry silence, though when Serge was called out by a secretary he turned to Ella and said: 'I shall tell the Tsar. He must make Serge enlarge the area, otherwise there will be a disaster. It's utter madness!'

Ella was worried by the idea of so many thousands being crushed into a small space and bravely brought the subject up again when she thought her husband was in a good mood. It was no use. His face set, and speaking in tones of condescending affability – which he knew she hated – said: 'Now, my dearest little one, remember that while you have an exceedingly beautiful face, you also have an exceedingly small brain, and I would not wish you to strain it, puzzling out problems which you don't begin to understand.'

On the whole, Ella was now much happier in Moscow than in St Petersburg, and she was coming to love, if not the Orthodox Church, then the churches and chapels of the old city. She often drove out in her little dog cart on afternoon voyages of discovery into the poorer districts. On nearly every journey she found an unknown sanctuary where an atmosphere of goodness pervaded the air, to be inhaled with the smell of candles and the scent of incense.

She realized that she would never understand theology: it did not mean anything to her. All she was capable of was good actions – which she was not yet allowed to perform – and private consultations with God, who, she believed, received and answered her prayers when she begged for strength to continue her life of concealed unhappiness. These journeys helped her to fill the empty hours, and then, all of a sudden, the coronation was only a few days away and the Tsar and Tsarina had arrived in Moscow for the rehearsals.

Tired as she was of ceremonies, Ella played her part in the coronation rituals, walked in the right place and made her correct obeisances, but it was as if she was watching a friend acting in front of an audience. Yet she realized that to others the coronation was a splendid and popular success, apart from the usual rows with Marie Feodorovna, and that its magnificence amazed the world. She was struck by how much better Nicky looked on horseback, and wondered if his shortness was the cause of his lack of confidence and his habit of never disagreeing with the advice of his ministers and courtiers, even though, swayed by the opinions of a late visitor, he would frequently carry out policies exactly contrary to those to which he had earlier agreed.

In the Cathedral, Ella noticed an incident which was afterwards vigorously denied. It happened when Nicholas, the crown on his head and wearing the imperial mantle, walked towards the Grand Altar to be consecrated as Emperor. The collar of the Order of St Andrew had fallen off his mantle on to the ground. She saw the Chamberlain move quickly, pick it up and hand it to the Minister of the Court, Count Vorontzov, who somehow hid it under his robes. She was not the only person to notice, for Miechen had given a stifled gasp of horror and crossed herself.

That evening, her ladies-in-waiting asked her if the story was true, and also whether a pin had pricked Alix, causing a drop of blood to fall on her ermine. Ella shook her head. Two days later, Sandra told her that the ill omens were a subject of excited discussion and dissection in Moscow and would, in a few days, be common knowledge in Vladivostock and Bokhara.

The next day the scene was set for Serge's triumph on the Khodynka Fields where, at eleven o'clock, the Tsar was to start the distribution of gifts. The day was to be completed by an enormous ball at the French Embassy to cement the friendship of the new allies.

In the early morning, Ella was woken by steps walking up and down the passage and the opening and shutting of doors. The noise was so unusual that she peered round her door to see Serge standing in the passage at the top of the stairs.

'What is it?' she asked fearfully. 'What has happened? Where are you going so early?'

He turned to her and smiled. 'I have to go to the Khodynka Fields. The crowd is out of hand. It is nothing to bother about; the people's excitement merely shows their eagerness not to miss the Tsar's distribution of gifts.'

The morning was full of rumours, but Ella was told nothing officially and, as usual, got her information from her ladies-in-waiting. The first rumour said the Cossacks had charged the crowd to prevent the storming of the booths. Later, they heard how the army had not filled in old trenches and many of the crowd had fallen and broken their necks. It was soon clear to the horrified household that a major disaster had occurred, and at nine o'clock Ella received a sealed, unsigned letter:

I hear you are not aware of what has happened; you must be anxious to know the truth. Early this morning an untrue rumour spread through the crowd, unwisely confined in a limited area, that the souvenirs would soon run out. This made those at the back, fearful they would go away empty-handed, press forward towards the area of distribution. The Cossacks tried to restrain them, but the pressure from behind grew irresistible and the crowd surged forward, treading unknown numbers to death. The situation is under control. The crowd has been allowed to spread out and the Emperor will formally start the distribution of gifts at two o'clock instead of eleven.

Serge came back at twelve, stiff, trembling and pale. He shouted: 'The whole thing's the fault of that damned old fool, Vorontzov, who said there wouldn't be enough gifts to go round.'

At two o'clock, Ella and Serge stood behind the Tsar on the imperial platform. All appeared peaceful, with no sign of blood or bodies. But she noticed tension among the grand dukes and heard Alexander remarking loudly to the Tsar: 'You know, thousands are dead – the last bodies were moved only half an hour ago. Do you know where they are? You are standing on top of them. They had to shove them under this daïs, otherwise they would have been lying in front of you in rows like dead pheasants.'

Nicky turned petulantly away, and Ella looked at Alix, who was standing erect and stern-faced. After a grim, short opening speech and the presentation of the gifts to a small number of peasants, the ceremony ended. Ella wished to go and comfort Alix, who looked so stiff and proud, her red face set in a repelling mould, but she had second thoughts, although guessing that beneath the childish façade her sister was miserable and on the verge of tears.

At the Governor's Palace, nobody could speak of any subject but the numbers crushed to death. It became unbearable and Ella shut herself in her room and tried to read. It was no good, and in desperation she drove in her pony trap in the opposite direction to the crowds, to a dark little church where she sat alone in a back row. If she could do nothing, at least she could pray for those who had died in pain, for the mothers who had lost their children and the children who had lost their parents. She wished, with all her heart, that Serge would have allowed her to go to see the bereaved families.

Her prayers seemed useless compared to the practical advice and medical aid she could have organized. She knew that Alix would feel the same, but was certainly confined by the same traditions. Ella decided that, if the ball took place, she would defy etiquette and tell Alix to visit the survivors. For while her sister usually hated advice, she had looked so desperately unhappy on the daïs that only by visiting and helping the survivors could she mitigate her pain. How good it would be for her to meet the stricken. To see their sorrow would broaden her outlook and give her great understanding, checking her possessive selfishness and breaking into the isolation in which she and Nicky now lived at Tsarskoye Selo.

In a way, Ella was envious of Alix, who was not confined to a role of passivity, as she was by Serge, since any regret or sympathy shown by Ella would be taken as criticism of her husband's mismanagement. She could only pray, but to pray when all her body was crying out to help was not enough.

She looked around her refuge, the Chapel of St Cyril, which Vladimir, before she left St Petersburg, had told her to visit because it was the only fourteenth-century church in Russia which had frescoes painted by an Italian. Perhaps pleased by her unusual interest, he had told her at length the strange story of a stray Italian painter who, bypassing Byzantium with its frozen iconic art, had arrived in Moscow and covered one church with the art of his own country before disappearing without a trace, leaving not one seed of his skill behind. All that remained were mouldering frescoes of singular interest.

Ella had never liked Vladimir since the day, in Hesse, when she had seen him bullying Serge, and to begin with, after her marriage, she had hated the way he shouted at and harangued everybody but, as happened so often in Russia, she later found how beneath the angry verbosity there lay a man of sensitivity, and after her move to Moscow, he inspired her with interest in many secret shrines. She thought, as she looked at the frescoes, how little she knew about painting. It would never have entered her head that the painter was an Italian. The pictures looked so faded that she wondered how anybody could tell who had painted them.

The largest remaining unspoiled painting was in the apse, where poor Jesus hung, nailed and bound to a cross. The thief, on Our Lord's right, was a muddle of greeny-black, but the fresco on his left was undamaged, and she could clearly see a soldier on horseback beneath the thief's cross, lifting his thick stick to bring it down repeatedly on the sufferer's broken shins. These the painter had already flattened into a red mass, and Vladimir told her to examine them carefully, for not in the art of the East or West would she ever see legs so broken and flattened. Neither should she ignore the skill of the painting of the body above, jerking in hopeless agony.

Ella had thought the description so unpleasant that, while loving the chapel, she had carefully avoided looking at the tortured figure. But, today, the hundreds of candles lit for the Tsar's celebration illuminated the grim scene, and she found herself examining not only the figure of Christ but also the breaking of the legs by the evil-looking mounted soldier with his loathsome stick. How well the artist had caught, all those years ago, an act of revolting cruelty. At last she pulled her eyes away and regained her peace by sitting with her eyes shut, but she could not help half-regretting that she had never suffered great pain to prove her courage. For all she knew, she might be a coward. Her doubts made her eyes stray back to the man on the horse: surely he had changed the position of his right arm?

Then, to her unspeakable horror, she saw him, with all his strength, smash his thick stick down across the flattened legs of the tortured thief, whose body jerked upwards as the knees shivered together. Thinking she had gone mad, she stared appalled at the blurred face of the mounted torturer, and as she looked, saw him take on an unmistakable likeness to Serge.

She dropped her prayer-book and muff and desperately edged sideways, tripping over the cushions, out of the pew, and ran from the church to stand for

163

a moment leaning against the outer door. Was she insane? Could there be another explanation? Nothing on earth would have made her look again at the fresco. The sudden shock made her long for comfort, but from whom could she seek it? Certainly not from Ivan of Kronstadt, or from Father Constantin. At last she thought of Zenaïde, and ordered her driver to go to the Moika Palace.

Ella wondered, during the short drive, whether she had made a sensible choice, for their friendship, intense to begin with, had since stood still. Perhaps they had loved each other too quickly, too dearly at Arkhangelskoye, and perhaps she had confided too much in her new friend, embarrassing her by a weight of secrets. Whatever the cause, although they remained friends, a barrier of embarrassment had stood between them, blocking confidence, leaving them detached, apart. They liked and frequently saw each other, but the original affinity had vanished, their friendship had become a pleasant formality.

Now her original trust and affection returned, and she could think of nobody else in whom she could have such faith. The transformation in the fresco had shocked her to the edge of the valley of despair, into which she knew she would fall unless she could confide in a human being who would not doubt her sanity.

The butler showed her into her hostess's sitting room, where Zenaïde was writing letters, but she jumped up at the sight of her friend's face, locked the door and, taking Ella by both hands, led her to a little sofa. Before she had even sat down, Ella started, in quick whispers, with downcast eyes, to get out of her mind the tragedy of the Fields, followed by the ghastly transformation of the painted soldier's face.

When she finished, Ella looked up with relief and burst into tears. Zenaïde saw she was better, a collapse postponed. Leaving her to cry, she went out and soon came back, carrying a tray, and they sat without speaking, drinking tea, until at last her friend spoke for the first time.

'Dearest Ella, I often feel I haven't done enough to help you, but since Arkhangelskoye we have been embarrassed, which was silly, as it ended our close friendship. But now I think I can help. You are ill. Unless you can get your worries out of your mind, you will get worse. I have taken a bold step and sent for a healer. You cannot be embarrassed by his questions since he is dumb.'

Ella wondered how she could communicate with a dumb doctor as Zenaïde continued, 'His history is curious. He was brought up, the son of poor serfs, on the estate of Prince Repin, but as a child he had the power of healing and became so famous in the district that his patron decided, although he was dumb, he should have medical training. To do so he had, of course, to learn to read and write, which was difficult and took a long time. The Prince persevered and sent him to a medical school, ensuring that he was specially instructed. Afterwards, he brought him back to his house and gave him his freedom and a laboratory of his own.

'The young man did not waste time, as the Prince's friends had prophesied, but spent years hunting for herbs in the woods and fields and, at the same time, cured many peasants, especially those thought to be possessed by devils. Success has not spoiled his simplicity, and he has always refused to take money or leave his cottage and laboratory on the Prince's estate.

'A few months ago, he asked if he could come to Moscow to be present in the

city during the coronation of the Tsar. I will leave you with him when he comes
– he will be here in a few minutes. I hope he will help, as I am sure he is a good
man and, as the peasants say, "touched by God".

'Oh, there is something else I must say just in case he disappoints you. If he
thinks he cannot help you, he will shake your hand and say he is unworthy and
leave you. I am sure he won't,' she added quickly, seeing signs of panic on Ella's
face. 'The only other thing is, don't call him "doctor". He only likes to be called
by his Christian name, which, stupidly, I can't remember.'

Half an hour later, they heard a gentle knock. Zenaïde opened the door and
in came an oldish, grey-haired man wearing a peasant's smock above thick
boots. Calmly he bowed in turn to them, sat down on the most uncomfortable
upright chair in the room, put his hands on his knees and waited. Ella noticed
his unexpectedly long, slender fingers, which ended in broken, dirty finger nails,
and his brown, deep-set eyes.

Zenaïde left them, and the healer lifted his hand when she started to speak,
conveying that he wished her to remain silent. She sat still and he stared at her.
At first she was not embarrassed, for his eyes, though penetrating, had the
kindly look of a loving, forgiving father watching his son play, ignoring the
boy's roughness and cruelty. Then the eyes changed and took on an impersonal,
searching look which made her aware that he was looking into her for an illness
as if for a hidden snake. She thought of Ivan, but thanked God that this man
looked kind and good.

After a while, he took out a slate and a piece of chalk and wrote on it in clear
script:

You are not ill but tired and unhappy. I will go back and send a herbal
mixture. It will calm you and do you no harm. Goodbye. I am honoured to
meet you.

Ella was surprised and could think of nothing to say except: 'Thank you for
coming,' but as she had hoped for more than herbal tea, she felt disappointed
and let down. Zenaïde soon came back, led her into her own bedroom and told
her to take a rest. The medicine would be brought by one of the Prince's
messengers and would arrive in half an hour.

'Meanwhile sleep, it is only half past five. You still have plenty of time to
change for this fearful ball, and my friend told me that if you will lie down you
will sleep.'

Ella thought she could not possibly do so, but was woken up by a gentle
shaking. She jumped off the bed, thinking she would be late for the ball and
Serge would be furious, but Zenaïde soothed her, put a little bag in her hand and
told her that the herbs had arrived with a note saying a spoonful should be
stirred into hot water and drunk after three minutes. Ella did as she was told,
and while she could not say she felt well, at least her desperation disappeared.
Relieved, she looked at Zenaïde and they both burst out laughing; it was
extraordinary how the only things which brought them close together were
calamities in Ella's life. After the laughter, she knew she could get through
the evening, and drove almost happily home in her carriage, hoping against

hope that the ball would be cancelled.

The grand dukes decided that the Tsar should hold the ball in spite of the fact – or because – Alix said it should be cancelled. The evening was ghastly. Serge smiled incessantly, as if to show he was not to blame and did not care what anybody said. Alexis and Vladimir shouted in defiant tones that the death of a few moujiks must not imperil the new friendship with France – famous tapestries and pictures had arrived from Paris – and to have cancelled the ball at the last minute would have had a detrimental effect on Russo-French relations, an argument rather spoilt by the Montebellos, the French Ambassador and his wife, repeatedly saying they feared the dance was a grave error. Paul was glum and silent, as if ashamed of himself, and Nicky and Alix walked round white-faced, red-eyed. At one moment Ella thought that her sister was going to burst into tears, and walked through the throng surrounding her to give her a kiss and whisper: 'Go to see the injured in hospital tomorrow.'

Alix was not surprised or angry, but offered Ella a little smile and sighed: 'I have already.' Ella knew that her gesture of affection had given her sister courage and stopped her from publicly breaking down.

On the way home, she shrank from Serge when he said, in an angry voice: 'The Emperor has been persuaded to ask Count Pahlen to hold an inquiry – nothing will come of it. Nicky will not dare to oppose myself, Alexis, Vladimir and Paul, despite his weakness. You need fear nothing.'

'Fear nothing?' she repeated slowly. 'No, I won't fear anything.'

The next morning Serge reminded her that they had to receive guests at an evening reception to thank them for their work in making the celebrations in Moscow a success.

'But Serge,' she said, 'surely we cannot say the trampling to death of countless thousands yesterday was a success?'

'That is an exaggeration. Perhaps three thousand died yesterday, out of greed. Otherwise everything went according to plan. I have every intention of thanking those who supported me.'

Ella was appalled. Yesterday, but for her herbs, she could not have faced the ball. Now she had to endure another ghastly evening, thanking those who had organized the death of three thousand poor people who had pushed forward out of loyalty to their Tsar and Tsarina. She took another glass of herbal tea and once again felt stronger.

The reception was to take place in the Kremlin, and Ella knew that it would be for her, as it was for officials and their wives, tedious and sad. She felt forlorn enough as it was, without having to face hours of talking to strangers. Looking about in desperation for someone familiar, she glimpsed the back of a man's head she knew but could not place. He turned, and there stood 'The Stranger'. He must have seen the look of amazement that came over her face as he gave a bow, as if to point out that their meeting should appear natural. Ella felt intensely excited: now she would discover his name, although it might not be easy to get it out of Serge, for he often replied to her queries by stating: 'I will not reply for two reasons. The first, it is a matter of no importance; the second, their identity is no concern of yours.'

They stood at one end of the room, greeting guests brought up by the chamberlains. Ella thought she must have repeated the same dull politeness at least a hundred times, and each time she was surprised how politely and gratefully her insincerity was received.

To make the evening more trying, she was constantly looking around for the stranger, and before long saw him talking to a chamberlain and moving forward. She began to prepare herself for their meeting. Officially, of course, they had never seen each other, so it was necessary for her to greet him without a sign of recognition or interest.

As he drew nearer, she felt giddy and prayed she would not make a fool of herself. Suddenly there he was, waiting to be introduced. Serge smiled in an unusually friendly way, pushed the chamberlain aside, shook his hand warmly and congratulated him on the lack of anti-royalist demonstrations before, mumbling a name like 'Azov', he turned and introduced him. Ella nodded in return, smiled at the man and said what a relief it was that the imperial visit had passed without a protest. Again he bowed and, when he lifted his head, looked at her with such passionate admiration that she knew he loved her, which explained why he had arranged the meetings and saved Serge's life. His behaviour at last became comprehensible if embarrassing, although she had to admit that in their private meetings he had always behaved with perfect decorum, which showed that she had dealt behind Serge's back with a man of importance in government circles, not a possible enemy.

Once he passed on she could not glimpse him again and wondered whether she had not dreamed the whole incident. However, there had been no mistaking the thick-set figure, looking more vulgar in evening clothes than in day dress. She decided, if possible, to find out more about his activities and what was his actual position, and saw her opportunity on the way back. As Serge was in a good temper, she asked in a casual voice: 'Who was the squat, ugly man with skin like a toad and a thick, black moustache?' (Serge was always pleased if she thought a man ugly.) 'And why did you congratulate him?'

Ella had chosen her moment skilfully, knowing that Serge liked the independence of his position as Governor-General and had, in the last week, resented walking behind the Tsar. Now, again, he was in his element, the most powerful man in southern Russia. Almost gently he replied: 'He is one of our agents who organize infiltration into the revolutionary movement. His knowledge is extraordinary. Last week he gave us the names of two hundred suspects to place in temporary custody. As a result, there was not one incident. But for bad luck at the Fields, all my plans would have succeeded.'

She knew he would be suspicious and angry if she asked another question, and had to be satisfied with the mumble which sounded like 'Azov'. She would remember the name by the Sea of Azov.

She went to bed happy, her conscience free of a nagging weight. Although Serge would be furious if he ever found out she had secretly communicated with one of his agents, all that the man 'Azov' had done was to try and save her obstinate husband's life. Her conscience was clear. On the other hand, she had discovered with embarrassment that he was in love with her. She must be very careful if she saw him again. But he had always treated her – even tonight – with extraordinary courtesy, and only his eyes had shown his secret. She was flattered to think that any man should be in love with her and would risk, without self-interest, helping her.

Nicky asked if he and Alix could stay a few days at Ilonskoye to rest after the tiring ceremonies. As usual, the entourage was so numerous that Ella did not have room, even with all her dashkas, to accommodate all the members of the imperial family, and Serge asked the Youssoupovs to put up the younger generation. Ella was sad she could not have Ernie to stay; he seemed nervous and full of artificial gaiety, while Ducky looked sullen and bored at his continuous attempts to be funny.

The house party at Ilonskoye made Ella feel old. Missy and Ducky, whom she still considered to be children, were both married, and Marie Pavlovna's sons, Cyril and Boris, whom she still thought of as schoolboys, had suddenly turned into splendid-looking young men. She drove down the day before Serge to prepare all the houses for her guests, and had to admit that she was full of forebodings. Alix was always uneasy and touchy outside her own home, Marie of Coburg was touchy everywhere, and Miechen hated to play a subsidiary role to the Tsarina. Altogether, it would be a challenging visit.

She put these tiresome thoughts out of her head and went carefully around the house, deciding how to please by careful positioning of bedrooms. When the difficult task was finished, she examined the greenhouses to ensure that all her family would have their favourite flowers in their rooms.

The visit began badly with Alix arriving with the corners of her mouth turned down, looking like Grandmama, except that she was twenty-four and happily married. Ella was annoyed when she paid no attention to the flowers or remarked on anything looking nice. Miechen asked Vladimir in a stage whisper, why was Alix always in a bad temper? Ella asked herself the same question. The popularity gained by her first pregnancy was being dissipated by a coldness and disapproval which Russian exuberance found damping. In Moscow, before 'Khodynka', she had seemed sad and cross whether she stood or sat, looking as if her only wish was to get away.

Marie of Coburg was certainly herself again. Ella had hardly recognized her at the coronation, in court dress weighed down with jewels, but at Ilonskoye she was back to her own individual style, wearing square boots and a hat pinned down only on the left side of her head. If the wind half-blew, it stood upright like a sail. She did not appear to mind and pulled it back again and hammered it down over her eyes as if she were driving a stake into the ground.

On the third evening of the Tsar's visit, Zenaïde gave an informal dance at Arkhangelskoye in the circular ballroom opening on to the garden. All day the sun had shone in a cloudless sky. Even though the Tsar was staying at Ilonskoye, Serge's authority continued to rule, which, coupled with Alix's disapproval, made the house so gloomy that Ella was delighted to get away and not have to preside at another meal full of awkward silences.

They set out in open carriages on a lovely early summer evening and stopped in the drive to listen to the nightingales. As they approached Arkhangelskoye, two gaily dressed gipsies stood by the roadside, a man playing his guitar and a pretty dark girl singing in a sad voice the song which Ella had heard in the theatre twelve years before:

> 'They say my heart is as the wind,
> I to my love am never true.
> Why then do I forget the rest
> And my heart but remembers you?'

They drove on slowly until, strangely, the words and music, instead of fading, became louder again and Ella saw, with delight, another pair of gipsies repeating the same music and words. The effect was enchanting, the pattern repeated again and again, with the last and best-looking pair of singers standing beside the front door.

As they took off their light wraps, Ella said to Marie of Coburg: 'Didn't you think it was lovely, driving down that river of music?' to which Marie replied: 'I can't see the resemblance. There wasn't any water.'

Zenaïde must have told the gipsies, after the imperial party passed, to return to the house and disperse in the garden for, throughout the evening, wherever Ella went, she heard gipsy music and singing, once or twice opposed by the voices of nightingales, the songs merging with the scent of the lime blossom in the warm air.

When Ella walked into the ballroom, she saw Ducky and Ernie, and Missy with her husband Ferdinand, the Crown Prince of Romania, and Vladimir's sons, Boris and Cyril, as well as Nicky's youngest brother George, about to start dancing a polonaise. She was startled by Missy. Her niece always looked so beautiful, but, tonight, Ella thought she had never seen a lovelier girl. She watched them dance, thinking how Ducky's darkness was the perfect contrast to Missy's fair beauty, while Boris and Cyril, although very young, gave an appearance of being tall editions of their magnificent-looking father. Both stood nearly six foot six, with straight noses, wide mouths and thick, pitch-black hair.

Ella sighed as she thought how splendid they looked and how flat-footed and clumsy and ugly Ferdinand seemed in comparison, with his large feet and nose and sallow complexion. She noticed how, when Missy danced with her husband, she carefully watched his feet and kept his body at a distance. But when she danced with Boris, her expression changed to one of smiling happiness as they gracefully moved together. Ernie was dancing with Ducky, and was, Ella could see, in one of his 'funny moods', but Ducky was looking bored and impatient with her husband's ceaseless chatter. When she danced with Cyril, they, too, made a splendid pair, and Ducky, who usually looked stiff compared to her sister, seemed pliant in his arms. Ella was enchanted by the beauty and grace of her two nieces and saw how, when Missy happily danced with Georgie, the Tsar's younger brother, Boris glowered with rage.

Her thoughts were interrupted by an invitation to dance, and she forgot relations and tragedies. Paul paid polite compliments and she felt young again, remembering their first friendship in Moscow. It was an evening when gaiety and music weaken the will, demanding submission to pleasure, and Ella felt intoxicated with excitement and delight.

Paul asked her to dance again, and afterwards they walked on to the terrace to hear the gipsies singing and to stroll on into the endless formal gardens where the statues shone in the moonlight. They sat down on a cushioned seat in a Greek temple without speaking, both remembering the slight romance in their past. The magic of the evening brought back Ella's love of life which she thought Serge had killed, and she felt contented and happy as they sat and watched the dancers through the big windows, and the white dresses and dashing uniforms moving slowly about the terraces.

Away from the house and music, she began to think sadly she would never be young again, when her thoughts were interrupted by two couples, Boris walking with Missy and Cyril with Ducky. Both pairs moved unaware, heads close, towards each other until they came face to face in front of the temple. Delighted, the girls burst into happy laughter, and Boris kissed Ducky and Missy kissed Cyril at the same moment as the sad voice of a gipsy woman pierced the air. She was singing a song they all knew, and the four joined hands and danced round and round in a circle singing. The music stopped. The circle broke up. Joined again into pairs, and with their heads together again, they walked on in opposite directions.

Ella had not known what to think. Certainly, as an older relation, she should have been shocked by their behaviour, but the way the four had danced and sung looked so romantic and natural that she said nothing and sat in silence until Paul, standing up, murmured a little sadly: 'Laisse-les, c'est si bon de les voir s'amuser, sait-on qui leur réserve la vie, on n'est jeune qu'une fois!'

With the gipsy music in the air, she could not disagree. When they returned to the ballroom she saw Ferdinand standing alone, moodily kicking a pillar. Ernie, on the other hand, was roaring with laughter in the centre of a group of young officers, before whom he was strutting about with twisted fingers, making a silly face. Ella thought her brother stupid and unkind. It was obvious that he was making fun of Willy's crippled arm. He never made fun of him to his face, and she remembered how the last time she saw the two men together Ernie had behaved quite differently, looking deferential and speaking in such an ingratiating way that she was ashamed of his obsequiousness.

In an ante-room they found Marie of Coburg, sitting like a square bulldog on a hard, upright chair, who immediately asked, 'Where are my daughters? No, you need not answer. I know. I will speak to them tomorrow.'

Ella and Paul smiled and both changed the subject by saying how tired Alix was looking. Marie began to talk, which meant that everybody listened. Paul drifted away, and Ella, leaning against a pillar, soon became aware of personal antagonism. She always hoped that her sensitivity made up for her stupidity, for while she instinctively had opinions – usually correct – when she was asked to explain them, she could never give a logical explanation but instead heard herself stammering out inanities. Tonight was a good example of her intuition. Without reason, she guessed that the Montenegrins intended to revenge her reprimand. Ever since she had told them to stop gossiping, they had kept their distance, only speaking to her at assemblies and balls, when they would flutter about, praising her beauty in voices edged with spite and dislike. Sure enough, across the room she saw the 'Black Perils' and wondered what piece of

170

nastiness they had thought up and how they planned to bring it – without speaking to her directly – to her attention. It must be something particularly unpleasant; they looked so pleased with themselves.

Almost at once, she guessed their plan. Their escort was the old, fat, walrus-moustached General Pashchilov who, as an unknown major in the Second Turkish War, had been asleep in his billet when a shell exploded on the roof. Pulled out of the ruins, he could hear nothing, although it was always his proud boast in quiet country houses that he was still able to 'hear the big guns'. Since he was a man of property, with connections at court, his deafness was overlooked, it was said, at the cost of half a regiment in the Caucasus, whom he slowly led on his charger through a valley in the mountains, unaware of a continuous attack by snipers. His courage under fire added to his reputation and ensured promotion. As a general, he found it necessary to be able to hear his junior officers' opinions and took a course of the new French system of lip reading. This enabled him usually to understand a word or two in every sentence, but as these were often in the wrong context, his replies rarely helped the questioner. After leaving the army, he sold his country property and bought a large house in Moscow, where he was squandering his fortune on entertainments which made up for his fatuity. His conversation was limited to such thundered phrases as: 'Are you sure? Interesting; I do not understand,' while to the timid pliant he would screw up his eyes, puff out his cheeks and bellow: 'You are talking nonsense, sir, utter nonsense.'

Ella watched 'The Perils' carefully manoeuvre the General into a suitable position before shouting their news in his ear, forcing her to hear, since she was trapped by Marie of Coburg, who showed no signs of drawing breath. Militza, the cleverer of the two, opened the conversation by telling a story which she knew would catch Ella's attention.

'Have you heard, General,' Militza screamed, 'of the sufferings of the Grand Duchess Constantine? No? Oh dear, I will shout a little louder as I would like you to hear, although it is too sad for words. The Grand Duke, as you know, is paralysed, but takes every day a drive through his park at Pavlosk and calls on a certain old friend of his whose name I am sure I can't remember, or rather never knew, but at any rate she is or was his favourite, if you know what I mean. Well, only yesterday he ordered his coachman to stop as usual at her house, but the man had received orders from the Grand Duchess and drove on. As Constantine could not move he had to suffer in silence. Cruel to him, don't you think?'

'Bitter after so many years,' echoed Anastasia.

'At any rate, when he arrived home his wife came to greet him as usual and he did not say anything until she kissed him, when he seized her by the hair and thrashed her with his heavy stick. Such a to-do, imagine! But of course, nobody dared stop him, and they say she is quite black and blue.'

'And too old to be whipped.'

'Even if she deserved it.'

'Too interfering, even if his habit was a bad one.'

'But shocking on his part, thrashing his distinguished wife.'

Ella was sure Militza knew she was listening, especially as she went on in an even louder voice: 'I must say I am surprised to see Ernie and Ducky here after all the scandal in Hesse. Everybody knows, they say.'

'I have heard it, too. So distasteful but certainly true.'

'Oh, undoubtedly. But even so, Ducky is married and united to him in God's eyes so it is her duty to respect her husband whatever he does.'

'Whatever he does.'

Ella knew she was intended to turn round, but decided the only dignified course was to pretend not to hear. She leaned further towards Marie.

'Such ill-fortune Ducky and Missy should stop for a drink of milk, but the details are too scandalous to discuss, don't you think, General?'

As the sisters had taken care to avert their faces, their escort, unaware he was addressed, remained silent. Ella saw, out of the corner of her eye, how Militza's anger was growing, and as she herself bent forward to emphasize her interest in Marie's conversation, the irate voices of the Montenegrins grew louder.

'Ernie, you see, was supposed to have gone shooting . . .' though here Militza made the mistake of allowing the General to catch a glimpse of her lips, and to his delight he read the word 'shooting'. It was too good an opportunity to miss, and he launched into a long story of shooting elks and bears in the north, the danger of the sport, the intense cold, the necessity of wearing special boots and the number of the animals he had killed. In vain, Militza tried to break through the avalanche of sounds. The General merely spoke louder.

At that moment, Nicky and Paul came up to speak to Marie. Ella, seeing her opportunity, tugged Paul's sleeve and they walked away. Militza, her purple swollen lower lip thrust forward, her black face twisted with frustration, was not to be denied and shouted triumphantly after them, her voice drowning the General's reminiscences, 'Ernie and the gamekeeper!'

Ella paid no attention. What dreadful creatures those sisters were. No wonder they called them the 'Black Perils'. And how stupid Alix must be to be taken in by such sycophants. Poor Ernie, poor Ducky. They were so young – they should never have married. The incident finished her enjoyment and changed the spirit of the evening. She felt like a spectator intruding on the young, but could not forget the two beautiful young couples singing on the terrace as they circled round and round. She felt sad never to have danced singing with a young man. Later, when she drove home with Serge and heard the sound of the guitars and the gipsy voices fading into the distance, tears ran down her cheeks as Serge sat in his corner, silent, unaware.

Whether she had drunk an unusual amount of champagne or because of the emotions of the evening, it took her a long time to fall asleep, while Serge, as usual, dropped off the moment he closed his eyes. When, at last, sleep crept upon her, it was only to find herself back at Arkhangelskoye, once again walking towards the Greek temple where, with Paul, she had watched her nieces and nephews dancing. This time she was holding the arm of an unknown man. They sat down and as she turned she saw it was the doctor. He took her hand without speaking, and, as they sat together, all her shyness vanished and she felt perfectly happy.

Looking around the moonlit garden, Ella saw a surprising group standing around the fountain, consisting of a gipsy guitarist, a gipsy singer, Boris and five young boys of seventeen or eighteen, obviously attending their first party. Every now and again Boris looked impatiently towards the house, while the guitarist played snatches of tunes. At last he gave a great shout of approval, and Ella saw a procession of footmen carrying a table, a tablecloth and champagne glasses and magnums of champagne on silver salvers. The table was put down, the cloth laid, the glasses arranged. The footmen bowed and retired and an animated discussion took place as Boris opened the magnums, the champagne bubbling out between his fingers. As she watched, Ella heard footsteps, and once again Missy and Boris and Cyril and Ducky appeared precisely as before, their heads close together, until they met joyfully. At that moment, the guitarist impatiently plucked a string. Cyril turned to Boris and asked him what was happening. He looked at the fountain and shouted in delight.

'Oh, I see, I am initiating five youngsters. They are drinking their first *charochka.*'

The guitarist began to play. As the gipsy girl advanced towards one of the young men, holding out a brimming glass of champagne, she nodded to him and sang:

> 'With wine of the scent of new-mown hay
> Let us fill our glass to the brim.
> Drink to his health to the break of day
> With the best of good wishes to him.
>
> 'With wine of the scent of new-mown hay
> Let us fill his glass to the brim.
> Drink to our health to the break of day
> With the best of good wishes from him.'

At the end of the charochka, the young man took the glass, drained it in one draught and put it back upside down on the silver salver. His friends, who had sung with the gipsy girl, cheered and clapped him on the shoulder. The champagne glass was filled again. Another young man took his place, and once again the gipsy girl began to sing. At the first sound, the four young cousins held hands and started to dance and, to Ella's delight, the doctor gently led her to join them. Cyril seized her left hand and they circled happily. When they came to the last four lines, they sang again: the men loudly, the girls and herself – to her surprise – in sweet voices:

> 'With wine of the scent of new-mown hay
> Let us fill his glass to the brim.
> Drink to our health to the break of day
> With the best of good wishes from him.'

Three more initiations took place before Boris pressed a note into the singer's hand, which, in a moment, vanished down her bosom. The gipsies bowed and disappeared. Boris waved to Cyril and led the laughing young initiates back to the lighted ballroom.

The six continued to dance, and twice the doctor, Cyril and Boris sang the first verse of the song and the three girls the last. All of a sudden, without warning, the circle broke into three couples, the two young pairs walking off into the darkness while the doctor led her down a path beside a wall to a door leading into the house.

Ella was puzzled. She knew the garden at Arkhangelskoye well and had never seen this entrance before, but she was not alarmed as her companion walked confidently forward and opened the door on to a long, high, empty passage, so dark she could not see the roof. In fact, all she could see was, far away, the shape of a door outlined by cracks of light.

The doctor put his arm round her shoulder and led her down the dark passage, fumbled open a little door, stood back and, to her delight, ushered her into the ballroom, where the orchestra was playing and couples dancing beneath chandeliers brilliant with hundreds of candles. Ella stood still, watching, aware that for the first time in her life she was going to dance with the man she loved. Her heart beat and she knew she was feeling and behaving like a silly girl. But she could not help her excitement. And it was not even silly behaving like a young girl, because at eighteen or nineteen young girls danced with young men they loved. She gripped the doctor's hand for reassurance, and his hand held hers gently but firmly as he led her out to dance. He put his hand round her waist as she looked up lovingly into Serge's eyes and saw the minute pupils coldly looking down. Her scream of terror and horror woke her husband, who reached out, shook her and asked what was wrong. She jumped out of bed to avoid his touch, muttered, 'A nightmare,' and ran into the bathroom, to sit before her dressing table, lay her face on her arms and cry.

But she would have cried harder had she known that for the following six years she was destined to be endlessly troubled by dreams in which the doctor, her nieces and nephews and Serge tormented her to the edge of madness, making her days as hard to bear as the nights. Twice during the first six months of those agonizing dreams she visited eminent doctors, and each time, when they asked her to describe her symptoms and the dreams themselves, she found herself unable to tell the truth. She tried sleeping potions, exercise, reading, late hours: nothing worked. Every night she was forced to enter another world.

The dreams pervaded her life, bringing an unreality to events which would otherwise have caused her acute unhappiness. Alas, Militza, a horrible gossip, was right: Ernie's marriage was a disaster. Ducky would scream at him that he had married her under false pretences since he was not a man, taunt him for his cowardice and love of arranging flowers, and then, frustrated, throw large vases at his head. She despised his cowardliness, his weak good nature and inability to argue without bursting into tears, and flung it in his face that he was considered a joke in every officers' mess throughout Germany. What could be more ridiculous than the Grand Duke of Hesse, a general in his own principality, a Colonel of Prussian and Russian regiments, running away at the sight of a horse. It was common knowledge that one of her black stallions at Wolfsgarten had chased him screaming up the front steps before it had taken a bite out of his tight trousers. Ducky called him 'Le Duc de Ridicule' and the name stuck. Both Ella and Alix regretted Ernie's humiliation and the public way in which Ducky flaunted – as Alix put it – her illicit love for Cyril. Of course, the romance and Ernie's humiliation were sources of endless stories, and everyone in Europe knew the marriage could not last, except for Grandmama, who had arranged it.

But at last even the Queen herself became suspicious, and sent for the Minister in Darmstadt, Mr Buchanan, to ask him bluntly what was happening. Embarrassed, he replied that since both the Grand Duke and Duchess had confided in him, he felt he must honour their confidences. The Queen, after a pause, nodded his head and declared that it would be the last marriage she would arrange.

The Montenegrins enjoyed themselves, telling Alix in shocked voices how abominably Ducky was behaving, cunningly conveying how it was believed in Hesse that she was pregnant again by Cyril. Alix would go red with fury, and soon there would be another row, since naturally Vladimir and Miechen supported their son, who, they argued, had only been nineteen when he was seduced by a married woman. Alix refused to admit that Ernie could be in the wrong: 'He has his little foibles – but what husband has not?'

To Ella's horror, Ducky's romance mixed itself up with her dreams and made her share their guilt, which, in the daytime, she doubted they felt. It was maddening to feel guilty when her own life was guiltless and they gloried in their open friendships.

As for Missy, the visit to Arkhangelskoye changed her life. She returned to Romania a woman, no longer the obedient, frightened girl who trembled when her husband's uncle, King Carol I, whispered. She had tasted adventure and romance and was no longer prepared to live as a prisoner with a blockhead of a bat-eared husband who never said boo to a goose. She was so beautiful that, wherever she went, all the young men fell in love with her, including, in Russia, her Page de Guard, one of whom by custom attended every visiting royalty. Alix, to express her disapproval, had Missy's pages changed every day to show how she could not be trusted for more than twenty-four hours, and was furious when Missy remarked: 'How lovely, I like change.'

Ella found herself endlessly dwelling on the lives of her nieces and the reason why they had become a part of her dream life. At the same time, a tiresome incident made her wonder whether one day, despite her prayers and belief in the goodness of God, she would go mad, for Serge's younger brother Paul fell unsuitably in love with a Madame Pistohcors and asked Serge if his children could live at Ilonskoye. Without consulting her he agreed, and told Paul to visit them whenever he wished. When Serge told Ella, she felt as if he had hit her in the face. Increasingly, she longed for children, and now to have to bring up another man's was surely too cruel.

Serge watched her with great attention when he told her his decision, and she thought the pupils of his eyes grew a little smaller, always a sign of his pleasure, when he saw how the idea hurt her. But there was no appeal against his decision, and soon Dimitri and Marie arrived at Ilonskoye and paid only occasional visits to their father. Ella found it impossible to be kind to them. She realized she was wrong and wicked, but how could she love children, even admitting their youth and defencelessness, whose presence reminded her of her greatest desire, which she now knew would never be fulfilled?

'Azov' however, was pleased about the children's arrival and wrote to her 'as long as they ride with your husband in his carriage he will be safe, as although the terrorists are determined to kill him, their idealism will prevent them from killing children'. Ella turned the letter nervously over and over, trying to decide what she should do, and eventually gave orders that the children should never go out with His Imperial Highness without her permission. The next day, she begged Serge to vary his routes and decided to drive with him herself whenever possible.

13

Between 1897 and 1899, Alix had two more children, both of them girls. With the appearance of each she became more and more anxious to have a son. Her later confinements were not as painful as her first, and Ella noticed how her sister no longed relied on her, but favoured instead a fat, stupid woman called Vyrubova, who fussed about, echoing her words, which at once made her a favourite. Vyrubova soon found out that Alix believed she was vilified by society and strengthened her own position by saying how unjust and unkind various friends were behind her back. This made the Tsarina certain she had found a true friend instead of a stupid schemer.

Alix's face had now set in an angry mould. How much, Ella wondered, was this due to her bitterness at her inability to have a son and her consequent unpopularity, for on each occasion when the cannons announced the birth of another girl, the peasants shook their heads, recollecting the journey behind the coffin, the blood on the ermine, the dropping of the collar of St Andrew, all of which had foretold how the Empress was a harbinger of ill-fortune.

Ella only once saw 'Azov' during her dream years, and found him full of gloom at Nicky's weakness and the rising tide of revolution. He emphasized that the continual persecution of the Jews could only result in providing brains for the revolutionary movements and, as he had feared, his earlier prophesies had come true and the persecuted were now banded together into an association called the Bund.

The Tsar's only reaction was to encourage his own wild royalist supporters to retaliate against suspected revolutionaries by intimidation and brutality. The most brutal of these groups, the Black Hundreds, consisted of the type of young men whom Serge had employed in hunting down Jews for sport in Moscow. To Ella, the news was the last straw. Her mind, stretched with pain, could not bear, on top of her dreams, having to worry about imperial atrocities. She wrote and told 'Azov' that she was sick and ill and could stand no more suffering. She was sorry, since she had come to depend on his information, but until she had recovered she begged him, with her whole heart, to leave her alone. He wrote back to say he prayed daily for her recovery and would only convey good news.

The character of Ella's dreams gradually changed, and her love of the doctor became entwined with the love affairs of her four relations. Sometimes, as she sat holding his hand, they would watch her cousins kissing, and afterwards she would turn to her beloved and say insincerely: 'Look how wicked they are,' but he would only stare more intensely into her eyes and grip her hands so hard that she cried out at the pain, which, at the same time, made her body shiver with excitement. One night, they saw Cyril and Ducky walking arm in arm through the garden towards a black door in the high wall, and the doctor took her hand as they ran as fast as they could after them. As the first couple approached the door, it swung open, but although the doctor and Ella flung themselves forward, it slammed in their faces. In desperation, they beat on the door, but it remained shut and Ella woke up exhausted, thinking how sad Ducky's behaviour must make Ernie.

All the next day, Ella thought of her poor brother. She understood why Ducky was exasperated with his uniforms and stupid vanity. On each of the next three nights, the same dream was repeated, and on each of the following days, she felt sick and desperate. She wondered whether, if she saw Ducky and Ernie together, she would feel better and perhaps help them as well. With Serge's permission, she wrote and asked Ducky if she could come to Wolfsgarten. Ducky wrote back that she would be pleased for her to do so. When Ella arrived, Ernie was in a state of wild excitement, rehearsing his translation of *Charlie's Aunt*, while Ducky looked miserable and ill from the effect of her second miscarriage, caused, Ernie said, 'through galloping like a madwoman while pregnant'. She had grown more beautiful, but Ella found her unable to look into her eyes. Not even her baby daughter consoled her, and she sometimes appeared to be gazing at the child with hatred. How ironic it was that when she appeared nightly in Ella's dream life she should seem to be so happy with Cyril.

Missy, more beautiful than ever, was staying without her husband, and said to Ella, smiling: 'I left my dullard at home.'

The two sisters dominated Wolfsgarten, disregarding Ernie, and every morning came down in tight riding clothes, leapt into their side-saddles and galloped, with a rush, out of the stables through the courtyard, out of the gate and far away into the woods, often not returning until after Ducky had missed an engagement. If Ernie remonstrated, she would say it was his fault as he had never told her, then blamed him for the dullness of her life and the provincialism of Hesse.

One morning she said to Ella: 'I know you are a saint, Auntie, but I am not, and I can't live with a man who is not a man, so don't think too badly of me. I have promised Uncle Bertie that I will not divorce until Grandmama dies, but the moment she is dead, I promise you that I will not stay one single day longer in this horrible little state. I know your brother is a nice and kind man, but what you don't know unless you are married to him is that he hates women, and that when he compliments me in public it's all pretence and hypocrisy. He should never have married. But I knew nothing of the world, and now here I am stuck like a fly in jam. Oh, it drives me mad.'

She had run out of the room then, shouting for Missy. A few minutes later Ella heard horses galloping out of the gate into the woods.

Ella began to realize that she was affected by Ducky's unhappiness, which was not dissimilar from her own, and perhaps Father Ivan would say that Ernie's wife would be redeemed as she was certainly sinning. For a day or two,

178

life was quiet at Wolfsgarten and Ella found she slept peacefully. Then, to her amazement, Cyril and Boris unexpectedly turned up, to be enthusiastically welcomed by Ernie. Ducky said nothing, but went a dead white colour. The sight of the two happy couples again changed the pattern of Ella's dreams, and she found herself as violently in love with the doctor as she had been years before in Darmstadt.

One night, as she walked with him in the garden behind Missy and Boris, the black door, for the first time, stayed open. They entered an unknown garden full of lilies were the doctor kissed her as she lay secure in his arms until an extraordinary peace flooded – there was no other word – through her, and all her doubts, repressions and fears vanished in a physical relief she had never known. She belonged to the doctor and nothing else mattered. The dream was a new torture, for when she woke up, happily thinking of her lover, content with the world, she saw the uncreased pillow and realized that her happiness was a mirage. She would never see the doctor again on earth, and was condemned to live with Serge, who could never kiss or love her.

Later in the day, when she saw Ducky and Missy in the garden, they said, laughing in unison: 'Oh Auntie, you are looking lovely.' She had blushed, as she could not help thinking herself a guilty accomplice, which was unfair, for how could she help her dreams? Neither was her daily embarrassment lessened when, each night, the door remained open and she and the doctor walked through and knew ecstatic happiness until she awoke happy . . . guilty . . . unhappy . . . her dissatisfaction lasting all day. She wondered how long she could bear her torments, and when she saw Ducky and Missy, she was envious – despite acknowledging the wickedness of her thoughts – of the freedom of their lives.

Once Missy said quite simply to her, 'Oh Auntie, why don't you have a gallant? You know, you are ten times more beautiful than I am!'

She stopped in her tracks and burst out laughing. There was something endearing about Missy's bluntness, and Ella thought she was not a sinner, whatever else she was. When she returned to Moscow she felt sad to have left the two untamed, beautiful sisters.

The night after her return, the doctor came and immediately understood her sorrow. He did not try and kiss her or take her into the garden. Instead, they sat hand in hand, talking of the two girls. Everything he said was so measured and sensible that she was reminded of him in the hospital and loved him more than ever.

Ella never thought of taking a lover. In her waking hours, she was married to Serge and would never break her marriage vows, but that did not stop her longing for the night, when she would meet her doctor. Despite condemning her thoughts and feeling guilty every morning, she realized that her self-absorption was destroying her character. She thought of nobody except herself. Her affection for Ernie had waned and she sympathized with Ducky. She was saddened by her lack of interest in the freedom of movement she had forced out of Serge. She went, without interest, to her charities and hospital committees, and forced herself to the poor districts, opening 'poor houses' and hostels.

The work she had dreamed of a few years ago seemed unsatisfactory, meaningless, its purpose destroyed by the intensity of her own self-dissatisfaction. If occasionally she felt an interest in the health of some poor invalid, or the need to see the Tsar about plans for the extension of a hospital, that very night, as if to frustrate her, she would be tormented by a new dream of the doctor. Once she was his helper while he performed an intricate operation. She stood and watched his skill with fascination, an indispensible assistant handing him the correct instrument at the right moment, but the next day was useless with love and regret. Alternatively her dreams would be so shockingly convincing that, when she awoke to reality and Serge in the Governor's Palace or at Ilonskoye, both of which she hated, all her good intentions disappeared beneath her deep unhappiness. It was no good confessing; she had nothing to confess, as she constantly repeated to herself, except in her dreams, and surely dreams could not be sins? Or could they be? When she felt such a blinding happiness she wondered whether she was not sinning in her heart. If she was, how could she confess such an unspeakable thought. She admitted to herself that she might be wrong, but she could not face telling her dreams to a priest.

By the end of the summer of 1900, the dreams had become unbearable, dominating her life, stifling her feelings. She knew that her Grandmama was slowly dying, but felt neither sorrow nor a desire to see her, or a wish to understand the implications which would follow after the passing of the sole link between the kings of Europe. Ella treated Serge formally and politely in public, but in her heart she hated him. They seldom spoke when alone, and he was frequently rude to her in public. During her illness, it never occurred to her to ask for his help. She knew that he was the cause of her troubles, but she never blamed him and often saw in his face a misery as intense as her own.

After each crisis, she tried to lead a normal life and would go through the motions of putting on her jewels and designing dresses for herself and her friends, but between herself and every activity there hung the veil of her other life. She realized that her brain was becoming disordered, and was uncertain of the borders of her dream world when, in the daytime, Missy or Ducky, who she knew were in Romania or Hesse, would appear as she sat in the garden or rested after lunch. They would come with Boris or Cyril and whisper to her in mocking tones to come, as the doctor was waiting. In the evenings, they would be especially urgent, and once, late at night, as she lay reading in bed as Serge went through his boxes, she heard a surprising knock on the door and said without thinking, 'Come in.' The door opened and Ducky peeped around the corner, beckoning with a sly, provocative smile. Ella turned to Serge, who was reading his papers. Trying to speak casually, she asked him, 'Did you hear me say, "Come in"?'

'No,' he said, not bothering to look up.

'Did you hear the door open?'

'No,' he said again. 'You must have been dreaming.'

Ducky winked at her and slowly closed the door.

When, at last, she fell asleep, the doctor came back with the other four and they danced and walked through the door. But one night the door remained closed, and the next day she felt nervous and ill. From that night onwards, she never knew whether it would be open or shut, and the fear and uncertainty worried all her waking hours. She swallowed her pride and tried a brain doctor; he was no help. She prayed desperately to God, and knelt for hours, gazing at pictures of Jesus, trying with all her heart to immerse herself in His goodness, but just when she thought she had reached a stage of peace, there would be Ducky or Missy looking over his head or winking by the side of an Apostle, or smiling over the Virgin's shoulder.

Once, in desperation, she visited a little chapel with a sacred icon which, she heard, had cured troubled minds. It lay in the woods, thirty miles south of Moscow. An old man, not a priest, but the keeper of the sanctuary, led her up to the altar, on which stood in a frame the miraculous picture of Our Lord sitting in a chair. The icon was crudely painted, and, looking at the rough, splodgy face, she found it hard to believe it was a good likeness. As she stared, the face changed: slowly the beard vanished and Our Lord turned into Boris, who stretched his hand outside the frame and pulled a naked Missy on to his knee. Ella burst into hysterical laughter. The idea of Missy coming into the picture was ridiculous, and even after she realized that Boris and Missy lived only in her imagination, she continued laughing. The caretaker's jaw dropped in amazement. He had never seen a grand lady behave in such a way, and his astonishment set her off again into peals of laughter. Terrified, he crossed himself and ran out of the chapel.

She stayed in bed for a few days after this incident, and Serge, worried by her white face and haggard appearance, insisted on her visiting his own doctor. Ella refused to speak of her grim fantasies to the cold man who gazed at her without blinking, but merely said that she suffered dreams and illusions and was unable to sleep. He ordered her to the Crimea, where the warm weather would do her good. On the way down, Sandra, who had now been with her for sixteen years, told her of a hermit or anchorite who lived in a cave on the cliffs near the monastery of St George and who was reputed to perform miracles. Ella did not reply for some time. If dead saints and images of Jesus did her no good, why go? And then she thought that at least the hermit was alive and Zenaïde's good man had momentarily helped her. Perhaps the living were more powerful than the dead.

'I will go,' she said, 'but I don't want to know what he is called. I may have to tell him things which I don't want anyone to know, and it would be easier if I don't know his name, as I can persuade myself he does not exist.'

Sandra had looked at her oddly, and Ella realized how even her closest friends had begun to think she was strange. She did not think so; she thought she was mad.

14

A week later, they visited the clifftop monastery of St George, and picked up a guide, who led them inland, across rough scrubland to the top of a chasm and down a rough staircase cut out of the rock, through tree tops to the hermitage. At the stairtop, Sandra turned to Ella and said in an embarrassed voice: 'I think I must explain. The hermit is said to be related to Alexander II.' She blushed and added, 'If you know what I mean.'

Ella, used to her friend's cautious evasions, remained silent. Preparing herself for a miracle, she did not wish discordant thoughts to upset her calmness. They crept slowly down the rough, uneven steps, pressing against the jagged side, Sandra occasionally squeaking with fear. At last they reached the bottom and followed a path between rocks and stunted bushes on to a narrow ledge which ran along the side of a cliff facing the Black Sea. Here, again, they pressed against the side, not daring to look down at the water washing against the rocks, and Ella could not help noticing, by fresh signs, how the anchorite used the path as a lavatory. Despite Sandra's little gasps of horror, she pretended not to have seen.

At last they cut into the cliff through a narrow doorway and, following a dim light, found themselves in a vaulted cave lit by two large candles which stood on a roughly carved stone altar, before which a man in a Russian peasant's smock was praying, the heels of his boots pointing in their faces. He paid no attention to their entry, and Ella, feeling faint from the steep descent and walk above the sea – she hated heights – leaned against one of the walls for support. She could see no chair or resting place, except a bench cut into the wall, covered by a thin layer of crushed straw.

Sandra, beginning to be nervous of her responsibility in the increasingly odd affair, coughed two or three times. For five minutes, the three remained unmoving: the holy man praying, Ella leaning motionless, Sandra fidgeting, making little noises, clasping and unclasping her hands. Then the sound of a distant bell made him jump up, cross himself, turn and bow, all in one movement. Ella straightened and he walked towards her, swinging his right leg outwards and passing a hand over his cropped head. Bowing again, he invited her to sit in the stone cavity, which he called 'my bed', and stood, an absent-minded smile on his face, as if he did not know what to do next.

Ella examined him carefully and saw that he was above medium height, thick-set, with a rather square face which looked as if every feature had at one time been squashed, while in his mouth all his teeth stood separated from one another, giving his smile an ogreish look, at variance with his brown, kind eyes. Her first impression was one of disappointment, as she had expected a pale, emaciated, ascetic anchorite, not a strong, eccentric, smiling man, bursting with good health and bearing no resemblance to her idea of a saint.

'I have heard of you,' he said, nodding his head, smiling, 'Imperial Highness, and consider you honour me by coming to my humble abode. I hope you will forgive my bad manners in not rising at your entrance. I was completing my prayers. I make a rule to do so, otherwise – poor sinner that I am – I would welcome any diversion as an excuse.' His eyes settled on Sandra. 'But perhaps it will be better if your lady leaves. I would prefer to be alone with you. I am clumsy and might tell you things which are disrespectful, and she would not like that, I am sure.'

As he spoke, he smiled apologetically at Sandra, and in his embarrassment nearly fell over his enormous feet, which, Ella noticed, pointed outwards.

He walked with Sandra to the entrance, swinging his leg out again, and as he wished her goodbye, said politely, 'Forgive my rough ways and my inability to offer you a chair, but there is a large, pleasant stone outside. Sit on it and you will enjoy the warmth of the sun.'

Sandra winced and Ella nearly burst out laughing, realizing that she thought the hermit meant the dirty stone outside the door. Sandra apologized before leaving, murmuring, 'I will never forgive myself if anything happens. I hate leaving you alone.'

Ella laughed. 'Don't worry, I'll be all right. Please go.' She knew the man was not dangerous.

When Sandra had left, the hermit sat down on the bed and went on, 'I would like to help you. Please tell me your life and your troubles – all of them – for by God's grace I can sometimes alleviate pain.'

Ella already liked and trusted the man; he was unlike the useless doctors who had looked at her across mahogany desks. At the same time, she thought that he was rather affected and, remembering her experience with Father Ivan, was anxious not to be embarrassed or insulted again. Plucking up courage she said, 'Please don't think I am doubtful or mistrustful, but I was insulted once, and I know so little about you that I don't want to talk about myself until I know you better. Please tell me about yourself and why you live in this cave.'

She stopped, embarrassed, but he only smiled and said: 'Of course, I quite understand your feelings of shyness. I will certainly speak of myself. But who has ever dared to insult you?'

She thought it a reasonable, if unwelcome, question, and told him of her last embarrassing visit to Father Ivan. He was particularly interested in his 'joke' on the dying man, making her repeat the details twice before he crossed himself and exclaimed, 'Mother of God! What a servant of the devil. How could the late Tsar have put you in the hands of such a man?'

A little later, he took a large silver watch out of his tunic, studied it carefully and said, regretfully, that it was again approaching his time of prayer. 'But I wish to help you and will certainly tell you my story if God agrees. So I will ask Him.'

He stood up, walked over to the altar and kneeled down. Ella could not help thinking him slightly ridiculous, and also wondered how he looked so strong and well if he lived in this awful cave. But perhaps she was wrong. Anyhow, she would wait until he had told her his story.

While he was praying, a grey-faced monk from the monastery walked in, carrying a leather bottle and pack, which he put down without a word and, ignoring her, walked away. She tried, by pointing, to convey that poor Sandra was waiting – hungry – outside, but the monk looked down and quickly withdrew. When the hermit finished his prayers, he sat down, put his face close to hers and said that God was agreeable to his relating why it was that she found him in a cave, overlooking the Black Sea, and also that he could only help her as long as she understood that she was not the only sufferer in the world. When he spoke, his face almost touched hers again, but she was not embarrassed, for although he looked ridiculous and ugly, she could virtually feel the kindness and good intentions coming out of his skin. But, to her surprise, instead of starting his story, he gave a grunt of pleasure and picked up the monk's provisions, saying: 'As Father Ivan said, we are all sinners.' He took the cork out of the leather bottle and handed it to her. 'But I fear I have no glasses.'

Ella drank from the bottle, and he opened the leather bag and handed her a slice of black bread white with salt. She nibbled while he ate his slice abstractedly, without speaking or answering when she asked whether Sandra could have something to eat as she sat on her rock outside. Not until he had finished the last crumb did he speak. At last he looked up and surprised her by asking, as he leaned forward and grinned, 'Were you a flighty girl?'

'No.'

'Why?'

'I suppose I was shy,' she managed to get out, wondering if he was going to be as impertinent as Ivan.

'Oh, please don't be embarrassed, because, you see, as a young man I was wild and headstrong and wondered if you had been as well. It was a great shock to my mother, as she had brought me up carefully, without the help of a husband. I was a religious child and from an early age was determined to enter a monastery at the earliest possible moment. Did you ever plan to become a nun?'

'Yes,' she said in an embarrassed way, and once again the beaming, ugly face was so close that she could smell his breath.

'There you are,' he said triumphantly. 'I knew we would find something in common.'

She shrank back, thinking, 'This is the last holy man I will visit.' However high her hopes, these meetings ended in disaster.

'Well, well,' he went on, leaning back. 'The trouble was that we both had second thoughts, didn't we? You can tell me more about yourself later. My story is that when I was young I fell in love with a blue-eyed, beautiful, dark girl. I watched her skating for many weeks. One day she skated with a young man. A little later she disappeared. I never spoke to or saw her again. But I was sad, so sad, when she vanished. I took up bad habits.

'Then, one day, nineteen years ago, when I was twenty-one and in the bedroom of a woman . . .' A shadow passed over his face as if it was painful for

184

him to talk of his memories. He repeated, '. . . in the bedroom of a woman, her husband returned and in righteous anger attacked me. I seized my clothes and tried to escape, and he chased me round the room. Oh, dear God, what a terrible scene! Somehow I got out of the door and reached the top of the stairs, when he jumped on me and we rolled down together, locked in each other's arms. When we arrived at the bottom, I was uppermost and he was dead.

'I ran back to my mother, who said, "It is unfortunate, but you are not to worry. I will arrange matters with the Chief of Police. You must go to Kiev immediately and stay in my brother's house until I tell you it has blown over." I did as I was told and went away, although the face of the dead man continued to haunt me. I stayed with my uncle, and two weeks later I received a letter, saying that my problem was over and I could return to my beloved mother. But that night God came and asked me if I was happy to ignore His commandment, murder a fellow man and escape punishment. I answered, "No," and he nodded and said that if I wished to save my soul and avoid eternal damnation, I should punish myself. I thanked him, and took the train to Moscow without telling my uncle, leaving my possessions behind, as I wished to sever myself from my past.

'I bought a peasant's clothes and boots, gave away my money to the poor, and decided to be punished by the man I had murdered. I prayed to him to come and sentence me, and he appeared with a sorrowful face, shook his head and said kindly but sternly: "You have always feared hardship and discomfort and pain. Get yourself to Siberia to suffer until I tell you God has forgiven you."

'I was puzzled. To go to Siberia you have to be a criminal, and if I admitted my crime, I would involve my mother and the wife of the man I had killed. But how else could I get there? And then God told me the answer, and I walked out into the street until I saw a policeman whose face I did not like. He had a round face with a black moustache, and was full of conceit and pride. I could not help laughing at my plan, as I was a humorous young man, and walked up to him and tapped him on the shoulder. When he turned round, I put my right foot behind his left and pushed him, and he fell over on his back in the dirty, wet street. He jumped up and came towards me, waving his police stick. I avoided him, as I was agile in those days, and tripped him up for the second time. He fell on his face and I laughed again.

'A crowd gathered, and four times he ran at me and each time I sent him sprawling. He looked so comic and dirty and mud-spattered, his face purple with rage. I could not stop laughing. But, without a warning, I was seized from behind and received a blow on the head and woke up with a headache in a police station.

'They questioned me for days on end. What were my motives? Why had I attacked the law? And, again and again, they asked my name and the names of my friends, and shouted with rage every time I replied that I had neither name nor friends. One morning, I was even taken to see a man of importance who was gentle and kindly and suggested that the incident was a stupid mistake, and that if I told him who had persuaded me to try and kill a policeman – for the policeman had much exaggerated his story – he would let me go. All I had to give him was a few names. I can see him now, leaning forward, smiling at me, showing his white teeth. But I shook my head and smiled back and said I had neither name nor friends.

'At length they threw me into prison in a solitary cell and questioned me every day, only allowing me to exercise for half an hour by myself. It was strange, but while I was in the cell all sorts of tappings and rappings went on as if to attract my attention, but I did not rap back, for I was a sinner and God had decided it was necessary I should receive my punishment without help from others.'

He stopped and gave Ella a charming smile which lit up his twisted face. But by this time she was judging him more cautiously, his story of his conversations with God having made her wonder if he was unbalanced.

'Later I was sent to the central prison in Moscow and questioned again for weeks. It was cold, damp and miserable in the cells, but, conscious that I had not suffered enough, I did not complain. Months passed. I asked for neither books nor pencils or paper, nor did I complain when I was starved or confined without exercise. Doctors visited me to find out why I had tried to kill the policeman. I only smiled.

'A few days after my questioning ended I was brought before a group of well-dressed men in smart uniforms, seriously sitting around a curved table, who asked what I had to say in my defence. I said, "Nothing." Then they said that I might regain my freedom if I named my accomplices, otherwise I would be sent to Siberia. I again smiled, at which their faces lost their well-fed looks and one of them told me I was sentenced by an adminstrative process – I do not know what that means to this day – to fifteen years' penal service in Siberia. As I desired the sentence, I was pleased.

'Several days later the prison bustled with activity and a blacksmith fixed irons, encased in leather, around my ankles, which did not hurt as I had hoped. Afterwards, with other convicts, I was taken into a room and had the hair on one half of my head roughly shaved.

'The next day we marched through the streets of Moscow, chains clanking, to the train to Nizhny-Novgorod, from where we travelled on a boat sailing down the Volga, through flat, dull country. Later, we turned up the River Kana, and eventually arrived at Perm, from where we travelled by train to Ekaterinburg. All the names will stay in my mind for ever. On the boat I borrowed a knife and, to begin my period of redemption, cut the leather off my irons to make them chafe my ankles, which swelled up to such a size I was unable to take a single step. At Ekaterinburg, I was examined by a doctor, who cursed and asked if I was a madman. He had difficulty getting the rivets out of my swollen, septic ankles and insisted that I should travel by troika on the next stage of the journey, instead of walking with the rest of the convicts. We passed a monument, on one side of which was written "Europe" and on the other "Siberia", which filled me with satisfaction, as I felt I had realized my intention and it would now be possible for me, by suffering, to save my soul.

'By the time I arrived at Tiumen, a posting station crowded with convicts waiting to be dispatched to their final destination, a meeting place of death and sorrow, my feet had swollen to such a size that I had to be carried into the crammed lazaret of the prison, where I was laid on a mattress on the floor. This made me feel privileged, as I believed that if I had been brave enough I would have remained with my fellow convicts. Despite the crush in the lazaret, the doctors treated my legs kindly until they gradually healed, which was unexpected, as men died around me day and night.

'After two weeks I was discharged as "recovered", although, as you see, I have still to swing out my right leg, and I was taken to a prisoners' cell which was very dirty. In the daytime I could hardly walk. I had nothing to do but examine the cell, which was thirty-five feet long and twenty-five feet wide. In the middle stood a wooden platform raised in the centre. The convicts slept on each side, their heads separated by a level top, three feet wide. Each man was officially allowed seven feet by three feet but, since it was spring, the cells were overcrowded, and as there was no room on the platform, many by necessity slept on the floor. I found the filth and stench nearly unbearable, and only consoled myself my remembering that I had come to Siberia to seek forgiveness for my sin.

'Remembering my purpose, I noticed on the first night that the space nearest the latrine buckets was avoided and the next night became the convict who lay nearest to it on the floor; and when, in the night, the tubs of excrement overflowed, I thanked God for the stench and discomfort inflicted on me. In this cell I became conscious that although every prisoner was of equal importance in the eyes of God, certain men thought otherwise and swaggered about wearing gaudy clothes, giving orders and receiving obedience. Nick-named Ivans, they ruled the convicts and made their own agreements with the Cossack guards. If men broke these agreements they died. I was afraid, and if they asked a question I shook my head and smiled to make them believe I was an idiot.

'Time passed slowly in Tiumen, and despite temptations from the devil I continued to sleep on the floor. But I was restless; every day men arrived or left or died. After a few weeks, which I survived by God's mercy, we went by convict barge to Tobolsk. An Ivan said it was modelled on the boats which traders used to carry slaves to America. It had two chambers below, with sleeping benches round the walls and in the centre, but minute open portholes made the air fresher, as the ship usually moved at night. The deck was like a divided birdcage: half for convicts and half for their women. Before we started, we bought food through the bars, our allowance being five kopeks a day to feed ourselves.

'The women's pen was next to ours. Many innocent women had accompanied their husbands, and it was sad to see them sitting mournful, crowded together. The vermin nearly ate us alive. We had caught bugs at the Tiumen, and, Mother of God, did they bite! The boat was clean and smelt of disinfectant, but we took the bugs with us and never changed clothes for ten days. They became very healthy and increased in numbers, and judging by the way they ate, bred many children and grandchildren.'

He paused and lifted his finger, and she heard the distant tolling of the monastery bell. Apologizing, he returned to pray at his little altar. Ella was relieved to be able to collect her thoughts. She had listened to him with difficulty. Once he had started to speak, his eyes appeared to look back into a past which she had never comprehended. Ever since she arrived in Russia, she had often heard of some wild young liberal or other whom she knew by sight having been sentenced to Siberia. Immediately she had conceived of them as thousands of miles away, sitting with books in a warm little room. She had never given a thought to their journey, never visualized them in irons, shut up in crowded, stinking rooms, sick, ill, covered with lice. She shuddered at her selfishness and self-pity. What did she know of suffering, disease and endless pain? Getting up quickly, she went and knelt by him and prayed for forgiveness and the strength to tell Nicky what she had learned. After a few moments her companion stood up, but she remained, trying to regather her strength. When she returned to her hard seat, she sat with her eyes downcast. At last she raised her eyes, looked at him and said: 'Do not spare me, please. I wish to know all your suffering.'

He gave no sign of having heard and continued, with his eyes looking beyond her: 'We passed several landing places and little townships where exiles landed to live in little settlements for the next ten or twenty years. At Tomsk, we finished our journey, and it was good to get out of the underground cabin and the exercise cage, for although I knew it was good for my soul, something in me cried out against being treated like an animal and peered at through bars. I knew it was wrong to resent treatment which I deserved, yet I was glad to get out of that barge, especially as three children of the prisoners' women had died on the journey and the sad wailing of their mothers could be heard all night long.

'My feet had quite healed by this time. They are great clumsy things with their own mind, as you can see,' he said, lifting a huge foot, 'and they decided to get well. I was glad, as the forwarding station was crowded to an extent you would not believe. The Ivans said it was built to hold 1,400 but 3,000 of us had to be packed in to wait, gamble and die. Like Tiumen, it was a camp of filth, sin and murder, and hopelessness for the weak and sick. Despite all my resolutions to bear suffering joyfully without complaint, I wished with all my heart to move on.

'At last we learned one day that our destination was Ust-Kara, of which I had never heard, and that the first stop was Irkutz, which was – my Ivan told me – 1,040 miles away. We walked twenty miles a day, and my legs, which had suffered so from the chains before, suffered no longer. In fact, although weighing five pounds, the chains caused no trouble if you tied them to a rope hanging from your belt. The women walked by their husbands, and it was quite a party along the road. We stopped to rest at the end of every stage at small resting places, where we crammed on to the familiar sleeping platforms, or on the floor, although the weather had begun to be cold. The air in those small stages had to be smelt to be believed. You are lucky, Gracious Highness, that you will never smell it. You know, life is strange, and some of the old convicts who escaped every spring to return in the autumn liked the air with its smell of mankind and food and excrement, and used to open their mouths and suck it in, and say it was like eating food. I welcomed it because the smell was so foul that I felt I was improved by my suffering, although it was only by intense devotion and prayer that I could make myself realize how fortunate I was to be in a position to prove I regretted my mortal sins.

'Our progress was difficult, and some died on the road and others died in our resting houses, when rain and sleet soaked us before the issue of our winter clothes and our only protection was a coarse linen shirt, a pair of linen trousers and a grey overcoat. When it rained – and it rained often – we were drenched to the skin, and the mud was in places a foot deep. I felt great sorrow for the women and children travelling in rude carts without springs, with no shelter and only a little wet straw to lie on. Many of the children died, and the mothers would scream and cry and one's heart went out to them. I lost both my shoes in the mud, as did many others. They were flimsy things and had done little good, and my feet soon learned to accept rough treatment and troubled me no more.

'I thought the journey would never end; we stopped at over fifty stages. At each of them we left behind the weakest of our party, for none of the cells had enough air, and all crawled with lice, who gorged themselves on the diseased, and since their next meal infected the healthy, the crowded lazarets stunk of the dead.

'Sometimes we picked up the sick from earlier parties, and occasionally small groups joined us, and at each stop we left some to die. By this time, all the prisoners had half-grown, half-shaved heads and beards, and filthy clothes and faces, so the guards could not tell us one from another. This was the time for which the Ivans had waited, and now they made many profitable deals, arranging for poor prisoners with short sentences or exiles to sell their names to rich prisoners with long sentences.

'The immorality was beyond anything I ever saw, and wives who had followed their husbands faithfully for 4,000 miles would find themselves sold for a few kopeks a night. You may ask why men sold their wives and their short sentences. The answer lay in gambling. Every night in the cells, in the stinking air, as I kept to myself on the floor, others gathered into little hellish circles around a candle to play cards. Again and again men would lose all their kopeks, and even their rations for the next day, and have to walk twenty miles without a bite of bread, but the next evening they would gamble and lose again, so that each day I found many in need to whom I could give half my rations, for I found I could survive on the other half.

'In the mornings, men who had sold their identities when drunk with vodka regretted their folly and wished to change their minds. It was their last day on earth: the Ivans, who had arranged the deal, would cut their throats. The guards would shrug their shoulders. How could they find the murderer among 150 silent, bearded men?

'After a few hundred miles I began to wonder whether I was dreaming. Each morning I woke up in a rest house on the floor, walked twenty miles, slept in another rest house with the same stench, the same black bread, the same cries in the night, the same disturbed sleep as men stepped over me on the way to the excrement tub, while, the following morning and evening, the pattern was repeated. I began to be cheery; I suffered so. At least, it is wrong to say that I began to be cheery, but rather that while I suffered most of the time, I was cheerful some of the time, and that by a miracle my health did not break down.

'But I must shorten my story or I will keep you here all day. At long last we approached our destination and crossed a river filled with great blocks of floating ice. I was full of fear that I might die before I had suffered sufficiently for my crime. But, again, God was merciful, and at last we arrived at our destination camp, which was called Ust-Kara and was near gold mines, or had

189

been until the workings had moved so far away that only healthy prisoners could walk to work.

'Here my room was a different size. It was eight paces long, seven and a half paces wide, and eight foot high, for I could not touch the black ceiling by lifting my hands above my head. The room had two heavily barred windows so encrusted with dirt that they could not be opened, and in a corner was a brick oven. The room was, compared to our last lodging, empty, since it contained only twenty-nine men with space for me to sleep on the wooden platform without displacing another man. To my surprise, I noticed that the old black logs had been whitewashed maybe forty years before, for you could see the remains of white near to the ceiling, but above the level of the platforms the logs looked red. I wondered who could have painted them such a curious colour, until I saw a prisoner squashing a bug full of blood on the wall.'

'Wait, please,' said Ella. 'Are you telling me the absolute truth?'

He nodded, a look of surprise on his face. She had to stand up again and walk backwards and forwards as she remembered the relish with which Serge had often said, 'He will not trouble us again for the next twenty years. He will be enjoying the Siberian climate.' Often, not to annoy him, she had merely smiled. Why had she never made the slightest effort to find out what happened to prisoners? She tried to imagine herself living in cabin with twenty other women and the logs red with blood. She clenched her fists and beat her cheeks, at which he started talking again in the same monotonous voice, every sentence sticking into her like a pin.

'Each prisoner was allowed one bath a week and issued with new boots. The food was better and more plentiful: three pounds of black bread a day, four ounces of meat, including the bone, a cut of brick tea and sometimes a little barley. But I found it hard to sleep on the dry platform after spending many nights lying on wet floors. Neither was I more comfortable, as the authorities provided no blankets. The camp was in a damp place and full of fever germs, judging by the number of my comrades who lay sick and dying. It was little comfort for them to know that the mines and all the gold belonged to the Tsar.

'I tried to love my fellow men, and comfort them, but it was difficult, for often they thought that if I said a kind word or asked them a question I was spying. Many times I was knocked down. At last my companions realized that I was no danger and began to show affection and treat me with kindness.

'The bugs I had brought with me found many new friends, and my blood was stolen from me every day. To the surprise of the guards, I volunteered to work in the distant mines, loosening with pointed pikes the gravel and clay which lay on the surface of an old rivulet, and pushing a barrel of the broken soil to the side of a washing machine, which separated the gold from the earth. It was uninteresting work, but it provided me with opportunities to help my brothers by carrying the heaviest loads. My help was often not appreciated, and my companions frequently grumbled at me for working too hard.

'After a while, I realized that my redemption was threatened by a worldly pleasure. Once a week, all our room enjoyed a steam bath. Oh, Imperial Highness, how can you conceive the wonderful relief of hot water cleansing your body and your soul! Afterwards, I would sit killing the bugs in my clothes

190

and thinking what strange things in life can make a man perfectly happy, for although I knew I would have to put on my wet clothes and cross the frozen yard and lie in damp clothes all night, it was worth while for the complete happiness and contentment which filled my heart as I sat in the hot steam, killing lice.

'So after a time I realized that by looking forward with such pleasure to my bath night I was avoiding my purpose of redemption by suffering: to look forward happily is not to suffer. I reflected sadly for many days on the weakness of my character and, after a hard struggle, made up my mind that I owed it to the man I had killed to forgo this wonderful pleasure. From then on, I would go into the bathhouse and quickly wash myself and my clothes and cleanse my body, for decency and not for pleasure, without luxuriating on the shelves in the beautiful steam. When I had finished, I would make my way sadly back to my room, remembering with bitterness the days when I had sat in utter happiness on the shelf. It was hard, oh so hard, and occasionally I had moments of weakness and lingered luxuriating. But the next day I would make up for my lapse by giving away my luncheon, hoping I would be forgiven.

'My life followed this pattern for three years, and I could see no future or end to it except for my daily work, but since that might have been God's wish, I never complained. Once a month, Major Pohulov inspected our quarters; he was a severe man. It gave us wrongful pleasure to see his face when he entered our rooms: the stench would hit him in the face and he would say, "Phah," and put to his nose a handkerchief scented with eau-de-Cologne. But only when I was ill did I see him inside, for it was the custom to line up outside in the yard in the cold, and after an hour of waiting he would walk quickly along the lines, inspecting us, looking very severe, but never speaking.

'On one of these inspection days, at the end of three years in the prison and nearly four years after my arrest, the Major stopped in front of me, screwed up his eyes and stood looking at me, then at a hidden object in the glove of his right hand and back again. At last he pursed his mouth, looked worried and walked on. However, a week later to my surprise our Cossack officer told me, one night, not to work the next day as in the morning an escort was coming to take me away and I should have a bath and collect together my few possessions. My departure created immense interest in Ust-Kara, and there was endless talk of what was going to happen to me. Late at night, my comrades in the next rooms knocked, one after the other, sending kind messages of farewell and hope, and trusting that God would stay with me. It touched my heart, the goodness of those rough men.

'In the morning, the gates opened and all the prisoners in the camp crowded to the windows and out of the doors, and a Cossack officer entered with eight men and I was marched away. As I left, the prisoners standing waiting in the yard bowed to me from the waist, which is the greatest compliment poor men who own nothing can give, and I was touched to the heart and sad at leaving a place which, despite many hardships, I had come to consider my home. To my surprise, after the prison was lost to sight, an officer came and walked by my side and spoke civilly and asked after my health.

'Because in the last four years no official had treated me with politeness, I was puzzled and remembered how, in a weak moment, I had sent a letter to my mother by a discharged prisoner to tell her that I was strong and well and to dismiss me from her thoughts. I thought she must have taken steps, for I knew her determination.

'As we drew near Kara, the Captain told me that orders had come from a high official in Moscow for me to be transferred to the political section for one further year's imprisonment before spending another year as a free exile in Ust-Kara and then regaining my freedom to return home. I was astounded, and the jump of pleasure my heart gave warned me that I had not yet suffered enough, and that while it would be more pleasant in this life to return to Europe, in the next I would regret the early reduction of my sentence.

'Confused by hope and guilt, I walked in a cloud and woke up outside the political prison, hidden behind a huge wooden fence, perhaps eighteen foot high, whose sharp points resembled giant pencils. I was surprised, on passing through the giant gates, to be greeted by a man who introduced himself as Captain Nikolin, Commandant of the Political Prisoners. In a friendly manner, he wished me good morning and said he trusted that I had heard of my good fortune, and that if I behaved well he might even be able to release me in ten months. I bowed to him but regretted having sent the postcard to my mother.

'The Captain told me that I was to sleep in the Nobles Room, though why it was so called no one ever knew, for no noble had ever slept in it. The living quarters consisted of four bedrooms, each containing sixteen men. In the same building was a small lazaret and a water closet. As it stood on a hill, the air was not damp, but otherwise it bore many sad resemblances to my former prison. We lay in chains on identical platforms and wore the same filthy clothes in disgusting rooms whose windows were cemented with dirt. Each man may have had more space in which to sleep, but this only gave the vermin more room to breed.

'But my companions, political not criminal convicts, greeted me with excitement and false expectations. Rumours in settlements spread like wildfire, and they believed me to be a wrongfully imprisoned political who had asserted his rights to leave the criminals. I disillusioned them, and they wished to know why I was moved. When I said that I did not know, they looked stupefied and gazed at me in amazement, certain of them with doubtful eyes, which made me realize that they suspected me of being a spy. I laughed and told them to have no fear. "I promise you, I am an ordinary convict who knocked down a policeman in Moscow four times." When they asked yet again why, I said: "I wished to go to prison as I killed a man and escaped justice and hoped to redeem myself," after which they looked at me with respect, for every Russian understands the trials of a sinner.

'My new companions belonged to a different class of men and treated me with kindness, but they talked, oh how they talked, and argued endlessly about books of which I had never heard. I can remember the name of only one – *Socialism and the Political Struggle* – but they all had names like that. And it wasn't only politics which they argued about. They would disagree about every subject under the sun, and oddly enough those who argued most appeared to me to be those nearest in agreement to each other.

'Their appearances confused me as well. The gentlest mannered advocated terrorism and organized revolt by the peasants; the fiercest and roughest argued against violence. When they were not arguing, they sat talking and placing bets on every subject on earth, some of which could not be decided for seven years. When the time came to settle an old bet, I noticed how the winner would argue that the loser should not pay, and the loser would argue that he should, and so it went on. They showed great kindness to me, and appeared to be good men, apart from their belief in throwing bombs.

'I was given more to eat than at Ust-Kara. We received three and a half pounds of bread and six ounces of meat a day, salt, barley and a portion of brick tea. We cooked alternately, and endlessly discussed our next meals. I settled into my new life easily, although in many ways the days passed more slowly than in the convict camp, for politicals, forbidden to work, never leave their camp. Their whole world was the prison, the little courtyard and the soldiers' barracks contained by the huge surrounding pencils far too high to see over.

'Months went by, and one day Captain Nikolin told me at an inspection I only had two months to serve before I became a free exile. I was surprised, and when I said my prayers that night I was about to add, "Amen," when the face of the man I had murdered appeared and said, more in sorrow than in anger, "Did I not say I would appear to you when your sin was forgiven? Ask yourself, have I come?" I replied, "No," at which he looked at me severely and said, "Understand, I am nothing in the eyes of the Lord God. He is the only judge of sinners. His words are my words and he has not said you are forgiven. I say to you, wait until you have received the word of God, for it will avail you but a short hour if you return before your sins are washed away."

'He made a sign of the cross, and I saw him no more. His words made me understand that it was God's wish I should stay in prison and save my eternal soul, but how? I opened my mind, and, as always, when man opens his mind to God, an answer came: I should try to escape, but in such a manner that I would be caught and severely punished for my selfish forgetfulness. I thought of two men in our camp, one named Berezniàk and the other Sanhedrin. Both had escaped two years before, and after their recapture were chained night and day to wheelbarrows. Berezniàk never complained, but as the chain of the barrow was short, I thought he must be in perpetual discomfort. Surely to be chained like a dog would reduce my pride and be a fit punishment for my sin? The decision made, I fell into a peaceful sleep.

'The next morning I woke refreshed and waited, idly brushing a path in the yard. At nine o'clock the front gate was opened to allow the entrance of the new Cossack guard. Immediately I rushed at them, although my fetters prevented me from moving fast, and as I am a big strong man, as you can see, I knocked down two of the soldiers before I was overpowered.

'Ah, how they beat me with their fists and rifle butts – you can see the scars on my face,' and he thrust his face forward and pointed to the scars which Ella had already noticed.

'I began to wonder if I would be beaten to death, when the thrashing stopped and, to my amazement, I saw one of the officers beating the men who had beaten me. I was hauled to my feet and marched before the dumbfounded

Major, who could not understand why I had done such a stupid thing only two months before my release.

'He walked up and down, tugging his beard, shouting with anger that I had complicated his life and set a terrible example, and that he had no alternative to confining me in the solitary cells. Eventually he calmed down and said he would see that I was not denied my food ration, as was the custom, but that he could relax discipline no further. I remained silent and could see he thought me a madman. At last he shook his head in anger and clapped his hands for the soldiers to march me off to the cells, where I stayed in discomfort for a month, hoping I was pleasing God, sitting frozen and cramped.

'At the end of my sentence I was taken again before the Captain, who said: "I have received orders from Moscow that you are to be treated and punished as an ordinary prisoner and have decided that, for the next three years, you will be chained to a wheelbarrow. After that," he said, rubbing his hands, "your case will be reviewed."

'When I returned to my room with the wheelbarrow, my roommates received me with great kindness and prepared a special meal of my favourite dish, *pirog* – a pie made of flour and rice and mince. I was touched, knowing that they had all gone without meat the day before to save up enough for my welcome-home feast, believing that I was starved. I forced myself to eat, and you should have seen the pleasure in those good men's eyes.

'I found the barrow difficult at first, for I would forget my new companion, who could give me a severe jolt. Berezniàk told me that I should regard my barrow as a favourite dog and pat it kindly when it was good and beat it when it was bad. I followed his advice, and do you know, I became very fond of my new pet and never once corrected it severely? Neither was it an uncomfortable bed mate, for my next-door neighbours gave us more room. Berezniàk told me that he found it unbearable when the Cossacks looked at him with scorn, but I never minded how they looked at me, and amazed them by carrying on conversations with my barrow, which made them tap their heads and regard me as an idiot, though others crossed themselves.

'The winter passed quickly but in the spring I had a terrible bout of homesickness, for when I was a convict working in the mines, time passed quickly and I enjoyed my walks to work but, tied to a barrow and unable to see beyond the stockade, I longed with intense passion for freedom. And do you know what caused it? The call of a cuckoo. It may seem silly to you, dear lady,' and he again put his face close to Ella's.

With an intense effort, she avoided leaning back and smiled.

'But if you have been shut in a box for years, the sound brings back to you the world of freedom, and I thought of sentimental things long forgotten: of walks in the country, the garden behind my mother's house and the blue-eyed girl skating. Oh, how I longed to skate again. My passion was unbearable before I understood that my frustration was part of God's just sentence. I told my companions afterwards of my restlessness and wild desire to follow the bird, and they told me how every year the voice of the cuckoo calls to prisoners to escape and how there was in the exiles' village an old man who, when a younger prisoner, would escape each year at the first cry of the bird and live in the forest on nuts and berries until, when winter returned, he would come back and stand at the door of his prison. At last he became too old to bear the hardships of sleeping on the hard earth, and before the bird spoke he would go to the Prison Commander and ask to be locked up until it ceased its unbearable taunts.

'After two years, and without warning, my barrow was taken away and, do you know, I missed it at night? It was as if a companion had deserted me or I had lost an old friend. It was the same with my clothes. Every now and again we received a new linen shirt and a pair of linen trousers, but although my old clothes – which never left me night or day – had turned to rags, they had become a part of my personality, and on the first day when I wore my new clothes I thought sadly of the old ones.

'After my separation from my barrow, I have no memories of my last two years in prison until the time of my release drew near. If you are confined in a room for eight years, you live a life of repetition and everyday events are copies of the day and the week and the year before. But before I was released, I was nervous that I had not suffered enough and would be forbidden to leave by my victim. Plucking up all my courage, I prayed and waited, fearful of having to attack the guard again, for despite my resolutions, I was sick to death of our prison yard. But this time he came and told me I had paid my price and could leave, and then after a few years as a free exile, return to the world to work for others.

'On my last evening, I gave a party of farewell, and oh, what a feast we had. For months I had saved up a little money out of our allowance of a few kopeks a week and ordered good meat and, secretly, vodka, and do you know, we had a real blow-out? I was sad, on leaving, to see envy in my friends' eyes. It was extraordinary to step out of the gate and know I was half-free, yet after a few yards I was so frightened that I nearly ran back again. After years in which the limit of my vision had been thirty yards, the world was full of dangers and precipices and I was full of fear of many things. Oh, it was a strange feeling, gracious lady; one I hope that you will never know.'

As he spoke, he put his head on one side and looked at her quizzically, as if considering the possibility of her imprisonment.

'Well, I was now a free exile, allowed to go anywhere in a confined area. They gave me a little house with three quarters of the roof remaining and otherwise in good condition. I moved in to put things in order before winter came along. For, you see, the authorities always arrange by either extending or shortening your stay in prison, to let free exiles out in the spring. This is not from kindness, but to give them a few months to rebuild, before the winter, some tumbledown shack which has become available through the tenant going home or blowing his brains out.

'It was a long time before I could walk more than thirty yards in one direction without beginning to turn, and sometimes, when I paid visits, and was thinking deeply, I would walk thirty yards and turn and walk backwards and forwards until I realized my error. But I won't dwell on this period, for it was one not of suffering but of waiting. I knew most of the free exiles from our prison days together, and in such an enclosed society, a new face – even if it is an old face – is a welcome addition and subject of conversation. It was strange to see a woman again after ten years, and when I felt the touch of a soft hand like this' – and he wouched her shrinking hand with his finger tips – 'it gave me quite a start and brought back forgotten memories.

'The married exiles received from the Government a grant of a few wretched kopeks a day, but even so, they would entertain guests with ceremony. The housewife would lay a little cloth and carefully place a teapot on a tray of old boards and sit down at the head of the table and serve tea in chipped cups, in a delicate manner which brought tears to my eyes. One of my new friends was called Mrs Chernyavsky. She had followed her husband to Siberia for a political offence. Later he refused to swear allegiance to Alexander III, and as a punishment was sent, in mid-winter, to northern Siberia. They rode in a springless cart which became caught in a storm, one of those terrible storms when the wind cuts like a knife through your thickest clothes. Nothing his wife could do kept her baby warm, and when they arrived at Kransnoyarsk, the baby was dead in her arms. And believe it, dear lady,' and he put out his hand and squeezed hers as if for comfort as tears came into his eyes and his crooked face twisted with unhappiness, 'the poor man was kept waiting two hours outside the prison with a mad wife and a dead baby in his arms before he was allowed to enter. When I heard the story, she had recovered and was giving me tea, and as usual I said the wrong thing and asked him – he was writing as usual – why he had refused to swear allegiance to the Tsar Alexander III since it would have saved his baby's life. It was an unfortunate question, for she burst into tears and he jumped up and stamped backwards and forwards, shouting that nothing would make him abandon his principles.

'But I learned afterwards that he had abandoned them in the end and that his baby died all for nothing, for after his wife had recovered from her madness, they sent them both to a Yakurt settlement. The Yakurts, you know, are nearly animals and sleep in the same room with cows for warmth and only drink milk and smell terrible and never let exiles out of sight, and for eight months the Chernyavskys lived like animals, without a friend for over a hundred miles, with only sour milk and cheese to eat and never once a bath, until the husband thought he was going mad and swore allegiance to the Tsar. But, you know, I noticed how those who have the strongest political beliefs and talk the most about their duty to mankind are the most selfish of men and do the least for others. They never understand that the intensity of their beliefs is conceit; this was true in the prisons and outside in the settlements, and I am sure it is the case in the world as well.

'But despite my tactlessness, I made many friends among the women, whom the cruel, dull life aged and tired. I found I could help them, for although I am not clever, I can read and write and I taught the children their ABCs and made swings on the branches of trees, and sledges and slides. But when spring came, the cuckoos called again and I longed for home with a terrible intensity. I was cleverer than the old convict who returned to prison: I put wax in my ears.

'After four springs I was free and began the long march home. And so, sixteen years after I had left my mother's house, I walked in at the front door again. But before I tell you what has happened since, I must ask God's advice about the questions I should ask.'

196

He turned and went and knelt at the altar in a manner which made her think he was ostentatiously turning his heels towards her. All the doubts which had been mounting in Ella's mind as to his sanity returned. Was she prepared to tolerate this twisted saint prying into her life? If she allowed herself to go through the agony of his questioning, could he help her? To begin with, she had listened to his story with awe, believing him to be a good, brave man and determined not to be put off by his unattractive appearance and wet face. But as he continued, while she did not disbelieve him, she several times wondered doubtfully if his ostentatious piety, shining eyes and moist forehead did not suggest an unhealthy enjoyment of his ghastly experiences. Was he, she wondered, despite her determination to believe in his goodness, one of those men who enjoy suffering?

Her thoughts produced a flash of memory of a conversation: 'Never feel sorry for saints – they love their suffering, and if they escape return for more.' Surely it was unnecessary to choose every night to lie by a disgusting excrement tub? The idea made her sick, and she shuddered as she looked at his back. And what was the purpose of uselessly attacking Cossacks to ensure that he stayed years longer in a Siberian prison? How did that help either his mother, who was left alone for sixteen years, or the wife of the man he had killed? What practical help had he given to either? If his history illustrated his idea of goodness, what advice would he give her? She dreaded he might suggest a public humiliation.

And he smelt. She had pretended not to notice, but when he put his face near to hers his breath positively reeked – she was certain – of spirits or vodka. The air in the cave was filthy. She envied Sandra, sitting on a rock in the sun, and so quietly, without saying a word, she stood up and began to creep out. She had not gone far when the holy man's voice rang out clearly, 'Goodbye, gracious Imperial Highness, I am honoured at your visit and comprehend your silent departure. But fear not my advice – I shall give you none. But I have spoken to God and he tells me that your present troubles are nearly at an end. You will be helped by the death of an old woman. Soon afterwards, your dreams will end. Go with my blessing, and know that I am not as bad as you think.'

Ella was uncomfortably startled at the way he read her thoughts. She hoped that, repelled as she had been by his repulsive characteristics, she had not misjudged him. How stupid she was to mind how others looked. She regretted her silent withdrawal and went back, crossed herself and knelt by his side and prayed for both their souls. When she had finished, she got up and left him kneeling, mumbling prayers, oblivious of her. She walked out of the cave, leant against the cliff and gulped the air with relief at escaping from the fetid atmosphere. As she sidled nervously along the filthy path, avoiding looking at the sea, she saw that the sun had disappeared behind dark clouds as a cold wind blew from the Black Sea. At last she found Sandra, sitting and shivering on a fallen tree trunk. Ella apologized and asked if the sun was warm.

'Oh,' said Sandra with a brave smile, 'it would have been lovely if the sun had shone.'

'Did the monk give you food or drink?'

'No, but I am sure it would have been very good if he had.'

15

A week later, a telegram arrived to say that Queen Victoria was sinking fast. If Ella wished to see her grandmother alive, she should hurry to England. Grandmama was dead when she arrived, and she did not feel as sad as she ought to have done, the funeral seeming unimportant compared with the intensification of her horrible dreams, which mixed up her grief for her grandmother with her sorrow for herself. When she saw Ducky and Missy before the funeral, she thought that she might faint. Surely they had not come to haunt her now? When they kissed her, she clung on their arms to make sure that they were made of flesh and blood. Ernie, in lower spirits than usual, asked her to come to stay with him on her way home.

When she arrived in Hesse, Ducky was packing her things and said, quite naturally: 'As I have often told you, Ernie is an inadequate husband and I have remained tied to him for seven years against my will out of respect for Grandmama. Now that she is dead I am leaving as quickly as I can.'

Ernie was downcast and told his sister that he hated Ducky. 'She was never fair to me and was horrid after we married and never tried to help me. She even set fierce horses on me whenever she could, and laughed at my uniforms. She could not see I had to wear them or that they looked beautiful. I'll be glad when she goes. My ministers know what she's like and hate her and think a divorce without scandal is possible. But Ducky is so beastly and indiscreet, and makes up such horrid lies, I know she'll try and create one.'

Ella felt sorry for her brother. She knew that he was, beneath his bitterness, kind and sweet and gentle. At the same time, she agreed with what Victoria wrote:

Ernie should never have married such a fiery, impetuous girl, brimming with life. Goodness, I could have found plenty of fat, dull German princesses who would have been happy to put up with what Miechen calls 'his little foibles' to be his wife. Now we must find him an ugly, safe woman who will be a good mother to his children.

Ernie begged Ella to speak to Ducky to ask her to be discreet and stop spreading awful rumours about him. The next morning, she went early into her bedroom and said: 'Please be kind to Ernie, for while he was a bad husband, you must admit he is a kind man.'

Ducky burst out laughing and said: 'Oh dear, once I am free I will tolerate him, but I cannot bear the way he goes on imploring me to be nice. If only he would hit me or say I was horrible I would not mind, but all he does is cry and wring his hands, which infuriates me, and I lose my temper. I promise you that when I go – and I am joining Cyril in two weeks' time – I won't say a word against Ernie. He honestly isn't worth talking about, you know. I think you'll find that I will change when I marry again. You have always been kind to me Ella, and never criticized because, I think, you understood my difficulties. So please rely on me to be good when I go, but while I am here, I cannot promise anything. But wait, you can tell him that I will promise to keep my temper as long as he doesn't use the words "horrid" or "nasty" or "beastly" again. There, that's a bargain,' and she flung her arms around her sister-in-law and kissed her.

Ella's dreams that night and in the succeeding weeks became sombre nightmares. The weather was always dark and cloudy and the habits of her young relations changed. They no longer sang or danced but sent the gipsies away, and Boris would shout in anger if a nightingale sang. Instead of laughing gaily in the beautiful garden, they hung about in black clothes, whispering together in dark passages before beckoning to her. When she walked towards them, they always led her into a vast, empty, dark room and vanished. Terrified, she would run round the room trying to escape, but could never find a door, and would wake up screaming and stay awake, hopelessly weeping.

Perhaps her greatest sorrow was the change in her lover. She had come to think of him as the doctor again. He had grown cold and distant, and if he still loved her, why was he so sad? One night when, for the first time in many weeks, they were walking hand in hand in the garden, he took her into his arms, pulled her to him, clasped her to his breast, stared into her eyes and said: 'Goodbye, Ella, I love you but I will never see you again.' Then he walked through the black garden door and slammed it in her face. Desperately, she tugged at the handle, knowing she would never again enter their secret garden. Heartbroken, she screamed to him to come back, and the noise woke her up. Luckily, she was in Moscow, alone in her bedroom, but it was impossible to stay in bed. She paced up and down in her dressing gown, wondering whether her phantoms might one day allow Serge to have her shut up.

That afternoon, she was taking the chair at a hospital meeting when a terrible lassitude crept over her and it was all she could do to keep her eyes open, which made her wonder if she was developing influenza. But her lethargy continued as she dressed for dinner, and she could not have cared less what she wore or how she looked. At dinner, she had to pinch herself to keep awake. Immediately afterwards, for the first time in her life, she sent for her carriage, pleading a terrible headache. Serge told her to take a pill and let her drive home alone. Had she slept on the way back? At all events, she had pulled herself upstairs to her bedroom in such a state of exhaustion that she was hardly able to take her clothes off before collapsing into sleep.

The next thing she remembered was Sandra shaking her shoulders and looking at her anxiously as she asked: 'Are you all right? It's eleven o'clock, and the maid could not wake you, and you never ate your breakfast.'

Ella said without thinking: 'Yes, I am all right,' and then she realized that a weight had lifted from her mind. She had slept for twelve hours without dreaming.

'Oh, I understand,' she said suddenly, thinking of the doctor's farewell.

'Understand what?' asked Sandra.

'Oh, nothing,' said Ella in embarrassment, 'or rather, I mean I was just tired. Please send me a cup of tea – I don't want anything to eat,' and she walked towards the bathroom.

Sandra started to speak, but Ella shut the door and looked around with reopened eyes. The glass looked like a glass, her toothbrush a toothbrush. Reality had returned. She touched things, pleased at their solidity, and, shaking her head to make sure she was not dreaming, washed her face with cold water. Back in her bedroom, she saw on her breakfast table a telegram pinned to a note which stated it had arrived last night. It was from Ernie with the news that his divorce from Ducky had been approved by his ministers.

She never dreamt again. Her long nightmare was over. She had come to hate her love, and prayed never to see the doctor awake or asleep again. It took her a month to be sure that she would at night rest and not fall into a second frightening life. Terrified that the dreams would return, she decided to have a holiday to ensure her break with the past was complete. Since Ducky had left, she decided to go back and try to comfort poor Ernie. Victoria wrote that he was 'quite perky again', and he had written to say how his council in Darmstadt had behaved very well and that Ducky had given up little Sunny without a qualm.

When Ella arrived, Ernie told her again how relieved he was to be rid of Ducky, who was a rotten mother and only pretended to love art nouveau, really admiring nothing but her beastly horses and Cyril, 'who is about as big and stupid as a horse anyway'.

His face took on a petulant look as he continued: 'It was so unfair to me, having miscarriages just through galloping about like a lunatic. Now she's gone I will take a little rest for a year or two, and then will marry a cosy princess who will do as she's told and won't give me any trouble because she will be so grateful I've married her. I am fed up with the beauties who think of nothing but themselves.'

He stopped. His self-pity vanished and an expression of intense interest came over his face as he changed the subject. 'I say, let's stop talking about Ducky. Are all these extraordinary stories true about Alix and the "Black Perils"?'

'What stories?' Ella asked, embarrassed at her ignorance.

Ernie, too excited to be interrupted, went on: 'Well they all say that ever since Marie was born, Alix is desperate to have a son, and the "Black Perils" – or your friends, the Montenegrins – are Alix's best friends and take her to séances and fortune tellers and crazy priests and holy men. Now they have got hold of a madman called Koliaba who is a epileptic and lies on the floor gibbering and foaming at the mouth. But Alix thinks "God is visiting him" and listens to his gurgling and spitting and announces he is "inspired", and believes it, because he has told her that she is going to have a son. Isn't it unkind of the "Perils" to make her look so silly?

'And what of Monsieur Phillipe, who is said to be a French butcher, of all things, from Lyons, of all places? Of course, he is one of the Montenegrins' protégés as well. And would you believe it, Militza says that when he wears a hat he becomes invisible and anyone who is with him as well? The other day, in the Crimea, she cut old Felix Youssoupov. Afterwards, when he asked why, she said that the butcher had his hat on and so she was invisible and he would not have seen her if she had smiled at him. Did you ever! I mean, they are the limit, aren't they? And do you know, the "Perils" have a mad sister called Xenie who thinks she's a chicken, a black one I should think, as they get darker every year. And they say that Nicky's not much better and consults a ouija board before making a decision, and the joke is, it is said he needs a new board.'

He looked at her sharply. 'Tell me, why haven't you heard these things? You like to know what goes on, even if you are a saint.'

Ella could not help smiling; her brother was so silly. However, if Ernie knew so much, Alix must have been very indiscreet. She decided to go and see her in St Petersburg. It was idiotic believing in fortune tellers and table turning. She had been to them herself, like everybody else, at the beginning of her marriage, but soon realized how they never did any good.

16

Ella, dreamless in St Petersburg, began to live again. It was strange – as if she had slept for years – but she found that, by going to dine with Miechen and keeping quiet, she soon learnt everything that had happened. Apparently Ernie had for once told the truth. Alix had become great friends with the Montenegrins and their magicians and was determined to have a son. When Ella went to see her and begged her not to worry, Alix drew herself up and announced coldly: 'I am not worried. Monsieur Phillipe has given me his word, so the matter is not in doubt. And he is supported by Koliaba, a saint whose sacred sayings only I can interpret. I've already made the little boy's clothes. We are going to call him Alexis.'

Ella said she was pleased, and her sister stopped looking angry when they discussed who Ernie should now marry.

Later in the year, Alix was devastated with disappointment by the birth of little Anastasia and cried in Ella's arms. Nicky was worried, and said he was going to send Phillipe back to France and Koliaba back to his monastery. But Ella realized how he hadn't changed in her blank years and remained entirely under Alix's thumb.

After her visit to her sister, she lunched with Miechen, who had become her friend since she tactfully conveyed Serge's message and, to Ella's surprise, kept the whole embarrassing affair a dead secret. Ella was grateful, as Miechen loved gossip, and to keep quiet on such a fascinating subject must have caused her to practise unwelcome self-control.

At the end of the summer, Ella returned to St Petersburg to see her sister once more before opening a new wing of a hospital. She found Alix ill and withdrawn and discontented, but still in love with Nicky, who adored her. But their self-sufficiency had drawbacks, for it caused Alix to retire entirely from public life and to look angry and resentful when she was forced to appear. She looked hurt when Ella said that she was going to stay for the first time with Miechen, and conveyed that her sister was acting disloyally to both herself and Nicky. Ella smiled and said, 'Oh no, Alix, it is best for us all to be on good terms, isn't it? You are my sister, I love you – she is only a friend.'

Alix's face set in hard unyielding lines. It was extraordinary how little she had changed. Ella had seen that look a thousand times in the nursery.

During her visit to the Vladimir Palace, she made a new friend in Miechen's daughter Helen. Ella could never resist beauty in any form, and this girl, with her heart-shaped face and huge blue eyes, was not only lovely, she also had a mind of her own which had broken the most ridiculous of imperial rules: limiting grand duchesses at balls only to dance with partners printed on official lists. Helen refused to make a list and declared firmly that she would only dance with those who asked her. A complaint was made to the Tsar, but as he could never resist her simplest request, she got her way. Ella sighed in admiration, remembering the boredom which the lists had caused her. Vladimir was kind, explaining rather than shouting. At once she liked him, which made her realize how weak and pliable she was.

After two nights in St Petersburg, they moved to Tsarskoye Selo in time to celebrate Miechen's name day. Ella looked forward to the party with enthusiasm. It was her first outing since her shadow had lifted.

Over a hundred guests sat on cushions, beside long white tablecloths laid upon the ground beneath an awning. Footmen handed round enormous tins of caviare, giant croutes of *foie gras* filled with huge black truffles especially imported from Querchy, cold turkeys, chickens, sturgeon and salmon, followed by dishes of fruit and strawberries covered with Jersey cream. Champagne and dry sparkling Schloss Metternich stood on the cloths in silver ice buckets, with bottles of Château Yquem to drink with the strawberries. The feast was concluded by cheese from France and Germany, handed round on wooden platters, while footmen poured out glasses of Château Lafitte.

At various places in the surrounding wood stood tables laden with iced drinks and liqueurs so that her guests could after lunch separate into friendly groups. The lunch sounded pretentious, but was informal and charming, and Ella enjoyed watching the enormous amount of food which the German Ambassador was able to swallow without a sign of distress. Afterwards, Miechen and her friends sat down beneath the trees around green baize tables and played bridge, while her children and their friends danced on a wooden platform to gipsy music.

Ella did not want to dance or play bridge, and she carried two cushions to a small space beneath a large pine tree surrounded by bushes. She felt sleepy after her heavy lunch, and the last thing she wanted was a forced conversation. As she sat drowsily, half-awake, half-asleep, she heard laughter from the other side of one of her guardian plants, and the sound of chairs knocking against the bottom of a table followed by thumps, rustling, the clinking of glasses and the scent of cigar smoke. She listened, annoyed that she could not recognize the owners of the voices. They did not seem to be saying anything interesting, and she was dropping off again when a rather thick German voice woke her up with a jump.

'I quite agree with your great Tsar – "The English are all Yids". Look at Afghanistan. It is emphatically in your sphere of interest. What right have the Yids to insist you keep out of a neighbouring state which is full of marauding bandits who molest your countrymen? And when you kept the peace and respected Afghan neutrality, what did the slimy little hypocrites do but walk into the country themselves and incite the tribesmen to fight? And don't forget that at the Kouchka incident British officers led the Afghans against your army.

Pfffof. . .their hypocrisy makes me sick,' and the speaker made a gurgling noise before continuing, 'Now they plan to contain your expansion in the Far East and are planning to sign a treaty promising aid to Japan if another country attacks her. What right have they to stop the Tsar from preventing those yellow monkeys from overrunning his great country?'

There was a chorus of agreement, and Ella guessed that the voice belonged to the hungry German Ambassador, the supporting voices to young officers.

'My Emperor would like to see you take Port Arthur and consolidate your position in Mongolia, and now, thank God, the English have made fools of themselves in South Africa and can't pretend it's immoral for you to civilize yellow monkeys when they have killed thousands of Dutchmen!'

Another voice, surely not of a soldier – it sounded rather high-pitched and querulous – broke in: 'What I can't understand is British fears. How do they think our army could possibly mount a campaign through the Pamirs, or even through Afghanistan?'

'You are wrong there,' shouted the German Ambassador. 'You are wrong there,' he repeated fiercely. 'I consider – and my military attaché does the same – Russian troops are the finest in the world, finer, I say indiscreetly, than our own. They could mount a campaign in the Sahara Desert.' The remark was greeted with delighted cheers. 'Look what you have done,' the voice went on, 'look how, in the past fifty years, you have conquered territory the size of North America without defeat, making the rest of Europe jealous. The English and French robbed you of your rightful gains when you beat the Turks. No, no,' the Ambassador said, rolling the words over his tongue, 'my money is on Russia. I think the English will find you know how to teach them a lesson or two, and the way the Japanese are behaving, you will have to teach them a lesson as well. Long live the Russian army!'

The toast was followed by a great shout and a clinking of glasses.

Ella sat wondering whether the Ambassador was drunk, when the noises suggested that he had stood up and moved away. No sooner was he out of earshot before, to her surprise, a hubbub of approval arose, revolving around the hypocrisy of the English and how they would one day learn a great lesson when the Russian army walked over the Himalayas and took India. But for the moment there was a lot of tidying up to do in Mongolia, and putting the Chinks in their proper place. As for the yellow monkeys, they needed a lesson, and judging from their stupidity, they'd get it soon. A voice proposed, 'The Tsar!' and the glasses clinked again.

After the loyal toast, they stopped speaking in pompous voices and turned gaily to discussing the prettiest girls in Moscow. They teased each other about their conquests, and when the name of Helen was mentioned, one voice cried, 'The Goddess!' and another laughingly declared that she had now displaced the sad, ageing Grand Duchess Serge as the reigning beauty of the Romanov family.

Ella shivered when she heard the words 'ageing' and 'sad'. She was thirty-seven, which, she supposed, to young men seemed old – and she was sad. She felt hurt, and a longing to look in a glass to see if her face deserved to be so unkindly described. Perhaps she was conceited and vain, and it served her right to be told the truth. But she was nevertheless upset and could not rest. She knew that she was behaving ridiculously but she felt offended.

When, late in the afternoon, they returned to Tsarskoye Selo, she went immediately to her glass and, carefully examining her face from every angle, saw why they thought her 'ageing and sad'. Her eyes had a melancholy, withdrawn look and her lips had tightened and lost their colour. She imagined herself looked at by a stranger for the first time, and decided that her face was drained of the vitality which shone out of Helen's young features. Sadly, she admitted that the young men had spoken the truth and nodded in agreement to her reflection in the glass.

17

When she returned to Moscow, Ella found a letter from 'Azov' asking if he could arrange an audience. She opened the envelope slowly. The letter failed to stir her feelings, and she realized that she was sinking into despondency. She was barren, her youth was over, her beauty dying, she was not allowed – by order of Pobedonostsev – to build her own school, church and hospital, without which she could accomplish little lasting good. She felt sorry for the Jews, for the assassinated, for herself, and loathed her powerlessness, for she knew that Nicky and Serge had made up their minds to limit her activities. She felt useless and empty and disregarded the letter.

Her despond lasted the whole autumn and into the next year, and was undisturbed by the murder of the Minister of the Interior, Sipyagin. His successor was announced – a man called V. K. Plehve. Ella had seen him for years at receptions, sidling about and giving the impression that he was determined to speak to Serge, who, to begin with, ignored him, but later received his advice with condescending politeness.

The week after his appointment was announced, Plehve came to Moscow and stayed at Ilonskoye for a weekend. She re-examined him and decided that her first impression was unchanged. He was ingratiating, but this did not make up for his sly, fat face and small eyes and a general air of insincerity which she found repulsive. He was polite – too polite – to her, and positively cringing to Serge.

At Ilonskoye, Serge told her he was delighted with the Tsar's new appointment. 'He is a man after my own heart who recognizes that those sections of the community behind the revolutionary movement should be purged and destroyed.'

When Ella asked whom he meant, he replied furiously, 'The Jews and Freemasons – they work hand in hand.'

Somehow Plehve stirred her out of her apathy and brought back her sense of guilt. How could the Tsar appoint such a creeping sycophant who had no beliefs beyond those which would conveniently advance his own career? She asked Serge how he could trust such a man. He angrily told her to wait and see and she would find out.

She found out in 1903, when Serge came back elated one evening and told her a pogrom had occurred in Kishinev: 'I think it has taught the Jews a lesson. The more who emigrate the better, and Kishinev – if they have any sense – will send them scuttling out of the country.'

At first, the papers reported the pogrom as a minor event, but as the weeks passed it was built up into an international incident by questions asked in the British Parliament and the American Senate. Journalists flocked to Bessarabia, and Serge blamed the fuss 'on that cursed paper *The Times*', which had stirred up the whole thing with lies. But Ella knew he was worried by reports that Nicky was embarrassed by the publicity, and Alix wrote indignantly that Victoria had made contact from London, asking, 'How can I defend Nicky against the unending stories of atrocities and killings reported in the London papers?'

One day, Serge flung an American paper in front of her. 'Look at the lies they tell!' he shouted.

It reported a mass meeting in New York City at Carnegie Hall on 27 May 1903, addressed by Grover Cleveland, an ex-president of the United States, who had made a measured attack on Russia's treatment of minorities, and pointed out that the United States was not guiltless, comparable violence on a smaller scale having the previous year been practised in Wyoming against the Chinese, while anti-Italian riots had occurred in Louisiana. Only a few sentences of the ex-President's speech were reported. The rest of the front page was covered by a sensational speech by Isidore Singer, claiming that a woman had had her breasts cut off and was later disfigured in a way not to be described, while a little girl of nine was torn into two pieces. A third girl, Shaga Sarah Panasky, had nails driven up her nostrils into her skull. To end the catalogue, he stated that a carpenter had been bound to a board and his own saw used to cut off his arms and legs. Ella put the paper down, unable to read such details.

'But it's not true?'

'No,' Serge said furiously. 'It is a gross exaggeration. They mention hundreds dead. Our information is that under fifty died. But it will soon blow over.'

It did not. The American press published letter after critical letter, and further large protest meetings took place in Louisiana and Philadelphia. The Tsar, fearful of unpopularity, was worried, but Serge stoutly maintained that the pogrom was a success.

Ella at last wrote a note to Anton, saying she would be grateful if he could tell her where she should have her broken violin mended. She felt now that she must know what was actually happening. A month later she received a long letter.

It is with great pleasure that I hear of your recovery. No day has passed without my praying to God that He would be merciful. But enough. I believe I am correct in understanding that you would like me to convey to you what has happened in the last few years, and since, at the time of writing, I am setting off to Paris, I am sending you a written estimate of the situation today.

At the moment, the Empire is filled with discontent. This is inexplicable to the Tsar and his family. He points out the advances made in Russia during his own and his father's lifetime; the extension of the railways, industrialization, the expanding economy and, despite the land problems, the quiescence of the peasants. Why, then, the Tsar asks, are the revolutionaries more active than ever? The answer must be an internal culprit. He looks around, and, with

207

Pobedonostsev at his shoulder, his eyes fix as usual upon the Jewish nation, who, it must be admitted, have since the establishment of the Bund in 1897/8 played an active part in industrial unrest and the organization of strikes for better wages. The Tsar, prevented by world opinion from carrying out what he calls 'the conclusive policy, genocide', has decided to put 'local pressures' on Jewish communities still outside the Pale in an attempt to force them to emigrate.

'Local pressure', you see, is the Imperial name for pogroms. Here I would like to explain that, since the beginning of history, kings and ministers responsible for the government of countries have again and again diverted attention from the unpopularity of their administration by working up a discontented populace either against an imaginary external enemy or against an unpopular minority within its boundries. This campaign at Kishinev is of especial interest in that it marks the repetition of a pattern of anti-semitic riots in Bessarabia, conceived by Pobedonostsev and intended to be enforced by V. K. Plehve, with the knowledge of the Grand Duke Serge and the compliance of the Emperor.

Repetitions of the pogrom at Kishinev will occur again in the coming years in Odessa and Kiev and other cities with large Jewish populations. In the case of Kishinev, the ground was prepared by attacks on Jews in a local paper which pandered to the jealousies of the indolent peasant and hardworking trader. A journalist called Khrushchevan, a disciple of Pobedonostsev, was the local instigator of the campaign, and his articles were clearly intended to create bitter antagonisms between the Russians and the Semites.

In 1902, the accusations changed from the general to the specific, and when, at Easter, the police discovered a murdered young Christian boy in a well, Khrushchevan distorted the facts in his article, declaring – uncontradicted by the local authorities – the young man to be a victim of Jewish ritual murder and warning every mother of the danger threatening their children. Again the authorities declined to contradict these fantasies. In the beginning of this year, when another man was found murdered, Khrushchevan declared the case to be a repetition of the previous year, and repeated that the murder of young Christians was an important part of Jewish ritual. His story was so blatantly untrue that he was forced to withdraw his accusation, but in such a manner as to leave behind the impression that his retraction was because of the power of Jewish financiers shielding their guilty brothers.

By now, feeling in the town was becoming dangerous and was added to by a death in the nearby town of Dubossory, where a broken-hearted Christian girl employed by a Jew took poison when she was deserted by her lover. She was taken to a local Jewish hospital, where, before dying, she told the police the reason for her attempted suicide and the guiltlessness of her employer. At her funeral, a government official pointed out how frequently Christian girls died before the Jewish Easter festival, and when the Chief Rabbi of Kishinev asked the Orthodox Bishop to deny such an untruth, he was met with a refusal.

It was now apparent that the pogrom was planned to begin at Easter, and during the preceding weeks, anti-semitic pamphlets which were circulated around the town showed Christ crowned with thorns and bore the message of God's punishment upon the iconoclasts. At the bottom of each poster was written clearly, 'Printed by the Committee of the Confessors of the Holy Synod at St Petersburg, 4 February 1903'. This encouraged doubtful peasants to believe that the persecution of the Jews was directed by the Holy Synod with the compliance of the Tsar.

Jewish citizens asked for and were given assurances that they would be protected in the event of riots.

Yet, on the night of 18 April, an unusual number of policemen appeared in the streets, telling questioners that their purpose was to prevent the entrance of vagrants from surrounding districts. Despite this assurance, all night long peasants entered the town. However, by now the Jewish population had regained their confidence, the first day of the Passover having passed without the threatened attack. The Chief Rabbi, however, was still nervous, and gave orders at the close of services throughout the town that the congregation should keep to their houses to avoid trouble. Such was their confidence that many Jews disregarded the advice and walked peaceably about the streets. They regretted their action when, at precisely midday, a number of boys between twelve and sixteen attacked isolated individuals, chased them to their houses and broke their windows with stones. At three o' clock, a number of men, all of them wearing red shirts, began to chant, 'Death to the Jews, beat the Jews.'

The crowd then split, obviously according to plan, into twenty-four divisions, to cover the twenty-four districts of the city, each group consisting of fifteen men. As they reached their allotted areas, they smashed open doors, stole all they could carry, beat any who dared to offer resistance and attacked and raped young women. At five o' clock a Jew was thrown out of a tram and beaten to death. Throughout all this tumult, the police remained inactive.

On Monday morning, the pogrom recommenced, and it is said, but not proven, that officials issued to the rioters axes, iron bars and clubs. In any case, the mob was in possession of new weapons and avoided the mistakes of the previous day when a Christian newspaper had been sacked.

When the Jews woke up, they found distinguishing marks on their doors and not one Christian's house was attacked when bands of men with carts arrived to take away furniture. The rioting continued. Jewish representatives visited the Governor, who pretended to give instructions to the inactive police. It had been stated in various papers that hundreds of Jews died. This is not the case. But forty-two innocent Jews lost their lives, while somewhere in the neighbourhood of seven hundred others suffered serious injuries. Stories of rape and deliberate torture have been verified, and at least six men and women went mad from fright or torture.

Thanks mainly to a reporter of the English *Times*, the riots aroused enormous interest throughout the world, and the officials could give no answer as to why the local police stood passively watching the rioting and murder. The consequent uproar has caused numerous journalists to visit the city, and while this has resulted in journalistic exaggeration, international pressures on the Tsar have caused him to appoint a new Governor of

Bessarabia, Prince Urosov, a man of courage and integrity. He has moved quickly and already a number of men have been arrested as criminals and put on trial. It is doubtful whether their sentences will be severe.

That is the situation at the moment, but the authorities remain far from having learned a lesson since identical preparatory steps to those which laid the foundations of the Kishinev riots are occurring in other cities. I can state with certainty that there will within the next two years be pogroms, financed with money from Pobedonostsev and circulated by the Union of Russian People, in the cities of Kiev, Odessa and other centres of Jewish population. Nor, as Pobedonostsev says, is 'the policy of Russification rusting', and other minorities, such as the Armenians, will receive the same treatment. The authorities are holding up their hands and saying that they are guiltless; that the riots express popular feeling. This is half-true, but the Holy Synod excited that feeling and planned the riots. Those who pretend innocence are compounding guilt by hypocrisy. I have told you the bald truth. Watch and observe whenever my prophesies are fulfilled.

The letter made Ella shudder, and, to her infinite distaste, Kishinev was for weeks the whole subject of conversation. Of course a number of Serge's friends said that it was one of the best things which had ever happened and that a few more displays of similar patriotism would increase the emigration figures. Serge would reply to such remarks with a smile, but Ella found it very difficult not to defend innocent people, although she knew that her arguments were dismissed. Her only recourse was to bite her tongue hard, which, her mother had told her years ago, was the best way to take your mind off an irritating argument.

Fashions fortunately change, and to Ella's relief Japan next became the object of interest. She had not forgotten the German Ambassador's speech at Miechen's picnic. Afterwards, Alix had told her, with surprise, how well Willy was behaving, which made her deeply suspicious since his actions had always been guided by his own interests. Both Alix and Nicky hated the Japanese because, when Nicky was as a boy on a world tour, a Japanese lunatic had tried to kill him. Ever since, he had referred to the nation as a collection of 'yellow monkeys', his description being accepted as the only way in which you could describe such ignorant little savages. She heard Serge say at dinner that the army and navy believed war to be inevitable. As usual, Ella could not understand the political arguments and why it was that, if Siberia was empty, Russia's frontiers must be extended. Trying to understand, she asked Serge to explain. After a moment's silence he told her to mind her own business, but added, as if it was an unanswerable argument, 'If the Tsar plays his cards right, China will in twenty years be reduced to a sphere of Russian influence.' Neither was she reassured to get one of Alix's staccato letters, full of abuse about Japan. And the same evening, as Serge was looking through his papers, he shouted at her: 'Certain reports say the yellow monkeys are planning to declare war on us without notice. How like the little devils. By the way, we have made contingency plans and the Emperor has decided that you should organize private resources to help provide the troops with clothing and food if war breaks out.'

Ella sat upright with delight. The idea of actually involving herself in something positive made her hope that war would be declared soon. At last she would then be able to do something practical and be something more that a useless chairwoman and 'poor visitor'. But then, on second thoughts, she hit her forehead as if to drive out the wicked idea that she should welcome the deaths of thousands of men merely to satisfy a selfish wish. All the same, she listened with increased interest to conversations, and found the commonest belief was regret that England, America and even their new ally, France, would never allow them to invade Japan, so the war could not last long.

A week later she went to stay in St Petersburg and found Alix pregnant again, this time more certain that she would have a son. Ella kissed her and asked Nicky about the possibility of war. She could not understand his incoherent reply, which blamed Germany, England and France. 'All I can say is that those yellow monkeys in Japan are asking for trouble, which they will certainly get if they insist on interfering with my plans.'

Ella was even more confused after dinner with Miechen. The British Ambassador told her that the crisis was the result of German meddling. 'I hope that both sides will agree to arbitration, and if not, in my view the wisest course is for you to keep Manchuria and leave them a free hand in Korea, for in the event of any other country entering the war on your behalf, the United Kingdom has a treaty to support Japan. The matter is serious. Restraint is essential.'

Alexis, on the other hand, roared: 'The time for talking has passed, and I can't wait for my ships to send their yellow fleet to the bottom of the sea, and then they will look damned silly with no way of supplying their troops.'

Shortly before Ella went to bed, the French Ambassador came up and stated: 'France is a loyal ally to the Empire and I hope war will be averted.'

Anxious for a clear answer, she asked why.

He made circles with his right hand and said: 'The Trans-Siberian Railway is not completed. The battlefield will be six thousand miles from St Petersburg, under a thousand from Japan,' and then he changed the subject.

Ella returned bewildered to Moscow, to find Serge confident and belligerent, organizing the transfer of rolling stock from the west to the east. He was furious and amazed when, on 6 February, Japan attacked Russian forces without any declaration of war, and then on 9 February sank the cruisers *Koriets* and *Varyaga* and attacked Port Arthur. The bad news was put down to treachery, but Ella was too busy to consider explanations and worked day and night, organizing the conversion of passenger into hospital trains and a large body of women of all classes into a working party to provide clothes, comfort and provisions for the troops going eastwards by train.

After the initial surprise the war appeared to hang fire without any serious exchanges. And then, on 12 April, Admiral Makarov's flagship hit a mine and sank with all aboard, except for five men, one of whom was miraculously Cyril. Alix wrote in her curious style:

Nicky thinks sinking disastrous. A good man, best of admirals. All will miss him.

But the serious land fighting did not begin until May, when the Japanese advanced in strength on Port Arthur.

Ella regretfully admitted that she had never been so happy since her marriage and enjoyed her defeat of Countess Kleinworth, who had tried to insist that aristocratic women ought to work in different rooms from the merchants' wives and daughters. She decided to allow no snobbery and arranged alphabetical seating to mix the classes up. Immediately the atmosphere was pleasanter and everybody got on well.

After six months, she had collected so many voluntary workers that every state room in the imperial private rooms at the Kremlin (except for the Throne Room) was being used to deal with enormous quantities of salted fish and food and to produce huge bales of bandages, disinfected dressings, boots, shoes, slippers, gloves, sleeping bags, ground sheets, thick socks, coats, underclothes. She even welcomed unskilled volunteers, to pack and tie up hundreds of boxes to help the soldiers at the front.

During the following months, everything seemed to start to go wrong and rumours began to get to Moscow of shortages of precisely those items which she had packed and sent off in enormous quantities. The first excuse was the gap in the railway line after Lake Baikal. But in the spring the lake was navigable by boats, so the excuse was dubious. Complaints increased. To Ella's amazement, even her new hospital trains complained of a shortage of blankets.

The reports were repeated in letters which arrived regularly from the front to her women. At first they expressed gratitude, but then regretted the small quantities arriving from Moscow, which puzzled Ella until a merchant's daughter, who had a brother in the army dealing with supplies, produced one of his letters which said that the last consignment of food and clothing, although correctly labelled, contained nothing but stones equalling the weight of their original content. In fact the only commodity which unfailingly arrived untouched was the canvas churches. By a coincidence, she received after luncheon the same day an unsigned note:

Your supplies are not leaving the station. Pay an unexpected call.

Ella felt the blood rising over her eyeballs, clouding her vision with red specks, and could neither move nor speak for a moment as she stood paralysed with anger. Who could be so despicable, so unspeakably vile as to steal the provisions, clothes and boots so desperately needed by men fighting for their Emperor?

A consignment had left early in the morning and would be at the station now. Without putting on a hat or coat, she sent for Sandra, who was in charge of the wool department, and drove to the station, where, paying not the slightest attention to the astonished guards, she walked on to the commandeered platforms.

The confusion was appalling. Piles of ammunition – boxes of rifles and machine guns and dismembered field guns – lay about without method or order. A few soldiers wandered around in pairs, rifles slung over their shoulders. One goods train stood with doors open, while navvies lackadaisically filled the trucks with what looked to Ella the lightest boxes they could find.

Only by threatening a fat major, who appeared wiping his moustaches and nearly fainted when she told him her name, was she able, after two hours, to find the originally neatly labelled boxes from the Kremlin, dispatched so proudly a few hours earlier. They lay littered over the floor in an unlocked sorting room, their holding ropes cut, their wooden tops broken open. She noticed, standing apart, four large wooden boxes criss-crossed with new planks and labelled 'Food Stuffs'.

'Open these,' she demanded of the major, stamping her foot with rage.

He stood with his mouth open, motionless.

'With this,' she said, seizing his sword and pulling it out of its scabbard. 'At once.'

Like a man in a dream, he did as he was told. The reopened cases were half-filled with sacks full of stones. That morning, she knew, they had contained barrels of salted herring and large cheeses.

Trembling with rage, she sent for the station commandant and paced up and down until the reply came he was ill. She asked for the second-in-command, and continued pacing. At that moment, two large doors opened from the street and a black-bearded man walked in, leading two large horses pulling an empty dray. When he took in the strange scene, he led the horses round in a circle and out of the door again.

'Stop him!' she shouted. But nobody moved. Again she stamped her foot in impotent rage, and as there was nothing else to do, paced furiously until another door opened and in came a young, good-looking colonel in blue uniform, who walked up to Ella, saluted and said he was the second-in-command and at her service.

She pointed to the packages and told him their original and present contents. Sensing sympathy, she asked him simply whether the station was in the hands of brigands? He pursed his lips and remained silent before sending, in a sharp voice, for two men, and telling the major he was excused. A pale young lieutenant arrived and nervously saluted, but listened with such glazed eyes to the colonel's questions that Ella did not believe he understood what was happening until an untidy captain bustled in, giving him courage. They both talked at once, appearing to tell the officer that they had only acted under orders, which made Ella even angrier and say she would tell her husband and ask for an inquiry.

The colonel spoke to her in his quiet voice for the first time. 'I would welcome an inquiry – it is high time. I have taken the liberty of sending for your coat. I see that it has arrived,' and, taking it from an orderly, he placed it over her shoulders. Moved by his kindness, Ella felt tired and allowed him to lead her to the waiting carriage.

Serge looked indignant when she told him her story, and said he would inquire into such a shocking matter, but when she told him how the young colonel had also said he would welcome an inquiry, she was surprised by his furious reaction.

From that day onwards, Ella insisted that her consignments were accompanied by a personal representative who demanded signatures for each numbered package. Another personally delivered all their packages to the hospital trains.

213

At the end of six weeks, Serge said calmly: 'An inquiry was held, but nothing could be proved.'

'But somebody must know,' Ella almost shouted at him. 'You can't open hundreds of crates without somebody seeing or noticing.'

Serge for once quietly agreed, and said he would make further inquiries, but after a month Ella realized she was going to learn nothing more. Still furious, she determined to find the traitorous thief herself, whether Serge helped or not.

She thought of 'Azov', whom she had not thanked for his 'Kishinev' letter. The matter had seemed irrelevant compared to the war. But now, once again, she needed his help and wrote a long letter explaining the scandal.

He replied by the next post, suggesting she called at the merchant Voronsky's house to ask his wife to organize a group of women to knit underwear for the soldiers at the front. She agreed, and wondered if he would have changed as much as herself. She could not have seen him for seven years! Ella smiled at the comedy of their meetings, first at Anton's house, where the poor little man had played the violin to convince his neighbours of the innocence of her visit; now in a merchant's palace in Moscow, where she was greeted by an exceedingly pretty woman of thirty with an olive skin and slanting, expressionless eyes, who led her into a richly decorated drawing room, where patterns of men's shirts and underclothes lay grotesquely draped on the blue velvet cushions. She asked Ella to select the most suitable patterns, which she guaranteed to produce in large numbers. Calmly, without embarrassment, they made their choice, and Ella wondered, not for the first time since the start of the war, whether the educated middle class were not only cleverer but more civilized and abler than the ruling class. She remembered how her mother had reached a similar conclusion in Hesse.

After the choice, Madame Voronsky led the way to a small library where 'Azov' was sitting writing letters. Certainly he was stouter, his jowl bigger, but, to her surprise, he looked at her with the same respectful adoration in his eyes. How stupid she was to be relieved, but she had not forgotten the pain and shock of the overheard conversation which had left her a lingering sadness, although her war work was transforming her character and giving her a strength she had never known. She looked at him without embarrassment or fear as he sat opposite her, thanked him for his note, told him the situation at the station and asked him who was the traitor responsible for such blatant robbery.

'My husband cannot find out, so I have come to you. Did you know this was going on? Do you know who is responsible?'

'Yes,' he said. 'Immediately you began to send by train large consignments of saleable goods, a percentage remained in Moscow. Now, about a third is retained and sold in the open markets. I did not believe it was my place to inform you of the details until I heard that the matter had been brought to your attention, when, to save time, I advised you to visit the war goods depot. Practically everyone in the station is doing well out of the enormous supply of freight going east. This includes the major and the commandant, who was made ill by fright at your discovery, but not the colonel you distrusted, who has since – as a penalty for honesty – been moved east himself. Without question, while

214

other intermediaries have and are making money out of the war, the chief beneficiary is your husband, the Grand Duke Serge.'

She stood up, holding hard on to the table, but as she felt the blood go out of her head, sat down quickly. At last she heard herself say in a mild, conversational tone: 'I don't believe it.'

He looked at her sadly. 'I can't prove it, but why would I lie to you? For many years, the Grand Duke, like his predecessors, has benefited from taxes on goods travelling east. The custom is continuing; it is as simple as that.'

'Oh,' she said, putting her hands over her eyes. 'He should be punished. He must know that stealing from the troops is the same as killing men.'

She pulled herself up, stopped talking and left, returning not to the Kremlin – she felt too ashamed and bitter – but to the Governor's Palace to think.

Clearly, she could say nothing. Serge would deny her accusation. How could she tell the Tsar and betray her own husband? She had known that he was evil, but not so tainted and rotten that he would steal badly needed supplies from men fighting for his own beliefs. She must be practical, let Serge know that she guessed the truth, in the hope that fear would curb his greed. That was something. Circumstances forbade more.

She carried out her plan, and Serge listened nervously and walked out of the room. That night, for the first time since her illness, she took a sleeping potion and dreamed of 'Azov' sitting at the round table, looking at her and gradually growing bigger and bigger until he burst, covering her with blood.

She woke up terrified that the shock of Serge's treachery had driven her back into her old nightmare world. But, after drinking a glass of hot milk, she started laughing at how ridiculous 'Azov' had looked as he swelled bigger and bigger, and immediately fell into a dreamless sleep.

Next day her original lady-in-waiting, Anna, who had married a Stroganov, asked if she was feeling ill. Ella shook her head and toured every room and department, encouraging her women to work harder, checking delays, praising, blaming, stimulating. At last, alone in the great building with no one to cajole, she sat late into the night, writing letters of thanks to her voluntary helpers outside the Kremlin, including Madame Voronsky. She returned to the Governor's Palace after midnight and went to bed without speaking to her husband.

The war continued, and when Ella visited St Petersburg, Nicky said the position was satisfactory. Yet while it was true that the Japanese had not taken Port Arthur, the imperial army had suffered heavy casualties at Chinchow, while the returning wounded in her Red Cross trains told stories of shortages and lack of ammunition and inefficiency.

Sandra picked up a newspaper one day and said: 'Oh dear, I suppose I am stupid, but I can't understand why we are fighting for the Liaotung Peninsula or Liaoyang, wherever they might be.'

Ella told her that she didn't think she was stupid. She had found, talking to soldiers in the hospitals, that not only had they not known what they were fighting for, but that they had not known where or who they were fighting, since they were given no maps and all the towns had incomprehensible names.

The battle of Shaho in August was claimed as another victory, but all that

Ella knew was that her hospital trains could not carry all the wounded and the field hospitals telegraphed for more tents. With each battle, whether it was called a victory or a tactical withdrawal, the returning wounded appeared to be more disillusioned and resentful of suffering for a cause they could not understand.

The news of the naval operations sounded bad as well, perhaps because it was impossible not to notice when ships disappeared. But still Port Arthur held out, and the Baltic Fleet sailed for the Far East in October, under the command of the nervous Admiral Rozhdestvensky. His nerve gave way immediately and disastrously off the Dogger Banks, when his majestic ironclads found themselves surrounded by a host of little ships. Believing every rumour, the Admiral decided he was under attack from Japanese submarines and opened fire on a fleet of little English fishing boats.

Luckily his men's aims were as wild as his judgement: only one vessel was sunk, but the action enraged British opinion and only an apology averted war. What could not be averted was the ridiculous aspect of a Russian admiral firing and missing fishing boats believed to be submarines. The whole European liberal press laughed at the Tsar and his navy. Leading articles asked what route the Admiral conceived the submarines had taken. Had they gone through the Suez Canal? How had they powered themselves for 15,000 miles? How maintained their disguise?

Alix was furious at the laughter and wrote that it hurt Nicky's feelings more than the loss of any battle in the war. But worse was to come: Port Arthur unexpectedly surrendered on 2 January.

Ella was spending New Year with Nicky and Alix, who appeared to be the only people in Russia not overwhelmed by dismay. Both took the catastrophe so calmly that Ella wondered whether reality existed for them beyond the nursery walls and their obsession with the new baby boy, Alexis. Alix feasted her eyes on him, and they both stared at the child, like peasants at an icon. Even Serge noticed Nicky's carelessness, saying, 'I don't think he cares a damn what happens to the Empire so long as that bloody little boy is all right.'

Before returning, they spent one night with Vladimir and Miechen, again to Alix's extreme annoyance. Ella noticed for the first time an unexpected side to her brother-in-law's character: a passionate love of Russia. His eyes filled with tears as he said: 'The fall of Port Arthur was a stab in my heart, and due entirely to the appointment of that brainless coward, General Stoessel, as Commander of the fortress.'

He told her of his agony at the conduct of the war.

'If Nicky was going to fight, he should have waited another year or two until the Trans-Siberian Railway was completed. But what could have been greater folly than dividing the command? Admiral Alexeyev knows nothing of land fighting, and anyhow is over sixty, while Kuropatkin has been a paper soldier for years. Both men hate each other, and their only qualification was and is that neither of them has ever contradicted Nicky. So it's not surprising if the whole conduct of the war has been a shambles, and it nearly kills me seeing that Nicky cares more whether his wretched little son has a cold than if Port Arthur falls.'

He sat looking at Ella and without eating a mouthful.

'I don't know why, but I am going to confide in you. You cannot imagine what an agony my life has been. I had to watch an elder brother, who was an idiot, make every mistake under the sun, and now I have to watch his nephew, who is half the man his father was, let the Empire fall to pieces under his hands. You have no idea what a terrible fate it was to have been for years the heir to two simpletons. Can you wonder I gambled, can you wonder I drank? But enough. We can only pray that the Baltic Fleet will win a miraculous victory in the China Sea. Though imagine sending out Rozhdestvensky, who is frightened of a mouse. Bring me some more brandy!'

Ella had never realised the sensitivity and patriotism hidden behind Vladimir's loud voice and overbearing manner, and thought it a pity he was not the Tsar.

Before she left, Vladimir said: 'Ella, I am fond of you now, and I think you should prepare for Serge's resignation. He has persuaded himself that the answer to our inefficiency in Japan is the iron hand and the Russification or destruction of the minorities. Nicky agrees, but has not the courage to enforce his beliefs, and Serge says he will have his way. I can't see either of them giving in.'

Ella's first reaction was selfishly to wonder whether she would have to give up her war work. Perhaps Vladimir was wrong: it was no good getting unnecessarily alarmed. Serge had talked of retiring for years. A week later he resigned.

Ella was horrified. She was pleased to move to the Nikolai Palace, but who would manage her Red Cross trains and her band of helpers in the Kremlin? If she was not there, who would check the treatment of the wounded in the hospitals? She had no conceit, but she knew that, for at least six months, she would be irreplaceable. Nicky wrote and asked her to stay on for the moment, adding:

I have written to Serge regretting his decision and assuring him I fully understand his position. After fourteen years of unceasing work it will take him several months to wind up his affairs.

Anxiously, she looked around to see if she could find a replacement, and on 5 February wrote to Nicky:

I think I have found the ideal person, of whom I am sure you will approve. At the moment she has not obtained her husband's agreements. I am sure you will agree it is wiser not to mention her name. Meanwhile, I am only too happy to carry on, especially as Serge says it will take weeks to collect his papers together.

Ella was touched by the number of her 'women' and nurses who begged her, with tears in their eyes, to stay, and was glad to be able to tell them that she would not be leaving yet.

18

February the 17th, 1905, was a busy day. In the morning, she spent an hour at the Red Cross headquarters, examining the position of the hospital trains on their long journey back from the war. Afterwards she visited, for the remainder of the morning, a series of rich merchants to try and raise the money needed to keep the hospital trains and tent hospitals fully equipped with the most modern drugs and equipment. A large luncheon for the same purpose followed, and again the generosity of her guests, some of whom had travelled a thousand miles, exceeded her expectations.

At 3.30 she planned to visit her chamberlain's wife, 'Beta' Mengden, who was ill in hospital. In the few minutes between her engagements, as she sat, unusually smartly dressed and bejewelled, writing to a rich merchant of Odessa a letter of thanks for his generous contribution, the sudden rattling of an explosion shook the windows. Standing up, she felt her heart twice change its beat. She knew that Serge was dead.

She stood motionless before deliberately placing her crystal and gold pen down on an enamelled holder and walking across the room to kneel before a gilded marble-topped table, in the centre of which stood a silver cross bearing an ivory carving of the Agony of Christ. She was infinitely touched by the figure's suffering and prayed for courage and strength to live through the coming days. As she knelt, she ran the curved ends of her long, white fingers over the ivory, receiving consolation and hope that her prayer would be answered. Crossing herself, she rose to her feet as the blood started to run again through her veins. She was about to move away from the table when a thought struck her. Putting her hand to her throat, she unclasped her choker of four rows of matching pearls and laid them on the table before the crucifix. On the necklace, she placed her engagement ring, a clasp of pearls set with diamonds, and a Fabergé gold and enamel watch which had, for many years, hung from her neck on a golden chain.

The little collection made an ostentatious, gleaming pile. She paused and thought, her fingers on her lips, before picking up the jewels and stowing them away in the back of a drawer. Opening a cupboard, she selected a coat, threw it over her shoulders, walked out of the room, and slowly down the great staircase, holding on to the wooden bannister of the iron railings.

The hall was crowded with silent servants in various states of dress and undress, staring vacantly up at her. Heedless, she walked towards the front door, which the dazed doorman, his teeth chattering with fright, hurriedly flung open, and walked down the steps, followed by young Marie's fluttering French governess, Mademoiselle Hélène, wearing a man's overcoat.

Before they had sat down in the sleigh, the driver cracked his whip and the horse dashed off at full speed, turned to the left beyond the steeple of St John. Mademoiselle Hélène, clasping and unclasping her hands, murmured in dismay that she had not put on a hat. Ella, hatless, turned vacant eyes, half-smiled but said nothing. As the horse galloped along in the rutted snow, the sledge bumped up and down, throwing the two women together.

After driving for two minutes, they arrived at the Spassky Gate. Outside it lay the shattered remnants of her husband. The immediate area of the vast square had already been turned by the crowd, standing in a silent circle, into a theatre of death. One horse lay dead. Another stood quietly bleeding, on three legs, nudging at the snow with his nose, hoping to find grass. A few yards off the coachman lay face downwards on the ground, both his legs at eccentric angles as he scratched at the snow with bloody, gloved hands.

Ella stepped out, her face still impassive, and examined, without visible emotion, the relics of the blood-stained area. She looked about as if searching for something which she eventually found, as two soldiers ran out of the Spassky Gate, carrying an army stretcher. She told them where to put it down and walked on to the snow, gaped at by the crowd detained by the excitement of the tragedy. A leg of her husband lay twenty yards off, driven by the force of the explosion into the snow. Tugging it out, she covered her hands and dress with warm blood.

For perhaps half an hour, she searched minutely, in dead silence, until she had picked up every visible piece of the man whom she had married twenty years earlier, and gently laid them on the stretcher. When she had finished, her skin was pale, her lips tightly compressed, while her auburn hair had fallen, dishevelled, over her face.

Nothing could detract from her beauty, which made the crowd, now a stolid mass, sway and emit sighs of sympathy and admiration. She spoke only once to General Lamey, her late husband's secretary, asking him to go back to the Palace and tell the children to stay inside and in no circumstances to look out of the windows.

Having examined the snow to see whether any part of Serge remained uncollected, she covered the remains with soldiers' overcoats and ordered the stretcher to be carried to the chapel of the Monastery of the Miracle, next door to her Palace. She walked slowly behind, her head upright, moving with extraordinary grace and followed by the shuffling, lamenting crowd.

The soldiers laid their burden at the foot of the altar, ignoring a boot which protruded from under the coats and dripped blood on to the white stone floor. With a composed air, Ella sent for her nephew and niece, ordered that the service should begin when they arrived, and herself sank to her knees beside the litter, her mauve dress gleaming brightly in the light of candles hurriedly lit by trembling priests.

A little later, Dimitri, now fourteen, and Marie, fifteen, both white-faced and trembling, came hurriedly into the church and sat down in the front pew. Ella made a sign and the priest began his quavering chant without music. The responses sounded in rough, discordant voices from all parts of the chapel as the crowd, increased by the addition of the household of the Grand Duke, knelt without coats on the cold floor.

At the end of the service, the congregation rose in silence, all eyes watching Ella with the excited interest common to observers of death or tragedy. As she stood up, she stumbled, and the new Governor of Moscow moved forward quickly to give her his arm. She walked slowly towards the door, only stopping when the children moved slowly towards her. Holding out her hand, she said simply: 'He loved you both,' and, shocked, repeated the phrase again and again.

The mourners drew closer round as she stood repeating the phrase, and gasped with fascinated horror as they saw the blood on her mauve silk dress, and the flesh in the nails of her left hand, which still grasped the medals blown off his chest. Nobody knew what to do. The crowd stood spellbound. At last the children moved to either side of their aunt and, each taking an arm, guided her back to the Palace and slowly upstairs to her bedroom.

As the bedroom door closed behind them, Ella fell back into an armchair and closed her eyes, quickly opening them again as she called for telegraph forms to send to her near relations. To her stunned mind, the house seemed full of whispering, as if all the people who had ever lived there were telling each other of the sad event. She wished she could think of some practical action to avoid sitting, hopelessly inactive. She thought of the tragedy, remembered the injured coachman and asked if he was dead. Words ran to and fro until the answer came back that he was in hospital.

'Order my sleigh,' she said. 'I will go to him.'

As she drove towards the hospital, she tried to think rationally, but gave up the attempt, finding that her mind was out of control, working in jerks, presenting pictures of the past which came and went without cause or reason. At the hospital, the President of the Board was waiting, flustered and important in a top hat, to present her to Chiefs of Departments. She forced herself to give a brief, embracing smile before asking impatiently to be taken to the coachman's bedside.

The old man, who had served her husband for twenty years and earlier worked for his father, lay, his skin the grey-white, ebbing colour of death. She put her hand on his forehead and took it away again quickly when she noticed her own bloodstained fingernails. Slowly, he opened his eyes and looked weakly at her.

'How is His. . .' he began very slowly, when she interrupted, easing his last moments.

'Oh, quite all right. He sent me to see how you are,' and she gently made the sign of the cross over his forehead.

The man closed his eyes and he mumbled words suggesting relief.

She stood back – there was nothing else to do – and returned to the Palace to give orders that they would dine as usual at eight o' clock. Her nephew and niece should change; she would not. It seemed to her that, in wearing the dress still besmirched with blood, she was retaining a contact with her husband which she had never had during his lifetime. She looked at her hands, changed her mind, took a hot bath and ordered her clothes and shoes to be burnt.

The children ate little, she nothing. After dinner, she began to open a pile of telegrams and told her secretary to send replies. Once she had finished, she climbed up to the children's rooms. They sat on either side of a big wooden table, and she could tell by their embarrassed looks that they had been talking of what was going to happen to them now their uncle was dead. She felt it her duty to ease their worries and, speaking with an effort which she tried not to show, told them how her husband had regarded them as beloved consolations for the children he had never had, continuing, in a tone of voice which she hoped expressed love, to assure them that she would now devote herself to their education.

'This being the case, it is time for you, Marie, to go to bed,' and added, smiling, 'But before you do, we will all pray together for your uncle's soul.'

After she had kissed Marie goodnight, she sat talking to Dimitri and told him how difficult it was for a childless woman not to be jealous, and how consequently, she had not been as nice to them as she should have been. Now that Serge was dead, she would try to be a kinder and better aunt. The boy nodded gravely without speaking and before bursting into tears. She was disconcerted, and could think of nothing else to say except goodnight. An hour later, she looked into their bedrooms. Both lay sleeping soundly, with peaceful looks on their faces.

Having stood looking at Marie and wondering whether she could ever like her, Ella walked downstairs to her own dressing-room, opened her cupboard and took out a thick black velvet cape, a black hat and veil. Waking the sleeping night porter, who jumped as if he had seen a ghost, she then left the Palace and walked to the monastery next door. In the chapel, she found, to her relief, that the stretcher, with its saturated coats, had been replaced by a coffin. She forced herself to look over the side and saw that while the remnants of Serge's face were sheltered by white muslin, the rest of the body was covered by a square of gold brocade. Four soldiers stood at the ends of the coffin, their fixed, trembling bayonets catching the light of hundreds of flickering candles, their eyes rolling with fear at the apparition in black. Disregarding them, she knelt against the altar rail of a side-chapel and asked God to forgive her sins.

Without bitterness she remembered her past life, her youth, the sad story of her twenty married years and how suffering had given her the strength of character to go through in frozen silence, without a tear, the terrible task of collecting the pieces of her husband from the snow. Was she an unnatural, sinful woman to feel no regret at the death of a man who had become unendurable to her? Was she wrong in believing that by retiring from the world and devoting herself with humility to the services of the sick and poor, she could ameliorate the guilt of having shared without protest the life of a cruel and evil man?

Without warning, an idea leapt into her mind. Was Serge's death her fault? Could she, in error, have spoken inflammatory words that might have encouraged his assassins? She was able to think of nothing. The only time when she had expressed horror and distaste was to 'Azov', after she discovered that

Serge was selling her war supplies. 'Azov' was a trusted member of the security force. Was she not guilty, rather, of never having criticized her husband? God alone could tell. Yet, as she knelt at the altar to pray that Serge was in God's merciful hands, she looked at herself dispassionately and decided she was a weak, not a bad woman, who should have had the courage to leave her husband nineteen years before.

Part Four
1905–1918

1

Despite having stayed in the chapel, praying for her husband's soul until she heard the clock strike four, Ella woke up with a start at eight o'clock, thinking of 'Azov'. She remembered, with an unusual distinctness, the way he had looked at her when she was angry with Serge for taking the stores meant to go east to the troops. Had she said then that no one was fit to live who could behave in such a way? She racked her brains, but could not remember her exact words. The uneasiness remained. What if 'Azov' were a traitor? Had he looked at her in a curious way as he asked, 'Do you mean what you say?' At the time, she was too angry to notice his question. Thinking back, she was aghast. Could he have understood that she thought Serge unfit to live?

Too worried to stay in bed, she walked backwards and forwards before deciding to get dressed and find 'Azov'. She changed her mind again: what if he admitted connivance? How could she look at and talk to the man responsible for the death of her husband? Thoughts jumped about in her head: she must be brave and face the truth and go to see her husband's murderer, Kaliaev, in prison.

She rang the bell, ordered her carriage and arranged for Count Mengdon to inform the Prison Governor that she would be arriving at the fortress at 9.30 and wished immediately to see the assassin alone. Her maid, trembling with fear, went down on her knees, begging her not to go. The man would murder her; he was a madman. Ella quietly told her to do as she was told.

On arrival at the prison, she found the Governor, looking embarrassed, wearing a long overcoat, and guessed from his face that he had hurriedly put it on over his underclothes. He tried to persuade her that the visit was both incomprehensible and dangerous, and might cause unfortunate misinterpretations, but if she insisted on refusing his advice, he could assure her that soldiers would be at hand to come immediately to her aid. She smiled, ignored his advice and asked to be led to the cell. With reluctance, he summoned the Chief Warder, who led her down dark passages, past countless iron doors with peep-holes, and at last opened a door, holding above his head a lantern to light a dank, dark cell. Apart from this, the only light in the room came through a grating half-obscured by dirty glass set in the immensely thick stone walls close to the ceiling. A man, lying on an iron bed in the corner with his back to her, turned and half sat up, blinking in the yellow lantern light. She could see that he

225

was under normal size, with delicate hands and a thin white face darkened by the shadow of a beard. Everything about him was peaceful and gentle, except for his eyes, deep-set in his head, which made him look like an unshaven skeleton.

He spoke first and asked her, forcing violence into his voice: 'Who are you? What do you want?'

She answered in what she hoped was a gentle tone: 'I am the wife of the man you killed yesterday. Why did you do it?'

Kaliaev at once poured forth passionate words about liberty, democracy, the rights of all men to be equal, the tyranny of the Tsar and the cruelty of her husband's rule in Moscow. She remained silent, examining him with care. There appeared to be nothing even faintly Semitic in his appearance.

'Are you a freemason?' she heard herself asking.

'No, why should I be? Tell me what you want. I am a Democrat and . . .' he repeated his earlier diatribe against the Romanovs.

He began to shiver before he had finished talking and she could see how it was only with a great effort that he was keeping himself under control. She could not help thinking that there was a nobility in his appearance and behaviour. He showed no fear, declined to abase himself, apologize or ask for mercy, and clearly he believed in his own mad ideals. Reluctantly, she found herself admiring the man. Speaking very slowly she then asked: 'Have you ever heard of "Azov"?'

'Azov?' he said, in a voice expressing such unrehearsed surprise that she knew he was telling the truth.

'Yes, Azov.'

'Azov? I have never heard of anyone of that name.'

'It may not be his right name,' she mumbled in confusion, 'but it is a name something like it. He is short, thick-set, forty to fifty, sallow-skinned with a black moustache. I pray you, tell me if you have ever heard of him.'

'Azov?' he said again. 'And yet you describe Azev. If that's who you mean, he is a traitor to our society and it would be my duty to do to him as I did to your husband. Why do you ask?'

'Oh, it doesn't matter.' The words rushed out with relief. She had heard what she wanted. She stood, feeling silly and inadequate, wondering how quickly she could leave, and added, without thinking: 'Is there anything I can do for you?'

He looked at her as if she were mad, and she felt she would like to have eaten her words and was glad no one had heard them. But what an idiot he must think her, coming to see him and making such fatuous remarks! All she wanted to do now was to get away from this man, who sat on his iron bed and stared at her in surprise.

Gathering her wits together, she said: 'May God forgive you and make you realize that all you believe in may not be good.' She looked in her bag, took out a holy miniature, pushed it at him, opened the door and ran out of the cell, nearly falling over a posse of kneeling soldiers armed with thick wooden truncheons. Now it was her turn to shiver and shake all the way home, but she was filled with an enormous relief that Kaliaev was as much Azev's enemy as her late husband's. What a fool she had made of herself.

226

The next morning, Ella considered her spontaneous action and changed her mind. She had done the right thing. Without questioning Serge's murderer, she would have been haunted for ever by the lingering doubt that unwittingly, by stupid thoughtless words spoken in outraged anger, she had unintentionally brought about her husband's death. Kaliaev's angry words that he would like to kill Azev filled her with relief and joy. She thanked God that she could begin her new life without a shadow from the past perpetually hanging over her future.

2

After the funeral, Ella collected all her jewels together and placed them on her bed. Then she made four piles: one for Marie, one for Dimitri, one to sell and one to return to the Tsar. The task completed, without a wince of regret she told her maid, who burst into tears, to make four parcels. Two, the children's, the maid was to take to the bank to remain there until they attained their majority; the third, mainly heirlooms, was to be given to an imperial courier with orders to convey it to the Tsar at Peterhof; and the fourth, and largest, she would sell, but to whom? After some hesitation, she sat down and wrote a letter to Ivan Blok, explaining her plan of withdrawal from the world, and saying that she hoped he would excuse her writing, but that since she was always helpless in financial matters, she knew that if she disposed of her remaining jewels, they would make an inadequate price. Her reason for the tiresome request was that the proceeds would be devoted to the poor of Moscow. Could she place the matter in his hands? Two days later, she received a reply sympathizing with the Grand Duchess in her great sorrow, and assuring her the correspondent was honoured by her letter and would do everything in his power to ensure she received a fair price.

A few weeks afterwards, she received an enormous cheque for the jewels, over double the valuation which Fabergé had placed on them. She thanked Ivan Blok profusely and asked him if he would do her one other service. Her life's desire was to establish a convent, a school, an orphanage, hospital departments and an emergency station on the other side of the river, and herself a new sisterhood of dedicated women to look after and succour the poor. A month later, he replied that he had bought her a large block of land on the southern bar of the River Moskva, along the Great Ordynka.

> The price is reasonable and would only take up a fraction of the money brought in by the sale of your jewels, and you should have more than enough money left to complete all the building you mentioned. I will be pleased to help you at any time.

Despite this good beginning, Ella knew that two impediments stood in the way of her turning her dream into reality. Neither would be necessarily easy to overcome, and both might hold up her plans.

The first was the attitude of the Holy Synod, for although Nicky was said to be tired of Pobedonostsev, she knew that feeling ran strongly against the creation of a sisterhood of active, working nuns, dedicating themselves to mixing with and saving the souls of the poorest, most savage sections of the communities who lived, starved and often died, in the slums. The idea of women exposing themselves to squalor still appalled the old-fashioned, who, she knew, would fight to the last ditch to keep pure women in their proper place: in convents or nunneries. She was prepared for a long and tedious battle, and her chief consolation was the promised support of Nicky and her belief she would be able to persuade him to overcome opposition by his reluctant use of his authority.

The second obstacle was her guardianship of her niece and nephew, who were still only fifteen and fourteen. How could she retire from the world until they were established in life? Dimitri, although only fourteen, was the lesser problem. He was about to begin his military career, and as Nicky loved him like a son, he spent a large part of his holidays in Peterhof. Marie, although a year older, was a greater problem. She had the power to delay all Ella's plans. What was to be done? Ella had bitterly resented Serge agreeing that the children should live with them after his brother Paul's morganatic marriage, when he was forced by Nicky to live abroad. At the time, she had realized how her resentment of his decision had given Serge a twisted pleasure, and this had made her, despite every effort, dislike the children. From the beginning, her husband's behaviour had added to her dislike. He would talk to both in kind, affectionate tones which he never used with her, and while he punished them himself, he delighted in overruling her punishments and taking their side. His behaviour added to her antipathy, which, she admitted, was wrong, strove against and was unable to overcome.

Gradually, she began to like Dimitri; he was gay and charming, good-looking and wished to please. Marie was another matter. She was a rather plain, graceless girl, shy and gauche, difficult to teach, often sulky and cold. Worse, she would sometimes look sentimental and gaze at Ella before coming out with some unexpected embarrassing compliment, such as, 'Oh, Aunt Ella, you are looking beautiful tonight!' spoken in such a sickly, vulgar way that Ella had no alternative to crushing such bad taste by telling her sharply: 'Please do not make personal remarks.'

Afterwards when she blamed herself for her unkindness, she realized that her cold anger was caused by the knowledge that no daughter of her own would have made such a remark, or, if she had, would have put it in a different way. Even if she was unpleasant and unfair to the girl, it was only because she felt certain that Marie was stupid, shallow and sly. After seeing the children's sorrow at Serge's death, she had felt guilty and made overtures to Marie, which the girl had sulkily refused. Ella soon gave up trying, her dislike returning, her annoyance increased by her fear of the maddening consequences should Marie obstinately refuse to marry soon, for as long as the girl remained under her charge, there would be no hope of Nicky overruling the Synod. The girl had it in her power to delay for years all her plans and designs. Ella wondered at what age Marie could marry. Certainly, fifteen was too young. Ducky had married at sixteen, and Missy when she was only seventeen, and she remembered with pleasure Mary of Coburg saying how princesses should marry early. She did not wish to be accused of pushing the child off, but there was no doubt that it was perfectly normal for girls to make early engagements and marry when they were seventeen. She could write to both Victoria and Irene, who relished match-making, and ask them to make a list of suitable young men. The decision left her feeling uneasy, but she indignantly pushed her doubts aside. She knew that her ambitious ideas would help towards emancipation of women in Russia and would draw attention to the thousands of poor who lived in the criminal slums of the city. Such plans were of greater importance than the problem of when a tiresome girl married.

Her mind made up, she wrote to her sisters and left for England to study the rules of various Anglican convents, whose working lives she hoped her sisters would emulate in Moscow. During the journey, she repeatedly tried to read Russian, Italian and Spanish books which dealt with the faith and history of the many branches of the Catholic Church. She found the endless hair-splitting and religious beliefs impossible either to understand or to wish to understand, and although the outlook of the majority of orders was far less narrow than the restrictions imposed by the Greek and Russian Orthodox Churches, she found their concentration on meditation and continual prayer at variance with her own idea of practically working for God, and so abandoned all attempts at imitation, excepting the Poor Clares, whose work over the centuries she found both practical and touching.

On her return from England, she was told that current unrest had encouraged the Holy Synod to try and persuade the Tsar that her religious plans were revolutionary and undermined the Tsar's position as head of the Church. It was disappointing and unfair; all she wished for was to collect together a number of women of all classes who were willing to give up a worldly life to alleviate the terrible results of poverty, the very cause of the revolutionary dissatisfaction. It was true that she did not want to be tied by stringent strings to the orders of the Holy Synod, who believed that women should be sheltered and remain ignorant of the crime and disease which inevitably sprang from poverty and slum life. She wished for her sisters to be able to devote themselves to all work, face all tasks, however daunting, and by facing and trying to alleviate the sad lives of the poor, to bring them into closer contact with God.

She realized now that Nicky's original support was waning and noticed he went out of his way to avoid meeting her. Then there arrived a message from Alix, asking her to come to Tsarskoye Selo. When she arrived, her sister started the conversation by regretting that Ella had given so many jewels to Dimitri and Marie, and not returned them to Nicky to give to his own daughters. But what worried her even more, she continued, was that she had heard rumours of her sister planning to establish a convent outside the accepted traditions of the Holy Synod.

'Please, Ella,' she said stiffly, 'change your mind. Nicky is worried in these terrible times – when his authority is attacked from all quarters – about coming into conflict with Orthodoxy.'

Ella had quietly asked Alix whether she realized that all she wanted to do was to carry out her mother's beliefs, which Alix had always agreed with, and surely nothing could be wrong with that. The reply flustered her sister, who changed the subject, but when, at lunch, Ella noticed how Nicky was avoiding her eyes and looking down at his plate even when talking about little Alexis, she knew that his early promises of support meant little and she was facing a long and difficult tussle. She continued to search for a Christian sisterhood with rules that she could adopt and which would be acceptable to Orthodoxy.

In February 1906, she realized that she had been a widow for a year and that her plans, about which she endlessly thought, were so far nothing more than drawings on paper. She tried to discuss the matter with Miechen, who frankly said that she wasn't interested and told Ella sharply that, while she had been selfishly concentrating on her own future, the Tsar's position was being threatened by events which she had not bothered to notice or understand. Had Ella forgotten how, in the previous June, the crew of the battleship *Potempkin* had mutinied, while the Russian fleet was destroyed by the Japanese in the Far East, and in December Russia had ceded Port Arthur? During the winter, a strike in St Petersburg was only squashed by troops, and now, in the New Year, riots and rick burning were occurring all over Russia. There had been pogroms in Kiev and Odessa, and the Tsar had been forced, by public opinion and the disloyalty of the Grand Duke Nicholas Nikolaevitch, to establish a Duma or Parliament which was to meet for the first time in St Petersburg in May. When all this was happening, how should Ella, she asked sarcastically, expect Nicky – or, indeed, anyone else – to bother about her plans?

The defeats which Miechen mentioned worried Ella less than the tiresome problem of Marie. Ella had received replies from both Victoria and Irene on the subject of her marriage. Victoria's letter was annoying, reminding Ella that they had both, as children, decided that girls ought to be allowed to marry whom they liked, and surely, anyhow, Marie was too young and backward to be married yet. Irene, on the other hand, answered twice, saying the first time that she would look round carefully and let Ella know more soon. A month later, she wrote again to say that she had made progress and had in mind a young man whom she thought would be suitable, Prince William of Sweden, the second son of the Crown Prince. Surely, however, before he paid his respects to Marie, she should be presented in society, since otherwise would there not be talk of her being married out of the nursery? Ella thought this good advice, and by good fortune knew the answer, for she had heard the old Grand Duchess Constantine was giving a ball for her granddaughter at Pavlosk and knew, the Duchess being famously mean, that if she offered to pay half the costs, Marie could certainly share the ball with her granddaughter. As soon as she made the proposal, she knew that her calculation had been right by the look of pleasure which passed over the Grand Duchess's face. She must have seen Ella notice, for she put on a pious expression and said: 'Of course, I will be only too pleased to help the poor child. After all, she has been motherless since she was a baby, and was abandoned by her father.'

To Ella's surprise, Marie, although only sixteen, appeared to be transformed at the ball. Her sulky look vanished. She spent the evening dancing and laughing and was positively snowed under by favours, which made Ella decide that it would be wise to refuse any future invitations on her behalf until she was officially engaged.

After their return to Moscow, Ella found waiting for her a third letter from Irene, saying that William of Sweden was having second thoughts and wished to see photographs of his intended bride. Ella sent for the most fashionable photographer – the portraits needed to be flattering – and watched to make sure that Marie put on a pleasant expression. To begin with, the tiresome girl posed sullenly, holding a bouquet of flowers as if it were a hedgehog. Ella saw that this would never do, and brought the subject round to the party at Pavlosk and how pleased she was to see Marie being given so many favours and how well she danced. At once the girl's face lit up, her whole expression changed, and within ten minutes Ella was sure that enough satisfactory photographs had been taken.

She was right. They duly pleased William, who arrived a few weeks later. He was an exceedingly tall, thin young man, with a melancholy expression, a stoop and the narrowest shoulders which Ella had ever seen, though she consoled herself by noticing that he had beautiful eyes. He seldom spoke, but if he did his voice was gentle and depressed. He never invited conversation, and when she spoke to him, he took a long time to reply and never smiled. Ella realized that he was primarily interested in Marie's money, but this, she told herself, was a good thing, since he would not dare fall out with Marie, to whom she was prepared to give a generous dowry.

She had spoken only vaguely to Marie about William's arrival, without implying that he was in any way to do with her future, telling her only to dress up in her best clothes and come down to tea. Marie, Ella realized, had definitely changed since her success at the ball, and she stared at William quite openly, with a look of puzzled interest on her face. Neither of them said a word, and the wretched Prince spent most of his time gazing down his nose, so that Ella became afraid that Marie might not have noticed his beautiful eyes.

To Ella's relief, he told her later in the evening that if the preliminaries could be arranged – by which he meant that if Marie received a large dowry – he would be honoured to ask for her hand. She kissed the Prince and almost ran off to her niece, who turned pale at the unexpected news. Ella looked at her shocked face, felt guilty and told her niece that she only desired her happiness and she could think the matter over.

A few days later, Marie developed a high fever, which made the doctor insist she should stay in bed. Dimitri was sent to bed as well when he said that his sister's illness was caused by her fear of having to marry the Swede. The illness was embarrassing, for William obviously longed to have a definite answer to allow him to go home. Luckily Victoria, who was staying, had changed her mind, and now agreed that William would be a suitable bridegroom and that the sick girl was well enough to make up her mind. Ella explained to Marie that William could not be kept waiting any longer, and that she must realize that if she did not marry, she would have to live alone once Dimitri had entered his military college. The news appeared to upset the girl, but, to Ella's annoyance, she said at last that while she might accept the proposal, she would not marry until she was eighteen in 1908, and then only with her father's agreement. This was embarrassing, and Ella then had to explain that when Marie's father abandoned his children, the Tsar had taken parental responsibility out of his hands, and after Serge's death, had made Paul's children her wards.

Sensing that her niece's resistance was weakening, Ella asked before leaving: 'Can William come and ask you for your hand tomorrow?'

Marie paused a moment, turned her head away and said, 'Yes,' in a resigned voice. Delighted, Ella kissed her and went away, a weight off her mind, and told William to go and propose without delay.

He was accepted. After dinner, when Ella went to offer her congratulations to her niece, the girl annoyed her again by insisting that, whatever the Tsar said, she would not marry without her father's permission. A few weeks later, Paul wrote to sat that while he reluctantly agreed to the engagement, his daughter was too young to marry and should wait until she was eighteen. To Ella's further irritation, she received a letter the next day from Marie's grandfather, the King of Greece, who also wrote that in his opinion the marriage should not be rushed. Ella found such delays exasperating, but could only agree, and the marriage was arranged for the spring of 1908.

Frustrated but relieved, Ella thought that now the girl would definitely be out of the way in eighteen months, and she could turn her undivided attention to persuading the Holy Synod to agree to her plans. The matter was not, however, as easily settled as she had hoped, for, when William came again to Moscow, he and Marie had nothing whatever to say to each other and the already limited enthusiasm she had for him had waned. After this unsuccessful visit, Marie went to St Petersburg to see Nicky, which worried Ella, who made Miechen promise not to give a dance for her, though she could not refuse to allow her to go to the lunches and dinners which her sister-in-law incessantly gave, and where Marie would meet all sorts of unsuitable young men.

While her niece was away, Ella decided to undergo a minor operation, which, the doctors said, she could have in her own home and then be well again in a few days. She wrote to Marie, telling her the news. Unfortunately, the letter remained unposted and was given to Marie only as she arrived at the station on the morning of the operation. Marie was pleased at her aunt's illness, thinking it offered a chance of getting out of a loveless marriage to a dull, pompous young man. The day after the operation, without saying a word to her Aunt Irene, who had come to help nurse Ella, she wrote to William saying that she was too young and unsure of herself to marry him. He replied at once, stressing the awkward consequences of her change of mind and asking her to reconsider her decision. Marie, backed by Dimitri, was adamant that she would not marry against her will.

Ella, who remained in bed on Irene's insistence, the operation having been more serious than the doctors expected, quickly heard the news of Marie's rejection of William, and the two sisters had a long discussion on how to make 'the silly girl' change her mind. Irene, annoyed at the cancellation of her plans and seeing Ella upset at the idea of having the girl back on her hands again, decided to be firm with Marie and told Ella to leave it to her. Ella was doubtful. Irene was such a fool. Yet she had no wish to browbeat the girl herself, and so thankfully agreed.

That evening Irene, instead of the nurse, took Ella's temperature and said it was alarmingly high. Immediately the doctor was sent for and, after a talk with Irene, shook his head and said that the Grand Duchess must have received a great shock which had undermined her recovery and made her illness take a dangerous turn for the worse.

Late that night, Irene went and woke up Marie, who was startled to hear the news of her aunt's collapse. Irene sat on her bed and said: 'Marie, I must have a talk with you. I was going to in any case, but my darling sister's critical illness has made it essential. I must speak more frankly. Do you realize that, in first accepting and then refusing William, you have behaved in a most thoughtless and inconsiderate way to a young man you had encouraged to love you dearly? This is not all. You have offended the whole Swedish royal family and sullied the honour of the imperial Russian family into which you had the good fortune to be born. Perhaps you do not realize the damage which your father did to the Tsar by marrying – I am afraid I will have to speak to you frankly – a loose woman by whom he already had children. Now, on top of that, you choose by your thoughtless, selfish conduct to make trouble between two nations who it is important should remain friends. Marie, stop crying and listen to me carefully. Not only are you causing a rift in international politics, you are endangering my sister's and your aunt's life. Are you prepared to accept the entire responsibility for her death? Oh, do stop crying and realize this is the question you must ask yourself, or do you only think of yourself? If so, you should be ashamed. You are a selfish child, you know. Have you forgotten how your aunt took you and your brother to live with her after your father chose to abandon you? I have heard that you complained of her strictness. Can't you understand that she was determined to bring you up to respect your position and not to behave to others as your father behaved to you? And remember, after your father's behaviour, it will not be easy to find you a husband. Your aunts and I only found William with difficulty. And now you behave in this way! Stop crying, I tell you. The time to do that is if my dearest sister dies.'

Irene paused. She felt that the interview had gone exceptionally well and that Marie would now be agreeable to behaving sensibly. She therefore adopted a more tender approach and said: 'After all, Marie, you are very young, and perhaps you haven't understood the implications of all your actions and how you are unwittingly endangering your loving aunt's life?'

Marie cried even more and said she would do whatever Irene wanted.

The next morning, when Irene went into Ella's room to take her temperature, she said triumphantly, 'It is a little down,' before telling her sister of her long rewarding talk with Marie, who had at last realized that she had made a silly mistake in turning down such a nice young man. Irene next produced triumphantly a letter which Marie had written to Ella, apologizing for her stupidity and hoping that William would forget and forgive her refusal, written when she was excessively worried about the health of her dear aunt, whose illness was still worrying her.

Ella, who knew she had never been seriously ill, did not like the look of triumph on Irene's face, which reminded her of childish triumphs over grooms and tiresome cousins. She hoped that she had not been too brutal with the poor girl, but comforted herself that the marriage was in Marie's best interests, for once Dimitri had left for his military academy, she could only have led a miserable life alone at home.

Irene stopped Marie coming to see Ella for three days, and spent them assuring the girl of the advantages of an early marriage and the horrible plight of unmarried princesses. By the time Marie met her aunt again, she was taking a brighter view of the future, which allowed Ella to return to her own ambitions with an easy conscience.

3

Ella's next step was, at the invitation of Alix, which she thought it unwise to refuse, to tour the nunneries of Holy Russia. It was a depressing business, the buildings reeking of incense. The nuns seldom looked serene or happy, but appeared to Ella to be inferior women who had been put out of the way. It was true that they got up early and worked hard, but they were not allowed to teach or nurse, and instead dug fields, ground corn and continually prayed standing up. It appeared to her that every action which they performed was intended to blunt their senses and destroy their beauty. Their clothes were made of a hideous, badly cut cloth; their veils were so thick that they could hardly see through them; their shoes reminded her Marie Coburg's. Ella could not imagine what was the point of women making themselves unhappy when, by helping others, they could gain happiness. Neither could she see why they must make themselves look more hideous than God had made them, or that God could have meant women to avoid even an elementary knowledge of men and so make nursing out of the question.

Afterwards, she made a further tour of establishments in England and Germany, eventually deciding to revive an old order of deaconesses with their customs modernized to allow them to work in God's service all day without the constant interruption of prayer times. When she returned to Russia, she began to plan her buildings on the Great Ordynka. Ivan Blok advised her that Chussev was the most imaginative architect in Moscow, and so she sent for him. He, in turn, suggested she should get Nesterov to paint frescoes and he, too, agreed.

In February 1907, Ella again took stock of her affairs. The foundations of her buildings had been laid and building was about to begin. She made it perfectly plain to Alix and Nicky that, if her sisterhood was not acceptable to both him and the Holy Synod, she would give the church to them to do what they liked with. When Alix heard this, she smiled and looked happy and was very nice to Ella, which made her realize how unsure of herself her sister was, and how necessary it was for her contentment always to be praised and told of her importance.

Marie was to be married in a few months, and during the course of the winter Ella had allowed her to go to one of Countess Kleinworth's balls. It eased her conscience, and now, if anyone accused her of marrying Marie out of the nursery, she could reply that she had been to two dances.

This was the bright side of her life. On the other hand, the Holy Synod continued to prove as intractable as ever, and she had not yet decided what to call her sisterhood or precisely what rules her sisters would have to follow. During the past year it had struck her that she knew little of what had happened and what was happening in Russia, and sometimes she thought that she was escaping too much into her own world and plans and becoming ignorant of events. Twice during the past two years she had received letters from Azev, but on each occasion she put them unopened in a drawer. The last had come only recently, and it occurred to her that if she read them she might get an impartial view. His first was written in December 1905 and described the disasters of that year, starting with the massacre of the workers outside the Winter Palace, followed by the mutiny on the *Potempkin* and ending with Russia ceding Port Arthur to Japan. Azev had written:

It is now said in Russia that Count Witte pulled off a miracle and by his own personality turned American opinion from sympathy towards Japan to sympathy for Russia, and is now indispensible to the Tsar. Do not believe it, the Tsar never forgives success and I am sure he will dispense with Count Witte's services within a few months. And don't forget, when the Tsar signed the October Manifesto in which he promised power to the Duma, this was on the advice of Witte, which is another reason why he will never forgive him. He could not do without him last year as the Empire was on the verge of chaos with outbreaks of arson and terrorism all over Russia. But the Tsar will get rid of him.

Azev's second letter, written at the end of 1906, proved the accuracy of his prophecies. Witte had been replaced on 5 May by 'the old, inadequate Goremykin'. The first Duma met on 10 May and was dissolved, after two and a half months of wrangling, on 21 July. Azev continued:

It is said that the Tsar will gradually become dependent on the Duma. I do not think this is likely – he has not lost his belief in autocracy – but he has acted shrewdly in making Stolypin prime minister. He is the only man with the power and character to stamp out terrorism by giving the terrorists their own medicine. It augurs a bloody outlook, but he may well succeed. He also plans a system of land reform and the creation of more and more prosperous farmers; maybe if he has twenty years he will succeed. It is an optimist who would give Russia that time. Beneath the surface of the life you see there is poverty and cruelty. Modern communications are creating a new Russia and modern thoughts have replaced the old belief in the inviolability of the Tsar.

Ella looked at the words. Certainly Azev was clever, but she could not really take in what he was saying, and when she read through both letters again, she realized that she did not understand their meaning. She realized that the happenings of the world would, until she had achieved her ambitions, be of no interest to her. She was sure it was her own fault, but she could not see what she could do about it.

4

Marie was married in April 1908. Only with difficulty did Ella face the wedding: the same faces, the same ceremonials, the same remarks about how happy the couple looked, ignoring their apathetic interest in each other. At long last it was over. Marie was off her hands and she was free to start building. She liked Chussev; he appeared to understand her wishes and was planning a large church to be dedicated to the Virgin, a chapel for her sisterhood, whatever it might be called when it was finally approved, a large hospital, a dispensary for every-day use, a hostel for the old and penniless, a religious house for the resident priest, an orphanage, guest rooms, a house for guests and, next to it, three small rooms plainly finished for herself to live in. Nesterov had shown her a sketch of his planned frescoes, and of his designs for her nurses' grey robes, and for white robes for her use on state occasions. She thought they looked plain, dignified and beautiful.

The group of large buildings was to be surrounded by trees, lawns and flowering shrubs. All her life she had loved plants, and felt shocked by the ugliness of the areas surrounding convents and monasteries in Russia compared to the beautifully kept gardens she had seen in England and France. Her love of gardens and her belief that they should be a part of life she owed to Grandmama. When they were young the Queen had insisted that every Sunday evening at Windsor, all the children should be called together to hear half an hour's reading from an instructive book. Nearly always Ella and the others fidgeted and made faces and kicked each other and did anything to mitigate the boredom, but one day some old parson had read to them Bacon's essay 'Of Gardens' with its emphasis on the importance of beauty. Directly he began reading, Ella had become fascinated, and from the early days of her marriage, when she had started to plan her retreat from the world, it was always, in her mind, set amid beautiful trees and flowering shrubs. After all, if her sisters were going to work, as she hoped, in the filthy slums, they should surely have a place of beauty where they could sit and recuperate.

She had also decided to hold prayers in the morning and evening to leave the days free for work. With some doubt, she bowed to the custom that women dedicated to God should be vegetarians, but was insistent their food should be hot, and made Chussev alter his plans so that the kitchen directly adjoined the dining room. She knew that the Holy Synod had its spies and that her decisions were immediately brought to their notice, and that if, as she would have wished, she gave the sisters meat, it would be a weapon in her enemies' hands. Secretly, however, she told Chussev to ensure that the ranges could be adapted for every type of cooking. She had decided that her rules should be based on the London convent of the Little Sisters of the Poor, but when she presented the rules to the Holy Synod, they protested against the introduction of Protestantism into an Orthodox country and flatly refused her proposal.

During the spring of 1909, she wrote to Azev and asked him the best method of getting her own way. She felt sick and tired of arguing, and was now uncertain whether Nicky would ever support her. Azev thanked her for her letter and replied:

I have, of course, been aware of the intrigues. You have many enemies. The most powerful is Hermogen, Bishop of Saratov; there is no way in which your present intentions will ever be acceptable to the Holy Synod. Pobedonostsev planted his own acorns and they have grown up as conservative as himself. His followers desire no change. Your ideals, however concealed, will be anathema to them. Your hope therefore lies in the Tsar establishing your foundation by an imperial decree, but, as you know, he is reluctant to make any decision without the advice of the Tsarina. The question is how you can persuade her to persuade him. I have thought the matter over carefully and believe you will fail unless you practise guile. Forgive my worldliness; you will achieve nothing unless you face the truth.

I believe that you should come into the open with your ideas, but tell your sister they are based not on the Sisters of the Poor in London but on an inspiration you received during visits to the Zossima Hermitage, for which your sister has the greatest affection and which she has honoured with her patronage. Years ago, the Hermitage had a sister order of deaconesses, and the members of the order still hanker for its return, although, of course, they would not dare to make such a request to the Holy Synod. If you go and have discussions with the fathers at the Zossima Hermitage, I believe you will receive their moral support. The Tsarina visits it every year, and I suggest that you go before her annual visit, which will take place in September. After your visit and before hers, you should tell your imperial sister that, after a long talk with the fathers of the Hermitage, you have decided to try and revive the old orders of deaconesses. Say that, nothing more. When Her Imperial Majesty makes her own visit, she will be certain to discuss your plans and will, I believe, be told that such an order was once an adornment of the Russian Church and that its passing is regrettable. See her again immediately after her return and present your plans to the Holy Synod, who will turn them down as inconsistent with the rules of the Orthodoxy. This decision, especially if the Tsarina is informed that it was advocated by Hermogen, whom she particularly dislikes, should then be presented to her by yourself as a direct contradiction of her wishes, besides being historically incorrect and taken out of dislike for your and her German background.

I advise you to add that you believe their decision to be an insult, not only to you but to her, and that an insult to her is an insult to the Tsar. While you

239

do not matter, the Tsar should never be insulted. My belief is that if you follow my advice, you will succeed in your endeavours.

Ella followed Azev's advice, and Alix returned from her visit to the Hermitage with more enthusiasm than she had ever before shown for Ella's plans. At the end of the month, the Synod turned them down. Alix was furious, and Ella, remembering Azev's letter, said that while it did not matter hurting her, and she remained content to try and continue to please the Synod, wasn't the Synod's rejection of her scheme basically an insult to Alix herself, and if it was an insult to her, wasn't it also one to Nicky? Alix went red with anger, and, for the first time in her life, Ella watched her scarlet hands with pleasure. After that, she felt that the battle was won, for although she knew that it would take Nicky a few months to come to a decision, Alix would go on at him until he did what she wanted.

5

In October, she wrote a letter of thanks to Azev, saying:

I cannot tell you for what I am thanking you, but all I can say is that, on the unmentionable matter, you have been a great help to me. I shall never forget it and wish one day that I may be of service to you.

His reply was unexpected:

Your Imperial Highness, I estimated as I sat down to write this letter that I have been corresponding with you for nearly twenty years. Circumstances enabled me to tell you, upon occasions, certain facts concerning yourself and your late husband which, I believe, mitigated the dangers and difficulties of your lives. When I felt I had helped you in any way, I was filled with a greater delight than any other actions in my life ever brought to me. Never was my heart moved by such happiness as at the concluding sentence of your recent letter, conveying your gratitude and hoping to repay my poor kindness. I must sadly tell you that the opportunity can never occur. I leave my beloved homeland for ever during the next few days, to spend what can only be the poor remnants of my life in other countries.

Before I leave, I would like to fulfil the assurance I gave you many years ago, the first time I ever met you in Anton's house, that I would explain to you the motives behind my actions. Upon occasion I have felt over the years that your natural delicacy alone prevented you from asking me questions, and I am sure I have puzzled you with the mysteriousness of my knowledge and our sporadic meetings.

The first occasion on which I actually saw you was not at Arkhangelskoye, but in St Petersburg, on 16 December 1886, two and a half years after your marriage. On that evening I was, having called with a message to one of my superiors, returning to my home on foot, and was walking along the quay opposite the British Embassy when I saw a crowd, kept back by the police, surrounding the glass porch which protected the front door. Obviously the Ambassador was giving a dinner as carriages were lining up before the porch, discharging their distinguished owners and moving on.

I was a lonely young man with nothing to do except work, and I crossed the street and joined the crowd. I knew, from experience, that the best place to stand was next to the Embassy wall, since it was then possible to see, through the glass sides of the porch, those descending from their carriages. I took my place and noticed some stirring of excitement in the crowd, and a self-important policeman standing in the middle of the road, looking down the street. All at once he turned towards his men, shouted to them and made a threatening gesture at the crowd, who, used to such treatment, paid no attention. An extremely smart carriage, with outriders wearing the livery of the Grand Duke Serge, drove up and stopped in the porch. The footmen leapt down and stood on either side of the door, and you stepped out of the carriage. For a moment I thought I was going to die as the blood burst my veins, and then, for a moment, you stopped and everything stood still as I noticed the sweet smile you gave to right and left before walking through the doors. How long did I see you? A few seconds at the most, and yet how many times have I relived the scene of the arrival of your carriage, your descent and the exact manner in which you looked from right to left. I could describe precisely what jewels you wore, how your hair was done and the colour of your dress shining in the gaslight.

I must have stood there for a long time, idly leaning against the wall, until I excited suspicion and a sergeant and two of his men came up and asked me rudely for my papers. I showed them my badge, which sent them quickly away, and I continued to stand. I don't know whether I hoped that by some miracle you would come out again. To be leaning against the building you were in was enough. I realized that until I had seen you, the past had meant nothing. My actions, early successes and hopes I now saw as mirages. Without you the future was meaningless. I, who had been a young, ambitious, self-satisfied man, became in a moment a nullity. I was aware that our paths could never truly cross, yet I knew that unless I devoted myself to you, nothing in my life would be worth living.

As my life began when I saw you, my early life is irrelevant, except to enable you to understand my background. I was a young Jew, son of a tailor born in the Pale, and brought up in Rostov-on-Don. Bored to tears by wailings and family prayers, I entered the Orthodox Church at the age of twenty. To begin with, although I was not religious, I was an idealist, and I sympathized with my young revolutionary friends, although I thought them stupid. One day I was furious to hear how a ridiculous manifesto, which they had let me read, had been seized by the authorities and that I was in danger of arrest. Fortunately, I had a little money and escaped to Karlsruhe in Germany, following friends who had already fled. They bored me to death, talking and making plans, sitting up late, burning with idealism, running out of money and scrounging from their friends and their families at home, and often ending up in prison for debt.

One day, in a café, I was sitting late when a man came and sat down by me, introduced himself, told me my name and exactly what I had been doing since I left Russia, and finally asked what I thought of my friends. I realized that he must be a Russian agent. I was so sick and tired of my associates' stupidity that I told him he had nothing to fear from them since they were incapable of damaging anyone except themselves. He then asked if I would write a report. Since I knew that none of my friends could ever return to Russia and would waste and die in Karlsruhe, I wrote one into which I put all the venom born of my idleness, stating what idiots they were.

A month later I was asked to enter the Okhrana. I thought why not go into the secret service? I have never told the man who questioned me that I do not believe in reform in Russia, and if I enter the service, at least I will have a chance of seeing whether the administration I dislike is as corrupt as my former colleagues.

Three months later, I arrived in Moscow. I soon found the Okhrana to be as inefficient as the dreaded revolutionaries, and it was difficult to choose between them for stupidity. Some of my colleagues could hardly read or write and seemed without the most elementary understanding of the characters of their adversaries.

My success was meteoric, and within two years I was the private secretary of the head of the Okhrana branch in St Petersburg, and since my chief was a lazy man and left for home early every day, I was able to acquaint myself with the secrets of the capital. Sometimes he would not even come into the office and I would visit him in his house. In fact, it was returning from one of these occasions that I saw you for the first time and had my life turned upside down.

The next day I woke up thinking of you and went to a shop to buy a large blank sheet volume, the first of many. They contain, I think, every picture of you ever published in Russia.

The other change which you made in my character was bringing about a determination to succeed in any and every way so that somehow I might become acquainted with you, and although I realized that the acquaintance would be slight, to me this was an end enough. That year there was a change in the administration and I put it to my new chief, who was a man with good connections and no talents, that I might establish a close contact with my old revolutionary friends and infiltrate myself into their ranks, and so supply him with information. This I did, and as I rose in the Okhrana, so I rose in the revolutionary movement by telling them that I had infiltrated the Okhrana. I intended to maintain my ideals and only renounce to the authorities those men whom I considered to be animal assassins or nihilists, killers without purpose. I seldom betrayed sincere men of good intentions. Equally, I only gave revolutionaries opportunities to kill or corrupt stupid men in the police and secret service.

I therefore had knowledge of plots on both sides, and came to consider myself a somewhat godlike figure. But the chief purpose was to put me in a position where I could see and know you and give you advice which justified my living. I saw my chance when I heard of the Grand Duke's acceptance of the Governor-Generalship of Moscow, and since then, every meeting with you, every letter from you, has been a treasure to inspire and uplift. When you were ill from 1895 to 1901, I watched over you from a distance. I prevented numerous plots against the Grand Duke Serge, and made it a rule that any man who threatened you both died. This was the period of my greatest success.

Then, in 1901, it seemed for a moment, as a result perhaps of some action on your behalf, that a number of my terrorist colleagues became suspicious of how many of them ended up in Siberia. This was necessary because of the hatred for your husband, and so I came to be distrusted in hazardous quarters and needed to arrange for a number of successes by the revolutionaries against the most inefficient of the police and tyrannical of my official colleagues. I can say, without guilt, that I organized in 1903 the death of the Minister of Agriculture, and in 1904 the death of Plehve, the Minister of the Interior.

I must tell you that I was aware of the plot against your husband. You will remember how I warned you earlier to take care, and as the danger increased, so I had official warnings sent to him. On the morning of his death, a letter was delivered to him, telling him on precisely which spots in Moscow men waited to kill him. All I can tell you is that I could not have done more to save his life, at a considerable risk to my own.

You grieved for your husband after he was dead, but I think he wished to die. Although I hated him with all my heart as an evil man, he was brave and proud and could not conceive of himself retiring to St Petersburg to work as an ordinary Grand Duke when he had, for fourteen years, been emperor of the south. I think he avoided my warnings because he wished to die, and I wish you never to believe that I planned his death; I was only mixed up in the planning so as to be able to warn him exactly what to avoid. It is a strange thing, life. As I have just written to you, I am sure that your husband was sick of living because he loved working for Russia. I see myself in the same position.

In a few days or weeks or months, at the most, my double role will be made public by the revolutionaries, and what I thought were godlike actions in the public good will be presented to the nation as squalid murders. I must leave, and there will be no pleasure for me in my life until I die. In this letter, I would like to tell you that I have not been honest with myself or those I have dealt with. I have betrayed friends who put their trust in me and have, without remorse, seen them die for what I believed was the good of my country. To you alone I have been faithful, and for twenty-five years I have loved you with the whole of my heart; a crueller punishment than that I should live in another country from you I could not devise.

This is my last farewell. You are the star of my world. If I had the chance of living again a life of hopeless love with only occasional glimpses of unearthly joy, I would take it every time. That is the measure of my love.

The letter dropped from her fingers on to the sheets. Were her torments never to end? Was she ever to be haunted by her unconscious sins? She lay back and waited for the pain of hopelessness to return and haunt her good intentions, but it never came. Slowly she realized that her past no longer had the strength to hurt her. Her belief in the present and future was too strong.

She picked up the letter, painstakingly reread every word, got out of bed, tore it into little pieces and threw them into the waste-paper basket. She felt sorry for poor Azev. Whatever else he had done, he had truly loved her. Her sorrow was interrupted by thoughts of her plans for the coming day. She picked up her diary, opened and closed it, opened it again and saw that she had time to confess to her new friend, Father Mitrophan, between 11.00 and 11.30. The decision taken, she carefully considered her other appointments.

She made her full confession of her remarks about Serge on the hour. At 11.22 she was given a small penance for deceiving her husband in her mind, and received absolution. At twelve o' clock she was discussing with Nesterov the exact locations of his frescoes in the chapel of St Martha and St Mary.

6

Ella never forgot Azev, and she followed his advice. The Holy Synod again rejected her attempts to meet their objections. In March 1910, Nicky, by an imperial decree, established Ella's foundation. Five weeks later, Archbishop Triphoni gave the veil to her and twenty-two followers, who ranged from Princess Marie Obolensky to Barbara, one of her maids. Their father confessor was a white-bearded, simple man, the son of a peasant shopkeeper. Unquestioning, full of faith and fearless, he seemed to her to be the perfect choice, and her belief was reinforced when he soon made it plain that he regarded her as an ordinary sinner and told her he proposed to treat her exactly like his poorest parishioners.

Ella woke up the day after the ceremonies with a feeling of excitement and expectation which she had felt when, as a young girl, the Queen had given a dance for her and Victoria at Windsor. It was strange to feel happy again, after so many years of waking up haunted by some terror or fear. Now she could start afresh in the poorest, saddest, most vicious area in Moscow, whose centre was the infamous Khitrovna Market.

The area was built on an inadequately drained swamp. Nearly all the houses were built of rotten wood, without foundations. It was known in Moscow by its shape and peculiarities as the 'Bowl of Vice'. In winter, a low, fetid mist lay over the area, and it became impossible to see more than a few damp yards. In the spring, when the thaw arrived, it was not unusual for one or two of the inhabitants to disappear for ever into the mud. In summer, the mud was turned into a thin, damp crust by humidity, which made the rotten houses steam as if on fire. In this swamp town lived the dregs of the Empire: criminals, escaped prisoners and exiles from Siberia. There were no schools, no hospitals, no parks or playgrounds. The heart of the slum was the market, which every day was filled with stalls providing food and every conceivable type of merchandise, mostly stolen goods.

The square was surrounded by colossal cement blocks of apartments with hundreds of little windows, built by speculators after whom they were proudly named, determined to make money out of the poor. When the Chief of Police heard that Ella was encouraging her sisters to enter the 'Vice Bowl' to try and combat the appalling squalor and disease, he came to see her in the little sitting room, almost empty of furniture except for two chairs which faced each other across a plain table. He sat down, a large, bald man with a gigantic head and eyes which constantly darted all around the room, showing astonishment that anyone in their senses who had so much could choose so little. He had an ingratiating way of speaking, when he wished to be pleasant, and would push his head back towards his neck so that its size was increased by his double chin. He told her that one of his officers, whom she had asked to lecture, had informed him of Her Imperial Highness's plan, and so he had taken the liberty of coming to beg her to reconsider her decision to enter the five cement buildings which surrounded the Khitrovna Market. Was she aware that they were warrens of vice in which dwelt women of low reputation, and, what was worse, men who lived upon them? Into these buildings the curious sometimes strayed. If they were foolish enough to have money on them, they often disappeared. The police could do nothing. Each house was ruled by a collection of men who policed it in their own way by simply murdering those who disobeyed their orders. Surely Her Imperial Highness was not prepared to risk the lives of her young ladies in such a place?

Ella said simply: 'The purpose of my foundation is to do good, and surely the place to start is in the worst place. And I may tell you, I plan to enter these buildings myself.'

The Chief of Police slapped his face in irritation. She became certain that he was afraid he would be blamed should anything happen to her.

He leaned forward, and opened his mouth wide and said: 'Imperial Highness, I must tell you more. In these houses are criminals, sellers of stolen goods, murderers who live in flats with secret doors or skylights into other rooms. It would be as easy for us to catch a criminal in the Khitrovna flats as it would be to catch a rat in a haystack. One raid was tried under my predecessor. He set out to catch eighty notorious criminals, and ended with one criminal and two missing policemen.'

Ella smiled again. She found herself disliking the man intensely, and purposely spoke words which she knew would exasperate him: 'The greater the danger, the more we are needed.'

The Chief of Police started fidgeting in his chair. Would Her Imperial Highness therefore do him one favour? Would she not go into the second floor of the Yaroshenka Building? Was she aware – for she could not know – that one whole floor was devoted to the beggar women of the city?

'They are more dangerous than any man. They have their own territories in the town, and if an outsider from the country by mistake begs on their ground, they often beat them with flays until they die. Your Imperial Highness, please do not consider going there yourself, or even sending one of your sisters as I have heard you plan to do. Think of the effect if one of them were killed!'

Ella did not answer. The Chief of Police, encouraged by her silence to think she was heeding her advice, continued: 'You have no idea what devils those harpies are. You know, in the whole of the "Bowl" about half the children die at childbirth. Of the remainder, large numbers are sold to the beggar women of the city, for, you know, nothing touches the Russian's hearts like an ailing child. The most diseased and deformed go to the House of Yaroshenka. You would not believe it,' he continued, this time slapping his cheek with disgust, 'but they pay most for babies without arms or legs, or for those with diseased eyes. They really bring in the money. Then they will take up their position with these little wretches at some street corner, and to keep the baby crying, will sit them on a drawing pin. One inspector told me that the most successful beggars, the users of the most malformed, may get through forty or fifty babies in a year. The infants die like flies in the winter.'

He clenched his fists in the air as if he were killing a mosquito.

'No, Your Imperial Highness,' he continued with an ingratiating smile, 'please listen to my advice and avoid such a place. There is plenty of good to be done in the new buildings in the new parts of the town where some of the streets have even been paved with cobblestones. I will be pleased to show you round any time you like.'

Ella wondered whether she had ever disliked a man more, and rising to her feet and giving him a little bow she said: 'I would like to thank you for coming today. We were uncertain with which task to begin. Now you have told me. I thank you.'

Vexed beyond endurance, the Chief of Police smacked his cheeks with both hands and, looking depressed and worried, bowed his way out of the room.

When he had gone, Ella put her hands on the table and sat thinking. She had realized that if what the Chief of Police had told her was true, she would get no support from his forces and that twenty-two women without the law behind them could clearly do nothing. She decided to collect evidence and then go to see Alix, not Nicky, and ask for a special body of police and soldiers to be formed without delay, to seize the harpies in the streets, try them and send them to Siberia.

For three weeks, she sent her sisters round the streets of Moscow, observing the women beggers to see if such awful stories could really be true. They were, and every day her girls brought back reports of women sitting at street corners, each with a baby coughing or screaming beside her, and since it was now spring, the horrors of the many limbless or malformed children were fully exposed to the public. Every evening she received reports, and once a week all her sisters sat round the big, communal room, trying to decide what they should do and how they might persuade one who had never seen such sights to believe them.

At the second of these meetings, Sister Elizabeth had an idea. Her father owned a large store in Moscow, which sold all sorts of modern devices that he brought every year from England and America. She said he had recently brought back from the United States a camera less cumbersome than the usual types, and lighter to carry. She knew that if she asked, he would lend any number of them, and then they could have the evidence in print.

Ella was delighted, and asked if anyone else except Elizabeth understood photography. Two girls, Zenia and Tatyana, said they did. The three were immediately chosen to do the work.

Later, when Ella, after half an hour's praise of little Alexis, told Alix about the monstrous trade, she had in her bag fourteen photographs – enough to break any woman's heart – showing starving, deformed and crippled babies on the verge of death and being used as lures by the harpies.

Ella was wise, for when she told Alix her story, her sister's face closed up and

Ella saw she was determined not to worry Nicky about such a matter. She was not surprised when Alix said coldly: 'Naturally, my dear, I have inquired into these allegations, and Nicky has been assured they are untrue,' to which Ella replied: 'But look at these. I know the police are lying to Nicky. It is wicked of them. He should know the truth.'

Alix looked at the pictures, and her reaction was, again, exactly what she had expected, for although obstinate and excitable, she was at heart a kind woman, and the terrible catalogue of photographs made her go red and white in turn. 'Oh Ella,' she said at the end, 'what should be done?'

'Well, I have found where the worst of the women live. I think that if Nicky appointed a temporary force of a few hundred police and soldiers, they could arrest these fearful creatures and do what they like with them. Anyhow, I feel it will stop the custom of purposely deforming babies to sell to beggars to make money.'

Alix pursed her lips, gave a little nod and said: 'I am sure Nicky will do what I wish on this matter. Those who have lied to him will be punished. It is treason for officials to lie to their Tsar.'

For the next month, the three girls quietly took photographs and Ella made lists of the exact position in which the beggar women kept their stations. By the end of the month, they had amassed an accurate dossier of 650 women, of whom no less than 450 lived in the House of Yaroshenka. Ella went into the neighbourhood herself once, but it was no use; nobody spoke to her. Afterwards, she sent for Barbara, who, she knew, despite her grey robes, was able to get information out of anybody. She came back with a frightening story that many of the beggar women only needed to work with their strings of babies for two years before they had enough money to retire to the suburbs and build a cottage.

At the end of the month, an officer called Levitsky arrived in a uniform which Ella had never seen before, and said he had special orders to act on her information. He was a clean-shaven, determined-looking man, and appeared to be literally astonished when she gave him, carefully written out in a notebook, the exact places where 650 harpies sat. She also told him of the floor in the Yaroshenka building where so many of them lived, and gave him, with photographs, the names and addresses of many of the women who came round several times a week, carrying two or three deformed babies to act as suitable replacements for their dead predecessors.

Levitsky looked at her with open admiration and said he would take her information away and study it, though he had never expected such help and efficiency. Would it be disrespectful for him to suggest that Her Imperial Highness (despite her calling herself Sister Elizabeth, the inhabitants of Moscow still insisted on referring to her by her original title) would have made the most efficient police officer in the city? Before leaving, he said he would return in a few days and tell Ella his plans.

By special orders of the Tsar, no fewer than fifty drays were hired for one day and 500 men of the Chevalier Guards were asked to work with the police. Such a thing had never before been heard of. By the end of the day, over 700 women had been arrested, and, within a week, dispatched by special order to Siberia.

Ella became a heroine, and money for the new charitable buildings which she was planning in other parts of the city poured in. The Tsar was openly grateful, and, curiously enough, even the citizens of Khitrovna seemed relieved. As one notorious murderer remarked to Sister Marie: 'You cannot like a baby being ill-treated, however bad you are, can you?'

7

One unforeseeable consequence of Ella's triumph was the enormous interest which the affair raised, and visitors claiming the most tenuous friendships with any of the sisters began to appear at the convent. The large church was packed every Sunday, and visitors constantly thronged the garden, which Ella had intended to be an area of rest and relaxation for her sisters. Another effect which particularly annoyed Ella was that there was a positive rush of enthusiastic young women, with recommendations from many of the greatest families, asking to be accepted as novices. Curiously enough, Ella found it quite easy to choose who she would be prepared to take and who to send away. The latter were usually girls who had bright eyes and ecstatic looks on their faces and were full of conversation about their desire to give themselves to God. Ruthlessly, but politely, Ella said no, but these interviews took hours of her time, and then an incident made her resign, leaving the selections to Sister Marie.

She was sitting in her room one morning after turning away 'an ecstatic fool', when a beautiful, dark-haired girl came in, looking exactly like the nun she had seen years before in the church at Marburg. Ella was too surprised to rise to greet her, and sat staring, it seemed, into those same eyes which had bewitched her in the past. She pulled herself together and asked the girl to sit down and whether she was prepared to devote her whole life to others without thought of herself.

'Yes,' said the girl, 'because every night a man with the face of Jesus comes to me and tells me he is my husband.'

Ella blushed scarlet, remembering her own dreams, and told the girl that the reason was not enough. She should go away and come back in a year's time if she still felt the same way. As she made the suggestions, she found herself going redder and redder, and the girl, with her beautiful dark eyes, seemed to look at her as if she knew what she was thinking, and the eyes seemed to laugh when Ella said she should consider marrying and having children of her own.

Relieved of her interviews, Ella took stock of her sisters and noticed how thin and pale many of them looked. She had them examined by the doctor, who told her quite simply that they were undernourished, the work and strain which they had faced over the babies having weakened young girls not used to ceaselessly walking about the streets and coming back only to eat vegetables. Now the convent was well thought of, Ella could defy the Synod, and she decided to change their diet. While she remained a strict vegetarian, she insisted on her girls having meat every day except Wednesdays and Fridays, when they had fish instead. Almost at once she was made aware of anger replacing exaggerated praise for her initial sucess. A letter from Alix asked if it was wise to flout a tradition, held by the Russian Church for a thousand years, that women who dedicated themselves to Christ never ate meat. She wrote back that her primary consideration needed to be the health of her girls, and 'while it was possible to pray on vegetables, it was not possible to work on them'. After she had sent the letter off, she rather regretted her phraseology, because she thought that Alix, who hated that sort of thing, might think she was trying to be clever.

The change in the girls was extraordinary, and instead of flopping down exhausted in the evening after a meal of soup, carrots or rice, and falling asleep at their prayers, they seemed to gain twice as much energy. She was conscious that this innovation was nevertheless seized on, not only by Alix but all her traditional critics, who had always argued that she was mad and her experiment would end in disaster. Ella was so used to reverses in fortune that she ignored the drastic manner in which the visitors disappeared, the church emptied and the garden again became a place for rest and peace.

It was at this time, when she was facing criticism and unpopularity, that one of her girls, a young peasant called Sister Vera, who had worked ceaselessly and hard against the harpies, came to her and said she had discovered the existence of another terrible network, this time in a street behind the Bulin building, which faced the Khitrovna Market. Vera had made the discovery by accident in the market when she saw a small girl of twelve leaning against the side of a stall, sobbing her eyes out. The child's hopeless grief upset Vera. She asked the child what was wrong, but the little girl, who was dressed up in a white communion frock, was too frightened to say, although Vera guessed, from a few stammered answers, that she was frightened out of her wits. Vera led her back to the convent and put her to bed, where she started to tell such a frightening story that Ella was sent for. She found the child, whose name was Anna, on Vera's bed, still trembling, her face buried in the pillow. It had taken them a long time to get everything out of her. At last they had discovered that the child was the daughter of poor parents, who used to come with their farm produce from the country every Friday to Moscow. One day, she said, as she was sitting up in front of the cart alongside her parents, a woman in bright clothes had asked her mother to get off the cart and whispered for a long time in her ear. Her mother had said, 'No,' and repeated it three times, but the woman was insistent, and eventually her mother said she would ask her husband.

During the next week, Anna noticed her father staring at her and then looking at her seven younger brothers and sisters sitting in their ragged clothes round the sparse dining room table. The day before their next visit to Moscow, at the evening meal, when the soup had been more than usually thin, he had banged his fist on the table and shouted to her mother: 'I agree, it will be a mouth less to feed. It's a lot of money.'

The next morning her mother, without looking her in the eye, told her to pack her few belongings, as she was going to stay with her aunt in Moscow.

252

'Which aunt?' Anna had asked.

Her mother snapped at her to close her mouth and do as she was told; she would soon find out.

The cart was loaded and they drove into the city again, where, at the same place, the woman in coloured clothes was waiting. The mother had roughly pulled Anna off the cart and put her hand into the other woman's, who firmly gripped it. Then she had seen her father also get down and come and talk to the woman, who put a purse into his hand, which he rubbed between his thick fingers, as if he was counting the contents. Eventually he nodded his head, her mother kissed her on both cheeks and ran away, her father waved his hand without looking at her and the cart had trundled on down the street. Anna was left alone with the woman, who told her to call her 'Mama', and promised that if she behaved she would have fine new dresses to wear instead of her filthy old clothes. Anna said she was at once terrified of her. Vera very gently asked her why, and the girl looked puzzled and said she had bright red hair as if it was on fire, and 'while she smiled all the time Mother was with us, she stopped as soon as Mother went away, and jerked my arm'.

The girl was then led, petrified, through unknown byways to what Vera later learned was a modest-looking house behind the Bulin building. 'Mama' had opened the door and pushed her up a flight of stairs into an astonishing room which had small windows and the softest carpet she had ever trodden on. It was furnished with three big sofas, covered in the most beautiful red material she had ever seen, and surrounded by golden tables on which stood beautiful, bright brass gas lamps. On another big, shining, wooden table stood a collection of bottles and tall glasses.

After 'Mama' had shown her the room, stroking the gilded furniture and running her hands – and making Anna run her little hand – over the velvet covers, she had led her down a passage into a bedroom with six beds with six white sheets and eiderdowns. On them sat five girls of about her own age, or even younger. Anna said that she thought they were all sisters at first, since they wore identical, neat little dresses. The woman told the other girls to look after her, and on no account to allow her to wave from the barred window. The girls, who all had different coloured hair, had been quite friendly, and when Anna burst into tears they laughed at her and told her to 'cheer up' since 'it was much better here than at home'. You had a comfortable bed to sleep on and did not work hard every day, wore pretty dresses, and what happened was no worse than being beaten by your father, or his doing the same thing to you.

After a few moments another strange woman, without teeth and entirely dressed in black, came in and took her away, undressed her, put her into a bath and washed her from head to foot. The woman then put all her clothes into a basket, and when she protested said they were 'fit for nothing but burning as they are full of lice'. Anna was indignant; she had never had lice.

The next day, Anna was given a delicious breakfast of a boiled egg, all to herself, and then a funny little man with curly hair came in and took her into the bathroom with a big basin. He washed her hair gently but thoroughly, and told her she must have come from a good family as she did not have any nits. Then he snipped away with scissors and brandished a hot iron, which badly frightened her but gave her a lot of pretty little curls, so she could not help feeling pleased with herself.

For lunch they ate chops and a sweet pudding, and as much cheese as they wanted. Anna had never seen half as much food in her life. During the afternoon, the girls went out one by one at different times, and always came back with one or two silver roubles. Eventually she plucked up the courage and asked them what they had to do for it, and they told her: 'Just do as you're told. It doesn't take long. Once a week, "Mama" takes us out and lets us buy what we want, and she also keeps money for us in a book, so that when the time comes to go home, we will have good dowries, enough to buy a horse and four cows. It's not a bad life.'

At about six o' clock, Anna was herself taken by 'Mama' into a room she had not seen before, with cupboards full of every type of dress for children, even little sailor suits, and was told to put on a little white communion dress which had a white veil, and promised that if she was a good girl she would be given ten silver roubles. She had never heard of so much money and could not help thinking of what she could do with it. She was shown into the red drawing room, where a big, fat man with a white, pointed beard and large watery eyes was sitting with a brown drink by his side. He got up and said how pleased he was to meet her, and he hoped that she would be a good girl and call him 'uncle'. He did not at all look like her uncle, who farmed next door to her father, and she shook her head and said nothing. Then the fat man had smiled and said he was glad that she was not a violent child, went to the window and talked under his breath to 'Mama', who was smiling all the time again, before taking Anna by the hand and leading her down the passage into another room which had thick curtains drawn across one wall and was lit, as far as she could remember, by only two tiny candles. The furniture consisted of two chairs and a large bed.

After having told this much, Anna refused to say any more and burst into tears again, and Ella held her hand and asked whether she had been hurt, and she said no. When the fat man had kissed her, she had opened the door and run into the corridor just as 'Mama' was opening the front door to another old man in uniform, leaning on two sticks, who was being held up by a man with powdered hair in livery. As Anna dashed out, she had knocked the sticks over, which had made 'Mama' scream with rage and run after her down the steps, before she escaped into the market. Then the kindly lady had found her and brought her here.

Ella knew by now that money alone counted in the Khitrovna area and that the police frequently took bribes. This was a case where she would have to use her relationship with the Tsar, and she went at once to the police station and asked to see one of the men who had helped her earlier. She described the place and what had happened, and saw a look of fear and embarrassment come over his face as he asked her to leave the matter to him. She guessed what that meant and said no, either he would send some policeman with her or come himself, or she would go herself with her sisters and release all the girls. The officer looked appalled, and she knew he could never allow her to risk her life. Reluctantly, he called two policemen, and they followed Vera to the locked door and rang the bell.

The door opened with the clink of a chain, and a powdered, white face looked out from beneath a pile of henna curls. The policemen moved forward and whispered. 'Mama' said something shrill in a frightened voice. They whispered again fiercely and she opened the door. They all walked in and up the stairs into the sitting room with the velvet sofas which the little girl had described, and then through it and down the passage to the bedroom, which, once again, after a show of resistance, 'Mama' was forced to open. The room was clean and newly painted and all the windows had red chintz curtains to match the red carpet. Five girls of between eight and twelve were sitting lazily about, most of them looking at picture books.

Ella looked at them with horror and received a shock. All but one of the girls looked as well and happy as well-fed schoolgirls. The exception was a child who stood with downcast eyes. She looked again at the other four; they appeared healthy, had neither hard faces nor brazen eyes and stood up politely, looking surprised. Ella was wondering what to do when 'Mama' burst into tears, flung herself on the ground and said she was a poor woman who had always looked after her children well. Ella felt dumbfounded at the sight of the apparently happy children, who showed no signs of their sinful life, and, feeling cheated, she moved away.

Turning to one of the policemen, she asked him if he would ensure that the old woman was prosecuted and the girls returned immediately to their homes. Here, again, Ella's preconceptions were upset. Four of the girls burst into immediate floods of tears, and two of them literally screamed at her. They did not want to go home to be whipped by their mother and hit by their father, to receive nothing to eat and sleep on a straw mattress full of lice. They wanted to stay with kind 'Mama'. Ella felt exceedingly stupid, and the old woman, thinking her weakening, started to claw at her dress, begging for mercy, crying out that the girls' tears showed how well she had looked after them.

Trying to conceal her confusion, Ella turned to the policeman and again asked for an assurance that the woman would be prosecuted. He looked back at her in an embarrassed way and asked whether he could come and see Her Imperial Highness that evening. Of course, he would ensure that the girls were sent home if only they would tell him where they lived, and of course he would close the house and take 'Mama' to prison, but there were certain aspects of the matter which she should understand, and he held up a leather book with a lock. When 'Mama' saw it, Ella noticed the expression on her face turn from cringing servility to fury, and with a scream of rage she jumped at him, clawing at the book. He stood back, extended his fingers over her face and shoved her hard across the room, to fall screaming and sobbing on the floor. At once all the girls began to sob in unison, and Ella could not wait to get out of the house, relying on the policeman's assurance that the woman would be arrested.

That evening, at seven o' clock, he was shown into her little, bare study, and they sat looking at each other across the table. Then he took the key and passed her the unlocked book across the table, asking her politely whether she would take a quick look at the first few pages. She turned them over, to find them devoted to three members of the imperial family. On them was written the age of the girl which each wished to see, with height and build, colour of hair, type of dress, and the style of shoes or little boots which should be worn. Ella wanted to throw the book on the floor, for, apart from her late husband's relations, the book was full of the names of many men whom she knew, members of the Duma, court officials and governors, and she realized at once the police would never be able to prosecute such names.

She sat back and looked at the policeman: their eyes exchanged a mutual look of embarrassment. At last she had an idea, wrote down the names of the three members of the imperial family and then went through the rest of the book, selecting nine names from among those who she thought would be the richest in Moscow. She returned the notebook to the policeman and asked him what had happened to the girls. He said that they were still in the apartment and obstinately refused to say where they lived since they insisted on staying with 'kind "Mama" '. Ella then asked what he was going to do with her. He replied that it was a difficult question.

'I have sent some of our officers round, and they have found certain pieces of furniture in the room which have certainly been stolen. She will be charged as a thief and appear before the severest magistrates, who will almost certainly send her to Siberia.'

That was all. There was nothing else she could do, and by now Ella realized that it was in everybody's interests for the affair be kept as quiet as possible.

During the next week, she made appointments with the three of her husband's relations, and, visiting each in turn, informed them that she was aware of their activities in the house of Bulin. With a little smile, she said that since they had shown such interest in children, she had come to ask them for a cheque to pay for the girls' education at a convent school outside Moscow, and also for sufficient money to provide them with a dowry, to be given to the girls when they married. At each place she left with a large cheque in her hand.

She looked at her list: it contained six aristocrats and three merchants. She knew all of the former, and with considerable embarrasment made the same delicate demands. Each paid up immediately. Next she called on two merchants, who immediately thought that it was her intention to tell their wives. They went on their knees, begging her not to destroy their married lives. She assured them that she had no wish to see their wives. All she desired was money to educate the girls in Christian surroundings and to try to undo the spirit of evil idleness which had been implanted in their minds by selfish men. Gratefully, they had paid her enormous sums and bowed her all the way to the door, thanking her for her kindness.

Ella was so accustomed to success by the time she came to make her last call that she was convinced she would be treated with the same kind of terrified respect and expected the old trader to go down on his knees like the others. His reaction was quite different. He stared her straight in the eyes, which she found embarrassing, for she knew that it meant discussing subjects she still did not like thinking about. He asked her to repeat what she had said, and listened to her without showing any sign of confusion or guilt. When she had finished, he asked her what good she thought she was doing. There were many other places of exactly the same kind in Moscow, and he was aware of the names of the men who frequented the Bulin flat. She must also realize that the Tsar could and would never allow the matter to turn into a major scandal involving members of his family. Was it not, he asked, staring coldly, unusual for Her Imperial Highness to seek money to prevent disclosures? Was there not another word for such activity?

Ella found herself blushing, with no way of retaining her dignity. She stood up quickly and walked out without looking back.

The matter ended in a way very different from how Ella had hoped. Nothing remained secret in inner Moscow society, and soon her sisters told her how they were being embarrassed by the exaggerated rumours which went round the town. As usual, these distorted the truth out of recognition, and Sister Marie told her of a story, repeated to her family, that one of the Grand Duchess's girls had been caught in a brothel. The wild rumours caused pleasure and excitement, and to Ella's embarrassment, the next week the parents of Sister Tatiana called on her and said they wished to withdraw their daughter from the convent, for while they had expected her to do charitable work among the poor, they had not expected her to go searching round brothels and mixing with the filthiest people in the lowest areas. It took Ella over an hour, in which she had to tell them the exact story, to convince them of the truth and send them away alone.

8

The next embarrassment was a letter from Alix, phrased almost as a demand and requesting her sister to come at once to St Petersburg. When she arrived, Alix gave her the coldest kiss she had ever received, and said that Nicky was upset by the whole business. All sorts of damage had been done to members of the imperial family by Ella's escapade. The word 'escapade' annoyed Ella so much that she could hardly sit still. It suggested that she had done something wild and stupid, when all she had done was to rescue one poor girl who was being violated by a lot of rich old libertines. Alix hoped that Ella would now confine herself to doing conventional good. By this she meant looking after the poor and sick and nursing the ill, and not going round stirring up hornets' nests of trouble.

As usual, Ella was placed next to Nicky that night at dinner. Of course, he never dared to say a word, pretended to be pleased to see her and behaved as if he had no idea why she had come to visit them. Each time she saw him, she realized he was growing to be more and more under Alix's thumb, and that the life of both of them centred round little Alexis, who had fallen over playing some game the day before she had arrived and was now lying in bed with an agonizing swollen arm. This was perhaps responsible for Alix's rudeness, which Ella secretly found intolerable in a younger sister, but when she saw how, at meals, Alix sat miserably at the head of the table, hardly bothering to listen to what her neighbours said, and only came to life when someone suggested she could consult a new miracle worker, a Hungarian doctor who had achieved startling cures, Ella realized that her sister's mind was affected by her son's illness.

Miechen, who had grown to be even more formidable since Vladimir's death, was frank about her sister-in-law and said: 'Ella, you're her sister, can't you do anything?'

'The trouble is that she is so miserable about little Alexis that she takes it out on everybody else, including, I hear, you.'

'Without being rude, that doesn't matter, but what does matter is that she wants to blame the rest of the world for her suffering, and her endless worrying and unhappiness are slowly emasculating Nicky. He no longer has a mind of his own and gives in to her all the time. To work in her household has become a nightmare, as she is always dismissing people out of hand for no reason except

258

that Alexis is ill. I only hope that she doesn't start interfering with politics, for then not even the Prime Minister, unless he is one of her creatures, will last a moment.'

The morning before Ella left for Moscow, she was surprised to receive, at nine o'clock, a note brought by a mounted corporal of the Horseguards from Count Fredericks, Minister of the Court. After briefly expressing his gratitude, the count continued:

> May I express the earnest hope Your Imperial Highness will honour us by lunching with myself and my wife today. I hope you will forgive my deplorable manners in asking you so near to the time, but circumstances are responsible for my lapse. If you would see the way to accept, might I ask the honour of an audience afterwards? It would be a great help for me to hear the latest news from Moscow.

Ella was surprised. She had known Fredericks ever since she had come to Russia. All his life he had been a courtier, becoming Master of the Horse under Serge's elder brother, Alexander III, and later being appointed Assistant Minister of the Court under Count Vorontzov before succeeding him as Minister when his resignation was accepted after the disaster in the Khodynka Fields. Fredericks's appointment as Minister of the Court had caused an uproar. He was not considered to be sufficently aristocratic. It was pointed out that the founder of his family was a Swedish prisoner who had stayed on in Russia. One of his descendants had made a huge fortune banking in the time of Catherine the Great. His grandson, Fredericks's father, was a soldier and had ended his career as General A.D.C. to Alexander II. Ella disagreed with his deprecators and thought that Nicky had for once made a good decision, for she always found Fredericks to be a man of absolute honesty. Mienchen constantly criticized him for never arguing with Nicky's decisions, but Ella knew that nobody could argue with Nicky and Alix's plans and hope to remain. It was much better that they should be served by a scrupulously honest and decent man who did not hold his own political opinions.

At all events, he soon proved his worth. It was always said that he had two great virtues: he was honest and was never shocked, and therefore was invaluable when it came to dealing with and keeping secret the scandals and escapades of the imperial family. Ella knew that he reported to Nicky twice a week and, noticing the two lines under the word 'hope', realized that it must imply he had been commanded to see her. She wondered what for, and hoped it was not to tell her bad news, since he was always said to carry out the unpleasant tasks which the Tsar could not face. All the morning she wondered whether, after the scandals brought to light by the release of the imprisoned girl, Alix had persuaded Nicky to curtail her convent's activities. She tried to pray, but found it impossible; went for a walk, but found her steps always led home. In the end, she just sat and waited.

The Count, for some years affectionately known as 'the old man', had never changed the house in which he had lived when he was Master of the Horse. It stood exactly opposite the huge Horseguards Palace, on the other side of the vast parade ground. Ella had never known Countess Fredericks well, but had always thought she appeared rather bitter, which seemed surprising, considering that she was lucky enough to be married to such a nice man. It was an old-fashioned, cramped house with numerous small rooms.

Fredericks, except for state occasions, always wore simple clothes of some indeterminate military origin, and had an extraordinary moustache which grew out sideways five or six inches on either side of his mouth of its own accord, without any pomade or attention. She remembered that such moustaches were called 'handlebars' in England, and had always been considered comic. She noticed he had grown much balder and was stooping, and that his rather nondescript, slightly sheepish face was a rather grey colour, which her nurse's training associated with heart trouble. His heavy, lidded eyes, however, still shone bright and kind.

Lunch was a very simple affair of only three vegetable courses. The Countess apologized in an angry voice, and said that her cook could have produced many other excellent dishes but that her husband had said the meal must be short. She could only apologize.

Ella suddenly remembered how Miechen had said; 'I don't blame her, for although the old man is the most powerful figure in Russia, he likes to play it down and pretend he is just a simple citizen with a dislike of power, when it is what he lives for. Everyone kowtows in admiration of his simplicity. It is rather bad luck for his wife, as part of his pretence is to make her go on living in a poky little house where she cannot give balls or entertain properly, especially as he is enormously rich. But he is mean unless he can spend money ostentatiously in the service of the Tsar, or in a way which shows what a good man he is. And so, poor thing, I really think she has a reason to complain, for while he is the Russian Brutus, nobody bothers about her, and wherever she goes she hears how lucky she is to be married to such a good, simple man. You're so kind yourself, Ella, that you probably won't understand why she is irritated by his deliberate humility. You know, women don't like living in their husband's shadow, especially if everyone praises him all the time for denying her the position maintained by every one of his predecessors' wives.'

Ella tried to please the Countess by saying how nice she had made the house, but all she replied was: 'It is so difficult, you see, for we have to entertain all the time, but as we can only ask a few people, we made endless enemies who daren't dislike Fredericks and so take it out on me.'

After lunch, the Count took her into his little library on the first floor, where they sat on two old wooden and green leather chairs, looking out over the square, with a table between them. After he had apologized for such simplicity, they sat down and he turned and looked straight at her before raising the lids of his kind, brown eyes.

'May I dispense,' he said, 'with all formalities? I am not stupid enough to think that you have not guessed there is a purpose in asking you to my table today. You are, of course, correct in guessing what it concerns.'

She realized that his eyes were watching her acutely to see whether she was denying any of his hypotheses. She merely nodded.

'The fact is that it's my business to keep peace in the imperial family, and this

260

often means my having to say things without permission, which is what I am going to do today. To be honest, the Tsarina and the Tsar are both very upset by all the publicity that your convent has caused in Moscow, and I have had, if you will excuse the soldiers' term, a devil of a time quietening two of the Grand Dukes, for there is no doubt about it, you stirred up a wasps' nest. I admire you too much not to wish this vendetta against you to end, because I hear such wonderful stories of what you are doing and have done, but if antagonism builds up against you, it will, I fear, damage your reputation and limit your opportunities, and that is the last thing I want to see.'

Although he had not spoken anything but generalities, Ella realized that Alix had asked Nicky to restrict her, or, at any rate, to warn her that her Order could be restricted unless she behaved more moderately. It really was an annoying example of Alix's jealousy. There was no good in getting angry; she needed to keep the old man as a friend so that he could warn her if it was planned to take steps against her. She knew, by now, that neither was it any good talking to Nicky or Alix. If this visit had taught her anything, it was that Alix's personality had overwhelmed Nicky and she would have to avoid offending her own sister. It was a pity.

'I would like to thank you,' she said simply.

The old man just nodded, still looking at her and weighing up whether she had fully understood the implications of his discreet words.

To further reassure him, she went on, 'I would like to say that the publicity of the babies was, I think, unavoidable and did good. The second case was just bad luck, and really also unavoidable. How could I not come to the rescue of a girl caught up in such shocking circumstances?'

The old man smiled and said: 'I agree it was unfortunate. I just hope the same sort of thing does not happen again, for, as I have said, I have always admired you intensely and would hate to see your work constricted.'

There was relief in his voice, and Ella thought how strange it was that while she could never understand what authors wrote, she could always comprehend the finest niceties of court etiquette and language. Anyhow, she realized that she was only to be given a warning and would be left alone for the moment.

She stood up and told the old man how pleased she had been to see him, how grateful she was for his help, and he at once became so deferential and self-deprecating that she wondered if Miechen wasn't right and it would be rather annoying to be married to a man with tremendous power who pretended all the time that he was a nobody.

9

When Ella returned to Moscow, she found the scandal still being talked about in a tiresome, exaggerated way which made her life so unbearable that she decided to go to Darmstadt to stay for the first time with Ernie's second wife and their young children. She knew it was weak to run away, but she had never pretended to be a saint, and had thought that the scandal would have died down while she was at Tsarskoye Selo and St Petersburg. She was wrong, for the affair had instead brought to the surface the long-held belief that she was good but mad. From the Synod came unveiled criticism of her wearing the elegant, grey robes which Nestorov had designed, and it was suggested that her sisters' working clothes should be changed to conventional black. She absolutely refused, but realized bitterly that unless she was careful, her followers would grow nervous if they found themselves watched and becoming objects of suspicion.

She told Sister Marie to concentrate in her absence on nursing, looking after the sick, the schoolchildren and the orphange, and for the moment to avoid the horrors of the Khitrovna. She felt depressed, misunderstood and hurt, and wondered whether Russians did not prefer evil to good. It seemed to give them more pleasure.

Directly she had crossed the frontier, her spirits lifted. She was convinced that everybody needed holidays, and on the journey through Germany wrote to Sister Marie to say that each of her sisters, however far away they lived, was to have two full weeks a year holiday in their old homes and the travelling time was not to be counted.

As Ella approached her former home, she wondered how different it would be. Victoria, as she had promised, had found Ernie a suitable wife, a Solms-Hohensolms-Lich, who, she said, was 'exactly what Ernie needs in that she is plain and infinitely grateful he had married her, and though there is a good deal of the governess in her, I think she is sensible enough to understand Ernie's difficulties and she certainly won't forget functions and behave like Ducky'.

Apart from an occasional meeting – they had married during her period of mourning for Serge, and illness had twice prevented earlier visits – Ella had never really got to know her new sister-in-law, who had dutifully produced two sons. In the old days, when Ella arrived, if Ducky was out she would soon come flying into the room in her riding habit and throw herself into Ella's arms, saying: 'Oh, Auntie, I am glad to see you,' and though she would sometimes fly into furious rages, there had been about her a tempestuousness and wildness which Ella always found entrancing.

. Ernie's new wife, Eleonore, had changed from being a nervous, fat, not very young spinster, always jumping up to help, into a self-satisfied looking matron whose nose seemed to have grown with her importance, though her mouth was thin, her chin sloped away and her hair was of the indefinite blond-red colour which went with the pale, freckly skin that Ella had never liked.

Eleonore received Ella graciously and led her to her old room in Wolfsgarten, on the way picking off the ground a fragment of paper and a pencil lying on a piece of furniture. The house was absolutely spotless, and in Ella's room, instead of great jugs of wild flowers picked in the woods by Ducky, stood three new cut-crystal vases, each filled with sixteen tulips of one colour, looking formal and unhappy on little squares of muslin with lace edging. The books which Ducky used to leave lying about to shock her, such as *The Yellow Book* and the work of Beardsley and Beerbohm, had all vanished and been replaced by two new sets, each bound in brown leather, of Goethe and Schiller. By her bed was another square of muslin, and on it a jug of water with a glass beside it, both again covered with muslin with little blue beads hanging down at the end of pieces of lace.

Giving a quick glance at Ella to make sure she had recognized the welcome change of taste in the room, Eleonore, who, Ella saw, was very large from behind, showed Ella her old bathroom as if she had never been there before, and discreetly left her. Ella at once ran to look out of the window across the tops of the trees of the surrounding forest. She had always loved the romantic view. The window was covered with frosted glass; no one could see in or out. She winced with annoyance. Nobody could possibly have seen in unless they had been sitting in the top of a tree. She quickly blamed herself. What did it matter if Eleonore made Ernie happy? But by the time she had left, she was not sure. Everything was perfectly run in what Ella, despite her charity, could not help thinking was a bourgeois manner. But was that enough? All the gaiety had gone out of the house. Eccentricity had been replaced by dull formality; life was too correct, in precisely the way her mother had hated.

Eleonore entertained neighbours every day, and to Ella's amazement, Aunt Schönburn, whom Ernie had never ceased to mock in the old days, came to stay for two nights. All the other guests seemed to be relations that she had not seen for years, who knew, without a moment's hesitation, the name of every sixth cousin, the family names of their husbands and wives and the exact number of their children. It was a maze that Mama had avoided and Ernie scoffed at, and now here he was, not the laughing, mocking figure of his youth, but a serious, rather fat, ageing man with a prim, proper and, Ella had to admit, immensely boring wife.

Ella especially missed certain faces among the servants: a drunken footman, whom Ernie had insisted on keeping for years because he made him laugh, had gone, and so had an Irish housemaid who had somehow strayed into Hesse and stayed there, an ageing fixture unable to speak a word of German. Yet what worried her most was the change in Ernie himself. Even in the worst of the

Ducky days, he had kept his humour, and to the very end, although he and Ducky fought and she was openly unkind to him, he was still recognizable as the boy she had known. Now something had happened: he had become conventional and sad and had lost the essence of his personality. When he spoke, Eleonore would listen to him politely but did not appear to take him seriously. When he made a joke in a feeble imitation of his old gaiety, his wife would give a superior little smile and change the subject. Ella could see that she was in command and had managed to make her brother ashamed of himself. She noticed how he was treated, even by the servants, with a deference edged with contempt. Ella sadly wondered whether Victoria had made a good choice and, in choosing the embodiment of all the Germanic virtues, had not sentenced Ernie to living with a woman whose crushing conventionality, natural dullness and iron, hypocritical morality had reduced him to a sad, ignored, guilty shadow in his own home. The thought made her angry, and she could not help wishing that some busybody would tell her sister-in-law one of the most popular private jokes in Europe: a conversation which had taken place in Baden-Baden between Mrs Keppel and King Edward. It was shortly after Ernie's marriage, and Uncle Bertie had asked what she thought of Ernie's new wife.

She had replied: 'Sir, it would not be proper for me to reply,' and added, after a moment's pause, 'What was it that Henry VIII called Anne of Cleves?'

Uncle Bertie had looked vacantly at her for a moment before spluttering with laughter, 'My God, "the Flanders mare" you mean? Well, in this case Ernie has married a Hohensolms horse.'

The King was delighted with his joke, which became, in two or three days, common knowledge in every European court. It caused great pleasure, as it was the general opinion that Eleonore, who had for years been ignored as an unmarriageable spinster, was, after her surprising marriage, far too pleased with herself.

Ella found life at Wolfsgarten so staid and dull that she spent much of her time in her bedroom or in the forest thinking ruefully about herself. She had been upset by a letter from one of the younger and more impressionable sisters saying how she missed her leader and saint. Being called a saint annoyed Ella more than anything, for she knew she was not one. If she had been, she would have dedicated herself to the Lutheran Church as a girl, and although she had never forgotten her experience at Marburg, she had soon had a curiosity of life which had made her wish to live, but now here she was grumbling to herself about the past. Was she making the most of the present? And had the scandal driven her back into a weak, passive role? Had it been weak of her to flee to Darmstadt? She felt guilty, and made at Wolfsgarten two resolves which she promised on her knees to maintain: personally to nurse the worst cases and to prepare the dying for death. It worried her that sinners and even ordinary good people should have the true state of their health concealed from them and die unconfessed and unprepared to face their future life.

She could not help being pleased with the welcome which she received on her return. It was unanimous and touching, and almost immediately a chance arose to enable her to show the strength of her dedication. A man was brought into her hospital, suffering from severe burns from running into his blazing house to try and recover his few possessions. He was poor and, like so many peasants, fearful of hospitals. To begin with, he had merely hidden his agony and covered the worst part of his body with dirty bandages. Eventually, however, he was taken by his wife, terrified at his pain, to the hospital. The doctors who examined him diagnosed acute septicaemia. Large areas of his body were suppurating and it was extremely unlikely that he would live. Ella insisted on nursing him herself. Every morning and evening she would dress the affected areas of his body, which stank so terribly that she had difficulty preventing herself from fainting as she cleaned the wounds. Gradually, under her unceasing care, a miracle occurred, and Ella had the satisfaction, after six weeks of ceaseless work, of seeing the man recover.

She felt it to be a decisive moment in her life. She alone knew the battle which she had fought against repulsion and her desire to run away from the stinking flesh. Every moment seemed endless, and she knew that if she had once paused for even a minute in her dressing of the wounds, she would never again have returned to this poor, revolting body. Each day she had to force herself to finish a ghastly task and, when it was over, to live in dread of the next dressing.

When, at last, she realized that there was nothing else she could do, she felt a wave of relief, and then one of guilt for merely having followed her chosen vocation. Then a thought struck her: had she at any time, when she was holding her breath and using the whole of her self-control to hide her revulsion, felt any affection for the man, an actual desire to help him? How could she, when all her impulses were to run out of the room? The memory disconcerted her. Had she merely done it, not for the sake of humanity but to prove that she wasn't squeamish? At least, she thought, she was honest with herself and knew she had shown strength of character, proved she could perform her next task: the preparation of the dying for death.

Ella knew that Marie thought her policy of truth unnecessary and unkind, and that if a human being had only a few days to live, then they should spend them in as pleasant and carefree a way as possible. But Ella decided that the dying must prepare themselves to meet Our Lord and admit their sins, not necessarily to a confessor but to themselves. Sometimes it was difficult, for she noticed how nature deliberately conceals the truth, and how the most hopelessly ill patients with incurable ailments often talk of the future, unaware that they have none. Ella disillusioned them, being convinced that it was necessary for every soul to prepare itself by prayer and contemplation for meeting the Creator, and that it would be wrong to allow anyone to go unprepared to their death, even if it made their last days on earth unhappy.

Ella was so certain of being right that she did not dread these final meetings, for once the sufferers had been shocked by surprise or had sobbed their hearts out, they would come round to a state of acceptance, from where, slowly, she guided them towards acknowledgement of their sins. The last stage was prayer and remorse and preparation for their final journey on earth. Once, a few months after her return from her unhappy visit to Wolfsgarten, she had what nearly amounted to a quarrel with Marie over her treatment of a young girl whose father was a drawing master and who was suffering from consumption. She lay, pretty, with dark red hair and a dead white skin, designing dress after dress, which reminded Ella of her past and made her sympathize with the young beauty. During the first week, the girl had no haemorrhages and continually talked of future plans for when she was better, and how difficult it would be to persuade her mother that she should work for her living. She wanted, above all, to design ballet costumes, but realized that was perhaps a difficult dream to accomplish and that she might have to settle for working for a dressmaker's. Ella looked at her and studied carefully her leather book full of coloured drawings, and saw she was unusually talented. She promised to help her.

The next day the girl had a haemorrhage, but was by evening sitting up again with her pad on her knees, her eyes glittering, her face dead white, feverishly designing a long, mauve evening dress. Ella was touched, because she had told the girl how this had once been her favourite colour. But, worried that the girl had ignored the haemorrhage as irrelevant to her recovery, Ella asked the doctors how ill she was. They said that her lungs were riddled with holes and the next serious haemorrhage could well be fatal.

Ella decided to prepare her for death. Surely it was her duty to give the girl a chance of attaining a state of grace by the realization of and regret for her sins and selfishness? It would be wrong for her to miss this opportunity by falsely believing she was going to live. She had sat down by her bed, taken her hand and told her the truth. The girl looked at her with large eyes, twice the size they had been the week before and gradually opening wider and wider as they filled with horror. Then she had buried her head in the pillow and burst into floods of tears. Ella sat, stroking her head. Gradually the girl's sobs ceased. She sat up and said: 'I don't want to die – I have never lived. It is so unfair. There is so much I want to do. Why should I die when everyone else I know is going to live? I don't believe in God and never have,' and she collapsed again into tears.

Ella sat with her every day, trying slowly to persuade her she had an eternal soul, that otherwise there was no meaning in life and she must prepare herself for joining her Maker for ever by purging herself of her sins and not wasting the last of her few days on earth. The next day Ella noticed that she lay without moving her eyelids, flushed and red, while the drawing pad had disappeared from the bed. One of the sisters said that she had asked for her drawings to be burnt. Each time that she saw Ella, she asked her with passionate interest why should she believe in afterlife. Ella would gently reply that it was a question of faith, and asking questions was a good sign, for it showed, without her realizing it, how she was seeking the truth. The girl would merely lie back with closed eyes, out of which tears ran down her white cheeks. Ella would pat her head, tell her to be brave and walk away.

On the fifth day she died in Ella's arms, coughing blood, worn away to a white-skinned skeleton. Before her last spasm she had looked up and said, in a despairing voice: 'I hope you're right, but I don't feel you are. I still believe I have missed everything I would have liked to see, but in case you are, I have confessed all my sins.'

A final rush of blood had spurted out all over Ella's sleeve. Without wiping off the blood, she knelt down and prayed for the girl's soul, and had the comfortable belief that her prayers would be answered. What evil could the poor girl have done?

That evening, Sister Marie came in to give her usual report on the events of the day. It was her business to tell Ella if any member of the community, down to the lowest charwoman, had any problem, and of any trouble or need of her presence in any of the schools or orphanages or old people's homes. She also presented the lists of those in hospital, specifying the state of their health and marking with a red asterisk those near to death. Ella had always liked Marie Obolensky, even when she was a young girl. It had undeniably made her work easier to have as chief assistant a woman whom she had known all her married life.

As she was looking through the hospital list, she saw that the name of the red-haired girl who had died during the afternoon was blotted out by red ink. Ella looked up at Marie to say how sad she was about her young friend, but did not speak out of surprise at the look on the usually friendly face. It was obvious that Marie was moved by some strong emotion. Her lips were close together and her face had set in hard lines.

'What is it, Marie?' she asked in surprise.

The reply came out in a flood of words, half-prepared, half-spontaneous, sentences at times spoken so quickly as to become incomprehensible though the meaning was plain. Marie wondered whether Ella realized, ever since the scandal of the young girls, how her character had altered. A few of the senior sisters had discussed it among themselves the other day. It was as if, out of anger, she had lost her gentleness, formerly the part of her character which they most admired. Then, during the past week, Marie had to confess that she had been shocked, something she never thought could have happened, by the unkindness – no, the insensitivity – of Ella's behaviour to the dying red-haired girl. Was it conceivable that God could wish for a young girl to be made unhappy and frightened, and have her condition worsened, by the unnecessary information that she was to die. Why tell her? Surely God would in His mercy already have known of the young girl's sins, without her needing to be frightened in her last hours into making up stories which had never happened, and crying out in her sleep, 'I must remember or I will go to Hell.' Surely frightened, garbled recollections, created by a frightened imagination which had overcome truth, were not fitting thoughts for a young girl about to die? Marie made the sign of the cross and stopped abruptly.

Ella was horrified. Was this true? Were the determination and zeal she had felt since her return merely reactions and frustrations ? Was it anger, not the desire to bring the dying in a correct mood to the steps of eternity, that had made her so strict? Was it also to contain frustration and anger that she had bathed the suppurating wounds of the burned man? She had wondered at the time about her own feeling. Now she had an explanation. She was grateful to Marie, and asked her to come closer, then held out both her hands and put them round her neck and pulled her head down and kissed her on both cheeks. After that, without another word, she continued calmly to go through the reports.

Directly she was finished, she went to confess to Father Mitrophan, and explained to him precisely her anger at what she considered to be Alix's treacherous behaviour, followed by the warning from old Count Fredericks that restrictions might be imposed upon her community's work. Then she confessed her cowardliness in running away to Hesse, where she had felt guilty that she was becoming a figurehead and not the simple working sister she had always prayed and hoped to be. She described her feelings as she daily cleansed the putrified flesh, and repeated every word which she had said to the red-haired girl.

Father Mitrophan sat in silence in his box for several minutes, and then told her that she was wise to have come to him, for frustration was a form of pride and, as such, a serious sin. He said she had nothing to confess about the burnt man, but had, in his view, sinned grievously in her treatment of the dying girl.

'It is wise to show the way to repentance, and perhaps wise to be truthful to those who are in a state to accept the truth, but to frighten a dying girl out of her senses is not putting her on the right step to meet God. I saw her the day she died, and the sins she confessed to me were, I am sure, out of fear, tangled imaginings rather than genuine regrets. Sister Elizabeth, you should curb your pride.'

He gave her a stiff penance.

She went away and that night gave herself the extra punishment of praying an extra two hours on the cold floor by her bed. The next day she called all her sisters together and publicly thanked Marie. Having pointed out her sinful failing, she advised them all to judge her as a sinner and be aware of how easy it was to fall into the trap of pride. Then she dismissed them and sighed as she saw, by their looks, that they admired her more than ever.

10

From 1910 to 1914, the original community, the associated schools, hospitals, orphanages and old people's homes now scattered round the city, all thrived. The original antagonisms slowly disappeared. The goodness, bravery and kindness of Sister Elizabeth's followers enabled them, in their unmistakably elegant grey robes, to enter even the worst slums. Ella was proud of her success, but maintained it was owing to the character of the girls rather than to herself, who was now, of necessity, frequently confined to organization and raising money, although, whenever she heard of ghastly situations, she would go, safe and admired, into the evil world of the Khitrovna. Each morning when she woke she thanked God for her utter happiness.

During these years she came to realize the bitter unhappiness of her sister and deplored her own selfishness in having ignored, through concentration on the creation of her foundation, Alix's plight. She, Nicky and their children, lived in sad seclusion in Tsarskoye Selo. Alexis's disease had made his mother miserably unhappy and guilty at producing a crippled heir to the throne. Ella saw that she should forgive her sister's late rudenesses and accept that she suffered so much she hardly knew what she said and, in her pain, struck out in every direction. Nicky was as helpless and hopeless as ever, and for the sake of peace gave in to all of Alix's demands that he should stand firm against every reform, deny the Duma power and insist that his autocracy, despite his promises, remain undiminished. Ella believed that Alix's insistence on resisting all innovations arose from her irrational fear of any compromise being taken as a sign of admission that her beloved boy would not live to succeed his father.

It was, in any event, impossible to argue with either Alix or Nicky, and Ella tried to soften her sorrow by making them take more interest in the four girls. At once Alix asked her not to interfere and the idea had to be given up, but not before Ella had won their friendship and become disturbed by their innocence and ignorance, which was not surprising, considering the way they had been brought up, immured from the world. Ella remembered, years before, Nanny Eager complaining about the bad effects of the unnatural restriction of the children's lives, and saying: 'You wouldn't be believing it, but Olga had never been in a shop until we all stayed in Darmstadt. She was eight, you know, but she couldn't understand the toys were for sale and thought they belonged to other children. And, you know, she still thinks the Tsarina's milliner is " a kind woman to give us all those lovely hats". She won't have it she's a saleswoman.'

Ella looked amazed, and the Irishwoman said quickly, in her insincere brogue: 'Not that she isn't forward in other ways, of course,' and, as if proving a point, continued: 'The little girls actually thought the Japanese were monkeys for years, and when Tatiana was introduced to the Prince of Siam, the silly thing said – and wasn't I embarrassed – "You are no prince, you are a monkey." It's not natural, keeping them all together. It doesn't bring the elders on. They should have friends of their own age.'

The imprisonment continued. The children never had any competition. What was worse, their adolescence was made confusing as well as confining, for Olga, when she was sixteen, was allowed to go to small dances in Livadia, but then had to return to the nursery to be treated in exactly the same way as Anastasia, who was still a child. Ella was surprised that Alix, who had loved her clever governess, Miss Jackson, insisted on her children's teachers being old-fashioned courtiers, but decided it was a result of her wish to possess those she loved. She would rather keep her children backward than share them with clever, modern teachers.

A more serious matter was represented by the holy man, Gregory, now called Rasputin, and the scandalous innuendoes published in every periodical and newspaper. Even the respectable journals suggested that Alix's friendship with Rasputin was not normal and that the Tsar weakly allowed his wife to make a fool of him. Moscow was full of such gossip, and Sister Marie thought it her duty to report what the other sisters heard.

When Ella visited St Petersburg in the spring of 1912, she stayed with Miechen, who, now that Nicky and Alix never left Tsarskoye Selo, was the undisputed leader of society and consequently friendlier and nicer. Ella asked her what was the source of all these lying tales, and what sort of man this Rasputin was, adding: 'I saw him once, years ago. He seemed only a typical Montenegrin holy man.'

Miechen had laughed and replied: 'Well, I am always accused of making unpleasant remarks about Alix, which, I may say, is quite unnecessary, for she does herself more harm than ever I could do, even if I wished it, which I don't, but I am not going to say anything about him because I suggest you see him yourself. He is definitely a more domineering character than that dreadful Monsieur Phillipe, who Nicky actually raised to the rank of a general, and the other holy men and lunatics who have been hanging round ever since Alix came to Russia and made friends with the Montenegrins. The holy ones only have to do one thing to gain her favour: say what she wants to hear. I am not going to say any more. But wait, I know Rasputin is going tomorrow to the Kleinmichels' reception, so we will go too and you can make up your own mind. I will send a message that we will come. I need not tell you that she will be delighted, and you can have a decent dinner for once, instead of spending the evening eating carrots and reading Thomas à Kempis.'

Countess Kleinmichel welcomed Ella, saying it was a great honour to receive the saint of Moscow, but Ella did not listen because she was looking carefully at Rasputin. He appeared better dressed than the last time she had seen him. He still wore simple moujik's clothes and boots, but was cleaner, although his greasy hair hung down on either side of his lined face, while his beard looked straggly and unclipped.

When he was presented, he bowed low, and as he lifted his head, opened his eyes wide, stared and blatantly tried to convey some message. Ella's experience in Moscow had given her a new insight into the ways of so-called holy men, and when she stared back, rejecting his influence, she saw his eyes falter before he looked away and bowed to hide his embarrassment. She watched him, whenever she could, for the rest of the evening, and saw that while he looked happy, compelling and commanding when he was talking to women, especially pretty women, with men he fidgeted and spoke in a loud voice, and looked uneasy and shifty, as if anxious to get away. She noticed that he had a charming smile, but his vague, meaningless phrases, which carried across the room, were those of an uneducated, pretentious peasant, over-anxious to impress, and she wondered how Alix could believe in his cleverness, which had nothing to do with his animal powers of healing.

When they arrived, she told Miechen of her surprise, and begged her to explain privately what was happening. It was unpleasant to live in Moscow and hear every sort of story without knowing the truth. Miechen replied she was willing to tell Ella everything, but she must promise never to repeat a word to Alix since this would only cause a terrible row.

'Actually, I was sure you would ask me, so I have looked up all the papers I was shown last year and I can tell you as much as anybody because poor Peter Stolypin had the Okhrana investigate his life, and he gave me their and his conclusions last year, shortly before he was murdered.'

When Miechen mentioned Peter Stolypin, Ella noticed tears in her eyes and, without thinking asked: 'Why do you look so sad?'

Her sister-in-law looked at her sharply before saying in an exasperated voice: 'You know, my dear, I have now a great affection for you, but sometimes your saintly unworldliness gets on my nerves. Great men and events mean as little to you as the first snowfall. I believe you are unaware that, after 1905 and 1906, when we came to the brink of revolution, the Empire would have disintegrated had it not been for the strength of Stolypin. He was accused of brutality in subduing the revolutionaries, but all he did was to punish violence and murderers and bring back peace and order, while his plans that the peasants should own their own farmland will, I believe, if it has time, change the face of Russia and create a prosperous, loyal peasantry, the greatest safeguard a Tsar could have. And now he has been killed, and you ask me why I look sad. Well, I look sad because the strongest man in Russia has been slaughtered and there is no one else who will stand up to Nicky.'

She smiled then, her whole face softening at the sight of Ella's embarrassment.

'Really, I have only told you what you should know. Anyhow, let me get back to that horrible monk and the extraordinary fact that, the day before Stolypin was killed, Rasputin, when he saw him drive by in a carriage, shouted after him, "Death is riding behind you!" which was inexplicable. But Rasputin was never the wicked man that he is now said to be. All Stolypin's investigators could discover was that he once stole a horse when he was young and dabbled with the Old Believers and other sects, though it could not be proved he was ever a

Khlysty, or practised flagellation , sensual rites or the self-infliction of wounds like some members of those eccentric sects. They found that he had powers of healing animals and peasants of minor complaints. Indeed, he is a typical holy man, but, at the same time, a braggart, liar and fighter.

'Certainly he drinks, and debauches women, to whom he was and is exceedingly attractive, but not in any straghtforward way, for he often seduces them by using a kind of hocus-pocus of pretending that he is testing their moral strength or some such nonsense. He is quite old, you know. He must be fifty now, and until four years ago, when he stopped Alexis's bleeding, he had lived for forty-five years without committing greater crimes than stealing that horse and continually getting fighting drunk. You know, he has been married for nearly twenty years, and is a good father to his three children, whom he visits twice a year. His wife is fond of him and calmly dismisses his unfaithfulness with the simple sentence, "Gregory has enough for us all." And Ella – I hope you will forgive me for being frank, but you asked my opinion, and it is interesting – even though he has possessed dozens of women, none of them have held it against him when he has left them after only making love to them once or twice. Neither could the investigators find any of his women who would complain that he had been cruel to them. So, really, he isn't an ogre. Stolypin said that while it is true that his friendship with Alix had done her immense harm, nobody seems to have realized she has, in turn, done him immense spiritual harm, for he was, before he knew her, only a harmless holy man, moving from place to place, living from hand to mouth.

'He has never stolen or cared for money, and when he has a large sum, he immediately gives it away to the first beggar who asks him. Stolypin thought that he definitely has had a good effect on Alexis, having the sort of calming power which reassures children and calms women and releases Alexis's tensions, which are one of the causes of his internal bleeding.

'Stolypin added: "You cannot pretend Russian magic does not exist," but he could not see how things will get worse every year, for already Rasputin's character is deteriorating, and as Alix grows more dependent, she spoils him more and more. Recently she has written idiotic letters to him, and has even been encouraging her girls to write as well. The more she favours him, the more she corrupts him. The worse he behaves, the more he is attacked, as are royal favourites always. The consequence is that when he defends himself against those who she tells him have attacked him, it is called meddling in politics. Actually, he is merely retaliating against those who want to get rid of him, which is understandable, for Alix's behaviour has placed him in the centre of a vicious circle. The trouble is that Nicky, whose life has been an unending agony ever since Alexis was known to be ill, not unnaturally likes Rasputin because he keeps Alix quiet and so gives him a bit of peace, and, you know, when Alix is peaceful, Nicky is perfectly happy, for he loves her more than anything in the world.

'And so, although Stolypin gave Nicky, before he died, all the facts about Rasputin's women, orgies, fights, drunken stupidities and mad boasts, none of which Alix allows herself to believe, he guessed that Nicky wouldn't show her his proofs, because it would have meant the end of his peace, and he hasn't. It all comes down to the fact, I am afraid, that their world is confined to the nursery at Tsarskoye Selo, and as long as there is peace there, and Alexis is well, neither of them care what happens anywhere else, even if thousands are killed.'

Ella heard with relief that her belief in her sister's innocence was confirmed, the Moscow stories having no foundations, but she could not help wondering what was going to happen in the future.

'Is there no way to make Alix realize the harm which her stupid friendship with Rasputin is causing?'

'I don't think so,' said Miechen. 'The trouble is that Alix has put a stupid, God-touched peasant into a position of eminence and can't see how his only virtue is his healing powers, absolutely refusing to believe that when he is drunk he lies about their relationship. Thanks to her generosity, he is surrounded by scum, including spies, so Stolypin told me, put there by Willy to find out everything they can, which has been a good deal, for Alix asks his advice and tells him everything. But you can't altogether blame him, for neither Alix nor Nicky, having raised him to a powerful position, has ever handed him a kopek, so he has to live by what people give him and he is naturally generous and indiscreet. His indiscretions and political advice madden Ministers, and even his friends, for he is an uneducated, debauched peasant who can hardly write. Naturally, the honestest of them protest, and point out that the state secrets he relates to followers seriously damage imperial interests and allow the Germans to be aware of everything that happens at court. Any criticism makes Alix blind with rage and causes her to beg Nicky to rid himself of these loyalists, whose objection to Rasputin's treachery she represents as impertinence to the Tsar. At the moment she has only one idea: to place in positions of power those who are willing to support her friend. Soon we will only have as Ministers wretched men like Goremykin, with no qualifications except loyalty to the moujik. War grows more likely each year. If ever there was a time when the Empire needed its best men, it is now. Thanks to Alix, we are getting the worst. I don't know if you can do anything. Perhaps you might be able to persuade Alix to see him only when Alexis is ill. That would do some good, but I am afraid she'd be furious with you.'

Ella sat thinking, and then said slowly: 'I think I should say something, but I'll have to pick the right moment, for poor Alix's unhappiness makes her prickly even with me.'

But whether it was through disinclination to upset her sister or circumstance, Ella never found the opportunity, and soon returned to Moscow to immerse herself happily in her work to the extent where she had little time to think. And then, in the winter, came celebrations of the centenary of the Battle of Borodino, which Ella thought was rather embarrassing, as the Tsar came to Moscow and thanked God, before more than 100,000 people, for the victory over the French, at that moment Russia's closest ally.

In 1913, Rasputin momentarily fell out of favour, and a passionate, detailed and embarrassing attack was launched on him by Ileodore, a monk formerly one of his greatest admirers. Ella persuaded herself that Rasputin might disappear without her having to face the meeting.

In the early part of the winter of 1914, Ella went to Livadia, which Nicky had rebuilt and then had furnished by Maples in London. It struck her as extraordinary that anybody could think of living with that pale, shining furniture. Nicky showed with such pride the new decoration, that she found herself agreeing it was lovely. She had had a letter from Victoria, saying she would come with Ella on a tour of the holy shrines and convents late that summer, but, in the meantime, she should surely speak to Alix, for even in England everyone believed the rumours about her close friendship with the monk. The letter was decisive. Ella decided that she must face her sister. But, the next morning, news arrived of Gregory having been stabbed by a prostitute in his home town and being unlikely to live. At this time Ella knew she could not say anything, for Alix was lost in hysterical grief. Gregory had become her god. Once she said: 'You know, he has told me that he has heard from the Almighty that after he dies the Romanovs will not survive for six months. He never lies, so I must believe him.'

As the days passed, it appeared that neither the wound – which would have killed an ordinary man – nor a day-long journey across rough roads to hospital, had proved fatal, and he was slowly improving. Ella had a letter from Alix, stressing her relief and violently attacking the enemies of her friend, who openly displayed their disappointment that he had not died.

In July, Victoria arrived, and they had to make up their minds whether, in view of the likelihood of war, it was wise to set out on their tour. She said that Louis, who had been First Sea Lord since 1912, was practising for the first time the full mobilization of the British Fleet and was convinced that England would be fighting by September and that Winston thought it would start earlier. But Victoria said both of them had been making the same prophecy for years, and that if she had listened to them she would never have left England. She had discovered that all the Ministers were going away as usual, and Margot Asquith was sending her daughter to Holland on the 26th, so why should not she travel as well? Sir Edward Grey always appeared to settle matters peaceably at the last moment, and, after all, they had known Willy all their lives and he had always bullied and threatened. Surely he would not be mad enough to encourage Austria to follow a policy which would entail fighting France and Russia, and probably England as well, for behind all this bristling and boasting he was a weak, vain man, and Alix and Nicky certainly did not want a war. Did it make sense that Russia would fight over Austria dominating Serbia? For the past seven years, the Balkans had been in turmoil and the pessimists had wrongly prophesied war. Finally reassured by hearing how the British Ambassador in Russia had booked tickets for a holiday in England, they started their journey down the Volga in an imperial river boat at Nizhny Novgorod, stopping and visiting shrines and convents near to the river. Ella was happy to be with her sister again. They had long, inconclusive talks about Alix, and both agreed that Rasputin was to blame. He could not be expected to change his character or way of life suddenly at his age, but it was a great pity he had not died of his wound.

Despite her best intentions, Ella could not look at her niece Louise; she was so ugly. It was curious: she did not mind dressing a septic wound, but she was repelled by the poor girl's face. She said a prayer. It was no good – her eyes would not turn towards her. She admitted a sin.

After ten days, they left the Tsar's boat and separated, Victoria and poor Louise wishing to tour the Ural Mountains. The first she heard of the situation changing was that Nicky had ordered the mobilization of the Russian army. Nobody seemed to know why.

Ella continued on her journey, visiting convents beyond Perm, only to be woken on the morning of 2 August by Sister Varya bringing in a telegram to say that the Germans had declared war on Russia the evening before. Ella went down on her knees and prayed silently and with all her heart that her own country would be defeated, and, to Sister Varya's amazement, ended by saying out loud: 'Thank you, God, that I did not marry Willy.'

On the way back by rail to Moscow, to Ella's astonishment, patriotic crowds gathered in their thousands at the stations to cheer the Tsar's sister-in-law, and each time she was asked to say a short prayer for the victory of Pan-Slavism to the multitudes, including passengers and porters, who knelt in dead silence on platforms and low roofs as she asked, at the top of her voice, for God's aid. She had lost her voice by the time the train reached Moscow, but had come to understand why Nicky had been forced into confronting Austria. Millions of Russians believed that the Austrians intended to destroy their defenceless Serbian cousins and demanded a holy war. She realized that this passionate belief would overcome Nicky's weak resistance.

11

When Ella returned to her convent, she knew that the happiest time of her life was over. She saw she would no longer be allowed by circumstances to live quietly with her sisters, seeking out cases of ill-fortune and misery, educating children and looking after the old, but that once again, as in the Japanese war, she would be dragged into the imperial effort. She remembered how, ten years before, the opportunity to help in the war had meant for her the end of years of unhappy idleness, but this time it was different. She felt she was abandoning practical, necessary good works to mix herself up with the dreaded inefficiency of the army machine. She knew that the country was unprepared, and anyhow, although she had accepted the Russian way of life, she could not but dislike the brutal fact of Russia now being at war with her own countrymen.

There was one good thing. Ernie had told her last year that, because of his pacifism, he had told Willy he could not fight himself, although Hesse would support a war in every possible way. His plea was understood and he was put in charge of hospital trains. How odd it was, she thought, that she would be in charge of hospital trains on one side, looking after Russians wounded by the Germans, while Ernie was on the other, looking after Germans wounded by the Russians.

The following week she went to St Petersburg and saw Nicky, who told her, in a voice which could not conceal his excitement, how when, on the declaration of war, he had appeared on the balcony of the Winter Palace, the whole packed square had gone on its knees before wildly applauding him. Alix said the peasants had shown they were as one behind their Emperor, but had whispered to Ella, when Nicky was out of the room, 'Gregory is against the war. He says it is a great mistake and that many will die, but I support Nicky. He did not want to support Serbia at first, and I don't think he would have done if Gregory had been here. But Sazanov and the Pan-Slavs persuaded him he had to fight. Perhaps it is God's way of uniting Russia behind their little father and showing the peasants how they need him to curb Willy's madness.'

Ella said nothing. She could not understand why Austria had given an ultimatum to Serbia which they could not accept. She could understand, having seen the depth of Slav feeling, why Nicky had to support and even fight Austria, but why had Willy supported and encouraged Austria, which meant that Germany had to fight Russia, and consequently France and England? Even in

St Petersburg, nobody had explained her doubts. But war was declared and she must work for her adopted country. Olga and Tatiana already wore nurses' uniforms and looked forward to their nursing as if it were a treat. Ella tried to explain to them the horror of war, but they looked at her with the blank eyes of uncomprehending children and she realized, once again, that they had not grown up.

Before Ella left, she asked Nicky if he would be making any changes in his ministry. He looked at her with the frightened face which he sometimes put on when an unexpected question was asked. She said she had wondered, as Goremykin was seventy-four and known to be in poor health, and the strain might be too much for him.

'Is that all you have heard?' asked Nicky suspiciously.

'Yes,' she replied, and he looked relieved. She could not help wondering whether an old man of seventy-four, who never had an opinion of his own, was the right man to lead the Empire into war. At the same time, she had hoped that the Minister of the Interior, Maklakov, would be changed, for although she never mixed herself up with politics, she knew that during the past two years this pigheaded Minister had constantly told the Emperor how he should put every obstacle in the way of the local councils who were striving to train and organize Red Cross units. Maklakov insisted that the plan was a dangerous innovation against the spirit of autocracy and the authority of the Emperor, and hence was revolutionary in nature. She could not help thinking it was a pity that Nicky was not changing such hopeless men when the whole of Russia had shown it was behind him and wished only to be led in the right direction.

She returned sadly to Moscow, and set about the reorganization of supply trains. Remembering from last time the terrible trouble which the railway and Lake Baikal had caused, she asked the station master what problems he would have to face on this occasion. He lifted his hands in exasperation.

'We have been told to move two million men. I don't see how we can, but we'll try.'

For the first two weeks, nothing happened. The inactivity was in marked contrast to the Western Front, where the Germans poured through Belgium into France. Paléologue, the French Ambassador in Russia, was known to be desperately imploring the Emperor to create an eastern diversion, as Paris was in danger of falling. Then, on 17 August, General Rennenkampf was attacked by the German General François. To the general delight, François was pushed back, and in a battle two days later, Rennenkampf defeated the Germans again and continued to advance into East Prussia. At the same time, General Samsonov – Ella was painfully having to learn all these new names and positions – was advancing from the south from Warsaw.

Toasts were drunk every night to the advancing Russians, and it was claimed that they would be in Berlin within three weeks. Then, all at once, silence fell, the only news being that Rennenkampf was continuing northwards without much opposition, the papers triumphantly announcing that the German Commander-in-Chief, Prittwitz, had been replaced by an old general called Von Hindenberg. Suddenly, out of optimism, without warning, came news that the Germans had avoided Rennenkampf, fallen on Samsonov, who had shot himself, and annihilated his army at Tannenburg. No attempt was made to conceal the disaster, and the Grand Duke Nicholas announced: 'God has visited us with a great misfortune.'

The whole of Moscow grew confused and frightened. How could apparent victory have turned into disaster? Ella, hearing that the British Ambassador, Sir George Buchanan, was in Moscow, called to see him. She had known him for years, as he had been the tactful Minister in Darmstadt when Ducky was married to Ernie. He personified, for her, the qualities of England which she had always admired: courage, straightforwardness and discretion, and she asked him without hesitation what had happened. He received her with old-fashioned courtesy, and then told her he had known her for so long that he knew he could trust her implicitly. It would be a relief for him to speak to Her Imperial Highness, on whom he could rely to be discreet. He had first-hand reports from the front, which indicated that General Rennenkampf had made the mistake of not keeping in touch with the enemy and had allowed a beaten army to regroup under new commanders.

'As for Samsonov, he seems to have divided his army in an unwise manner, but he had in the fighting been at a terrific disadvantage because of his stretched supply lines, for during the last twenty years the Germans have covered East Prussia with carefully thought-out railway lines, designed not to take people from one town to another, but to reinforce troops from north to south or west to east.'

Sir George continued: 'On the advice of our military attaché, I have several times asked His Imperial Majesty if he was aware of the military advantage which this would give to the Germans in the event of war, and have also pointed out to him that since the Russian railways have a wider gauge, it would be impossible for his soldiers to use their own railway transport on the German reilway lines and that this matter should be seriously considered. He assured me that he would speak to his generals about the matter, but nothing, I know, has been done, and as a result, what could and should have been a great victory has been turned into defeat. I fear that your losses will exceed 150,000 men, and that is a conservative estimate.'

Ella told him how her trains could not move yet, despite her daily visits to the converters' yards. He stood up and walked up and down.

'I am afraid your difficulties are those of the whole Russian army, but, with respect, the greatest loss which your soldiers will have is not the shortages of hospital trains, important as they are, but of guns, rifles and ammunition. I fear that when the war is continued it will be found that, as the two armies come face to face on level territory, the Germans will have four pieces of artillery to one of yours. As for the supplies, my military attachés can see no way in which ammunition and food can be brought up, if there is food and ammunition to bring up. I can say to you what I can say to no other member of the imperial family: that Russia has gone into this war without enough trained men, without organization, without adequate artillery or supplies of shells, and that, even after the defeat of Tannenburg, no lesson has been learned. With the exception of the Grand Duke Nicholas, efficiency is unknown in the highest commands, and the trouble about him is that he is hated by the War Minister, Soukhomlinov, who would place the defeat of the Grand Duke before that of the Germans or Austrians. But there is one thing which your soldiers have which is of inestimable value: that is bravery. They will go anywhere. One unfortunate aspect of this is, however, already apparent: the officers are going into battle standing up while encouraging their men to crawl. Consequently, their casualties have been disproportionate to those of their men. This is a disaster: there are gigantic reserves of men, but a minute reserve of officer material, and however brave the men are, without officers they will not fight well. The Tsar should tell his generals that they cannot afford chivalry.'

He came and leaned towards Ella and looked down, a sad figure of rectitude, caring desperately for the Russian losses. Without thinking, she asked simply, 'Why are things so hopeless?'

Sir George for a moment looked surprised at her question, then, turning his pale eyes on her, he replied: 'It will be a relief to tell you that I will not even ask for a pledge of discretion. I know you will not repeat my words.'

He paused.

'You know, I have been here since 1910, and it has been my duty, taking into consideration the German preparations for war, to examine impartially the internal position in this country. It has been a difficult time for me, for it has seemed to me that the country has been undermined by pointless change and strife. When I arrived, Stolypin was Prime Minister. In many ways, he was a great man, and had his land reforms had time to mature, they would have transformed the country. In 1911, I received news that the Tsar was to replace him in response to antagonisms at which I must ask you to guess. Before he could be dismissed, he was murdered and fortunately replace by Kokovtsev, but then, in the same year, Lulkyan, the Minister of Religion was replaced by Sabler, a strange choice, and Bishop Hermogen, a man respected throughout all western Russia, was banished by imperial decree, while Bishop Anthony of Tobolsk was exiled to Tiba. The public considered that these last three decisions were made by Rasputin. In the same year, the Minister Makarov returned to the Emperor certain letters written to Rasputin, of which you may have some knowledge. These letters were causing immense damage to the imperial family, but all that happened was that Makarov was replaced by an old-fashioned autocrat, Nikolaslakov. Luckily, the Prime Minister, Kokovtsev, remained. If he was not a man of Stolypin's stature, he was honest and sincere. He was dismissed in February of this year and succeeded by Goremykin, who is seventy-four and whose career has thrived on agreeing with every word of those placed above him.

'I give you these bare details to explain to you why, in the four years of my stay in this country, the fabric of the government and the fabric of religious stability have both been fractured with unforeseeable results. Perhaps even worse have been the divisions among the military. The two dominant figures in this period have been the Grand Duke Nicholas, for whom I have unlimited respect, and the War Minister, Soukhomlinov, for whom I have no respect, and, to make matters worse, during the past nine years there have been no less than six Chiefs of Staff whose main purpose has seemed to our military attachés to be to undo their predecessors' works. At the beginning of the war, thank God, the

279

Tsar chose the Grand Duke to be Commander-in-Chief but, to mollify Soukhomlinov, he then made the Grand Duke accept General Yanushkevich as his Chief of Staff. The War Minister has one fault: he will never admit he is at fault. Although he has not stockpiled enough ammunition and has not an adequate supply of rifles, he will not admit it, and both I and the French Ambassador have tried to persuade him to accept advantageous sales from the United States. He has declined. I feel certain that, at Tannenberg, the Germans hopelessly outgunned your soldiers, while the position of the wounded frankly terrifies me. The War Minister has allocated three surgeons to every 4,000 men.

'I spoke to you earlier about the German railways being strategically placed. You have another disadvantage. In all Germany, the main roads are laid with stone. In Russia, they have no foundation. You are therefore asking your soldiers to fight with limited artillery and no reserves of ammunition against superior artillery, strategic railways, metalled roads and unlimited ammunition. Russia alone has courage, and by courage alone she first made advances in the north and prevented a German breakthrough after Tannenberg. And what is more,' added Sir George, 'it has enabled them to advance into Galicia, and so far our information is that not only are they defeating the Austrians in battle, but that large numbers of Ukrainians, Czechs and Poles are coming over to the Russian side. That is good news, but what frightens me is that when the serious fighting breaks out in the spring, the War Minister will not have enough artillery or ammunition or, even more importantly, rifles, to take on the enemy on equal terms.

'I have no more to say. I am sad at what I have had to say. Meanwhile, you can help. Do all you can to get the local Red Cross units brought to the front. On them the weight of saving lives will fall. You will find that when your hospital trains return you will hear more sorry stories. Get the Red Cross to help you.'

Ella felt so moved that she could not speak, but stood up, then walked out of the room without saying goodbye. She knew Sir George would understand her emotions. A footman was standing outside the door, and in the high, gaslit corridor, she noticed, as she walked past, that he made a sign to a man at the end of the passage, who immediately disappeared. Before she had reached the top of the great stairway, she heard a rustling noise behind her and, turning round, saw a large, overblown woman with a fat, purple face covered with white powder, a large mouth, huge white teeth and her hair fluffed up all over her head into little curls. Ella immediately understood the footman's movements. They had been stationed to call Lady Georgie, the Ambassador's wife, a gushing, self-satisfied woman who, to everyone's delight, Serge had once over-turned in a boat at Darmstadt. She broke at once into a full flood of conversation.

'I am so delighted by chance to meet Your Imperial Highness. You will know that I have opened a British Colony Hospital for wounded Russian soldiers, and volunteers of the best possible type have come in from every side. Sibyl Grey, who I think you know, was one of the first to join us. I only hope that Your Imperial Highness will honour us with a visit one day, although we are all aware of your time-consuming good works.'

At that moment, a rather pretty younger edition of the Ambassador's wife came running breathlessly down the passage, looking as if she had just changed into her best dress.

'Ah, here is Meriel to welcome you,' said Lady Georgina in a surprised voice. 'She, of course, works full time, and this is her first day off for weeks.'

Meriel made the lowest possible curtsey and gave Ella one of those dazzling smiles usually seen on the faces of girls of eighteen. Surely, Ella thought, the girl was at least twenty-five? Lady Georgie was off again about her war effort and the price of linen, and how quickly Englishwomen learnt nursing. Ella could only stand still, remembering how Alexander III had said that while ambassadors are bearable, their wives are unbearable, being nobodies until they are fifty and then giving themselves insufferable airs. Ella was in a bad temper when she finally got away, and agreed with Alexander III. It was sad, for Sir George had made her feel the English would be true allies.

But when she returned to the convent, all the feelings he had inspired in her returned, and she sent for her sisters and decided to start yet another hospital for the wounded troops. She would go and raise money the next day. Meanwhile, they must increase their numbers, and if any of those there wished to go to the front, they had her blessing, but they must not leave until they had trained others to take their place.

By the end of the next day, Ella agreed to the renting of a palace for the duration of the war and had raised enough to begin alterations immediately and build three operating theatres and change the water supply. Then she decided to go and see if she could persuade Alix to see that the local branches of the Red Cross were drafted to the front.

On her arrival at the capital, she was told that Miechen had taken over the leadership of the women's war effort, and had insisted that all wounded soldiers from Tannenburg should be brought to St Petersburg. The consequences were frightening, the result being over 100,000 maimed scattered across the city in houses and palaces, while unfortunately the doctors had no lists of their whereabouts. The result was that many soldiers were dying of gangrene and lack of correct attention. She wondered why Alix had allowed it. She understood when she saw her, dressed up as a nurse, talking of nothing but her own nursing feats. The hospital in the Palace of Elizabeth at Tsarskoye Selo was to be hers alone and the single contribution she was prepared to make to the war. She willingly abdicated all imperial responsibilities to whoever wished to fill them. Alix proudly told Ella how she had shaved the leg of a wounded man before an operation. When Ella asked who was to organize the Red Cross and the women of St Petersburg and avoid a repetition of the chaos after Tannenburg, she said, vaguely: 'Oh, Miechen, of course.'

Ella was, for a moment, too surprised to speak. She knew how they disliked each other, and how deeply Alix resented Miechen's salon, which, she considered, undermined her own position, and here she was at the beginning of a great war calmly handing over authority to her. She looked carefully at Alix and saw she was unmoved by her unconcious abdication, which illustrated how much her sister's life had contracted. Her world began and ended with her family at Tsarskoye Selo. Nothing outside it mattered. She and Nicky remained aloof from the world with their backward girls, their sick boy and doubtless, when he was well again, the monk Gregory. How could Nicky understand the movements or the shortages? She felt a cold anger for her sister, and left without a fond word, but, she was certain, Alix noticed nothing.

As Ella was walking downstairs, she stopped. She must say something. She walked back, and to Alix's obvious surprise sat down by her side. She leaned over, took her sister's hand and said: 'Dearest, it is a mistake to leave so much to Miechen. She will,' she said, speaking very slowly, 'be inefficient and proud and you will get the blame. Already I have heard that she is giving herself airs. You must take over many of her activities, at least in name, otherwise she will say you are incapable and spread even worse rumours about you and Gregory.'

Alix flushed and stood up and kissed Ella. 'You are right. I will do what you say. I had forgotten what an evil woman she is.'

Then, without the slightest warning, she threw herself into Ella's arms and cried out through her sobs: 'I worry every moment of the day and night about Alexis, and Gregory is still wounded and cannot be here to help. But I know it is all a test, a terrible test, and if I have faith, one day he will be well and Emperor like his father. To give away anything is to give up faith. That is why Nicky must rule. That is why I must make him rule. I love him so.'

Ella ran out of the room.

12

Winter stabilized the battle fronts, except for constant skirmishing, which filled the ambulance trains and made Ella increasingly impatient with the time it took to convert her carriages. By December, only three out of twelve were in use. Every day she continued to visit the railway yards, and every day found tiresome reasons for complaint, always arising out of the haphazardness of the Russian mind. She found it almost impossible to persuade the foremen to plan work in an orderly fashion. For instance, a large operating table would be firmly screwed into the floor and would then have to be unscrewed again to allow the necessary cupboards to be placed against the wall. Such stupidities made her intensely irritable, and cold and cross with her sisters, and unable to feel, out of frustration, affection for even her relations.

One of her cousins by marriage, Oleg, son of Constantine, was killed and brought back to be buried on his father's estate near Moscow. Oleg's sister, Titania, was doubly upset, as her husband was also reported missing. Ella sat for a long time, talking, trying to explain to the distracted girl that if both were dead they would meet again before long.

As she talked, Ella knitted Titania a little woollen hood and gave it to her as a parting present when she said goodnight after they had prayed side by side for the dead brother and missing husband. Titania burst into tears and tried to throw her arms around Ella's neck, but found herself pushed away with the brusque remark, 'Don't do that.' Ella never knew why she had behaved in such a cruel way. All she knew was that she felt it necessary to repel any ostentatious sign of affection. Not understanding the reason for her new coldness of heart worried her.

The last three army trains were ready for service in the spring at exactly the time when a German offensive was launched in the extreme north and a German-Austrian attack in Galicia. Ella spent a week checking every detail of the supplies. Every conceivable requirement was sent, including six sets of mobile operating theatres designed by herself which could be carried even into the inaccessible Carpathians. The operating table, the disinfectants, metal containers of chloroform, bandages and splints, steel instruments, crutches, stretchers and a collapsible tent could be carried in satchels by eight orderlies. Ella was pleased with herself.

The day the trains left, it was apparent that the southern army, in danger of becoming cut off, was in full retreat through the mountains. The telephone was now working between the front and Moscow, and Ella had insisted on a direct line to the Red Cross headquarters so she could be sure of her trains arriving at the most convenient places. At the end of three days, they had still not appeared, but she was assured that this was because of heavy armaments moving south. She waited another day, then went to the station. The Commanding Officer swore that everything was in order and they must be somewhere along the line. Ella was not satisfied, and insisted on going to the station master's office to see whether he had any knowledge of the position of the trains. The station master, a fat little man with a waxed moustache, appeared confident. Yes, he would produce the book, and yes, he should be able to tell her their approximate position.

The book was produced and she saw that the three trains had been sent to Sebastopol in the Crimea. The station master examined the writing, and at once sent for a head clerk, who traced the handwriting to an old man who had come back to work to help his country. He appeared, trembling with terror. Yes, he admitted the error. He had been writing to his daughter that day who lived in Sebastopol. He threw himself at her feet. She asked him to get up and go away and asked the station master how, once the original mistake had been made, no one had questioned it. What possible use could three hospital trains filled with medical supplies be in the Crimea, hundreds of miles from any fighting? Surely someone must have checked the destinations and queried the trains' departure to a peaceful area?

The station master shrugged his shoulders. It was the train drivers' fault as well. He could not conceive why they had not brought such orders to his attention. Anyhow, they would be dismissed; it would never happen again.

Ella returned almost ill with frustration, and when she got back rang up the station master and said that if he did not have the trains found and diverted to their correct destination within a week, she would telephone the Tsar and ask for his dismissal. She blamed herself for not having checked every detail. How could Russia win a war when nobody cared what happened? But, at least, in this war here was one honest mistake.

The next day other hospital trains began to return from the front and to remind her of Sir George's warnings. Some men recounted how their artillery was only allowed to fire three to five rounds a day, while their regiments were decimated by an endless barrage from the German guns. The army was retreating everywhere.

At this time of acute depression, Ella became conscious for the first time of personal unpopularity and that her nationality was now being held aginst her. Twice as she walked in the area near the Khodynka, men jumped off the pavement to avoid her and spat at her feet. Another time, she saw a woman whispering to little children, who then ran up to her and shouted: 'German go home! Traitoress go home!' Alix sent her broadsheets in which she, Ella, Marie Pavlovna and Costantine's wife, all German by birth, were caricatured as spies, and an enclosed letter saying, 'My Friend says I belong to Russia with both my heart and soul so I do not heed these lies.' Ella threw it on the ground, but thought she must go and comfort Alix, who was alone, since Nicky was in

Galicia. This absence meant that for the first time since their marriage the two would be separated on Nicky's birthday, the 6th, a sacred moment to Alix, who never forgot an anniversary.

She arrived in Petrograd on the evening of the 6th to bad news: General Von Mackensen's army had broken through. Alix said she had heard on good authority – 'though I am not saying from whom', and she gave Ella an angry look – 'that casualties so far are between three and a half and four million, and yet the army is fighting as magnificently as ever. And oh, Ella, I forgot, Nicky was very pleased with your message. Look, he has not felt neglected on his birthday,' and she handed to Ella three telegrams headed 'Starva' (the Russian equivalent to the English G.H.Q.).

Stavka, 5 May 1915. Have just arrived safely. Lovely weather. The woods are now quite green and smell delightfully. I am just off to church. Thanks for telegram. I embrace you tenderly. Nicky.

Stavka, 6 May 1915. I am very touched by your lovely presents and good wishes. Am sorry that we are not together. I thank Ella. I kiss you and the dear children fondly. Nicky.

Stavka, 6 May 1915. Again I thank you warmly for your good wishes. Be kind enough to thank our Friend for his moving words. After great heat and a night's downpour, it has become much cooler . . .

Ella sat silently reading the telegrams, and then read them again. How extraordinary of Nicky to send such telegrams in the middle of a battle in which thousands of his soldiers daily died. How strange of Alix to consider them normal.

It was a difficult week for Ella, as Alix was obsessed with Alexis, who had fallen and hurt himself. One evening Tsarskoye seemed full of whispering and furtive glances, and when Ella sat in her bedroom, going over plans for the extension of her hospital which avoided spoiling the garden, one of Alix's ladies-in-waiting came in, looking embarrassed, and talked almost incessantly for two hours, changing the subject with startling rapidity but never drawing breath. After a while Ella only half-listened and continued to examine her plans, having realized that the lady-in-waiting was making sure she did not leave her room. Rasputin must have arrived secretly to comfort the little boy.

All the week the news was bad. The Przemysl Fortress was suffering a bombardment so shattering that its evacuation became inevitable, and every day Alix serenely told Ella such bad news as: 'Von Mackensen has reoccupied Lvov, the capital of Galicia'. Ella felt sorry for Alix, but was glad to be leaving the next day, her sister's calmness and happy concentration on her family seeming sinful when so many men lay dying on battlefields for her husband.

After lunch on the 12th, Ella planned to leave Tsarskoye for St Petersburg to catch the night train. She admitted to herself that she was leaving as soon as she could. To her surprise, Alix was radiant.

'I have good news from Nicky,' she said, and handed Ella another telegram.

Stavka, 12 May 1915. Warmest thanks for news and dear letter. Divine weather; the lilac has come out in bloom. I am leaving at two o'clock. I kiss you tenderly. Nicky.

Ella quickly kissed her sister goodbye, though Alix appeared oblivious to her fond farewell and said vaguely: 'Do come again some time.'

The next week, in Moscow, the Chief of Police visited Ella and told her anti-German riots had occurred and she should not walk alone in the streets. He was stationing policemen in the grounds. She decided to travel the next day to the station by car, and had the window smashed by a stone. Her grief was so deep that she felt as if a knife had been driven into her heart, but she made herself understand her tormentors' point of view. After all, she was a German, and so was Alix, and stories had appeared in all the newspapers of how Russians had been beaten and tortured in Berlin. She increased her own attention to the sick, quadrupled the number of her sisters; and as the summer went on, gave over the administration to Marie and, herself, perpetually nursed the seriously wounded. She often questioned the men as soon as they came in, and before they had any idea of who she was, as to the conditions under which they were fighting. Their replies appalled her. Not only had the army almost run out of artillery shells, but the German artillery daily destroyed whole companies and regiments so that new men had to be sent in to the line. Two batches of patients told her that in their companies only one man in three was armed. Despite this, their orders were to advance carrying sticks, and to seize an armed companion's rifle when he was killed.

In early June, Ella received another communication from Alix, a copy of a letter to her from their cousin Daisy, who was wife to the Swedish Crown Prince. It stated how Willy had written to her, saying he had heard from Ludendorff that the spectacle of the Russian infantrymen unceasingly charging, often unarmed, the German lines was the bravest and most terrible sight he had ever witnessed in battle. Underneath, Alix had written, 'It makes me proud.' Ella wondered how she could feel proud when the deaths of hundreds of thousands was being caused by a shortage of weapons. She was working so hard that she fell asleep and woke up to find the patient she was sitting with had died.

Two days later, Sir George, dapper and old-fashioned as ever, came to Moscow, and to her pleasure visited her at the convent. He said: 'I have come to give you good news, and then, when I have given it, to ask you a favour. To begin with, at last the Tsar has taken advice from the Grand Duke Nicholas and Rodzyanko and Lvov and many others. They have made him see at last how Soukhomlinov's inefficiency was costing thousands of lives. Luckily, Sazonov had proof of the War Minister having lied to him. So he is going, and also Malakov, who is as reactionary as it is possible to be. They will both be replaced by good men. Others to leave include Sabler, a friend of Rasputin's. There lies the danger, for the Tsar made decisions and changes which will be unpopular with Rasputin and consequently with the Empress. I gather that he was already expressed regret at taking the decision without her advice. Rasputin is put out and prophesying doom and has already announced to his gipsy friends, and indeed anyone who cares to listen, that he will have his revenge on the Tsar by making the Empress insist that he take over the command of all the armies from the Grand Duke Nicholas.'

Ella started to exclaim, 'But that is impossible – Nicky is the Tsar, he's not a general!'

'Why do you think it impossible? Rasputin is a transparent man with simple ambitions to remain in the position of power which he has won by his ability to cure the Tsarita. He boasts out loud of his plans, and both the Germans and the Allies know them. He has stated that in a few months the Tsar will take command, because he knows it is exactly what he has always wanted to do and that it makes sense from his point of view. With the Tsar at the front, the Tsarina will do exactly as he wishes, and all he wants is for his friends to be in power so as to maintain his position. Already we have information that he has persuaded the Tsarina to convince the Tsar that the Grand Duke Nicholas is planning to take his place, and the woman Vyrubova tells the Tsarina everything which Rasputin wants to hear. Naturally there is universal discontent, for I should say that the Russian army has already suffered, as far as we can estimate, three and a half million casualties in nine months, and it is easy to blame the Grand Duke, although Soukhomlinov is the culprit. Yet the danger, as I see it, is that the Tsar will persuade himself it is the right thing to do, especially since it was his original plan. The favour I have to ask you is that you try and dissuade your sister – for it is believed you are the only person who can change her mind – from this mad plan.

'Let me say again, the changes this month will, in a year transform your army, but until the snow comes it will face nothing except further retreats and disasters, for which the Tsar, if he becomes Commander-in-Chief, will be held wholly responsible. At the same time, it will necessitate his absence from Tsarskóye Selo, and consequently Rasputin will be the increasingly corrupt power behind the Tsarina. So the Tsar will not only face unpopularity as a soldier, but also contempt – I cannot soften the word – as a husband, which will undermine his position to a degree which will invite consequences I hardly dare to contemplate. I ask you again to try and convince your sister of the terrible position in which it will put her beloved husband, and to try and make her distrustful of Vyrubova, who is, we understand, entirely dominated by Rasputin.'

Ella sat silent, and then said simply: 'I hate all this underhand talk, and if I did not know you well enough, I would not think of such a thing. But honestly, I think Alexis's illness has unbalanced her mind. I don't think that at the moment, out of her worry, she knows what she is doing or understands what is happening. But even so, I cannot believe she will plan such a stupid idea. Even I can see it would be utter madness and I can't understand politics. But if she is trying to persuade Nicky, I am prepared to tell her the truth, if nobody else will, though please do not ask me to do such thing unless that awful man looks like persuading her to agree with his wicked plan.'

Sir George stood up and bowed, leaned forward and kissed her hand before leaving without another word. Ella thought it was clever of him; he must have realized her reluctance. Yet her promise made her feel disloyal and unhappy. Thinking back to her visit to Tsarskoye, she realized how much Alix now listened to Vyrubova, a fat, stupid character whom Alix adored out of guilt for having insisted she marry an unsuitable husband. Ella thought that you only had to see the woman's face, with its small mouth and tiny eyes, to realize she was an untrustworthy sycophant, and if she was indeed under Rasputin's influence, then it was surely very bad news.

13

Over the next two months, Ella shut her ears to gossip and politics. Indeed, such was her unpopularity in the town that she only walked out of the convent at night, and then only to see patients in ill-health, or those about to die. In the daytime, when she wished to visit the soldiers' hospital, she used an old cab.

Even in her army hospital she found a change of atmosphere. Sometimes, when she went into a room, she would notice how a group of undischarged soldiers would stop talking and avoid her eyes, averting shamed faces, sometimes not even saying good morning. The matron would usually look embarrassed and stammer that they were victims of German propaganda and it was her belief that 'they are spreading wicked rumours not only about Your Imperial Highness but the Tsarina as well, and they are, also, believers'.

Ella was relieved to find there was less pessimism about the military position, and that the great German offensives, while scoring bloody successes, had not achieved a breakthrough. Shortages of arms remained serious, but it seemed as if the military position was improving, with supplies getting through for the first time. Yet still the casualties grew at a frightening rate. She was often able to forget, in taking over the sickest cases, her own problems, and never, if possible, gave herself a moment to think.

One morning in August, Ella was informed that a young man had called to see her from the British Consulate. He presented her with a plain, untitled envelope, in which, on a blank sheet of paper, was written: 'The change in command which I told you about will soon take place.' Ella was amazed at such an irregularity, so unlike Buchanan, and startled, wrote a note saying she would be leaving for Tsarskoye Selo the next day. When Ella arrived she thought she had never seen Alix looking so well. She lost no time in starting her carefully rehearsed speech with saying she had heard Nicky was to become Commander-in-Chief.

'Surely this is dangerous?' she concluded.

For a moment, she saw a wavering look in Alix's eyes and tried to emphasize her point.

'And surely, not only will he be in danger from the enemy, but at home his opponents will take advantage of his absence. He is the source of all decisions and should be here.'

'Let me speak,' said Alix fiercely. 'Are you aware that ever since the beginning of war he has had total authority over all the armies and all the war areas, which now include Peterhof? Those powers were provided for the Commander-in-Chief because Nicky intended to command his armies at the start of the war. He was pursuaded not to. He will now have greater power than ever before.

Alix was standing upright, her eyes gleaming.

'Wait,' she said, 'you ask me to tell him to return. Let me show you what I have written to him,' and she picked up a whole bundle of papers and threw them into Ella's arms. 'Read my letters, I am proud you should know what I think of him, what I tell him. I will take away the last sheet,' and she pulled one sheet away from Ella and turned it upside down. 'But read the rest. Understand my faith, my belief, my determination. We will win by strength, he leading his armies, I protecting his interests and the future Emperor's here. Ella, read my letter. I am sure you will understand why God wishes him to lead his army.'

She kissed her sister and left Ella feeling as embarrassed as if she had opened a private door. She took up the first letter and read:

Tsarskoye Selo, 22 Aug. 1915

MY VERY OWN BELOVED ONE,

I cannot find words to express all I want to. My heart is far too full. I only long to hold you tight in my arms and whisper words in intense love, courage, strength and endless blessing. More than hard to let you go alone, so completely alone. But God is very near to you, more than ever. You have fought this great fight for your country and throne, alone with bravery and decision. Never have they seen such firmness in you before and it cannot remain without fruit. Do not fear for what remains behind. One must be severe and stop all at once. Lovey, I am here. Don't laugh at silly old wifey, but she has 'trousers' on unseen and I can get the old man [the Prime Minister] to come and keep him up to be energetic. Whenever I can be of the smallest use, tell me what to do. Use me, at such a time God will give me strength to help you, because our souls are fighting for the right against evil. It is all much deeper than appears to the eye. We, who have been taught to look at all from another side, see what the struggle here really is and means; you showing your mastery, proving yourself the Autocrat without whom Russia cannot exist. Had you given in now on these different questions, they would have dragged yet more out of you. Being firm is the only salvation. I know what it costs you and have and do suffer hideously for you. Forgive me, I beseech you, my Angel, for having left you no peace and worried you so much, but I know too well your marvellously gentle character and you had to shake it off this time, had to win your fight alone against all. It will be a glorious page in your reign and Russian history, the story of these weeks and days, and God, who is just and near you, will save your country and your throne through your firmness. A harder battle has rarely been fought than yours, and it will be crowned with success, only believe this. Your faith has been tried – your trust – and you remained firm as a rock, for that you will be blessed. God anointed you at your Coronation, He placed you where you

290

stand and you have done your duty, be sure, quite sure of this, and He forsaketh not His anointed. Our Friend's prayers arise night and day for you to Heaven and God will hear them. Those who fear and cannot understand your actions, will be brought by events to realize your great wisdom. It is the beginning of the glory of your reign. He (Rasputin) said so and I absolutely believe it. Your Sun is rising and today it shines so brightly. And so will you charm all those great blunderers, cowards, led astray, noisy, blind, narrow-minded and false beings this morning. And your sunbeam (Alexis) will appear to help you, your very own child. Won't that touch those hearts and make them realize what you are doing and what they dared to wish to do, to shake your throne, to frighten you with internal black forebodings; only a bit of success out there and they will change. They will go home into clean air and their minds will be purified and they will carry the picture of you and your son in their hearts with them. . . All is for the good as our Friend says, the worst is over. . . when you leave, shall wire to Friend through Anya and He will particularly think of you. . . Tell me the impression if you can. Be firm to the end, let me be sure of that, otherwise shall get quite ill from anxiety. Bitter pain not to be with you. Know what you are feeling and the meeting with N. [Grand Duke Nicholas] won't be agreeable. You did trust him and now you know what months ago our Friend said that he was actingly wrongly towards you and your country and wife. . . Lovey, if you hear that I am not so well, don't be anxious. I have suffered so terribly and physically overtired myself these two days and morally worried (and worry still till all is done at Headquarters and Nikolasha gone) only then I shall feel calm. . . you see they are afraid of me and so come to you when alone. They know I have a will of my own, when I feel I am in the right, and you are now – we know it – so you make them tremble before your courage and will. God is with you and our Friend for you – all is well – and later all will thank you for having saved the country. Don't doubt – believe, and all will be well. . . The Lefts are furious because all slips through their hands and their cards are clear to us and the game they wished to use Nikolasha [the displaced Grand Duke] for. . . Now goodnight, lovey, go straight to bed without tea with the rest and their long faces. Sleep long and well, you need a rest after this strain and your heart needs calm hours. God Almighty bless your undertaking, His Holy Angels guard and guide you and bless the work of your hands. . . I always place a candle before St Nicholas at Znamenje for you and shall do so tomorrow at 3o'cl. and before the Virgin. You will feel my soul near you. I clasp you tenderly to my heart, kiss and caress you without end, want to show you all the intense love I have for you, warm, cheer, console, strengthen you and make you sure of yourself. Sleep well, my Sunshine, Russia's Saviour. Remember last night, how tenderly we clung together. I shall yearn for your caresses. I can never have enough of them. And I still have the children and you are all alone. Another time I must give you Baby [Alexis] for a bit to cheer you up. I kiss you without end and bless you. Holy Angels guard your slumber. I am near and with you for ever and none shall separate us.

Your very own wife,
SUNNY

Ella felt frightened and knew now that Alix was mad and had become a bewitched eastern mystic, believing in omens and charms, without a mind of her own. She finished the letter with embarrassment, realizing that Alix had, by mistake, left her intimate farewell behind.

Yet she was also filled immediately with a cold and terrible rage, and leaving Tsarskoye Selo without a word of farewell, went to Miechen in Petrograd, where she ordered a sleeper to Moscow and said she had a severe headache and would stay in her room until it was time to catch the train. Then she locked her door and paced up and down, unable to stay still for anger. Her sister was not mad: she was selfish, possessed by her own little life and loves. That was all she cared for or thought of, and such selfishness was sin. How many casualties was it that Sir George had told her Russia had suffered during the last year? Four million men. It made her sick to think of such numbers maimed or dead or imprisoned for this sister of hers and her wretched little husband, who was too weak ever to say no to such a vile, useless creature. Her mind turned to the poor men, blinded, limbless, useless for the rest of their lives, who had passed through her hands, and remembered one young boy of twenty-two who had come back without a leg and his manhood. She had seen him cry and turn his back to avoid her eyes. Later, he had told her he was a farmer engaged to be married. Now he did not know what he could do. Later still, she had seen him sitting carving the heads of walking sticks, and he had smiled at her. Why should he and others have ruined their lives for such a wretched pair who talked condescendingly about 'our people' and thought only of themselves and the spoilt, diseased son and the bloodsucker who claimed he could cure him?

She found it impossible to sleep in the rocking train, anger at her sister's carelessness of the millions of dead keeping her awake. At one time she dozed off, but it was only to dream of the maimed, smiling young man. And then she saw him sitting by a samover in a typical hot little peasant's room, with dozens of carved sticks standing in a corner which he knew he was unable to sell. Her sorrow woke her up and, for the first time in her life, she felt utterly alone and irrelevant to God, whose purpose she could not understand in allowing so many millions of young men to die or only to live half-lives in pain. She longed to see Ernie and Victoria, but one was an enemy in Germany, the other in England. She realized that the days she had spent helping and sympathizing with the wounded and dying had emptied her of affection and left her with a sense of duty without pity. She had exhausted her love on strangers and could not replenish it without seeing those she truly loved. All that was left to her of the whole past was Alix, who, for the moment, she hated with her whole heart. As she lay hopelessly awake, she doubted the existence of God, goodness and heaven. Her doubts made her feel like a shell, emptied of hope and life.

As soon as she returned to the convent, she sent for Father Mitrophan and confessed the hatred in her heart. She dared not confess her lack of belief. A serious look came over his face as he told her that God was love and to deny His wishes was to sin, however great the provocation. For the second time since she had known him, he gave her a stiff penance, and after she had repeated twenty times a long prayer for forgiveness for those who harboured hate, she felt her anger soften enough for her to write to Sir George at the British Embassy and tell him of the failure of her visit.

14

A few days after Ella's return, a young, large, fat, red-faced man called Robert Bruce Lockhart called and asked to see her alone. Only when they had retired to her little sitting room did he produce a plain envelope which, he said, the Ambassador had given to him before he left Petrograd. It was unsigned, but she knew it was from Sir George when she read the words:

> You have only told me what I feared, but I would like to thank you for your effort and to tell you I understand the pain it must have caused you. I only asked you because I thought the matter of absolute importance, and his decision closes the last door of opportunity for creating a respected government that had a chance of satisfying the country and bringing good government to this long-suffering nation. I ask you to listen to this young man whose views, of course, are his own, but I have asked him to speak with a frankness my training has forbidden me.

Lockhart was a surprising envoy of an ambassador. She gazed at the young Scotsman, but did not wish to be ill-mannered and, remembering Buchanan's extraordinarily good judgement, said: 'How kind of you to come. How this war changes conventions. Please tell me your news.'

Lockhart blushed with pleasure and started off with such well-rehearsed sentences that she realized he had learned them by heart, but his Celtic enthusiasm soon overcame his confused shyness and he began to speak with a passion that refreshed and moved Ella.

'When the Tsar agreed to the creation of a special defence council, there was hope. All the best elements in Russia would have come together to provide administrators in a constitutional government which would have given confidence to the nation. The parties of the Duma were prepared to come together for the first time since 1914. The Mensheviks would have worked with Kerensky's labour party. Shulgin could have represented the nationalists, Milyukov the cadets. All would have given up their traditional hopes and compromised to work for victory. The socialists would have criticized, but with relief, as there was general agreement that abuse of power was destroying the country. But things could be put right. Look at what honest co-operation the Congress of Trade and Industry is already beginning to achieve. It would have been possible for the Tsar to agree to a constitution which would have united almost all, except the extremists.

'Now, having excited and disappointed expectations, he goes to join the army, leaving Rasputin to block progress, grasp greater power, frustrate honesty, and sanctify autocracy. Those who will not resign and who protest at a system they cannot stomach will be dismissed, and those who have supported the Tsar as a constitutional figure of power will be treated as his enemy. God knows the type of men we will get in their place. They will only need one qualification: the ability to say yes. The pity is that if the Tsar had created a cabinet of elected representatives with defined authority, he could have retained great power. In promising only to deceive and giving nothing, he will destroy himself and the State.

'I will next tell you of an incident which you will scarcely believe. Do you know that before one of the meetings which the Tsar was having with Rodzyanko, the Tsarina made him comb his hair with a dirty old comb of Rasputin's to give him strength to resist wicked inroads on autocracy? That fool of a woman, Anna Vyrubova, who is too stupid not to repeat what injures those she sincerely loves, says that when the Tsarina gave him the comb, he looked at the greasy, long hairs stuck between the teeth and took out his handkerchief to pull them out, at which the Tsarina attacked him and asked him if he was mad to diminish the strength of the implement which would give him courage. With her own fingers she threaded back the greasy hairs. Then she stood and waited until he combed his head three times before sending him off, with her blessing, to break his promise.

'How can you blame those who oppose a ruler who is guided by such dirty magic? You know, the sad thing is that there is a good side to Rasputin, but every day it is decreasing. I know, for there is in his house a waiting room and it has for months been the duty of a friend of mine to send different representatives daily to find out what is going on. The Germans, I may say, do not even bother to change their agents. I have seen reports from other sources, and all paint a sordid and extraordinary picture. Anyone who calls is shown into a waiting room which is so crowded that there is not room for half the occupants to sit down, and every day generals, contractors and swindlers stand about, waiting to beg favours, promotion, contracts and cancellations. Ready money is openly displayed. There are a few exceptions to those who wait. Notable among them is a dubious banker, Rubinstein, a man of most unsavoury reputation, who always walks straight through into one of the inner rooms. But, in the outer room, the rich crows are pressed against honest old peasants, who in turn press against young girls and richly dressed, veiled society women whom he sometimes comes and takes into his bedroom for a few minutes, after having loudly whispered indecencies in their ears. You know, it is said that many of his female visitors come from the highest society. This belief has arisen because so many of his visitors are veiled. It is not the case. The police have had many of them followed, and they report that they are veiled because they are so ugly that Rasputin would not ask them into his bedroom if he saw their faces. Certain respectable women have come, and resisted him, and been turned out in disgust.

'It is true that contractors and swindlers openly pay him money, but, apart from the comparatively small amounts which he sends home regularly to his wife and children, he never keeps any. He gives the rest away – and, again, you have a strange quirk in his nature – to the truthful and deserving. He asks a begging peasant a simple question or two and knows at once if they are telling him lies, when they get nothing. In short, this is the room where contracts are made and cancelled, where the Tsar's authority is pledged and honoured, where the army's plans are discussed and disclosed and Ministers' decisions overturned, and where the owner is frequently drunk, indiscreet and indecent, and occasionally kind to the poor.

'Sometimes he will come into the room and shout that he won't see another person that day since he is tired, but they are to return, for the Tsarina will grant him every favour he asks. Then he will tell them some lie of his familiarity with either the Tsarina or one of her daughters. All fear, all discretion, has left him during the past month, and God knows how he will behave when the Tsar is at the front, for however badly he behaves, he has only to say he is a repentant sinner to be forgiven. Would you believe it?'

'Yes,' said Ella, 'I believe you.'

Lockhart looked surprised at Ella, and stumbled over his next few sentences before regaining his Celtic confidence.

'To me the most extraordinary part of this whole affair is that not once has Rasputin received a penny from either the Tsar or Tsarina. How do they think he lives? On what? The Tsar has been told a hundred times that he takes bribes, but ignores the information. The Tsarina thinks God provides for him and that it would be indecent of her to give money to a holy man. Alas, they are both living in a world which has no boundaries of sense, and now the last chance has gone of doing away with that room. Instead, it will become the centre of the Empire, the only place in Russia where the Tsar's intervention can be ensured. I hope I have not said too much,' he said, embarrassed again.

He looked so brash and young and clever that she went up and made the sign of the cross on his forehead. He seized her hand, almost roughly, and kissed it. She saw the tears running down his cheeks as he stood up.

When he had gone, Ella's loneliness remained. She went into the garden where the trees she had planted had already made an oasis and remembered her excitement when she planted them, and how she had looked for a combination of trees that would soothe and please. She remembered how once, when she was staying with Nicky and Alix just after their marriage in the Forest of Skiernivice in Poland, she had found in the garden a great weeping birch which dropped its branches with the greatest delicacy on to the lawn. Once you entered the tent of the tree, the sun, shining through the leaves, gave an enchanting effect of soft, changing light. It was the biggest birch she had ever seen, and the leaves the smallest. When Nanny Eager saw it later, she said: 'Surely it's the fairies' tree.' Even when Ella had stayed there in her unhappy years, the shelter of the tree comforted her. She had asked the gardener for a seedling.

The next time when she came to stay, three years later, she had been shown her young tree in a terracotta pot, already standing nearly three feet high and throwing out graceful little drooping branches. She had taken it back to

Ilonskoye and had, the first year, watered it herself as it stood in one of her favourite places down by the river, firmly supported by a bamboo stake. When she planned her garden in the convent grounds, she had moved it again, now eighteen feet high, in a farm cart, and replanted it with loving care alone in the centre of the garden. It had always been called her tree and it grew with an almost magical swiftness, and so, by 1910, she was able to sit in its shade, surrounded by dappled light, and to find peace and rest when she was tired and angry. Often she had touched the silver bark and gained reassurance from its almost human presence.

She decided to go and sit beneath it again on a little wooden chair, to see whether it would bring back her peace of mind. She pushed the falling branches aside, sat down and looked up. The tree was perhaps now thirty feet high, but there was no sunshine to be glimpsed through the top, and her old feelings of peace had gone. She touched the bark, calling back the past. Peeling off a little bit of silver, she crushed it in her fingers. It meant nothing. She walked out through the branches and examined the lilac bushes she had planted in a long row, facing her first little hospital's ground floor. The leaves looked tired and old and were beginning to fall. She tried to imagine them in spring, their flowers blooming white and purple; no picture came into her mind. It was the same wherever she went in the garden. All the trees and shrubs, whose positions she had carefully chosen and which she had manured and watered that first dry summer, creating, she had thought, between herself and them a perpetual relationship, now meant nothing to her. Had she lost not only her friends and relations but also her love of nature? It was sad, and as she returned to her little room she felt as if she were walking through a graveyard of dead friends. She sat and thought and understood how, if she had emptied herself of life by working for others, there remained no alternative but more work. That evening she asked eight of her original sisters to come and tell her whenever there was any section of the community which they should help. There was a moment's silence, and then Marie said that large numbers of Jews were living in the Khodynka with starving families.

Ella understood at once. When, in the first year of the war, the Germans had advanced in the north, General Yanushkevich had tried to emulate the policy of Kutuzov in 1812 by emptying the countryside in the neighbourhood of the battlefields. As the front advanced, he had refused to change his policy and the army had deliberately driven back before it the entire living population of the border areas, including about two million Jews from the Pale and Poland. Their position was, she had heard, frightful, for technically they were not allowed to leave the Pale and settle where they had in fact been driven by the army and where the antagonistic villagers persecuted them. Ella had heard how their retreat was marked by a trail of dead old men and babies, as, for two years, they lived by their wits.

Already millions of roubles had easily been collected to resettle Russian peasants, but far less had been done for the Jews. Fortunately, many of them had illegally entered Petrograd, and others had gone south to Odessa or disappeared into the countryside but never, she had been told, to Moscow, as a consequence of the memory of her husband, the Grand Duke Serge. Apparently, however, this information was wrong, and when she visited the Khodynka the next day, followed ostentatiously by two huge policemen, she was shown house after house in which Jewish families were crammed, suffering from disease or starvation, for already the price of food was rising to an alarming extent. She did not enter any of the houses, since she saw terrified faces looking out from behind curtains at her policemen. The next day she went back into the past and revisited the rich Jews who had helped her before and who now did so again. In exasperation, she asked one young industrialist who had been particularly generous and appeared to be bursting with energy and efficiency: 'Why have you done nothing for your own countrymen?'

He replied simply: 'The answer is because the police would have arrested them and broken up any hospital or school which we founded. You must realize that you can do what we cannot.'

When Ella discussed, that evening, her proposal for a hospital in a large house on the verge of the Khodynka, which, she had noticed on her way back, was for sale, Marie suggested she write to the Tsarina asking for her agreement. Against every instinct, she wrote, and a week later received a letter:

Thank you, Ella, for your letter. You have my blessing and that of my Friend who says you are and always have been a good woman and he regrets you will not see him. But Ella, next time here talk to him, will give you strength. Alexis is well now under his guidance and, missing Nicky, I could do no good without him.

Your loving sister,
Alix.

So yet another hospital was founded and Ella hoped that she would be moved by the joy of curing sick babies. To her dismay, however, she found herself one day watching a little girl of five die, and feeling horror because she felt no horror.

In February she received another strange letter from Alix:

E [meaning Ernie] is coming from Hesse without, of course, W [the German Emperor] knowing, to see Nicky. E made overtures for peace before and Nicky refused to send anyone to see a man he had sent to Stockholm last April but now our Friend has said he should come himself. My Friend says Nicky cannot agree to peace but to see Ernie would be leaving open door. I ache and long for Nicky so if anything comes of plan E will be here two weeks. His visit of course secret. No one to know. Would love to see you. Will fall on his neck and kiss him. Ah, if I had the patience of my beloved husband!

Your old
Alix

Ella wrote back that, much as she would love to see her sister's visitor, the unpopularity of the Germans was so great in Moscow that if the meeting became known, prejudices would destroy all her work, and anyhow, Nicky was so resolved that she was sure the meeting would come to nothing. The country

298

was still determined on the war, and she was pleased there had been no great defeats since he had taken over the high command.

Ella determined to get through the winter ignoring, as far as she could, events outside her own charities. She rose every morning at six, prayed until seven and then came to the most distasteful part of the day: paperwork dealing with questions, especially of her new Jewish hospital, the Governor of Moscow seeming suspicious of every detail of every patient, demanding names of the father and mother of every baby. After that, she would take some biscuits and water. Marie had thoughtfully bought up from a Petrograd grocers their whole stock of Carrs' Water Buscuits, which, she knew, Ella loved, and had placed them in huge tins to remain fresh. Then would come the hours of visiting the convent, the school, the hospital. It was almost unbelievable, now that everything had expanded, that the problems which she had every day to face were not ones of importance, but of stupidities such as who had broken the thermometer or which maid was responsible for cleaning the blackboard. It was hard for her to keep her temper, and she was always quite exhausted before her lunch of dried biscuits and fresh fruit.

After lunch she went out, first in her old cab, and when the snow came, in an old covered sledge which Father Mitrophan had bought second hand. Even then, as she crossed the short space from the pavement to the hospital or a school, she would sometimes receive venomous remarks, referring to herself and her German sister. At about five o' clock, she would come home and drink a cup of her favourite Earl Grey tea, of which Marie had also laid in a colossal chest. Then, refreshed, she would insist on what she called her hours of service, when she would perform the dressings of her sickest patients. After that, she would once more take tea with a little honey in it, and then talk to Marie for an hour before she prayed again before retiring to her stark little bedroom.

After two or three months, she thought that a sense of feeling was returning and she was helping the sick out of her desire rather than from duty. She was relieved. Then, in February, once again her regular life was disturbed. To her surprise she received a letter from Miechen.

Dearest Ella, you have not been very friendly lately and I am sure the fault is mine as Vladimir, when he was angry, always said I was a selfish, insensitive woman. Whatever I have done to offend I regret and ask your help in a time of trouble.

It concerns Boris. He is now thirty-eight and has led for years the life of a debauched bachelor without attempting to settle down. Now the war, thank goodness, seems to have changed his outlook and he realizes his wasted life. He has fallen in love with Olga and somehow has come to a sort of understanding with her, though how he has managed to see her, I can't understand. Anyhow, she is the first person he has ever wanted to marry, and he tells me – and if I am sure of one thing it is that he understands women – that she reciprocates his feeling. But Alix has ferreted her thoughts out of her and at once came down against the marriage on every count she can think of. 'He's too old', 'he's debauched', 'he's unreliable', and so on, and the other day she came to see me and said, in as offensive a way as she could, that the two should not meet. This concerns me, as I genuinely think he has lived long enough to know if he is in love, and, after all, Olga's twenty-one this year and has already, as you know, turned Carol down mainly because he was not a Russian. What I fear is that Alix is determined, at all costs, not to break up her family, and, indeed, she has managed well so far, keeping them with minds of children of ten or eleven. However, it is that innocence which appeals to Boris. Would you believe it, the other day Olga said she could not meet him one afternoon because she and her three sisters had promised to go and play with two of their friend's babies. I don't think even your saintly self would have done that when you were twenty, and there is something frightening to me about four girls of fifteen to twenty-one going off in a group to play with babies!

Anyhow, I gather Olga is still seeing Boris occasionally and surreptitiously and cries each time they part, but then says something unconsciously unkind like 'Mama thinks you are wicked', or asks why Mama says 'you can't have a husband fourth or fifth hand or more'.

I have tried not to be angry, but it never put her off Nicky that he was second hand, for she is a liar if she says she knows nothing of Kschessinka. Can you help? I am desperate. I have the feeling that if this goes wrong Boris may give up. It is hopeless, this Russian system of rich young grand dukes with nothing to do.

Ella sighed. She was fond of Olga, but she could not disagree with Miechen's comments on the girls being young for their age, or that Alix was keeping them back because she could not face the break-up of her family.

Regretfully, Ella read the letter again and decided she would have to try and do something. It might not only be Boris's last chance, but Olga's as well, for the girl seemed nervous and unhappy. She went to Tsarskoye Selo under the pretext of asking Alix's advice about a further expansion of her hospital, for although Alix never, by any chance, listened to what Ella said, she liked thinking she was giving advice. Her sister was talking with bated breath about her friend and how, once again in the autumn, he had saved Alexis, who had started bleeding and would have died without him. She went on to describe others of the great man's cures and his belief that military attacks should be launched on the southern front.

Ella sat listening, and, at last, the subject of Boris came up.

'I won't have it,' said Alix. 'Think of the awful set his wife would be dragged into – bankers and society people, the Orlovs and such types all intriguing, making fast conversation she could not understand.'

Ella asked quietly: 'Have they come to love each other?'

Alix's face went red, and out of interest Ella looked down at her hands, and saw that they had as well.

'The girl thinks she has feelings, but she is a child, she is not yet twenty-one – how can she tell what she thinks? I don't know how Boris dare ask a poor, fresh young girl, eighteen years his junior, to live in a house in which many a woman has shared his life. I know Nicky will agree, since for him to allow an inexperienced young girl to have a husband fourth or fifth hand or more would be wrong.'

Ella did not know what more to say, for she saw her sister had made up her mind. She asked gently if perhaps Olga at twenty-one ought to see more people, as then she would realize that Boris was too old for her, adding: 'Of course, it's the war really which has stopped her going to dances and seeing men of her own age.'

Alix began to go red again and told Ella that Olga, as a nurse, saw every type of young man and what she had seen had in many ways made her old for her age, but still, in others, she was young and pure and should not be polluted by Boris and his fast friends. Ella saw that she could not help in the matter and told Miechen exactly what had happened, saying she was sorry she could do nothing more. Now, in turn, she had to face her sister-in-law's anger and hear her say how Alix was not going to think of letting her girls marry until they were thirty when no one would want to marry them. Personally, she was pleased in one way by Alix's decision, as she would hate to have her as a joint grandmother to her grandchildren.

Ella pretended not to hear. Then Miechen changed the subject. What on earth did Ella think of the new Prime Minister, Sturmer, whose appointment was to be announced tomorrow? Ella said she had heard nothing of it. Miechen overflowed. Hadn't she heard that Goremykin had seen the Emperor yesterday and been treated with his usual kindness? But, as he left, an equerry handed him a message that at twelve o' clock he would be succeded by Sturmer, a cowardly villain who nobody had ever conceived could be Prime Minister. Miechen said she had not yet got to the bottom of why Goremykin had been sacked. It was something to do with another rogue from Rasputin's underworld called Manulov, but other people had been mixed up with it, as, by now, the devil was surrounded by so many crooks, the latest joke being that he kept not a salon, but a saloon bar. Another extraordinary thing was apparently that Sturmer was going to summon the Duma, which Goremykin hadn't dared to do, though why Rasputin wanted it reopened was incomprehensible. It was full of his bitterest enemies. She had been told he was advising Nicky to make more promises that he did not intend to keep, and to quieten down suggestions that he was to blame for its closure.

As Ella was leaving, Miechen asked if she minded being hated as a German. She said she certainly did.

Miechen went on: 'You know, it is not surprising. Rasputin's house is full of German spies who repeat everything which they hear back to Willy and we get the blame for it. German agents all over Russia excite the working man against the imperial family, and it is said that the police daren't touch them. We live in such a madhouse now, I can't see where it will end.'

15

Although she had been brought up with simple tastes and a small allowance, Ella had never, since her marriage, thought of money. Serge insisted she should buy what she wanted, and gave her presents of jewels at least twice a year during the twenty years of their married life. Even after his death, when she parted with most of her fortune, she had enough left generously to endow her convent and hospital and schools and still leave substantial sums to give to the poor. Consequently, it was not surprising if she had lost any understanding she might have had of the value of money, especially since, whenever she made appeals for help to build and endow new schemes, she never experienced any difficulty in raising the necessary sums. Therefore when, from the beginning of 1915, Sister Marie began to warn her that all goods were more expensive, and that since she was giving away three times as much as before the war, she should realize how her capital was disappearing, Ella paid no attention, always persuading herself that every new expenditure was a special case. When Marie continued to nag and surreptitiously put accounts on Ella's desk and begged her to economize, she began to be annoyed, and at first gently and later curtly declined to discuss the matter until a future date.

For the first time in their association, they began to get on each other's nerves. At last Marie, one Monday morning towards the end of June, asked Ella to come with her and see the chief chef, who was responsible for the expenditure in the kitchen which fed the hospital, the school and the convent. She was too surprised to say no, and on the way wondered guiltily whether the chef was planning to leave after all these years, and if it was her fault for neglecting the kitchen staff for her new responsibilities. To her relief, when they arrived he led them into a small store room where, on a table covered with a linen cloth, stood a number of plates. On the first was a square of butter. A foot to the right stood another square, less than half the size. Behind it in large letters was printed:

These two figures represent the amount of butter which could be bought with 50 kopeks in 1914 and which can be bought with 50 kopeks today.

Behind stood more comparisons, illustrating how fat and meat had trebled in cost. Salt had risen to five times its 1914 value, and flour to two and a half. Underneath one table stood two boots; on the other, one boot without a toecap.

Ella could not think of what to say, and looked from one to the other while the chef hoped she would forgive him for reviving a method used by St Cyril to illustrate the poverty of peasants. He hoped it would explain how it was now so expensive to feed so many people, and why it was difficult for them to clothe themselves. Ella said she understood, and thought to herself that only in Russia would a chef prove his case by reviving a legend of a saint. Surely the person who had behaved badly was Marie, and she gave her an angry look, but, surprised by how firmly her friend stared back, she realized the fault was her own because she had always refused to listen to complaints.

She thanked the chef and his cooks and walked round the kitchen, commending them on their cooking and admitting she had not paid enough attention to them and asked if they would accept her apologies. They gaped at her, and she remembered how Serge had told her that a Russian would never understand if members of the imperial family admitted they had made a mistake.

As they left, Marie suddenly tugged her sleeve and said: 'Forgive me, but I have another nasty shock for you. Our banker is waiting in my sitting room.'

Ella's first reaction was, again, to be angry, but once more she admitted it was her fault. She had buried her head in the sand. The banker was not the old grey-haired figure she expected, but a man of fifty with thick, black hair and piercing eyes which never allowed her to look away as he explained, simply, that if her expenditure on her charities and convents continued at their present rate, she would have no money left in two years' time. It was true that numbers of people had given large sums of capital, and that her community had been left legacies as well, but the cost of living had doubled and she should realize her capital had halved in value and was now decreasing faster every month. At the same time, a number of her friends, and even members of the imperial family, who had, for years, paid annual contributions, in the last year made no gifts. He regretted his insistence on seeing Her Imperial Highness herself, but he felt it was only honourable to draw her attention to the unpalatable facts. Now that she had achieved her object, Marie looked shamefaced and asked to come and explain and apologize, but Ella said: 'No, you were right, I was wrong. I refused to read the statements you gave me or listen to you, and unless you had done something drastic, I would have gone on avoiding the truth. Tomorrow I shall go and see Monsieur Haritonenko; he has always been helpful and I hope he will help me again.'

The Haritonenkos' colossal palace stood on the far side of the Moskva, opposite the Kremlin. The family, the sugar kings of Moscow, possessed a stupendous fortune, and Ella knew that her old friends and relations looked down on them as vulgarians, but nevertheless went to their parties and justified themselves by not asking them back. Since the war, their receptions and balls had been grander than any of those given by any member of the nobility now that the Youssoupovs no longer entertained, and Miechen had christened the present head of the family 'Monsieur' to distinguish him, she said, from the merchant class. The name had stuck and seemed to please him. He was fifty, clean-shaven with fleshy cheeks, a hooked nose, a thin mouth and a large chin: the delight of caricaturists as a symbol of capitalism.

303

He had always helped Ella, and, a few months before they had met again in her convent hospital, where he was visiting – an unusual action for a Russian employer – his chauffeur who had crashed near by. When he heard that the man was receiving free treatment, he had looked at Ella with respectful surprise, and eventually told her if he could ever be of assistance he would be honoured to help. She saw the time had come, and sent a message that she would call next day in her capacity as a servant of God.

She noticed, with pleasure, the abundance of beautiful flowers in the palace, mitigating the new gold and marble. When she was shown into his room, the sweet scent of geraniums was so strong that she felt nostalgic and dizzy and thought for a moment that she was going to faint as he shook her hand. He must have thought the same, for he put both hands forward as if to catch her, but she looked down and pulled herself together as he led her to a pair of wooden chairs, with a table between them and facing over the river. Once they had sat down, she saw that for such a large man he had minute feet. She explained to him how she had learned for the first time that her money was running out, and that while she had not come to him for aid, she had come for advice. She did not mind about herself, but she could not bear to think of her own carelessness and extravagance being about to destroy the institutions which, she knew, helped the poor and wounded.

He put his left hand in front of his eyes, half-clenched his fingers and examined his nails. Then he said: 'You know, I don't want to confuse you with figures, but since the war, while wages have risen by double, the cost of food has trebled. Things will get worse.'

'Why?' she asked.

He looked rather embarrassed and waited a moment before replying slowly: 'The uncertainty.'

'Uncertainty of what?' she said.

He put his hand on the end of the arm of the chair and gently stroked the wood.

'You have asked me an awkward question, Your Imperial Highness. Do you wish me to give you a truthful answer?'

'Yes,' she said, 'because I see that I cannot isolate myself from events as I have tried to do.'

'Well,' he began, and started talking slowly at first, but, as he continued, his indignation grew, his voice became thicker, losing all refinement and delicacy of expression. 'I fear you may not like what I say, but the truth is that the country believes the government centres around Rasputin and the men he appoints. I can only tell you that I would not employ Sturmer as a sweeper in one of my factories, and the same may be said of every single appointment he has made. You know, as a tradesman – and although my father made all this. . .' he waved his hand in a circular movement, '. . .that's what I am – I am told things you don't hear. Perhaps I can illustrate the width of the present chaos by showing how today isolated honest administration can become as damaging as maladministration.

'Let me explain. Until a few weeks ago, the War Office was run by General Polivanov, an honest man who I would like to have working for me. He succeeded Soukhomlinov and found everywhere corrupt confusion. For instance, I knew we were selling sugar to military camps that had ceased to exist, the sugar then being resold for a large price by some man whom I won't name. At the front, a platoon of twenty were being issued with six rifles and a hundred rounds of ammunition and expected to fight all day. Neither could our few big guns fire more than six rounds a day. Polivanov set about remedying the shortages, not only by converting the factories to armament production and co-operating with the local councils to do the same, but by buying considerable quantities of arms from England and France, which his predecessor had refused to do because he was too proud to admit inadequacies.

'At the same time, the railway system was working in a most haphazard manner, as I understand you found yourself on one occasion. To improve armament deliveries, Polivanov commandeered more trains, and our troops are now, for the first time, adequately armed and have artillery support. But the unforeseen cost of this isolated efficiency was – as only a businessman would have foreseen – an immediate shortage of rolling stock. It was bad enough last year, but this year even more trains have been taken to maintain the offensive which began on 4 June, and, I gather from where we are sending our sugar, extends from the Pinsk Marshes to Romania. The supplies are now reaching the troops, but with the result that there will not be enough rolling stock to circulate this year's good harvest, to Moscow and Petrograd.

'I repeat, the efficiency of the military machine has caused consequences neither thought of nor understood. Excellent, no doubt, from a purely military point of view, but causing prices to rise, shortages of food and dissatisfaction of the working class, who will find it difficult to get enough to eat. The matter could have been and should be put right by putting both the millitary and civilian railway chiefs under the authority of a board which takes the need of the country as a whole into consideration. That's what I would have done as a businessman. That's what the Duma planned. That's what has not been done, and the result of General Brusilov's successes will mean extra problems. A lot of territory has been gained, which increases demands. I gather that 100,000 prisoners have been taken; they will have to be looked after and fed, and with our own severe casualties, these will have to be brought back and reserves taken up to replace them. Unless I am mistaken, this will mean more commandeered rolling stock and less food and more discontent in Moscow.

'It is the same with the local Red Cross units. They are run by local councils and have taken over from the medical services. They are efficient, and the army could not have done without them. The local war committees are the same: they have done splendid work producing munitions. But both of them work for the army. Nobody is bothering how the millions of workmen and their families in the towns are going to live.

'I mentioned reserves. The army has two million now behind the lines in depots. It is outright silly, since there are not enough arms for the fighting men, let alone this useless, untrained mass. They are useless, you know. The officers who should be training them are dead, and there are no spare rifles to train them, so what can you expect? And what a lot they eat! More meat in a week than folk get in a month at home, and so much of our sugar that they must eat cakes all day. I would not believe what I was told about one of these depots and went to see with my own eyes. The stories were true, every one of them. In the camp, 40,000 men sat eating their heads off, commanded by eighteen officers – eighteen I promise you – and only two of them have ever fought. The men are discontented, bored, useless, and won't know what to do when they fight. It's madness, stark staring madness. The Germans and pacifists and socialists are dropping pamphlets like leaves, and as the men have nothing to do, they believe what they are told.

'Well, when I saw this stupidity I got some of my friends together: Politov and others with big interests. We went and saw the Tsar and pointed out the folly of feeding two million useless reservists, and all the rest of what I've been saying, and added that every single day that the civil railways remained in the hands of Sturmer's officials, we have to bribe somebody to get freight cars. Couldn't he authorize the creation of a transport authority to control the excesses of the army and the corruption of the politicians? Otherwise, we told him, there wouldn't be enough food in Moscow or Petrograd.

'He looked shocked and agreed with us, and promised we would have our way. And what's happened? Nothing. And what will happen? There won't be enough to eat in any big industrial town.

'Another thing I had forgotten – you know, in Petrograd there are 150,000 untrained men guarding your. . .' he paused and added quickly, '. . .Tsarina. Not one regiment I'd rely on. I would not like my wife to be in their hands.'

He took out a delicate silk handkerchief, wiped his face and sat back. Ella was pleased to see how, when he was angry, he forgot who she was and called her 'you', and had been about to say 'your sister' when he remembered in time. Now that he sat back he was the sugar king again, but while he had spoken, lost in passion, he had been a simple Russian peasant patriot telling her the truth. She saw he was smoothing his hair down. When he noticed her looking, he smiled in confusion and said: 'You know, when I lose my temper my hair stands on end. It makes me feel a fool.'

'No, no,' Ella said, 'you have no idea how grateful I am to you.'

She wished she could have said something in praise of his honest patriotism, but she could not think how to put it. He apologized for talking so long, but honestly he felt better now, he said, and asked her how he could help her. She replied that he had already done so, but she would like further personal advice on how to keep her convent and hospitals running. All the new casualties meant the beds were full again, and money was running out.

He looked at her, and she was pleased to see he had again forgotten everything except her problem.

'Well, it is as simple as this. As long as it's believed Rasputin is running the country, and as long as you have a dishonest fool as a Prime Minister and dishonest Ministers, and as long as the army gets all it wants, there is going to be more uncertainty, more corruption, more inefficiency. And, as I told you to begin with, what costs a rouble now will cost three roubles next year. I am sorry I have not come to your problem yet, but I get so worked up; forgive me.

'As to yourself, however, I've thought about your charities: you've got too many. It's quite simple – you should try to limit your activities and give the new hospital you have started on the edge of the Khodynka to the Jewish community. It is an economic strain which you can't afford and they can.

'On top of that, you should limit your expenses by staying in your convent. You know, the anti-German rioting last year will be repeated again soon, on more savage lines. I have spoken to some of my fellow industrialists, and we are prepared to take over the administration of the schools and hospitals and all your charities lying outside your compound. I am afraid we will run them on very different lines, but we believe that the expenses can be cut in half without unkindness. We should be able to continue for two or three years. More than that I cannot promise. I wish I could see into the future.'

As he showed her out, she noticed again how the furniture and mirrors were overgilded and ostentatious, but she forgave him everything for his passionate patriotism, and as he stood in the doorway, she made the sign of the cross on his forehead with her finger. He looked surprised, and in a spontaneous movement made as if to kneel at her feet. Their eyes met with mutual embarrassment as he saw she had noticed his peasant's reaction and the quickness with which he had checked himself. Perhaps to make up for it, he gave her an imperceptible bow. She smiled and knew they parted friends.

Ella told Marie of the conversation afterwards and they could not see any alternative to his advice. In a way, it was a relief: both had too much to do. For the first time, Ella realized that the situation was not only serious but hopeless, and that if Rasputin continued to control Alix, the whole of the Empire might collapse. Why was nobody doing anything? And then she wondered whether they were, and if it was only her determination to concentrate on her work and ignore their conversation when they dutifully visited her that prevented her from realizing that they had been trying to ask her something. Certainly she had in the last two months received surprising attention. Dimitri and Marie, whom she had not seen for years, had both called and begged her to go and visit Alix in Moscow. Miechen had written of her fears of revolution if Nicky did not dismiss Rasputin. Paul, who she had only seen twice since his morganatic marriage, had appeared, looking old and ill and sad, on his way to the front, and said how worried everybody was about 'the man of God's' influence. Even Boris had appeared and slapped his leg and said Alix was mad. She had pretended not to hear, but five minutes later he repeated himself. She pretended she had to deal with an urgent case and left him.

She had listened to all the others politely, and then put everything they said out of her mind, but now the oddity of the visits struck her. What had they said and what could they do? Surely they were not suggesting that Nicky should be replaced – if so, by whom? Alexis was too young; Nicky's brother Michael was hopeless; and next came Cyril, married to Ducky, and how could you have a divorced Tsarina? It was wild talk, that was all. But, at the same time, she felt uneasy, as if something was going wrong. It was indisputable that Nicky had made a terrible mistake in allowing Alix to fall under Rasputin's influence, but only Ella knew how obstinate she was. Perhaps all that the rest wanted was for her to go and tell Alix she was destroying the Empire. But what would be the good of that when she never listened to her anyway? On the other hand, if there was some sort of plot, could it be to make Nicky abdicate and put Alix in a

307

monastery? Ella tried to remember where she had heard the rumour. Was it from Boris? She could not remember; she heard wild rumours every day.

In the morning after her visit to Monsieur Haritonenko, she woke up feverish and ill. The doctor said she was suffering from exhaustion, overwork and strain. She nodded coldly at him and fell asleep for twenty-four hours. The next day, she said she had recovered, but the doctor was insistent on change being essential if she wished to continue to run her convent. He ordered her to Livadia for three weeks, where she found delight in the warm Crimea, in the vineyards and the garden with its roses flowering for the second time in the season. Her body took possession of her, demanding that she should not worry but allow it to recover by rest and peace. Usually overwhelmed by guilt unless she was busy, she felt guiltless. It was as if she had been given a holiday before a heavy task, and she lay comfortable in bed, happy not to move. Some days she went for little walks and sat in the shade and shut her eyes, listening to the birds, and every evening she sat by a wall, looking out over the sea. For the first time since she was a child, she was happy and contented doing nothing, forgetful of every worry, careless of her convent and the tragedy of the world.

The mood lasted for three weeks, and she returned to Moscow feeling strong and determined to face whatever the future had in store. She thanked God for her strength, for when she returned she found that Marie was now unable to reassure the sisters. They had become nervous, frightened of the changed attitude of the patients, and Marie lamented that one of the girls told her a patient had walked out before he had recovered, saying: 'I am not going to stay in a place belonging to one of the "German witches".'

The casualties must again have been enormous, for every hospital was crowded, and, to her anger, silly, kind Sister Barbara told her, looking as if she was repeating good news, that all sorts of stories were coming out of her old foundations, saying that Haritonenko was running them in a meaner manner than before. The patients, Barbara said, were having to endure less nurses per patient, and some of the nurses who still belonged to Ella's Order were full of grumbles and asked for a delegation to see Ella. She received them and told them coldly that it was their business to think of the wounded and not of themselves, and that if they were not prepared to sacrifice their comforts, she would be pleased if they would retire from her Order. They looked sad and surprised that Ella had not welcomed their complaints. She said goodbye to them without a smile.

The problem of the patients was not so easily solved. They grumbled all day, and some of them actually pulled out their stitches to avoid returning to the front. They were nearly all boys who had not the slightest desire to fight, and whose only wish was for the war to end so they could go home. They said that imperial casualties were enormous and the war going badly, which was confusing, as the War Office claimed 300,000 prisoners had been taken and the Austrian army overwhelmed. Marie told her that even the soldiers had heard that Nicky was to resign, the Tsarina be confined in a monastery and Alexis made Tsar under a regency council including Ella. Marie said that after all Ella's imperial visits in the autumn, not only the girls in the convent but even the maids and porters believed the story as well. Ella thought that it was ridiculous, and said that when she had time she would go to Tsarskoye to find out what was happening. August was a bad month, when four of her sisters fell ill and she had to work all night herself. Not until mid-September was she able to telephone Dimitri and ask if she could stay with him and see her relations. She thought he sounded horrified at the idea, but had to say yes. She arrived on 20 September.

The first question which Dimitri asked was, 'What do you think of the news?' and was astonished she had not heard. One of the worst of the ones he called 'the mad monk's creatures', Protopopov, was to become Minister of the Interior. There was an uproar. Rodzyanko, the remaining Ministers except the monk's followers and practically the whole of the Duma had protested. Protopopov was known to be a useless, dishonest, servile little man whom Rodzyanko had used and even sent on a deputation to England, because he knew he would only do exactly what he was told. Apparently, when he was appointed, he was as surprised as everybody else and said to Price Lvov: 'I am delighted – my highest ambition was to be a vice-governor, and now here I am, the second most powerful Minister in the whole Empire.'

Rodzyanko, who thought he was still his creature, told him what to do, but immediately found that Protopopov had deserted him for where the power lay: in Rasputin's reception room. Dimitri said that the only good thing about him was his admission that he was a friend of the monk's, since Sturmer and all the other Ministers pretended they did not know him. Protopopov made it quite plain that he thought Rasputin was a wonderful man to have appointed him.

The worst part of the matter, Dimitri said, was: 'The man, Protopopov, is actually mad, and since I can discuss medical matters with my nurse-aunt, it is common knowledge in Petrograd that he has for years received treatment by various doctors for syphilis. His behaviour lately has been so peculiar that it is now believed the disease has reached his brain, for would you believe it, the first thing he did on becoming Minister of the Interior was to rush around trying to borrow – he could not even wait to have one made – a costume of the General of Gendarmes? The force is now under his authority. I swear it is true, and when he appeared in the Duma, he was dressed up in a General's uniform much too big for him, and trailing a huge clanking sword. He was greeted by roars of derision by the whole assembly and could not understand why. This is the man who is to reorganize the railway system and provide food for Petrograd, and the Minister who Aunt Alix swears will be the saviour of the Empire. Good heavens, Sturmer is bad enough. You know, many of your casualties last month resulted from his idiocy. He made the Romanians fight, which was the last thing Alexeyev or Sazonov wanted, since it was known they had no organization and would collapse. And so they did, and our left flank was exposed. God knows,' he ended bitterly, 'how many hundreds of thousands of lives the monk's appointments have cost Russia, but none of them are as bad as Protopopov.'

Ella was aghast, but, determined not to be diverted from her intention, told Dimitri how she had been annoyed to hear it said that she was to be on the Council of Regency after Nicky had been deposed and her sister sent to a monastery. He changed the subject quickly and said he was so glad she had come to Moscow. His father was ill, so he had arranged they would dine at

Miechen's. He had not asked his stepmother, especially not to offend her. Miechen and Boris and Cyril and Sister Marie all looked forward to seeing her and reassuring her.

At dinner it became plain that the others had been told to keep quiet and leave the talking to Miechen. She told Ella how actually, at the moment, all was going well, perhaps because Nicky never interfered with his generals but went for long walks every day. It was also true that over 350,000 prisoners had been taken, but the real trouble lay behind the line, in the big towns, where the workers, many of them socialists and Bolsheviks, were not having enough to eat, 'and God knows what will happen in the winter, because the man whom Rasputin has chosen to bring food is this ghastly little madman who is incapable of doing anything except say yes'.

The disastrous truth which Ella should understand was that Nicky appeared unable to stand up to Alix, who was mesmerized by the monk.

'In view of this, you must see that it is not surprising if there has been loose talk of *coups d' état* by the army and us. I won't deny we had a family discussion. It was necessary. The Empire is falling to bits, and all because of a possessed, drunken, debauched monk who has assumed imperial powers and only thinks of preserving his position. How could we not discuss this? But we did not find a solution. After all, Michael's weak-minded, and next is him. . .' and she pointed to her son, Cyril, '. . .who is married to Ducky, and it would be difficult to have a divorced woman as Tsarina.

'Please don't think I am unaware of what people say,' ended Miechen, staring hard at Ella as if she had been spreading rumours. 'But, again, how could we not discuss the matter? What if Nicky was killed at the front? The monk would have tried to make the Tsarina regent, which would have meant he was Tsar. Then we would have to fight, or Alexis would have been his prisoner for life. So, of course, in case that happened, we discussed a council of regency, and everybody suggested that you, Ella, should be a member. Surely you are not prepared to blame us for that?'

She looked at Ella, half-persuasively, half-triumphantly, as if she knew she had pleaded an unanswerable case. Ella didn't say anything, but could not help admiring Miechen. She had known exactly what her objections would be and had refuted them before she had mentioned them. At the same time, she did not believe that she had told the truth, for she had spoken like a lawyer and the others had not said a word, but had sat nodding their heads in agreement as if the whole thing was planned. Some plot must have miscarried. She would never know exactly what had happened, but clearly it had been abandoned or gone wrong. She said quietly that she was relieved, because she would never have had anything to do with deposing Nicky or shutting Alix away. Rasputin was a different question; he was obviously an evil, wicked man, and although she should not say such a thing, it was a tragedy the woman's knife had not killed him.

'Exactly,' said Dimitri so loudly that everyone looked at him.

At the end of the evening, Miechen said: 'I want you to know, Ella, that all of us are loyal to Nicky and Alix, but all of us hate Rasputin and believe everything should be done to make Alix get rid of him. Rodzyanko's going to see Nicky or her, and later Dimitri will, and even Zenaïde Youssoupov has said she'll come, and any number of others. Buchanan swears he will speak tonight, but I don't believe him; he's in with the revolutionaries. And even Paul says he'll talk to Alix.' Paul gave a gloomy nod. 'Alix is the one that matters. If all the others fail, will you go?'

Ella said: 'Yes, not that it will do any good.'

After she had spoken, she sensed that everyone in the room thought what a typical remark from that cold, pious, depressing old nun. Sad, she rose to her feet, and Dimitri said he would drive her home. When she said goodnight, she thought they all looked relieved, but Dimitri cheered her up by saying he had been amused by her face when Miechen was telling lies.

'Of course, you are right. She was lying, but she always is when she tries to be pleasant; it's an infallible rule.'

To change an embarrassing subject, Ella remarked how sad she had been, dismayed to see so many beggars and haggard women hanging about the streets when she arrived: 'It looks worse here than in Moscow.'

Dimitri laughed and leaned forward and told the driver to change direction. Ella was pleased; there were two or three degrees of frost and it was a beautiful night to drive about the city, even with the Cossacks clattering along at either side.

To her surprise, they stopped at an enormous hotel. The porter knew Dimitri and dashed down the steps. They walked up the stairs of the Astoria, and he led Ella across a high, gilded hall to huge glass doors which jumped open as they walked into a gilded restaurant packed with young soldiers and girls, old soldiers and jewelled women. The whole room gave an impression of champagne, rich food, glittering uniforms and evening dresses. At one side an orchestra played and couples danced. Dimitri stood, holding Ella's arm, and whispered in his mocking voice: 'Are things worse than Moscow?'

Ella looked with horror around the room. Had these useless rich not seen the poor in the streets? She felt herself going cold with dislike and disapproval.

Something in her appearance, or perhaps the agitation of the waiters round them, caused the eyes of the whole room to turn to them; even the band fell silent, the dancers still. Everybody stared at the pale, legendary Grand Duchess with her large, beautiful eyes, and Ella turned and said: 'Let's go.'

The room remained silent until the doors had closed, when everyone started talking at once. On the way back, she began gently to cry, and Dimitri, without looking at her, said: 'I know what you mean. It can't go on like this, can it?'

16

The new casualties from Romania were of an unusually horrible nature. No less than seven men had both legs shot off, and had she not sat up with them night after night, she thought they would have died. Her holiday in the Crimea had given her a strength which enabled her to go almost sleepless, and she wondered if it had been God's intention that she should rest and be ready for such a trial. Then she asked herself why should God anyhow allow these poor boys to be maimed for life, fighting in a country they had never heard of?

Gradually, to the amazement of the doctors, all of the legless men began to recover, and Ella moved them into a corner in one of the wards and sent one of her sisters into the Khodynka to find a woodcutter who could teach them how to carve images. She came back with an old Lithuanian, who showed her his tray of wares, and she told Marie to buy them as models, and ask the man to come every morning to teach the cripples. The effect on six of them was miraculous, and two weeks after they had appeared to be dying, they were sitting carving away, already making passable images. But the seventh man was hopeless; three or four times he cut his hands, the last time so badly that the doctors insisted his implements should be taken away, after which he lay with his face in the pillow and three days later died. The doctors remarked, with the scientific interest which custom causes to replace pity – she had caught it herself when dealing with hundreds of ill men – how it was strange a man should die not from having both his legs blown off, but from a broken heart at being unable to copy a wooden image.

Ella read no newspapers and asked to be told no news, but over her hung the vague dread of the interview with Alix. In the middle of the month, young Bruce Lockhart appeared again. She thought he had grown fatter. His undeniably Scottish face gave her such pleasure, reviving old memories, and all at once she wanted to hear from him what was going on. He replied that at the front of the line it was holding, but, internally, the German agents continued to undermine the industrial workers and receive help for agents, pacifists and all those who were now against the war, which she should know was almost every town dweller. Since the offensives, the drain on the railway service had become almost intolerable. Hanbury Williams, who was with the troops, had passed through Moscow the week before and had told him that, at a conference of quartermasters held by Alexeyev, it had come out that the army now needed no less than 2,676 wagonloads of victuals and fodder for the horses per day, which filled four hundred trains, and that this would not only continue but would increase in the foreseeable future, since it was planned in the winter to bring more recruits into the line.

And so there was no way for the food problem of the industrial towns to be improved. It was said that the Empress herself and Rasputin were also aware of the danger and had some plan for rationing, but that there wasn't any food to ration, and the feeling of the lower against the upper classes was rising in intensity. Twice a week from the surrounding countryside hundreds of peasant carts drove into Moscow to the market place next to the poor quarter. There, all the goods were at once bought up by the upper classes and the hotels, the wretched poor having to make do with the bottom of the barrel.

'By the way,' said the young man, blushing, 'you know, I was in the Astoria the other night when you and the Grand Duke Dimitri came in for a moment. I don't know if you noticed, but everyone fell silent.'

Ella said she had been embarrassed and told him it was Dimitri's idea to show her how luxury went side by side with the starving people on the streets. He did not seem to hear, but went on: 'You know, it was extraordinarily interesting; I understand now the way the peasants think about the Tsar, for when you both came in, no one spoke or said anything, and yet, within two minutes, the band and the dancers had stopped and we were all staring at you as if you belonged to another world, which you appeared to do. When you went out, it was as if the room was empty, and then I noticed people shaking their heads, crossing themselves and drinking champagne at the same time. Honestly, I saw an old red-faced general making the sign with his glass and then gulping champagne, and I promise that one of the women dancers let go of her partner's hand and genuflected. You are a legend, you know,' he said naïvely.

'How about the strikes,' said Ella, 'are they likely to be bad?'

'Each time they are better organized and getting worse as inflation goes up by 15 per cent a month, but what are the poor devils to do?'

'I am worried about the army,' she said. 'They don't seem to want to fight any more. By the way – please never repeat this indiscreet question – does the Emperor ever give orders at the front?'

'No, our attachés say he attends conferences but never speaks. He astonishes his staff even after a year, for every day he goes for long walks, moving so quickly that no one can keep up with him, and, at the same time, he notices any strange flower or bird. And if, in the evening, the news comes through of a disaster, or occasionally of a victory, it doesn't seem to interest him as much as what he saw on his walk. That's why. . .' and then he pulled himself up.

'Why what?' said Ella. 'Tell me what you were going to say.'

'Well,' he said, 'I won't repeat names, but I can't believe that, in the capital last week, you could have avoided hearing of the bungled Palace revolution. There are plots on in the army too, and if the Grand Duke Nicholas had agreed, he could be the regent of the little boy now. But the strange thing is that, despite all his loyalty, the Tsarina still hates him because he told Rasputin he would hang him if he went to the front, and although I am sure she knows he has been loyal to her and refuses to scheme, it doesn't redeem him in her eyes for hating her monk.

'You know, the Russians can't keep a secret. They enjoy the drama of knowing something which nobody else does so much they cannot keep it in. When Lord Kitchener was coming here in the spring, I was sent for by the Ministry and told, as the Consul-General, in absolute secrecy, having to swear not even to tell my wife. Well, within a week, seven foreign correspondants had rung up asking me on which day I was expecting him! I went to see Benjie Bruce, in case the Ambassador might think I had been indiscreet, but he told me that the Tsarina is told everything by the Tsar and passes it all on to her friend, including secret documents, and the closest secrets are soon public knowledge.

'I am rambling on, but do you know, General Alexeyev found out that the Tsarina had in her possession one of his plans of advance? Only two copies had been made; one for himself and one for the Tsar. He went straight back and changed his plan and said out loud: "That explains why so often, whenever we plan a secret attack, the Germans seem to be ready for us." For all we know, the Germans may have learned about Kitchener from that source, and so decided to kill him. Nobody seems to care, but now the commanders-in-chief don't show the Tsar anything secret, and there's a joke at headquarters that the way to deceive the Germans is to let the Emperor have one of our plans and then do the opposite. It was unbelievable to me at first, but you get used to anything.'

'I don't,' said Ella, and stood up. 'I am grateful to you for what, after all, has been gossip, and I think in the end you have been more indiscreet than I was, but I was starved. Suddenly I wanted to talk to someone. I am not the cold, unpleasant woman everyone makes out, you know, and your being Scottish warms my heart. The way you look and talk, and the way your hair stands up, and the way you walk as if you were alone on a hill and knock into people, all remind me of your people, who I once knew and loved.'

Lockhart appeared to be too confused to say anything, so Ella continued: 'You think there are going to be strikes this month? You know, feeding the poor wounded here is becoming impossible.'

'Yes,' he said, 'and I think workers will strike all over Russia, and I am not even sure that the troops behind the line will be able to subdue them.'

Before he left, Lockhart said: 'Your Imperial Highness, please forgive me for forgetting to call you that all the time' – she made a gesture – 'but I am making a list of all those who have been discharged or dismissed since the war. Would you like to see it?'

'I don't know,' she said. 'I don't really know what I want. I did not wish to hear any news, and yet I have talked to you. Neither do I feel any pity any more for my patients. When they come in, I look at them just as the doctors do and think, he'll live or he'll die, and the sad thing is that I am nearly always right. I find it frightening to have lost my sense of pity. I did once before, though it came back, but now I know it never will again. I have seen too many dying men.'

In the beginning of November, Ella received from the young Scot a hastily written note:

You will see nothing in our Moscow papers but on 29 October all Petrograd factories struck. On the 31st two regiments were called out by Protopopov to aid police to subdue strikers. They fired on police, not on strikers. Regiments dispersed by Cossacks obeyed officers for first time doubtfully. I fear loyalty of army is uncertain. A very dangerous sign.

At the same time, Ella heard Zenaïde had seen Alix and been ruthlessly snubbed. Paul was ill and would not be able to go and see her yet. Ella had never felt so hopeless in her life, as she knew something dreadful was going to happen.

Ella had forgotten about Lockhart's visit when a letter arrived by hand, written on plain paper and dated 15 November.

Your Imperial Highness,

I enclose with deference a list I have made of the most contentious changes in government since 1914. I have left out numerous minor appointments and those which didn't seem relevant to the present disastrous position of the country.

As you will see, there have been in this period of 34 months no less than six Ministers of the Interior, one lasting for only eight weeks. This office is responsible for the internal running of the country and for the supply of food. How could it work efficiently when no minister has been there long enough to understand the diverse problems?

The chart illustrates that until the departure of the Tsar for the front he ordered the changes, including the dismissal of Malakov, Minister of the Interior, Shchervatov and the Procurator, Sabler. All three were ardent supporters of autocracy and opponents of the delegation of power of local councils and the Red Cross. The local councils have kept the country running despite the deterioration of the responsible Ministries, and the Red Cross have organized the most medical services at the front; the army could not have done without them.

The dismissed Ministers also opposed the creation of the Defence Council which was to co-ordinate the efforts of the army and co-operate with the civil authorities. However, after the dismissal of the Grand Duke and the departure of the Tsar to the front, the chart clearly illustrates that the subsequent changes made at the request of Rasputin were directed against those he disliked or believed threatened his position. I have not included a number of reputable ministers who have served the Empire to the best of their ability but who, since they refused to obey directions – even orders – from Rasputin, have found their powers reduced and their advice ignored. The Empire is in effect now controlled from his house by his nominees, whose sole qualification is unquestioning subservience and obedience to this unstable character.

You will see that I have traced only one of the dismissals to Her Imperial Highness the Tsarina, who, I believe, insisted on the dismissal of Sazanov because she was convinced his plans for a semi-autonomous Poland would have reduced the Tsar's, and in the future the Tsarevich's, autocratic authority. I would also draw your attention to two appointments, or unofficial appointments, of men with criminal backgrounds.

Thank you for so kindly receiving me. Will you forgive this letter from a blunt and sincere Scotsman? You have inspired me as you do all who you know. I hope your advice will be taken before it is too late.

Yours sincerely,
R. B. L.

PS. You should know that on 9 November the army executed 150 rebellious soldiers in Petrograd. Strikes are continuing.

Ella carefully studied the names and realized gratefully that Alix's association with 'My Friend' and her influence on the appointments were tactfully glossed over. She was shocked; how could she have ignored the perpetual changes? How could the Empire and the war be governed in such a way? She realized completely for the first time that the Tsar and his government had destroyed themselves. Once she accepted facts from which she had previously averted her eyes, her thoughts became certainties and she knew that there would be a revolution and herself would die. She prayed for courage and dignity and health in the meantime, to look after those under her care.

On 22 November, to the amazement of everyone, including himself, who had just finished a friendly interview with the Tsar, the Prime Minister was dismissed from office. Ella picked up Lockhart's sheet and added the name Sturmer to the changes, and two days later filled in the name of A.F. Trepov as his successor. Trepov was an honest man, but, Dimitri wrote, he had taken the post reluctantly, and the monk and Protopopov would continue to rule with Alix's support. At the end of the week, Zenaïde Youssoupov, passing through on her way south, told Ella that she had seen Alix, was not asked to sit down and after a few moments was dismissed icily with orders never to return. The next day, her son Felix telephoned as she was about to go to bed. He sounded passionate and urgent. He had to see her. She said calmly: 'Now don't be excitable, but come at five o' clock tomorrow, and remember, restrain yourself.'

That night Ella remembered the events of Felix's birth three years after she came to Moscow. Zenaïde, certain he would be a girl, had actually bought hundreds of pretty little dresses and was dismayed when he turned out to be another son. Ella had often wondered whether his mother's thoughts had influenced the baby, as he had been a very feminine child whose antics drove his father nearly mad with rage. Ella had always liked him, for even as a child he had charm. Serge had not, for the little boy, with a sly, innocent look, always fingered her husband's stays, exasperating him, especially as Zenaïde always laughed. Later on, there had been a great scandal when he had dressed up in his mother's clothes, worn her jewels and performed in a cabaret as a singer, before he was recognized.

His life had changed when his brother Nicholas was killed in a duel in 1909. When she heard the news, Ella rushed to Zenaïde's bedside, even though, at the time, she had withdrawn from life, working to get her convent accepted, hoping she could help the stricken woman who had adored her elder son with a passion she felt neither for her husband nor for Felix. She was in bed when Ella arrived, with brain fever. When Ella came into her room, the sick woman seized her

316

hand and put her finger on her lips. Ella understood, said nothing, but knelt by her bed. From then onwards, every day, morning and evening, the two would pray silently together and when, after two months, Ella returned to Moscow, Zenaïde wrote to say that her presence and understanding had given her faith and the belief that 'I will see my dear dead boy again. I can never express my gratitude.'

Ella was pleased with the letter; twice Zenaïde had saved her from desperation.

In 1913, to Ella's surprise, Felix fell in love with Alexander's beautiful daughter Irena, and after the Tsarina's opposition was with difficulty overcome, they married in 1914. Since then he had always helped Ella with money, and frequently with practical help. Sometimes he would prance in unexpectedly and tell her how he loved her, and was she in need of anything? And give her, to raise money, a diamond or a valuable ring he had found hidden away in the Moika Palace.

'You saved my soul,' he would say, smiling. 'You are a much better judge of those in need than I am, so we'll get married,' and he'd push the ring on her finger.

The day after his telephone message, he came leaping in with a whole bag of Fabergé boxes, threw them on a table and, without waiting for her thanks, shouted in his excitable way: 'Russia is being destroyed. I know you knew all about Miechen's silly plot, and rightly had nothing to do with it, but did you know that when my dear, broken-hearted mother, despite her shyness, went to see Cousin Alix about the monk's evil influence, she was turned out without being asked to sit down, and told that the Tsarina hoped she would never see her again. How dare Cousin Alix talk to her like that, even if it isn't really herself speaking, because she's become his zombie?'

Ella said: 'Yes, Felix, I think you're right, the man is evil but Alix won't listen. Everybody's tried and I'm going, as well, to see her or Nicky. I would not forgive myself if I didn't try, hopeless as it will be. I imagine Zenaïde felt the same way.'

He hadn't answered but had jumped down from his chair and walked to and fro, shouting – waving his arms, almost screaming – 'Something has to be done about him! I'm sure Cousin Alix is under his spell and is not to blame. I know, as I've visited his house several times. Once he looked at me with powerful, wicked eyes and I was mesmerized and would have done anything he wanted. Then I pulled myself together. But Cousin Alix is a weak woman and lives for Alexis and has always loved madmen, but she's gone too far. It is intolerable. Something must be done, and don't forget . . .' and he went white and shook with rage, '. . . she never asked Mother to sit down. I am sure he told her not to.'

He looked at his watch. A totally different expression came over his face, sly intense excitement replacing anger and rage. He jumped up, flung his arms round Ella, kissed her and said she would be his second wife – she could not help laughing for he was so charming – and dashed away. She thought how difficult it must be for Irena to be married to him. When he had gone, she found a letter on her desk.

Dearest Holy Sister,

I get so excited I can never put things clearly but what I want you to know is I think, and everyone thinks, you are the best woman in Russia and you should go and tell Alix to get rid of him. You are so powerfully good you might be able to get rid of the loathsome mesmerist but you'll have to work hard. It's the last chance, otherwise something will have to be done. However, I have faith in you and am, and always will remain,

Your loving zombie,
Felix

In the beginning of December, Paul was ill again, and from every side Ella received notes that she alone might avert a catastrophe by persuading her sister to get rid of her friend. Ella wrote and asked if she could see Nicky, which was now the only way of seeing Alix, for while those who asked to see her were refused, her inquisitiveness ensured that she saw those who wished to see her husband. This behaviour increased the cruel gossip of Nicky's emasculation and total acceptance of domination by his wife.

Ella was received by Alix in her mauve drawing room in Tsarskoye Selo, of which she had always been so proud and about which Miechen was always so sarcastic. Immediately she entered the room, Ella knew that her sister, whose face looked swollen but haggard, was irritated to have to waste time on her. She sat down, determined to speak in the tactful way she had planned for months, to tell her sister, without giving offence, how her relationship with the monk was misunderstood. They sat in silence for a few minutes which seemed a long time, until Ella realized that she would have to start the conversation since Alix was not going to inquire how she or her convent were, and would merely sit on, silent and unwelcoming. Ella, upset, made a remark which she had not planned: 'What a pity the Romanians came into the war. My patients tell me it was the cause of many casualties.'

Alix replied in a harsh voice: 'Under Nicky all is well, despite obstinate generals. My friend says victory will come.'

Again there was silence.

Ella began again: 'How is Alexis?'

She watched her sister carefully, and saw her eyes soften with love, and then harden again, as if she had decided Ella was trying to get round her, and she was not going to be taken in that way.

'Often well,' was her terse reply.

How strange, Ella thought, it was to see Alix, whom she had known as a little girl, changed into a possessed woman, furious, deranged, caring for nothing except the health of the boy and the maintenance of the power of the man she believed healed him. Ella wondered whether her love for Alexis was now a custom rather than a reality, and if Rasputin had stolen her affection from the boy himself, or had, at any rate, managed to associate in her mind any threat to himself as a threat to the boy. Again there was a silence. Ella thought that she had never been to such a hateful meeting in all her life, but she had no alternative to going on.

'Alix,' she said, in her calmest voice, 'I have come to say something you may

318

not like. I know how you love Alexis, and I am sure if I'd had a son I would have loved him as you do.'

'No children,' said her sister, almost in triumph.

Ella paid no attention and went on with her rehearsed speech: 'Naturally all your thoughts are for him, and of course that makes you respect your friend.'

She got out the last word with enormous difficulty, but it seemed to her it would show she bore no antagonism to the man, evil as she knew he was, 'And of course I understand why you want to have him near you and Alexis, as I know he cured him when nobody else could staunch the bleeding. Whatever happens, I don't think Gregory should, on any account, be more than a day's distance away in case of any accidents. But I must tell you, and I think you know yourself by all the horrible articles in the newspapers, that your friend is misunderstood in the country and all sorts of lies are told about his habits, which are, unfortunately, believed, and therefore, though it is unfair, he harms you, Nicky and Alexis.'

Alix's face had by now gone red and her eyes begun to protrude. With difficulty, Ella made herself not look at her hands and continued in the calm voice with which she had found she could soothe delirious men: 'I am sure things are exaggerated. I believe, for all your sakes and the country's, he should move away from Tsarskoye. If he journeyed by train, I know of a monastery thirty miles from Moscow, hidden in the country, but only one and a half miles from the railway line. A siding could be made, a telephone line run directly to your room and a special engine and carriage wait there permanently, so that if anything happened he could be with you in a short time. I know you think I am interfering, but the lies have harmed you, and the wounded men who are coming back have nothing like the enthusiasm they had, and wish for peace, and listen to the socialists, who wish to undermine Nicky and Alexis's position, so please think of my idea.'

Alix drew herself up and delivered her answer in a flood of words: 'My friend will not be moved. He is the good spirit of Russia, a link between God and the Tsar. As for danger at the front, I have told Nicky to be strong, that is answer. Russians respect strength, admire strength, have had their greatest days under strong Tsars. Nicky must change, become Ivan the Terrible, Peter the Great, the men under whom Russia grew to greatness. Those who oppose should receive the knout, generals, politicians, all.'

Ella was shocked at the way Alix spoke, and at her fragmented incoherence, which suggested an unsettled mentality. Clearly her mind was affected. Rasputin had destroyed her; there was nothing she could do.

She stood up and moved forward to kiss Alix, who moved back and rang a bell and told the footman to bring Olga and Tatiana, who were off duty.

'We will escort you to the station to say goodbye. I ask you not to visit us again till victory comes, which will be when Nicky shows his strength. God has conveyed this message to me by my Friend.'

The two girls came running into the room, excited to see their aunt, but their smiles vanished as they saw their mother's face. They did not even dare kiss Ella, but ran away again to get their coats.

It was a short, embarrassing drive to the imperial platform. Nobody spoke or moved, except Alix, who incessantly stroked the furs over her legs with one hand. When the carriage stopped at the imperial platform, they all got out and Ella saw Alix look at the surrounding officials and guards and noticed a look of annoyance cross her face as she realized that she would, for propriety's sake, have to kiss her sister. She did so with the movement of a pecking bird. The nervous girls, looking like frightened children, kissed her with averted eyes. She got into the train, and before sitting down, looked out of the window. The carriage had gone.

17

The next day Ella left for a monastery near Saravo. She had dreaded her interview with Alix. Now that it was over and she had understood what she had known but not admitted – that her sister was no longer in control of her senses – the discovery shocked and demanded a rest for her to recover her equanimity before returning to work in her own convent. She had visited the monastery years before, and remembered how it stood old and peaceful, set in a clearing surrounded by woods. When she arrived, she knew she had chosen well. Here she could admit Alix's condition and realized that Nicky would never contradict his wife's whims, however disastrous their consequences, and accept instead that he had hidden from her at the front, allowing the despotism of Rasputin to continue and abdicating his power to his wife's increasingly drunk and debauched favourite, a state of affairs which could only end violently at the hands of his family, starving workmen or the undisciplined army.

Ella had to decide whether, if Nicky was replaced and Alexis made Tsar under a council, she would serve as a member. It was a cruel decision: the ailing boy would be separated from his mother and his healer, although she might insist on Rasputin being allowed to visit Alexis if he was ill. She knew that her sister would regard her acceptance, even of an appointment where Ella could help her son, as treachery. But Alix was deranged! It was all so complicated, so difficult. She hoped that she would, in the peaceful atmosphere of Saravo, receive guidance to make the right decision; but would true guidance come, for she had begun to wonder whether what she had previously taken to be divine guidance was not merely a persuading of herself that God wished her to do what she wanted?

Tired by the strain of the events in Petrograd, she rested for two days, conscious that she was not yet in the right state of mind to make a decision, enjoying walks in the woods where snow covered every leaf and twig of the birch trees, whose usually silver stems appeared to shine with a golden lustre in the pale winter sun.

On the third day, as she returned from an afternoon walk, she sensed an unusual excitement. As she approached the monastery she saw to her surprise a nun leaning out of a window staring, her hands shading her eyes. All at once, the nun abruptly disappeared and was replaced by the Mother Superior, who, leaning her head forward, also shaded her eyes, then disappeared in turn while other faces could be seen pressing their noses against the windows. When Ella opened the wooden door in the surrounding wall, she saw the Mother Superior hastening down the path towards her, her head down, zigzagging sometimes off the path into the snow. They met half-way between the gate and a side-door, and through trembling lips Ella heard the news: 'The monk Rasputin has been murdered!'

The word, 'Good,' came into her mind, but she said nothing and made the sign of the cross, not for the dead man, who would no longer ruin her family, but for her sister, though she was unable to stop herself saying: 'I wonder if anyone else will be able to cure Alexis now?'

The Mother Superior gaped at her incomprehendingly, and Ella told Sister Barbara, who was fluttering around as if a calamity had occurred, to arrange for them to leave for Moscow as soon as possible. When she arrived, Marie was full of stories and had even spoken to Lockhart. It looked, although no one was certain of what had happened, as if Rasputin had been murdered in the Youssoupov's Palace, and Felix, Dimitri and Purishkevich had been there, but who had actually killed him, no one would say. Felix and Dimitri had both, it was said, been confined to their houses, and the Tsar was returning. Without thinking, Ella sent a telegram to Dimitri, sending him her good wishes and saying she was praying for him. She did not communicate with Alix.

Every day the rumours increased, but, to Ella's surprise, many of the soldiers in the wards said bitterly that 'their monk' had been killed because he was a peasant who had tried to look after the people and stop the war. After Nicky's return, it was announced that Dimitri was to be exiled to the Persian frontier and Felix sent to one of his estates. Miechen, of course, was active, and had organized a petition, signed by most of the imperial family, asking for Dimitri's pardon. Paul wrote: 'I must warn you – Alix somehow heard of a telegram you sent to Dimitri and regards it as a disloyal betrayal.' Ella did not mind and hoped that with the monk dead Alix would regain her sanity and allow Nicky to appoint a Ministry of the best men.

But, on 13 January, when new Ministers were appointed, it appeared that Alix had only allowed Nicky to appoint the favourites of her lamented friend. So, from beyond the grave itself, those 'the monk' had appointed to protect him were reappointed, even though the one reason for their appointment no longer lived.

There appeared to be no hope now. The shortage of food had increased exactly as Haritonenko had prophesied. The rouble decreased in value every day at the same time as riots daily caused loss of life from attacks on the starving protestors by the Cossacks. The untrained reserves who had moved up to the front openly discouraged their companions from fighting, and all Nicky did was to calmly ignore all opinions except Alix's. In Moscow, the hospital was short of food, but this did not stop scribblings appearing on the outside walls, accusing the 'German witch' of hoarding.

Sadly Ella realized that the last chance of reform and the creation of a good administration had gone. Her opinion was shared by every responsible politican of the right and left, by the imperial family and even by Nicky's personal appointments on the Council of Ministers. On the 9th, Trepov was allowed to resign as Prime Minister, only to be succeeded by Prince Golitsyn, an ill, weak old man. He paid no attention, did everything he was told, and praised Protopopov, who was so disturbed by the personal attacks being made on him that he was said to have suffered a series of fits. Miechen's belief that Nicky spent so much time at the front to get away from Alix was frequently quoted, and it was argued that the sooner he went back to his pretended command the better, for while he could occasionally assert himself on paper, whenever he was with Alix he did exactly as he was told. Apparently, immediately after the murder and Nicky's return, Alix had a hole knocked through her wall and a wooden staircase built, which descended to a listening platform placed just below the ceiling in Nicky's reception room, so that she could be certain that he remained obedient. The first to notice this innovation before it was finished was his brother-in-law Alexander, one of his relations whose advice he occasionally took, who arrived from Kiev immediately after Nicky's return and insisted on an interview with his sister-in-law, at which he told her bluntly that 'there must be a change and a new constitution, or you will ensure it is not the people who are encouraging revolt against the government, but the government who are ensuring that the people revolt against it. I repeat,' he had shouted at Alix, 'one cannot govern a country without listening to the voice of the people.'

Nicky, frightened that Alix would be upset by her huge brother-in-law, collected Olga and Tatiana and walked in to save her from embarrassment. It was the first in a closing round of protests from despairing politicians, old friends and diplomats, who all insisted on giving warnings of coming calamities to the Tsar. One by one, members of the imperial family, the French Ambassador, Rodzyanko, the president of the Duma and Buchanan came, spoke and went. Lockhart said that the British Ambassador had read his speech to Benjie Bruce before he left to see the Tsar. A dignified, correct, ageing man, for once he put his trust in a personal appeal, trembling with emotion as he spoke it: 'If I were to see a friend walking through a wood on a dark night along a path which I knew ended in a precipice, would it not be my duty, Sir, to warn him of his danger? And is it not equally my duty, Sir, to warn Your Imperial Majesty of the abyss that lies ahead of you? You have, Sir, come to the parting of the ways, and you have now to choose between two paths. The one will lead you to victory and a glorious peace – the other to revolution and disaster. Let me implore Your Majesty to choose the former.'

Bruce had congratulated him, remarking that such words might move a stone, but Buchanan had shaken his head: 'It all depends. If he asks me to sit down, there's hope; if he receives me standing, there's none.'

He returned almost in tears; the Tsar had stood and listened coldly to his passionate words. There was no hope. All the pleaders agreed that the Tsar was worthless, empty and had irrevocably handed his powers to his wife. None of them had any doubt that, behind the curtain on the balcony, reclining on a chaise longue, lay the Tsarina, listening to every word to make certain that her husband remained firm and was not persuaded, by alien oratory, to give away a mite of his son's historic right to one day succeed to the autocratic rule held by his father.

The plea which most infuriated Alix was Buchanan's. It was said that the curtain shook with her rage. The Tsarina had never liked the Ambassador and regarded his contacts with members of the opposition party as a sign of his treachery. Yet after she had overheard his desperate plea to the Emperor to allow a new constitution which would have confounded all her hopes for her teasured son, he became a loathed enemy to be dismissed like her friend's opponents and she tried to get Nicky to insist he should be recalled. Nicky, for once, prevaricated; it would mean a row with Georgie and would upset the allies, and while he did not say no, Alix, who knew his weakness and fear of offending his relations, saw that he would not agree before he returned to the front. So she changed her tactics and ordered Protopopov to inform the Tsar that he knew Buchanan was actually encouraging the radical movement to revolt and had been seen in false whiskers at a secret rendezvous with the Bolsheviks.

The Tsarina immediately spread her story to astonished members of the family, who, even though they did not like Buchanan, only quoted her statements that the dignified Ambassador had put whiskers over his moustache as another sign of her madness. Paul wrote that Miechen had also lost her senses and told the appalled Rodzyanko that 'the Empress should be annihilated'. But what worried him more was the food shortages and daily riots, the rumours that even the Cossacks' loyalty was wavering at the daily orders from Protopopov to cut down frozen, starving men, women and children in the streets. The incessant butchery was beginning to disgust men who had never hesitated to obey orders to commit atrocities on behalf of generations of Tsars to whom they had given unquestioning loyalty. If this was how the Tsar's loyalist soldiers felt, Ella could see no way to avoid a revolution. It would mean the end of all her work, and probably her death, and when she prayed and felt herself unable to communicate with God, it did not stop her believing that it would be better to die and suffer oblivion than continue to see her sister turned into a monster, daily ordering Cossacks to cut to pieces the poor, innocent and hungry.

18

[From 18 January 1917, the Grand Duchess Serge kept a diary which mysteriously appeared in an auction room in New York in the 1960s and is not available for inspection.

Only excerpts relevant to the main story of her life have been included here, and many references to her garden, her convent and the weather – a favourite subject of imperial diarists – have been omitted. When she writes 'L', she is referring to the late Sir Robert Bruce Lockhart, who was in charge of the British Consulate in 1917. The letter 'C' refers to a M. Courtois, a representative of the French Ambassador, Paléologue, whose exact position in Moscow has never been ascertained; 'V' to Vyrubova; 'P' to Protopopov; and 'K' to Kerensky.]

THE DIARY

18 January 1917

It is my wish to fill time with activity, and I have decided to write a diary of these times.

Here things are bad. Not only is it difficult to provide enough food for our patients and orphans but, for the first time last week, we have been faced with a shortage of wood and had to reduce the heating. This has had an ill effect on some of the patients, and two of the elderly suffering from asthma have died, but as they were in ill health, it would be unfair to attribute the blame wholly to the lack of heating.

This afternoon Mr Lockhart came to see me and told me he has been ordered by the Ambassador to see me twice a week to keep me informed of the news. Monsieur Paléologue, who was present when Buchanan gave his instructions, has also quietly planned to send a Monsieur Courtois, whom he described as 'a member of my unofficial staff', to visit the convent once a week. Both called today and advised me to consider closing down my charities. I have told them simply that it was my intention to stay here whatever happened. C merely nodded and said that was the answer he expected me to give, but started arguing and gesticulating in a typically French way and told me of the shortage of wood in Petrograd and how the Embassy there is unheated, and how the only person able to get fuel is Kschessinka.

I really could not see what this had to do with me and told him so sharply, but he misunderstood me and thought I was angry at being compared with this woman, who, he then told me, had led a very different life from my own and not in a thousand years would he have compared her to me. I said I was aware of the difference, but as he still seemed to wish to go on talking, I had to stand up and say I had an appointment.

No news from Alix, but both representatives told me there are food riots every day in Petrograd. Here, although there are shortages, things are not quite as bad.

Monday, 22 January

L called with news of Alix which annoyed me. Apparently last week Prince Kurakin, who has for years been a member of Alix's magic circle, rang up Protopopov and informed him that he had raised the ghost of Rasputin. I never liked Kurakin. He always had the sepulchral voice of a grim Lutheran pastor and was always stopping and standing still and saying he was looking into the future or the past or anywhere but where he was. I found him silly; my sister was always taken in. But L says V and P now every evening have séances at which they ask the ghost questions and take the answers to Alix the next day. Apparently Rasputin says all will be well if the Government remains unchanged and firmness is shown with the rioters. So Protopopov persuades Alix that this is what must be done, although L says he evades responsibility if the advice is bad by saying that the policy was Rasputin's and not his.

I tried to pray for Alix; it was no good.

Monday, 29 January

French, British and Italian delegates have arrived for a conference. I only pray they will be told the truth. Our patients are getting difficult to deal with, are rude to the nurses, and one of them spat at me. I pretended not to notice and went and sat down by his bed and asked him about his mother and his wife an children. I think he repented, for before I left he reached out his hand and gripped mine so hard I nearly cried out. His eyes had tears in them. I was touched. Later, I asked about his wound and found he was one of six patriots with bullet holes in their feet; apparently large numbers of men are wounding themselves in this manner in order to be sent home. How unhappy they must be to behave in this way.

[There is an unexpected gap in the diaries until 1 March. In this period, in the middle of an intensely cold winter, the country was ruled by the Tsarina and Protopopov and was marked by discontented strikes and riots caused by shortages of bread and wood and a decrease in the value of the rouble.]

1 March

Tonight I admit I have been dishonest about writing this diary. Now I must truly admit that whenever I tried to pray, I found my mind straying, going over ways in which the present disasters could have been avoided. This was an admission that my old belief that all suffering was for good, I could no longer accept however hard I tried. Why this endless slaughter, why should God wish for quantities of grain and food to rot in warehouses in the south because the Government is so inefficient they cannot be moved to big cities? I cannot now believe it is God's wish that millions should suffer for a few to grow rich by bribes. I had always thought He was all seeing and that not a hair could fall out of a man's head without his knowledge; now I believe I was wrong for I cannot accept that He chose the deaths of millions of men, and the responsibility is not His but that of the family into which I married. I cannot divorce myself from their guilt by pretending that death and chaos is His will, not mine and theirs. I believe that is why, when I try to draw close to Him, he repels me for the punishment he is justly meting out to those not Himself who are responsible.

These are not deep thoughts and are of no interest to others, but they break my faith into pieces. And so I decided that every night, when I prayed, if I could get no answer, I would not waste my time writing down my poor thoughts.

4 March

We are lucky in Moscow: it is icy cold; but in Petrograd the temperature is below zero, food and wood are short and L quoted a saying going round the town that 'only the corrupt are warm, as God is giving them a foretaste of the heat of hell'. The people are so hungry for food that they queue up outside the bakers, and two nights ago four young women with children determined to sleep outside a bakery all night to ensure they were the first to enter. In the morning, three of them had frozen to death.

6 March

A surprise visit from Monsignor Theophanes, Bishop of Viatka. I received him coldly. He was a friend of Rasputin's, but he seemed sensible. He says that those who have stayed at home are not discontented, but the many wounded soldiers returned to the front are full of revolutionary ideas and have lost their faith. The influence of the clergy has ceased to exist. His village priests who haven't left their villages, know nothing and appear ridiculous and ignorant to returning soldiers full of new ideas. He told me another thing: a source of violence has been caused, of all things, by the new cinematograph houses, which show scenes of murder and violence; and he insists – for I was disbelieving – that motion pictures have set terrible examples to the poor peasants, who have never ever seen violence exhibited as exciting and heroic.

He is also worried by a further vice of which I knew nothing: the taking of morphia. The trouble is that, because of the number of casualties and insufficiency of beds here in Petrograd and in Kiev, hospitals have had to be scattered all over the country in large houses where doctors and orderlies and hospital clerks, whose example is of importance, dose themselves with the stuff, which makes them inefficient, lazy and dishonest. They spread the habit among their friends, and the result in small country towns is appalling. A decline in the status of the Church and the official classes has a serious effect on the community. The Bishop says he can do nothing about the morphia, but he believes in reforms in the Church and in an improvement of the salaries of priests.

7 March

A man with appalling burns has come in. When I saw them, I jumped. He reminded me so of the first patient I ever treated. The burns were similar and septicaemia had spread. I have taken him as my special patient. Years ago, I remember how the smell of rotting flesh made me sick. I no longer notice it. I pray for his life now.

Apparently nearly 50° of frost in Moscow. Many engine and boiler tubes burst. Monsieur C told me 57,000 railways wagons have jammed in the snow. It can only worsen the food situation. He also told me Princess Leon Radziwill is giving on Sunday a large and brilliant ball. Everything is to be as before. I am making no comment.

8 March

Vanya, my burn patient, suffers unceasingly. I have given him morphia, but there is a shortage; somehow Marie gets just enough. At the moment we can only feed the patients. Yesterday I temporarily closed the school for all except my resident orphans until the spring. We now rely on food brought to us by peasant farmers in their carts. I bless them.

9 March

Vanya still in pain, but it appears most burns are healing except his left leg and hand. I don't like the colour of either. The doctor says that with my help he may pull through. Food riots, with twelve killed here in Moscow.

11 March

Vanya's burns improving on chest and stomach and left hand. I asked the doctor to examine him again. He says I can work miracles, which makes me worried.

Eight police killed in Petrograd. Princess Radziwill refuses to cancel ball, but Boris is the only member of imperial family going.

12 March

Vanya's leg deteriorating. Dress it three times a day. All other wounds healing. Desperate. In evening, riots and shooting, and demonstration shouting curses at me.

13 March

I woke up at six and went at once to see poor Vanya. I had seen him in the night, and thanks to morphia he slept. I turned back the bedclothes with dread and saw the same, no better, no worse. I am using a new balm from the country which Sister Vera sent for. She said her mother used it and it works miracles. I hope so; I am sad for him. He never complains, however great the pain, and smiles at me and often holds my hand.

L in evening arrived late, bringing news from Petrograd. Volhynian Regiment of the Guard mutinied and killed officers. Alix safe. Marie says revolution has broken out. I am still worried about Vanya.

18 March

Operation took place on leg. Question is now whether poison has been contained or will spread. Michael abdicates – Provisional Government formed. Riots in Petrograd, riots here. Nicky said to be prisoner in his train. Poor Alix.

19 March

Vanya's holding on, but temperature has risen. He held my hand and smiled. Doctor says no need for priest yet, but I had long talk to see if he has any bad sins on his mind. Nothing. Nicky still held in train, Alix at Tsarskoye surrounded by friendly troops, behaving with dignity and bravery. One of girls has measles.

21 March

Vanya no better or worse. Temperature 102°. Doctor shook head for first time. Small crowd came again outside walls and shouted abuse at German witch. Officers massacred at front. Baltic Fleet revolts.

23 March

Vanya's leg black. No alternative to operation. Doctor doubtful about his heart. I pray all afternoon to God to save a good brave man.

24 March

Operation in morning. Still surviving – temperature 103°. L called at six o'clock to say Nicky has reached Tsarskoye Selo. Also Cyril has gone over to Bolsheviks and has raised red flag on his palace. He was a nice boy with good in him. I cannot see that one side is better than the other.

25 March

Watched Vanya sinking all yesterday. Called priest midday. I am sure he was happier after I sat with him until 3 a.m. Died peaceably.

L says that Nicky and Alix are to go to England with the children when they are better. That will be best place for him if he feels he can go, as Georgie was always his closest cousin and best friend. L also said none of family except Paul have tried to do anything for Nicky. I think I understand why.

28 March

There is talk of peace and L says Germans are triumphant and will take much

Russian territory, but Soviet minister Kerensky to fight on. I can't understand. I am for peace.

31 March

I hear the so-called Rasputin metropolitans and bishops have been sent to a Siberian monastery – Pitirm, Macarius, Varnava – I forget the others. The more I think of this revolution, the more I understand it: Russia had to be cleansed.

Rasputin's bones have been taken away and burnt. How I hate this hate.

2 April

I hear the opinion is Provisional Government rules only in Petrograd. The Bolsheviks are undermining them. L gave me a long talk about the army pouring back from the front shooting their officers; no discipline. Germany advancing everywhere. Apparently Kerensky is still for war, but the soldiers are refusing to obey orders coming from him and have shot generals.

5 April

Apparently Prince Lvov is to be Chief Minister and Kerensky, who L says is a strong man, is to be Minister of Justice and is the man responsible for guarding Nicky and Alix.

6 April

An outbreak of ptomaine poisoning in the hospital, I fear owing to some of the meat peasants had brought us, which we have to accept or starve. Many ill, two dead. Stayed up all last night, plan to sleep four hours tonight, otherwise I become forgetful and useless. L called to say Mr Bruce, head of British Chancery, had sent message in diplomatic bag saying the Ambassador is anxiously awaiting recovery of Tsar's children, who all have measles, so the family can go to England. The German Emperor has offered the ship immunity from submarine attack. Unfortunately, news of their impending arrival has produced indignation in radical circles, in the House of Commons and in the newspapers, but Kerensky is determined to keep his word and allow them to leave. Hot-heads want to try them, but he has given assurance they will go. I thought how lucky Georgie is such an old and firm friend of Nicky's; they always looked so alike. But ought Nicky to leave?

10 April

Poison outbreak abating, but has, alas, caused six deaths in infirm patients.

14 April

Marie has cold. I always miss her when she is ill. L called to say Bruce was coming to Moscow to ascertain the situation in the city and was anxious to call on me. He is arriving on the 15th and asks to be received in audience the next day. Of course I agreed.

All patients quite recovered from outbreak, but I have given instructions the chef must personally inspect all meat himself.

Mr Bruce called and I could see at once he was ill at ease as he fidgeted in the chair when paying unnecessarily long respects. Then he came to the point. On the 12th, Sir George had received a telegram from London saying the British Government had reconsidered its position and withdrawn their invitation to send a destroyer to Murmansk to pick up the imperial family. He said he was with the Ambassador when he received the telegram, which literally staggered him, and in a shocked state he took it into Lady Georgie's and his daughter Meriel's sitting room. After half an hour, he came out and told Bruce to come into his study, where he read the telegram, and told him personally to draft a ciphered message to the Foreign Secretary, asking if the King was aware that the Government's refusal to accept the Tsar and his family could amount to signing their death warrant. The Provisional Government was shaky and ill-organized and the Bolsheviks, although momentarily weakened, 'are gaining strength every day. I wish to emphasize it is solely due to Kerensky's influence that the offer to allow the Tsar to leave was made. It is unlikely permission will be given again. I am anxious the King should be acquainted with the exact position.'

The next day, the message came back that the event had been considered at the highest levels. A decision had been made and would not be changed. Bruce said that once again the Ambassador was overcome and remarked: 'From years of reading telegrams I fear this means the decision is the King's and not the Government's. God help those poor children.'

Bruce said the Ambassador was particularly upset as he had, only a few days before, sent Nicky a message saying the imperial family would be granted refuge in England. 'He told me to acquaint you with the true facts as, though he can never tell another person, he could not bear you to think he hadn't done his best. He told me to say in sending me here that he is breaking every rule of his service for the first time in his life.'

Mr Bruce himself was on the verge of tears, and went on to say how Meriel told him that when her father had come into the room, he had sat down and put both hands to his forehead and said: 'My God, the King must be frightened. That's the truth of it. He must be afraid.'

Mr Bruce looked at me and I tried, as I have learned to do by much practice, calmly to decide what should be done. I thought how I would behave and was sure that if I was given the chance, nothing would make me leave Russia; it is where I belong and I am, in part, responsible for what has happened. The same must apply to Alix and Nicky. Surely they should not think of going? But the children are another matter. Olga is twenty-one this year, and Alexis, the youngest, only thirteen. In no way can they be held responsible for the past. All of them are innocent.

I looked at Mr Bruce, who was sitting across the table with embarrassment all over his face, as if expecting me to break down, and said to him: 'I think the Tsar and Tsarina should stay. Surely the Labour parties and the revolutionaries in

England would accept the children?'

His mouth fell open with surprise. I could see that my idea astonished him. He said: 'Well, well,' and paused before saying weakly: 'Would the Tsar and Tsarina be prepared to separate themselves from their son?'

I said: 'If not, could not a request be made to the Government that those children who wished to leave should be granted the right to enter England?'

Once again he was amazed, and all he could do was mutter something to the effect that he would put the matter to the Ambassador.

I thought about it afterwards, and believe my suggestion is the right one, but I fear Alix won't, out of selfishness, let Alexis and the girls go. It would cause no trouble in radical circles in England. The English are notoriously sentimental about children.

19 April

I received a letter from Mr Bruce, thanking me for seeing him, and saying that out of sheer stupidity he had forgotten to mention that Alix, Nicky and the three children are all improving and Kerensky ensures they are well treated.

22 April

Marie came to see me early to say we really must consider the wisdom of leaving the outpatients' door open all day. Yesterday Sister Helen had been alone in the dispensary and two men had come in, obviously in a queer state. They had laughed a lot and clung to each other and leaned over the counter and said something unspeakable. Then one of them started to climb over the counter, but by good fortune Father Mitrophan had come in to get iodine for an orphan's cut. He took the men by the scruff of the neck, which made them laugh even louder, and threw them into the street, still screaming with laughter. He rubbed his hands and sent Sister Helen to bed. She had a lucky escape, as the men were lunatics; the asylums have all been opened. I said that in no circumstances was any sister to be alone in the outpatients' room, and it should only be open from ten till two. I went to see Helen with Father Mitrophan, who, when I had finished speaking, asked us all not to move and went away and came back with a large handbell and told any of the sisters to ring it if they were in danger. He becomes fierce if anyone threatens them. He then told them not only to ring the bell but to hit anyone who assaulted them with it as hard as they could on the head. 'It's a church bell, and I'm sure God will see it strikes down sinners.'

We all laughed, but afterwards the story made me sorry for the poor lunatics; what will happen to them, wandering laughing round Moscow in the intense cold with nowhere to go and no hand to welcome them? But I knew I could not reprimand Father Mitrophan. He is a man, and a strong presence in the background, which gives the women a false sense of security.

24 April

I looked in on the dispensary at eleven o'clock this morning. Everything was neat and tidy. Then the door was pushed open, and in came half a dozen men, unshaven with short hair. I saw at once that this time our visitors were not lunatics but criminals, who last week were set free as well. The poor men looked filthy and must have slept out, or in an outhouse. Again I thought how wicked to let men free with nowhere to go.

One of the ringleaders was drunker than the others. His beard was filthy on one side and clean on the other, as if he had been sleeping in the gutter.

'We have come to see the German woman!' he shouted.

I stood forward. 'Here I am.' I could see he was playing a part and was not a bad man at heart, and how can one judge anyone fairly who has been shut up for years?

'You are, are you?' he said. 'Well then, clean my wound.'

The sisters gave little gasps of horror, and I said it would be 'my pleasure', at which the man lifted up his tunic, which was held up by a friend behind, and started to undo the belt of his trousers. I heard Father Mitrophan, who was behind me, move. I knew that the brave old man would soon attack them, so without turning round told him to stand still. The man, who had been doubtfully holding up his trousers, seemed to make a decision and pulled them down to his knees. He was wearing nothing. He took a step forward to try and shock me. I was not shocked, for I saw on his groin a black blood clot. I asked the sisters to get a table, and in the shrinking way which makes me often despair of them, they pushed one into the middle of the room. I told him to take off his trousers and lie on the table while I dressed the wound. At once he tried to pull his trousers up again. I saw I would have to be severe with him, pushed him towards the table, made him lie down and told the sisters to take off his boots and trousers, than sent for a razor, hot water, disinfectant and dressings. While they were coming, I told the girls to get soap and hot water and wash his feet.

The man was now lying on the table, his eyes rolling with embarrassment. I smiled at him and put my hand on his forehead. It was wet and dirty. I sponged it. His followers had become quiet and sober and were standing stupidly behind him, pushing closer together like frightened sheep, which showed there was no real harm in them either. When everything had been brought, I washed away the blood, shaved around the wound and bathed it with hot water and disinfectant for some fifteen minutes. He gave a little groan whenever I touched him, and each time Father Mitrophan told him 'be a man'. Actually, the wound looked worse than it was, and when it was cleaned and dressed I had no doubt that, if he looks after himself, he will be all right.

When at last I was finished, he jumped off the table, pulled up his trousers, pulled down his tunic and went back to his companions, where, naturally, he tried to recover the dignity he thought he had lost.

'Who are you?' he said in a puzzled voice.

I replied that I had told him, and made the sign of the cross towards him. He said nothing, but I could see he was wishing to thank me. But one of the men at his back whispered: 'It is the German woman all right – you can tell by her voice.'

They stared at me without speaking.

Father Mitrophan moved forward and I was afraid he was going to hit them, but he only opened the door and stood glaring as they filed out, looking at the floor, and then, despite my orders, he shut and locked it, put the key in his pocket and walked away.

26 April

I had a talk with Father Mitrophan about the need for him to be more charitable. I thought he was going to burst, and then he looked at me and said: 'I never thought I would say such a thing to Your Imperial Highness, but you need a man about the place and I am better than nothing.' It was funny.

8 May

To my embarrassment, the story, with every sort of exaggeration, about my dressing the prisoner's wound, has somehow got round and many gifts have come in from the country districts. The chef told me, with glee, that he had received five fine young pigs.

12 May

Just as things were becoming normal again, the chef asked for an appointment at ten o'clock. Two of the pigs had been eaten, but for the first time the vegetable truck had not arrived. What was he to do? He was prepared to buy vegetables from hoarders, but it would be expensive.

At that moment, there was a great noise from outside and a banging on the church door. I told everyone to go back to their duties and went and opened the door. Outside stood three big lorries full of men with red scarves and badges pinned on their shoulders, several of them waving red flags like schoolchildren. A group of men came towards me. I could see it was their intention to insult, as they spoke without taking their cigarettes out of their mouths, and said rudely that they were going to search the convent to take the hidden arms away and arrest the Prince of Hesse if he was here, and if they found ammunition I would also be arrested and taken away.

I saw once again that I was having to deal with frightened children, and after looking straight into each of their eyes, which made them uneasy, I asked for a few minutes' grace to prepare myself. Then I went to find Father Mitrophan and told him not to ask questions or get angry, but to go and get all the sisters as quickly as he could into the chapel to attend a farewell service as I was leaving. I told Barbara to pack warm clothes for us both, as she had made me promise to take her wherever I go. It didn't take very long, and then I returned to the men, who still had cigarettes in their mouths, and asked them if, before they searched the house, they would do me a favour and come to a short service of farewell which was to be given for me?

They looked stupefied, which showed they were true peasants, and immediately took their hats off. And then three of them put their rifles down and looked at the two others, who then threw theirs down rather angrily. I led them into the chapel and knelt and prayed for their forgiveness, for my sisters and for Marie to have the strength to keep them together, and for dear Father Mitrophan to keep his temper and not get killed.

I need not have feared; his voice was breaking with tears and he looked so noble with his white beard that I am sure his honest presence affected the men, for I heard strange voices joining in at the back when he asked the congregation to sing a 'Te Deum' for those going away.

After it was over, I went to the men and told them I would go to my room and wait for them with Sister Barbara and my baggage. Would they please now go and search every available place in the building, but remember two things: that we had sick and dying patients on the premises, whom I hoped they would treat with care, and a separate room used for infectious diseases, which already contained an occupant suspected of having typhoid fever. I would have the doors opened wide but, I suggested, for their own good, they should not go in. They stared at me as if I was mad. I left them and sat in my little room. I wondered if I would be happier in prison. For a long time I had known that I have been chosen by God to suffer, and until I have done so, like the hermit long ago on the Black Sea, I will not be forgiven.

But it was not to be, for when the men came back they had the embarrassed look on their faces of those who wish to apologize but don't know how to speak. However, they admitted that they had only seen invalids and sick children and neither Ernie nor ammunition were to be found.

L telephoned later in the day to see if I was all right and told me he had informed representatives of the Government of the outrage. He is a help and appears to know everything that happens.

13 May

I hope for a peaceful day, but three men called to apologize for the soldiers, who, they said, had no authority to arrest me. I said nothing. They then suggested I move for safety into the Kremlin. I asked them how I could possibly look after my patients and orphans from anywhere but here?

18 May

L called and said Kerensky was the only man in the Provisional Government; the rest were useless aristocrats or placemen, but the trouble was that he was seldom in Petrograd and spent his time at the front, trying inefficiently to continue the war. He has managed to make some regiments fight, and they have even had successes. This has helped the Western Front, where the British and French are hard pressed, but his ideals stop him 'squashing' the Bolsheviks, who are in league with the Germans and have won over the recruits already since the country is sick of war.

I found this so confusing. I long for peace, but what if William won? I wish I understood politics; my thoughts are too confused.

21 May

Food is suddenly arriving with regularity by lorry, so perhaps the three men who came to see me have positions of power.

16 May

Typhoid is confirmed in the city, but our patient is better. Apparently, owing to maladministration, all the city drains damaged in the March riots are blocked and unmended and water supplies are now polluted. We have to boil even lettuce. Food supplies are satisfactory, but likely to be difficult in the coming winter.

L came to see me and tells me that though Kerensky is a magic speaker and can sway an audience, his efforts to get the army to fight are proving a failure, although such numbers are still under arms that the Germans are said to have recalled divisions from the west. Quite unnecessary, he thought, as Knox in his last report said the army was finished as a fighting force.

28 May

Weather the warmest I have ever known for May and typhoid said to be increasing. L said extremists are making demands, supported by some members of the government, to put Nicky and Alix on trial, but Kerensky remains loyal.

Tuesday, 4 June

I have received a message that the Swedish Minister will be calling on me in week's time.

11 June

Heat intolerable, typhoid worse in city.

The Swedish Minister called. He had come with a message from Willy, 'who believes' – he looked all round the room before finishing his sentence – 'the Provisional Government is falling to bits and the Bolsheviks are certain to take their place, in which case not only will the Tsar and Tsarina be in danger, but also yourself as it's their plan to destroy the whole of the imperial family'.

He went on: 'If you wish to leave now, as I strongly recommend, arrangements can be made, but it will be increasingly difficult to leave later.'

I thought for a few minutes about the offer, and how nice it would be to see Victoria and Ernie again. It is nearly three years since I saw her – the longest separation of our lives – but I knew there was no question of going and told the Minister my life had been in Russia and here I would stay. To my annoyance, I felt rather good about my decision when I would have been wicked to have accepted. How easily we praise ourselves!

13 June

The heat is unbearable. I had to change my clothes three times today.

15 June

Woke up with a headache. Got up with difficulty. Felt shaky and feverish, and at six o'clock sent for Marie to tell her to stand by the door as I was certain I had somehow caught typhoid fever. Barbara alone was to look after me. I put everything in Marie's hands and said that if I died, she was to continue as long as she could, but if our affairs became hopeless, she was to go to the Crimea. The little money I have at the bank is entirely at her disposal.

[During the next six weeks there are no entries in the diary. For a month, Ella was seriously ill and Marie faithfully looked after her as all the sisters pleaded to be allowed to help. Marie said later that Ella had lain still most of the time, without thinking, and the doctor was worried at her placidity, which would not enable her to fight death. But she recovered slowly and was on her feet again in August.]

1 August

It is strange, I have no memory of the last six weeks. I feel like Rip Van Winkle, a story our mother read us of a man who went to sleep for years. I have asked my sisters, who have been little saints to me, and they say I slept most of the time. I still feel weak, and when I wake up in the morning I sometimes think I am at Ilonskoye and will go out into the garden, and then all the present comes back to me. The doctor says that we are lucky not to have had cholera, but the Provisional Government is utterly hopeless. There is no authority anywhere and the drains have not even been mended. The coming winter should end the outbreak.

5 August

I feel stronger and walk daily in garden, sitting for hours under my tree. Marie seems to have managed well, but I noticed two of the sisters' uniforms are dirty. I think that this is the first sign of my taking interest again.

11 August

L called. Marie had tried to put him off, but he insisted it was a matter of the greatest importance. When he arrived, he gave a start of surprise, so I fear I must have changed for the worse. He said he had come to tell me of an event which might have caused me concern if I had heard it from another source: on the 14th, Nicky and Alix and the children are to be sent to Tobolsk. He went on that Sir George often sees Kerensky, who has told him he is sending them not in an imperial train – that would be asking for trouble – but in wagons-lit, and is allowing them to take with them wine, baggage, pictures and their jewels, one butler, one steward, one wine steward, ten footmen, two valets, seven cooks, a nurse in case Alix or Alexis is ill, and even a barber in case Nicky feels his hair is too long, as well as their favourite courtiers who are well enough to go. L says it is ridiculous. To ensure their safety, K sending another train behind full of soldiers. The move is entirely for their sake, as he doesn't believe he'll be able to protect them any longer near Petrograd. They are to stay in the Governor's house. K thinks it is the safest place they could be.

I asked L if he would get a letter to Alix. He said he would personally give it to Kerensky, but that did not mean it would ever arrive.

16 August

Gradually taking over again in the hospital. Marie has done very well, but some of the rooms were not as clean as I would have liked, and I found dust under the beds. We are beginning to get short of medical stores. I feel depressed and wonder if I should not send away two of my sisters, who appear nervous.

28 August

L called to say Kerensky has made his second fatal error – the first was while I was ill in July and the Bolsheviks attempted a *coup d'état*. He put them down but refrained from destroying them. Now, when General Kornilov has tried to bring off a right-wing *coup* by marching his troops into Moscow, Kerensky has asked the Bolsheviks to help him oppose the troops and put himself in their hands. L says the trouble is he is a kind-hearted idealist, but unfortunately is opposed by Lenin and Trotsky, two merciless men of genius. He thinks Kerensky will soon disappear.

10 September

We are greatly troubled by numbers of rats. Received a short note from Alix sent two weeks ago to say they have arrived and their quarters are exceedingly cramped.

21 September

L came to see me. He was looking downcast and is to return to England. I looked at him and saw he was troubled and asked why. He said: 'I am being relieved . . .' then he burst into tears. I sat still and waited for him to recover, when he told me he had fallen in love with another woman and neglected his wife. Sir George had warned him in the kindest way to give her up, but it was no good; he had gone back. I told him we all give in to temptation in one way or another and I would like to thank him for all his many kindnesses to me and he would be sorely missed. I gave him my blessing. He almost burst into tears again. I was sad to see him go; he has been useful in bringing news. Without him I would have known nothing – the talkative Frenchman soon disappeared. As he was leaving he turned. We looked at each other and I am sure both knew that we would never see each other again.

1 October

I have had to make a decision that we will take no more patients; the food supplies are so uncertain. I miss L and his cheerfulness, and I know nothing of what is happening. Marie hears rumours that Nicky's old mother escaped to the Crimea with Miechen and that Paul is a prisoner in his own house in Moscow, but the source of her information makes it both unsatisfying and worrying.

15 October

Nothing but riots and killing. Things are so dangerous I have allowed no sisters out this week.

28 October

The Bolsheviks have risen in Petrograd. Sounds of shots all day here. No one allowed to leave convent ground.

10 November

A rumour that Moscow is to be new capital and the Government is to sit here. The Bolsheviks are active everywhere. Food is almost impossible to procure. An old patient died because of the lack of correct antidote.

20 November

Churches attacked by Bolsheviks. Priests torn from their altars and thrown into street. Apparently their intention is to stop all religion. We have not been persecuted yet. I have had long talk with Father Mitrophan, and told him he must not resist if he is pulled out of our church. We cannot have an unseemly fight. He should follow Christ's teaching and turn the other cheek. All I can get from him is a promise: 'I will try.'

25 November

Today a horrible scene that will haunt me as long as I live. The foot of a farmer peasant called Yermolai was crushed by the wheel of a runaway cart in 1911 or 1912, and he was taken into my hospital in great pain. He remained brave and uncomplaining. All his toes except the smallest had to be amputated, and I offered to help his family during the three months he was in hospital. But they were proud country people and his wife and eldest son brought their produce in every week he was here. When he left, he made that servile Russian gesture which I hate of throwing himself at my feet. I turned away and kept my back to him until he stood up, when I explained to him that in the eyes of God all men are equal and no one should abase himself before another. Ever since he has supplied us, before the war with delicacies, and since the war began with the fruit and vegetables we so badly need, and occasionally pigs. I always ask to be told when he calls and go and speak to him. He is a funny looking little man, almost as broad as he is tall, with a mop of silver hair and a perpetual smile on his face. His wife is hard-faced, never smiles, and they have four children. The whole family appear to work happily, and I often think of them as an idyllic peasant family. He never complains and always thanks God for his good fortune. I like to see him, for he makes me feel better.

Almost the first law which the Bolsheviks made when they took over was the prohibition of sales to private individuals, but Yermolai, when he heard of it, put his big, square forefinger on his nose and pressed it flat, winked and said that if he called at five in the morning, the police would still be in bed, and if we did not mind getting up that early, he would still continue to deliver two big boxes of apples to us every week. Somehow, his never go bad – mine do.

For the first week all went well, but since Marie has the idea that I should not be woken up early, I did not see him last week to thank him. Yesterday I said I should be called at four and would meet him at the gate at five, and nobody except Barbara was to come with me. We opened the wooden gate into the back yard and stamped our feet and walked in the street, which was pitch dark, except for my own oil street lamp, which always burns oposite to show that the hospital is open. Almost exactly on the hour we heard the distant rustling of a sleigh and the thud of horses' hooves drawing nearer, but we couldn't see a thing until we saw the red eyes of a horse, followed by the sleigh, rushing into the patch of light. Yermolai pulled up and doffed his fur hat, jumped down and started to lead the horse through the gate, when there was a sudden shouting, and three men with red badges on their shoulders and rifles with bayonets fixed came running up and seized him, shouting that he was a traitor. One of them pushed the poor man against the wall of my convent and held a bayonet to his throat, jeering that he would never help the 'German witch' again. I walked forward and asked him to have mercy, but he told me, in coarse words, to get off, and gave Yermolai a cut on the side of his neck with his bayonet, telling him he would pin him to the wall if I didn't mind my own business. Luckily, I don't think he knew me.

Barbara burst into tears, so I told her to go inside, as 'tears help nobody'. There was nothing I could do but watch and pray. I saw that the other two men were hacking Yermolai's horse out of its traces, and when they had succeeded, it jumped in the air, ran a few paces, and then stood still, looking at his master. The man holding the bayonet at his throat lowered his rifle and told Yermolai to go on standing against the wall or he would be shot. The three began whispering together and laughing in a horribly drunk way before two of them jumped on to the sleigh to examine it. They gave a whistle of pleasure to find a young pig and four large rabbits, threw them out of the sleigh, but looked disappointed at the three boxes full of apples which he had so proudly brought us. But the fruit gave them an idea, and they pelted Yermolai with it as he stood against the wall, laughing when they hit him. The scene looked devilish in the dim light, and the men like bearded fiends. Not the least sinister thing was that the apples shone green in the snow. When there was nothing else to throw, they found, to their delight, a small basket of eggs, and one of the men held the bayonet against Yermolai's throat while the others thrust a whole egg in his mouth and then hit him on the jaw. Afterwards, they opened his coat front and pushed the rest in and hit him in the chest.

I tried to pray hard for those men as they walked back to the sleigh, while my poor friend stood quietly aginst the wall as if nothing had happend. Again the three men started whispering together while the horse stood like a ghost, puzzled, stock still. Then they went round the other side of the sledge and heaved with all their might until it fell over and the bags of grain which Yermolai was taking to the market fell out all over the street. They looked in triumph at their victim, but he said nothing, remained unmoving. This irritated them, and they walked over and prodded him with their bayonets and said it was lucky for him they were tired and going home or they would have taken him to the police station. I thought they would go now, and believe they would have done if the horse had not distracted them, for the poor animal, seeing nothing was being thrown, perhaps thought the worst was over and walked slowly towards his master.

The leader turned to the other two and said something which made them all shout with laughter. Then he picked up an apple and all three of them walked towards the animal, making the noise which peasants do when they talk to horses. When they had drawn close the man very carefully put out his hand flat with the apple on his palm in front of the horse, who bent down, flapped open his lips and took the apple in his teeth, crunched it in half and put his head down to eat the rest. At that moment, the other men let off their rifles close to his ears. The noise was so loud and sudden I almost fell backwards, and the poor animal reared up on his hind legs, just like the Austrian horses used to do, turned round and galloped away. Yermolai gave a terrible cry and dashed out of the light after his beloved animal. The men laughed loudly, and whether that was the last straw or he realized that in the dark he would never find the horse, Yermolai suddenly appeared again in the light, running, roaring with rage at the nearest soldier, who waited until he was near him and then moved forward and smashed the butt of his rifle into his mouth.

They stood silently, looking down at him as he lay still, then on tiptoe they walked away from him, picked up the pig and rabbits and disappeared. The whole scene had I thought lasted an hour, but when I looked at my watch I could just make out that it had taken ten minutes.

I went to get Father Mitrophan and, waking up all the sisters and the eldest boys, told them to put on their snow boots and thickest clothes. Then we all put as much of the wheat as we could into the split sacks, picked up the apples, and somehow righted the sleigh, pushed it through the gate and shut it, while others carried poor Yermolai into the hospital. He looked as white as the snow, and every time he breathed a bubbling froth of blood came out through his mouth. But luckily, only his jaw was broken and eighteen teeth knocked out. The doctor says he will survive, as such an accident is nothing to a peasant. He worked quickly on him, terrified that the police might come and drag him away, but perhaps the criminals didn't want to be questioned about their plunder, as nobody has come.

Yermolai could not speak after his jaw was set, although he kept making signs until Father Mitrophan guessed that he wanted to draw something and gave him a slate and a piece of chalk with which he drew a rough horse. I saw at once that he was worrying about the poor animal, and while he did not mind the pain of his broken jaw, he dreaded the loss of his friend.

I told Father Mitrophan to go to the rear door and leave it open in case the animal wandered back, and he came back grinning and nodded at Yermolai and shouted at him what a good horse he had. When he opened the gate to look out, the animal had pushed his way in. He would personally see that it received a large helping of grain from the sleigh and then would go to the market to send a message by one of the farmers to Yermolai's family that they were not to worry.

I used to pray for those with hate in their hearts. Now I must pray for myself.

26 November

I have not, out of embarrassment, written all the truth about yesterday. When the horse came back, I put my head on Father Mitrophan's shoulder and burst

341

into tears. Tonight I asked Marie to forgive my stupidity and emotionalism, but I had been very tired. She told me, and I always insist that she speak to me as Victoria used to: 'You make a mistake in always being perfect. People think you are cold and without feelings. After yesterday, those who respected you will love you.' I answered truthfully: 'I have to look and behave coldly because I can't be natural, I don't know why.' Afterwards I hated myself for talking in such a way.

Christmas Day

Despite the statement that the bells were not to be rung and no one was to go to church on Our Lord's birthday, many bells rang and thousands of men and women took their own candles and went to their own churches and, strangely enough, there were few incidents, although, as far as I can understand, our new rulers kill whoever they wish. Nicky's reign looks peaceful compared to what is now happening.

Our own church was full, and Father Mitrophan walked round the streets later and said that even some of the Bolsheviks had gone to church and, for the first time in two months, he did not see a dead body in the streets

10 January

Yet another visitation, this time by a group of twelve men who said they represented the new authority and produced a signed paper, stating it was a search warrant. Again they looked for ammunition and asked if Ernie was there, which made me laugh, for it is unlikely he would have been spending the last two and a half years hiding in my convent. They demanded to see even my bedroom, and insisted that I show it to them myself while they measured the walls with tapes. Of course, they found nothing, and appeared quite startled at my bare little room, straw mattresses and hard pillow, which they all felt in turn, shaking their heads in amazement.

They left behind them one man who tried to explain to me what communism meant. I said that the ideals were noble and differed little from the Church's, at which he became angry and said the churches had sucked the blood of the people. I told him that perhaps that was true in some cases, but surely men should be allowed to worship God, who had created us, and surely the watchword of the revolution was freedom, and how did a believer hurt anyone by going to a chosen place to pray by himself? He is the first Bolshevik I have ever met who made me understand what the best of them desire.

17 January

A lorry of provisions and medical supplies arrived. It must be the young man's influence. We are able to take in more patients again, but I do not know for how long. Every night there is shooting in the streets, every night men are killed, and every day churches are closed and boarded up, but, for some reason, we are allowed to offer freedom of worship. I can't understand why, but often I feel that I don't understand anything and my brain is going to collapse.

28 January

Two grey-faced men who looked like what Serge called scornfully 'middle class intellectuals' came in with ledgers and took down the names and addresses of everybody in the hospital and orphanage. I knew that they were the sort of men with whom I would not get on, so I asked Marie to help them. I was soon sent for and asked for the orphans' fathers' names and where each had come from. I told them often from the streets or on our doorstep, so we had no idea. The elder of the two men, who said his name was Lermentov, asked how we had decided what the orphans should be called, and I said that we had once run out of ideas and that one of the sisters, who loved reading, had gone and got a book of Turgenev's, and we had called two little forsaken babies after characters in the book.

'Which characters?'

'I forget . . . Oh yes,' I said, hearing Marie whisper, *'Fathers and Sons.'*

'You made no effort to find out their real names?'

I began to get angry. How could we? All we knew was that they had been left on a bench in the park, surrounded by warm blankets.

'You called them "Nikolai Kirsanov" and "Pavel Kirsanov?"'

'Yes, you can see – it is written down.'

'Why did you choose the name "Kirsanov" before others in the book?'

'I have no idea.'

'Have you treated them differently from the others?'

I had to bite my lip not to get angry, and said in my coldest voice: 'All the orphans are treated in the same way.'

The senior leaned forward: 'I suppose you never thought of calling them "Bazarov"?'

'Why on earth should I call them "Bazarov"?'

'Because,' he said, getting angry, 'he is the only idealistic character in the book. The "Kirsanovs" were bourgeois reactionaries.'

That was enough.

'Please understand that I have never heard of the name "Bazarov" or met anyone with that name, neither do I want to, nor have I ever read the book from which the names were selected. Gentlemen, I am a busy woman. Forgive me if I leave you to do useful work.'

I walked out. They asked to see me again; I refused. Marie repeated to me that the men had remarked: 'A typical Romanov, full of pride.' I nodded. I was furious to have been questioned like a convict about twins for whom I had cared for five years.

16 February

Father Mitrophan went for a walk today. He says he was stared at with fear. He saw an old friend, who beckoned him into a side-street and told him to change his clothes when he went out. Of course, he said he wouldn't. Then he was told that Moscow is in a state of terror: men shot every day, even socialists of fifty years or anyone who protests at the killing. The prisons are full of those awaiting trial, but there are no trials. We live here like the besieged in a castle. Last night I sat up with an old man. I fear that my faith is failing. When he died, I felt uncertain whether he had an immortal soul. If I lose my faith, I will have nothing, but my lapses are rare.

21 February

Moscow is to be the capital city of Russia from the beginning of next month. My faith is stronger.

23 February

The Health Commissariat – what a dreadful name – delivered medicines today. The local depot provides us with small quantities of food once a week, but now, every day, we have to know exact numbers in hospital and orphanage. This is impossible because of the deaths and recoveries. Strange men come and are rude to my girls. It is becoming intolerable. I think they are trying to drive me away.

25 February

Another nameless man called to say that at a future date the care of the orphans will be taken over by the State, implying that I had not looked after them. The three sisters in the orphanage cried all evening.

4 March

A large ambulance drawn by two horses arrived without warning to collect four of our patients and take them to a State hospital. Marie came rushing in. 'Who are we to send? Why are they tormenting us?' I decide on two young men, one with a broken leg, the other with an eye infection which has already been cured. Both are ready to be discharged. I also sent one old man with sleeping sickness, and another who never knows where he is, so he won't notice. Marie says she will pretend to be upset as she is sure their object is to hurt us.

14 March

Shooting all day time. The baptism of the new capital!

28 March

Some other men in grey called, but gave no names. It seems to happen every day. They both had watchful eyes, which is new in Russia. They told me that Alix, etc., at Tobolsk wish me to join them. I have instinctively expected such a call, and say that although I will go where I am sent, my place is here. They go away, I fear not for long.

In case I am taken to Alix I get ready. Say goodbye to Marie, divide a small sum of money between myself and Barbara. Say goodbye to Father Mitrophan. We both cry. He still has his goodness and faith untouched and says we will meet again.

344

I say goodbye to my patients. Alas, my pity has gone. They mean little to me. Honesty does not excuse my coldness. A tearful goodbye from sisters. They cry and sob until I think I will be lucky to leave them, although I know they are all good, unselfish, dedicated girls.

21 April

The last four days I have spent half my time walking in the garden leaving much of my work to Marie. I have tried, in looking at the now fine trees and bushes and already budding lilacs, to recapture my original enthusiasm. It worked once before; not now. The convent belongs to the past. I know that my trials are coming. I only wish that to meet them I felt as strong as I once was. I feel I am living in a dream and will wake up when I leave.

22 April

I write this in a 'wagon-lit' compartment on the way to join Alix and Nicky. Our Letts guards set out to be rude. They opened our door every hour and looked in, leering. We were only given two hours to leave the convent by uniformed men, with two sisters. I said I only wished to take Barbara. They looked at a document and stated I have to take two. Barbara said she will take Krivovna, who never speaks. Luckily we were ready. All our packing done, and Krivovna took only a small bag. Why I have to take her I can't imagine. Say goodbye to Marie, dear Father Mitrophan, no others; could not bear more futile tears. I cannot bear emotional scenes and I am so glad the waiting has finished. All day I shut my eyes, praying that I will face the future with courage. Barbara has kept looking out of window saying 'Oh' and 'Ah' at nothing. I hope I will keep my temper. I feel reborn, the past is dead and a great trial ahead, and then I realize that I am weak and old.

23 April

The journey could apparently take a week or more, but the soldiers now leave us undisturbed following a piece of good fortune. The sergeant came in last night, looking bad-tempered, rubbing his cheek. I asked if he had toothache. He nodded crossly. I told Barbara to open the medicine chest, which Sister Helen had insisted I took. It is full of little drawers, all neatly labelled. I found 'Toothache', made the sergeant sit down and open his mouth. I examined his teeth with a dentist's mirror and saw clearly an exposed nerve in a rotting tooth. I plugged the hole with cotton wool soaked in white liquid labelled Co^e. He came back in half an hour, relieved and grateful, and ever since we have been left alone. No door opening or laughs as we walk to our washroom.

24 April

Dressed sergeant's tooth.

25 April

I think only of arriving, then I know I am to be tested. Dressed sergeant's tooth.

26 April

Barbara looks out of window and says in amazed whisper 'Oh', 'Ah'. I looked out and saw a horse. Krivovna has not spoken yet. Dressed sergeant's tooth twice.

30 April

We arrive tomorrow night. I can't help comparing this journey with my first visit to Russia with Papa, lilies and saluting soldiers, but I believe I was unhappier then. Sergeant came in, beaming, declaring his tooth cured.

1 May

Our train stopped outside a station, and we were marched blindfolded to a strange building, a monastery or convent I think, where we were given a very uncomfortable cell to sleep in. Silence if we ask about Alix. As I have no hopes, I have no fears. Our friendly Letts changed for Russians with red badges, intentionally bad manners and a fixed idea that I will have to eat what they give me. At dinner, they slapped down a plate of horsemeat and looked angry when I refused. I ate only bread. I feel tired and ill. Write to dear Father Mitrophan, saying I have arrived safely. Write to Patriarch Nitikhov, asking if I can have a vegetable diet. Leave letters unstuck. A blank wall faces my window.

2 May

Black stew slammed down again. Still hungry. Ate only salt and bread.

5 May

I sleep and dream all will be well. I will die brave.

8 May

We are in a nunnery. Nuns have orders to still bells and ignore our existence. Mother Superior insisted on seeing us, but knows nothing of Alix or where we go. I feel weak; sleep most of day.

15 May

Vegetable soup for the first time. I think they thought I was going to die.

17 May

We are to go by train tomorrow to Ekaterinburg. Still tired and feel ill through never being allowed to walk in open air. Barbara says Alix and Nicky are there; I can't think how she knows.

18 May

We arrive after many hours at E. Our blinds drawn before we reach the town.

19 May

We sleep in a small, cold office. Turnips and milk for breakfast, which is a treat. Where and when will my journey end? I have heard no futher mention of Alix. I was led here by lies.

20 May

Last night our guards told us not to undress – we would be travelling. They were right. At ten o'clock we were placed in hideously uncomfortable, jolting vehicles which bounced us about on a mattress for hours. Early this morning we arrived at a place called Alapayevsk and were dropped by a square building, once a school, so bruised we could hardly walk. Inside, eating breakfast, we found Serge's namesake, Serge Mikhailovich, and the sons of another cousin, Constantine Constantovich, Joannchik, Igor and Constantine, as well as a very good-looking young boy who is, I was told later, Paul's morganatic son, Vladimir Paley. They all stood up politely in horrified amazement; I went quickly to my room. How strange, being shut up with one I have always refused to see. But I was pleased to see Joannchik.

I am sure I have come here to die. Why, otherwise, should they have collected us here by lies and pretexts? I have known my death is coming. Again I hope to . . .

21 May

I fell asleep while writing, slept for eighteen hours and dreamed I had arrived late at one of Nicky's shooting lodges and met the usual party. We planned a picnic in the woods. And then I woke up and realized we are prisoners in a school-house.

21 May

For the last two nights I was too tired to care, but today I have to face the problem of three of us sharing a smallish room. The girls went out last night while I undressed, and I was asleep when they came back. But I see it is difficult for all nuns – and I include myself – to be seen undressing and washing. I must see if we can get some sheets and make bed curtains to give us privacy for dressing and washing. Alas, no baths, only tubs. I am making a little shrine in one corner.

How odd it is to be among relations again after seven years! I was pleased to see Joannchik. I have heard that Helen, his wife, is also in Siberia. He has always been laughed at and considered a ridiculous ninny, but only because he is gentle and hates killing animals and has always been a faithful and good husband. I had hardly ever met his two younger brothers, Constantine and Igor. They grew up after I went into my convent, but they were sweet children. Serge Mikhailovich I have always thought an unhappy man: unhappily married, unhappy in his faithlessness. It was always said that one of the reasons why our artillery was so inadequate was because he was corrupt. I believe this was a result of his stupidity, but my opinions are unfair – I don't know him. Lastly, there is little Vladimir Paley. I can never forgive Paul for leaving his legitimate children behind to live with this boy's mother, but the boy looks nice, and while I cannot forgive Paul, now that I have spoken to Vladimir I will continue to be kind to him.

Barbara has found out already that we are allowed to send letters, and Vladimir recently had a letter from Paul, but I knew last night, when I arrived here, that all our deaths must soon occur. I hope they are preparing themselves. I will help them.

Although I was exhausted when I arrived, I now remember clearly the dismay on my relations' faces. There they were, five men sitting comfortably round a table, smoking and talking, when in came three nuns. They all leapt to their feet with that look of guilty embarrassment which men have when they are talking together and a woman comes in. I can't help smiling at how dismayed they must have been to think I would now be taking every meal with them and destroying their easy companionship. To put their minds at ease, I wrote a note, gave it to the silent one and told her to take it to Serge. I told him I would be having breakfast and dinner in my room, but upon occasion, if they agree, would join them for tea. We have the meals at strange times: breakfast at 1 p.m., tea at four and dinner at seven.

After I had put their fears at rest, I decided to devote the day to prayer. As I have written, in the last month I have been prey to doubts and losses of faith, but today, when I knelt at our little shrine whose centrepiece is a little icon Nicky sent me after he abdicated, all my doubts cleared away and I realized that thoughts other than acceptance of an almighty God are false temptations. Faith alone is what counts, and it is not for us to question the events of the world but rather to accept even the worst of things as a plan of God to strengthen us through suffering. All my life, even in the period of my terrible dreams, I have always imagined voices talking to me, and I am sure that this morning a voice said: 'You have gone through much, but I will be with you to the end. Prepare yourself and those with you for a solemn change of lodgement.'

I shut my eyes even closer and it seemed to me that God in the form of Jesus was with me.

I continued to pray. I confessed again all my secret sins, admitting I had been unforgiving to Paul and that, in Moscow, I was a sinful person not to have seen his wife. I shall try to be kind to his son. I even admitted my impatience with Barbara in the train when she said 'Oh' and 'Ah' whenever she saw a cow or a tree. When I had admitted all that I could think of, it seemed that once again I came into the presence of God, who had forgiven but was at the same time gently suggesting I should make it clear to those who were to die with me that if they wished to be received into his presence, they should admit and repent of their sins.

My first thought was rebellious. Why should I not continue in this blessed state of grace? But I remembered it was my duty to think of others, and in front of God dedicated myself to this last task, happily worshipping in the rays of His strength and glory. I believe I reached a state of communion I had never known before. Perhaps I was unwisely elated, but I felt so lightheaded, certain and confident that I determined to start my task of saving my relations' souls and went into the room, where they all sat around a samovar. Again all the men jumped up, and all except Joannchik looked dismayed. I sat down and was full of pity that they knew not God. I knew I must speak at once. A force stronger than caution made me, although a small voice said that this is not the time or place. I stood up and made the sign of the cross and said: 'For seven years now I have given myself to God, and never until today has He accepted me as His own. He has told me that we have come to this place to die. It is His will you should know, and His will I should help you to prepare yourselves by honesty and admission of your sins for the solemn change of lodgement which lies before you. May I ask if we can all pray together, and after, you should come to me and let me try and offer you some of the knowledge which God's grace has given today.'

I felt almost unearthly, elevated and full of God's power, but when I looked at them I saw the only face which looked kindly at me was Vladimir's. I was lifting my hand to take his, to teach him of heaven's glory and the goodness which still filled me, when Serge stood up and said, in an angry voice that shattered my feelings: 'I hope my sainted cousin will forgive me, but I am going to make my own solemn change of lodgement by going into my own room. We have to face the future in our own way, which, as far as I am concerned, is not her way.' He went out. Igor and Constantine burst out laughing, Joannchik seemed embarrassed, and only Vladimir looked at me kindly as I stood still with surprise.

It was strange, but I felt exactly as if I had been punctured and the air was going out of me like a pricked balloon, leaving me little better than a ragged piece of crumpled rubber. Tears came to my eyes as I recovered and said: 'I am sorry, I will leave,' and was walking towards the door when Joannchik stopped and said: 'Ella, do not mind Serge. He is always bad-tempered. He hasn't a bad heart, but I think you have made a mistake in thinking we are as good or are ready to be as good as you. I know that you believe what you are saying, but I don't think you ought to push the others. Let them come to you on their own. For come they will, Serge as well. No one has ever been able to resist your charm and goodness.'

He made me feel better, and I realized I had made a mistake and that nothing is as easy as it seems. I had felt so full of goodness: I could work miracles. I was wrong. I thanked Joannchik and went sadly back to my room.

In a few moments, there was a knock on the door and in came Vladimir who said he had come to talk to me. I said: 'Of course, sit down,' but as the only two chairs in the room were part of my little shrine, there was nowhere for him to sit, except on my iron bed, where he was too embarrassed to settle. But I patted the mattress and he began to talk and told me he was only nineteen and loved music more than anything in the world, and composing songs and writing the words. He longed for the war to end and added 'Did you mean it when you said today that we are all going to be killed?' If so, he wondered why his father and mother were still allowed to live at Tsarskoye Selo.

I repeated that what I said was true, and he should be honest with himself and sensible, and confess his sins and meet God with a clean heart. He sat thinking and at last said, of course he had committed sins: 'I will write you a little poem in which I put them down, and then I will confess them all to the ugly father who comes once a week to see us.' He went out gaily, as if the whole thing was a joke. The young are so brave.

22 May

The sun was shining, and apparently we are allowed to go out walking without restraint. My dinner last night was disgusting. Goodness knows what the soup was made of, and I wondered if we could not grow our own vegetables. I examined the ground on the other side of the school-house and found a large patch of earth and a little wooden hut with tools inside – it must have been a kitchen garden once. Later I found Serge alone in the sitting room. He looked embarrassed and told me that the others had gone for a walk in the meadows. I said: 'I am sorry about yesterday, I won't mention it again, but I hope if you ever feel like it, you will come and talk to me. You know, I had a marvellous feeling of ecstasy yesterday and I had to try and help you all.'

He gave a twisted, embarrassed smile, but I went on: 'I have come to talk to you about other matters. For weeks I've hardly had anything to eat, and I see there is a large plot the other side of the school where the caretaker must have grown vegetables. Will you help me to make a garden? It will help us take our minds off the future and I long for fresh greeneries. The cook Krivovna has told me she can easily find us plants and seeds. Let's set to work and make a kitchen garden! You were a general in the army; it is for you to give the orders.'

He twisted his mouth up again. I thought he was pleased, and he must have said something, for that afternoon everyone, including the orderlies, worked. We cleaned a sizeable patch, digging in turn and pulling up weeds and burning rubbish. Everyone laughed, and the servants behaved very well, while Krivovna worked unceasingly, pulling up weeds with amazingly quick jerking movements. We all felt healthy and tired, and it was not until I got to my room that I realized how exhausted I was and fell asleep for three or four hours; and now that I have woken up I am not sure I shall sleep again, as both the girls are snoring. I wish I did not mind.

29 May

All this week we have been working, and I have persuaded the men to weed and clean and relay the stone slabs in the centre courtyard, so everything looks neat and tidy. There is another space by the front door where some creepers are falling over rotten posts. I got the boys to take them out, and then they cut down some saplings while one of the guards stood with a gun pointed at him.

The kitchen garden is planted with rows of cabbages, lettuces, spinach, carrots, radishes, onions, beans, peas, cress, and two other plants I don't know, all growing at a terrific pace. The courtyard is clean and tidy, and the three youngest have made a pergola over which I hope the creeper will climb. When the hot weather comes, they can sit there peacefully, for I have told them that no women will be allowed in the place. All this working together has made everything so pleasant that I think they have forgiven my outburst and have, for the first time in my life, done what I always wanted to do: plant seeds. I was always vain. In the past, I thought of my beautiful fingers, and I fear that vanity was always a weakness in my character and that I love beauty too much. Even now, when I pray at night and see my dirty, cracked nails, I have a momentary shock before I smile.

No one has come to talk to me.

30 May

Vladimir came and told me he had seen the Father, whom I have not mentioned before, I suppose because he's so useless. He is a poor, benighted countryman who was educated in one of their dreadful seminaries and is married to another priest's daughter and has seven children. I can see that Serge has, as a joke, bribed him to tell me what a good man the Grand Duke is. It is a pity to have such a poor ally, and when Vladimir asked him if he really could convey his confessions to God, he asked him if he was joking! I blame myself greatly for never having persuaded Alix to get the Church reformed. I think that if I had been less proud and treated her tactfully, I might have persuaded her to be firm with the Synod.

1 June

It is amazing, the speed with which vegetables, and indeed, every living thing, grow in the Russian spring. They seem to leap into the air.

2 June

Lovely weather. I look at the plants at least twice every day and will be unhappy when the beautiful rows have to be broken up. The carrots grow fastest.

3 June

Joannchik came. For the first time I noticed his slyness, about which the family always complained. He looked out of the corner of his eyes and said he had confessed all his sins except one. Would it not be unfair to Helen to confess a sin detrimental to their marriage? I told him he must be honest and confess to the Father the next day. He looked disappointed. I think less of him.

4 June

The men had baby carrots fried in oil, I carrot soup; a delicious change. Our first 'vegetable garden' meal.

5 June

Joannchik came to me, shaking and in a terrible rage. It appears he went to confess yesterday. When he had finished, he saw the priest winking at him. He was furious, but said nothing, as he thought he must have imagined such an improper gesture. But this morning at breakfast, Serge said how his servant had told him the priest was drunk on vodka at a celebration last night and entertained the company with the Prince Joann's confession. Of course, Serge was delighted, but I sent for the priest and told him I would report him to the patriarch. He grovelled and wept. I sent him away. A man who makes public jokes of secret confessions cannot belong to God.

6 June

I told my sisters how the priest had behaved, and then asked them to pray with me to see if God wishes me, as a deaconess, to take confessions. We all prayed and later agreed it was God's wish. After I mention that I will receive confessions and grant absolutions, nobody speaks.

A new section of Austrian Bolsheviks has taken over as guards for three days. They are familiar and insulting to the men.

Last night, at midnight, I heard loud laughter in the passage. The guards had entered Serge's and Vladimir's room and mocked them. Serge was very angry.

7 June

The tiny radishes are edible and delicious with lots of salt. Igor and Constantine asked Barbara if they could see me, and came in all hands and feet about eleven o'clock. They asked me if I could confess them, and I said it was for them to decide, but, regretfully, I thought I was a better alternative than the priest. They confessed. I gave them stiff penances, for their faults were those of boys loosely brought up who took their pleasures without consideration of the effect they could have on others. I blessed them both, and we prayed together for courage. They went out looking pleased, and I feel that they wrongly regard me a sybil who has relieved their fears. It was not what I intended.

9 June

I woke up early and walked out of our little prison into the garden, to find a guard with a basket cutting our vegetables. He had laid his rifle on the earth beside him. I walked up behind him and said quietly, 'I am a vegetarian,' and was going to add that he would be wise to follow the same diet when he jumped into the air as if he had been shot, seized his rifle, dropped it into the earth, seized it again, and fled round the house. I had not intended to frighten him, merely to tell him what to eat.

11 June

Serge's servant, who finds out more than all of us put together, says that Nicky and Alix and all the children are still in Ekaterinburg, so I must have been close to them.

15 June

I was asked to dinner and sat next to Serge. They had brought some Caucasian wine and insisted I drank a glass. It was against all my principles, but they were so merry and regarded the thing so much as a treat that I accepted and drank a glass with them. I had forgotten how good wine was. It seemed to course through all my veins and I felt happier and much more at ease.

Serge sat on my left, Joannchik on my right, and I soon saw why I had been asked. Serge wished to speak to me, but being too proud to come to my room, placed me next to him at dinner. He drank a lot, and I sipped at a second glass as he told me how he had always felt stupid because, when he wished to say pleasant things, his shyness made his sentences come out unpleasantly. I saw that he wished to say something else, and at last it came out. Even in the war everything had gone wrong. Soukhomlinov had starved the artillery, Serge had repeatedly protested but had received much of the blame. He had been too proud to complain. And then he added quickly: 'In the war I often found myself praying to God, but it was not to your narrow, limited God, but a God who would praise a man who admitted his own errors and faults and knew he was responsible for them, and this to me is nobler than leaving your sins on priests' shoulders and walking away to do them again.'

I said I understood his point of view, and was sure God would as well, for it was my belief that only those who concealed from themselves the truth are sinners. I said I would pray for him, and he should not worry, for what he had told me meant he was a good and honest man. He looked surprised and pleased, thanked me, and at once turned his back until the end of the meal. For the rest of dinner I talked to Joannchik, who had taken a glass of wine but who, I noticed, only put the glass to his closed lips, and each time the bottle passed pretended to refill his glass without putting in more than a drop. He is going bald now, and his nose is twisted slightly to one side, and his eyes are close together. I know he has been a good husband and does good things, and if I had to say what causes me to distrust him for the first time, having liked him all my life, it is that he is too polite, which is not a good reason.

21 June

The guard has changed, and, alas, we have the Austrians again. For the second time they set out to be abominably rude to Serge, who at once sent off a telegram of complaint. All of us have had to give up our possessions and what little valuables we have, and the men have also had to give up their clothes and wear the ugliest things imaginable, though, for some reason, myself and my sisters are allowed to keep our robes. I pleaded also for the icon which Nicky gave me, and they studied some papers and eventually nodded. Barbara says that Krivovna, the cook, told her that special orders had come from Moscow that I was to be treated differently to the others. If I had known at the time, I would have asked to change my clothes.

Our lot is to be harder. We are completely confined now to the house and kitchen garden and cannot go outside this area unaccompanied, except once a week to church. Barbara said that they were the most familiar and unpleasant guards she had ever met, worse even than the first lot. I did not answer, but Krivovna suddenly said: 'I don't agree.' As she never speaks, our surprise ended the conversation.

23 June

The guards more offensive than ever, and broke into Serge's room for the second night running, obviously drunk.

24 June

Vladimir came to see me. The curious thing is that when I arrived I was so weak I just took the relations for granted and paid little attention to their appearance, but when he came in today, I noticed for the first time how tall and gangling he is, his arms too long, his feet always getting in his own way. His black hair is long now, and when he gets excited it falls over his eyes. With his straight nose and firm mouth, he will, when he is a man, be very good looking, and his face has a mobility which is even now affecting. His dark eyes are kind and sincere, and it makes me sad, for I am sure he has not long to live. Anyhow, he came in today and asked me if he could have another talk. I said yes. He sat down without embarrassment on the bed and said he really had been trying to think of his sins, as I was so anxious he should shed them before his death (and here he gave a sweet smile), and he supposed he had stolen some apples once, and twice he had taken books from houses because he hadn't finished them, and certainly his nanny had smacked him sometimes when he was a child, but he could not remember what for. He really could not think of anything wicked he had done, though he was sure he was selfish and very forgetful, but what he would really like to discuss was not his beliefs but mine, for he could not understand them.

He realized that his knowledge of religion wasn't deep, but he would like to know certain things. What did I believe happened after death? I said: 'If we repent, we're welcomed into heaven.'

'And what happens then?'

I hate these sort of arguments, because I always get caught out, so I said: 'Well, that depends on God's wishes; I always believe we may come back to earth again to be given another chance.'

'Really?' he said, quite excited. 'Tell me how that works. I never could remember figures, but I believe that at the time of Christ there were only about 20,000 Jews altogether, and the whole population of the world was only a few million as everybody spent their time killing each other. I also read somewhere that there are more people alive today than ever lived in the world before. I mean, why did God suddenly decide to step up the population and change the whole nature of man, for we were savages, you know? I am afraid I cannot believe in God. I mean, Darwin seems so much more sensible.'

I didn't say anything, so he went on: 'For instance, why, when God created man, did He make him a newt or whatever we were to begin with, and waste millions of years before we became human?'

I said: 'One can only have faith. Can't you understand? We are not intended to know many things, but we have to believe in God's goodness.'

Vladimir shook his head. 'Dear Aunt Ella' – for I have told him to call me that – 'perhaps you can explain to me another thing. Why did God send His Son down to save us but allow Him to be crucified? Why didn't He save Him? It always seemed to me so weak, sending Him down and then letting His career be cut short just when people were beginning to listen to Him.'

I said gently: 'He died to save mankind.'

'But how did He save mankind? I mean, poor Jesus suffered agonies on the Cross, and the only effect was a Christian symbol of a tortured man which

354

brought intense cruelty into the Christian religion. For instance, we have been killing and torturing Jews in Russia ever since for that reason. His agony didn't help them, did it? And because Jesus suffered, Catholics, especially in Spain and Italy and France, and Orthodox Christians like ourselves, used to torture thousands of people to make them believe in our false conception of Him. I mean, look at the Spanish. In South America, goodness knows how many thousands of poor natives they burned to death to make them believe statements He never made, and they even tortured their own people for the slightest variation of beliefs. And we were nearly as bad. Look how we have tortured the Old Believers and other sects! I mean, it would have been wiser if God had allowed Jesus to live longer and make things plain. I repeat, why let Him be killed at thirty-two when His teachings were still contradictory and confusing? How much better for Him to have lived a long life, defined his beliefs and died happy and at peace, a loved, respected grey-beard instead of a young, nearly naked, tortured man on a cross illustrating God's personal cruelty, for if I'm in agony, I don't see how it helps, do you? Anyhow, I think God made a tremendous mistake in making pain and death the symbol of Christianity, justifying war and persecution. You don't think that as Jesus was dying in agony, He wanted that to happen, do you?'

'No, no,' I said, shivering with unhappiness, 'He preached the reverse.'

'Well then, wasn't God a fool to kill him off so soon? Admit that!'

'Oh, Vladimir, it upsets me when you talk like this.'

'But you must listen, Aunt Ella, and please don't say like other . . . other . . .' He hesitated, and I realized he had been about to say 'older people'. He went on formally: '. . . of your generation. I have been reading Ibsen and Shaw.'

I said: 'I wasn't going to say anything of the kind, for although we used to love acting as children, I always thought Ibsen was so gloomy. I never liked his plays, and I've never understood Shaw either.'

'Well, anyhow, let's get back to my point. I am sorry, but I do want to be persistent. Do tell me why God sent His Son to proclaim who He was and then die. Why was He not allowed to do more? I mean, just providing a lot of bread and fish for a crowd wasn't much, especially as the Bible never said the fish was cooked, and if it wasn't, unless you're a Lapp or an Eskimo, a meal of bread and raw fish would be uneatable, wouldn't it? And if He could bring one man back to life, why not thousands? That would have made people believe in God. And why, if He said faith can move mountains, didn't He move a mountain? I've seen hundreds of pictures of the Holy Land, and the mountains look so dry and bleak I should have thought the people would have been jolly glad to have some of them moved out of the way. It would have shown how powerful His father was, and everybody would have listened to Him. And lastly,' he said, putting up his hand to stop me, as I was about to tell him it was easy to think such things if you are clever, but what right had he to judge God; but I didn't speak, and he went on: 'And lastly,' he repeated, 'if God wanted to save mankind somehow by suffering, why didn't He go down and get crucified Himself? I mean, I was taught by all my tutors and schoolmasters that you had to face problems yourself and not pass them on to other people, and it seems to me that if He'd had himself crucified and borne all the pain and died, and then leapt off the

Cross and walked about and moved a mountain or two, His enemies would have been confounded and the power of good would have been proved. As it was, I believe Jesus was so furious at the way He had been treated that when He rose to heaven he remembered what His Father had done to Lucifer and decided the cruel old muddler now deserved the same treatment himself. So He pushed him over the side and Lucifer caught him and made him chief crucifier in the third circle. As for poor Jesus, I think He must have been trying to do good ever since. But the days on the Cross had so exhausted Him, He never had enough power again to make His earthly followers carry out His gentle teachings. And has not the conduct of Christianity been the reverse of this good man's teaching? I don't want to be rude, but look at your own position. Ever since you came to Russia, you have served a Church whose actions have, for hundreds of years, contradicted the preaching you believe, and which has, in your lifetime, persecuted Jews in Kishinev and dozens of other pogroms. Why do you believe in God through such a weak middle man? And would Jesus, if He had been strong, have tolerated the methods of the Catholic and Orthodox Churches?'

I was feeling desperate now. These are the sort of 'clever' arguments which I detest, but I could not go on saying 'faith', so I turned to my personal experience and told him how Jesus had come to me the other day and illumined my life.

He looked at me carefully before he answered: 'Well, we all discussed your experience, and Serge said that when he was on the Galician front, a platoon of men got cut off and rejoined the army after having two weeks with nothing to eat but a few berries. When they came in, they said Jesus had led them back, and they had seen Him walking barefoot in the snow with a staff in his hand. All of them swore it, and Serge thinks that this is what happened to you. You were half-starved when you came here and you imagined the whole thing, and honestly, it can happen again as you only eat about two carrots a day. Please don't think I am being rude, Aunt Ella, but it is so odd that you, who I love now and know are good, can believe a religion which is so cruel and makes God out to be a ridiculous pedant who will only accept those who, regardless of their goodness or badness, follow certain ridiculous rules like confession. I know that sophisticated Orthodox zealots will deny it, but this is what the Synod wishes the peasants to understand.

'Please, I'm sure I've contradicted and repeated myself, and I'm not going on any more, and I don't want to upset you, but there is one last question I want to ask. If our object is all to be good, how, when we are all in heaven being good – among other millions being good – are we to go on being good? I mean, I know it sounds like a riddle, but unless we are all going to lie happily asleep all day, I can't see how there can be goodness without badness! I mean, after all your efforts, you surely don't just want to lie about grinning when you die.

'But I won't go on. I am afraid I'm what you would call a wicked atheist, but can you explain how there can be goodness without badness?'

I hate this sort of talk, and started to cry, at which Vladimir came and put his arms round me – and for once I didn't resent the comfort – and he said: 'Oh, Aunt Ella, I am sorry I have been selfish and stupid, but since you told me I am going to die, and since I really want to live and do things and create music, I have been trying to believe you, and I know you're right in some ways, for you are so good yourself. You know, we all think you are wonderful, even Serge, for the way you leave us alone and are kind to everyone and inspired us to make the garden. We all love you, so don't pay any attention to my outburst.'

He kissed me on the forehead, the first time any man kissed me kindly since Serge in the forest at home all those years ago.

After he left, I tried to dismiss his arguments, but they worried me until I prayed, when, again, I knew that God exists and that is all we are meant to know. There is a choice between good and bad, but what appears bad may be good, for who can know His intentions? I felt cheered afterwards.

25 June

I must believe or I will have no reason to live. Sometimes I remember my brother-in-law, the last Emperor, saying Hesse blood was rotten. His mother was a Hesse, but then I remembered Uncle Bertie had said she wasn't. Perhaps the Emperor was right. Alix has set a terrible example. This place builds gloomy thoughts.

26 June

Yesterday's depression has gone.

27 June

The vegetable garden is a mass of growth. Every plant has thrived, allowing us a different choice each day. The men have made paths and bordered them with stones, so it looks nice and neat. I think the work has helped them, because, apart from the garden, there is nothing else to do, and it is pleasant even when we are watched by men with guns, who now, every night, break into Serge's or Vladimir's room. I have a feeling that it will not be long. Curiously enough, Vladimir's logical arguments have strengthened me, so easily could I push them aside by the power of prayer.

1 July

I was sitting in the garden when Serge came and sat down in the clumsy manner shy men have. His hair is grizzled and his face lined, and he looks like an old English colonel, yet he's never at ease. He is, I think, a man of action who is unhappy when he's idle, but if anything goes wrong, he quickly takes charge and makes the right decision. In a way, he is the most English of all the family: no graces, awkward and dependable. I was wrong about him. He told me that everyone will behave well, except Joannchik, who is frightened.

3 July

The imprisonment is beginning to have an effect on our nerves. Barbara is touchy, and Igor and Constantine had a ridiculous row, each claiming the other snored. Curiously enough, the two who remain calmest are Serge, who I like better, and Valadimir, who share a room with their servants. But now Vladimir's has been taken away and only Remez is left. Yesterday, the Russian corporal stared in the most blatant way at poor Barbara, and even seemed to brush against me on purpose if I meet him in the passage. The corporal came in at lunch yesterday – the poor men are now limited to 28 pounds of meat a week – and, walking round the table, suddenly took Serge's fork out of his hand, stuck it in a bit of his meat and ate it, then gave him back the fork. I am glad he played his trick on Serge, who is old and experienced, because if he had done it to Igor or Constantine, I think they would have hit him. As it was, Serge politely pushed his chair back, stood up and made a gesture inviting the guard to sit down in his place. The man was dismayed. He had probably looked forward to a fight and instead was made a fool. All he could do was turn his back and say: 'Huh, I wouldn't sit in your seat,' before quickly leading his men away.

When we were sure they were all out of earshot, we congratulated Serge, and Joannchik even went and got a bottle of wine and drank his health, as usual going too far.

But the bad treatment has an advantage: it brings us all closer together and stops disagreement among ourselves.

7 July

I must be very stupid, because I had never realized until today that the room in which we sit is Igor and Constantine's bedroom. I admire them, for every morning they make their iron beds and push them against the wall and place pillows to look like cushions. Then they put all their things away and set out chairs so it looks as much like a sitting room as possible, although, alas, the room will always remain a bleak schoolroom and they are like two overgrown schoolboys.

8 July

Krivovna was taken away with the others when we were closely confined three weeks ago. She is an odd girl. When she was told to go, she showed no emotion, packed her few things and made for the door. I suggested we should say a prayer together. She shook her head and walked out without saying a word, and Barbara said she walked past her in the passage as if she had never seen her before. I only bring this up because, today, when Barbara came fluttering in with my breakfast, she told me that Krivovna is now living with one of the Austrians. I find it hard to believe. Barbara said the Austrian is deaf. I have never heard her make a joke before.

10 July

Vladimir called. He, unlike the others, never seems to have moments of gloom, and I asked him today if he ever felt unhappy. He laughed, tossing his hair back.

'Oh, Aunt Ella, I know what you mean, am I afraid of being shot? The answer is no, because I cannot believe I am going to be. I feel so full of life and have so much to do, it is impossible to imagine being snuffed out like a candle. You know, I had always tried to base my life on a passage of Hertzen's, which I am sure you have read, about living intensely.'

I said no, I hadn't.

He said: Oh, I have known it by heart ever since I was sixteen. It's too long to quote to you, but he says you should live every moment of your life as if it was your last.

'Well, I am still trying to live like that. I write poems every day, but I haven't shown them to anyone because, without being rude, I know you don't like poetry, and it is an unpleasant feeling when you put your heart into a poem and a person you admire does not understand it. But,' he said, changing the subject, 'I hear you have been making drawings?'

'Yes.'

'Do show them to me.'

Rather shamefacedly, I produced them. He was astonished when he saw that nearly all my sketches were of evening dresses He asked me why on earth I drew such things in this place, and whether I was going to renounce my vows. I said no, of course not, but, strangely enough, I had lately often thought of the dresses I wore which never quite satisfied me, and I realized here, of all places, what had been wrong with them, and so I drew them as they should have been. I have to so something, and now everything in the garden is growing it is so much less fascinating than when we were making it. But that is always the way.

I like Vladimir so much, and so, to please him today, I asked him to send my respects to his mother. He blushed like a schoolboy, and then stammered would I add a few words to a letter he was writing to his mother and father. With difficulty I agreed. I like him so much.

13 July

Serge came today – calling is almost formal – and said one of the few guards he has made friends with shook him by the hand when he went off duty, said it was an honour to have known him and that he wished he could have served him in happier days.

'I think,' he said, walking up and down, 'it means the end as far as we are concerned. I don't know why, but I sense it and I feel that others do as well. We are all so polite and nice to each other now.'

I thought he was right, for Igor and Constantine had gone out of their way yesterday to say what a wonderful gardener I was. This afternoon I suggested that the men dig a whole new bed of earth as the garden is now fully planted. I came and watched, but could not help noticing that, although they dug quickly, it wasn't methodically. They did not take the weeds out as they had done before, and their jokes and laughter seemed forced. Joannchik stayed in his room. His face looks green and he is always looking over his shoulder. I think he has started to squint. It is strange. Years ago, I liked Joannchik as a good, kind man and looked down on Serge. It is now the other way round.

17 July

Before going to bed last night, I prayed at our shrine as usual, first with

Barbara, and then alone, and at once felt myself tranesposed into the same feeling of ecstasy which I experienced on my arrival. Once again, I was in a divine presence who had come to tell me He would aid me in my final worldly agony. As I prayed, my chief sorrow was not for myself but for poor Vladimir; why should a youth so full of hope be what he described as 'snuffed out'? But I knew, although I am sad, that I should not question. Suddenly I moved into tomorrow afternoon and carts had arrived to take us away. As we moved off, I led the singing of psalms and hymns, and as we lined up in a row to be shot, I led the singing again, as we died praising God. All of a sudden, in the air, flying and looking down, I saw myself and the others in the forest, lying dead, twisted on the ground. I rose higher and higher, until only by screwing up my eyes could I pick out where we had been. And then I looked up and my eyes stared into a blinding brightness. I remember nothing more, and I must have fainted, for it was early morning and Barbara had gone to fetch the hot water.

As it was my last day on earth, I went out at dawn and looked at the garden. It was a lovely morning and everything seemed fresh and green and luxurious. The trees stood in full leaf, dropping heavy branches, and dew sparkled on the grass. I sat down on a little seat and again fell asleep. I find it strange to write this, but I thought I was in heaven. I remember nothing else until twelve o'clock, when Barbara appeared, dead white and trembling, and said a Bolshevik called Peter Startsev had arrived with several supporters and said we would be moved tonight. In the meantime they would relieve us of the last of our possessions. He ordered us to come into the guard room. Joannchik was then taken away. After half an hour, he returned trembling, and said they had been through his room with extraordinary care, prising up the floorboards, slitting open his mattress and pillows after taking all his money, and even his wedding ring, which, he said, was luckily loose, or he was sure they would have cut his finger off. However, he had found out that it is Startsev's intention to transfer us all this evening to Verkhne-Sinyachikhenskii.

It was Igor and Constantine's turn next. Serge remained undisturbed, but I suddenly told the surprised guard that I was going to my room, and asked Vladimir to come with me. At once he sat down on my bed, tried to smile and said: 'Well, Aunt Ella, I see you're right and my dreams were silly pretences. The thing is that I thought I wouldn't be frightened, and I wasn't, but I am now, because I don't want to die – I am nineteen!'

Here he burst into tears, laid his head on my lap, and I stroked the back of his head.

'It is so unfair. I had made myself believe I was going to live and that makes it worse.'

He cried with his whole body for five minutes, and I could feel him pressing his fingers into his temples as if he were trying to control his grief. At last he seemed to quieten down and I felt the stiffness go out of his body. He stood up, turned his back on me, wiped his eyes and then turned round, smiling, and said: 'Well, if Hertzen said it is essential to live every moment of one's life as if it was one's last, it is most important for one to live one's last moment well. I have tried to live well. I shall now definitely die well, and it is thanks to you, dear Aunt Ella, for if there hadn't been a woman here whom I loved, I couldn't have wept, and if I had not wept in private, I would have broken down in public and looked silly. That is all I am going to say now, and I will address you formally in public, otherwise I might cry again. I can only say thank you.'

He rushed out of the room. It was my turn to weep.

At five o'clock, Startsev, who had finished ransacking every room and taking every penny from the others, opened my door without knocking. He then said: 'I think you will have heard you are to be moved tonight or tomorrow morning. I have brought with me a travelling cloak which you are to wear over your robes. I must now ask you for your jewellery.'

'I have none,' I said simply.

'No jewellery?' he said in an angry voice. 'Your wedding ring will do then.'

'I gave my wedding ring away when I retired to my convent over seven years ago.'

'Have you no personal jewellery or possession of any kind? It doesn't need to be valuable,' he said in an annoyed voice.

My eye at once turned to the little icon which Nicky had sent me after his abdication.

'Ah,' he said, striding over, 'this is yours?'

'Yes, but must you take it?'

'Yes,' he said with satisfaction. 'It is very necessary.'

He did not slit my mattress, and in fact seemed in a better temper, and did not ask me for my little stock of money, but said politely: 'I am afraid I have to request you to leave your room, for unfortunately my men have to go through Sister Barbara's things and I am afraid you are needed in the guard room, but only for a few minutes. I will come with you. Please don't be frightened.'

I went calmly with him, determined not to be upset, wondering what insults lay in store. To my surprise, the only other person in the room, except for Startsev and his men, was a woman sitting by herself in a corner, shaking with fear. I had never seen her before. She looked about my age, only was rather fatter and was certainly not a peasant, although she was in old working clothes. Startsev told her to stand up, which she did with difficulty, assisted by one of the men. I really could not imagine what she was so frightened about; I had no wish to hurt her. I put out my hand to bless her, but so violently did she jump back, as though I had been going to hit her, that she and the men supporting her nearly fell over. Startsev laughed and said: 'I didn't know the merchant class lived in such fear of the Romanovs.'

I went back to Barbara, who was in floods of tears and now in peasant dress. I said that if she had been forced to change her clothes, I would like to do the same, but when I complained, Startsev said, 'All in good time,' and left the building.

Back in my room, Barbara began to be hysterical, and I could not comfort her, finding out that what had upset her was the indignity of having to change her clothes behind a curtain while men were in the room. She repeated her story twice, screaming so loud that I thought of my medicine chest, and was pleased to find that while the drawers had all been opened and the instruments taken, the medicines remained. I found what was labelled 'Calming water', and gave her such a strong dose she soon fell asleep.

Startsev has issued orders that we should dine an hour early. It was a sorry meal, even though everyone tried to be cheerful – all except Joannchik, who seemed to have shrunk even more, and this time asked for and drank several glasses of wine. Igor and Constantine drank some, but Serge, who is usually the heaviest drinker, and Vladimir, refused a single glass. None of us could be natural or pretend not to understand what awaited us. We ate little, and the only time when there was animation was when Vladimir said, quite gaily: 'I hope we go soon.'

Everybody agreed loudly, but instead we were ordered abruptly to go to our rooms, where I found Barbara awake again and crying. I was wondering what to do when Vladimir knocked on the door and said: 'I asked Startsev, and I am sorry to say we are starting at eleven.' I looked at my watch: it was seven o'clock. Four unbearable hours remained. I lay down and tried to contemplate. It was no good. I looked at my watch again: two minutes past seven. I went to the medicine chest and took some calming medicine. Like Barbara, I soon fell asleep.

I was woken up out of a deep sleep by a rattling at the door. Looking stupidly at my watch, I saw it was eleven o'clock. The door opened. A man shouted impatiently that the carts were ready. Two of the princes were waiting. Would the woman called Barbara hurry?

'What about me?' I asked.

'Oh, you are staying. Come on,' and he went and shook Barbara and lifted up her little case.

I couldn't move with horror and astonishment, and stood helpless as they hustled my poor friend out of the room. 'They're taking me away!' I heard her cry in the passage, while I stood, realizing that all my beliefs were lies, my ecstasies imaginations. My only wish had been to die. Now I was to live. I felt as if my stomach was full of lead.

And then Barbara was back in the passage, crying: 'I won't go! I won't go until I have your blessing.'

I spoke as clearly and as loudly as I could through the door: 'Please let Sister Barbara in. I promise you I will say one prayer and return her to you. It will not take a minute, then she will go with you. Come with her, if you like.'

Barbara came stumbling in. I said to her severely: 'Be courageous,' and led her, with the men walking just behind us, to my iconless shrine. I knelt down and told her to repeat my words:

'Oh Lord, give me, a poor sinner, the courage to face less suffering than your own beloved Son, and may I come before You knowing myself a poor sinner who has tried to serve You. I know it is but a brief step I am taking, but I pray You to give me courage to take it alone, receiving courage from my faith in the life everlasting.

I chose words which would comfort her. They no longer held a meaning for me, and I followed them with now meaningless gestures.

I touched her hand, kissed her on the forehead, made the sign of the cross and gave her to the guards. Once again, the door was shut. I was alone with my desperation, disturbed only for one moment by Vladimir shouting: 'Goodbye, Aunt Ella, I hope I see you soon!' I heard his steps vanishing, ran to the window, opened it to hear the stamping of horses' feet and the unmistakable squeaking noise of badly oiled axles. There was a cracking of the whip and jingling sounds, and, it seemed to me, the sound of wagon after wagon driving away. I had planned that they would sing a hymn of triumphant belief; they went in dead silence. I flung myself on my bed, crying, miserable at being alone, at having deceived myself over having imagined what had not been there; above all, over having wasted my whole life worshipping a God who, if He exists, is a loathsome, cruel torturer. I wept bitterly. I have never, in all my unhappy life, felt such despair, and as I write these words I know that the beliefs and hopes which guided my life are dead.

18 July

At three I was woken by a bang. I slept again. At six o'clock a voice shouted that the wagon would be ready in half an hour, and added: 'You are going to be taken to Perm to see your sister.'

I noticed he said 'my sister', and wonder what has happened to Nicky. We set off in a horrible wagon, and I sat up in front, where you are thrown about less. Two soldiers with rifles sat behind. It hasn't rained for a week, and the dust was unbearable, getting in every crevice in my clothes. Luckily, before I left, I had been given a linen towel to cover my veil, and found I could lower it to keep the dust out of my eyes.

The journey was a continuation of my nightmare. The roads were full of holes, the wagon springless, the horses lethargic. Every now and again one of the wheels would fall into a hole several inches deep, almost shaking my teeth out. We stopped at one o'clock in a valley by a stream, and I was given some sandwiches full of meat, which I refused, and a number of little tomatoes, which I could swallow; but after the shock of yesterday, my sense of taste has vanished.

We started again, hoping to reach Perm by nightfall, but as we were going through a broken-down little village the right wheel went into an enormous hole and broke the axle and we had to spend the night in a peasant's cottage. It looked clean, but I was still so tormented by my thoughts, and how I could survive without the force which had guided my whole life, that I could not sleep. And then I heard a pattering. I wondered if it was raining outside, but realized that the drops were falling inside and on to me. How could it be raining in my room? A drop fell on me; I put out my hand and caught a bug, and remembered how the horrible little things creep up the walls to drop on their victims. I woke the guard and told him that, as it was a warm night, I was going to sleep in the back of the wagon – he could chain me down if he wanted, but I was not going to stay to be eaten by bugs. My determination must have impressed him, for he led me to the cart and, to my astonishment, lay down in the middle of the dusty road and went to sleep.

It is now seven o'clock. I dread the coming day.

19 July

A hopeless morning. First of all, a carpenter came and spent a long time looking at the wheel before going away to get a piece of wood. Then he disappeared to fetch nails. It never entered his head to get everything at the same time. Even the guards became irritable and began threatening him with bayonets, but it wasn't until three o'clock that we set off. Luckily, the peasant's wife, who was a kind but dirty woman, let me see her garden and gave me some ripe apples.

We set off on another dusty, bumpy drive.

On the way, the guard told me we were going to Perm. I asked him if Colonel Romanov was there. The men laughed. 'If you mean the Tsar, they say he is dead. I don't know; one hears a rumour a day.'

My mind is frozen, and I heard the news without any emotion and asked: 'Is his son with his mother?' The man shrugged his shoulders and we jolted on until darkness fell and he began to curse.

At last we saw lights in the distance and came into the outskirts of the town, but by now it was late and nobody was about. The guard stopped twice, and once went into a house, where a candle shone through the window. He did not learn much. We continued to drive round and round until, at last, we saw another cart travelling in the opposite direction. Our driver shouted and the answer came back: 'You are not far. Take the second right and go down Pokrovskaya Street and stop when you come to Obvinskayast Street. The house is at that corner, immediately on your right.'

At last we arrived. The guard jumped down and I, covered with dust and bruises, followed. The man lit a lantern and hammered on the door for an age before a sleepy man appeared and wouldn't let us in until he had received, through the chained door, documents which he studied for a full ten minutes by a flickering candle. At length he reluctantly undid the chain, and after more argument my guards said goodbye, and to my surprise asked for a blessing. I shook my head, and they looked so hurt that I made three meaningless gestures. The sleepy doorman led me up some stairs and down a corridor to a door of unpainted wood, against which lay two soldiers asleep. After they had been roughly shaken awake, the door was opened, the lantern was thrust into my hand and I was pushed through. The door closed; by lifting the lantern I could see I was alone in an empty passage, high, cold and bleak with an uncarpeted wooden floor, four doors down either side and a window at the end. I didn't know what to do, so I opened the first door on my left, and again lifted the lantern high in the air. I heard a rustle of bedclothes, but the shaking light, swaying and flashing, prevented me from seeing what made the noise. Then a voice asked: 'Is that Aunt Ella?'

I saw a mass jumping out of bed and running towards me. The next moment Anastasia had thrown herself into my arms, almost knocking me down, and making the lantern sway dangerously. I managed to put it on a table and said I must sit down. She led me to her bed and began asking questions. Did I know what had happened to Papa and Alexis? I told her I had just come from Alapayevsk, and asked how long they had been there.

'We have only just come, but Papa and Alexis were taken away. We do not know when they are joining us, and it has had a terrible effect on Mama. You know, before Gregory was killed we thought she was getting funny, but afterwards, when we were sent to Tobolsk, she was much better, like she was long ago. It was as if, once Papa and Alexis had abdicated, she had them both. I oughtn't perhaps say all this, but now she rambles and talks so that we don't know what she means, though the others will tell you. We have all got our own room. They are high – they will be cold in winter – but they are nice now. Come and see the others. Oh, Aunt Ella, they'll be so pleased to see you.'

She seized the lantern and ran down the passage opening doors, and soon the other three girls were hugging and kissing me and I noticed, for the first time, that their hair had been cropped. They looked strange.

'Where is Alix?' I asked.

Olga put her hand to her lips. 'Shhhh, she's sleeping, we must not wake her. You will see her in the morning. For,' she added, putting a little watch in front of the lantern, 'it's two o'clock. I'll get you some milk and then you must go to bed. Goodness, you're covered with dust! They bring us hot water in the morning, and there's a spare room you can have. Anastasia and Marie, light some more candles and get it ready while Tatiana and I have a word alone with Aunt Ella.'

When the other two had gone, they asked me again if I had news of their father, and I said no, and repeated what I had told Anastasia.

'We heard you were with the others at Alapayevsk, but we didn't know if it was true,' said Olga. 'Where are they?'

I looked down and said: 'I don't know.'

They were silent. Olga said: 'It's so awful, but go to your room now, Auntie, and I'll get your milk and you will see Mama in the morning.'

I don't know what to make of everything, but as I finish writing this, I am feeling tired for the first time and it may be I will sleep. It will be a wonderful relief.

20 July

I woke up at eight, my eyes red with dust, and looked out of the door. To my delight I saw there was a bath outside my room, with four big cans of hot water. I have never had such a wonderful wash in my life and began to feel real again. I could not help noticing that I was covered with big bites, and longed to throw my clothes away, but as I have only one spare set, I pushed all my dirty clothes into the bath, hoping the beastly little things would drown.

I walked out of my room and could hear a clatter and the chink of plates at the end of the passage, as if the girls were in the kitchen. Only one door in the passage was unopened. I unconsciously said a prayer, knocked and went in.

Alix was sitting on her bed. Her eyes rested on me fully a minute before she said slowly: 'It's Ella, isn't it? I suppose you've come about more money for your convent?'

'No.'

'I never approved, you know. I thought it was wrong to spend so much. It is imperial money you spend – Nicky's money – and Russia respects the iron hand rather than kindness. They understand strength, which I hope Nicky is showing now. I cannot understand why he does not come, and Baby with him. I had a long talk with our friend last night, and he told me all was well, our parting would be rewarded, and Nicky and himself would come together soon. I don't know what I would do without Gregory. He gives me, every night, a message from them. I thought it was him last night, come to hold me in his arms, secure, safe, loving. It was only Gregory, with messages. Not enough. But I hope he is showing strength, sending disloyal to Siberia, behaving like Peter and Ivan the Terrible. I know it is necessary, but I miss him so badly,' and she burst into tears.

I tried to hold her hand but she went on: 'It was all the Duma's fault, and Witte and Stolypin, trying to steal Baby's inheritance.'

Alix relapsed into silence, her eyes looking down. She paid no attention as I left the room.

When I saw Olga, I realized she was no longer a girl but a woman of twenty-three, with little wrinkles round her eyes. Her cropped hair had taken much of her beauty away, as she hasn't a good-shaped back to her head, but she is still pleasant looking, her square face redeemed by clear skin and large, kind, candid eyes.

'Now, my dear,' I said, 'before we talk about the future, please tell me what happened to Tobolsk, because I have really heard nothing since you left Moscow.'

Olga put her left hand to her eyes and made a gesture of tiredness as if to push back hair which was no longer there.

'Oh, Tobolsk . . . well, it was crowded, but it was curious – I have hardly ever seen Mama and Papa so happy. You see, Mama hadn't had Papa and Alexis to herself for two years, and she had never really had Papa to herself since they were married. Ever since I grew up, she was making desperate attempts to stop the constitution from changing, which she thought was unfair to Alexis, and of course she worried about his health every moment of her life. And then, of course, Gregory's death made her despair, but after the abdication, she seemed to calm down, become normal again, stopped continually worrying and trying to stop Papa doing things, as there wasn't anything he could do. As for Papa, I think he was happy too. You know, both at Tsarskoye and Tobolsk I have never seen him so cheerful as when he was cutting wood. I think he hated being Emperor, and it was the first time since his father died that he had not been asked to make decisions every day. The guards at Tobolsk were not too bad, and two messages came from Cousin Willy, telling Mama not to worry as he was making special arrangements with the Provisional Government. He wished her to know he would never allow his blood relations to come to any harm.

'But there was one man who worried them both. He was called Malakov, I think – I may be wrong – anyhow, he came from Uncle Ernie and he told Mama, in absolute secrecy, that Cousin Willy's plan was to get Alexis recrowned Tsar, and then Uncle Ernie would come to Russia to act as Regent. Apparently, Cousin Willy was making other of his relations kings of Finland and other parts of Russia. It was really stupid of Uncle Ernie to send such a message, for it made Mama quite furious that he should both take both Nicky's place and Alexis away from them again. When she told Papa, which she had been told not to do, I have never seen him so angry. He could not bear to think of separation from Alexis. It was the first time I've ever seen him nasty. He said the whole thing was typical of Ernie. "For twenty years before the war he changed

German uniforms twice a day, but when the war came along, he was against fighting, but, of course, once Germany defeated us, he immediately drops all his anti-war scruples and now plans to eat the fruits of victory and sit as a German puppet using Alexis to rule the Russian people." It really upset them both.

'Later on, when Yakovlev arrived to take Papa to Ekaterinburg, to our amazement, Mama left Alexis behind and went with Papa. Tatiana and I thought she must have gone because she was terrified that one of Uncle Ernie's men would get Papa alone and persuade him to agree to Alexis becoming Emperor with Uncle Ernie as Regent. I am sure Papa wouldn't have done, as he despises Uncle Ernie, but it showed the extent of Mama's terror, that she was prepared to leave Alexis when he was ill. Then, at Ekaterinburg, it wasn't so bad to begin with, but twice we were pestered by Cousin Willy's agents telling us not to worry. I think the guard found out and made life even worse.

'Then, at the beginning of the month, when Kerensky was defeated, a man came specially to tell us, again secretly, that Cousin Willy had a promise from Lenin, the chief of the Bolsheviks, that we wouldn't be harmed. It was after that that it got awful, with the guards tormenting us in the coarsest way, while Mama would keep on trusting Solovyov, just because he was Gregory's son-in-law, even though Dr Bodkin and Papa said they didn't trust him.

'Ten days ago, a dreadful man called Yurovsky took over guarding us and we were intolerably insulted. They even took the lavatory doors off. I've never seen such brutes. A few days ago, we were told to get ready to move . . .'

'How strange,' I said. 'It's so like what happened to us.'

' . . . and to cut all our hair off, which we hated, because it makes us all ugly, and to wear peasant clothes, which is silly, because we don't look like boys or peasants. And then Papa and Alexis were taken away in a motor car and we haven't seen them since. On the 17th – that is a date I can remember – we were all put in a train with the blinds down and brought here. When Maria heard that Papa had gone with Alexis, we dreaded telling her, but it was as if, when she heard, something broke in her head, for she reacted quite differently from how we expected and, after thinking for a moment or two, said he must have gone back to the front and taken Alexis as usual. Their uniforms would be on the train and he was going back to be a stern Tsar: it was sternness the Russians loved. And then she was like that on the journey and after we got here, and, as you've seen, she hasn't changed. But, you know, what is worrying me most is Anastasia and Tatiana. I can look after Mama, and Marie's no trouble – she's so good-natured – but Tatiana and Anastasia say that they're going to escape, and when I try to frighten them by saying they might be caught by those terrible soldiers, they say they'd rather be caught than go on living shut up without seeing a soul their own age, as they have done ever since the revolution, a year and a half ago. Oh, Aunt Ella, I'm frightened they'll escape. Do talk to them.'

21 July

I talked to Tatiana and Anastasia: Tatiana tossed her head and said she could not stand it and couldn't promise anything, and Anastasia smiled artfully and said she was sure she could get away. I told her of the terrible dangers, but she just laughed and said, 'You don't know how cunning I am.'

I find I am writing such unpleasant things about my family that I shan't write for a few weeks, to see if I can help them, but as all the belief has gone out of me and there's no conviction in anything I say, I can't feel myself able to influence people as I used to. It is a terrible effort to be with Alix, but I must try, I must try.

1 August

I have broken my resolution because Tatiana has shown me a newspaper which says, briefly, that Serge and the others escaped when the Czechs attacked Alapayevsk on the night of the 18th. This is a lie! I was there and no one attacked me. It's funny I was not mentioned. I wonder if that fat, frightened woman took my place, and if William is helping us? We will be a sad family if we ever get away.

1 September

There is no change. Olga remains good and Marie is, I think, a little simple; but Tatiana and Anastasia are always whispering and going downstairs, and I have heard them talking to men at the door. I know it is wrong.

Alix is no better; she just sits and every day tells me she has talked to Gregory the night before, and that Nicholas and Alexis are at the front. 'All will be well if he is firm' – and then she repeats the whole story all over again. I make myself listen three times, and then I leave her, and she shows no emotion whether I come or go.

2 September

Tatiana tried to escape, but was brought back. The result was that a decision was taken to move us to 'safer quarters', and yesterday, at nightfall, we had to walk down Obvinskayast Street for a hundred yards and move into a vaulted basement which had mattresses on the floor. There is no privacy here. I have to close my mind to stop thinking what is happening. Tatiana is in tears, Olga still good and saintly; Marie is the only one who seems to take everything cheerfully, and Anastasia is still determined to escape.

22 September

Anastasia escaped yesterday and there is a furore. The guards came down and shouted at us. Tatiana cried and told them she hoped she would get away. Marie seemed to take it as an everyday event. I think she has a mind of a child of ten. I couldn't sleep for thinking of the dear, stupid girl, loose in these terrible times. What I worried about was that I was not worrying but making myself worry. How could I not care?

23 September

Tatiana this morning told us – I thought triumphantly – that Anastasia hadn't succeeded, and the poor girl was caught on a railway line and beaten up by soldiers.

24 September

Anastasia has escaped again. A Dr Utkin was sent for and treated her for minor injuries. Her guards thought she was really hurt, and left her alone to sleep. This morning, she was gone, nobody knows where. Olga burst into tears. Tatiana looked angry and then cried. Maria laughed and said she hoped she was all right, and sat fiddling with some little bricks. We hear that hundreds of soldiers are looking for her.

1 October

Tatiana says Ekaterinburg has now been taken by the Czechs. I have never understood what the Czechs are doing here. Our guards are nervous and only talk to Tatiana. Alix still says she is visited every night by Gregory, who repeats the same message. I have nothing to read and nothing to do. I try every day to make my mind blank.

1 November

No change. I cannot get myself to write.

8 December

We have moved again. The Czechs are advancing. I do not know if I have got the date right; there is no way of telling. We are in a place called Glazov, a horrible village with filthy huts. I don't care where I am.

10 December

We are to be moved again. We have one kind guard called Sivkov, and two others unkind. Sivkov says we are to go to Kazan.

12 December

Arrive in Kazan, although names mean nothing to me now. Olga quietly cried and came to me and told me, on the journey, she wished to be a nun. I said, 'Oh no,' before I thought. She backed away from me and has looked hurt ever since.

Tatiana talks to the guards in the corridor. I think I am getting confused about events.

17 December

We are living in what was once a political prisoners' room in Kazan. It is surrounded by a blank wall. I still talk to Alix every day and hear the same stories.

Sometimes I go into a trance of nothingness, and when I wake up she is saying the same thing. Tatiana angry, and shouts at me for no reason. Marie only laughs. Olga lies weeping.

18 December

I have found an occupation. The wall which guards us is made of cement. There is a place where the cement has fallen off, showing rubble behind. I find that, unless it is snowing hard, if I stare into this patch of rubble, which has a red brick in it, I go back into the past through a hole which appears in it, and stay for hours in England or Darmstadt.

Two days ago I had a long talk with Grandmama. She dismissed her Indian servant and I told her that all the things she had heard about Serge were true. She tapped the ground with her stick and informed me I had never taken her in with all my lies, but she admired me for telling them; in her view it was a wife's duty to defend her husband. She wanted me to know that she had never liked Serge and was always against the marriage. She actually wrote to the British Ambassador, Sir Edward Thornton, asking his advice, and he wrote back that he could find no reason why I should not be married to him, so what could she say or do to help me?

30 December

Still everything the same, and still on clear days I can go through my wall. I relive many happy days of the past. Today I went riding with Victoria up the yew avenue, and we sat and talked about what will happen to us.

10 January

I went to my wall and stared, and at once it appeared to me that a large hole appeared and I was pulled through to find myself back in bed again in Khoroz. Serge lifted his whip and I only managed to squeeze through in time before he hit me again. It was very frightening and several times I went to see if the hole was open and he was following me, but it was dark and I could see nothing. I pray he won't get through.

1 February

I have forgotten my diary. I have been in England at Osborne and in the woods around Heidelberg. Next week I think I will go to the dances in St Petersburg again. I remember so well my jewels. I loved them so much, although I pretended not to. Now, when I put them on, I don't pretend not to love them.

20 March

I am told . . . I went through the wall into the hospital, and decided that after I had watched the doctor operating, I loved him. I cannot think why I never told him before. I wasted my time. I'm not going to this time.

6 May

I had a fight with Victoria last week. She said I would have been happy if I'd had children. She could not understand why I could never have been happy with Serge. She goes on saying that I was. Why does she also want to hurt me? I was so upset I decided I would not go through the wall if she was going to be unkind to me.

[May the 6th was the last dated entry in the diary, by which time her handwriting had deteriorated.]

Undated entry

I am frightened. I have spent so many happy months going into my hole, and now it is growing smaller and sometimes I have difficulty going through. When I feel sad and depressed, the blankness of the wall enters my mind and my brain is overwhelmed by grey fog through which I can see nothing. But today I wish to say I went through and found I was in the Boucher coach going to my marriage. How stupid I was at the time not to enjoy every moment! The people cheered and waved flags from all the windows. Afterwards I walked through the Winter Palace on Alexander's arm. I remember how tired and confused I was, why I can't remember.

Undated entry

I felt better today after being ill for so long. I thought I would go to Livadia. I asked Alix if I could go to her house. She was very kind and said, 'Of course.' When I arrived it was warm, and as usual I at once felt better. I went down to the sea to the landing stage below the house. The landing stage was there; the sea had gone. I looked everywhere, but it was nowhere. I told Alix when I came back, and she made me sit by her and hold her hand while she comforted me. At last I put my head in her lap and went to sleep.

Undated entry

The hole is closed. I cannot get through. All is over. The surface of the wall is hard and grey. But Alix has become kind to me and is better herself. I need her until I can go through again. It should not be long. It must be something to do with my illness. She stroked my head last night. I felt happy and slept. When I woke up I explained my worries to her. She listened. She never used to. I feel closer to her than I have done for years, and, you know, she talks to me whenever I go to her, and sends Gregory away. It is a good sign. It means she's getting better and kinder.

[This entry was the last written in the diary. On the following pages, it appeared as if a child had drawn swords and spears and axes, and afterwards rough circles with thickened joins where the ends met.]

Epilogue
1946

Epilogue

In the summer of 1946, the chairman of the Politburo, Joseph Stalin, ordered an investigation into the whereabouts of the remnants of the imperial family. He remembered his surprise in 1920 when Lenin had calmly informed him: 'While without compunction I ordered the execution of Nicholas and his son, I felt myself bound by a private promise I made to the ex-Kaiser to spare "the German women", Alexandra and her sister.' When he saw the surprise on Stalin's face, Lenin repeated that he had given his personal word, and although the necessity of keeping it had disappeared with the Kaiser's defeat, 'I cannot forget that but for provision of the train I would not have been able to return to Petrograd at an essential moment. Consequently, I inquired into the where-abouts of the remnants of the imperial family and received the reply that they had, since the end of 1919, been secretly imprisoned in Kazan, that the ex-Tsarina Alexandra and her sister Elizabeth were considered by their jailers to be deranged, and that of the three surviving daughters, the eldest was an invalid, the second hysterical, and the third simple. I therefore decided that they should be exiled to Siberia, in the vicinity of the area in which I was once imprisoned, remote enough to avoid notice or enable escape, but clement enough not to cause death.

'After consideration, I chose a valley in the east of central Siberia in the neighbourhood of Murminsk. A small river runs through its centre, and an unsuccessful attempt was at one time made to establish a penal gold mine there where the wooden ruins of a prison remain. The valley is ice-bound for seven months of the year. It is surrounded by forest and unviolated by a road. I gave firm orders for a wooden house to be built on the exact site of the old prison. The work has been carried out by members of the landed gentry from Siberian prisons, encouraged to work hard by an assurance that if the house was completed by 21 September they would be released. It was completed on 1 September. On the 2nd, the whole work-force was shot.

'I have given the chief of the local tribe three orders. First, as long as one of the prisoners survives, a large stock of wood is to be delivered before the cold weather and a smaller load in the spring. Secondly, sufficient quantities of dried fish, meat, flour, dates and figs are annually to be provided by the local Soviet, and delivered at the same time as the logs. Thirdly, he should arrange to kill any occupant of the valley who tried to escape, and on the death of a survivor inform the Soviet, so enabling supplies to be downgraded.'

After Lenin died, Stalin was too busy to bother with the exiles, and it wasn't until 1946 that he asked Beria to find him a suitable envoy to visit the valley. When he heard that a young man of thirty-six called Paul Bykov had been chosen for his efficiency and discretion, he asked to see him. Bykov, who years later described the interview, stated this was to annoy Beria, who disliked his staff receiving orders from any authority but his own. (Precise, bespectacled, professional, and resembling in appearance his later mentor Beria, Bykov in fact fled to the West after the death, in 1953, of Stalin and the subsequent disgrace and death of his chief. He related the story of this experience one evening, in a natural and authentic way, to an interrogator while he was still subject to investigation. It was considered to be a curiosity interesting enough to end up in the tray of a then Minister of State at the Foreign Office in London, but its present whereabouts is unknown.)

At any event, Bykov was received by Stalin in his small white room in the Kremlin where, as he trembled with fear at the extraordinary honour being paid him, it was explained to him that the history of the banishments was an illustration of Lenin's wisdom and sense of honour. Stalin continued, in a surprisingly friendly voice, to say how the memory of the exiles was only revived by a question asked him at Yalta the year before by Churchill as to the ultimate fate of the imperial family. At the time, he merely changed the subject, but afterwards realized he was ignorant of the answer and now wished to know if any of the family survived.

Beria's office gave Bykov details of the Romanovs, and he learned that if she was still alive, the wife of Serge would be eighty-two, the wife of Nicholas seventy-four, and Alexandra's surviving daughters fifty-one, forty-nine and forty-seven respectively. He was able to reach M —— by train, and then drove nearly a hundred miles in acute discomfort to the small provincial town (which he constantly refused to name) that provided the tribesmen with the food supplies. There he was informed by a frightened official that the rations continued to be supplied twice a year, the man nervously adding that nobody ever visited the valley because the local tribesmen claimed to have instructions to kill any trespassers. He had only recently been appointed, otherwise, of course, he would have officially visited the valley himself to ensure that none of the family had died. Bykov asked whether any visit had ever been recorded; none had. The next day, 20 August, he was driven in an American jeep to a meeting place on the edge of the valley's surrounding forest, where he was forced to mount an agile Tartar pony by his tribesman guide. (While Bykov also continually declined to name the tribe, they would almost certainly have been of Asiatic or Tartar origin.) They then set off on an uncomfortable climb up the small mountain range, followed by an even more uncomfortable descent.

When they reached the valley floor, Bykov insisted on dismounting, and they continued several miles alongside a shallow river full of large stones. He remembered the scenery as dismal and sad, the surrounding black forest, the brown, burnt, stony ground and the melancholy river all combining to create a gloomy impression. Eventually he was shown a small square log house, and after climbing a hill saw his destination forty or fifty yards in front of him.

Outside the house stood three wooden chairs, the left-hand one empty, while a large woman with a rather florid face and a mass of untidy white hair billowing out from under an old straw hat sat in the middle. On her other side was a minute, grey-haired woman, with a scarf arranged around her head, and arms like the bones of a skeleton sticking out of her coarse peasant's costume. Bykov noticed with surprise that the large woman was talking not to a woman on her right but to the empty seat on her left.

When they came within about ten paces of the house, the large woman put up her hand and said: 'Stay there, I am discussing matters of great moment with my friend.'

She continued to ignore Bykov and to his annoyance the tribesman guide bowed down low, even though the woman paid no attention to him either, and went on talking, occasionally pausing as if she were listening to a question, then answering at length. The little woman on her right sat absolutely still, gazing in front of her with blank eyes, and Bykov said he could think of nothing to do but stand and look awkward. After keeping him standing for ten minutes, the large woman stood up, put her hand out to nobody to be kissed, said, 'Farewell, I will see you tomorrow,' and then turned towards Bykov, beckoning him towards her. When he was only a foot or two away, he stood still and she put out her hand for him to kiss. To his amazement, he found himself kissing it – he never understood why – and quickly looked round to see if his companion had noticed his reactionary behaviour. To his relief, saw the guide had again prostrated himself on the ground before jumping up and running back to the ponies.

Then the large woman spoke: 'Have you any news from the front? Because, as you see, my friend has told me all is well. He is my comfort, but I still wait longingly for my love and my Baby to come back. But as it is, I have another baby who makes me happy for she is kind and does everything I tell her and never contradicts me, like the good girl she is.'

She turned and looked at the little old woman, whose eyes very slowly turned to Bykov as if she were obeying the other without understanding why or what she saw. Bykov said, speaking very slowly, that he wondered if he could come into the house, as he had orders to check their documents.

'Oh, you come from Nicky! Documents, always documents. Go and get them.'

Bykov had to admit that he walked nervously into the house, for he had seen no sign of the three daughters and wondered whether he wouldn't find their skeletons inside. The first room on his left was empty, except for two narrow iron beds, but on his right was a kitchen in the wildest disorder, with, on one side, boxes of unopened meat and fish and dried fruits. On the table stood two plates. One contained a neat pile of date stones; by the other, were a number of fishes' heads and tails, covered with flies. He said the room was so revolting and smelt so disgusting that he had an intense desire to escape, but he made himself go into the third room, which, from the plan he had been given, he knew was another bedroom. This was tidy, and contained a hanging cupboard full of women's old clothes, and two beds separated by a plain wooden chest of drawers. The sheets of each looked filthy, almost black, and the room stank, but both beds were perfectly made. He was standing, looking amazed at this contradiction, when the large woman with the hat, whom he now thought of as the Tsarina, appeared at the door and said proudly: 'You have seen my beds. My grandmother always taught us to make beds. I always make mine, and now Baby's too, and do it so much better than the servants.'

They stood looking at each other; Bykov had no idea what to say. At last he repeated himself: 'I have come for the documents.'

'Of course, from the front. Come!'

She led him into the fourth room. At one time it had clearly been another bedroom, for it also had two beds, both beautifully made, the sheets not black, merely grey with dust and brown with little pools of sand. The Tsarina pointed to a chest of drawers and said: 'All the documents are in there.'

Bykov opened all the drawers, but found only a few papers and an old leather diary, which he put into a canvas bag that he carried over one shoulder. Then he suddenly realized that he had not seen a candle of any kind in the house. Did this frightening pair spend the long winters without any lights? The smell of the house overwhelmed him, and walking quickly past the kitchen, he went out of the front door, only to be met by the odd pair, who seemed to be standing waiting for him, some rolls of knotted twine from the packing cases lying between them.

The Tsarina said: 'Now that you have collected the documents, you can go, but before you do so, I would like to show you Baby's garden. For years, you know, she planted trees which the girls brought us from the hills, but they all died. But still she worked and worked and made her garden. You will see.'

She led him behind the house, and Bykov said that, to his bewilderment, he could see no sign of any garden. A gigantic pile of wood was stacked against the kitchen side. That was all, except for a huge, circular heap of stones roughly piled to a height of perhaps four feet. In the centre of them was a declivity. Bykov, who was so astonished that he did not know what to do, stood still until the Tsarina gave him a gentle nudge.

'Yes, that's her garden. Baby carried all the stones. All her trees died, but she made this shelter and an apple tree grew in the centre. See?' She turned and called back over her shoulder: 'Baby, don't you want to show him your garden?'

Bykov turned and saw the little old woman standing behind them with the same vacant look on her face. But – and he declared his mouth fell open at the sight – one end of the pile of knotted twine which he had seen on the ground was fastened around her thin little neck, while the other, eight feet away, was held in hand of the Tsarina, who, as she received no answer to her question, gave a little tug at the string. Although the little women's – he could not think of her as the beautiful Grand Duchess – head was jerked forward, she did not move.

'Ah, Baby's in a bad mood today, but walk up and see her apple tree.'

Bykov found himself stumbling up the stones, which, he said, were roughly formed into the shape of an inverted saucer. At the apex was a hole half-full of fallen stones surrounding the stump of a withered and dead tree. That was all. He looked back. The Tsarina must have hauled her little companion to her, for they stood watching him, or rather the little woman's eyes looked in his direction.

'Is the tree well?' shouted the Tsarina.

'Yes, very well.'

'It is very well, Baby. You clever girl, to make something live when all their apples died.'

Bykov, who was no countryman, slithered painfully down, scraping the skin off his ankles, determined to leave as quickly as he could and not go too close to them again in case he found himself once more forced to kiss the Tsarina's hand.

He looked at his watch and said, in what he hoped was a brisk voice: 'Well, please forgive me, but now I have the documents I must be getting back.'

'Goodbye,' said the Empress without interest, going into the house.

Bykov looked back once, and saw the little woman was still standing motionless, though at that moment she must have felt a hard pull, for she was jerked backwards, lost her balance and nearly fell over, before turning and following her sister.

On the return journey, Bykov tried to ask his guide questions by signs and single-syllable words. As far as he could make out, the two married daughters came down twice a year to collect their share of the food, while Olga had died years before and was buried by the river. He noticed that darkness was falling, and at the same time felt both exhausted and exceedingly hungry while seeing no possible chance of himself getting home before nightfall. He plodded on despondently until they reached the edge of the forest, when his guide pointed out to him a flickering fire and he learned that he was now expected to sleep in the open. He went to bed hungry, having been offered only sour milk and a steak which his guide had thoughtfully tried to make tender and succulent by placing it for the day between the saddle and the pony's back. It was a long, chilly night, and as he was not prepared to sleep under filthy sheepskins, he crouched uncomfortably by the fire, every now and then throwing fresh logs on the embers, and reading Ella's diary. He decided that she was a spoiled and stupid woman and had clearly been mad now for twenty-five years.

After another long and painful ride, he returned in a savage temper to the little town, where his mood so frightened the local officals that he soon found the presence of the ex-Empress and her sister to be an open secret, the elopement in 1921 of Tatiana, and a year later of her sister Marie, for whom she had found a husband, also being local knowledge. That the two girls had now become typical old tribeswomen, hardly distinguishable from their husbands' people, was considered a romantic story. They had borne between them at least sixteen children. Their girls had grown up strong and handsome – several of them had already married and produced great-grandchildren for Alexandra Romanov – while the boys, on the other hand, remained undersized, good-natured and idle. Alexandra Romanov, treated with awe, paid no attention to the loss of her daughters, took no interest in their children nor gave signs of pleasure on their occasional visits. Elizabeth Romanov was considered to be with God. Daring boys from the town would, in the summer, make expeditions to 'the holy ones', and creep close enough to hear the endless conversations addressed to the empty chair, and watch, with horrified fascination, the little old silent woman led by a piece of tattered twine.

In Moscow, Bykov described every detail of his trip to Beria, who listened with an expressionless face and occasionally took notes. Two days later, he sent for Bykov and told him that for some inexplicable reason Stalin wished to see him in the Kremlin again.(Bykov told his interrogator that Beria never forgave him his two interviews with Stalin, which, in the end, saved his life, for, missing promotion, he was not considered important enough to share his senior colleague's fate.)

Once more, Bykov was shown into the little room with the couch, and this time the two sat opposite each other across a desk as Bykov was ordered in gruff tones to tell his story, which was listened to in absolute silence. When he had finished, Stalin went and sat on his couch, took out his handkerchief, threw back his head and shook and shook, his body twisting in some sort of ecstacy. It was obvious, to the terrified young man, that the President was having one of his renowned silent fits of laughter, as, every now and again, he paused to wipe saliva off his moustache with the red handkerchief held in his thick, short fingers.

Bykov started to tremble himself. He knew that those who saw the great leader in moments of weakness usually disappeared. He tried to look down, took out his own handkerchief to wipe his wet forehead, but checked himself, thinking the action might be regarded as a piece of deliberate mockery. He sat in silent agony, his eyes examining every detail of the material of his trousers until, at last, to his immense relief, the great man spoke again in a hoarse, happy voice: 'Just think of it, the Tsarina leading the Grand Duchess Serge around like a dog on a string!'

The idea set him off again, and amid his convulsions he pointed to the door, ordering Bykov out to leave him alone, undisturbed, to enjoy the magnificent joke of the comic fate of his two old adversaries.

Appendices

Appendix 1: Facsimile letter from Lord Stamfordham

(This letter to Sir William Lambton is of particular interest for the way it illustrates the strong anti-German feeling which dominated the policies of King George V and culminated in his overruling his government's decision to offer hospitality to the imperial family.)

BUCKINGHAM PALACE

Septr 24. 1914.

My dear Billy.

I am writing to ask you, if occasion arises, to contradict a rumour which has reached me from Head Quarters, that the King has been going out of his way to visit & to be kind to German

Prisoners — Psychologists
must explain why
War stimulates the
lying propensities of
the mind !
H. M. has seen no german
prisoners (& has no desire
to see any of them!)
except (1). When he visited
his own sick & wounded
soldiers at Netley Hospital,
he found in a ward

3

Some wounded German,
Officers & men who had
arrived that morning:
naturally he & the Queen
spoke to them & I believe,
tho' I was not there
myself, His M. did say
that they were to be treated
like the other patients.

(2). At Sister Agnes'
Hospital he saw 2
German Officers &
entre nous, he thought
it was a mistake there
being there — Voilà tout.
I believe Cabinets

Ministers have been to
see the prisoners.
It really is too bad
for such lies to be
made into a grievance
against the King —
You know, but I do not
wish it to be made
public, how the K.
loathes the Germans
& is often too outspoken
I have just read one
of your letters: they
are all most interesting.
How I wish I could
run out & see the life you

BUCKINGHAM PALACE

lead: it must be
strenuous—! What one
cant grasp is the
enormous extent
of ground over
which the fighting
is going on — The King
& Queen are going to
Aldershot Friday —
Tuesday & they will see
100,000 of the new
army — Splendid

material 9 fancy
but they will take
time to make — You
are short of officers:
but these new battalions
have hardly any!

Yours afford well
been reshuf
Stamfordham —

Appendix 2: Extract from a letter from Sir Clive (later Lord) Wigram

(This letter to Sir William Lambton, when military Secretary to Sir John French, from Sir Clive Wigram, Assistant Secretary to King George V, is dated 9 April 1917. Originating from a member of the King's household, it contains the strongest expression of the King's opinion on his first cousin's plea for sanctuary ever published.)

You have probably heard rumours of the Emperor and Empress of Russia, together with many Grand Dukes, coming to England to find an asylum here. Of course the King has been accused of trying to work this for his royal friends. As a matter of fact His Majesty has been opposed to this proposal from the start, and has begged his Ministers to knock it on the head. I do not expect that these Russians royalties will come, but if they do their presence here will be due to the War Cabinet and not to His Majesty.

Of course the public mind has not forgotten His Majesty's association with the Tino clique, and the visit at a critical moment to Windsor of the Grand Duchess George together with Prince Andrew of Greece. There is no doubt that Their Majesties lost ground over this.

I wish too that the House of Lords would quickly pass this Alien Princes Bill, otherwise the unseen hand for not doing so will be attributed to the King.

Another point I think would be advisable is the revoking of the Marriage Settlement Act, and allowing English Princes and Princesses to marry pure Britons. To my mind now is the time to do this, before it is forced by public opinion, when people will say that Their Majesties were compelled to do this and did not act voluntarily when they might have done so.

The position in Russia causes much anxiety. The extreme Socialists have too much influence to allow the Provisional Government to take proper charge. The Russian Navy in the Baltic is in a deplorable state, and directly the ice melts I should not wonder if the Germans try an invasion scheme on the Russian right.

Appendix 3: Letters of the Tsaritsa to the Tsar, 1914–16

(The following further letters of the Tsarina to the Tsar illustrate her increasingly unsettled state of mind in the war years.)

No. 6

Tsarskoje Selo, 23rd Sept. 1914

My own beloved Darling,

I was so sorry not to be able to write to you yesterday, but my head ached hideously & I lay all the evening in the dark, In the morning we went to the *Grotto church* for half of the service & it was lovely; I had been before to see Baby! Then we fetched the Pss. G. at Anias.

My head already ached & I can't take any medecins now, neither for the heart. We worked from 10-1, as there was an operation wh. lasted long.

After luncheon I had Schulenburg who left again to-day, as Rennenkampf told him to hurry back. Then I came up to kiss Baby & went down & lay on my bed till tea-time, after wh. I received *Sandra Schouvalov's otriad*, after wh. to bed with a splitting headache. Ania was offended I did not go to her, but she had lots of guests, & our Friend for three hours. The night was not famous & I feel my head all day – heart enlarged – generally I take drops 3 or 4 times a day, as otherwise I could not keep up, & now I cant these days. – I read *Doklady* in bed & got on to the sopha for luncheon. Then received the couple Rebinder from *Kharkhov* they have my *stores* there & she had come from Villna where she had been to bid goodbye to her brother *Kutaissov*. He showed her the Image I had sent the battery from Baby & it looked already quite used it seems they daily have it out for prayers & before every battle they pray before it – so touching. –

Then I came to Baby & lay near him in the half dark whilst *Vlad. Nik.* was reading to him, now they are playing together, the girls too, we have had tea up here too. – The weather is bright, in the night almost frost –

Thank God the news continues being good & the Prussians retire. The mud hunted them away. *Mekk* writes that there are a good many cases of cholera & dissentry in *Lvov* but they are taking sanitary measures. – There have been difficult moments there, according to the papers; but I trust there wont be anything serious – one cannot trust those Poles – after all we are their enemies & the catholics must hate us. – I shall finish in the evening, cant write much at a time. – Sweet Angel, soul & heart are ever with you.

No. 400

Tsarskoje Selo, Dec. 13th 1916

My own dearest Angel,

Tenderest thanks for Your dear card. Am so anxious (as you have no time to write) to know about your conversation with that horrible *Trepov*. I read in the paper that he told *Rodzianko* now, that the *Duma* will bee shut about on the 17-th till first half of Jan. Has he any right to say this, before the official announcement through the *Senate* is made? I find absolutely not & ought to be told so, & *Rodzianko* get a reprimand for allowing it to be put in the papers. And I did so hard beg for sooner & longer. Thank God, you at last fixed no date in Jan. & can call them together in Feb. or not at all. They do not work & *Trepov* flirts with *Rodzianko* all know that, 2 a day they meet – that is not *decent* – why does he make up & try to work with him (who is false) & not with Protopopov (who is true) – that pictures the man. Old *Bobrinsky* loathes the *Trepov's* & knows their faults – & he is so utterly devoted to you & therefore *Trepov* kicked him out. My Angel, we dined yesterday at Ania's with our Friend. It was so nice, we told all about our journey & He said we ought to have gone straight to you as we would have brought you intense joy & *blessing* & I fear disturbing you! He entreats you to be firm, to be the Master & not always to give in to *Trepov* – you know much better than that man (still let him lead you) – and why not our Friend who leads through God. Remember why I am disliked – shows it right to be firm & feared & you be the same, you a man, – only believe more in our Friend (instead of *Trepov*). He lives for you & Russia. And we must give a strong country to Baby, & dare not be weak for his sake, else he will have yet harder reign, setting our faults to right & drawing the reins in tightly which you let loose. You have to suffer for faults in the reins of your predecessors & God knows what hardships are yours. Let our legacy be a lighter one for Alexei. He has a strong will & mind of his own, don't let things slip through yr. fingers & make him have to build up all again. Be firm, I, your wall, am behind you & won't give way – I know He leads us right – & you listen gently to a false man as *Trepov*. Only out of love which you bear for me & Baby – take no big steps without warning me & speaking over all quietly. Would I write thus, did I not know you so very easily waver & change your mind, & what it costs to keep you stick to Your opinion. I know I may hurt you how I write & that is my pain & sorrow – but you, Baby & Russia are far too dear to me. What about *Sukhomlinov* & *Manuilov*. I prepared all for you. And *Dobrovolsky* – a sure man – & quicker get rid of *Makarov*, who, do at last believe me, is a bad man. God give me the power to convince you – its harder keeping you firm than the hate of others wh. leaves me cold. I loathe *Trepov's* obstinacy. There were lots of paris in the *Duma* that *Pitirim* wld. be sent away – now he got the cross, they have become crushed & small (you see, when you show yourself the Master) & more one finds it right *Princess W.* was sent away. – You never answered me about *Balashov*, fear, you did nothing & *Frederiks* is old & no good unless I speak firmly to him. – Such a mistake not to have closen the *Duma* 14 & then *Kalinin* could get back to his work and you wld. see & talk to him. – Only not a *responsible cabinet* which all are mad about. Its all getting calmer & better, only one wants to feel Your hand – how long, years, people have told me the same – 'Russia loves to feel whip' – its their nature – tender love & then the iron hand to punish & guide. – How I wish I could pour my will into your veins. The Virgin is above you, for you, with you, remember the miracle – our Friend's vision.

391

Soon our troops will have more force in Roumania. – Warm & thick snow. – Forgive this letter, but I could not sleep this night, worrying over you – don't hide things from me – I am strong – but listen to me, wh. means our Friend & trust us through all – & beware of *Trepov* – you can't love or venerate him. I suffer over you as over a tender, softhearted child – wh. needs giding, but listens to bad advisers whilst a man of God's tells him what to do. Sweetest Angel, come home soon – ah no, you have the Gen., why not before, – I cant grasp; why the same day as the *Duma* – strange combination again. – And *Voyeikov*, has that also fallen through?–

Oh, dear, I must get up. Been writing Xmas-cards all the morning. Heart & soul burning with you – Love boundless, therefore seems harsh all I write – pardon, believe & understand. I love you too deeply & cry over your faults & rejoice over every right step.

God bless & protect, guard & guide you. Kisses without end.

Y. truest
Wify

Please, read this paper & Anias too.
If a lie – have *Rodzianko's* uniform taken off.

No. 401

Tsarskoje Selo, Dec. 14th 1916

My beloved Sweetheart,

. . . That paper I sent you yesterday, *Rodzianko* himself wrote – he has no right to print & distribute yr. conversation & I doubt it being literal as he always lies – if not exact then be the Emp. & at once have his court-dress taken fr. him, don't ask Frederiks' or *Trepov's* advice, both are frightened tho' old man wld. formerly have understood the necessity, now he is old. Already one spread in town (*Duma*) that the nobility in Novg. did not receive me, & when they read that we even drank tea together they became crushed. About *Kaufmann* one is very pleased – you see, yr. firmness is appreciated by the good – so easy to continue when once begun forgive me tormenting you with these letters – but only read the 2 telegr. I wired to you, you will hear fr. *Kalinin* again & he begs to close the Duma – do it, don't stick to the 17-th – time is money, the moment golden, & if dawdled over difficult, impossible to catch up & mend again. – I do hope its not true *Nikolasha* comes for the 17-th – formerly it went perfectly without *Vorontzov* – that has nothing to do with the Caucasus, our front here. Keep him away, evil genius. And he will mix into affairs & speak about Wassiltchikov. Be Peter the Great, John the Terrible, Emperor Paul – crush them all under you – now don't you laugh, noughty one – but I long to see you so with all those men who try to govern you – & it must be the contrary. Countess Benkendorf was so outraged by Princess W.'s letter, that she made a round of visits to the older ladies in town, Princess Lolo, Countess *Vorontzov* etc. telling them her opinion & that she finds it a disgrace to what the society has come down to, forgetting all principles & begging them to begin by strongly speaking to their daughters who behave and talk outrageously. It seems to have had its effect, as people speak now of her, so they realise the letter was really an unheard of one, & not such a charming one as some try to pretend. Katoussia W. also wrote to me, but after reading I tore it. And here the contrast, telegr. fr. '*Union of the Russian People*' asking me to give over things to you. – One is rotten, weak, immoral society – the other, healthy, rightthinking, devoted subjects – & to these one must listen, their voice is Russia's & not society or the *Duma's*. One sees the right so clearly & they know the Duma ought to be closed & to them *Trepov* won't listen. If one does not listen to these, they will take things into their own hands to have you and more harm unwillingly may be done – then a simple word from you to close the *Duma*, – but till February, if earlier – they, will all stick here. I cld. hang *Trepov* for his bad counsels – and now after the papers *Kalinin* sent *Voyeikov* with those vile, utterly revolutionary *representations* of Moscou *Nobility* & *'Unions'*, wh. have been discussed at the *Duma*, how can one keep them even one day on still – I hate false *Trepov* who does all to harm you, backed up by *Makarov*. Had I but got you here again – all was at once calmer & had you returned as *Gregory* in 5 days, you wld. have put order, wld. have rested yr. weary head upon wify's breast & Sunny wld. have given you strength & you wld. have listened to me & not to *Trepov*. God will help, I know, but you must be firm. Disperse the *Duma* at once, when you told Trepov 17-th you did not know what they were up to. – I should have quietly sent *Lvov* to Siberia (one did so for far less grave acts), taken *Samarin's rank* away (he signed that paper fr. Moscou), *Miliukov, Gutchkov & Polivanov* also to Siberia. It is war and at such a time interior war is high treason, why don't you look at it like that, I really cannot understand. I am but a woman, but my soul & brain tell me it wld. be the saving of Russia – they sin far worse than anything the *Sukhomlinov's ever did*. – Forbid *Brussilov* etc. when they come to touch any political subjects, fool, who wants *responsible cabinet*, as *Georgi* writes.

Remember even Mr. Philippe said one dare not give constitution, as it would be yr. & Russia's ruin, & all true Russians say the same. Months ago I told *Sturmer* about *Shvedov* to be a member of *Council of the Empire* to have them & good Maklakov in they will stand bravely for us. I know I worry you – ah, wld. I not far, far rather only write letters of love, tenderness & caresses of wh. my heart is so full – but my duty as wife & mother & Russia's mother obliges me to say all to you – blessed by our Friend. Sweetheart, Sunshine of my life, if in battle you had to meet the enemy, you wld. never waver & go forth like a lion – be it now in the battle against the small *handful* of brutes & republicans – be the Master, & all will bow down to you. – Do you think I shld. fear, ah no – to-day I have had an officer cleared out fr. Maria's & Anastasia's hospital, because he allowed himself to mock at our journey, pretending Protopopov bought the people to receive us so well; the Drs. who heared it raged – you see, Sunny in her small things is energetic & in big one as much as you wish – we have been placed by God on a throne & we must keep it firm & give it over to our Son untouched – if you keep that in mind you will remember to be the Sovereign – & how much easier for an *autocratic* soveriegn than one who has sworn the Constitution. –

Beloved One, listen to me, yes, you know yr. old true Girly. '*Do not fear*' the *old woman* said & therefore I write *without fear* to my agoo weè one. – Now the girlies want their tea, they came frozen back from their drive. – I kiss you & hold you tightly clasped to my breast, caress you, love you, long for you, cant sleep without you – bless you

Ever yr. very own
Wify.

No. 403

Tsarskoje Selo, Dec. 16-th 1916

My own beloved Treasure,

... Only one thing just torments me, *Gregory* & *Protopopov* – the Duma not to be called together before Febr. so as to give them time to disperse, wh. is more than necessary, they are in a "group" a poisonous element in town, whereas dispersed over the country nobody pays any heed to them nor respects them. – Olga had a Committee yesterday evening, but it did not last long. *Volodia Volkonsky*, who always has a smile or two for her – avoided her eyes & never once smiled – you see how our girlies have learned to watch people & their faces – they have developed much interiorly through all this suffering – they know all we go through, its necessary & ripens them. They are happily at times great babies – but have the insight & feelings of the soul of much wiser beings. As our Fr. says – they have passed heavy "*courses*". *N.P.* took tea, told heaps about Odessa & the battalion, Olga Evgen. etc. – Full of Petrograd horrors & rages that nobody defends me, that all may say, write, hint at bad things about their Empress & nobody stands up, repr. mands, punishes, banishes, fines those types. Only *Princess V.* suffered, all others, *Miliukov* etc. go free. Yes, people are not to be admired, cowards. But many shall be struck off future court-lists, they shall learn to know in time of peace what it was in time of war not to stand up for ones Sovereign. Why have we got a ramoli rag as Minister of the Court? He ought to have brought all the names & proposed how to punish them for slandering your wife. Personally I do not care a straw – when I was young I suffered horribly through those injustices said about me (oh how often) – but now the worldly things don't touch me deeply. I mean nastinesses – they will come round some day, only my Huzy ought really to stick up a bit for me, as many think you don't care & hide behind me. You answer about *Balashov* – now why did you not have him severely written to by Fred. – I am not going to shake hands with him whenever we meet, I warn you & I long to fling my fury into his face; little snake – I have disliked him ever since I set eyes on him, & I told you so. He thinks his high court rank allows him to write vile things – on the contrary, he is utterly unworthy of it. – Have you said that Prince Golizin is to have his court rank taken fr. him – don't dawdle deary, do all quicker, its the Danish Bummelzug – be quicker in acting strike out people fr. court lists & don't listen to Fred. protests – he is frightened & does not understand how to deal at the present moment. –

Now forgive me, if I did wrong, in asking *Kalinin's* opinion about the list you sent me. As we trust him (he came for ½ an hour to her yesterday). I asked her to find out what he knows about the people. He promises to hold his tongue that he saw the names of the candidates. – Only above all begs *Makarov* to quickly leave, without putting him into the *Council* of *the Empire*, others neither were put there, & don't need *Trepov's* letter, believe our Fr's advice & now Kalinin's too – he is dangerous & completely holds *Trepov* in hand, others, *Zhevakhov* for instance knows it too. – He spoke a while ago to *Stcheglovitov*, who finds *Dobrovolsky* whom he knows – excellent in that place. I think you would only be right in naming him. I know Dobrovolsky is much against the reorganisation of the Senate as projected, (I think agreed to in the *Council of the Empire* & now presented to the *Duma*) – says it will be as bad & left as the *Duma*, & not to be relied upon – he told me that, when I saw him. I only spoke about the Senate & Georgie's committee then. –

Send for *Kalinin* as soon as you arrive here & then *Dobrovolsky* to talk to & name

394

Stcheglovitov quicker – he is the right man in the right place & will stick up for us & permit no rows. Yr. *order* has had a splendid effect upon all – it came at such a good moment and showed so clearly all yr. ideas about continuing the war. Fancy, poor Zizi was so upset, *Miliukov* in his speech spoke about *Lila Narishkin (Lichtenstein)*, spies etc. & said she was a lady in high function at court confounding her with Mme. Zizi. Poor old lady heard that it got into small papers in the country, the *Kurakins* came all flying & she had to explain to them – her *supervisors* full of horror, a general in the army, – how can we keep such traitors near us (always a bite at me & my people!!) – so she sent for Sazonov (*Miliukov's* bosom friend), & told him to explain all & to insist upon his writing in the papers that he was lead into error. It will appear in the "Retch", & now she is quite calm again. They touch all near me. *Lila N.* is at Astoria, & being watched by the police. – Poor old *Stcheglov* died this night – better for him, he was so ill! I am going to get hold of Ressin one of these days & tell him to pay attention to his officers – Komarov, was always with them, he never, & the tone has become very bad & even left – its the most difficult reg. as so mixed & therefore needs a head to keep them well in hand & guide them, & one does not speak well of them at all. The men don't like him because he is hard – but the officers he does not a bit occupy himself with. – Just had old *Shvedov*, fancy, when he told *Trepov* he was to be a member of the *Council of the Empire* by your & my wish, he answered that it did not concern him what orders Sturmer got, he did not hear it from you.

He brought me the list on one paper of all the members & we can look at it together & strike out & add on new ones. Hates Kaufmann, says he said very bad things, strike him off – now one must come with the brush & sweep away the dust & dirt & get new clean brushes to work. –

Warmest thanks precious letter. Poor dear, will be tired to morrow – God help you – only military & no political questions. All wild about your *order*, the Poles of course intensely so. –

The kitten has climbed into the fireplace & now sneezes there. –

Glad, you saw *Bagration* – so interesting all about his wild men.

"*One must not speak*" – "*with tiny will*" but a wee bit weak & not confident in yourself & a bit easily believe bad advices. – Now – I bless, hug, kiss you, my one & all. God bless & protect you.

Ever yr. very, very own tiresome   Sunny.

(SOURCE: Empress Alexandra, *The Letters to the Tsar, 1914–1916*, Duckworth, London, 1923.)

Appendix 4: List of officials discharged or replaced, 1914–16 (see pages 314–16 of text)

		NAME OF DISCHARGED MINISTER OR OFFICIAL	POSITION	REASON	REPLACEMENT
(1)	1914 Feb. 12	KOKOVTSEV	Prime Minister	Dislike of Rasputin	GORYMEKIN (senile)
(2)	1915 June 16	MALAKOV	Minister of Interior	Disagreement with Tsar	PRINCE SHCHERBATOV
(3)	1915 June 20	SOUKHOMLINOV	Minister of War	Inefficiency, shortages of armaments	GENERAL POLIVANOV
(4)	1915 June 25–30	SHCHEGLOVITOV	Minister of Justice anti-war	Disagreement with Tsar	A.A. KHVOSTOV
(5)	1915 June 25–30	SABLER	Minister of Religion (Procurator Holy Synod)	Disagreement with Tsar anti-war	A. D. SAMARIN
(6)	1915 Aug. 26	GRAND DUKE NICHOLAS	Commander-in-Chief Imperial armies	Desire of Tsar lead army	TSAR Chief of Staff ALEXEYEV
(7)	1915 Aug. 30	DZHUNKOVSKY	Assistant Minister of Interior	Persecution of Rasputin	BELETSKY
(8)	Sept. 20	PRINCE SHCHERBATOV	Minister of Interior	New appointment Supported by Rasputin	ALEXIS KHOSTOV (nephew of A.A. Khostov)
(9)	1915 Sept. 20–30	SAMARIN	Minister of Religion	Rasputin	VOLZHIN
(10)	1915 Sept. 20–30	KRIVOSHEIN	Minister of Agriculture	Rasputin	NAUMOV
(11)	1915 Sept. 20–30	RUKHLOV	Resignation	Unknown	A.F. TREPOV
(12)	1915	Unknown	Assistant Minister of Religion	Rasputin	ZHEVAKOV
(13)	1915 Oct.	No old post VLADIMIR	Metropolitan of Petrograd	Rasputin	PITIRIM
(14)	1916 Feb. 2	GOREMYKIN	Prime Minister	Tsar's acceptance of inefficiency	STURMER

	NAME OF DISCHARGED MINISTER OR OFFICIAL	POSITION	REASON	REPLACEMENT
(15) 1916 March	ALEXIS KHVOSTOV	Minister of Interior	Rasputin	STURMER, Additional office
(16) 1916 March	GENERAL POLIVANOV	Minister of War	Rasputin	GENERAL SHUVAYEV (Tsar's appointment)
(17) 1916 April		Secretary to Premier	Rasputin	A known criminal and blackmailer MANASEVICH MANUILOV
(18) 1916 July	NAUMOV	Minister of Agriculture	Disgusted resignation	
(19) 1916 July	RELEASE OF POSITION BY P.M.	Minister of Interior	Unknown	A.A.KHVOSTOV
(20) 1916 July	A.A. KHOVSTOV	Minister of Justice	Rasputin	A.A. MAKAROV
(21) 1916 July 24	SAZANOF	Minister Foreign Affairs	Fear of Empress he was giving up Tsar and Tsarita's rights in Poland	STURMER
(22) 1916 Sept.	A.A.KHOVSTOV	Minister of Interior	Insistence on persecuting Manuilov, who would have implicated Rasputin	PROTOPOV
(23) 1916 Sept.	KLIMOVITCH	Director of Police Dept.		
(24) 1916 End Sept.	No known predecessor	Unofficial assistant to Minister of Interior	Signed documents declared illegal due to K's criminal past	KURLOV

Appendix 5: The basis for the doubts concerning how the Tsarina, her daughters and the Grand Duchess Serge died

The presumed deaths of the Tsarina and the Grand Duchess Serge have become established legends built on repetition and wishful thinking which bear little relation to fact. In 1976, Anthony Summers and Tom Mangold published, after five years of intense and detailed research, *The File on the Tsar* (Gollancz), which produced a mass of deliberately concealed evidence supporting the doubts, first expressed by Sir Charles Eliot, British High Commissioner in Siberia, concerning whether the Tsarina and her daughters were massacred in Ekaterinburg in July 1918. The following extracts from his report to the Foreign Minister (in the archives of the Foreign Office) speak for themselves:

> On July 17th a train with the blinds down left Ekaterinburg for an unknown destination and it is believed that the surviving members of the Imperial family were in it.

> It is the general opinion in Ekaterinburg that the Empress, her son and four daughters were not murdered but were despatched on 17th July to the north or west.

This was a first-hand judgement by a man, noted for his exactitude, who visited the scene six weeks after the so-called massacre and inspected the murder room. Towards the end of his report he wrote:

> Also hair identified as belonging to one of the Grand Duchesses was found in this house. It therefore seems probable that the Imperial family were disguised before removal.

Later investigations found four women's hair, identified by the royal valet Chemodorov. The concealment was necessary because the Bolsheviks appear to have had two seemingly contrary purposes: to ensure that the local population thought 'the Romanov women' had died, but also to be able to assure the German command and the Kaiser that they were alive, since in the period from July to August 1918, Lenin could not afford to offend the yet unbeaten Germany, which had held Russia at its mercy since the signing in March of the treaty of Brest-Litovsk.

But enough. I do not wish to get involved in an argument on evidence. All that can be said for certain is that the bodies of the Tsarina and her daughters were never found, and that despite attempts to persuade them otherwise, many of the inhabitants of Ekaterinburg believed that only the Tsar had been shot. Yet the world demanded certainty and drama, and the massacre story fitted both bills at the same time as satisfying the extremist Bolsheviks as well as the White Army as a justification of the brutality of the new regime. Once Sir Charles and the original investigators, Nametkin and Count Sergeyev, had been replaced, Sokolov, the last investigator, and General Diterikhs supported the massacre, took up a fixed attitude, omitted or changed evidence which contradicted (as in the case of Galliard) their opinion in a manner reminiscent of the Dreyfus scandal.

Even greater uncertainty surrounds the death of Ella, or the Grand Duchess Serge, near Alapayevsk. All that is known for certain is that she was the companion in prison of the three sons of the Grand Duke Constantine, Prince Paley, the morganatic son of the Grand Duke Paul, and a cousin and namesake of her late husband's, the Grand Duke Serge Mikhailovich. The known facts are that, on the evening of 17 (18) August, all the prisoners disappeared. Later that night, Soviet troops shot a peasant and made a claim, believed by few, that the grand dukes had been rescued by the advancing 'White' Czechs, but made no mention of the Grand Duchess. On 8, 9 and 10 October, after the arrival of the 'White' relieving force, the bodies of seven men, stated to be the Romanovs and two servants, and two women – one stated to be the Grand Duchess, the other her maid Barbara – were extracted from a mine, but never officially identified. Later, post mortems were carried out on the bodies.

Out of these bare facts has grown a myth, usually told in sickly prose, which has been endlessly repeated along the following lines. A lorry draws up at the school-house. One by one the condemned climb in; on the journey they sing the 'Magnificat'; on arrival at the mine they are thrown one by one alive down the sixty-foot shaft, with the exception of the Grand Duke Serge, who is *clumsily* shot in the head. The Bolsheviks throw down grenades and leave. However, near by in the wood lurked a loyalist priest, Father Seraphin, and friendly peasants, who crept close to the mine and heard, for the rest of the night, loud singing of hymns which continued growing fainter until the victims died of starvation. A little later, the Whites arrived and hauled up the bodies. The Grand Duchess's veil was torn and a strip used to tie up Prince Joann's arm.

Father Seraphin, 'a man of means', recognizes the Grand Duchess and bravely decides to take her and the faithful maid, Sister Barbara, thousands of miles across country to Peking. They set off at the beginning of winter, with the coffins tied by ropes to horses, and after marching thousands of miles for two years through mud, snow, deserts and mountains, arrive in Peking with the coffins so battered that they have to be changed. The new coffins are then opened in the presence of the Orthodox priests of Peking, and the body of the Grand Duchess is found to be uncorrupted. The report of the priest's amazing journey reaches the London papers. Lady Milford Haven sees the item, and the body ends up, where it has since been venerated by successive generations, in the Church of St Mary Magdalene on the Mount of Olives, Jerusalem.

The Grand Duchess was undoubtedly a good woman, her life a long saga of good works and suffering, and there is no reason why her body should not be venerated. But is it her body? Even a cursory glance at the myth, which, in the last years, the late Lord Mountbatten, the Grand Duchess's nephew, sought to perpetuate as a tablet of truth, must cause doubts and raise questions. Why, for instance, has Chapter 26 of Sokolov Report, which dealt with life at Alapayevsk, the journey to the execution at Sinyachikha, the executions and the autopsies, been carefully neglected? It is published as Appendix 6, translated for – as far as I know – the first time from Russian into English, although it has always been available in French. The content of Chapter 26 contradicts nearly every belief of the myth-makers, who apparently concocted their story from distorted family gossipers who had never been near Ekaterinburg or Alapayevsk, such as the late Prince Christopher of Greece, who is remembered – if he is remembered – for his flippant, rather vulgar, anecdotes. Why he should be considered an authority on the massacres is odd, to say the least, since he never set foot in Russia during First World War, and was in Switzerland at the time of the Grand Duchess's presumed death. Neither was he an eminent historian. His memoirs suggest an overgrown schoolboy who records, with delight, an evening spent hiding under tables in his sister's house in Harrogate, squirting syphons of soda water at ex-King Manuel of Portugal. That his vague, third-hand gossip should come to be accepted as established fact is grotesque.

The myth says that they sang the 'Magnificat' on the journey to the mine. The inquiry produced a peasant, Alexander Samsonov, and his friend, who met a column of ten or eleven wagons travelling towards the mine which passed them in dead silence.

The myth says that all except Serge were thrown in conscious.

The autopsies reveal that all the bodies had been hit with blunt instruments on the skull.

The myth says they sang until they died of starvation.

The autopsies reveal that they died of haemorrages of the brain.

In fact, the endless, biased memoirs of the Romanovs and their supporters, and the neglect of the twenty-sixth chapter of the Report, have allowed a saintly legend to displace truth.

It is after the discovery of the bodies on 8, 9 and 10 October that the ridiculous becomes supreme, culminating in the miracle march. Readers of Peter Fleming's *Adventures in Tartary*, about a journey made in the early 1930s, will know of the difficulty which two young people faced with no coffins and with adequate money.

But anyway, why should Father Seraphin have gone to Peking on foot with the coffins on ponies when he could have boarded the Trans-Siberian Railway, a branch line of which ran from Perm to Ekaterinburg to the coast, and was at that time under the control of Admiral Kolchak, who had organized the body lifting, the inquiry into the autopsies and the burial of the four Romanov men in the crypt of Perm Cathedral, as well as their later movement to the Convent of Chita. It is here worth remarking that according to Paul Bulygin, Father Seraphin was not a mendicant, as the myth suggests, but the Superior of the monastery of St Seraphin of Sarov, which explains his presence in the area. But he still leaves unexplained why he set off in mid-winter on his unlikely trek. The answer to that is quite simple. He did no such thing. He went by train, according to Countess Alexandra Olsoufiev, for many years the Mistress of the Grand Duchess's Robes, who states in her memoir, written just after the event but ignored by the myth-makers:

In the time of Admiral Kolchak, a pious hand collected her mortal remains, and they were transferred first to Harbin and then to Peking. At the time of writing, I hear that owing to the efforts of her sister, Victoria, Marchioness of Milford Haven, they have been conveyed from Shanghai to Port Said, and from thence to Jerusalem, where they will rest in holy ground in the church of St Mary Magdalene, near the Judgement Gate, dedicated to the memory of the Empress Marie, wife of Alexander II.

We now come to a puzzle. Why, once the body arrived in Harbin some time at the end of 1918 or early 1919, did it disappear for a year and a half until it turned up in Peking? A glance at the map will show that Harbin was ideally situated to send the coffin by sea to Jerusalem, so if this was Father Seraphin's object, why did he go several hundred miles to Peking, and what did he do in the year that he spent either in Harbin or Peking with his incorruptible body?

This makes one ask whether the Grand Duchess actually died with the others. In Footnote 7 to Sokolov's Chapter 26 he writes: 'I will try to explain why the fate of the Grand Duchess Elizabeth Feodorovna is not mentioned either in Beloborodov's telegram nor in his official newspaper announcement'; but nowhere later does he try to explain the singular omission.

The supposed photograph of the Grand Duchess bears no resemblance to her appearance in life. This could have been the result of her physical deterioration after spending seven weeks in the bottom of a damp mine after receiving two blows with a metal object on the head and then dropping sixty feet down a timber-littered shaft. As the pre-autopsy photographs of the other Romanovs do not bear any resemblance to their photographs in life either, it is likely that they also suffered physical deterioration. But the question must be asked, if the bloated body photographed was the Grand Duchess's, which afterwards became the subject of an autopsy, how did it turn up two years later, unmarred and uncorrupted in Peking?

Was the body hers? Was she in fact alive, the body in the mine belonging to a fat, peasant woman put in her place, with an icon pinned on her chest? The icon on her presumed body is surprising since for seven years the Grand Duchess had never worn an ornament. Surely, before she is made a saint, it would be wise to examine the miracle-working body in Jerusalem to see if it was subject to ornamentation or plastic surgery. There was much in common between the supposed death of the two sisters. The Barina mine was said to contain the Tsarina's jewels and bones which were never examined or the bones proved to be human. The Grand Duchess was found in a mine wearing a recognizable icon. The chairman of the Oblast Soviet, Beloborodov, was mixed up with both murders, and his telegrams suggest that he organized each event. In both cases, the Soviet appeared to ensure that all knew that the Romanov men had been killed, yet in both cases, reticent statements were made concerning the Tsarina and her sister.

Summers and Mangold put forward the theory that the Empress and her daughters lived on, thanks to a pact made between Lenin and the Emperor William to keep the German women alive, and they cited witnesses interviewed by 'White' interrogators – suppressed by Sokolov – who claimed they had seen her and her daughters in Perm after she was supposedly dead. Their argument is strengthened by the Soviets' behaviour towards the Grand Duchess and their unexplained avoidance of stating that she was dead. This suggests that when the Soviets mentioned the German women, they were referring not to the Tsarina and her daughters, but to the Tsarina and her sister.

As I say, all is now supposition, but the answer may still lie in the Houghton Museum of Harvard, where an untranslated mass of evidence remains. It is to be hoped that some scholar will set himself the task of helping to solve a problem which entwined the two sisters in the uncertainty of their deaths. Until that day, Bykov's story remains uncontradicted.

Appendix 6: Chapter 26 of the Sokolov Report

The murder at Alapayevsk of the Grand Duchess Elizabeth Feodorovna, the Grand Duke Serge Mikhailovich, and the Princes Ioann Konstantinovich, Konstantin Konstantinovich, Igor Konstantinovich, and Prince Vladimir Pavlovich Palei.

In the summer of 1918, in the town of Alapayevsk, Verkhoturskii Uezd, Perm Guberniya, not far from Ekaterinburg, the Grand Duchess Elizabeth Feodorovna, the Grand Duke Serge Mikhailovich, and the Princes Ioann Konstantinovich, Konstantin Konstantinovich, Igor Konstantinovich, and Prince Vladimir Pavlovich Palei were being held prisoners.

During the early hours of 18 July 1918, they all disappeared from Alapayevsk, and in the morning the Bolsheviks pasted up notices throughout the town that they had been stolen away by the 'White Guard'.

The populace did not believe these notices, but, under the weight of terror, did not dare to take action.

On 28 September, Alapayevsk was liberated from the Bolsheviks.

The military authorites appointed Officer Malshikov to undertake police investigations.

The court investigation started on 11 October, in the hands of Member of the Court Sergeyev.

On 7 February 1919 it was transferred to me [Sokolov] together with the case of the murder of the imperial family.

This is what the investigations determined:

The prisoners arrived in Alapayevsk on 20 May 1918, and were accommodated in the so-called 'Napolnaya school' on the edge of the town. This is a stone building consisting of four large and two small rooms with a system of corridors.

The corner room to the left of the corridor was occupied by the guard. Further along the same side of the corridor were three rooms. In the first lived Serge Mikhailovich and Vladimir Pavlovich Palei with their servants Feodor Semyonovich Remez and Krukovskii. In the next room lived Konstantin Konstantinovich and Igor Konstantinovich. the corner room was occupied by Elizabeth Feodorovna and two sisters of the Order of Martha and Maria who were in her service: Varvara Yakovleva and Ekaterina Yanysheva. In the corner room on the right side of the corridor lived Ioann Konstantinovich, in the next, the footman Kalin, and the next room was the kitchen.

Gelmersen, the doctor of Serge Mikhailovich, arrived later, and moved into the school.

No one commissar was appointed to oversee the prisoners. Authority over them was manifested by many Bolsheviks who had served with distinction at Alapayevsk. These were:

1. Grigorii Pavlov Abramov (chairman of the Sovdep)
2. Ivan Pavlov Abramov
3. Mikhail Ivanov Gasnikov
4. Mikhail Leontev Zayakin
   (Members of the Sovdep)

5. Dmitrii Vasiliev Perminov (secretary of the Sovdep)
6. Nikolai Pavlov Govyrin (chairman of the Cheka)
7. Pyotr Konstantinov Startsev
8. Pyotr Aleksandrov Zyryanov
9. Mikhail Feodorov Ostanin
   (Members of the Cheka)

10. Vasilii Petrov Postnikov (a judge)
11. Ivan Feodorov Kuchnikov (leader of a Red Army brigade)
12. Efim Andreev Solovyov (judiciary commissar)
13. Vladimir Afanasev Spiridonov (administrative commissar)
14. Serge Alekseev Pavlov (military commissar)
15. Aleksei Aleksandrov Smolnikov
16. Egor Ivanov Sychev (Bolshevik worker)
17. Vasilii Pavlov Govyrin
18. Evgenii Ivanov Naumov
19. Dmitrii Petrov Smirnov
20. Ivan Dmitriev Maslov
21. Vasilii Pyabov
22. Mikhail Nasonov
    (Bolshevik workers)

All these were Russian people, residents of Alapayevsk and its environs.

The guard always consisted of six people: Magyars, Red Army men, local workers appointed by the Sovdep or Cheka.

One Krivovna, serving the prisoners as non-resident cook, her assistant Pozdina-Zamyatina and the worker-watchman Startsev «1» testified that:

KRIVOVNA: 'The rooms of the Princes had only the simplest bare essentials: plain iron beds with stiff matresses, a number of plain tables and chairs. There were no soft furnishings. Towards 1 p.m. I would prepare breakfast, at four tea was served and at seven – dinner . . . The Princes occupied themselves by reading, went for walks, worked in the kitchen garden adjoining the school. With the permission of the Red Army duty guard, the Princes would go to church and for walks in the fields which start behind the school. These walks were without guards. The Grand Duchess Elizabeth Feodorovna occupied herself by drawing and spent long periods in prayer; her breakfast and dinner were taken to her in her room. The other Princes would gather for breakfast and dinner in the room of Serge Mikhailovich, which also served as the communal dining room.'

POZDINA-ZAMYATINA: 'In the month of May, when I was serving the Princes, they had freedom enough: they could wander without hindrance in the meadow by the school, they worked in the kitchen garden and went to church. All the Princes and the Grand Duchess worked in the kitchen garden, with their own hands digging vegetable and flower beds. They also cleaned and tidied up the courtyard, creating a clean and cosy place where the Princes frequently drank tea in the open air, read and chatted.'

STARTSEV: 'Occasionally the Princes would walk in the corridor. With one of them, already turning grey (I do not know his name) we would have long conversations. The Prince would demonstrate that universal equality was an impossibility, quoting the 'parable of the talents'. Concerning land redistribution, the Prince would say that land also varied, and therefore it was difficult to divide it equally and fairly among all the working people. The prince would complain of rheumatism in the legs and say that only massage eased the pain . . . The conversations were of a pleasant peaceful nature, so that the Prince expressed his satisfaction and stated that he was only able to converse occasionally, as the guard were for the most part hooligans.'

How did they relate to the prisoners?

Krivovna testified that: 'The Red Army men, guarding the house, were a mixed bunch. The good ones were sorry for the Princes and were attentive to them, but the bad were coarse and argumentative and even addressed the Princes as 'comrade'. On some three occasions the Austrians were on duty. These Red Army men were the very coarsest, and at night almost every hour they burst into the rooms of the Princes and carried out searches. The Grand Duke Serge Mikhailovich protested against these pointless disturbances, but no notice was taken of his complaint. I pass this on from the words of the Grand Duke himself.'

On 21 June, the life of the prisoners suddenly deteriorated: a prison régime was implemented, and their belongings and money were taken from them.

Krivovna testified that: 'Over about a month the situation of the Princes rapidly deteriorated: All their property was confiscated: shoes, linen, clothes, pillows, gold articles and money; they were left only their underclothes, shoes, and two changes of linen. From the same time all walks beyond the school fence were prohibited, and they were prohibited from making any purchases at the market. To feed the Princes it was decided to send in prepared food from the soviet, but later I was permitted to cook for the Princes from my own store; I guess 28 pounds of meat, 15 pounds of millet and one bottle of hempseed oil per week.'

There is no shadow of doubt that the change took place on orders from Ekaterinburg.

On 21 June, the Grand Duke Serge Mikhailovich telegraphed:

Ekaterinburg. To the President of the Oblast Soviet. On the orders of the Oblast Sovdep we are from today under prison régime. For four weeks we have lived under the surveillance of the Alapayevsk Sovdep, and have not left the school and its courtyard except to attend church. Not knowing any fault in ourselves we petition for the lifting of the prison régime. On behalf of myself and my relations in Alapayevsk, Serge Mikhailovich Romanov.

Judiciary commissar Solovyov inquired the same day by telegraph:

Military [telegram]. [To] Ekaterinburg Oblast Soviet Should the household [servants] of the Romanovs be considered as arrested [?][Should we] allow them to leave [for any] reason[?] 4227 Alapayevsk Sovdep Sender E. Solovyov'«2».

What brought about the change in the regime?

In the Summer of 1918 the Grand Duke Mikhail Aleksandrovich was in exile in Perm.

During the month of June he disappeared.

This was the motive of [the] Ekaterinburg [authorities] for the introduction of the prison régime at Alapayevsk.

In reply to the telegram of Solovyov, Beloborodov telegraphed to him on 22 June:

[To] Alapayevsk
Sovdep
Your discretion [concerning] the household [servants] Nobody to leave without permission of Dzerzhinskii [in] Moscow Uritskii [in] Petrograd Ekaterinburg Oblasoviet stop Inform Serge Romanov that imprisonment is precautionary measure against flight in view of disappearance of Mikhail [from] Perm

Beloborodov «3»

The transmission copy of this telegram appears in photograph No. 134.

All who were not relatives were separated from the prisoners. Only Sister Yakovleva was left with Elizabeth Feodorovna and Remez with Serge Mikhailovich.

On 17 July at twelve o'clock [midday] chekist Pyotr Startsev arrived at the school with several Bolshevik workers. They took from the prisoners their last remaining money, and told them that they would be transferred that night to the Verkhne-Sinyachikhenskii works, roughly 15 versts [16 km] from Alapayevsk.

The new arrivals sent the Red Army men away from the school and took over from them. At this time Krivovna was preparing dinner. She testified: 'The Bolsheviks hustled me over the dinner; I served dinner at six o'clock, and during dinner the Bolsheviks kept hustling: "Finish your dinner quickly. At eleven o'clock we are going to Sinyachikha." I started to pack some groceries, but the Bolsheviks told me to wait, that I could bring them tomorrow to Sinyachikha.'

Late that night grenade explosions and gunshots were heard near the school building. This caused consternation in the town. Many saw Red Army men deployed in line some distance from the school, who were later led right up to the school itself.

The nature of the hoax was even then clear, not only to many townspeople , but also to the very Red Army men in the line.

Four of them were held «4». I will limit myself to the testimony of Yakim Nasonov:

'About three in the morning of 18th July the alarm was raised in our barracks: the White Guard were attacking. We rapidly gathered, dressed and armed. We were led to the Napolnaya school, in the vicinity of which we were deployed in line. We were led to the Napolnaya school in the vicinity of which we were deployed in line. We remained in the line about half an hour, and then moved up to the school itself. We saw no enemy of any kind and did not fire a shot. Commissar Smolnikov stood on the porch of the school, swore and said to us: "Comrades we'll catch it now from the ural Oblast Soviet because the Princes have managed to escape. The White Guard have taken them off in an aeroplane."

'Peoples Court Judge Postnikov was also present, with "a big book in his hand", and conducted an investigation into the flight of the Princes. About three to four days later people were beginning to say that the commissars were deceiving the people with their story of the abduction of the Princes, and that the Princes had actually been murdered by them.'

On 18 July at 3.15 in the morning, the Alapayevsk Sovdep telegraphed to the Ekaterinburg Oblast Sovdep «5»:

Military [telegram]. [To] Ekaterinburg. Ural administration. On the morning of 18 July at 2 o'clock a band of unknown persons under arms assaulted the Napolnaya school where the Grand Dukes were accommodated. During the gun battle one bandit was killed and apparently there are wounded. The princes and household [servants] succeeded in escaping in an unknown direction. When [the] Red Army detachment arrived the bandits fled in the direction of the forest. None were captured. Search continues. Alapayevsk ispolkom. Abramov. Perminov. Ostanin.

On the same day at 18.30 [6.30 pm] Beloborodov telegraphed:

Collective [telegram]
   Moscow two addresses [to] Sovnarkom [to] President Tsik Sverdlov
   Petrograd two addresses [to] Zinoviev [to] Uritskii Alapayevk Ispolkom has informed [us] of the assault on the morning of 18th by an unknown band on the premises where the once Grand Dukes Igor Konstantinovich Konstantin Konstantinovich Ivan Konstantinovich Serge Mikhailovich and Polei [sic] were being held under guard stop notwithstanding resistance the Princes were abducted stop there are casualties on both sides search in progress stop 4853. Predoblasoviet [president of Oblast Soviet]

Beloborodov «6»

This telegram appears in photograph No. 135.
On 25 July 1918, just such an announcement by Beloborodov was placed in edition 144 of the Perm *Izvestiya*:

The Abduction of the Princes

The Alapayevsk executive committee informs us from Ekaterinburg of the assault during the morning of 18 July by an unknown force on the premises where the once Grand Dukes Igor Konstantinovich, Konstantin Konstantinovich, Ivan Konstantinovich, Serge Mikhailovich, and Palei were being held under guard.

In spite of the resistance of the guard, the Princes were abducted. There were casualties on both sides. A search is being carried out.

Chairman, Oblast Soviet Beloborodov – «7»

The first clue was given by Krivova: they were preparing to take them to Verkhne-Sinyachikha.
Another incident also helped.
No long before the abduction of the Noble Prisoners, an Alapayevsk peasant Ivan Solonin was preparing to get married. He ordered of [another] peasant Aleksandr Samsonov some kumyshka (samogon) [illicit spirit] for the wedding. Samsonov accepted the order and went into the forest with the neccessary supplies to prepare the kumyshka.
However the wedding fell through, and the mother of the bride, the disappointed mother-in-law, to avoid paying Samsonov for his work, went to the Cheka and denounced him for preparing illicit spirit.
Samsonov's friends, having heard of this, searched him out in the forest and warned him of the danger that threatened.

Samsonov stopped working and returned to Alapayevsk by a round-about route.

He rewarded his benefactors with a quarter of the kumyshka he had made, and they drank it there and then.

Late that night they set off for Alapayevsk. They travelled the road leading from Alapayevsk to Sinyachikha, and met a column of 10-11 wagons, with two people in each, without coachmen in the boxes. They all speak of the meeting with a single voice.

Here is the testimony of Trushkov «8»: 'The whole column was coming from Alapayevsk towards Sinyachikha and I came across it about the fifth versta [5.3 km] from Alapayvsk. There were no cries, no conversation, no songs, no groans; absolutely no sound I could hear. They all proceeded quietly and calmly.'

The Sinyachikhenskaya road rivetted the attention of Malshikov. He studied it and came to the conclusion that the solution to the mystery should be sought in the mine situated close to that road.

He soon noticed that one of the old shafts of the mine was scattered on the surface with fresh earth. He carried out excavations.

The shaft was 28 arshins [19.9m] deep. Its walls were clad with planks. Inside were two sections: the working shaft, through which ore was removed, and the machine shaft, where the pumps stood for the removal of water. Both sections were cluttered with a large quantity of old planks, lying completely at random.

At various depths in the shaft Malshikov found bodies: 8 October Feodor Semyonovich Remez, 9 [October] Varvara Yakovleva and Prince Palei, 10 [October] the Princes Konstantin Konstantinovich, Igor Konstantinovich and the Grand Duke Serge Mikhailovich, 11 [October] the Grand Duchess Elizabeth Feodorovna and Prince Ioann Konstantinovich.

The bodies were clothed. In their pockets were found various household articles and their papers, which they always carried with them during their imprisonment.

On the breast of the Grand Duchess Elizabeth Feodorovna was an icon of the Saviour with precious stones. To my knowledge, the Emperor prayed before this icon before his abdication, and gave it afterwards to Elizabeth Feodorovna. On the reverse is the inscription 'Palm [Sunday] 13th April 1891'.

In photograph No. 59 it is on the left of the top row.

The shaft had without doubt been blown up with grenades.

The bodies were displayed to the public and were recognized.

Here are the results of the autopsies «9»:

The body of the Grand Duchess Elizabeth Feodorovna: In the cranial cavity, on dissection of the skin, bruises were exposed; in the forehead area [a bruise] the size of a child's palm, and in the region of the left parietal bone [a bruise] the size of an adult's palm. There are bruises in the cellular tissue, the muscles and on the surface of the cranium. The skull bones are intact. A bruise is visible in the dura mater of the parietal area.'

The body of the Grand Duke Serge Mikhailovich: 'On dissection of the cranial skin in the left parietal area [there is] a bruise in the muscle and cellular tissue; in the right parietal bone there is a round hole the size of the groshina ($\frac{1}{2}$ centimetre in diameter); the channel of this wound runs downwards and backwards. On removal of the cranium, on the inner surface of the right parietal bone there is a hole 1 centimetre in diameter corresponding with the first; around the hole are splinters of bone. In the dura mater there is a disruption of the fabric in the form of a [not quite] round hole corresponding with the holes in the skull bone.'

The body of the Prince Ioann Konstantinovich: 'In the region of the right temple, on dissection of the skin, a bruise is visible in the muscle and cellular tissue, which occupies the whole region of the temple. On removal of the cranium a bruise was exposed in the dura mater in the same right temple region. There is a bruise within the thickness of the muscle over the whole of the frontal chest wall. In the cavities of the pleura is an extensive haemorrhage. In the abdominal region, on dissection of the skin, a bruise is visible in the thickness of the muscle and fatty tissue, which has spread over the whole frontal wall of the stomach.'

The body of the Prince Konstantin Konstantinovich: 'On the parietal is a large torn wound in the skin running from right to left, with a length of 9 centimetres and a width of 3 centimetres. Two centimetres behind this is a second torn wound 2 centimetres long. On the right temple and parietal (bones) and on the parietal itself is an extensive bruise the size of a palm. On removal of the cranium a bruise was discovered on the dura mater, the parietal and the occiput. In the thoracic cavity, on dissection of the skin, a large bruise was found which has penetrated the muscle and cellular tissue of the front wall of the thorax.'

The body of Prince Igor Konsantinovich: 'In the cranial cavity, on dissection of the skin, a bruise [was found] occupying the whole right hand half of the forehead; [There is] a crack in the bones of the skull starting in the centre of the upper edge of the right orbit and running along the centre line of the frontal bone. The crack runs rearwards into the (posterior fontanelle) and on to the occiput. On dissection of the cranium, the brain [was found to be] a grey mass. On removal of the brain, [a] crack was seen running over the upper wall of the right orbit to cross the (internal occipital protruberance). In the thoracic cavity, on dissection of the skin, a large bruise was found, which has penetrated the muscle in the lower part of the front wall of the thorax. On dissection of the abdominal cavity, a large bruise [was found] in the thickness of the abdominal wall.'

The body of Prince Vladimir Pavlovich Palei: 'In the cranial cavity, on dissection of the skin, [was found] a large bruise occupying both parietals and the occipital regions. On dissection of the skin about 4-5 cubic centimetres of blood ran out . . . On dissection of the cranial cavity a haemorrhage [was found] under the dura mater in the occipital region. The rearward parts of the brain are a gruel-like red mass. In the thoracic cavity [is] a large bruise in the thickness of the muscle and cellular tissue of its front wall.'

The body of Fyodor Semyonovich Remez: 'In the region of the chest muscles [is] a severe bruise, which has spread over the whole thoracic cavity . . . [There is] a haemorrhage in the region of the right pleura. . . In the region of the right temple, on dissection of the skin, a large haemorrhage [was found]. A bruise has spread over the entire occipital region . . . Under the dura mater in the region of the left temple [there is] a haemorrhage.'

The body of Varvara Yakovleva: 'On dissection of the skin of the head a bruise was found in the region of the right temple, and a second bruise in the occipital and parietal regions. The bones of the skull are intact. There is blood in the sutures. On removal of the cranium a bruise was found under the dura mater in the occipital region . . . On dissection of the skin a bruise [was found] in the region of the sternum.'

The bodies of the Grand Duke Serge Mikhailovich, the Grand Duchess Elizabeth Feodorovna, the Princes Ioann Konstantinovich, Konstantin Konstantinovich and Igor Konstantinovich are illustrated in photographs Nos. 136-140.

Experts have determined that the death of the Grand Duke Serge Mikhailovich was caused by 'a haemorrhage into the dura mater and disruption of the brain tissue as a result of a gunshot wound'.

All the others were thrown alive into the shaft, and their death was caused by 'haemorrhages as a result of their injuries'.

Judiciary commissar Efim Solovyov, chekist Pyotr Startsev and sovdep member Ivan Abramov were captured«10».

Many other murders lay on the conscience of Solovyov. He murdered, by the way, the local priest Father Udintsev. A hardened criminal, Solovyov affirmed that he was absent from Alapayevsk on 17 and 18 July, which, however, was refuted by the investigation.

Startsev and Abramov saw everyone who took the prisoners to the shaft on the morning of 18 July and everyone who remained by the school and simulated the assault of the imaginary 'White Guard'.

Their names are given above.

In photograph No. 141 are shown:

Efim Solovyov (1), Grigorii Abramov (2), Nikolai Govyrin (3), Mikhail Ostanin (4), Aleksei Smolnikov (5), Sergei Pavlov (6), Dmitrii Perminov (7), Egor Sychev (8), Mikhail Nasonov (9), Vasilii Postnikov (10).

The imaginary 'bandit', whose body was found near the school after the removal of the prisoners, turned out to be a peasant from the Saldinsk works. He was seized beforehand by the Chekists and was for several days held at the Alapayevsk Cheka.

Startsev explained that the murder of the noble prisoners was on orders from Ekaterinburg, and that Safarov came from there specially to handle it «11».

Is it possible to doubt this?

No more than one day [24 hours] separate the Ekaterinburg murders from those at Alapayevsk.

There they chose a disused mine to conceal the crime. The same method [was used] here.

There they tricked the imperial family from their quarters with a lie. They used the same method here.

Both the Ekaterinburg and the Alapayevsk murders were the product of the one will of the same people.

Appendix 7: Two modern medical opinions

In order to obtain a modern opinion, I wrote to Dr Roger Williams of King's College Hospital Medical School, asking if he could recommend an expert. He gave me the following general opinion:

> With respect to the injuries suffered by the Russians, all the bodies showed evidence of severe traumatic injury to the skull and brain. Although normal consciousness may be retained following very severe trauma causing skull fracture, cases 2, 5 and 6 were almost certainly unconscious from the time of their injuries, since these were particularly severe and in the latter two instances brain substance was also apparently grossly damaged. Cases 1, 3 and 4 may have remained conscious following their injuries, although this would probably have been for a short period only.
>
> The bruising of the abdominal wall and the thoracic injuries described in cases 3, 4 and 5 would be compatible with a fall from a considerable height (or with previous injury caused by a blunt object). Although there is no mention of fractured ribs in the post-mortem reports, there can be little doubt that these injuries could have been extremely painful and would have made it difficult, if not impossible, to summon help.

Dr Williams recommended me to Her Majesty's Coroner for Greater London (Western District), Dr John Burton, who has kindly compiled details of the injuries which he sent on to Professor Bowen, Professor of Forensic Medicine at Charing Cross Hospital, who in turn sent me the following opinion for publication:

COMMENTARY ON THE FINDING OF THE BODIES AT ALAPAYEVSK OF THE MEMBERS OF THE RUSSIAN ROYAL FAMILY IN THE SUMMER OF 1918.

The bodies were recovered from various levels from the shaft of the mine which suggests they were disposed of by means of being thrown down one after the other. The identification was by papers and clothing and there is no mention of disturbance of tearing of the clothing which might occur following an explosion of a hand grenade.

There is therefore no evidence to confirm the statement that the shaft had been blown up with a hand grenade.

1. *GRAND DUCHESS ELIZABETH FEODOROVNA* (a) Bruising of scalp on the forehead on the left side in two areas 2-3 and 3-4" across respectively. Bruising also

present in the underlying temporal muscle.
(b) There was no fracture but a right subdural haemorrhage or haematoma had occurred.

Comment: Survival could have occurred for some hours, if not longer, after infliction of blows, which were probably two in number, on to the left side of the scalp.

2. *GRAND DUKE SERGE MIKHAILOVICH* (a) Bruising on the left side of the head.
(b) Fire armwound of the right parietal region with no mention of exit wound or finding the bullet on examination.

Comment: This is an exceptional case because it was the only victim who was shot. Could this have been because he was a chief complainant as to their somewhat harsh treatment earlier on in captivity, or possibly did he try to run away?

3. *PRINCE IOANN KONSTANTINOVICH* (a) Bruise right side of the head into muscle tissue and a right subdural haematoma.
(b) Bruising of the muscles of the chest and abdominal musculature.

Comment: This is the first of the series of 5 cases where this unusual degree of trauma of the chest wall and abdominal tissues is found. There is no mention in the cases above (1) and (2) possibly because no further examination of the body was done (i.e. other than the head) or simply because it was not present. It suggests some quite violent trauma occurred to the abdominal and thoracic tissues, if it was true bruising, probably punching in the chest and abdomen or it may even have been some post-mortem change in the tissues which was mistaken for bruising. The cause of death here is Right Subdural Haematom in the same way that death occurred in Case (1).

4. *PRINCE KONSTANTIN KONSTANTINOVICH*
(a) Laceration of left side of skull, 9 x 3 cm., with a second one behind it 2 cm. across (side not stated).
(b) Right temple and parietal bruising 3–4" across and an underlying subdural haemorrhage extensive enough to involve most of the right side of the skull.
(c) Bruising on the front of the chest.

Comment: These are serious injuries and clearly following a blow on to the uncovered skull, probably with a blunt instrument.

5. *PRINCE IGOR KONSTANTINOVICH* (a) Bruise right side of forehead.
(b) Fracture over top of skull from the edge of the eye to the back of the head, right side.
(c) Second(?)fracture over upper margin of orbit, or is this a re-description of (b)?
(d) Large bruise on the front of the chest an abdominal musculature.

Comment: This is the first case of fracture of the skull: death was probably due to brain damage. The description of the brain in all these cases is not very satisfactory.

6. *PRINCE VLADIMIR PAVLOVICH PALEI*
(a) Right subdural haematoma with ? injury to the brain, contusion.
(b) Large bruise on the front of the chest.

Comment: Death due to subdural haemorrhage; difficult to estimate the time it occurred following infliction, probably several hours.

7. *FEODOR SEMYONOVICH REMEZ* (a) Large bruise in chest tissues and muscle and haemorrhage into the chest space.

(b) Large bruise in right temporal and occipital area.

(c) Bruise in region of sternum (probably same as (a) above). There is also a left subdural haemorrhage which caused death.

8. *VARVARA YAKOVLEVA* (a) Bruise in the right temple and a second bruise in the occipital and parietal regions but no fracture of the skull although blood was present in the suture lines with an occipital subdural haemorrhage.

(b) Bruise in the region of the sternum.

Comment: There is somewhat sketchy description of autopsy findings but, even so, two distinct types of lesions or injuries were seen. In all cases except (1) and (2) there were unusual bruises of the chest wall. It seems more than likely that all the victims except the Grand Duke Serge Mikhailovich, who was shot, were beaten on the head with a blunt instrument, probably through their head coverings, i.e. presumably at the time they were wearing a hat, with the possible exception of Prince Konstantin Konstantinovich, who was beaten across the head in such a manner that lacerations occurred which would have been unlikely to occur if he had been wearing a hat.

Following blows to the head, bruising occurred into the scalp tissues, subdural collections of blood developed, i.e. between brain and skull, which produced coma and mounting pressure, resulting in death.

The chest and abdominal injuries are more difficult to explain. As mentioned, they may have been due to blows or punches to the front of the body.

The findings indicate that it is likely that, following fatal assaults, the victims were thrown down the mine shaft. It is difficult to assess from these reports, particularly taking into account the clothing and warmth, the time interval between injury and death. I am presuming that several months occurred after death to the time of autopsy and that a doctor with some pathological training carried out the autopsies.

David A. Ll. Bowen, M.A., M.B., B.Chir.,
F.R.C.P., F.R.C.P.(Ed.), F.R.C.Path.,
D. Path, D.M.J.
Professor of Forensic Medicine,
University of London.

Appendix 8: Source notes

A. *Comments on the Grand Duke Serge*

Some readers may feel that I make the Grand Duke Serge unrealistically unpleasant. The following extracts show what relations, contemporaries and historians thought.

(a) The Grand Duke Alexander Michailovich (his nephew by marriage), *Once a Grand Duke*, Garden City Publishing Co., New York, 1932, pp. 139–40.

Uncle Sergei, Grand Duke Sergei Alexandrovich, played a fatal part in the downfall of the empire, having been partially responsible for the Khodynka catastrophe during the coronation of the year 1896. Try as I will, I cannot find a single redeeming feature in his character. A very poor officer, he commanded the Preobrajensky Regiment, the crack regiment of the Imperial Guard. A complete ignoramus in administrative affairs, he held fast to the general governership of the Moscow area, which should have been entrusted to a statesman of exceptionally seasoned experience. Obstinate, arrogant, disagreeable, he flaunted his many peculiarities in the face of the entire nation, providing the enemies of the régime with inexhaustible material for calumnies and libels. The generals visiting the messroom of the Preobrajensky Regiment listened with stupefaction to the chorus of officers singing a favourite song of Grand Duke Sergei, with its refrain consisting of the words – 'and peace, and love, and bliss.' The august commander himself illustrated those not very soldier-like words by throwing his body back and registering a tortured rapture in his features.

(b) Richard Charques, *The Twilight of Imperial Russia*, Phoenix House, London, 1958, p. 44.

In 1891–2 the grand-duke Sergey Alexandrovitch celebrated his appointment as governor-general of Moscow by the summary expulsion of some twenty thousand Jews from the city. In an even more candid gesture of persecution, the adoption by Jews of Christian first names, a normal proceeding in educated families, was declared a criminal offence.

(c) Alexander Ular, *Russia from Within*, Heinemann, London, 1905, pp. 76–9.

He accordingly reaped a harvest of vast estates, exclusive appanages, and a multiplicity of handsome sinecures with their corresponding perquisites. His annual income exceeded £320,000. As, however, he showed the mania for

413

dissipation common to all his family, and the gratification of his lusts cost him incredible sums, he was perpetually in pecuniary difficulties, and did not hesitate to become a party to bureaucratic peculation, which he was supposed to repress by his authority.

His departure was also due to a more delicate affair. Serge refused the renewal of a licence to a lady who conducted perfectly respectable dancing classes, which were attended by young girls of good family. The establishment was in a flourishing condition. Serge, incited by his erotic mania and lust for money-making, invited the lady in question to arrange 'assignations' for him with some of the prettiest of her pupils. As she indignantly refused to have any dealings of this nature, he tried to blackmail her and demanded a large sum under the threat of accusing her of being a procuress. She still refused. The licence was withdrawn and this gave her the opportunity of explaining the affair to some of the members of the aristocracy, who conveyed the story to St Petersburg. The Tsar was furiously angry, and this was Serge's last act of blackmail.

Sadism, along with money, was his ruling passion and from his youth up this vice had preyed upon him. The commencement of his official career was marked by an especially reprehensible display of his passions.

He founded and conducted a Society for Pilgrimage to Palestine, the treasury of which, being richly endowed by donations of a somewhat compulsory nature, enabled a few peasants to be sent annually to the holy places, and also, incidentally, filled up the great breaches in the Grand Ducal exchequer. At the same time he purged the Orthodox Holy City of the assassins of Christ. He next extorted several hundred thousand roubles from certain rich Jews who were affected by his law of expulsion.

To one of their deputations he declared that 'all Jews ought to be crucified', but he was open to accept money, and subsequently expelled only those who could not advance him large sums without receipt. In connection with the law of expulsion, however, he introduced two highly characteristic exceptions.

One was in reference to young Jewish girls. These are only admitted to live in Moscow if they inscribe their names on the registers of prostitutes, and this involves medical visits, along with frequent affronts, from so-called 'doctors' and 'inspectors'. His Highness sometimes deigned – in the interests of good government – to assist in these private visitations. The other exception referred to little Jewish boys employed as apprentices or as grooms. All other classes of Jew being useless at the residence of the Tsar's Uncle, it was a matter of course that they should be driven back to their Ghettoes in the south-west of Russia.

(d) Henry W. Nevinson, *The Dawn in Russia*, Harper, New York and London, p. 13.

On February 17th the Grand Duke Sergius, Governor General of Moscow, uncle of the Tsar, conspicious for his cruelty, and, even among the Russian aristocracy, renowned for the peculiarity of his vices, was assassinated as he drove into the Kremlin.

(e) Count Witte (Formerly Prime Minister and Chief Economic Minister), *The Memoirs of Count Witte*, Heinemann, London, 1921, p. 377.

Among the most implacable enemies of the Russian Jews was Grand Duke Sergey Alexandrovich, the man who, by his ultra-reactionary and near-sighted policy, drove Moscow into the arms of the revolutionists. The measures which the Grand Duke adopted against the Jews of Moscow the Committee of

Ministers refused to sanction, so that they had to be passed either by special commissions or directly by Imperial decrees.

B. *Note on the Montenegrins*

Those who wish to have a further picture of the conversation of the Montenegrin Grand Duchesses should read the account of the French Ambassador, Paléologue, in *An Ambassador's Memoirs*, Vol. I, Hutchinson, London, 1924, pp. 22–3.

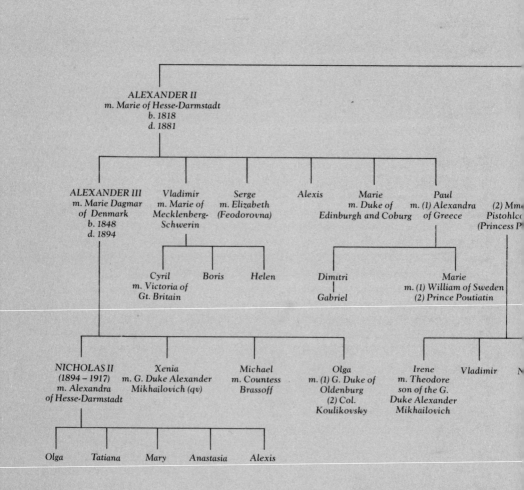

ALEXANDER I

ALEXANDER II
m. Marie of Hesse-Darmstadt
b. 1818
d. 1881

ALEXANDER III
m. Marie Dagmar
of Denmark
b. 1848
d. 1894

Vladimir
m. Marie of
Mecklenberg-
Schwerin

Serge
m. Elizabeth
(Feodorovna)

Alexis

Marie
m. Duke of
Edinburgh and Coburg

Paul
m. (1) Alexandra
of Greece

(2) Mme
Pistohlc
(Princess P

Cyril
m. Victoria of
Gt. Britain

Boris

Helen

Dimitri
|
Gabriel

Marie
m. (1) William of Sweden
(2) Prince Poutiatin

NICHOLAS II
(1894 – 1917)
m. Alexandra
of Hesse-Darmstadt

Xenia
m. G. Duke Alexander
Mikhailovich (qv)

Michael
m. Countess
Brassoff

Olga
m. (1) G. Duke of
Oldenburg
(2) Col.
Koulikovsky

Irene
m. Theodore
son of the G.
Duke Alexander
Mikhailovich

Vladimir

N

Olga

Tatiana

Mary

Anastasia

Alexis

Elizabeth
&
Alexandra